bed Duke Wallenstein by his collar and yanked him backward. Behind the fallen guard, she could see one of Rossbach's companions with his sword now in his hand.

Ellie hauled Wallenstein back into the telephone room. She just had time to slam the door shut in Rossbach's face. Wallenstein was now rising to his feet. Unfortunately, in his own personal suite, the Duke wasn't carrying his sword.

Ellie stooped over and rummaged through the big tool chest that had been in the room for weeks now. An instant later, she came up with a modern Crescent wrench—Len's 12-incher—as well as a two-foot cheater pipe. She tossed the pipe to Wallenstein and hefted the wrench. It wasn't much, but it would have to do.

Wham!—and the door came off the hinges. Rossbach and another man started pushing through the doorway, their swords level.

WHAM! WHAM!

Both of them sailed through the opening, as if shot from a cannon, their swords flying out of their hands. Ellie had seen the erupting exit wound in one man's belly. That *WHAM* had been a gunshot.

She stared through the open, shattered doorway. She could see Edith Wild standing in the salon, now. The big woman's face was contorted with anger and she was holding a modern-style revolver in both hands. ***WHAM! WHAM!*** Now that Ellie wasn't completely overwhelmed by adrenaline, the sound of the gunshots seemed ten times louder.

Ellie heard a man shout something. A protest of some kind, perhaps, or a plea for mercy.

Fat lot of good it did him. ***WHAM!***

Wallenstein was smiling thinly and stroking his badly scarred jaw. "A pity there are so few American women." he announced. "If I had an army of you mad creatures, I could conquer the world."

—from "The Wallenstein Gambit"

RING OF FIRE

Edited by
Eric Flint

RING OF FIRE

This is a work of fiction. All the characters and events portrayed in this book are fictional, and any resemblance to real people or incidents is purely coincidental.

Copyright © 2004 Eric Flint

All rights reserved, including the right to reproduce this book or portions thereof in any form.

A Baen Books Original

Baen Publishing Enterprises
P.O. Box 1403
Riverdale, NY 10471
www.baen.com

ISBN-13: 978-1-4165-0908-0
ISBN-10: 1-4165-0908-9

Cover art by Dru Blair

First paperback printing, October 2005

Library of Congress Cataloging-in-Publication Number 2003021801

Distributed by Simon & Schuster
1230 Avenue of the Americas
New York, NY 10020

Production by Windhaven Press, Auburn, NH (www.windhaven.com)
Printed in the United States of America

Contents

Preface

Eric Flint

The stories in *Ring of Fire* are all based in the alternate history setting I created in my novel *1632*, which was further developed in the sequel I wrote with David Weber, *1633*.

Producing "spin-off" anthologies as part of a popular series has a long and venerable history in science fiction, of course. But, in at least two respects, this anthology is different from most such—and the two differences are related.

The first difference is obvious: It is very unusual to produce a shared-universe anthology when a "series" consists, so far, of only two novels. Doing so would seem premature, since the setting really isn't all that firmed up yet.

But that was exactly why I wanted to do it so early in the game—which leads me to the second difference:

1

In most shared-universe anthologies, as a rule, the stories are tangential to the main line of the story as developed in the creating author's own novels. They might be excellent stories, in their own right, but they rarely have much if any direct impact on the logic of developments in the series itself. The reason is simple. Authors are generally reluctant to have other authors shape their own setting, and the contributing authors to an anthology respect that and design their stories to be somewhat "off to the side." The stories are *in* the setting, but they do not really affect the setting very much.

That is not true of *Ring of Fire*. The stories in this anthology all feed directly into the development of the series as a whole. They are not simply part of it, they actively *shape* it.

Indeed, several of them have already done so. Many of these stories were written before Dave Weber and I wrote *1633,* and we deliberately incorporated them into the plot of that novel. For example:

The characters of Tom Stone and his children, who appear in *1633* and will be major characters in the upcoming novel *1634: The Galileo Affair,* are first introduced into the series by Mercedes Lackey in her story in this anthology, "To Dye For." (*1634: The Galileo Affair* is co-authored by me and Andrew Dennis, and will be published in April of 2004. Andrew is another of the authors in this anthology.)

The interaction between the Earl of Strafford and Dr. Harvey, which occurs in *1633,* presupposes a prior visit to the time-transplanted town of Grantville. The story of that visit is told here, in S.L. Viehl's "A Matter of Consultation."

Dave Weber's story "In the Navy" provides the background for the creation of the new American navy, which was such a prominent part of *1633*.

The character of Gerd, who appears in *1633* as one of Captain Harry Lefferts' men, is first introduced into the 1632 universe in Greg Donahue's "Skeletons."

A number of the other stories here lay the basis for future developments in the series. That is most clearly evident with my own story, the short novel *The Wallenstein Gambit*. The events depicted in that story will be central to most of the future volumes in the series. The story is not "on the side." It is right smack in the middle of the series as it continues to unfold.

Furthermore, the basis for *The Wallenstein Gambit* was, to a considerable degree, laid in this anthology by three other stories: Dave Freer's "A Lineman For the Country," Jody Dorsett's "The Three Rs," and (most directly) by K.D. Wentworth's "Here Comes Santa Claus."

Andrew Dennis' "Between the Armies" lays much of the basis for our forthcoming novel *1634: The Galileo Affair*. (As does *1633*, of course—the character of Sharon Nichols who figures prominently in *1633* is a major character in *The Galileo Affair*.) Some of the characters developed by Deann Allen and Mike Turner in their story "American Past Time" will also appear in *The Galileo Affair*.

Virginia DeMarce's "Biting Time" lays the basis for a novel which she and I are working on, which will both continue the story she began as well as link it to the story line I develop in *The Wallenstein Gambit*.

To one degree or another, that is true of every story in this anthology. Many of the characters you first encounter here will reappear in later volumes of the series—and sometimes as major characters in their own right.

I wanted to produce this kind of anthology early in the series because I wanted, as much as possible, to capture something which is usually missing in alternate history series:

History is *complicated*. It is not the story of a few people, it is the story of an immense number of people—each of them full individuals in their own right, each of them having their own greater or lesser impact on developments.

In the nature of things, fictional series—like biographies—tend to give the illusion that history marches more-or-less in lockstep with the actions of the main characters of the story. That's almost inevitable, given the very nature of narrative. But it *is* an illusion, and I wanted to avoid it as much as possible in the unfolding 1632 series.

Yes, Mike Stearns and Rebecca Abrabanel and Jeff Higgins and Gretchen Richter and the other major characters I created in *1632* will continue to be major characters in the series. But they are not Greek gods and goddesses. They are simply people—and what happens to them will, in the end, be deeply affected by the actions of a Jewish jeweler in Prague trying desperately to prevent one of the worst pogroms in history, a small town Catholic priest undergoing a crisis of conscience, and a woman in late middle age who simply decides to found a school.

And . . . enough. Welcome to the *Ring of Fire*.

In the Navy

David Weber

"I'm telling you, Mike, we can do this!"

Mike Stearns inhaled deeply, counted to ten—*no, better make it twenty*—and reminded himself that the President of the United States couldn't go around throttling overenthusiastic teenagers. He told himself that rather firmly, then reopened his eyes.

"Eddie," he asked as patiently as possible, "do you have any idea how many people walk through this office every week—every day, for that matter—with projects that absolutely, positively just have to be done Right This Minute?"

"But this is *different*, Mike!" The wiry, red-haired young man on the other side of Mike's desk waved his hands. "This is *important*!"

"That's exactly my point, Eddie. They're *all* important. But important or not, we only have so many up-timers with the sorts of skills to make them work. And this—" Mike thumped a solid, muscular palm on the lovingly executed sketch plan Eddie had laid on his desk between two tall piles of books "—would require skills I doubt any of us have to begin with. Besides, can you even imagine how someone like Quentin Underwood would react if I handed whole miles of railroad track over to you for a 'crackpot scheme' like this?"

"It's not a 'crackpot scheme'!" Eddie said hotly. "This is exactly how the Confederates built their original ironclads, with rolled railroad rails for armor back during the Civil War."

"No, it's not," Mike replied patiently. "It's how you *think* they built them, and that's—"

"It *is* how they built them!" Eddie interrupted. "My research is solid, Mike!"

"If you'll let me finish?" Mike's voice was noticeably cooler, and Eddie blushed with the fiery color only a natural redhead could produce.

"Sorry," he muttered, and Mike was hard pressed not to chuckle at his expression. Eddie Cantrell, especially in the grip of one of his effervescent enthusiasms, was prone to forget that the Mike Stearns he'd known all his life had become President of the only United States that existed in this Year of Our Lord Sixteen Hundred and Thirty-Two. Which was fair enough, Mike supposed. There'd been enough times over the last year or so that *he'd* thought he was living in a fever dream instead of reality.

"As I was saying," he continued after a moment, "I don't have any doubt at all that this plan of yours," he thumped the sketch on his desk again, "represents one hell of a lot of research and hard thinking. But the truth is that you don't have any better idea than I do of what sorts of hardware it would take to build the thing. Or, for that matter, who do you think is going to do the stability calculations? Or figure out its displacement? Or design a steam plant to move a boat this size and weight? Or even have a single clue how to take command of it when it was built?" He shook his head. "Even if we had the resources to devote to something like this, we don't have anyone here in Grantville who has any idea how to build it. And I've got too many other projects that people do have a clue about to justify diverting our limited—*very* limited, Eddie—resources to building some kind of Civil War navy."

Eddie looked away, staring out the office window for several seconds. Then he looked back at Mike, and his expression was more serious than any Mike recalled ever having seen from him before.

"All right," the young man said. "I understand what you're saying. And I guess I do get carried away sometimes. But there was a reason they built these things back home, Mike, and Gustav Adolf is going to need them a hell of a lot worse than Sherman or Grant ever did."

Mike started a quick reply, then stopped. Just as Eddie had trouble remembering Mike as anything more impressive than the leader of the United Mine Workers local, Mike had trouble thinking of Eddie as anything but one of the local kids. Not quite as geekish as his friend Jeff had been before the Ring of Fire deposited their hometown in seventeenth-century Germany, but still something of an oddball in rural West Virginia. A computer nerd and a wargamer who was passionately devoted to both pastimes.

Yeah, Mike thought. *A geek. But a wargaming geek. He may be short on experience in the real world, but he's spent one hell of a lot more time than I have studying wars and armies and . . . navies.*

"All right, Eddie," he sighed. "I'm sure I'm going to regret this, but why is 'Captain General Gars' going to need ironclads so badly?"

"Because he doesn't have railroads," Eddie replied. "That's why rivers and canals are so important to his logistics, Mike. You know that."

Mike nodded slowly. Eddie was certainly right about that, although the youngster hadn't been present for the meetings at which he and Gustavus Adolphus had discussed that very point.

"Without railroads," Eddie continued, "the only way to move really large quantities of supplies is by water. That's why successful seventeenth-century military campaigns usually stuck so close to the lines of navigable rivers. I know we're talking about building steamboats and steam-powered tugs for that very reason, and that should help a lot. But the bad guys are just as well aware of how important rivers are as Gustav Adolf is. When they figure out how much more efficiently he's going to be able to use them with our help, they're going to start trying really hard to stop him. And the best way for them to do that is to attack his shipping on the water, or else build forts or redoubts armed with artillery to try and close off the critical rivers." The teenager shrugged. "Either way, seems to me that something like an ironclad would be the best way

to . . . convince them to stay as far away from the
river bank as they can get."

The kid had a point, Mike realized. In fact, he
might have an even better one than he realized.
The major cities of most of Gustavus Adolphus' so-
called "vassals" and "allies" also happened to lie on
navigable rivers, and altogether too many of those
vassals were among the slimiest, most treacherous
batch of so-called noblemen in history. Which meant
that in a pinch, an armored vessel, heavily armed
and immune to said cities' defensive artillery might
prove a powerful incentive when it came to honoring
their obligations to the Confederated Principalities of
Europe and their Emperor.

None of which changed a single thing where the
incredible difficulties of Eddie's proposal were concerned.

Eddie started to say something else, then closed
his mouth with an almost audible click as he realized
Mike was gazing frowningly down at the sketch.

The vessel it depicted would never be called graceful.
It was an uncompromising, slab-sided, boxy thing which
sat low in the water, and its gun ports and a thick, squat
funnel were its only visible external features.

"You're right about how important river traffic is
going to be," Mike admitted as he ran one blunt fin-
gertip across the drawing. "But this thing would be an
incredible resource hog."

"I know that," Eddie acknowledged. "That's why I'm
only suggesting building three of them. God knows we
could use as many as we could get, but I knew going
in that there was no way you were going to give up
enough rails to armor more than that."

"No way in the world," Mike agreed with a grin which held very little humor. "Quentin would scream bloody murder if I gave you enough rails for *one* of these things, much less three! And he wouldn't be alone, either. It's going to take years and years for us to develop an iron industry that can produce steel that good. But that part I could handle . . . if I thought we'd be able to build the damned things in the end."

"Look," Eddie said, "I admit that a lot of that plan is based on the best guesstimates I could come up with from my reference books. At the same time, some of those books are pretty darned good, Mike. I spent a lot of time researching this period when Jeff and Larry decided we just had to do a Civil War ironclads game." He chuckled. "I always was the navy specialist when it came to game design.

"But that's not important. What matters is that it's a starting point. If you can find someone else, someone better qualified to take my notes and my reference books and turn them into something we can build, I'll be delighted to turn them over. You're right. I don't have the least idea how to figure displacements or allow for stability requirements, and I know the designers screwed up the displacement calculations big time for a lot of the real ironclads built during the Civil War. There was one class of monitor that would've sunk outright if they'd ever tried to mount their turrets! So maybe my enthusiasm did run away with me. But it's more important that this gets done and that it work than that it gets done *my* way."

Mike tipped back in his chair and considered the face across his desk. It was the same face it had always been, and yet, it wasn't. It hadn't changed as much as Jeff Higgins' face had, perhaps, but like every face in Grantville, it had thinned down over the course of the last winter and its sometimes short and always monotonous rations. Eddie had always been wiry; now he'd lost every ounce of excess weight, yet his frame was well muscled from hard physical labor. More to the point, perhaps, that face was no longer as young, as . . . innocent as it had been, and Mike felt a pang of deep, intense pain for the loss of Eddie's last years of childhood.

But a lot of people had lost a lot of things, he reminded himself, and it looked as if Eddie was doing a better job of growing into the reality he faced than Mike had realized when he came bursting into the office. His pride in the concept he'd come up with was obvious, yet it was equally obvious that his offer to turn it over to someone else who might be better qualified to make it work was genuine. Unfortunately, there was no one in Grantville who *was* better qualified. The skills a project like this would call for weren't the sort that were in much demand in a West Virginia coal mining town. To make it work, they would have needed someone with some real expertise in mechanical engineering and heavy fabrication, not to mention running complicated industrial projects. Better yet, someone with some genuine experience with boats and ships. Best of all, someone with some idea about how a real navy worked.

Someone like—

Mike's thoughts broke off in a sudden mental hiccup, and he sat abruptly upright.

"What?" Eddie asked, and Mike shook his head the

way he'd shaken off the effect of a particularly good left jab during his days in the ring.

"I'm still not convinced that any of this is doable," he said slowly, contemplating Eddie through half-slitted eyes. "But if—*if*, I say—it is, then it's possible that there's someone right here in town who'd be perfect—" He broke off and grimaced. "Let me rephrase that. It's possible that there's someone right here in town who could actually make it work."

"There is?" Eddie looked puzzled. "Who?"

"The only person who has any experience at all with this kind of building project," Mike replied, and grinned sourly as Eddie's eyes widened in dawning disbelief.

"That's right," the President of the United States said in a tone which matched his grin's sourness perfectly. "I think we need to consult with my sister's esteemed father-in-law."

"Let me get this straight." John Chandler Simpson sat on the other side of a slightly battered-looking table in an Appalachian kitchen and regarded Mike through narrow eyes. "You're offering *me* a job."

"I guess you could put it that way," Mike replied in a voice he tried to keep entirely free of any emotion. His years of experience as a union negotiator helped, but it was still difficult. He'd seldom felt as much antipathy for another human being as Simpson evoked, apparently effortlessly, from him.

He sat back in his own chair, letting his eyes rest on the framed prints which brightened Jessica Wendell's friendly kitchen. He could think of very few settings which would have seemed less appropriate for a meeting with the one-time president and CEO of the Simpson Industrial Group, but at least Jessica's willingness to surrender her kitchen as an impromptu conference room had let him keep this meeting out of the public eye.

Not that the present confidentiality would help much when Mike's cabinet found out what they were discussing. He shuddered at the thought of how Melissa Mailey, for example, would react when she discovered that her President had been negotiating anything at all with their archenemy.

"I must confess," Simpson said after a moment in a poisonously dry tone, "that I find a certain degree of irony in this."

"I doubt you find it any more ironic than I do," Mike told him levelly.

"Maybe not, but after the way you turned me into some sort of Antichrist in the elections, I have to admire the sheer gall it must have taken for you to suggest anything of the sort."

"Gall doesn't come into it," Mike shot back, then shrugged his broad, powerful shoulders. "Look, Simpson, I don't like you very much. And God knows you've made it plain enough that you like me even less. But the simple fact is that there's no one else in Grantville who'd even know where to begin with a project like this one."

"Well, that's certainly a refreshing admission." Simpson's lips twitched in what, in another man, might have been called a ghost of a smile, but there was very little humor in his eyes. "I suppose I should be flattered that you're willing to grant my expertise in any field."

Mike felt his temper try to flare. He was, by nature, a passionate man, and learning the self-discipline required to control those passions—and his temper—had not come easily to him. But it was a lesson he'd mastered long ago, and although Simpson made it more difficult than most, he wasn't about to forget it now.

"We can sit here pissing in each other's soup all afternoon, if you like," he said instead, throwing the crudity deliberately into the midst of the conversation. "Or we can deal with the reason I came over. Which would you prefer?"

Something flickered in Simpson's eyes. For a moment, Mike thought it was the other man's temper. Then he realized it had been something else. A moment of . . . recognition, perhaps. Or possibly simply an awareness that Mike had no intention of rising to his jibes and giving him the satisfaction of losing his temper.

"Tell me exactly what you have in mind," the ex-CEO said after only the briefest pause.

"It's simple enough." Mike leaned forward in his chair, planting his forearms on the table. "Eddie Cantrell came to see me with the initial proposal. He brought along a stack of reference books, and it turns out that he's got an entire stash of other books we never guessed he had. I should've made a point of going over there and going through the Four Musketeers' library myself. Everybody in town's known for years that the four of them were absolutely buggy where military history and war games were concerned."

He shook his head, eyes momentarily unfocused

as he considered the treasure trove he and Frank Jackson had discovered in Eddie and Larry Wild's bookshelves.

"Anyway," he continued briskly, "Eddie has decided that we need a U.S. Navy, and he set out single-handedly to do something about it. Which is how he came up with this."

Mike took a sheet of paper from his shirt pocket, unfolded it, and slid it across the table. Simpson's eyes flicked to it in a casual, almost dismissive glance. Then they snapped back, and he smoothed the sketch's creases as he frowned down at it.

"Cantrell did this?"

"Yeah. He took a course in drafting over at the high school a couple of years ago. Not," Mike added dryly, "that it really prepared him for a career as a maritime engineer."

"I'd say that's a bit of an understatement." Simpson's attention was on the figures listed in the data block in the upper left corner of Eddie's sketch, and he seemed momentarily to have forgotten his obvious dislike for the man across the table from him. He studied the numbers for several seconds, then snorted in something very like amusement.

"This displacement estimate of his has got to be way low," he said. "And even if it weren't, there's no way he's going to get by with a six-foot draft!" He shook his head. "I'd have to do some volume calculations to be certain, but even at his estimated tonnage, this thing is going to draw ten or twelve feet, minimum, and that's too deep for riverine conditions."

Mike chuckled, and Simpson looked quickly up from the sketch.

"I said something funny?" he inquired in a voice which had suddenly remembered its frost.

"No, not really. But you did just demonstrate exactly why I'm sitting here this morning. Do you really think that anyone else in Grantville—or anywhere else in seventeenth-century Europe, for that matter!—could rattle off what you just did?"

"I suppose not," Simpson said after a moment. "Of course, you realize that it's been the better part of twenty years since I did any hands-on hardware work at all."

"Maybe so, but at least you did some once upon a time. And didn't your company have a piece of the Navy's shipbuilding program?"

"Not really. Oh, our electronics division was one of the second-tier contractors on the *Arleigh Burke*-class destroyers' radar systems," Simpson acknowledged. He didn't seem to wonder how it was that Mike had acquired that particular bit of information, and Mike was just as happy he didn't. The breach between John Simpson and his son Tom was a deep and apparently permanent one, and Mike had no intention of admitting that he'd discussed this offer with his brother-in-law at some length before approaching Tom's father.

"But that whole division was really outside our core petro-chemical business," the elder Simpson continued, "and we didn't have anything to do with the hull or the engineering plant. And I damned sure wasn't handling any of the engineering myself! I don't want there to be any misunderstanding on that. Translating this—" he tapped the sketch lightly "—into anything remotely resembling a practical warship would require skills I haven't used since before I ever left the Navy."

"There's been a lot of that going around lately," Mike replied without cracking a smile, and Simpson acknowledged the point with a grunt of sour amusement. He looked down at the sketch for several more moments, lips pursed, then returned his gaze to Mike's face.

"How much authority and support would I have?" he asked.

"As much as I can give you." Mike shrugged. "I'm going to have problems with my own people if I decide to push this one. Quentin Underwood is going to have three kinds of fits the instant he hears about it, and some of the others aren't going to be far behind. Especially not when they find out how many railroad rails we're going to be asking for! But that's not really the worst of it. What's really going to stick in their craws is the impact this kind of diversion of effort will have on all our other projects."

"They'd better get used to it," Simpson said, and his dark eyes sharpened as if to impale Mike. "And so had you."

"What does that mean?" Mike demanded, not quite able to prevent himself from bristling.

"I may not have the library your young Mr. Cantrell does, 'Mr. President,' but I've been something of a student of military history in my time, myself." Simpson's smile was cold. "Do you know what ultimately brought about the downfall of the Swedish Empire?"

"Gustav Adolf was killed," Mike replied.

"Yes, he was. But that wasn't what prevented the Swedes from making their empire stand up. His generals, and especially Torstensson, Baner, and Oxenstierna, had learned their trade well enough to take over from him. What they didn't have was the economy or the manpower to take on the rest of Europe head-on. That was what really devastated Germany during the Thirty Years War. The only way to raise the manpower the Swedes needed, especially when the French turned against them, was to hire what amounted to mercenaries. And then they had to find a way to pay for them."

He shook his head.

"Don't misunderstand me. Gustavus Adolphus and Sweden probably went further than anyone else in the seventeenth century in rationalizing their manpower resources and creating a standing army out of their own population. But the problem was that Sweden simply didn't have the population density to sustain armies of the size it needed. Just as it didn't have the tax base to create the revenues armies that size—whether raised out of its own population or by hiring mercenaries—demanded."

He shrugged.

"So, ultimately, the only real option Sweden saw was to attempt to make war pay for itself by plundering its enemies and extracting the necessary money in 'contributions' from the populations of the territory it occupied. Unfortunately, it turned out that there was only so much blood in the turnip . . . and it wasn't enough. Some historians still argue that the Swedish Empire really collapsed only when Charles XII finally lost to Peter the Great, but the fact is that it was ultimately unsustainable simply because it lacked the financial and population bases to support it, especially against the inevitable coalitions of nations with larger populations and deeper pockets. And whatever else we may have changed by arriving here, we haven't changed Sweden's demographics."

"I'm aware of that."

In the wrong tone, that sentence could have been dismissive, or a challenge, but it didn't come out that way. In fact, Mike was more than a little surprised by Simpson's analysis. Which, he thought, was probably because the man had shown absolutely no ability or inclination to analyze the social and political realities the transplanted Americans faced with the same acuity.

"In that case," Simpson said levelly, "it's time that you faced the implications. The *military* implications."

Mike started to reply, but Simpson's raised hand stopped him. It wouldn't have, if it had been the arrogant gesture of Management dismissing Labor from consideration. But to Mike's considerable astonishment, it wasn't. It wasn't exactly a gesture of warmth, but it wasn't overtly discourteous or dismissive, either.

"You've made your policies and political platform abundantly clear," Simpson said. "And you've also made it abundantly clear that you intend to put the platform you ran on into effect. I won't pretend I like that, any more than I'll pretend I . . . enjoyed the way you campaigned."

A core of anger glowed in his eyes, but, to his credit, he kept it out of his voice.

"I'll grant you the strength of your own convictions and your sincerity. I don't agree with you, and I hope to hell your social policies don't turn into a complete and total disaster, but that's a fight I've already lost. And I understand your position on the creation of a general . . . industrial infrastructure, for want of a better term. It may surprise you to discover that I actually agree with you, to an extent. There's no way the seventeenth century's ramshackle, top-down excuses for nation states could possibly hope to match the sorts of technological innovations we could introduce, any more than the Soviet Union was able to match the U.S.'s tech and industrial base back home. To match us, they'd have to become *like* us, and we saw back home what happened to the Soviets when they tried to do that."

Mike gazed at the other man with carefully concealed surprise. He and his cabinet had never made any particular secret of their commitment to spreading innovations as widely as possible, but he and his inner circle had never explicitly made the argument Simpson just had. Partly that was to avoid tipping their hand to any seventeenth-century opponent too stupid to see the sucker punch coming, but another reason was that even some of his own cabinet—like Quentin Underwood—would have had conniption fits if they'd realized just how much of his "secret technological advantages" he was willing to give away to bring it about. And Mike had never expected John Chandler Simpson, of all people, to recognize what he had in mind . . . or to acknowledge that his strategy made any sort of sense.

"Unfortunately," Simpson's chair creaked as he leaned back in it and folded his arms, "what happened to the Soviets happened during a *cold* war. Whatever our proxies might have been doing around the periphery, we weren't locked in a direct, life-or-death battlefield confrontation with them. But that's precisely the position Gustav is in right now, and if Sweden goes down, so do we."

"I'm aware of that, too," Mike said. "That's why we organized an army under Frank Jackson in the first place." He grimaced. "Not that sending up-timers out to get shot at is the most efficient imaginable use of their knowledge and skills!"

"Exactly," Simpson said. If possible, the industrialist liked Frank Jackson even less than he liked Mike Stearns, but once again, that seemed to be beside the point to him, and he leaned forward once more, stabbing the tabletop with an emphatic finger. "As a matter of fact, it's the worst *possible* use of their knowledge and skills. And sending them into the field, even with the advantages we can give them in terms of modern weapons, is inevitably going to lead to casualties. And every casualty we suffer is going to cost us irreplaceable 'knowledge capital.'"

"Are you suggesting that we refuse to risk any of our people and expect Gustav Adolf to foot the entire bill while we just sit around?" Mike demanded. He couldn't quite believe he was having this discussion in the first place, or, in the second, that it seemed Simpson had a brain, after all. The other man certainly hadn't given any sign of it during the constitutional debate or his campaign for the presidency!

"Of course we can't do that, either," Simpson replied. "But in the end, it's really going to come down to how effective an army Gustav can raise and maintain in the field."

"Wait a minute. Wasn't your entire original argument that he doesn't have the money or the population to support a big enough army whatever he does?"

"Yes, it was. But I didn't say anything about army size just now. What I said was that it came down to the *effectiveness* of his army. There's a difference between sheer size and combat power. In a way, you've already acknowledged that by using Jackson and his troops to give Gustav a qualitative edge at places like the Wartburg and the Alte Veste. But doing it that way wastes our most precious resource. What we have to do is to make that qualitative edge integral to Gustav's own forces. He's got to get his manpower requirements down, and the only way for him to do that is for us to take up the slack by providing him with superior weapons and the training and techniques to use them properly, so that his men make up in individual effectiveness what they lose in numbers."

Simpson paused and snorted suddenly with genuine humor, and one of Mike's eyebrows rose questioningly.

"I was just thinking about the presumptuousness involved in 'teaching' one of the greatest captains of history his trade," the industrialist explained. "But that's exactly what it comes down to, in the end. We've got to give him the tools and show him how to use them in a way which will ease the pressure on his population. Give him smaller armies, with the sort of waterborne logistical support your young Mr. Cantrell is advocating, and the superior weapons to let him defeat larger forces, and he'll have a genuine chance of surviving and holding this empire of his together. But the only way we can do that is to divert however much of our own resources and capabilities it takes to support those smaller armies. What it boils down to, is that we'll have to help him downsize—"

his eyes glittered with undisguised amusement as Mike stiffened in automatic resistance to the most hated verb in managerese "—and that will mean an inevitable slowdown in how quickly we'll be able to build up other aspects of our infrastructure."

Mike started to reply quickly, then stopped himself. Nothing Simpson had just said came as an actual surprise to him. God knew he and his innermost circle had spent enough time grappling with the same problems and the same limiting factors themselves! But no one else, not even—or perhaps, especially—Frank Jackson, had laid out the points Simpson had just made in such implacably logical order.

And he was right, Mike realized. It was a bitter admission, and only the tiniest edge of its bitterness came from the fact that John Simpson had elicited it. He turned his eyes back to Jessica Wendell's prints, and his lips tightened as he stared at them sightlessly.

He didn't *want* Simpson to be right. He didn't want to divert still more precious resources, and skill, and knowledge to the military. What Europe needed was medicines, a textile industry, steam or internal-combustion-powered farm equipment. It needed steamships, railroads, oil wells, and telegraphs. It needed widespread electricity, light bulbs, refrigeration, sanitation, sewage plants, and a food canning industry. There were so *many* things it needed—so many whose mere existence would undermine the aristocracy-dominated excuse for a civilization which was about to turn all of Northern Germany into one huge abattoir.

But to introduce those things, the up-timers and their seventeenth-century countrymen somehow had to survive long enough. And surviving had its own cold, uncaring imperatives. Imperatives, he told himself with what he knew was an edge of pettiness, perfectly suited to John Simpson Chandler.

"You're right," he admitted, and heard the reluctance in his own voice as he did so. "We've already been discussing possible weapon upgrades with Gustav and Oxenstierna—more 'building down' to something we can produce in quantity instead of trying to use our own weapons as some sort of magic wand."

"I'm relieved to hear it," Simpson said. "But it's going to be just as important to show them how to get the most out of whatever we can provide for them."

"I'm sure it is. Unfortunately, aside from a few youthful enthusiasts like Eddie and his buddies, we're awfully short on people who understand how to do that."

"I'm not surprised." Simpson drummed on the tabletop for a few moments, and Mike surprised an expression on his face which might almost been one of hesitation. If it was, it vanished quickly, and Simpson looked directly back at him.

"For what it's worth," he said, "I really am quite well grounded in military history. It's one of the few hobby interests Tom and I share." An undisguised flash of raw pain flooded through his eyes at the mention of his son's name, but his voice never flinched. "What we really need here is one of those historical reenactors—somebody who spent his vacations marching around in a Union Army uniform with a Springfield rifle-musket on his shoulder. But I assume we don't have any of those?"

Mike smiled crookedly. "Sure we do—probably a dozen of them, at least. The first battle of the Civil

War was fought at Philippi, not more than an hour's drive from here."

Simpson brightened visibly.

"I should have thought of that, but I suppose I simply assumed that the local population was too small to support many of them. I hope you're making them available to Gustav and his army? Someone with hands-on experience like that with nineteenth-century weapons, tactics, and formation drill would be worth me, Jackson, and Cantrell all rolled into one."

"I know," Mike agreed, but his tone was considerably less enthusiastic than Simpson's, and he grimaced irritably when the industrialist cocked his head in question.

"Our problem is that most of them have skills we need just as badly somewhere else. Down at the power plant, for example, or over at the mine. Dwight Rogers is a perfect example of the problem. He's been a reenactor for at least ten or fifteen years, but he's also the only man in town with actual up-time oil field experience, and that makes him critical to Quentin's oil project."

"I see." Simpson studied Mike's expression for several seconds, then shrugged. "I see," he repeated, "and I understand the problem. But I think you're going to have to consider this the first example of sacrificing infrastructure to survival. We *need* those men—need not just their actual skills, but also their ability to sell seventeenth-century professional soldiers on the concept that we can show them how to do their jobs better than they can now. In fact, you ought to have people like that in Magdeburg already, working with the Swedes there as military advisers."

"Um." Mike stared out a window while he chewed that unpalatable argument. It seemed to be Simpson's day for making him consider things he didn't want to think about, he reflected. And, once again, Simpson was right.

Damn it to hell.

"Okay," he sighed finally. "You're probably— No, scratch that, you *are* right. But I've still got to consider how many birds I can kill with each stone." He pondered some more, rubbing the tip of an index finger in slow, thoughtful circles on the tabletop, then nodded to himself.

"All right," he said, focusing on Simpson once more. "I don't know if I can make this permanent yet—we'll have to look at the competing demands on his time—but Jere Haygood's a reenactor, and a good one. He was also the senior partner of the one civil engineering firm we had here in Grantville before the Ring of Fire. Which means, of course, that there are at least seven things we need him to be doing simultaneously . . . including training other engineers. At the moment, though, he's heading one of the teams working with Gustav's engineers on improving the Stecknitz canal, which means he's already on the river. But if we go ahead with this project, you're going to need someone like him to help you lay out your shipyard, at the very least, right?"

"It would certainly be an enormous help," Simpson agreed.

"In that case, I'll send him a radio message and tell him to meet you in Magdeburg. You can discuss the engineering aspects of this whole idea with him, and there are enough other projects going on in and around Magdeburg that Pete McDougal probably really needs access to one of our better engineers on an ongoing basis, anyway. And we can see about having him assigned as our official liaison to Gustav Adolf's engineering corps. God knows we're going to need someone assigned permanently to that slot in a teaching role, if nothing else, and that should also get his foot in the door with the Swedish officer corps in general."

Simpson pursed his lips, obviously considering the notion carefully, then nodded.

"That sounds like an excellent idea," he said, and his tone was approving, if not precisely warm. "And it certainly does kill multiple birds with a single rock. Of course, he's still going to be so busy with other jobs that they'll undoubtedly interfere badly with his ability to function purely as a military adviser. On the other hand, once we actually begin providing Gustav's troops with better weapons, we'll just have to find someone else to assist him. Someone you'll be able to spare from other responsibilities then even if you can't spare him now.

"In the meantime, I would certainly be willing to make what *I* know myself available. And I wasn't always an engineer during my naval service. Unlike Mr. Underwood, my own early experience was in the combat arms."

"That might . . . be very useful," Mike said slowly, with what he hoped was well hidden caution. He had a sudden vision of Simpson ingratiating himself with the most conservative and inherently dangerous elements of Gustav Adolf's army. Or, even worse, the CPE's more reluctant German princes.

Yet even as the thought crossed his mind, he told himself that it was foolish. Conservative—maybe even reactionary—Simpson undoubtedly was, but the most reactionary twenty-first-century American imaginable was hopelessly and radically liberal compared to someone like John George of Saxony.

Which didn't mean that Simpson wouldn't do his absolute level best to build his own little empire if he had even half a chance. In fact, it would be asinine to expect anything else out of him. Whatever Mike might think of him on a personal basis, no one was successful at the persistently high level of industrial performance Simpson had demonstrated without being extremely capable himself. And that capability, especially in a situation like the one the up-timers faced, would inevitably attract power like a magnet if Mike allowed him to exercise it.

If.

Ultimately, he reflected, that was what it came down to. If Mike allowed his worst political enemy to demonstrate that there was an area in which he was truly and provably competent, it could have incalculable consequences for the future. But Mike was still in the position of a man with no choice but to run even faster to prevent himself from falling.

Besides, if I let a man like Simpson beat me just because there's one area in which he's competent, then I'll deserve *whatever the hell happens to me!*

"We'll have to think about that," he continued after a moment. "About the best way to make use of your experience and knowledge, I mean. But in the meantime, what about Eddie's design?"

"I think it has . . . potential," Simpson replied,

accepting the return to the topic which had originally brought Mike there. "It's going to need a lot of work to make it practical, but assuming that the Allocations Committee is willing to commit the resources and we can come up with the manpower and the funding, I think we can probably build them. Of course, once we do, we'll have to come up with crews for them, as well."

"I know." Mike gazed at the other man for a few more seconds, then inhaled unobtrusively.

"If I sign off on it, the Allocations Committee will, too," he said confidently. "I don't say it will be easy, but I'll bring them around in the end. But if I do, would you be willing to take charge of it?"

"Not without conditions," Simpson said after a moment.

"What sort of conditions?" Mike felt himself slipping into the natural stance of a negotiator, and a small smile flickered around Simpson's mouth, as if he felt the same thing.

"If I build them, then I command them," he said flatly. "It's not going to be easy, however much support you can give me. I'd have to build a shipyard before I could start building ships in it, and part of the job would have to include training the local work force I'd need. The same holds true for building crews to man them, as well. It's going to take time and careful organization to make any of this work, and I'm not really in the habit of involving myself in projects that fail. I refuse to oversee the expenditure of so much of our resources just to let someone else screw up and misuse the final product when I'm done."

He showed his teeth in a brief, fierce grin.

"So I suppose that, in the end, it comes down to how much you trust me, 'Mr. President.' Do you need my expertise badly enough to piss off 'General Jackson' and risk putting *me* in command of your navy?"

Mike met that flash of a grin with an unsmiling, level look of his own, and several seconds of silence hovered in the Wendell kitchen. Then the President of the United States smiled ever so slightly himself.

"Actually, I think 'Admiral Simpson' has a certain ring to it," he said.

"I can't believe this," Eddie Cantrell muttered under his breath. "*Simpson?*" He shook his head.

"Don't even go there, Eddie," Mike growled softly, and Eddie flushed as he realized that he hadn't spoken quite as much under his breath as he thought he had.

"I had enough trouble with Frank and Quentin—not to mention Melissa!" Mike continued. "You wanted your damned ironclads, and you're probably going to get them, so I wouldn't go looking any gift horses in the teeth, if I were you."

Eddie grimaced at the reference to "gift horses" and glowered for a moment at the flesh-and-blood horse whose reins he held. In his considered opinion, horses were a very poor substitute for motorcycles, and his posterior wasn't looking forward to the journey to Magdeburg.

"Sorry," he said, after a moment. "And I meant it when I said I'd be willing to turn everything over to someone else if they knew how to get the job done. But I gotta tell you, Mike—I'm not too crazy about putting Simpson in command of anything, much less the Navy."

"If we're going to do this at all, then he's the best man for the job," Mike said, just a bit more positively than he actually felt. "On the other hand, I'd be lying if I didn't admit that I'm just as happy he'll have you along for this little trip."

Eddie cocked his head at Mike, then nodded slowly.

"Gotcha," he said. "I'll keep the bastard honest."

"That wasn't exactly what I meant," Mike said somewhat repressively, already wishing he hadn't said anything about it at all. "Look, Eddie, you don't like Simpson. Well, I don't like him very much, either. But don't ever make the mistake of thinking the man is stupid or incompetent in his own area. Or that we don't need him just as badly as we need Nat Davis or Greg Ferrara. You're going along to help him find the right spot for his shipyard. You are *not* going along as some sort of Gestapo agent. Is that understood?"

"Understood," Eddie replied contritely, and Mike shrugged.

"Sorry. Didn't mean to bite your head off. But this is important, and we don't need anyone creating still more problems to overcome. At the same time, if you happen to notice anything you feel ought to be called to our attention, I expect you to do it."

"Understood," Eddie repeated in a somewhat different tone, and Mike nodded. He started to say something else, then broke off as Simpson came trotting around the corner on his own horse.

It irritated Mike that Simpson had already known how to ride when they arrived in Thuringia. Worse, the man rode Western-style, so Mike couldn't even put it down to an effete, socially pretentious thing like polo.

The beautifully tailored three-piece business suits which had accompanied Simpson to Grantville for his son's wedding had long since disappeared. The older man wore boots, denims, a flannel shirt, and a light nylon windbreaker against the late-spring chill of Northern Germany, and Mike was still a little surprised by how much the change in clothing changed the man's image. The John Chandler Simpson trotting briskly along the street looked very little like the supercilious city slicker who'd come to Grantville so long ago. This man was tall and broad shouldered—as tall as his son, even if he didn't have Tom's sheer mass of muscle. Then again, *no one* in the seventeenth-century was as massively built as Tom was. Which meant that "not as massive" certainly wasn't the same thing as "ninety-eight-pound weakling," and little though Mike might have cared to admit it, there'd always been far more muscle and far less fat on Simpson's powerful frame than many another senior up-time executive might have claimed. The recently past winter had wiped away most of the fat which had been there, too.

"Gentlemen," Simpson acknowledged them in brusque, no-nonsense tones as he reined in his mount beside them.

"Mr. Simpson," Mike replied. Eddie only nodded, but he clambered up into his own saddle. Not, Mike observed, with any particular grace. Eddie had learned to ride since the Ring of Fire, but only in the sense that he no longer fell off the horse whenever it stopped. At that, he was doing better than his friend

Jeff, but it was all Mike could do to keep himself from breaking out into laughter at Eddie's expression as he contemplated the long ride to Magdeburg.

At least the youngster would be spared the indescribable motion of a coach trip over seventeenth-century roads, and that was nothing to sneeze at. The main road to Magdeburg was slated for improvement as an urgent priority, but it was going to be a while before it could be accomplished.

"Don't forget to check in with the radio shack when you get there," Mike admonished, and Simpson nodded. Grantville's limited number of radio hams were busy training more operators and planning the construction of simple crystal sets to eke out and support the handful of modern radios which had accompanied them back to Thuringia. It was going to be a while before there were enough of them for more than purely limited use, but installing one of them at the new imperial capital had been a high priority.

"I guess that's about it, then," Mike continued. "We'll be waiting to hear from you."

Simpson gave him another not-quite-curt nod, touched his heels to his horse, and started off without another word. Eddie looked at Mike one more time, then shrugged and headed off—far less gracefully—in Simpson's wake.

By the time they reached Magdeburg, a few days later, Eddie had developed a new, even stronger, first-hand appreciation of the advantages of water transport in the seventeenth century. He would vastly have preferred to make the shorter trip overland to Halle and then travel down the river to Magdeburg, but there'd been a few unpleasant incidents along the river. Everyone agreed that they *thought* it was only isolated bands of brigands—probably mercenaries who were currently unemployed because Gustav Adolf had destroyed the armies to which they had once been attached—who'd turned to a little freelance river piracy to survive the winter. That was the official story, anyway. Personally, Eddie was none too certain that it wasn't a bit more organized than that. There were certainly enough German nobles who hated and feared the up-timer Americans' impact, starting with John George of Saxony, himself. It wouldn't surprise Eddie a bit to discover that one or more of them had been turning a blind eye to attacks on said Americans' barge traffic.

The situation was improving, in large part because Gustav had begun operating patrols of Finnish and Lapp cavalry—whose fearsome reputations were well deserved—along the more dangerous sections of the river. But for the moment, President Stearns and his cabinet had preferred to send their two-man shipbuilding force to Magdeburg by a more arduous but less adventurous route.

And "arduous" it had certainly been. Every muscle Eddie had seemed to ache with its own individual protest, but that background chorus was nothing to the throbbing ache in his thighs and buttocks. The inns at which they had spent their nights had been an experience of eye-opening unpleasantness in their own right, and he was uncomfortably certain that he had acquired all too many multi-legged insectoid boarders.

But at least they were finally here . . . not that "here"

was all that impressive. Magdeburg had been a largish city by here-and-now standards before Count Tilly's troops had massacred the population and burned the place to the ground in the worst single atrocity yet of the ongoing Thirty Years War. The nightmare event had rallied opposition to Tilly and the Imperialists from all over Protestant Germany and provided Gustav Adolf's army with one of the most chilling war cries of the entire war: "Magdeburg quarter"—the promise to be just as merciful to Tilly's men as they had been to the citizens of Magdeburg.

But Magdeburg's history, as well as its central location and its access to the Elbe River, had made it the inevitable choice as the capital of Gustav's new Confederated Principalities of Europe. The heaps of charred rubble surrounding the cathedral—one of the few structures in the entire city which had been spared the torch—had largely disappeared now, and reconstruction was well underway. The sheer devastation of the old city had given Gustav's architects the opportunity to design a proper capital, with a coordinated street plan of long, straight avenues and spacious squares, and the skeleton of the new city to be was plainly evident. But so was the sprawl of temporary quarters, thrown up in haste and without any apparent plan or order, for the work force laboring upon the new buildings and streets. And it seemed evident to Eddie as he gazed out over the site that the area outside the old city walls, where the foundations of the new factories and warehouses were going in, had not profited from the same degree of city planning.

"Quite a mess, isn't it?" Simpson remarked.

Eddie looked at him. The lengthy, arduous trip had

forced him to alter his opinion of Simpson . . . some. They hadn't exactly whiled away the journey in deep, philosophical discussion. In fact, they hadn't spoken to one another any more than they had to. But despite himself, Eddie had been impressed by how little Simpson had complained. Of course, Eddie thought resentfully, Simpson's posterior probably didn't ache quite as much as his own did. At the same time, however, Simpson was at least thirty years older than he was, and even though there had to be plenty of room for aches and pains in those extra decades, Simpson showed absolutely no sign of them.

Yet what had truly surprised Eddie was the calm, almost matter of fact way Simpson had accepted the primitive nature of both their transportation and their accommodations along the way. He'd expected the ex-CEO to demand the very best, and to throw temper tantrums if he didn't get it. But it hadn't worked out that way.

Simpson had displayed an amazing talent for hard, shrewd bargaining over the cost of their rooms every night—almost as if the money were coming out of his own pocket, rather than out of the funds the U.S. government had provided for the trip. And it had been obvious that he wasn't prepared to be fobbed off with anything less than the best the inns had been able to provide. Yet that "best" had fallen dismally short of anything he would have tolerated for a heartbeat "back home," and he hadn't said a word. In fact, he'd accepted the limitations of their accommodations far more patiently than Eddie had, and he'd actually tipped the staffs when they left.

Eddie wasn't quite sure what to make of that, but

it had at least cracked the armor of his preconceptions where Simpson was concerned. Not that he was prepared to surrender his distrust just yet. Simpson was still the arrogant bastard who'd tried to waltz into Grantville and take over the entire town. And he was still the slimeball politician who'd thrown in with the bigoted rednecks who'd opposed extending the vote to anyone who hadn't been born up-time. Which meant, by definition, that he was The Enemy.

None of which affected the fact that his observations summed up Eddie's own impression of Magdeburg quite handily.

"Calling this a mess is an insult to any other mess," he said, after a moment, and Simpson surprised him yet again with a dry chuckle.

"Oh, I've seen worse. Not very often, mind you, but I've seen worse. And given what they had to start with, I'm actually surprised they've done this well with it so quickly."

Eddie glanced at him speculatively. He'd been more prepared for Simpson to make some cutting remark about primitive construction techniques and lousy seventeenth-century architects. Instead, the older man's tone was merely thoughtful. Indeed, it might actually have been approving, mind-boggling though that possibility seemed to Eddie.

"Well," Simpson continued after a moment, "I suppose we should check in with the local authorities and get off a radio message that we've arrived. This way, I think, Mr. Cantrell."

He urged his mount into motion, and Eddie found himself—once again—following the rear end of John Chandler Simpson's horse.

◁◈▷   ◁◈▷   ◁◈▷

The streets of Magdeburg, such as they were, were a hive of activity. In fact, they were so busy that Eddie quickly decided to swallow his pride, dismount, and lead his horse. The journey from Grantville had been long enough for even his horsemanship to improve appreciably, but he knew his limits, and the first time one of the clattering, wooden-wheeled carts came rumbling unexpectedly out of a cross street, he knew he'd reached them. He managed to survive his horse's rearing protest at the sudden, frightening intrusion, but it was a very near thing, and he scrambled out of the saddle with far more haste than grace.

Simpson, on the other hand, simply sat there in the saddle, gazing at him with one quirked eyebrow. *His* horse, needless to say, scarcely even tossed its head. Eddie would have loved to put its calmness down to its innately placid disposition, but he knew it had far more to do with the hand upon the reins and the rider in the saddle.

Simpson waited until he was certain Eddie had the reins firmly in hand, then clucked gently to his mount and led the way through the bustling confusion of workmen, carts, freight wagons, occasional squads of Swedish soldiers, and street vendors. Eddie followed, glowering at the older man's ramrod-straight spine and feeling like a total doofus.

Stretches of the burned city's original cobblestones were interspersed with and crossed by muddy tracks—usually more puddle than mud, actually—and Eddie was grateful that he'd worn boots instead of sneakers. Nikes weren't exactly the footwear of choice when it came to wading through ankle-deep holes full of water and gooey mud.

Eddie hadn't seen so many people in one place, outside Grantville itself, since arriving in the seventeenth century. And the activity around him very nearly approached the frantic industry with which Grantville had expanded its housing to face the demands of the winter just past. The smell of smoke, the clatter of tools, the bellows of foremen, and the incredible smells of too many people crowded into too little space.

The smell bothered Eddie even more because it was so different from what he'd become accustomed to. He'd discovered, to his surprise, that seventeenth-century German notions of public sanitation were far better than he'd expected from his limited knowledge of history. Melissa Mailey had explained to him that was because he assumed that *British* history was synonymous with "history." It was in fact true that, as a rule, public sanitation in seventeenth-century Britain was just as bad as Eddie assumed—Edinburgh was especially notorious all over Europe for its filth, with London not too far behind. But most German towns had a long-established system of cleaning up public refuse, including human waste, with a class of people employed exclusively for that purpose. It was a system which Americans despised, since it involved relegating the caste of waste-haulers to pariah social status, almost like the caste system in Hindu India. Still, it normally served to keep the worst aspects of public refuse to a reasonable level.

The problem was that Magdeburg was, for all practical purposes, a brand new city. And one which, he suspected, had already been sufficiently "infected" with American social and political notions for the standard system of public sanitation to be functioning haphazardly at best. Not for the first time since the Ring of Fire, Eddie was discovering that social change, in the betwixt-and-between period, often had as many drawbacks as it did advantages.

So, he was more than merely grateful when Simpson finally drew up outside the hastily thrown together walls of a building two blocks from Magdeburg's temporary town hall.

Half a dozen Swedish musketeers stood guard outside the American "embassy's" entrance, accompanied by a single American in deer hunter's cammies and armed with a semi-auto Browning shotgun. The difference between the sleek, up-time weapon and the clumsy Swedish matchlocks was almost as marked as the difference between the Swedes' cold-eyed alertness and the American's obvious casualness.

Simpson dismounted slowly and handed his reins to the groom who came trotting around a corner of the hastily assembled structure to take them. The same groom collected Eddie's horse, as well, and Eddie was delighted to let him have it. Indeed, he hoped he'd never see the sharp-spined nag again.

But Simpson paid very little attention to the groom. He'd paused long enough to remove his saddlebags before he let the man take his horse, yet his attitude was very different from one he'd demonstrated when he and Eddie had stopped at one of the inns along the way. Then, he'd taken considerable pains to be certain that his mount would be properly cared for; this time his attention was fully focused on the sentries in front of the building.

No, Eddie realized. Not on all the sentries—only on Matt Lowry, the American.

Simpson's frown was not a pleasant thing to see. He looked, Eddie thought, like a man who'd gotten a sudden whiff of a three-day-dead skunk, and his own resentment rose in automatic reflex. Obviously, the rich bigshot from Pittsburgh could hardly contain his contempt for the hillbilly in front of him. Probably because Matt hadn't kowtowed properly in the face of Simpson's innate superiority!

Eddie waited for Simpson to say something, but the older man only pressed his lips firmly together and nodded to the trooper who was obviously the senior member of the Swedish guards. Then he slung his saddlebags over his shoulder and strode into the building.

"You're here to do what?" Pete McDougal asked.

Before the Ring of Fire, Pete had headed up the safety committee for the same United Mine Workers local union of which Mike Stearns had been president. Now he was Mike Stearns' personal representative in Magdeburg, at least until the rebuilding capital was ready for a larger American presence. Whether he was there as an ambassador to the CPE or to serve the interests of "Captain General Gars" was an interesting point, but McDougal had the natural diplomacy required to discharge both functions at once.

At the moment, however, that diplomacy appeared to be in abeyance.

"I thought my written authorization was clear enough," Simpson replied coolly.

"Well, I guess it is," McDougal admitted. He looked

at Simpson with obvious dislike, but his tone was reasonably courteous. "It just sort of took me by surprise. Nobody warned me you were coming."

"Somehow, I'm not surprised," Simpson said dryly. "Should I assume that that also means that Mr. Haygood has not yet arrived, either?"

"No, you shouldn't. As a matter-of-fact, Jere got here yesterday evening, but there was obviously some kind of screwup. He got the message to head on over, but no one told him exactly why he was supposed to do it." McDougal shrugged. "One of the problems with radio messages when you don't get to talk directly to the person who sent them to you."

"That sort of confusion is something we'd better get over," Simpson observed. "But at least he's here. And I trust that you'll be able to render us the assistance President Stearns assured me we'd receive despite the confusion?"

"I'll try," McDougal said. "But if Mike had warned me you were coming, I would've told him we're way too shorthanded already. I don't know who I've got available to assign as a local guide. Jere doesn't know Magdeburg any better than you do."

"What about Matt Lowry?" Eddie asked. He knew he should have kept his mouth shut, but the look Simpson had given Lowry had really rubbed him the wrong way. The notion of getting Matt assigned as Simpson's guide as a way to rub the old-so-superior bastard's nose in his dependence upon the hillbillies who surrounded him appealed strongly to the teenager.

"Can't spare him," McDougal replied promptly. "Frank—I mean, General Jackson," he corrected himself, glancing at Simpson from the corner of his eye

"—made it standing orders that we have to have at least one up-timer on guard here all the time. And Matt's picked up more Swedish than almost anyone else I've got."

"That's a wise precaution on General Jackson's part," Simpson said, and Eddie saw the surprise on McDougal's face. But then Simpson continued in a coldly dispassionate voice. "I can understand why his ability to pick up the local language would make this Mr. Lowry particularly valuable. It's a pity, however, that the language appears to be the *only* thing he's picked up from the Swedes."

"Meaning what?" McDougal demanded, his expression tightening with anger as Simpson's tone registered.

"Meaning that the Swedish troopers outside your front door are at least five times as alert as he is," Simpson said flatly. "It's pathetic. He's got twice the firepower of everyone else out there, and if it weren't for the Swedes looking out for him, anyone who wanted to would walk right past him. Or worse."

"Now just a minute!" McDougal said hotly. "Matt's been assigned here for over three months, and nobody's ever come close to getting past him! And unlike certain people," he very carefully did not glare pointedly at Simpson, "he was with the Army at the Alte Veste and the Wartburg. Did damned well there, too."

"He probably did," Simpson conceded, apparently completely oblivious to McDougal's dig at his own absence from both those battles. "And I don't believe I expressed any doubts about his courage or his willingness to fight. But there's a difference between guts and willingness and *discipline*, and discipline is what keeps a man on something as boring as sentry duty alert, effective . . . and *alive*. The Swedes have it; he doesn't."

He held McDougal' eyes levelly, and to Eddie's astonishment, it was Pete who looked away.

"Well, anyway, I can't spare him," McDougal muttered. Then he shook himself. "I'll have to see if I can find you a local. How good is your German?"

"Passable," Simpson replied, "but Mr. Cantrell's is better than mine." The calmly delivered compliment—if that was what it was—took Eddie by surprise, but McDougal only nodded.

"In that case, I think I can probably find someone. It may take a while, though. Do you have someplace to stay while you're here?"

"No."

"I imagine I can find you a room, then. We're still working on the living quarters of our 'embassy' here. I'm sure we'll get the whole thing finished up . . . eventually. But in the meantime, there's a sort of a boarding house for up-timers and some of the more senior Swedish and Scottish officers. It's more like a barracks, really, but it's only a couple of blocks east of here. We can put you up there."

"That will be fine, given the state of the local construction efforts," Simpson told him. "I suppose Mr. Cantrell and I should head on over and get ourselves settled in while you find us our guide. Will you go ahead and radio Grantville to confirm our arrival?"

"I'll take care of it," McDougal said.

"Thank you. In that case, I'll be looking forward to meeting Mr. Haygood and our guide." He nodded to McDougal, then glanced at Eddie.

"Come along, Mr. Cantrell," he said.

❖❖❖   ❖❖❖   ❖❖❖

As a citizen of the seventeenth-century United States, Eddie had become far more accustomed to walking than he'd ever been as a twenty-first-century American. Which turned out to be a good thing as he tagged along behind an obviously indefatigable Simpson, Jere Haygood, and their local guide, Dietrich Schwanhausser.

Haygood was a weathered-looking man in his mid-forties, with light brown-colored hair and hazel eyes. He wore work clothes and high-topped, laced boots which had undoubtedly been comfortably worn long before the Ring of Fire, and an old Army Single-Action Colt revolver rode in a black ballistic nylon holster at his belt. He was built on the lean and rangy model, and he moved with a quick, boundless energy that made Eddie tired just watching him. Simpson, of course, simply took it all in stride.

Eddie didn't know Haygood well—they'd never actually met before the Ring of Fire—but it had been obvious from the beginning that the engineer wasn't a Simpson admirer. He'd been civil enough, but that had been about all anyone could have said for his attitude.

Schwanhausser, on the other hand, had been another matter entirely. He hadn't lived in Magdeburg before its destruction, but most of his relatives had, and he'd lost them all. Apparently, that was part of what had drawn him to the reemerging city as it arose like a dusty, smoky, chaotic phoenix from its own ashes. The fact that he spoke more than passable Swedish and was already acquiring at least a smattering of English had made him extremely valuable to the new capital's local authorities, but McDougal had lured him away from them. Exactly how he'd done so remained something of a mystery to Eddie, but the two computers McDougal had been assigned from Grantville's precious supply of desktops seemed to have had something to do with it.

Whatever the reason for it, Schwanhausser had become one of McDougal's primary liaisons with the city government, and his familiarity with the endless construction projects which typified Magdeburg had proven most useful. The fact that he and Simpson got along like a house on fire (not, Eddie admitted to himself, perhaps the best chosen metaphor, here in the ashes of Magdeburg) didn't seem to be hurting things, either.

Eddie felt more like a half-forgotten appendage than ever as he followed the other three about. Simpson's German was considerably better than his comments to McDougal had suggested. It wasn't as colloquial as the German Eddie had been soaking up through his pores ever since he'd arrived here, and there were times when it sounded more than a little stiff, even odd, to a seventeenth-century ear . . . or to a twenty-first-century ear which had learned the language in the seventeenth, but it was quite adequate for his needs.

So was Haygood's. The engineer had started out following Simpson around with a somewhat martyred expression. Obviously, his most earnest desire had been to be somewhere else, doing something *useful*. But as the tour of possible shipyard sites continued, Haygood had become increasingly animated. Apparently, the engineer in him was sufficiently fascinated by the task at hand to at least temporarily overcome his antipathy for Simpson. By the time late morning had turned into midafternoon, he was waxing positively enthusiastic over the possibilities.

Eddie was more than a little surprised by that. And, if he was going to be honest, he was also a little disappointed. Not that he wanted the ironclad project to do anything but succeed, of course. It just . . . irritated him to see a good Stearns loyalist hobnobbing with John Chandler Simpson so energetically.

But if Haygood's reaction irritated Eddie, the way Schwanhausser seemed to respond to the industrialist bothered him on a much more profound level. It was as if there were some almost organic relationship between the two of them. One Eddie could sense but not really understand. Something which had automatically located them in relationship to one another in some sort of hierarchy or continuum Eddie hadn't even realized existed.

He decided he didn't like whatever it was. Part of that probably stemmed from his ingrained distrust of anything Simpson did and, especially, his suspicion of Simpson's empire-building tendencies, which made him uncomfortable with the easy authority the older man seemed to possess in Schwanhausser's eyes. But even more than that, he suspected, it was because he'd already seen quite a few seventeenth-century Germans who seemed to find the role of bootlicker a natural fit.

That was the one thing Eddie most hated when he encountered it. He supposed it would have been foolish to expect every German in the seventeenth century to be another Gretchen Richter, or even her brother Hans. And by and large, the majority of the

German citizens of the United States had done a remarkable job of adapting to the incredibly radical—by seventeenth-century standards—ideology and political freedoms the up-timers had brought with them. In fact, the way some of them—like Gretchen—had seized the twenty-first-century concepts and run with them sometimes frightened even Eddie just a bit.

But not all of them had adapted. Some of them had good (by their standards) and obvious reasons for disliking the bottom-to-top changes the up-time Americans had inflicted upon them. Those were the people who'd held positions of power and authority under the old order and found the notion of being held accountable by the subjects over whom they had previously ruled but who had now become their fellow citizens most distasteful. Yet some of those same former subjects seemed almost equally lost and unhappy. Perhaps it was because they feared the changes were only temporary—that the United States' enemies would succeed in destroying it after all. If that happened, there would undoubtedly be reprisals against those who had supported the new order when the old one returned to power. And in some cases, it was probably as simple as plain old uncertainty. A case of having learned the old rules of the society which was being remade all about them so well that they felt uncomfortable, even frightened by the ambiguities with which the new rules confronted them.

Whatever it was, Eddie didn't like it when he encountered it, and he'd seen a lot more of it since leaving Grantville. Maybe it was only natural for the people in the small towns and villages who so far had had little direct, personal contact with the up-timers to be less certain, more hesitant. He hoped that was all it was—that as the United States continued to expand outward from Grantville, its spreading influence would erode that hesitation and replace it with the same sort of often fractious independence he'd seen in Grantville itself.

But it hadn't yet, and one of the results was that sometimes an up-timer, even someone who still (in the privacy of his own mind) thought of himself as only a kid, found himself being deferred to and kowtowed to as if he were a natural born aristocrat. No doubt some of them enjoyed that, but it made Eddie's skin crawl when it happened to him.

Of course, he thought sourly, watching Schwanhausser and Haygood listening intently to Simpson, someone like Simpson probably ate it up with a spoon.

" . . . need deep water close to the bank," Simpson said as he and the other two stood side-by-side in ankle-deep mud, staring out over an Elbe River that was still high, wide, and murky with the spring floods. The up-timer gestured energetically at the water. "When we send them down the launch ways, they're going to have a tendency to drive downward into the mud if there's not enough depth of water."

"How many feet deep, Herr Simpson?" Schwanhausser asked. Simpson looked momentarily taken aback, but Schwanhausser smiled. "I have been learning your system of measurement," he reassured the American.

"You have?" Simpson looked down at the shorter German.

"Oh, of course!" Schwanhausser chuckled. "Many of our 'honest merchants' are screaming to the very heavens over the thought of adopting a truly universal standard set of measures, but the Emperor has made it quite clear that the entire Confederated Principalities *will* adopt your system. And it will be such a relief to deal in feet and yards which are the same from one end of the land to the other, instead of dealing with 'paces' which may be one length in Saxony and another in, say, Westphalia!"

"You can say that again!" Haygood snorted. "And what it's going to mean for engineering projects is even more important. For one thing, we're going to make damned sure that when we get around to building our railroads, 'standard gauge' means just that—*standard* gauge." He grimaced. "None of that business of every outfit building its own private set of rails to whatever gauge suited it."

Simpson glanced at the engineer and nodded.

"I actually hadn't considered that aspect of the rail extension project, Mr. Haygood. Of course, I'm sure that's only one small instance of ways in which true standardized units of measure are going to provide immense benefits. Although—" he turned to Schwanhausser "—I suppose I can see why some of your merchants might not find the prospect particularly delightful, even if that is incredibly shortsighted of them in the long term. But as far as our problem goes here, I can't really give you a definite answer until I know more about the design displacements of the ships themselves. Let's say that I'm probably going to need somewhere around twelve feet minimum depth."

"Um." Schwanhausser plucked gently at his lower lip in thought. "We should be able to find you that much water, Herr Simpson. But to get it, you may have to extend your . . . launching ways further out from the bank."

"Mr. Haygood?" Simpson asked, cocking an eyebrow at the engineer.

"That we can do," Haygood assured him.

"Well, in that case," Schwanhausser said, "I think this area here might meet your requirements. As far as I know, all of this stretch of the river—from there, at the corner of that factory's lot, clear down to that small point in the angle of the bend—is still available. That would give you a frontage on the river of—what? Perhaps two hundred of your yards?"

"More like two hundred and fifty," Simpson mused.

"Actually," Haygood said, casting his engineer's eye over the same distance, "it's probably about two hundred and seventy-five. Closer to three hundred than to two hundred, anyway."

"I will defer to your judgment," Schwanhausser said, then laughed. "I did say I was *learning* your units of measurement, not that I have already mastered them!"

Simpson chuckled slightly and turned his back to the river while he studied the terrain for several minutes. They were well outside the old walls of Magdeburg. In fact, they were beyond even the area already being developed for the new factories.

"I could really use even more frontage than that, actually," he said.

"We're only building three ships," Eddie pointed out. He tried very hard to avoid sounding like he was nitpicking, but from the expressionless glance

Simpson gave him he suspected that he hadn't completely succeeded.

"No, Mr. Cantrell," the older man said after a moment. "If, in fact, I agree to accept the responsibility for building your ironclads, they will most assuredly not be the only ships built here. At the very least, we'll be building additional tugs and barges. More importantly, don't you think it would be a good idea to provide a little something in the way of support for your battleships? In one sense, after all, it doesn't matter how powerful and well armored we make them, does it? If there are only three of them, then they can only be in three places at once, and I can assure you that we'll need to cover more than three places at a time sooner than you may expect."

"Well, yeah," Eddie said. "But right *now*, all we're authorized to build is the ironclads."

"Actually," Simpson said in a voice whose patient tone surprised Eddie, "we aren't authorized to build *anything* at this particular moment. All we have is President Stearns'—" he managed to use Mike's title without so much as a hint of sarcasm, Eddie noticed, and wondered if that was because of Haygood's and Schwanhausser's presence "—assurance that if he decides to support the project he'll succeed in obtaining authorization for it."

He smiled very slightly at Eddie's expression.

"Don't get excited, Mr. Cantrell. The President and I may not see eye to eye on a great many issues, but I don't doubt for a moment that if he decides to push the ironclads through, he'll succeed. In fact, I expect him to. And I also expect him to support my proposal to construct a fleet of timberclads to back them up."

"Timberclads?" Eddie could almost feel his ears perk up, and Haygood looked interested, as well.

"Precisely." Simpson nodded. "Timberclads should be survivable against seventeenth-century artillery. After all, they stood up reasonably well against nineteenth-century field artillery at the beginning of the Civil War, didn't they?"

"Yeah," Eddie admitted. "Of course," he added in a more challenging tone, "they retired the timberclads as soon as they could, didn't they?"

"Actually, they continued to use them throughout the war," Simpson disagreed. "Once they'd developed the capability—and had the time—to build better designed, more heavily armored vessels, they did build all of them they could. But the existing timberclads continued to serve in supporting roles until the very end of the war. And our problem, Mr. Cantrell, is that we're going to begin with the ability to build a very limited number of heavily armored units—by seventeenth-century standards, at least—but we're not going to be able to develop the infrastructure to build any *more* of them for quite some time. 'Building down,' I believe the President calls it, and rightly so. Which means that in order to project force as broadly as we're going to need to project it, we're going to have to accept the units we can actually build to do it with." He shrugged. "Timberclads should just about fill the bill."

"He's got a point, Eddie," Haygood put in. "A pretty good one, in fact. Timberclads may not be as good as 'proper' ironclads, but they'll kick the ass of any seventeenth-century 'warship' they run into. At least on a one-to-one basis."

Eddie turned the thought over in his brain, pondering it from several angles. And then, after a moment, he felt himself beginning to nod.

"You're right," he said. "I guess maybe I did get a bit too fixated on building the *Benton* or the *Tennessee*," he admitted in a chastened tone. "It's not like we're going to have to run the batteries at Vicksburg or anything anytime soon, is it?"

"Probably not," Simpson agreed. "Not, at least, in terms of facing concentrations of true heavy artillery. But don't look so downhearted, Mr. Cantrell. Timberclads should serve adequately in many instances, but there *will* be cases where properly designed, well-armored ships with heavy artillery are required, as well. In fact, the timberclads' actual function will probably be to carry out routine patrols and shipping protection. When it comes to an actual standup fight with a properly emplaced battery or fort, their job will be to back the ironclads up rather than get into the thick of it themselves."

He sounded almost as if he were genuinely trying to cheer Eddie up, although the teenager found the possibility unlikely.

"In the meantime, Dietrich," the older man continued, turning back to their guide, "I believe you're probably right about the basic suitability of the site. I'd like to get a little more of the river bank, if we can, and I'm going to need enough area running back away from the river for the yard facilities themselves and for barracks and a drill field, as well."

"And eventually, at least, we're going to want

someplace to put a decent drydock," Haygood put in, as enthusiastically as if the idea of a naval shipyard had been his own brainchild from the beginning, and Simpson nodded without looking away from Schwanhausser.

"That is probably possible, Herr Simpson," the German said thoughtfully. "It may be expensive," he warned.

"I suspect that if Gustav Adolf asks them politely, whoever owns it will be willing to be reasonable," Simpson said dryly, and Schwanhausser chuckled.

"I imagine they might," he agreed.

"Good." Simpson glanced up at the sun, and then down at his watch. It was an expensive electric job which, unlike most of the battery-powered watches in Grantville, continued to tick smoothly along. At first, Eddie had wondered if Simpson were buying additional batteries on the black market, but he'd been forced to give up that cherished suspicion when he realized that it was one of the kinetic-powered ones which used the wearer's motion to recharge its built in capacitor. Which meant, of course, that John Chandler Simpson possessed a modern watch which might run for decades yet.

Not that anyone needed a watch to guess what was on his mind just now, Eddie thought. The sun was settling steadily lower in the west in a funeral pyre of red and gold cloud.

"I suppose we should be getting back to our quarters," Simpson remarked, then grimaced. "I don't imagine the street lights are going to be very bright around here after dark."

"No," Schwanhausser agreed, and glanced back

and forth between the three up-timers. "In fact," he continued after a moment in a diffident tone, "the truth is that it isn't always safe for Americans to move about after dark."

"It isn't?" Simpson asked, and the German shook his head. The up-timer glanced at Haygood, but from the engineer's expression he didn't know any more about the local situation than Simpson and Eddie did, and the ex-industrialist looked back at Schwanhausser. "Is that simply because the local criminal element finds the lack of lighting . . . congenial to its efforts?" he asked. "Or is there some specific reason why *Americans* in particular should be on their guard?"

"It—" Schwanhausser began, then paused.

"Much of it probably is no more than desperation, darkness, and opportunity, Herr Simpson," he continued after a moment. "Even with all of the construction jobs here in the city, some remain who have no means of support. Some of those who lack work do, however, have families. We have enough criminals even without those circumstances, of course, but it has been much worse than usual this past winter. Armies, battles, and devastation do not contribute to social tranquility, after all.

"On the other hand, that situation seems to be improving now that spring is here and the pace of construction has picked up still further. But I fear that there is another danger, one I have not yet been able to convince Herr McDougal to take sufficiently seriously."

"Which is?" Simpson asked.

"*Richelieu,*" Schwanhausser half-snarled, and his head swiveled as if he were peering about for assassins. "Do not, whatever you do, underestimate that Frenchman, Herr Simpson! You and the other Americans are the greatest threat he faces, and he knows it well. Did he not attempt to murder your very children because he knew it?"

Simpson nodded slowly, and Eddie felt a chill which owed very little to the approach of night run down his spine.

"Well, then," Schwanhausser said, returning Simpson's nod. "Be warned. There are rumors of assassins and prices on American heads. No doubt such rumors would abound, whatever the truth behind them, of course. That is Herr McDougal's opinion, at least, and there is probably some reason in it. Yet I do not think that they are *only* rumors this time."

"That it," Bill Franklin announced, tipping back in his chair in front of the radio.

"Thank you," Simpson said. He was standing behind Franklin, unable to see his expression, but Eddie saw the radio operator roll his eyes. None of McDougal's staff liked the industrialist one bit. Of course, all of them were Stearns loyalists, and most of them had been solid union members before the Ring of Fire, which created two perfectly good reasons for their attitude right there. Simpson couldn't have been unaware of it, but he certainly didn't act as if he were, and Eddie wondered whether that was out of a sense of towering superiority which refused to acknowledge the slings and arrows of his social inferiors. That was what he'd written it down as at first, but he was beginning to question his initial assumptions. He didn't much care for that, because he liked things nice and clear, and he preferred for the people about him to remain if not predictable, at least consistent. The thought that there might be rather more to John Chandler Simpson than he'd assumed was particularly unpalatable, especially given the unmitigated jerk Simpson had shown himself to be during the immediate aftermath of their arrival in Thuringia.

Eddie wasn't entirely certain why he found the idea so distasteful. Well, he knew part of the reason—he didn't like Simpson, and he hated the very thought of finding something about the man to respect. The ingrained suspicion and hostility which were part of Eddie's self-identification as one of Mike Stearns' men undoubtedly played their parts, as well, he admitted frankly, yet he suspected that there was more to it even than that.

Maybe what it really came down to was that he'd never before encountered the combination in a single person of truly superior abilities with the capacity to make truly enormous mistakes. Intellectually, Eddie knew it was entirely possible for something like that to happen, but he'd never personally experienced it, and it was an affront to his teenager's sense of absolute right and absolute wrong. Worse, it made him wonder if *he* might be equally capable of screwing the pooch. Not a pleasant possibility at all, that!

"Will the commo link be manned all night?" Simpson asked after a moment.

"Well, yeah," Franklin replied. "'Course there's not much chance Mike—I mean, the President—is gonna be seeing this before sometime tomorrow morning." His voice was somewhat elaborately patient, although no one could quite have called it overtly discourteous.

"I didn't expect that he would," Simpson said calmly. "I was asking for future information, Mr. Franklin. If this project goes forward, I'll need twenty-four-hour communications capability, and I was simply wondering if it already existed."

"Oh." Franklin had the grace to blush slightly, but he didn't go overboard about it. "Yeah," he said in a much closer to normal tone, "we've got round-the-clock coverage. It's not like being able to pick up your cell phone, but we can usually get the message through without too much delay."

"Excellent," Simpson said, and nodded to him. "Come along, Mr. Cantrell," he said then, and stepped out of the radio room and headed back up the short hall towards McDougal's office.

He was finally showing at least some signs of fatigue, Eddie noticed, although they were still minor enough most people wouldn't have noticed at all. Nothing more than a slight limp on the right side—something even Eddie wouldn't have noted if he hadn't been following Simpson, Haygood, and Schwanhausser around all day.

"What do you think about the possibilities?" he asked as he followed the older man down the hall. He hadn't seen the four-page, handwritten draft of the message Franklin had just transmitted back to Grantville for Simpson.

"I think . . . I think it's possible, Mr. Cantrell," Simpson replied after only the briefest pause, then stopped just outside McDougal's office and turned to face Eddie.

"I don't say that I think it will be *easy*, you understand," he continued. "But assuming that the

President is as successful as usual in prying the necessary resources out of the Allocations Committee, and assuming that Gustav Adolf supports this as enthusiastically as I certainly expect him to and that Mr. Haygood's services are made available to us, initially at least, then I believe it should be entirely possible to set up our navy yard here in Magdeburg. Shipping all of the materials we'll need from Grantville will be a royal pain in the ass, of course, but I don't see how we could realistically expect to be able to build and launch them very much up-river from here. And the river itself is going to require quite a bit of improvement before we can move them freely, even operating from here instead of Halle."

"But you think the idea itself is really practical?" Eddie asked.

"Yes, Mr. Cantrell, I do," Simpson told him with a slight smile which, for some reason, made Eddie feel unexpectedly good. "Mind you, I can see quite a few aspects of your initial proposal which are going to require some . . . refinement, shall we say? But overall, I believe that it's not only a practical idea, but a good one."

"Does that mean you're gonna take the job?" Eddie demanded with an edge of lingering suspicion.

"Let's just say," Simpson said, "that my participation in the project is something of a prerequisite if it's going to succeed." He smiled again, ever so thinly, as Eddie stiffened. "Of course it is, Mr. Cantrell," he chided. "Or were you under the misapprehension that there was anyone else in Grantville who'd have even a clue as to how to make this work?"

It was truly remarkable, Eddie reflected as the ex-industrialist resumed his progress towards McDougal's office, how easily Simpson could go from making him feel obscurely pleased to absolutely infuriated with only two simple sentences.

Nor was Simpson finished infuriating people for the evening, either, the teenager discovered a few moments later.

McDougal looked up with something less than total enthusiasm as Simpson led Eddie back into his office.

"Is there something else I can do for you?" he asked.

"Actually, there is," Simpson told him, seating himself in one of the chairs facing McDougal's desk. Eddie started to sit in the other chair, then stopped. Sitting beside Simpson might seem to be ranging himself with the outsider against McDougal, so he chose to stand, leaning against the wall, instead.

"Oh?" McDougal sat back in his chair, his expression wary as Simpson's tone registered.

"I wanted to ask you about something Mr. Schwanhausser mentioned to me earlier this evening," Simpson said. "He advised us to be cautious about our movements."

"Not that again!" McDougal sighed, then shook his head wearily. "Was Dietrich bending your ear about Richelieu again?" he asked.

"As a matter of fact, he was."

"Well, he's just a little bit loony on the topic," McDougal said. He shrugged. "I guess it's not too surprising, really. He did lose most of his family when Tilly burned Magdeburg. A lot of the locals got pretty paranoid after that happened. Now they see murderers and assassins hiding in every alley, and of course the only person who could be sending them is Richelieu."

"So you don't think there's anything to his fears?"

"That Richelieu is sending assassins to Magdeburg? No, I don't think there's anything to that. And if he were sending them here at all, he'd be sending them after Gustav Adolf, not us. Which doesn't mean that there isn't enough 'street crime' here in Magdeburg to make it smart to stay alert."

"Have any of our people—up-timers, I mean—been attacked?"

"Jim Ennis got knifed about a week ago. Hurt pretty bad, in fact, though it looks like he's going to recover fully," McDougal said. Simpson looked at him sharply, and McDougal shrugged again. "Lucky for him, one of the Swedish patrols was passing through and heard him scream. He managed to run for it after the one stab, and the thief gave up and disappeared back down the alley when he saw the patrol. The bastard got Jim's wallet and his pocket watch first, though. Big windup railroad model, too, not battery-powered."

"So you think it was a robbery? A mugging?"

"What else could it have been? The guy demanded Jim's wallet and his 'jewels,' then stuck a knife in him. Sounds like a robbery to me." McDougal sounded a bit impatient, and Simpson snorted.

"Doesn't it seem just a bit odd to you that he stabbed this Ennis *after* getting what he'd come for?" McDougal looked blank, and Simpson shook his head. "I assume from what you just said that your Mr. Ennis gave the 'robber' what he'd demanded instead of trying to resist?"

"Damn straight he did," McDougal replied. "Jim's about fifty years old, and the first thing he knew about it was when he stepped around the corner and the bastard showed him the knife! What the hell would *you* have done in his position?"

"Quite possibly exactly the same thing," Simpson said. "But my point is that he did what this 'thief' of yours told him to. He handed over what the man wanted and didn't resist. And the 'robber' still chose to stab him. You said the Swedish patrol heard him 'scream,' not 'shout for help,' so I'm assuming that he hadn't even tried to summon assistance before he was stabbed."

"This isn't the twenty-first century," McDougal pointed out. "There isn't exactly a cop on every street corner, and there *are* some real hardcases and badasses hanging around here. Some of them would cut your throat for a nickel."

"I don't doubt it. For that matter, there were plenty of places back home where people would have cut your throat just as cheerfully for even less. But usually, Mr. McDougal—*usually*, I say—even around here thieves don't go around murdering people just for the hell of it. I'm perfectly well aware that there are exceptions to the rule. But it's still just a bit unusual, I'd think, for someone who's been able to get everything he demanded with only the threat of violence to go ahead and murder the person who gave it to him."

"Like I say, it's a rough neighborhood," McDougal replied. "People get knifed all the time, sometimes for no reason at all."

"Actually, people very seldom get knifed 'for no reason at all,'" Simpson disagreed. "There's always *some* reason for it."

"Maybe so, but there must have been dozens of locals who've gotten robbed, beaten up, or stabbed in the last two or three months, compared to a single up-timer."

"On the other hand," Simpson pointed out, "there aren't simply dozens of locals for each up-timer in Magdeburg, Mr. McDougal. There are thousands of them. Statistically, Americans—excuse me, up-timers—represent an extremely small sample of the total population. So if this was no more than a random street crime, the odds against the thief picking one of the literal handful of up-timers in Magdeburg must have been quite high, don't you think?"

"Look," McDougal said, "why don't you come right out and say whatever it is you're driving at, Simpson. What? You think I've just been sitting here on my ass ignoring some sort of master plot against all Americans everywhere? Is that it? You're accusing me of not doing my job?"

"I didn't say that," Simpson replied. "In fact, all I intended to do was to suggest to you that Dieter might have a point. Of course it's possible that Mr. Ennis was simply the victim of an armed robber with a particularly vicious temper. But it's also possible that the entire object was to make an assassination *look* like a robbery. That was all I came in here to suggest. On the other hand, now that you ask, and after hearing your reaction to my questions and my suggestion that you might want to be just a little open-minded on the question, I have to say that, yes, it does sound to me like you've been sitting on your ass—or maybe your brain—where this particular possibility is concerned."

"Listen, you—" McDougal began furiously, but Simpson only shook his head and stood.

"I didn't come in here to argue with you, McDougal. I came in here to try to get you to think. Obviously, whatever your other virtues—and I'm sure they're legion—may be, thinking isn't one of them. You do remember, as Dieter himself reminded me just this afternoon, that it was Richelieu who ordered the attack on the high school? The high school in which *your* children were students? Why do you think he did that? Richelieu is capable of total ruthlessness, but the man isn't a complete psychotic, you know. He attacked the school because of what it represents, and what it represents is *knowledge*. The information Gustav Adolf needs and that Richelieu fears even more than he does the Spanish Habsburgs. Well, he didn't get the high school, and he didn't manage to kill all of your teachers and all of your children in one fell swoop, but that's not the only place knowledge is locked up, is it? It's also walking around inside the brain of every single up-timer. And do you seriously think that Richelieu isn't perfectly capable of and willing to attempt to eliminate as many of those brains as he can?"

McDougal stared at him, jaw clenched, and Simpson snorted.

"Apparently you do. Well, I hope the people responsible for keeping your President alive are a bit more willing to think the unthinkable than you appear to be. I may not be one of his greatest admirers, but if I were Richelieu, the only person I'd want dead right now even more badly than I wanted Gustav Adolf that way would be Mike Stearns. You might want to pass that assessment along to him."

Simpson's voice was desert-dry, and McDougal's jaw unlocked enough to drop ever so slightly. Simpson observed the phenomenon and produced another snort, then glanced at Eddie.

"Come along, Mr. Cantrell. I'd like to find some supper before we turn in for the evening."

Dinner was quite probably the best meal Eddie had eaten since leaving Grantville. In fact, it was in the running for the best meal he'd had since the Ring of Fire, period. The "restaurant" was little more than a very large tent—or, at least, a tarp stretched across two-and-a-fraction walls of what would someday be a proper restaurant but which was currently still under construction. At least the kitchens seemed to be complete, and The Crown and Eagle Bar and Grill was obviously the establishment of choice for both the Americans—Haygood was already there when they arrived—and many of the Swedish officers stationed in Magdeburg.

The name was a nice touch, Eddie thought, and he rather suspected that The Crown and Eagle was a franchise of the owners of the Thuringen Gardens back in Grantville. It wouldn't be surprising, since everyone knew Gustav Adolf was planning to make Magdeburg his new imperial capital in Germany. The city was already a "boom town," and the boom was just getting underway. There was certainly something very up-time about the choice of names, and he recognized two of the bouncers from the Gardens. The food was just as good, too, and he tucked into the steak Simpson had decided to treat both of them to.

There were times when Eddie missed the twenty-first

century with excruciating poignancy, and memories of food had a tendency to bring them on. No pre-Ring of Fire American had been even remotely prepared for the change in diet imposed by their transition to the seventeenth century. It wasn't just the esoteric or "modern" foods they missed, either. It was the fact that the entire food distribution system, and the food *production* system, as well, was so damned limited compared to the one they'd grown up with. Steak, for example. It was generally available, but it cost an arm and a leg. Or corn-on-the-cob. They were lucky as hell that they'd had seed corn available when they were kicked back in time, but there hadn't been enough of it. Almost every kernel they'd been able to produce in the shortened growing season they'd enjoyed after arriving in Thuringia had gone right back into seeds, rather than onto people's tables. And tomatoes. Or avocados. God, Eddie had never imagined that he would have been willing to contemplate homicide for a couple of scoops of guacamole!

But at least The Crown and Eagle's cooks knew how to do justice to one of their extraordinarily expensive T-bones . . . unlike the cooks in the inns in which he and Simpson had stayed or dined on their journey to Magdeburg. Most of *them* had figured that the only way to cook beef was to boil it into a consistency which would have made decent cavalry boots. This steak, on the other hand, was done to medium-rare perfection (over an open-fire grill, of course!) and served up with nicely sauteed mushrooms, and a salad of very early bibb lettuce (courtesy of the up-timers) with a vinaigrette dressing.

There was even, wonder of wonders, a baked potato.

Potatoes had already been introduced in large parts of Germany before the Ring of Fire—to Eddie's surprise, since he knew that Frederick the Great had had to force them onto Prussia in the next century—but they were still something of a rarity. Of course, once he reflected upon the matter, it made sense that The Crown and Eagle would serve them, given that so much of the establishment's popularity stemmed from its "American cuisine."

Eddie luxuriated in all of them with shameless hedonism. In fact, it was quite some time before he was able to tear himself sufficiently away from gastronomic considerations to pay much attention to whatever else was going on about him.

" . . . so the point, you see," Simpson was saying to a pock-faced Scotsman who was obviously one of Gustav Adolf's officers, "is to eventually completely eliminate the pike from the battlefield."

"Och, mon, you're daft!" the Scotsman declared. "There's never a day musketeers could stop a hard charge of well-trained pikes without pikes of their own." He shook his head and thumped his beer tankard on the rough-planked table. "The King's already increased his proportion of shot to pikes to two-to-one, and that's higher than any of these stinking Imperialists. But any more than that, and we've nothing to stop t'*other* side's pikes with, and there's an end to it. It might be that if all our 'new weapons' could fire as fast as *yours* can there might be something in it, but they're not going to be able to, are they now?"

"I'm not sure exactly what sort of firearms are being considered, actually," Simpson admitted, and looked down the table at Haygood. "Mr. Haygood? Do you?"

"No, not really," the engineer replied after washing down a mouthful with a healthy swig of beer. "I understand that they're still debating the advantages of flintlocks and caplocks. I know which one *I'd* prefer, but the manufacturing end isn't my kind of engineering, and I've been kind of busy with other projects, I'm afraid. So far, I don't think anyone's even suggested the possibility of a breechloader."

"Given the difficulties in manufacturing proper cartridges—and, for that matter, fulminating powder and primer caps—I'd assume that you're going to be looking at muzzle-loaders of some sort, at best," Simpson agreed, and turned back to the Scotsman.

"I'm guessing that they'll probably be flintlocks, but the designs should include cylindrical iron ramrods and conical touchholes. In that case, your rate of fire is going to be considerably higher than it is right now, but you're right that it's never going to match that of up-time weapons. I'm sure that plans are already afoot to provide you with rifles, which will let you open fire effectively at greater ranges, so you'll generally have longer to shoot at an attacking enemy, but that certainly isn't enough by itself to guarantee that you can stop a determined charge.

"But you're missing at least part of the point, Captain. If you eliminate the pikes, then you can take the pikemen and issue all of *them* rifles—muskets, if you prefer—as well. And if your entire army is equipped with rifles and bayonets . . ." He paused. "Ah, they did mention bayonets to you, didn't they?" he asked.

"You mean that wee silly knife they're talking about hanging on the end of a musket?" The Scotsman shrugged. "Och, and won't *that* be useful against some bastard with a twelve-foot pike!"

"That 'wee silly knife' will be a lot more useful than you think, especially if your troops are trained with them," Haygood interjected. The Scotsman looked skeptical, and Haygood showed his teeth in a thin smile. "What happens when somebody gets inside your reach with a shorter, handier weapon?" he challenged. "Say, someone with a knife who blocks your sword to one side while he rams it into your belly?"

The Scotsman blinked, and it was Haygood's turn to shrug.

"Trust me, properly used, a bayoneted rifle is *very* effective in close combat. As it happens, I'm one of the very few up-timers who's had actual experience with the kind of weapons and tactics Mr. Simpson's talking about." He did not, Eddie noticed, explain that his "actual experience" was that of a hobbyist, and the Scotsman frowned.

"Mr. Haygood is correct," Simpson said. "For all practical purposes, bayonets will turn every single man in your entire army into a pikeman, if he's needed. And in the meantime, if *all* of your infantry are musket-armed and trained and disciplined to employ those muskets in mass fire that's properly timed, not very many pike formations are going to be able to close with them."

The Scotsman looked more thoughtful, but it was clear that acceptance still ran a distant second—or third—to skepticism, and Simpson cocked his head.

"Suppose that I gave your musketeers weapons

that could open aimed fire at a range of, say, three
hundred paces and expect to hit man-sized targets at
that distance. And that I got their rate of fire up to
four shots a minute, at the same time," he suggested
after a moment. "And suppose that your army had
nine thousand men in it, and that I organized them
into three firing lines, each three thousand men long.
And then suppose that I organized your musketeers
into ninety-six-man companies, each composed of
three thirty-two-man 'platoons,' and trained them to
fire by half-platoons."

The Scotsman was staring at Simpson, his eyes
almost crossed as he tried to follow what the American was saying.

"All right, now," Simpson continued. "If you've got
three thousand men in each line, then that means
that each line consists of thirty-one companies, or
ninety-three platoons, or a total between all three
lines of sixty-three companies and . . . two-hundred
and seventy-nine platoons, right?"

The sandbagged-looking Scotsman nodded, obviously
prepared to let the up-timer do the mathematical
heavy lifting, and Simpson shrugged.

"Well, the math is actually pretty simple. If your
musketeers can fire four times every minute, then
the total reload cycle for each man in your formation
is approximately fifteen seconds. So if half of each
platoon in your first line fires, and then two and a
half seconds later the second half of each platoon
in the first line fires, and then two and a half seconds after *that* half of each platoon in your *second*
line fires, and so on, your nine thousand men are
going to be sending the next best thing to fifteen

hundred rounds down-range every two and a half seconds. That's almost *thirty-six thousand* rounds per minute."

The Scotsman's eyes weren't crossed now—indeed, they were almost bulging, and Simpson shrugged again.

"But the total numbers don't begin to tell the entire tale, do they?" he inquired mildly. "Remember, fifteen hundred of them are going to be arriving every *two and a half seconds*. Effectively, there will be a continuous, unbroken wall of bullets pouring into any pike block foolish enough to try to close with your formation, which I should think would have at least a tiny bit of an effect on its morale. Obviously you've seen a battlefield or two of your own. How well do you think a formation of pikes would do when it came to holding its ranks and carrying through with an effective charge under those circumstances?"

"Carrying *through*?" The Scotsman shook his head as if he'd just been punched. "Mother of God, mon! If you're telling the truth about the range of these 'rifles' of yours, then it would take a good three minutes—at least!—under fire for the pikes to close, and that would mean—"

"That would mean that they were trying to charge through over one hundred thousand rounds of continuous fire," Simpson said, once again doing the math for him obligingly. "So if there were nine thousand pikemen, and if one third of the shots your men fired actually hit, you'd kill each of them about four times."

The American smiled thinly, and raised one hand, palm uppermost.

"Of course, that's under perfect conditions. It assumes that the terrain lets you see the target and begin engaging it at extended range, and that your rate of fire isn't affected by something like rain, barrel fouling, or something like that. And once the firing begins, smoke alone is going to cause individual accuracy to drop off pretty severely. But I think you see my point?"

"Aye, you might be saying that," the Scotsman said, and looked at Haygood, as if seeking additional confirmation of Simpson's claims.

"Mr. Simpson's description isn't exactly the one I would have used," the engineer said. "It sounds more like what the Brits did to the French during the Napoleonic wars than the sort of tactics I'm trained in. Of course, most of the differences are because the ones he's talking about would make the kind of tactics you're accustomed to downright suicidal. Which is why we developed better ones which were even more effective. Mr. Simpson's example was hypothetical, but in the up-time American Civil War, a battle was fought—*would* have been fought—with weapons very similar to the ones he's describing, about a hundred and thirty years from now at a place called Chicka-mauga, and in just two days, the two sides suffered over thirty-seven thousand casualties. And at the Battle of Antietam, in the same war, the two sides suffered twenty-two thousand casualties in a *single* day."

It was obvious to Eddie that no one had ever explained it to the Scotsman the way Simpson and Haygood just had—certainly not with the *numbers* the two of them had produced—and the officer stared at the Americans for two or three more seconds before he drained his tankard. Then he waved it at one of the barmaids for a refill and turned back to Simpson.

"And what other evil little surprises would you be suggesting?" he asked, leaning his forearms on the table and gazing at the American intently.

It was well past midnight before Simpson, Haygood and Eddie left The Crown and Eagle. Many of the Swedish officers who'd helped fill the restaurant had been thoroughly standoffish when they first arrived—no doubt because Simpson's reputation as an anti-German and anti-Swedish bigot had preceded him. Despite that, however, most of them had been listening when he began his discussion with the pock-faced Scotsman. And whatever his other faults might have been, it seemed that John Simpson had a definite gift for getting at the heart—or, at least, the nuts and bolts—of an explanation.

Even Eddie, with his wargamer's fascination with military history, wouldn't have thought of breaking down the numbers the way Simpson had. He would have just waved his hands and insisted that the weight of fire would have been sufficient to break the enemy's charge. Which would have overlooked the fact that the members of his audience, whatever theoretical faith they might have in Americans' technical ingenuity, were basing their understanding of what he was saying on their actual experience with matchlocks. No wonder they'd had such serious reservations about the possibilities!

But once Simpson had gotten the actual numbers across to them—and once the notion that Haygood really knew what he was talking about had percolated through their brains—virtually every officer in the restaurant had started easing closer and closer to the table the three Americans shared. And as they'd closed in, they'd begun to ask other questions, as well. *Lots* of other questions.

Simpson had done his best to answer those questions, and somehow Eddie hadn't been as surprised as he once would have been when Simpson frankly admitted, from time to time, that he didn't *know* an answer. When that happened, Haygood usually did, although there were times when even he had to admit he was stumped. Two or three times, Simpson actually turned to Eddie, drawing the younger man into the conversation when he rightly suspected that the question was the sort a war game enthusiast might know how to answer. But there was a difference between the explanations Eddie gave and those Simpson provided. Indeed, there was a difference between the answers that came from Simpson and those which came from Haygood, as well, and as Eddie listened to the older man, he knew what that difference was . . . and why it convinced Gustav Adolf's officers to listen so intently to the ex-Navy officer.

Experience. John Simpson had never served in the howling chaos of a seventeenth-century battlefield, yet there was something about his voice and manner, an assurance that he knew what he was talking about from personal, first-hand experience when he explained things to the hard-bitten officers of the Swedish Army. Not, perhaps, the same experience as their own, but experience nonetheless.

They kept him talking for hours before they let him go. And when they finally did let him take his leave, it was with nods of mutual respect unlike anything Simpson had ever seen in Grantville itself, before *or* after the Ring of Fire.

It would have taken a superman not to have been pleased and flattered by such a reception, and whatever else he might have been, John Chandler Simpson was *not* a superman. The after-supper discussion had to have been the most enjoyable single evening he'd spent since arriving as a less than eager guest for his son's wedding, and it showed. He was never going to be an expressive man, Eddie realized, yet there was a new liveliness in his voice and eyes as the two of them finally gathered up a Haygood who'd apparently had a beer or two too many and headed towards their quarters in the boardinghouse where McDougal had rented rooms for them.

It was blacker than the pits of Hell outside the restaurant. Eddie remembered how Mr. Ferrara had once complained, before the Ring of Fire, about light pollution and how it interfered with observations on their astronomy field trips even in rural West Virginia, but he hadn't really understood at the time. Not the way he did now.

Not even the endless months of the winter just past could have prepared him for the darkness which enveloped the one vast construction site which was Magdeburg. Dark as those winter nights had seemed at the time, Grantville at least still had electricity. Light bulbs were one of the items which had fallen under strict rationing controls as yet one more utterly irreplaceable twenty-first-century resource which had been taken completely for granted before the Ring of Fire. Because of that rationing, Grantville's homes and businesses and public places had seemed woefully dimly lit to up-timer eyes.

Compared to Magdeburg at midnight, however, Grantville at its dimmest had been lit up like downtown Las Vegas on a Saturday night. The inky blackness of the muddy streets and alleys between the half-completed walls of the buildings was broken only by occasional—*very* occasional—torches or lanterns. In many ways, the widely scattered pinpricks of light only made the darkness even denser by comparison, and Eddie buttoned his denim jacket against a chill night breeze as he followed Simpson out of the restaurant. Simpson, on the other hand, actually unzipped his light windbreaker, as if he welcomed the briskness.

It would have been easy to become hopelessly lost amid all of the heaps of brick, timbers, and other building materials, but they didn't have all that far to go. Besides, dark and confusing as most of the city might be, Pete McDougal had insisted that the United States' official headquarters had to be well-lighted—by Magdeburg standards, at least—at all times. That provided a visual beacon they could orient themselves upon, and they moved out briskly (or, at least, as briskly as Haygood's . . . cheerfulness allowed) through the muddy darkness.

Haygood was kind enough to provide them with an enthusiastic, if not particularly tuneful serenade, but Simpson wasn't in a very talkative mood. No doubt he'd used up a month or two of conversation after supper, Eddie reflected just a bit sourly. Eddie didn't feel much more like talking himself, though. He was too busy with his own ruminations, still trying to figure out how he felt about the surprising, apparently contradictory layers of Simpson's personality. And so the two of them trudged along silently through the deserted streets and alleys.

Except that they weren't quite "deserted" after all.

Eddie was so wrapped up in his thoughts that he didn't notice when Simpson abruptly halted. His first inkling that anything out of the ordinary was happening came when he literally ran into the older man's back. It was a much more substantial back than Eddie would have anticipated, and the wiry teenager bounced backward a step and a half from the impact.

"What the hell—?" he began angrily, but before he could complete the question, several things happened at once.

He and Simpson had just entered the faint spill of light from a lantern burning outside an alley mouth. It was the most feeble of illuminations, but clearly it was enough for the three men who'd been waiting in the alley to identify them. Eddie knew it was, although it took him two or three precious seconds to realize the fact.

"There!" someone hissed in German. "That's them—*get them!*"

Eddie was still gaping, trying to get a handle on what was happening, when he saw the gleam of naked steel and three burly figures coming straight for him. Confusion barely had time to begin giving way to fear and the beginning of panic as he realized Dieter Schwanhausser had been right to warn them. Whether or not the men in the alley worked directly for Richelieu didn't really matter. What mattered was that all three of them were obviously intent

upon shoving a foot or so of knife blade through one
Eddie Cantrell.

He opened his mouth to shout for help, even as he
stumbled backward another step. But that was as far
as he got before a hammer blow of sound smashed
his ears like a baseball bat.

The muzzle flash lit up the night like a lightning
bolt. Eddie had never before seen a handgun fired
in near darkness at very close range, and the brilliant
eruption of light stabbed at his eyeballs like a knife.
But if it came as a surprise to Eddie, it was far more
of a surprise to their assailants.

Eddie heard the beginning of a scream of agony,
then cringed as the baseball bat whacked him across
the ears again and another stroboscopic blast of light
assaulted his optic nerves. But that same flash of light
seemed to carve John Simpson out of the darkness,
and Eddie saw the nine-millimeter automatic which
had materialized magically from somewhere under his
unzipped windbreaker.

The city slicker from Pittsburgh had dropped into
a half-crouched shooter's stance, with the handgun
held two-handed, and the abortive scream of pain was
chopped abruptly off as Simpson's second shot hit the
lead attacker dead center, just above the collarbone.

One of the other assailants shouted an incredulous
curse and lunged desperately forward, but Simpson
didn't even shift position. Haygood was just beginning to claw at the revolver holstered at his hip
when Simpson fired again—twice, in a quick one-two
sequence that punched a pair of bullets into the tri-
angle formed by the would-be killer's forehead and
the base of his throat.

That one went down without even a scream, his throat and the back of his neck exploding in a grisly spray, Eddie noticed almost numbly, and the third man hesitated. It was only the briefest of pauses, and Eddie always wondered afterward exactly what the man had thought he was doing. He might even have entertained some notion of throwing down his knife and surrendering, but if that was what he had in mind, he didn't get around to it in time to do him any good.

Simpson's point of aim shifted, and Eddie had a fraction of a second to wonder how the man could possibly see what he was doing after the blinding brilliance of the muzzle flashes. Maybe he was actually closing his eyes—or one of them, at least—as he fired. Eddie didn't have a clue about that, but it didn't really matter, either. The nine-millimeter pistol barked twice more in that same, deadly rhythm. One shot hit the third attacker perhaps an inch above the heart; the second took him squarely above the right eye and slammed him back to slither bonelessly down the alley wall behind him just as Haygood's revolver finally cleared its holster.

Eddie Cantrell stood there, frozen in stunned disbelief. The entire attack couldn't have consumed more than five seconds. Probably less. But in those few heartbeats of time, three men had tried to kill him . . . and the stuffed shirt from Pittsburgh had killed all three of them, instead.

"Good morning, Mr. Cantrell."

"Uh, good morning," Eddie half-mumbled as Simpson greeted him the following day. The older man sat at the small, rickety table in the tiny "sitting room" of their shared quarters, carefully cleaning a Browning High-Power automatic.

It was the first really good look Eddie had gotten at it, and from the way the bluing was worn away, it was obvious to him that the handgun had seen a lot of use. It was equally obvious that it had been lovingly maintained during its lengthy lifespan, and Eddie wondered how Simpson had managed to conceal it so effectively that Eddie had never even suspected he had it.

"Are you ready for breakfast?" Simpson asked.

"Breakfast?" Eddie repeated, then swallowed heavily, remembering.

"Well, lunch, actually, I suppose," Simpson said thoughtfully, his face expressionless, although there might have been the faintest flicker of amusement in his eyes. If so, Eddie scarcely noticed as his mind replayed the previous night's events.

The sound of the shots, especially so close to the United States' "embassy," had brought two different Swedish patrols at a dead run. Not only that, but the sentries outside the embassy itself had responded almost as quickly, and, unlike the Swedes, they'd brought powerful up-time hand-portable lights with them.

Eddie rather wished they hadn't. He'd seen carnage and bloodshed enough for someone two or three times his age since arriving in Thuringia. He'd been there when Frank Jackson smashed his first Imperial army of mercenaries outside Badenburg and he and Jeff Higgins, Larry Wild, and Jimmy Andersen had faced down a second army of rapists and murderers who'd been their so-called "allies" with nothing but twelve-gauge shotguns and outrage. He'd been there at the

Wartburg, too—and at the Alte Veste. Despite his brash, often bubbling exterior, there were nights when nightmares spawned by the memories of those sights and sounds kept him awake, tossing and turning.

But whatever he'd seen, he was scarcely hardened against it, and the sight of what Simpson's shots had done to their targets on the way through had almost cost him his excellent supper.

McDougal himself had appeared on the scene in less than ten minutes, still buttoning his shirt while he stared down at the three twisted, blood-leaking bodies and the wicked looking knives lying beside them in the mud.

"So, Mr. McDougal," Simpson had grated, the harsh anger in his voice the only indication he seemed prepared to allow of his own adrenaline and fear, "do you still think Mr. Schwanhausser is *overreacting* to the possible threat from Richelieu?"

McDougal had flinched visibly from the bitter, biting irony of the question, but he'd only stared down at the bodies for a few more seconds, then shaken his head.

"No," he'd said then, not that he'd had much choice about it. "No, Mr. Simpson. I don't suppose he is."

There'd been quite a bit more after that, of course, before anyone got to bed, and it had been still longer before Eddie managed to drop off to sleep. Which was why he was so late rolling out.

"Uh, yeah," he said, shaking himself out of his thoughts. "I guess I am sorta hungry, at that."

He sounded a bit surprised, even to himself, and Simpson snorted. There was amusement in that snort, but not the harsh, dismissive sort of humor Eddie might once have expected. Indeed, in its own way, it was almost gentle.

"Well, give me a few minutes to finish up here, and I'll treat you to lunch at The Crown and Eagle," the older man said while his hands briskly broke down his cleaning rod and packed it and the other cleaning supplies away, then reassembled the Browning quickly and expertly. Eddie watched him, noting the smoothness of the practiced movements, and dismissed any lingering suspicion that Simpson had borrowed the handgun from someone for the trip.

"You had that all along, didn't you?" he asked after a moment.

"Yes, I did," Simpson agreed, not looking up as he finished reassembling the pistol and slid a freshly loaded magazine into the grip. "The Browning is an excellent weapon," he observed, "although the nine-millimeter round is a little short on stopping power, compared to something like the .45. On the other hand, with a hundred and forty-seven-grain hollow-point and about four-point-six grains of HS-6, it will do the job quite adequately."

"I . . . see." Eddie cleared his throat. "How long have you been carrying it?" he asked.

"For considerably longer than you've been alive," Simpson replied, and looked up at last with a slight smile. "There are times, Mr. Cantrell, when one should be a little cautious about leaping to conclusions, don't you think?"

"Yeah," Eddie said slowly, "there are." He paused, meeting Simpson's eyes levelly, then added, "I guess everybody should bear that in mind, shouldn't they?"

"I imagine they should," Simpson agreed after a moment, and something passed between them as the older man met the youngster's gaze equally levelly. Eddie wasn't certain what that "something" was, but he knew both of them had felt it.

Then the moment passed, and Simpson stood. He tucked the Browning away into the worn holster at the small of his back which Eddie had never noticed before, then nodded towards the door.

Eddie nodded back, and the two of them headed off towards The Crown and Eagle. Quite a few people looked at them—and especially Simpson—oddly as they passed, but the older man paid the curious no attention.

"By the way, Mr. Cantrell," he said casually as they approached the restaurant, "while you were sleeping in this morning, I went over to check with Mr. Franklin to see if President Stearns had responded to my message from yesterday."

"Oh?" Eddie glanced at him. Something about Simpson's tone sounded warning signals. "Had he?"

"Yes, he had," Simpson replied. "In fact, he informed me that he's accepted my recommendations and that he and his cabinet have authorized me to call upon Mr. McDougal for assistance in formally acquiring title to the land for our navy yard."

"*Our* navy yard?" Eddie repeated, and Simpson nodded.

"Yes. We're going to have to return to Grantville, of course. I'll need to spend some time with you and your original plan if we're going to work out a practical design for the ironclads. And we need to discuss with the President how many timberclads we'll need to add to the mix. And, for that matter, exactly what sort of priorities for resources—other than the railroad rails, of course—and manpower the Navy is going to require. And how we're going to organize that manpower and set up training programs."

"Why do you keep saying 'we'?" Eddie asked. Simpson cocked an eyebrow at him, and the youngster shrugged irritably. "I know you're going to tear my design completely apart and put it together all over again," he said. "I accepted that when I first proposed it to Mike—I mean, the President. So, okay, it wasn't a perfect design. I never claimed it was."

"No, it wasn't," Simpson agreed in a coolly judicious tone. "On the other hand, I'm sure we'll have time to work the bugs out of it. After all, it's going to take weeks—probably at least a couple of months—of organizational work before we can get back to Magdeburg and really start setting things up here."

"Dammit, there you go again with that 'we' stuff! Just because Mike sent me along on this first trip doesn't mean I want to spend my time sitting around in this mudhole while they build the city around us!"

"That's unfortunate," Simpson observed. "On the other hand, I'm sure there are a great many people who find themselves compelled to do things they didn't want to."

Eddie stopped dead in the street and turned to face the older man squarely.

"Just go ahead and tell me what you're so pleased about!" he snapped irritably.

"That's 'Tell me what you're so pleased about, *sir*,'" Simpson told him, and Eddie's eyes began to widen in sudden, dreadful surmise.

"I'm afraid so, *Lieutenant* Cantrell," Simpson informed him. "Still, I suppose it's only appropriate that the individual responsible for inspiring his country to build a navy in the first place should find himself drafted for duty as its very first commissioned officer. Well, second, actually, I suppose," he amended judiciously.

"B-b-but I—I mean, I never— You can't be *serious!*" Eddie blurted out.

"Oh, but I can, Lieutenant," Simpson said coolly, and showed his teeth in the edge of a smile. "Don't worry," he advised, taking Eddie by the elbow and getting him moving once more, "you'll adjust quickly enough, Lieutenant. Oh, and by the way, I imagine you'll adjust even more quickly if you remember to call me 'Admiral' or 'sir' from now on."

To Dye For

Mercedes Lackey

Tom Stone was lying flat on his back in the long grass in front of the geodesic dome, staring up at the sky when Mike Stearns and Doc Nichols showed up for the grass—as in, smokable grass—he'd promised them.

They arrived with a horse and cart, and one of the German boys driving; Tom had heard them coming for quite a while, but in his current state of flat-lined depression, it hadn't seemed important enough to get up just to greet them on his feet.

"Hey, Stoner!" Stearns called, when the hoofbeats and the creaking of the cart were getting pretty close. "Are you dead?"

Tom sighed gustily. "No," he admitted. "Catastrophically crushed, yes. Defeated, depressed, and debilitated. Out-of-time, out-of-luck, down-and-out. Bewitched, bothered, bereft and bewildered. But not dead."

He levered himself up out of the grass with an effort, for depression made his middle-aged body seem all the heavier, and clambered to his feet, while Stearns and the Doc watched him curiously. "Have you been sampling the product?" Stearns asked, finally.

He sighed again. "Would that I had, but not even a monster doobie, not even a full-filled bong of my patented West Virginia Wildwood Weed is going to make me forget my sorrows. I'd run off to join the Foreign Legion, but it hasn't been invented yet."

He took refuge from heartbreak in flippancy. What else could a man do, when he found the love of his life and lost her to something so stupid as money?

Doc Nichols looked completely blank, but a sudden expression of understanding crept across Mike's face. "Magdalena?" he asked.

Tom groaned; it was heartfelt. "Magdalena. Or rather, Herr Karl Jurgen Edelmann, whose considered opinion it is that I am no proper husband for *his* daughter."

"Ach, vell," said the German boy still on the seat of the wagon, "You aren't."

Tom gave him the hairy eyeball; bad enough that his feelings were exposed for all to see, but this commentary from the peanut gallery was adding insult to a mortal wound. "I resemble that remark, Klaus," he retorted bitterly.

"Vell, you *aren't*, Stoner," the boy persisted. "Vat haf you for to keep a guildmaster's daughter vith?"

"I am monarch of all I survey," Tom said sourly, opening his arms wide to include the geodesic dome he and the boys called home, laboriously built circa 1973 out of hand-hammered car hoods and scavenged windows by the founding members of Lothlorien Commune. The gesture swept in the two tiny camping trailers that had been added about 1976, the barn and now-derelict shotgun house that had been the original buildings on this property, and the greenhouse that Tom had made out of more salvaged windows.

"Und Magdalena vould haf better prospects elsevere," Klaus countered, stolidly. "You haf no *income*, Stoner. Effen der Veed, you gifs to der Doc."

Since Tom had heard all that already from the mouth of his beloved Magdalena's father, he wasn't in a mood to hear it again. "I am *not*," he growled, "going to make a profit off of other people's pain."

Klaus only shrugged, though Doc Nichols looked sympathetic. "Dat earns you a place in Heaffen, maybe," the boy said with oxlike practicality. "But on Earth, no income."

It was an argument Tom had no hope of winning, and he didn't try. Instead, he turned back to Stearns, changing the subject to one less painful. "The stuff I was going to sell before the Ring hit us was already bagged, and I've added everything I could harvest without hurting the next crop, Mike," he said, feeling his shoulders sagging with defeat. "Come on, give me a hand with it."

Stearns and Doc left Klaus with the wagon and followed Tom to the processing "plant" in the barn. Tom was Grantville's token holdover hippy, the last holdout of a commune that had been founded in 1965 by college dropouts long on idealism and short on practical skills—which basically described virtually every commune founded around that time.

"Maybe we can brainstorm something for you,

Stoner," Mike said, as they followed the mown path between the dome and the barn—Tom didn't believe in wasting time and ruining perfectly good meadow grass—which provided habitat for an abundance of tiny songbirds—with a mower if he didn't have to. Stearns didn't sound hopeful, though, and Tom couldn't blame him. After all, he was something of the town loser. . . .

"Forgive my asking, but since I'm not from around here, just what *are* you good at?" the Doc asked

"Other than the obvious?" He had to shrug. "Not much. I was a pharmacy major at Purdue in the late seventies, in no small part so that I could learn how to make mind-opening drugs for my own consumption. There were a lot of us like that back then. I kind of went on to graduate school for lack of anything else, then I lost interest in school and eventually ended up here."

Given that he hadn't been motivated to get a graduate degree, it hadn't taken a lot of persuasion to get him to drop out a year short of his masters degree to move out here, to what his friends and fellow freaks had decided to call Lothlorien Commune—although the fact that his old lady Lisa had been the one who urged the move also had a lot to do with it.

"So you followed the old Timothy Leary mantra, 'turn on, tune in, drop out'?" the Doc hazarded.

"Something like that. Some friends of my friends started this place—I think one of them inherited it from a relative. He left about 1984, and I haven't heard from him since, so I guess he's either dead, in prison or doesn't give a damn. I kept up the property tax payments, so maybe the brain cells that held the fact that he's the owner went offline." He swung open the barn door and they moved into the hay-scented gloom. At the further end was another of his scavenged-window greenhouses, but this one was his drying shed. "Now, of course, it's moot."

At first, in those early days, all had been well, surrounded as they were in a haze of high-grade weed and windowpane acid. But as with virtually every commune founded in the sixties and early seventies, by the time he got there, part of the last wave of the hippie generation, Lothlorien was showing early signs of disintegrating.

Part of it was having to deal with the reality of hardscrabble dirt-farming. All of them were city- or suburban-bred, and grand designs of completely organic farming quickly fell by the wayside under onslaughts of every bizarre bug known to the entomologist. From that slippery slope, it was a straight-down slide, and plans for a completely vegetarian lifestyle became necessity when all they could afford were rice and beans, and the only money coming in was from well-intentioned "businesses" that somehow never lasted very long. The leather-worker left after an argument with the hard-line vegetarians. The pottery was good enough, but no one around here would buy it. Macrame belts and pot-hangers didn't quite match that coal-mining couture. . . .

A total of three SCAdians bought the yurts. Beaded jewelry and embroidered shirts required a lot of time, and a boutique willing to take them. But most of all, businesses needed business-minded people to run them, and no one could stay motivated long enough to make a business work.

"You probably didn't need to bring the cart," he told them, showing them the pile of nicely-compacted kilo "bricks," hot-sealed in vacuum-formed plastic wrap, with pardonable pride in workmanship. *His* plants practically had resin oozing out of every leaf-pore, and they packed down beautifully. "Doc, don't unwrap these until you're ready to use one. They're exactly like flavoring herbs; air is your enemy."

"Right," Nichols said, hefting a brick and regarding it with reluctant admiration. "I suppose we're talking trial-and-error on dosage, here?"

"It's pretty hard to OD on grass," Tom pointed out. "Especially when you're using it medicinally. By the way, strongly flavored baked goods are the vehicle-of-choice for an oral vector, though I used to get good reviews on my spaghetti sauce."

Part of the reason for the collapse of Lothlorien was rebellion on the part of the women—who very soon found that a "natural lifestyle" meant unassisted child-rearing, childbirth aided only by Tom's hasty self-taught knowledge of midwifery, and nonstop housekeeping necessitated by the fact that there *were* no handy modern conveniences like—say—electricity. The chicks came and went, but in that final wave, Lisa bailed first, leaving Tom to solo-parent their son, Faramir.

Faramir. I must have been so stoned. How could that name ever have seemed like a good idea?

By the early '90s, all the women were gone, taking the girl-chicks, but leaving the other two boys born to the group with Tom "because he was such a good role-model." Elrond *might* have been his, but Gwaihir wasn't, and no one had *any* doubt of that, not with the kid's hair redder than a stop-sign. The only reason Tom was on the birth certificate as father-of-record was because the boy's mother was so stoned during and after the birth that she couldn't remember anyone else's last name.

By the time Gwaihir was born, Tom was no longer just the guru of drug-assisted meditation and provider of the sacred sacraments. Necessity and the fact that he was the *only* one with any medical training had made him the de facto doctor for the group, as well as midwife. More of a root-doctor than a sawbones, though he'd set broken bones in plenty, so long as the injury was pretty straightforward.

But with all of the old ladies gone, the rest of the guys lost interest in keeping things together. One by one, they drifted off, too, leaving Tom alone with three kids to raise. The three mothers never did come back even to check on their boys; he never knew why.

On the other hand—without a bunch of dopers lounging around, he had a lot fewer mouths to feed, and by then he wasn't bad at subsistence farming. The vegetable garden, the chickens, and the yearly pigs took care of most of their food needs. Wind-generators, one of the last things the commune had built together, brought much-needed electricity, and once Tom himself had gotten the greenhouse built, he was able to grow veggies all year long *without* having to fight bugs. He'd had a surprisingly green thumb, all things considered.

And of course—though by the time he and the kids were living here alone it was to bring in *much* needed money for the kids' needs, rather than to supply the group with smoking materials—that wasn't all he grew in there. A trusted friend had made a little pilgrimage to Holland once the greenhouse was operational, bringing back precious seeds, and Tom had been breeding the best of the best back every year. By the time it was just the four of them, he had some finest-kind weed flourishing amongst the zucchini.

"Want to see the greenhouse?" he asked, more out of politeness than anything else. Somewhat to his surprise, they did.

He was irrationally proud of the place, which had started life as the windows from every building that was about to be wrecked that he could scrounge, with a frame of similarly salvaged timber. That was before old barn-wood became such a hot item with decorators, and every time a tilting barn came down, he'd been there with the communal pickup and flatbed. Most of the farmers had been glad to let him haul it off.

"Damn," Nichols said, looking at the place from the inside for the first time. "How the hell did you manage to keep *this* under wraps?"

Made of barn-boards up to waist-high, with a relatively low eight-foot ceiling, he'd put windows with screens at the bottom where he could open them in hot weather, and solid windows for the roof. Now he'd segregated the pot plants at the rear, with the veggies and herbs up front—though in the days when the law might come a-calling, he'd mingled pot and beans, using the vines of the latter to screen the former.

He shrugged. "Stayed under the radar," he said. "Didn't get greedy. We didn't need a lot of cash to get along, so I didn't deal in more than that."

The boys had kept their dear little mouths shut, when he explained the economics of the situation in terms of toys, treats, and new clothing. An additional bribe—the promise of never telling *anyone* what their real names were, and signing them into the Grantville school system as "Frank," "Ronald," and "Gerry," made sure they wouldn't tell, wouldn't bring samples out to their friends, and wouldn't allow the friends *in* the greenhouse, ever. After all, as Tom knew only too well, peer-pressure among the male of the species is a dreadful thing, and a name can become a deadly weapon. "Gwaihir" was too funny for words, "Elrond" had any number of nasty permutations, and as for "Faramir"—well. Any idiot could quickly figure out just what sort of nickname would come out of "Faramir" in the mouths of a pack of boys.

No, Tom never grew too much and never sold it in or near Grantville. One of the former members of Lothlorien came and collected the crop four times a year, paying in cash, taking it—well, Tom didn't know where he took it, but it definitely went far, far away. It wasn't a lot of cash, but it was enough to keep them in shoes and T-shirts, Tonka trucks and the occasional Twinkie.

So yes, he managed to stay far below the radar, so far as the law was concerned. From time to time, he ventured out into legitimate mercantile ventures, but aside from the sale of eggs, they never amounted to much, and some were outright disasters.

Then came the Ring of Fire, and everything changed.

At first, he and the boys had just been concerned about surviving the experience. But—that was months ago. Survival was no longer the issue—thriving was.

It had not escaped him that suddenly he was the

only person in all of the New United States that was producing a pain-killer instead of consuming it. He'd never given up on the ethics that had brought him out here in the first place, and as soon as things settled down some, he brought himself and a sample of his crop straight to James Nichols, figuring that an ex-'Nam vet out of the 'hood was going to be a tad bit more open-minded about what had been going on in the greenhouse than the Law, and might be willing to intervene on his part.

As it happened, by then, the practicalities of the situation had not been lost on anyone who was in charge of Grantville, and though there had been some official growling and posturing on the part of the Law, it was all bluff and face-saving, and everyone knew it. Besides, it wasn't as if he was selling it.

"What I want to know is how you're keeping the kids out of the stuff," Mike asked, with one eyebrow raised. "Now that the secret's out, I can't believe you aren't getting midnight raids on your crop."

"Peer pressure," Tom said promptly. "I had my boys spread the word that the Doc here was going to prescribe it for the ladies who are having—um—" He blushed. "Monthly problems?"

"Not a bad idea. From what I've read, it's actually got fewer associated problems for that application than anything else around," Nichols admitted.

"Anyway, I let it be known via the kids that the crop is severely limited in quantity, and if there was so much as a single leaf missing, the culprit *would* be found and I would personally spread his name to all the women and let them take matters into their own hands." He'd been rather proud of that solution—having had to pacify the commune women himself when a crop came up short in similar circumstances.

"Damn!" Stearns laughed. "That's *harsh*!"

He shrugged. "I can't stop them from getting seeds and growing their own in the woods, but that's not *my* problem, that's Grantville's problem and you'll have to figure out how the town wants to handle recreational smoking yourself."

"Well, let's pack up and get out of here," Nichols decreed. "Good operation, Stoner."

Tom wasn't unhappy with the exchange, because it *was* an exchange. He *had* gotten something from Grantville for his contribution to the public good. Free electricity from the power-plant, some help with fixing things up around the place, including more insulation against winters that were undoubtedly going to be a lot harsher here than they'd been in West Virginia. The free electricity had allowed him to put the wood-walled extension he'd just added to the greenhouse under the powerful lights he'd bought specifically to grow enhanced pot, but never used, because his own power reserves weren't up to it. That made the Wildwood Weed a lot more potent, true medicinal quality, which made both the Doc and the dentist very happy when they tested and found it powerful.

"You got any more plans for the greenhouse?" Doc asked, as they loaded up with bricks to take them out to the cart.

"More medicinal herbs next, I thought—it makes a lot more sense to use it for things that no one else can grow or preserve, not without lights or protection from the harsh weather." He got a raised eyebrow from Stearns.

"Opium-poppies?" Doc asked carefully.

He shook his head. "I was talking to some of Rebecca's relatives. It's cheaper to buy the raw opium through them and crank out something approaching the morphine you're used to using, Doc. Something that you can inject without lumps clogging the veins of your patients, anyway, something with a consistent strength. What I had in mind was things like foxglove, hyssop, coltsfoot—I've got seeds in the freezer for a lot of stuff out of Culpepper's that I never got around to growing and using. Doctor Abrabanel will probably recognize a lot of them."

"I think we might have to put you on the town payroll," Mike offered.

But Tom shook his head. "You've got some regular pharmacists in town. One of them probably still has all his old compounding manuals, and between him, the chemistry teacher, Rebecca's dad, and the lab at the High, you've got more expertise and equipment than I have. This—" he waved his hand at the piled-up bricks in the back of the cart. "This is a public service. It costs me a little time. Grantville's giving me juice and help with the greenhouse when I need it, and the kids and I are getting medical and dental and that's enough. I'm no good at fighting, never was, so I'm useless for community defense. You've got to have analgesia and anesthetic, whisky isn't good enough, and since I'm not toting a gun, I owe it to the rest of you to do this as my share."

Mike Stearns laughed, and the Doc snorted. "You really *are* a holdover hippie, aren't you?"

"No income," Klaus said, gloomily.

⊰⊱⊰   ⊰⊱⊰   ⊰⊱⊰

The kids came home from school to find him mop-ing around, puttering in the greenhouse with some defrosted foxglove seeds. Frank unbent enough to give his old man an awkward hug. He looked just like his father had at the same age—skinny, puppy-dog eyes—well, except for the hair. Instead of Tom's mane, his boy had a buzz-cut, something that *he* couldn't understand. . . .

"We heard about it, Pop," he said, without specifying *it*. "Wish we could do something to help. Magdalena's pretty cool, I think she'd make a great stepmom."

"Stepmom, heck," Gerry said, a wistful expression on his round, freckled face. "She can *cook.*"

Tom's throat ached, and his chest felt squeezed with misery. What kind of cruel fate was it for him to find his soulmate four hundred years in the past, only to have her wrenched away from him? And the worst irony of all of this was that up until the moment that Tom had evidenced interest, Magdalena had been the "unwanted" spinster-daughter of her family—a victim of her times. Betrothed three times, all three of her husbands-to-be had met with nasty demises, and after that, a combination of a lack of suitors that met her father's rigorous standards and the reputation for being a romantic jinx kept her on the shelf.

Stupid, that was—she was clever, sweet-natured, attractive, and exceedingly well educated—the fact that she was over thirty shouldn't have mattered. They'd met quite by accident; she'd come along with her father when a group of guildmasters from Jena arrived as a trade delegation and Faramir had volunteered his old man to act as a guide for a small group that included her.

He'd never believed in love at first sight, and this wasn't it. It was, however, the attraction of kindred souls. Love came later. Not *much* later, but later.

And the irony was that if he'd just listened to *her* and let *her* handle her father, they'd be scheduling a wedding right now. *She* liked the commune, liked the boys, wasn't afraid of hard work, rather admired his public-spirited attitude—irony of ironies, because of *his wardrobe,* her father had *thought* he was rich. If he'd just let *her* handle it. . . .

"I dunno why you got as far as you did with her old man," Ron said callously, helping himself to a tomato—teenage boys took a lot of filling. "I mean, we're trailer-trash compared to the Edelmann family."

"Believe it or not, it was my T-shirts," he sighed. "Dyes like that, only the rich can afford—"

And that was when it hit him, and why it had taken so long, he couldn't imagine—except, maybe, that the Adventure of the Tie Dyed Festival Shirts had been something so traumatic that he had repressed the memory.

"Pop—" Frank said warningly. "If you're thinking what I think you're thinking—remember what happened the last time!"

"Yeah," Ron chimed in. "People want their shirts colored, not themselves!"

Which was what had happened, after a sudden heavy rain shower . . . rainbow-colored customers, dripping dye all over their pants, their cars, their friends. Not good. Not good at all. Lothlorien had folded the tent and snuck out the back way, leaving behind a lot of angry people looking for someone to strangle with tie-dyed rope.

The dyes got stored, the remaining shirts distributed among the rest of the commune, and no one, *no one* talked about it anymore.

"Yeah, but there's two things different this time—the big one being that I'm *not* stoned. Come on, give me a hand, let's see if the dyes are still any good!"

If they weren't—well, he still had some ideas, and he could not believe that no one else in Grantville had realized the profit-making potential lying around unused and dusty in the grocery, the hardware-store, and the pharmacy, *all* of whom had their own little racks of commercial dyes that no one had even *looked* at. This might work. This just might work!

"Mordants," he explained, as they headed for the barn, the loft of which formed the main storage facility for all the assorted flotsam and jetsam, useless for all practical purposes but too good to throw out. "That's what we need. Mordants."

"Sounds like an RPG villain," said Frank, holding open the barn door.

"Mordants are the things that chemically bind dye to fiber," he explained. "That was where I went wrong. I forgot about mordants." Then, shamefacedly, and because he had a policy of always being honest with his kids, "Actually, I was too stoned to remember about mordants."

That was when the unexpected happened, the thing that made every bit of the pain he'd gone through in the last several years worthwhile. Frank grabbed his elbow and stopped him.

"Pop," he said, looking straight into his father's

eyes (when had he gotten so tall?), his own honest brown ones the image of Tom's own, "Pop, you have not once, in the past fifteen years, been *stoned*. Don't think we haven't noticed. Once in a while, about half as often as most guys' dads drink a six-pack, you've been a little buzzed. Never when we needed you. Maybe the rest of the town thinks you're a doper, but *we* know better. Always have. You've been a damn fine dad, as good as the best, and better than most. No shit."

He was very, very glad for the whole honesty-policy then, because he honestly broke down and cried, and *they* cried, and everyone hugged. Then the kids got embarrassed and covered it by punching each other, he had to break it up, and they all went up into the loft to check on those dyes.

"The main problem is that I know what a mordant *is* and what it *does*," he continued, as he passed boxes of giant wooden beads back to Gerry, "But I don't actually know what any of them *are*."

"How hard can that be to figure out, Pop?" Gerry retorted. "After all, you made LSD in the sixties!" He screwed up his freckled face in a caricature of bliss. "Oh wow—like, taste the colors, man!"

Tom straightened, indignant. "I will have you know that LSD was a *sacrament*, not a—a—"

"Whatever." Gerry shrugged, and took the box out of his hands. "The point is, how hard can it be?"

"Alum?" the town pharmacist looked at him with a puzzled and peculiar expression. "Yeah, I have alum. Why?"

"I want it. All of it," Tom replied, trying to look

casual. "I've got a project. And I'll swap you a dozen eggs for every pound."

He'd already sent the boys around to corral every packet of dye and every bottle of food coloring in town. He'd decided, given the slim state of the family funds, he had to confide his plan to a few select movers-and-shakers. It was going to cost him later, in ten percent of the profit, but it was worth it.

A couple of days of research later—some of it in some pretty odd places, like historical novels—and he had his answer. The easiest mordant to get hold of and the safest to use was alum; alum had the added advantage that he could get more of it in the here-and-now once the last of the Grantville supply was used up.

A little dickering later, and he had his alum. And one more thing, his secret weapon—Magdalena.

His local fiber expert. She knew what he didn't—about fibers and dyeing, textiles and fabric, what would be profitable and what wouldn't. *She* suggested that he produce embroidery thread, *not* dyed fabric as he had originally planned. The town's relatively small stock of such things—Grantville hadn't had a hobby store—was long since exhausted by hundreds of color-starved handcrafters. Old clothing was being picked apart for the colored *threads,* for heaven's sake! If he could produce brilliantly colored, color-fast embroidery thread—he'd soon be as rich as her father had first thought he was.

That was what Magdalena said, anyway, and this time, he was going to let *her* run the show. Along with everything else in the loft had been skein after skein of fine cotton thread, bought surplus and mill-end, undyed cream and white and beige, meant to be used in a knitting machine that no one had ever been able to figure out. The machine itself was rusted into an unusable whole, but the cartons of thread had been right up there next to the boxes of dye. Later, Magdalena said, they would use fine-spun wool or linen, but this was going to be more than enough to prove to Herr Edelmann that Thomas Stone *was* going to be able to support a guildmaster's daughter, and any future offspring, in the style to which she was accustomed.

Two hours later, dye-pots a-bubbling, the games began.

The pigments were too precious to waste *any*, and dye-lots were not precisely an issue in the seventeenth century. The barn became a drying shed, with the bolts of cord from the macrame-business serving as clothesline, strung back and forth between the walls at just above head-height. When the bubbling pot held only dregs that wouldn't even produce a pastel, Tom went on to the next color, so that a literal spectrum spread itself across the twine. By the time he went to bed, exhausted, the barn was full—the barn floor looked like Jackson Pollock had come for an extended stay—and the tests he'd run on every new batch had proved that the dyes were *as* colorfast as anything contemporary, and more so than most.

He fell into bed, and for the first time in a week, really slept.

Edelmann didn't speak English; he left that up to his underlings, so Tom had recruited the sour and cynical Klaus. Somehow—he didn't ask how—Magdalena had persuaded her father to drive them all out to the commune in the Edelmann's own carriage. She and her father sat on the bench across from them; Magdalena with her eyes cast down and a deceptively demure expression on her face, her father wearing a frown. From time to time, he uttered something for Klaus to translate.

"He says dat he does not need to see dis farm to know it iss not sufficient to change hiss mind," Klaus would dutifully repeat in English. "He has done this as a favor to Magdalena, to make her be seeing dat dis iss impossible." Or, "Herr Stearns hass spoke vell uff you, but vords vill not support a vife."

After each such disparaging comment, Magdalena would murmur something to her father that Klaus did not trouble to translate. Klaus' glum expression would have dampened the spirits of a manic on the upswing, but Tom was armored in his secret, and kept smiling, something that clearly puzzled Herr Edelmann.

Edelmann's expression of disapproval changed only once in the walk from the yard to the barn, and that was when he dismounted from the carriage and was confronted with the dome. It clearly took him aback—but he recovered quickly. "A man vould go mad, liffing in such a place," he muttered, according to Klaus's dutiful translation.

Finally, they reached the barn, where all three boys waited, wearing their best—or at least, their brightest—outfits. Here Tom paused to make his own little speech.

"Guildmaster," he said, speaking slowly, giving Klaus plenty of time to make a thorough translation, "I can understand completely why you felt that I was not worthy of your beautiful and gracious daughter, whom God has endowed with so many gifts."

Behind Edelmann's back, Gerry made a gagging face. Tom ignored him.

"But there is one thing that you may not understand yet about Americans," he continued. "And that is that we all live by the proverb, 'Where there is a will, there is a way.' I vowed that I would find a way to prove to you that I *am* worthy of her. I swore that I would *make* myself worthy of her. I pledged that before I asked you a second time for her hand, I would *have* the means, not only to support her, but to impress you with my ability to rise to exceed anything you could demand of me in order to win her. And here, Guildmaster, are the first fruits of my labors—"

Frank and Ronald flung open the barn doors. He'd run an extension cord out there, and set up a couple of flood-lights, which now played on the display that he and the boys had set up for maximum effect.

The drying cords had been restrung, so that instead of lacing back and forth the length of the barn, they went back and forth between the walls from floor to ceiling. And draped over the cords, skein after skein after skein of the dyed cotton thread, forming an entirely new wall of color. He'd used up all of the cotton, though he'd only made a dent in the amount of dye he had stockpiled.

Edelmann stared. Klaus stared. Magdalena looked up at last, and smiled into Tom's eyes, and his heart turned over in his chest. There was a long silence.

Then Edelmann stepped forward and reached for one of the skeins to examine it closely. Slowly he began to ask questions. Was the color impervious to wetting? How quickly would it fade? Was this all of the thread, or did he have more? Was this all of the dye? Tom fielded the technical questions with ease, having been coached by Magdalena in what her father would probably ask. Questions about marketing the thread, he left to her to answer, which she did. Her father didn't seem to notice.

Evidently he was so used to being managed that it didn't impinge on his conscious mind anymore.

Finally, silence again. And when Guildmaster Edelmann turned back to face them, he was wearing an entirely different expression than the one he'd arrived here with.

"*Also,*" he said. "*Ja, gut. Und wann moechten Ihr beiden heiraten?*"

Tom didn't need Klaus's translation for that. Magdalena's shining blue eyes were enough.

Preliminary negotiations over, Tom handed his betrothed back into the carriage, following her father, and waved at them until the vehicle was out of sight.

Boxes of thread adorned the top of the carriage; samples to go back to Jena with her father. He pretended he knew what he was doing, all the time basically repeating what Magdalena had coached him to tell her father, while she sat modestly out of earshot in the carriage, pretending that she hadn't any idea what was going on between the men.

Magdalena was going to take care of negotiating the sale of this first batch, and Tom was perfectly content to leave that part of it up to her. He *knew* he didn't have a head for business, and she clearly did.

"Well, Pop, what are you going to do for an encore?" Ronald asked, when the carriage was gone.

"Another batch with wool instead of cotton—or maybe linen," he said, vaguely, still basking in the roseate glow of knowing that Magdalena was his, *his!*

"Yeah, but the dye we've got isn't going to last forever," Ronald persisted. "Probably not even a year, so what are you going to do for an encore?"

"What'dye think? He'll come up with something!" Frank countered, punching Ronald's arm. "After all, he made LSD by the gallon in the sixties! How hard can it be to come up with dye?"

"Dammit, I didn't make it by the gallon, it was a *sacra—*" he began, but all that reading up on dyes and mordants was still in the forefront of his mind, and Ronald's question suddenly made his brain lurch down another path.

Coal-tar dyes . . . Victorian coal-tar dyes . . . ummm. Reds, purples, good god, mauve! Damn! What a great way to get Porter to put a smoke-scrubber on the power-plant stack, a profit out of selling me the acid and the tars! Eco-sound and profitable! Oh, man that's not all—coal-tar salve, microscopy stains—Doc will canonize me—by god, I'm going to convert Grantville to Green yet!

He heard himself start to chuckle with glee, and the boys stopped their roughhousing to stare at him.

"You're right!" he said cheerfully, lengthening his steps into a stride as he headed for the dome, already planning his next course of research. "I made LSD in the sixties! How much harder can it be?"

A Lineman For the Country

Dave Freer

The Thuringen Gardens was, as usual, dense with people. After collecting his first priority at the bar, Dougal Lawrie looked about for his second priority: something to sit on that wasn't a saddle. The only empty spot he could see was at a small corner table with a solitary American at it. Dougal could tell that the man was an American by the teeth and the horn-rimmed spectacles. Well—what you could see of the teeth. He had a moustache that would have looked fine on the hind end of Shetland pony.

Dougal's blue eyes took in the scene. It was a case of stand or sit over there. He decided that the rotund morose-looking fellow was either a fighter or, more likely, a windbag. Well, the former didn't worry him, and he'd always found that he could shut up a bore.

He walked over to the small table. "I'll be sitting here then," he said. No point in delaying a fight if there was going to be one. He was tired. It had been a long ride from Halle to Grantville. He'd been on the road for two days. Then he'd had to stand around while Colonel Mackay read the messages, and hoped to heaven he wouldn't be sent off again tonight. Anyway, with beer at that price he wouldn't be staying long. Grantville was a boom town and bar prices reflected it.

The solid occupant nodded. "Can't stop you."

Dougal had none of Lennox or Mackay's awe for these Americans. Some of them were doughty fighters, to be sure. Their firearms and devices were near miraculous. But he, Dougal Lawrie, was a Supplicant, like the rest of the *Clann*, even if he had somewhat lapsed in his church-going these days. Too much respect bordered on worship. The covenant made it clear: Worship was due to God and no one else. And after all these years in foreign wars: respect was something you earned. If this American got too talkative he'd give him short shrift. Anyway he had things to think on, and he was looking forward to just relaxing. Being a dispatch carrier in troubled times and places meant most of your attention was focused on the countryside. There was no chance to let your guard down. He'd done that once. Damned near been killed for his stupidity.

After a few minutes of silence the American said: "Well, aren't you going to tell me how wonderful our guns are?" The American's accent was particularly impenetrable, but Dougal was good with languages.

Dougal took a pull at his beer. "Nae. They canna

ride dispatches." That should shut him up. He wanted to drink in peace and not sing praises to the wonder of sniper rifles. He'd heard enough of it in the barracks. The average trooper didn't understand that it took more than guns to win wars. It took the movement of men and materiel. And that rested with men and horses.

The slow smile spreading over the face of the American told him he'd guessed entirely wrong. "Well, maybe you Scots aren't all damned fools."

This was fighting talk, even if it was said with a hint of a smile. Dougal tensed. "We're no' stupid. We leave being fools to the *susunnoch*." These Americans spoke English of a sort but they did not have the Gaelic. The American wouldn't even understand the insult.

The American took off his glasses. Placed them carefully in a pocket. "Watch your mouth, sonny. You Scots are more Saxon than I am."

Dougal's eyes narrowed. "*Mo chainnt?*" Seeing the American was obviously trying to decide whether "my language?" was an insult or not, he continued. "You don't have the Gaelic do you? *Canan uasal mor nan Gaidheal.*"

The American snorted. "No. I don't speak your damned language. I'm no good with foreign languages." But he'd subsided somewhat. "Ma just used to call someone a Sassanach when she was mad at them. I asked what it meant once. I guess it stuck because she used it pretty darn often."

"So your mother was a Scot? What *Clann?*"

The American shook his head. "Ma was Irish. Came to the U.S. during the troubles. She had no time for the Scottish." He tugged at his horse-tail moustache. "Well. She didn't have much time for anyone."

"Irish, eh? I served with a couple o' the Wild Geese. None of them could drink."

The American took out his glasses again. Polished them and put them on. Drained his glass in one long moustache-foaming draft. "Really? 'Zat so? We'll have another round then, will we?"

Dougal drained his. "Aye. So long as you don't talk all the time. I have nae had a time when I could take a drink in peace for three weeks. And belike yon Mackay will have me off to Halle in the morning again."

The American was already waving his tankard at the barmaid. When she came over Dougal realized this was another old feud.

To work in the Thuringen Gardens you had to have a pretty fair grasp of English. Even the German customers tended to mix in a fair amount of English. It was a source of pride. Showed you were an old hand around here. Lawrie was willing to bet button-nose Hildegarde spoke English without effort.

"*Was willst Du, Du verdammtes rundes Schwein?*" Her comment was a source of some amusement with the miners at the next table. It was apparent that the American understood not one word.

"Two beers," he said grumpily, holding up two fingers and pointing at the empty stein.

She looked at him with perfect incomprehension. "*Wie Bitte? Was?*"

Dougal looked at his empty tankard. It was obvious that this game could go on until a man died of thirst.

"Mach das zwei Krüge. Und wenn Du sie schnell bringst, erzähle ich deinem Freund nicht dass Du diesem Amerikaner Augen machst." One of the reasons Dougal Lawrie did so much dispatch riding was that languages came easily to him. It made simple things like haggling for stabling or asking directions easier, and the receiving of oral replies a lot safer.

The barmaid had the grace to look embarrassed for a second. But she was a pert one, trouble looking for a place to happen, Lawrie reckoned. She was quick to recover. She made a showy little moue. "But you already know, mine darling," she said in thickly accented, but pretty good English. This got a shout of laughter and a whistle from the table next door, and let her sashay off smiling, without the tankards.

The American looked at the empty tankards. Sighed. "I never get service. These Germans give me the gyp. We'll have to go to the bar."

"She's bringing us a couple o' pitchers. Beer's cheaper like that. Which is good o' me, seeing as how you're paying."

The American sat back. Shook his head. "Okay. Hey, I can't talk their damned language. So what did she say to me? And what did you say to her?"

Dougal decided that a few beers was worth a bit of tact. "She asked what you wanted." No point in mentioning the rotund pig part.

"And you said?"

"I told her to bring us two pitchers. And if she made it fast I wouldn't tell her boyfriend she'd been makin' eyes at you."

The American snorted. But there was a smile

behind that moustache. "And you'd have to figure out who that was tonight." The pitchers arrived. He looked up, startled. "My God. You get service, Scot." He fumbled out his wallet and paid.

Lawrie contented himself with making a mental note of the barmaid. A bit on the skinny side for his taste, but worth remembering.

Lawrie poured his beer, watching the fine head form. "If ye cannot speak German, why don't you do your drinking across at the Club 250?"

"The beer is lousy," said the American. By the way it was said, there was more. He looked at Lawrie speculatively. He shrugged. "I got thrown out and told not to come back."

Lawrie took a long pull of his beer. Grinned. "Just about have tae get kicked out o' that rat-hole if ye want to be part o' human race."

The American tugged his moustache. "Yeah. But I thought a couple of them were friends of mine. And I organized their phone, dammit. I jumped 'em over the waiting list. I must have sixty of these *New Americans* yattering at me for phones. I haven't got the instruments even where they're inside the existing line network. Anyway. Name's Tanner. Len Tanner, Scotsman. What's yours?"

"While you're buying the beer, ye can call me Dougal."

By half past eleven, on a week night, Dougal could have found a fair number of seats at the Thuringen Gardens. But few tables with as many empty pitchers. It had been Len's idea to keep count. There were a fair number.

Len stared earnestly at him over his glasses and

wagged a finger. "'S not guns or newspapers or pol'tics that win wars, no matc . . . matter what Stearns says. 'S communications. The telephone . . . the net. God I *loved* the net."

Dougal knew what the telephone was. Even though Len had made this speech, at more length, six or seven times that evening, the *net* part was still a mystery. But it had been Len's social life. He had fixed telephone systems by day and spent his nights with this *net*. Beer was a poor substitute. But Dougal had ridden through firefights and across country with messages too often not to agree about communications. He nodded. "This telephone now, and the radio . . . they could save a lot o' horses." He had a feeling that he'd said that earlier too.

"Ha!" Len snorted so explosively his moustache stirred in the breeze. "I tol' them. But they din' listen. I sh . . . said: Where we going to get replacement telephones from, huh? Like gasoline . . . 'sential supply. Said they couldn't take 'em away. That we'd jus' have to fix. Y'can't fix 'lectronic and plastic crap. Jus' throw it away and get a new unit."

Quentin Underwood was tired and irritable. Grantville needed that coal mine. He gave it his best for sixteen hours a day on a lot of days, and the committee took up more time. They could at least let him have a few hours sleep. But the trouble was that some of the equipment they'd brought through the Ring of Fire was beginning to reach breakdown point.

The German "new Americans" were good miners, all right. But specialized technical staff was still primarily "old American," or "up-timers" as people were starting to call them. And in some cases they were few on the ground.

Sure, they were training up new kids, but some things took a long time. So at 11:30 P.M., when they had a goddamned problem, they still called the mine manager. This time they'd had to send a runner up from the blast-face, because the phone system in the mine was down again—and the shift boss couldn't find the telephone tech.

Underwood ground his teeth. He'd *love* to fire her. Of all the people on the mine payroll, Ellie Anderson would be at the top of his personal *downsize now* list. And thanks to the Ring of Fire it wasn't even an option. She was literally irreplaceable. And she knew it. They'd tried new American trainees with her. The men had left saying they wouldn't put up with being spoken to like that. Quentin couldn't blame them.

He drove down the empty street towards the Thuringen Gardens. Tanner hadn't been in his trailer, but he'd been in the beer hall earlier. Quentin just hoped he wasn't too drunk to be of any use. Well, even stone cold sober, Tanner wasn't a patch on Ellie "the terror" on the mine's exchange. Tanner had worked for the local phone company. The town switchboard was electronic. Safety regs had meant that the mine's switchboard was an old electro-mechanical setup, bought from Bristol when they'd upgraded to electronic systems.

Ellie had come with it. And God help them if ever she went. So the mine management shut up and put up. She'd order what she pleased—and they'd have to find it. Mind you, she was really amazing with the damn thing. She'd stand there, in among the clicking switching stacks and turn slowly like a terrier sniffing for rats. Then she'd lunge off, heading straight for the problem. She claimed she could hear when something was wrong.

The Thuringen Gardens was nearly empty, but yes, Len Tanner was still there. Sitting at a table full of pitchers with a lean, weathered looking fellow. One of Mackay's troopers at a guess. By the looks of the two of them those pitchers were empty. Underwood pinched his lips. Tanner, especially when drunk, had a reputation for being trouble.

"Evening, Len."

The only telephone technician who had been in the office on the day of the Ring of Fire blinked owlishly up at him. "We're going up in the world, Dougal ol' buddy. The mine manager come for 'a drink with us."

Well. He sounded affable anyway. "We've got a problem up at the mine, Len. Part of the exchange isn't working. And nobody can find Ellie."

Len snorted. "So suddenly I'm wanted, huh? Well get your sorry ass out of here, *sir*. I fall unner Bill Porter these days. You go ask him."

Quentin Underwood hadn't gotten to be a mine manager without learning to be effective. "Get on your feet, Tanner. I've got men underground whose safety relies on that system. You'll either come up with me now or I'll get the sheriff to cart you up there. And you can sleep it off in the cells."

It didn't look like it was going to work. Tanner started taking his glasses off. "Firsht you'll have to get to the sheriff, Underwood."

Then the trooper at the table put a hand on Tanner's shoulder, and said with a conspiratorial grin to his fellow drunk. "We'll be helping the man, eh Len, *if* he buys us a pitcher or two, next time. Anyways, I'm so fu' I canna take another drop."

It was quicker and easier than fighting about it. "Yep. I'll buy you a couple of beers—your call, but I need your help now. This is screwing up the blasting schedule. They're making do with runners, but that's bad for safety."

The trooper smiled. "Weel, now. I'd say a dozen was the going rate, but seeing as there are men in need we'll make it a half dozen. A special price for him, eh, Len? It's a bargain we have then, mister?"

Quentin noticed that Len had pushed his glasses back onto his nose. The man was grinning behind that moustache. He was also beginning to push his chair back. The mine manager knew how to drive a hard bargain. He also knew this wasn't the time for it. He nodded. "Half a dozen."

Len lumbered to his feet. "Ma always said Scots could do a goddamn deal with the Devil. Come on, buddy. Le's go fix his problems." The tech swayed to his feet. And so did the Scot. They looked like a real life version of Abbott and Costello—if you had given Abbott about a foot of moustache.

It wasn't worth arguing about. So what if he had a Scots trooper coming along for the ride? The man seemed adroit at turning conflict to his own profit. Maybe it would be useful farther down the line. "Come on. I've got the mine truck outside."

It was the first time Dougal had been in one of these American vehicles. He sat back against the seat. A man could get used to this. And it was fast. Damn sight faster than a horse. The lights . . . well they were a good and a bad thing. You could see the road, but you couldn't see into the darkness surrounding it. He'd done too many night-rides not to know how useful it was to be able to see off into the surrounding darkness. Still, at this speed you'd have to have some lights. It was as well to have them good, he supposed.

They came to a halt at the mine compound. The gate guard let them in and Dougal found himself being shepherded into a big windowless room full of stacks of machinery.

Len Tanner looked at it, with his hands on hips, swaying slightly. Sighed. "Go back to bed, Underwood. I'll try to dig this lot out of my memory. Damned dinosaur."

The mine manager cracked a yawn. "Do your best." He turned to the shift-boss. "Hein. If he needs to go into the mine, will you detail someone to guide him? Keep him away from the blast zones."

The beefy German nodded respectfully. "*Ja*, Mister Underwood. I see to it."

Then the two of them left. Dougal looked around at the setup. Machinery at this level he would never understand. He spotted a chair and moved over to it. "Weel, I'll get out o' your way. Unless I can do something?"

Tanner was already staring up at the charts on the wall. "Nah. Siddown. God, a T-bar system. I thought I'd finished with this old stuff forever."

Dougal sat down. My, but this chair was finely padded. This foam-rubber stuff was a long way up on horsehair. He leaned back. Instinctively, he reached for the mug on the table. It was full and still faintly warm. You didn't stay alive, riding dispatches across hostile terrain, by not noticing things, even small things. "Len."

The technician looked up, irritably. "Yeah?"

"Mebbe you should look at this." He tapped the cup. "Yon mine manager said the technician was usually here of an evening, but that she must have decided not to come in tonight." He touched the cup. "'Tis still warm, just. Would anyone else be in here, drinking a warm drink?"

Tanner felt the cup. Stuck a finger in the brew. Tasted. "Coffee! She's still got real coffee! You're right, Doogs. No way she'd have left this." He snorted. "So much for the goddamned mine management keeping their finger on the pulse of things. Let's go find out if her truck's still here."

As he spoke someone knocked at the door. It was a miner, by the overalls and head-lamped helmet. "Mr. Elsberg sent me, *ja*. Klaus Kleinschmitt. I am der Health and Safety officer."

"Take us to where Ellie parks her work truck."

"Pleez?"

Dougal translated.

"Oh. *Ja*. Come."

They walked across the compound . . . to an empty bay.

Len looked at it. "Oh, shit!" He turned to the Health and Safety officer. "You'd better get a search team. She's down there somewhere. Does she go out alone?"

"Pleez?"

So Dougal translated again.

"*Ja*. It is against the rules. But Fraulein

Anderson . . . she breaks the rules. She does what she likes, *ja*. And when we try to stop her, she swears terrible, and still does it. I go to Mr. Underwood, he just throws his hands up in the air." He sighed, and picked up his walkie-talkie. "I report this. The teams will be called out. But there have been no reports of any rockfalls or problems. You want to go anywhere else?"

Len pointed. "Back to the switch-room. I might be able to work out where the break is. She might be wherever that is."

Dougal was amazed at the turn of speed that the American put into his return to the switch-room. Drunkenness too seemed to have been pushed aside. They arrived a good minute before Klaus, who was attempting to talk on the walkie-talkie and follow them. When they got into the room Len grabbed the cup of coffee and drained it. "Hope that helps me think."

He then proceeded to prove, to the watching Klaus as well as the Scot, that he could both think and work hard when he had to. He was moving at a pace that had his moustache windswept. Dougal learned that *Weepstone bridge* and *ferret* meant different things to these Americans. Minutes later, Len was peering through his glasses at the map of the risers and cross-cuts.

"The break is hereabouts." He pointed. "On the old first cut. Good chance she'll be somewhere near there. Can you take us there? We might as well fix the damn thing anyway."

"Pleez?"

So Dougal translated.

"*Ja*. You vill come and collect the helmets and

overalls? And spick slowly, pleez. I cannot understand you so good. I read the lips, and I don't see
the lips."

Len tugged his moustache. "Yeah. Well, I'll take my
translator. Just need to grab some tools, huh?"

Ten minutes later they, and four other miners, were
climbing out of the vehicle into an alcove—in which
the mine's telephone systems' maintenance vehicle
stood parked.

Len Tanner blew out through his moustache. "Ladder's gone. Come on."

They went up a riser to the original cross-cut. Len,
despite his bulk, was leading the way. Dougal didn't
enjoy the feeling of tons of earth piled above him. It
felt as if the roof was pressing down on him. They
hadn't gone far when they heard a yell. At a dogtrot
they ran towards it.

She was a mess. Blood on her face amid the dust.
She'd been crawling.

Tanner ran to her. "Are you all right?"

The woman had startling red hair and rather glazed
eyes. And a totally uninjured mouth. "Fuck me. Yeah,
I'm having a real great time. What took you bastards
so long?"

"You didn't check in, *Fräulein,*" said Klaus, severely.
"We didn't know you were down here until Herr
Tanner told us."

She waved a hand vaguely. "Oh, piss on your rules.
I was in a hurry. If I have to wait for you bastards,
I'd never get anything done."

"You must obey—

Dougal had had enough battlefield experience to
know what he was seeing. He squeezed Kleinschmitt's

arm and said quietly. "She's been hit on the head, man. Leave it now."

Already two of the team had the stretcher ready. She pushed them aside. "Gimme a couple of shoulders. I've screwed this ankle." She hauled herself up on their arms. "Aw, shit!" She winced. "Not you, Tanner. You go fix it. It's the cable-tray maybe a hundred yards on. A fucking great piece of the ceiling fell into the tray. It, half the tray and the ladder came down with me when I got up there."

So Dougal Lawrie found himself unable to leave the pressing darkness just yet. He, Tanner, and one of the miners went on to fix the fault.

Looking at the splintered stone next to the fallen ladder, Len whistled. "If that whole thing had landed on Ellie, she'd a' been dead," he said quietly.

Dougal found himself a troubled man. If one piece of the roof could come down, could not others? The thought seemed to make the blackness blacker. Give him a moonless night of dodging moss-troopers on the open moor, rather. It didn't seem to affect Tanner. The man looked too round for the ladder—amazingly light that ladder was to carry a man that heavy—but he seemed comfortable up there.

"Bugger." Irritation from the ladder top.

"What's wrong, man?" Dougal hoped he didn't sound breathless. He felt it. Damn fool situations too much beer got you into. That was why he normally stuck with just one or two.

"I musta been drunk when I packed up. Haven't got my wire cutters, f'rchrissake."

Dougal reached into his gaiter and pulled out his *sgian dhu*. "This knife will cut near anything. Ye can even shave wi' it. I would nae give it to you to cut wire, but I need to get out of this place."

"*Herr* Tanner," said the miner. "Here is the plier of the . . . liddy Anderson. It must have fallen."

Len Tanner reached a hand down. "Yeah. Better than the knife. Pass it up."

Dougal saw that the light ladder could actually take the weight of two men.

A minute or two later Tanner came down, dusting his hands. "No point in testing it. No one in the switch-room. Ellie will be in the hospital by now. Let's get outta here."

Dougal was glad to oblige.

But, some fifteen minutes later, when they got back up to the switch-room they discovered he was wrong. Ellie had a bandage round her head, but she was very present. Her foot was up on the desk and she had a militant look in her eye.

Looking at her in the light, Dougal thought she was a fine figure of a woman. She'd cut and stook peats all day, he reckoned.

"I can hear you got it fixed," she said, cocking her head at the relay-stacks.

Len shrugged. "Yeah. Simple job. Why don't you get them to take you home, Ellie?"

"And leave you and your boyfriend with *my* exchange?" she sneered.

Tanner was principally interested in telecommunications. "Ha. What the hell would I want with this old dinosaur?"

The other part of her statement penetrated to Dougal. "Ye daft besom! We just gave up a guid nights drinkin' tae pull your tail oot o' the mess ye made.

I'm minded tae put ye o'er my knee an' gi ye guid hidin'. Have ye no brains or no manners?" He was quite angered and that tended to make his English a lot thicker than usual. Just about impenetrably thick, actually.

"I think I just got cussed out by a master," said Ellie, looking impressed. "What'd he say, Tanner?"

The telephone technician tugged his moustache. "Damned if I know," he said. "Ol' Doogs here can sound off in about six different languages," he said proudly.

Dougal was quick on the uptake. He realized that the way to deal with this particular woman was to be rude right back to her. He'd met a few troopers like that, but never before a lassie. No wonder the mine manager had sounded so uncomfortable about her.

The subject of his thoughts jerked a sardonic thumb at him. "Thought you didn't approve of all these foreigners. That we Americans should keep to ourselves."

Len Tanner looked uncomfortable. "Yeah, well. Dougal is a Scot. And I got used to it."

She snorted. "Realized you made a goddamn redneck fool of yourself, you mean."

Tanner's moustache began to bristle. "Ha. So where is your 'new American' assistant, Ellie Anderson? You can't handle the Krauts either."

Ellie laughed. "More like they can't handle me. I've been through three trainees. I don't mind Krauts, as long as they jump when I say frog. They bitch about my language to the boss."

"Ain't they figured out that your bark is worse than your bite yet?"

She raised an eyebrow. "That's what you think, walrus-face. And you watch your mouth about my switching gear."

He snorted. "You want me to be polite about stuff that came out of the ark? I work with state of the art electronic equipment . . ."

Now, by the flames in her cheeks, he'd really gone too far. "Tanner, you're so goddamn stupid! Your electronic rig is *so* superior. This is 'an old dinosaur.' Well, let me tell you this, walrus-face. Within three years that piece of plastic and electronics of yours is going to be nothing but fucking scrap. Something goes wrong there . . . you toss out the whole circuit-board and plug in another. Only you can't make transistors and circuit-boards. And you sure as hell can't buy 'em. But Ollie or Nat Davis's shop can *make* the mechanical switches here, if they have to. This ol' lady is gonna be the switchboard for the town. Hell, for the whole new United States. We've got ten times the capacity we need for this mine, or even this rinky-dink town. This is where it is gonna be at. So you better god-damn learn," she snarled.

"So your switching gear might outlast my switch-board. So what?" Len held up the telephone. "See this? Do you know what I do every goddamn day? Cannibalize broken phones, crap I'd have thrown away before, and try and make one working instru-ment outa two pieces of scrap. An instrument has an average life span in normal use of maybe five years. Ain't that many new phones around. In three years the network will be half the size. And in ten you might have three telephones working. But your 'ol' lady is gonna be the switchboard for the town,'" he mimicked savagely. "Big deal. Big fat hairy deal, Ellie."

Ellie stared at him. In silence. "You know, walrus-face, that's the first time I've heard you speak any sense."

"Stop calling me walrus-face!" he snapped.

Ellie snorted. "I'll call you any goddamned thing I please. But it's time I showed you something I've been working on. I figured out that they were going to run out of instruments PDQ. I guess I ain't the most diplomatic person around because when I tried to tell Underwood, he said it wasn't an immediate priority. Fucking jerk."

"Yeah. I tried to tell Bill Porter. He wasn't listening either. People take phones for granted. They don't even think of an existence without 'em."

She pointed at a metal cupboard. "Open that."

Inside stood what Dougal decided could be a fiendish new torture device for the Inquisition.

Ellie pointed proudly to the contraption. "We've got to reverse engineer. Downgrade. They've had to go back to blasting in the mine instead of using the continuous miners, right. Well, we can't make electret sets. So I've been workin' on this."

Dougal didn't understand it, but it certainly impressed Len. "Holy smoke! Edison would have been proud of you! Does it work?"

"Yeah, well . . . The carbon granule part was tricky at first, but I got it licked once I got Ollie Reardon to make me some decent diaphragms. I'm having a bit of trouble with the antisidetone network. But it works."

Len Tanner took a deep breath. "Okay. So I guess I made a fool of myself again, huh."

He didn't sound unhappy about it. He rubbed his hands together. "Heh. We're going to see an increase in subscribers again. Work our way up. Lines all over the new United States . . . Who knows? One of these days we may even have the net itself again. I kinda thought everything I knew about was heading for being history. Makes you feel so damned useless."

Ellie Anderson scowled. "It's not so simple. If I could get the fucks to listen to me. But when everything breaks down they'll want to listen. Maybe three years from now."

Len shrugged. "We can't talk to the bosses. It's not my line and it sure isn't yours. But I'm gonna put in some time up here. Refresh myself on this stuff. The instrument fixing is going to take a back seat for a while." He smiled evilly.

Dougal shook his head. "Weel. My head is starting to hurt. An' you understand this stuff, Len. I understand my way home tae my billet."

The next day Dougal awoke—as was his lifetime's habit—at first light, with something of a headache, and an idea eating away like a maggot at his mind. Three separate facts he'd picked up last night were connecting in his head.

Firstly, up at the mine was a device which was capable of carrying many more of these telephones than it did now. Secondly, the woman technician had made a telephone itself. It was large and clumsy compared to the phones the Americans had brought with them. But compared to a letter, a messenger and a horse, it was a grand thing indeed. The Americans might not see it as such, but in Jena or Saalfeld—any city in Germany—there'd be a stream of wealthy merchants and notables who would pay very, very well indeed, for such a device. And they'd be happy to take it right now, never mind waiting the three years that Old Americans would accept.

Never mind Jena, for that matter. Just among the new American families there'd soon be a demand if they knew that they could have such a thing. Of course New Americans would want the wonderful light phones that the Old Americans had. It might be a lot easier in one of the nearby towns.

It was however the third point that really was gnawing at him though: Neither Tanner nor the woman at the mine—Anderson—was any good at dealing with Germans. If you came down to it: neither of them was any good at dealing with people. As Mackay's dispatch rider, he understood how vital communications were. But neither of those two could have explained this. And neither of them had the business sense of a rabbit. And neither could deal with authority.

Dougal put his hands behind his head and let his breath hiss between his teeth. He spoke, to varying degrees of fluency, five languages. He could explain things. He'd had to—especially to men in positions of authority. And he did have the canniness to bargain and deal. This, if he could pull it together, had the smell of the deal of a lifetime.

He stood up. First Mackay. If the colonel had left his warm bed next to that pretty and deadly wife of his, he'd be in Staff HQ.

❦❦❦   ❦❦❦   ❦❦❦

He was, along with Lennox. Dougal Lawrie saluted. "Sir. Would you be having me return to Halle today?"

Mackay shook his head. "It's already too late to do anything about it, unfortunately."

Lennox twirled his mustachios. Dougal reckoned he had the length on Tanner, if not the breadth. "Nae purpose, t'whole thing. T'would o' done some guid if we'd had word two weeks ago. But th' barges are already on th' way to Naumberg. Now th' guns'll have tae go by road instead. Through Saalfeld, Kronach, and so on."

Mackay shrugged. "His Majesty did understand the communication problem. The message will have to go back, but there's no urgency. It's a pity we didn't have word earlier though."

Dougal Lawrie cleared his throat. "About that, sir. If I could have a word, sir?"

Lennox eyed him suspiciously. "This is nae' one o' your money-makin' schemes again is it, Lawrie?"

Mackay sat back in his chair, his infectious grin spreading. "He saved us a fortune in horseflesh last time, Lennox. Let's hear it, trooper."

Dougal knew that in some ways this would be his hardest pitch. "Well, sir, if we had yon *phone*"—he pointed to the instrument on the desk—"spread oot across Germany, we'd have done away with this problem."

Mackay smiled. "And trooper Lawrie could spend his time in the beer garden instead of in the saddle. Can't be done, Lawrie. I've talked to Mike Stearns about it. It's something they'd like to do. One day. But they've other priorities."

Dougal took a deep breath. "Colonel. If I could organize such a thing—without taking away frae their priorities, in a private way like—you'd have no objection? You know how many battles have been lost because of poor communications, sir. This could change that. And it would keep me out o' the saddle, sir."

He saw the wariness in Mackay's face. "And if it works, sir, ye'd be able to talk to Julie when you were away."

Mackay laughed and Dougal knew he'd won. "You're my most reliable dispatch rider, Lawrie. You're trouble in a troop, but a good man for detached duties. So if I can help it, you personally are going to be sitting in the saddle, telephone or no. There are places it won't go to and there are not enough of these radio devices to go round."

"Aye, sir. But this would nae need me tae leave your service. There's nowt in my oath that says I cannot have a business interest on the side, as it were."

Lennox snorted. "Y' already have, ye black-hearted moss-trooper."

Lawrie ignored Lennox. Concentrated on Mackay, hoping that the young man would not think too deeply on the affair with the gypsies and their current remounts. "Sir. I've the people who can do the job. They can no' deal with the Germans. They have no' the language nor the local knowledge. If I factor for them, the money will come from the Germans and the skills from these two. And we'll have telephones. They'll aid us in the war. The enemy cannot use them even if they capture the instruments, because the calls will all be routed through Grantville. It's a bargain, sir. A bargain in which Grantville wins, the other towns win, and King Gustav Adolf wins most of all. And ye've still got your dispatch rider. I just have a wee business on the side."

Lennox snorted. "Aye. And we can provide y'r time and horses too, eh, Lawrie?"

Mackay chuckled. "No doubt. But if he doesn't do this, he'll do something else. And we might get something useful out of this."

Dougal saluted smartly. "Thank you, sir. You'll no' regret it. If we can make it work, sir, ye'll talk to Mr. Stearns about a military appropriation?"

This venture was greeted with a shout of laughter from both men. "I knew that you'd be up to some scheme, Lawrie. Get along with you, but see you keep Lennox posted with your movements in case we need you."

Well, it wasn't a flat refusal, anyway. And he had permission to proceed. Dougal was smiling as he walked away.

He found Len Tanner frowning at pieces of telephone. "My head hurts," Dougal said by way of a greeting.

"Humph." Tanner said, looking up briefly. "So does mine." His voice was carefully neutral.

Dougal realized that what he was dealing with here was a man who was used to people being friendly . . . only when they wanted something. This was going to be trickier than he thought.

"Yon lassie up at the mine said something last night I wanted to ask you about. I've an idea o' a business venture I've a wish to go into. But I dinnae ken this phone business. I need some advice or she could sell me short."

Len Tanner laughed. "Ellie? She couldn't sell a drink to an alcoholic. She's got a nasty tongue and a hell of a temper. But she's rock solid honest, even if she'll snap your nose off for nothing."

Dougal grinned. "Ye sound as if you fancy her." And then, at the thoughtful look on the man's face, he realized he'd been more accurate in jest than he'd been when in earnest.

Len shrugged. "Her bad-mouthing doesn't worry me."

"Well. She is a fine figure of a woman," said Dougal respectfully. There are some lines a wise man doesn't cross. One of those is a fellow man's taste in women.

Len blinked through his glasses. "Yeah. I kinda thought . . . when we were cut off like this. Being the only two telephone techs and having something in common we might get together. Y'know. An' anyway. I've never had any luck with women. But I thought . . ."

Len fingered his moustache. "She said 'I got no fucking interest in a redneck walrus.' Y'know . . . it took me twenty years to grow this darn thing," he said resentfully, patting his moustache. "Anyway. Tell me about this idea of yours."

Dougal pursed his lips. "Weel. It's things you said last night, you and yon lassie. You got me thinking about not having to sit in the saddle all day. About that switch-room being able to cope with ten times the number of phones. And what you were saying o' phones all over the new United States."

"Yeah. Well, the exchange isn't *all* that big, but it

has a hell of a lot more capacity than they're using. But it won't happen for five, maybe ten years. Things have got to get settled and organized first, Doogs. They keep telling us that they've got other priorities. When you put that into my kind of language, that means they've got ten other places to put the money. Me, I think that's goddamn stupid, but they didn' ask me."

Dougal nodded. "Aye. It is stupid. Ye ken, things will get organized a lot faster if we have rapid communications."

Len nodded. "Yeah. Not much we can do about it though. People ain't inclined to listen to me. I've tried to tell Bill Porter. I kept getting this 'we'll get here but we have other priorities right now.' So. We'll just have to wait."

Dougal smiled. "What if we don't wait? What if we just do it ourselves?"

Tanner laughed sourly. "Are you crazy? Nah. I guess you just don't know, Doogs. It's real big bucks you're talking about. Forget it. And forget borrowing it. The Abrabanels pretty well control venture banking and that means big projects get chosen by the town. Mike Stearns ain't a bad guy, but he's set on a whole list of other stuff."

Privately, Dougal suspected that Stearns could be brought around to it by someone who was a better talker than either Anderson or Len Tanner. But that would not fit in with this Scot's plans. "If you're not interested in such a system getting started now . . ."

Tanner snorted. "Of course I'm interested. It just can't be done."

The salmon was chasing the fly. Now to set the

hook. Dougal held out his hands. "Well, if you canno' do it, perhaps I'd better talk to some o' the students at the high school. They're full of ideas. Also Mister Underwood. I can raise money from the German towns, even if I cannot raise it from the Abrabanels. As soon as I have a working line, I'll have investors queueing. All I need is one telephone to Jena or Saalfeld. I'll have them falling over themselves to buy shares. Well, it has been nice talking. Perhaps we can employ you one day. I'd rather have had you as one o' the owners, but . . ."

Tanner stood up and pounded on the table with a force that jumbled his miscellany of components. "Students! What the hell do they know about practical telephony? You need us! You need a wireman and Ellie's instruments. And forget it. We're not being your employees!"

"Aye? So you're in, then?"

Half an hour later they were sitting in Ellie Anderson's office, next to the clicking switch-stacks. Len Tanner was being more eloquent than he'd ever been in his life.

" . . . look, Ellie. We can either sit around and wait for it to happen and stay takin' orders. Or we can just do it. We end up with a phone system designed by telephone technicians and not goddamn bean counters."

Ellie looked suspiciously at Dougal. "So what's your share of this deal, you Scots cadaver? What do you bring in to it?"

"Something you cannot. *Ich spreche Deutsch.* And what's more, the notables o' the towns around here know me. They'll assume this is Mackay's business, which means King Gustav Adolf business, no' ours." He smiled beatifically. "Otherwise, if ye tried to do it wi' out me, ye'd have every petty official demanding a bribe or a tax. They'll no' try that on with what they assume is Royal business. Besides, I can deal with people."

Tanner nodded. "He's got a point, Ellie. Neither of us can speak to people. We ain't much good with Germans."

Ellie winced as she moved her foot on the chair in front of her. "Yeah. But what are Underwood and Bill Porter gonna say about this?"

Len gritted his teeth. "We're going to make 'em offers they can't refuse."

She snorted. Shook her improbable red hair. "I don't like the sounds of this. What are we gonna do? Take a cut in pay?"

"Nope," said Len Tanner sourly. "We're going to take on apprentices. New Americans. And we're going to pretend to like it."

Ellie put her hands to her head.

"And I'll do the negotiation for ye," said Dougal, in the very tone that he'd once used to trick Gypsy horse traders. "If it all works we'll be needing them. And I'll convince yon Underwood and is it . . . Porter?" Len Tanner nodded. "Aye, Porter, that ye'll no succeed and if they agree to the terms, they'll get the trainees they want. They'll think they're getting the better of you. By the time they ken it is the other way around it'll be too late."

Ellie smiled evilly. "Underwood would agree to hiring us three-quarters of the capacity of this board if he thought his dreams of firing me could one day be real."

Dougal smiled just as evilly in return. "And ye ken, if you train yon laddies or lassies well, why, we'll be able to hire them away frae Underwood. Then he'll have to bargain for our company's services."

Ellie Anderson shook her head and laughed. "Cadaver, I can tell that you'll end up owning the company. So my terms are that you call it Anderson, Tanner and whatever your name is, so people will at least remember we existed." Her eyes were suddenly bird-bright. "Your name doesn't begin with a T, does it?"

Dougal shook his head. "Lawrie. Dougal Lawrie."

Ellie sighed. "Oh, well. I guess I won't be one of the directors of AT&T, after all. There goes another ambition."

They sat in Len's chaotic trailer, surrounded by half a ream's worth of scrawled paper and the four computers that had been his life, once. Len was painfully aware that the place was a mess. Well, it had been a couple of years since anyone but him had been in here. And since the death of the net, he'd spent little enough time here himself.

"We'd need about twenty miles of three-hundred-pound-per-mile wire. Copper is still quite cheap, thank God. Poles every fifty meters. Insulators. Then we'll need some labor to put up the poles, and the wire. Say a team of five. We're talking months of work."

Len tapped the figures into the spreadsheet. His face got longer as they added new items. Eventually he said gloomily: "It doesn't work, guys. We're about a third over budget. And there'll be stuff we haven't even thought about yet."

Dougal tapped the rough map they'd been working out distances on. "Is it needful that we follow the road? And well, can we not get the farmers to put up the poles?"

Len considered it. He'd been a wireman. "They'd probably fall down in three months. And if we go across country we'd have to clear the trees. "

"Three months is all we need," said Ellie. "Look, our aim is one line to Saalfeld. Get tolls coming in and get investors. There's no way we're gonna have enough money to set up a telephone network." She grimaced. "Especially if every instrument we make is gonna take me a month."

Len knew she could do better than that. "We'd get around that. I reckon Ollie could do most of the parts for one in a day. If he did it production-line style, we'd get a lot more. Those phones sure aren't gonna be cheap. It'll work, though. But the poles, and the time and the labor—we can't get away from that."

The Scot looked speculative. "Do we have to put up poles?"

"Unless we can insulate the wire, yes. And then basically we'd have to bury it. Which would cost a whole hell of a lot more. It's got to be up in the air."

"We couldn't just attach it to the trees?" asked Dougal.

Len shook his head. "Trees move. And they grow at different speeds. And . . ."

"Y'know . . . he's right," interrupted Ellie. "We could

do that! We're talking about three months, Tanner. We can start replacing, putting up proper poles—even during that time."

Len tugged at moustache. "It won't look professional."

Ellie snorted. "Jeeze, Tanner! We're trying to get it up and running. The Germans won't know it's not professional, and the Americans—well, why should we care?"

Len sat back. Nodded. "Yeah. I guess we could do that. And I guess we can improvise so long on the insulators. They don't have to be glass as we were planning on. I figure a piece of tire should do the job. There's stuff down at the junkyard that is beyond retreading. But even cutting all the corners, me demanding leave . . . we're still going to be way short. Ellie and me aren't much by the way of savers, Doogs."

Dougal took a deep breath. "Ah, weel." He stood up and started undoing his shirt. "As well hung for a sheep . . . This idea had better work." He pulled out a money belt. "A tribute o' my faith. A mercenary trooper does nae earn much, but I've done a small amount o' horse trading."

He spilled some silver, copper and even one golden coin onto the desk. "My savin's over the last ten years or so. Will we do now?"

Len Tanner looked at the coins. At the weather-beaten Scot. The man wasn't young. He looked at Ellie, and she at him. Back at the pile of coins. The Scot's entire life-savings might add up to three hundred dollars. The two Americans looked at the Scot. Dougal Lawrie was plainly uncomfortable. "It's no' much," he muttered. "But it's what I've got."

"It'll be enough," said Ellie in her don't-even-think-of-arguing-with-me voice.

Len nodded. "Yep." He looked at the pile again. "Equal shares."

"It's no' equal to what you're putting in," said the Scot quietly. "Shares based on what we put in."

"We're *all* putting in equal amounts," said Ellie, harshly. "We're all putting in all we've got. I can find another grand or so."

Len nodded. He could always sell a computer. They were worth a fortune these days. It would be a shock to get more for a machine than he'd paid for it for a change. "Yep. Sounds fair."

The Scot looked embarrassed. "I'm no' dishonest. That's not right."

Len tugged his moustache. "He can take it or leave it, eh, Ellie?"

She nodded.

The Scot reached down and pulled a knife from his gaiter. Slit the stitching on his belt and squeezed out a golden coin. "A ducat. My last resort. If ye're going to do that, I canna hold this back, can I?"

The caravan was made up of a load-bed and the rear axle from a rusty scrapped truck. Ellie called it Fort Knox. They'd built it up to about six foot with rough timber and roofed it over. It had four low slit windows, just above the metal of the load-bed, and a ladder to a manhole at the top. As far as Len Tanner was concerned it wasn't secure enough. The forest still had loot-hungry deserters and other perils. Wolves and bears, too. At least those wouldn't steal the wire. They might eat the three of them in their narrow bunk beds, though.

The caravan's two oxen were an added aggravation. Len longed for a truck. But then he longed for even the relative comforts of Grantville. The only "comfort" he had was the new prototype AT&L carbon granule telephone, with the Tanner-built antisidetone transformer. It, and its battery, had pride of place in the crowded caravan.

The task had so far taken a week. It was more than just following the marked trees and poles that Dougal had had put up where there were no suitable trees. Every new wire attachment point was numbered. Len would attach the phone, call in, and Ellie would record resistances. If the line went down they'd be able to tell exactly where the break was by the resistance on it. It was tedious, painstaking work. Len was at the stage of wishing for some excitement. Wishing for better German linguistic skills, too. Dougal had been with them until two days ago, but the Scot had had to return to Grantville. The bulk of Mackay's troop were taking part in an exercise in Saalfeld, merely miles away. But Dougal was posted back to Grantville.

Dieter, the assistant Dougal had found him, was so eager it was painful. And he spoke fair to middling German-English. Len found he was coming to like the boy. But he was getting mighty suspicious about this *Waldross* term the kid kept using when talking to Ellie's trainee, Lilli. Still, he'd even managed to learn a few words of German. It was different when you wanted to. Having a purpose, having a dream, had made the year 1633 in Thuringia a great place to be. It had changed somehow from a curse to a place of opportunity. It had become a United States that had a place for him too, even if it meant learning a foreign language and working his hands raw at repetitive manual labor. Another four days should see them in Saalfeld, their first target city. A lot of business from Grantville was going that way these days.

They'd just settled in for the night when boredom suddenly became a very desirable thing.

The door-bolt was literally ripped out of the wood. And through it came barreling saber-armed men. Len never even managed to get to the shotgun beside him. Instead he was wrestling with a sword-arm. Then bar-fights came to his rescue. He grabbed a tunic and head-butted. He could actually feel the nose break. But someone else had seized him from behind. More hands, strong ones, and profuse German swearing. He kicked savagely and was rewarded by more cursing.

Ten minutes later he and Dieter were tied with their own precious wire as well as rawhide thongs and dragged outside the caravan, to where more men were throwing kindling onto the fire. Len was conscious. Dieter wasn't.

A pair of riders came up through the darkness. Two of the attackers hastened to hold bridles once they dismounted. The others saluted them respectfully. Len wished like hell he understood more German. One of the men who walked into the firelight looked as if he'd just stepped out of a palace rather than the darkness of the Thuringenwald. His clothes and cape were impeccable. His boots gleamed like mirrors in the firelight. He looked down an arrogant aristocratic nose at the scene. The other . . . well, he was one of those invisible people. Everything from his dress to his face radiated *ordinary, forget me*. They walked over to the prisoners. The elegant one looked at them in such a way that Len Tanner began trying to remember prayers. He snapped something in German at them.

"I can't speak German. *Ich nix sprechen zee Deutsch.*"

The look this earned him from the elegant one didn't bode well. "So. You are one of these American interlopers, *ja?*"

"Just what are you doing here?" demanded the plainly dressed man in perfect English.

"He is a spy, Weiman. *Ja.* Or a guard. Here to watch over the route of the guns. I think we will have the truth tortured out of him." It was said in English, while the elegant nobleman watched him under half-lidded eyes.

I'm expected to understand. To shit myself. Like it could get worse. But he knew it could.

"I'm a technician. I don't know anything about your guns. We are putting up the telephone line through to Saalfeld for King Gustav Adolf." As soon as he'd said it, looking at the man's face, Len knew he'd screwed up, badly. This man wasn't a bandit. Or even some local aristocrat. This was someone who both feared and hated the King of Sweden and Captain General of the United States. Whatever he was doing here was obviously aimed at hurting the King.

"You have just ordered your own execution." He leaned forward and grabbed Len's moustache, tugging. "I will singe Gustav Adolf's moustache via you. Captain Von Streml . . ."

The plain man held up hand "Wait, Graf. I wish more information from the prisoner."

Len knew that "Graf" translated roughly into the English "Count." It was apparent the count was not accustomed to being told to wait. But it was also apparent that this man Weiman held the whip hand. The Graf stayed the order.

Weiman turned to look at the two prisoners. "This telephone. I saw them on my visit to Grantville. You can make them?"

Len knew a lifeline when he saw one. "Between the two of us, yeah."

Weiman turned back to the graf. "I think the Emperor might like these men alive."

The Emperor! That had to be Ferdinand II of the Austrian Habsburgs he was talking about, Gustav Adolf's most bitter enemy. And earlier that day he'd thought 1633 was a time of opportunity. Well, if he could talk his way into letting him call Grantville . . .

"We need our gear in the caravan. And look, if the line gets broken the machines back in Grantville will ring an alarm. And if we don't call in every morning Colonel Mackay's men will come and check. You'll have to let us call in."

By the look in the eyes of Weiman, he hadn't succeeded. "We can deal with anyone who comes out. Most of Mackay's troops are not in Grantville. So, no, you will not call in and by great cleverness give some warning. You will now show us this telephone. A small device, Graf, but it allows them to speak across great distances."

Only when he was taken back to the caravan with a couple of flaring brands did Len realized that the AT&L carbon granule telephone was also a casualty of the fight. "It got smashed." The heartbreak in his voice made the count laugh.

"You can stay in here and enjoy it, *ja*." he said. He snapped something in German and Len found himself flung onto the caravan floor. A few moments later they tossed Dieter on top of him. The young new American groaned. Well, at least he was still alive.

The troops nailed the door in place.

It was a long, long night. Dieter had regained consciousness quite soon, much to Len's relief. There wasn't much he could have done for the boy, tied up like this. Outside they could hear several of the graf's men making use of the fire and devouring their precious rations. Their beer too. The fireside conversation grew louder. Of course it was all in German. Eventually Len had to ask Dieter. "What are they saying?"

The young man's voice was bleak. "They do not like the new United States, *ja*? It takes their peasants, their ancient rights. It weakens them. And now the graf, he waits for the big shipment of the new guns for Torstensson. They will ambush them here tomorrow. If they can, they will steal them for the Austrian Emperor. If not they will destroy them."

Len ground his teeth and went on with bending and flexing his bonds. Maybe they'd break. Not that that would do them much good. "And we just happened to be in the wrong place at the wrong time." He sighed. "Listen Dieter. You are an expert telephone tech. Between the two of us we make telephones. You got that, boy? That's what I told them. That's all that is keeping us alive right now."

Len began easing his way along the broken remains

of the telephone. In the ragged light of the brands he'd seen something among the ruins.

The battery.

Finding it in the dark, with his hands tied behind him was another matter. But eventually he located the squareness. And then, managing to sit up, keeping hold of it, against the back wall, to find the insulated cable. Getting it to his mouth was something that would have been best left for circus acrobats.

Len tried not to think about what biting the wire was doing to his teeth. And then he had to maneuver some more. Trying to manage a short behind your back, when your hands were tied was exhausting. And very difficult.

A spark told him he'd managed that short.

"What are you doing?" hissed Dieter.

"Tryin' to call home. I just hope Ellie's on the board, not your bit of talent."

Spark spark spark—spark . . . spark . . . spark—spark spark spark . . .

The battery died sometime after dawn. It had been a long night, and Len had no idea if the line to Grantville was intact. Or if anyone would hear it in between the sound of the switches.

The wagon train trundled forward toward the graf's ambush. From the slit window of their prison Len and Dieter watched, horrified and helpless. Oxen don't move fast. To Len, these seemed to be moving glacially. Sixteen heavy wagons especially built for transporting Torstensson's new gun barrels. Guns that could spell the difference in the war, neatly under canvas covers. And there didn't even seem to

be any outriders. At the moment the up-grade was
the image of tranquility. It was going to be murder.
And the aftermath, if those guns got to the other
side . . . would mean that the artillery advantage that
the Swedish forces had enjoyed would be over for a
while. Men, money and materiel still weighed on the
side of Emperor Ferdinand.

Len couldn't handle the waiting. The guards might
come and beat him up but the hell with it. He yelled.
So did Dieter, adding his bull-like young voice to
Len's.

No one came in. But the sound wasn't carrying
to the wagons.

Len saw the smoke-puff at the forest edge before
hearing the gunshot. Saw the cuirassiers begin to
charge out of the forest. Closed his eyes. He could
hear the pop of pistols.

The thin bright sound of trumpets made him open
his eyes again. The pop of cuirassiers' pistols was
replaced by the heavy, solid massed sound of shotguns.
Lots of them. Looking at the wagons now, Len saw that
the canvas—if it had ever been canvas—was ripped.
Firing in massed volley from behind the rampart of
cannon-barrels, the Grantville militia was tearing the
Austrian cuirassiers apart. There was a red head in
among those on the lead wagon. And riding down the
hill from the direction of Saalfeld were the bonnets
of Mackay's Scots.

Len grinned at Dieter's bloody face. The young
man grinned back. Len hoped Lilli wouldn't mind
a couple of missing teeth. The two settled back to
watch the Austrian raiders being shredded.

⋘⋙   ⋘⋙   ⋘⋙

Len massaged his wrists, his mind in some turmoil. Ellie had not only left her switch-room but had actually kissed him. Well, that was when she and Dougal had kicked in the door to the caravan. Now, she stood and shook her head at the smashed ruins of the AT&L Mark One. Awkwardly, he patted her shoulder. "We can make more."

She shook her head. "Maybe one day. But you came up with the real answer, Len. We've been over-engineering. We thought coming down to a Bell-type instrument was stepping down. Sure, it was a long way down from electret microphones and transistors. But it wasn't far enough. Any one of the machine shops can knock together a Morse-key in a couple of minutes. We need to go back to the telegraph. We can have the telegraph covering towns from here to the Baltic in six months."

Len sighed. "I guess the internet is a way off, huh? But I suppose you could be right."

Dougal nodded. "Aye. That she is. We were talking about it this morning. Look, you Americans expect to talk to people immediately. The rest o' the world—we're glad if we can send a message within three weeks. This telegraph will do a grand job."

"And once we've got the lines, well, then the step to telephones is a much smaller one, Len."

"Yeah. I guess. So did you figure out it was Morse code I was sending?"

She scowled at him. "You made that damned noise in my exchange for nearly ten hours. And I couldn't even tell you shut up. Three shorts, three longs, three shorts. Over and over again. Why didn't you tell us what was going on?"

Len shrugged. "That's all the Morse I know. Besides, my hands were tied behind my back."

Ellie smiled. It was a slightly nasty smile. "Bet you can't say that in a year's time. You'll even dream in Morse."

Len shrugged. "If that's what it takes to make AT&L fly . . . I will." He pointed to the rout below. "So how did you organize this? I mean the militia I can see, Mackay's troopers back from Saalfeld."

Dougal rubbed his butt. "There were horses before telephones, Len. And I've got a mort of an investment tied up in you. I couldnae let that go tae waste now, could I? It's going to cost you, mind. I have nae been in the saddle for months, and I'm damned sore."

Ellie shook her head at the third partner. "Lawrie, you're a fraud. Len, he led the scouting party, rode back to Grantville and then rode cross country to Saalfeld to find Mackay. He's been through about six horses, and been in the saddle just about nonstop since last night."

"Aye, but she was the one who got yon Stearns and his wife tae come up and listen to the tappin', to get it into his head where you were and why we needed tae scout it." Dougal grinned. "It wouldnae have been worth his life not to come up to the mine. Ye ken we've got some good out of this. Mike Stearns saw the value o' the idea no more than five minutes after Becky. We've got backing for the telegraph."

Ellie put an arm over Len's shoulder. "You're something of a hero, Len Tanner. Everyone in town is already talking about this." She pointed across at the hastily set up aid station. "Dieter is telling the militia nurse quite a tale by the looks of it. Story is going to grow, boy. You're going to be a popular fellow. Not bad for a man who didn't have a friend in Grantville three months ago." She looked at him quizzically but with an unusual tenderness. "And all it cost you is a black eye and maybe a couple of ribs. And blistered fingers."

Len blew through his moustache. "The truth is, Ellie, I did it to save my own skin, as much as anything."

Dougal grinned. "What they dinnae ken their hearts won't grieve over."

"And you, Len, are going to keep your mouth shut and let the lying Scots company spokesman do the talking," said Ellie firmly.

Len looked speculatively at Ellie. She'd kept that arm over his shoulder. "You wouldn't like to repeat that kiss, would you?"

Ellie actually blushed. "Not with that damn moustache, Tanner."

Len put a reflexive hand to it. Sighed. "Hey, Doogs . . . ya said that knife of yours was sharp enough to shave with. Lend it to me, will you?"

Between the Armies

Andrew Dennis

1

It was a bright cold January afternoon in Avignon.
An unassuming, long-haired, round-faced man in a
clerical soutane sat at a desk in a high chamber of
the Palais du Pape. He had the window open, for
the cool breeze. Outside, the winter sun cast a light
like crisp white wine on the Dom des Rochers and
glittered on the Loire.

Monsignor Giulio Mazarini, Canon of St. John
Lateran, Secretary to the Legate of Avignon—the
Legate, Cardinal Barberini, was in Rome to the minor
inconvenience of Mazarini's career—had found a quiet
spot to look over the latest intelligences. He did not

need to—he was between achievements, becalmed. The canonship was a sinecure he had held for some time, and his real work was diplomacy.

He had done, false modesty aside, good work for His Holiness and his Spanish allies—better to say, masters—in the Mantuan matter, even if others had sniffed at the self-aggrandizing behavior of a junior diplomat not thirty years old. Let them. If that battle had not been stopped before it began, the treaty negotiations would have become impossible, and even the botched peace that French mission to the Emperor had secured would have failed.

He had even risen from negotiating with Richelieu with credit: shaken hands with the man and come away with all his fingers. In truth, Mazarini had a high professional and personal estimate of His Eminence. Despite Mazarini's best efforts, the cardinal had taken the Pignerol valley as his price to keep French troops out of Mantua. A lesser man would not have had that much to show from bargaining with Mazarini. He had even found Richelieu pleasant and affable.

Mazarini had been rewarded for his work and now sought to anticipate his patron's next command. Hence his present diversion with the reports from the rest of Europe. Since the Swedish successes of the previous autumn, the main source of political and diplomatic information in Germany, the Society of Jesus and its devotion to regular reporting, had dwindled.

But not dried up. Information still came out. The reverses of the Catholic League made for intriguing reading—Tilly defeated, the Swedes looting Bavaria. Add to that the appearance of this new polity, claiming to be from the future, among the multifarious

Germanies. Even Mazarini could hardly find that news dull, whatever its credibility. From the future, indeed. There was certainly no shortage of lunatics in the Germanies—it seemed the Bohemian disease was a contagion.

Then, the latest from Caussin at Paris. The despatch of Servien—Chretien, not the Marquis de Sable by that name whom Mazarini had known in Mantua—to Vienna and Brussels by way of Thuringia, that was all too credible. A moment's thought to order the implications in his mind, and—

He opened the door to his chamber and bellowed down the stairwell. "Heinzerling! Get me a map of the Palatinate—no, maps of the whole Rhine. And get your fat German backside up here!" He shouted in French, the language the two had best in common other than Latin.

Shortly, from the stairwell, came Heinzerling's heavy footsteps. Although little worse than most parish priests, he was below the standards Jesuits expected even of an army chaplain. Either the Society of Jesus had some deeper use for him in mind or had simply ignored his raucous behavior and not dismissed him from the Society.

The latter was more likely. The last five years' frenetic re-Catholicization of the Germanies had seen the barrel scraped for priests.

Even so, nowhere was desperate enough to put Heinzerling in charge of a parish. Heinzerling had had to join the chaplaincy of Tilly's army. He had left that post carrying messages three months before and not been in any hurry to go back. For the time being Mazarini had appropriated him as aide-de-camp.

A disaster as a priest, he was one of life's better sergeants. Mazarini had learned the use of the breed as a cavalry captain in the Valtelline War. That Heinzerling was fluent in a dozen languages was certainly no disadvantage.

"Put that foul thing out and come here," said Mazarini, when Heinzerling shouldered the door aside and rolled in with a bundle of maps under his arm and his ever-present pipe clenched between his teeth, a habit he had picked up from English mercenaries in the Imperial army. "What do you know of Mainz?"

"I was born near there, why?"

"If you wanted to cut the Spanish Road from there, how would you do it?"

Unlike most soldiers, Heinzerling had some grasp of strategy. "Up the Mosel, or there're probably a couple of routes across country. More expensive, but quicker than besieging every damned fort from Koblenz to Trier."

"You think the Swede will do that?" Mazarini stared at the map, trying to squeeze more information out of it by sheer pressure of staring.

"If Wallenstein lets him, *ja*."

"So the Spanish have to—" Mazarini let it trail off. The implications for the Spanish if they lost their road up the middle of Europe were obvious from a single glance at the map.

"*Ja*, and they—why are we discussing this?"

"Don't tell me you don't read these reports before I do." Mazarini grinned to take some of the sting from his words. He had a simple arrangement with Heinzerling with regard to his duties to the Society: he could send reports to Satan himself provided he was an efficient aide. Besides, Mazarini had himself only narrowly avoided being talked into the Society which had educated him.

"Well, this Thuringia business, with Richelieu's man, is that it?"

"Exactly. We'll make an intriguer of you yet. Here, roll that out." The map showed the Germanies in more detail than he needed, and he had to hunt about a bit for the points he wanted. Mazarini stabbed his thumb, finally, at Leipzig. "Here, this is where the Swede knocked Tilly back on his heels."

"More, *mein' ich*. Tilly's not just knocked back, the old *teufel* is finished. Spent. I was there."

"Fine, whatever. But now the Swede is here." Mazarini drew his thumb south a little and west to the Rhine. "Mainz. Where, as you observe, he's right for an attack on the Spanish Road in the spring."

"Where he's right to get kicked off before a year is out if he does. Tilly's gone, fucked, but Wallenstein's not going to be so easy. The Swede's been running himself ragged for three years all over the Germanies. Before that, Prussia. Wallenstein's going to come roaring up the Donau, unbuttoning his britches as he goes to be ready to fuck the Swede."

"Quite. Now, in all this," Mazarini said, "why is Richelieu sending this other Servien to Thuringia, and not to Mainz? Mainz is the logical place if he wants to subsidize the Swede."

"These newcomers, it seems to me. They are definitely supporting the Swede?"

"Now you're getting it. They've got a regiment of the Swede's horse on hand, which I think counts for more than this nonsense about where they're from."

"You believe he'll take the opportunity?"

"Yes. Or, he will if Louis lets him. He will have the Swede supported on the Rhine, enough to hold off Wallenstein and still get a force up the Mosel. Spain will throw everything they have into saving their precious road. And this time there will be no way to stop it all with a convenient knife in the right set of ribs."

"They could—" Heinzerling paused. "No, you're right. No one the Spaniards can knife to stop the armies marching. It will all get a lot worse, *nicht wahr?*"

"A lot worse. Especially if Richelieu gets Spain mired in Germany and makes mischief elsewhere." Mazarini scowled at the map, as if willing Gustavus Adolphus away from the Spanish Road. That road had been instituted in days when the English were resolute in their heresy, rather than kissing Spanish diplomatic ass and leaving their shipping alone, inasmuch as a nation of inveterate pirates could bring themselves to do that.

The road was the land route from Spanish-held Genoa to Flanders, a hard road and an expensive one. *Poner un pica en Flandes,* they said, for anything difficult and expensive to just short of impossible.

"Don't know why Spain doesn't just abandon the Road. They haven't used it in ten years," said Heinzerling.

"That hasn't stopped them fighting for it. You forget, I was in the Valtelline for the last bloodletting. And the Mantuan business, for which that fathead de Nevers and his alleged inheritance was no more than a pretext. We kept that from a worse fight only by the Grace of God." Mazarini made a face. "Worse fight. Hah! Plague and fever and nearly three years of butchery." He trailed off, remembering some of the things he had had to ride past in cavalier finery. He had stuck resolutely to his clerical dress after that.

Heinzerling prodded, seeing his boss about to grow maudlin. "So what do we do?"

"Try to stop my good work being undone by Spaniard hotheads, that's what we do." Mazarini scratched his chin, although he had already thought it through. "We have to get into this before worse happens. Go, start packing, my German friend, you're going to be taking a trip home soon."

Heinzerling left and Mazarini turned his mind's eye to Thuringia and the problem of making contacts in this Grantville. Anywhere else, and the notables would be known to someone. A discreet question or two and the Church's formidable network of gossips would see that the information got to him.

So, instead, to first principles: if you want to know something about a parish, ask the priest. He began to rummage through the reports. The one that named the church in Grantville was among the earliest—the doctrinal lay of the land had been the first priority of the spies, given what it usually told about a local ruler in the Holy Roman Empire.

When Mazarini saw the name that church had borne when the town first appeared, he gaped for a moment. When he saw the spies' comment that it was clearly a heretic establishment as there was no such saint, he positively bellowed with laughter, slapping the desk in his mirth.

Heinzerling put his head back around the door as Mazarini was recovering, some minutes later. "*Ein* problem?" he asked.

"No, quite the reverse. I think there is more to the story about Thuringia than I was prepared to credit. You remember who we had in here last week? Who you had to 'escort' out of the Palais?"

"That *arschloch* down from Paris?"

"The very same." Mazarini turned the report around on his desk. "Here, look here."

Heinzerling looked down at the paper, his lips moving a moment. When he looked up, he was grinning. "*Ja*. Definitely from a far and strange time. Of course there is no such saint, he isn't dead. Yet. More is the pity."

"Oh, it makes too much sense not to be true." Mazarini choked while his belly shook again with laughter. "Saint Vincent de Paul. Oh, he should be, he should be. What do the French say of their priests? The shortest way to hell?"

"Is to be ordained a priest, *ja*."

"Quite so, and de Paul is trying to teach them their letters and to stay out of the whorehouses. The patience of a saint!"

Heinzerling's grin widened. "Would you mind that I tell him?" He was fighting to control his face, trying to reconcile the expostulating little man he had marched out of the Palais by the scruff of his soutane with the image of a plaster saint. With his name on the front of a church, yet.

Mazarini choked again, and then roared with another burst of laughter. "No," he said when he recovered, "In the name of God and all his Angels and Saints, including Saint Fucking Vincent, no. The wretched mendicant will simply increase his demands to match his new status. No, Heinzerling, you're going to

Thuringia. And I want reports on everything, you hear me? Everything."

2

Six months before, two newlyweds had walked out of Saint Vincent's, Grantville, after the novelty of a Methodist wedding service conducted in a Catholic church.

"Just got to change, then I'm ready when you are, Larry." The Reverend Simon Jones came back into the church from waving off the happy couple. "I intend to scandalize my flock by buying a beer for a romish idolater."

That was assuming Jones' congregation hadn't completely accustomed themselves to their pastor keeping company with a Roman priest, or that they were upset by his having borrowed St. Vincent's in order to have room for the guests at the wedding.

Mazzare grinned. "I looked it up. You've got more than a century to get drunk and chase the girls before Wesley comes to put you straight."

"Ah, touché." Only the day before Jones had twitted Mazzare about papal infallibility being anachronistic in 1631.

While Jones was changing in the sacristy, Mazzare cleared the more egregious litter from the church. The sacristy, the priest's green-room beside the sanctuary, concentrated the smells of the church: candles, floorwax, furniture polish and a hint of incense, the distinctive smell of Catholic churches everywhere.

The midsummer sun struck down through the

geometric stained glass. Too art deco for a church, not enough for a cocktail bar, Mazzare had once said of it.

Jones raised an eyebrow at the double handful Mazzare dropped into the wastebasket. "Couldn't that have waited for tomorrow?" he asked.

"I've got eight o'clock mass tomorrow morning. Mrs. Flannery, God bless her, comes in half an hour early to dust things. I doubt I could face her if"—Mazzare bent, and reached into the basket—"she found this."

He held up the offending object: one of Grantville's fine collection of now-anachronistic beer bottles.

Mazzare grinned, dropped the bottle back into the basket. "Bad enough I allow Protestants in here, without I allow drunken, littering Protestants in. And she'll say all that without opening her mouth. That woman can glare."

"Ah, now that was probably one of your own papists seeking to discredit the Methodist confession. Another romish plot."

Mazzare laughed. "I do wonder why I bother having anyone clean this place, you know. The amount of time I spend tidying up so I can face the ladies in question—"

"And well done for facing Irene Flannery at all."

"I'm sure she loves you too—I might as well do it myself."

"Have you considered a witch-hunt? They're all the rage these days," Jones said, holding open the door.

Mazzare stopped, frowned. "Now, don't even joke about that. We're right in the height of it here and now."

"Only, what, fifty, sixty years before Salem?" Jones nodded. He'd been doing some reading as well.

"About. One of yours, that."

"Eh?"

"Sorry. Protestant. Although in your case you can say 'before my time.' Come to that, does Methodism have any atrocities to its credit?"

"Other than three-hour sermons?"

"You know what I mean. It's the season for them hereabouts. Magdeburg." Mazzare paused, shuddered, went on. "The Inquisition. Forced conversions. Thuringia's Protestant this week."

"I heard. Still a fair few Catholics, though."

"Yes, but am I one of them?"

"Whoa there, big fella. This sounds serious." Jones felt a sudden start of alarm at the expression on Mazzare's face. He let the door swing shut.

"It is." Mazzare sighed. He leaned on the tall vestment chest with both hands. The summer sun was high. Through the stained glass, it lit the top of the vestments chest in a rainbow dapple almost too bright to look at. Mazzare stared into the glow for a moment.

"Troubles. And then some. Yes." He turned, leaned back against the heavy chest of drawers and folded his arms before he carried on. "No, it's—well, lots of things. You've seen the name out front?"

"Yes, what of— I see. He's still alive, isn't he? And this is only one of many shocks, I take it?"

"Well, it's the easiest one, just a little work with a paintbrush. That, and having to dust off my Latin to say mass in, and oh, how the old guard are loving that."

"I can imagine. Some of that Gregorian stuff is easy on the ear."

"Whatever." Mazzare waved aside the aesthetic merits of the Tridentine mass. "Simon, I didn't sign on for this. Here, the shop manual for this place, you've seen it before."

"Sure." Jones had seen the heavy, leather-bound volume Mazzare had picked up. It contained the liturgy for every conceivable service, office, benediction and mass that could be performed in a Catholic church. Jones had been particularly taken with the engagingly mediaeval Novena of Saint Blaise.

Mazzare let the book fall back to the table it had been on. "Heresy, every word of it, in this day and age. Just for the language it's in. I've got a catechism, the '92 one, that could get me executed, just for the suggestion that Protestants might be Christians too. That's what I signed on for, vowed to obey. Here and now, though, the orders are different. Damned if I do, damned if I don't."

Jones glared. "You snapped at me for lawyering?" he said. That had been Mazzare's response to Jones' last attempt to jolly him out of his gloom. "Look, Larry, if the pope's not infallible— If there's—well, what I mean to say is that what you've got there"—he jabbed a finger at the missal—"is the best the Catholic Church knew how to be up to, what, '98? The turn of the millennium in your own case. So take it forward. Look, the Inquisition won't get called in to Grantville if anyone around here can help it. They're in for the bum's rush if they turn up anyway. Just keep your corner of the Church of Rome as clean as you can."

"Can I do that?" Mazzare's tone said that he didn't believe it. "What do we do, Simon? Sit on our asses and pretend the word of God isn't being used as toilet paper everywhere more than three miles from this spot? What does that do to our parishioners, when some asshole, pardon my mouth, preaches a damn crusade because we're setting a bad example? Or do we just join in the lunacy?"

There was a silence between them for long moments, broken only by the refined tick of the sacristy clock. Jones said nothing.

"It's a tough one, Simon," said Mazzare into the silence.

Jones offered a face that, had he ever played poker, would have been a winner. Eloquence, polished before his own congregation, deserted him for a moment. What to say? Then it came. He pointed at a spot on the wall, where the only answer to his friend's worries was hanging.

Mazzare understood, laughed ruefully. "But," he said, "as the Irishman said, if you want to get there, you don't want to start from here."

Jones shrugged. "We've time to think. Come on, you old papist, there's a better use for the day."

Together they went out to find the party. The real trick would have been avoiding it.

3

The months passed, and Mazzare and Jones settled into something that was not routine. There were too many changes and shocks for that. But it was at least an accommodation with the life of twenty-first-century clerics transplanted to the seventeenth. They did not speak again of Mazzare's troubles, for the day-to-day hard work of pastoral responsibility for congregations that doubled and redoubled was enough to take the load off either priest's mind, just as five minutes of real stomach cramps will cure any amount of heartache.

It was February of 1632 before the issue arose again. The Reverend Jones answered the telephone late in the evening.

"I've had a letter, Simon." The voice was Mazzare's, abrupt as usual. He spent most of his time exhausted these days.

"Letter, Larry? Who from?" Jones had been half-asleep himself when the phone had rung.

"You remember we were talking about what'd happen when the hierarchy heard about me? I think the other shoe's dropping."

"Oh. What does it say? And who in particular is it from?" Jones sat up straighter in his chair.

"Guy name of Mazarini. He's a papal diplomat at Avignon."

"In France?" It was the best Jones could do. Mazzare was assuming he knew more than he did.

"Not for a while. Avignon's a papal state, this guy works for the head of it."

"Sounds heavy."

"Might be. Why don't you come over, we can have a chat while I think what to do."

Jones begged off until morning, when he made his way to Mazzare's presbytery in the quiet hours of the late winter dawn. Mazzare was already up and waiting.

"Someone I want you to meet, as well," he said, by way of greeting. "Father Augustus Heinzerling."

The priest in question was a short, wide, brawny-looking man, his shoulder-length hair and prize-fighter face clashing with his clerical dress. He nodded to Jones. "*Ein Ehre,* Herr Jones." He said it "Tschones."

"Pleased to meet you, too," said Jones, glancing across at Mazzare, whose face was impassive. "You come from Avignon?"

It turned out Heinzerling's English was reasonable, if German-accented and scented with cheap tobacco. "I am come presently from Avignon. I have the honor to be from Germany in my origins."

"I guessed," said Jones.

"Father Heinzerling is here in violation of King Gustavus' prohibition on Jesuits, it seems." Mazzare's mouth twisted, wry. "But we have freedom of religion here, so I think we needn't turn him in just yet. He brought Monsignor Mazarini's message for me. Here, before we go any further. I've written out a translation."

Jones took the two sheets of paper, one a heavy, ragged-edged sheet with wax seals and pale brown ink and the other feint-ruled with Mazzare's neat handwriting. Neither version was a long document.

"Doesn't say much, does he?" said Jones when he had finished reading. "Would be honored to make your acquaintance, interested in discussing matters theological. There's more?"

Mazzare grinned, although there was no humor in it. "Tell him, Father Heinzerling."

"The monsignor is a diplomat. He hath seen implications in Grantville"—he gave it the French

pronunciation—"and Sweden. He would have correspondence with Grantville in the hope of a present
peace."

"You'll raise this with Rebecca?" Jones looked to
Mazzare for that.

Mazzare nodded. That was a given. "There's more,
though, Simon. Tell him, Father."

Heinzerling nodded. "Richelieu has sent his man
Servien to Wien and thence to Grantville. Thereafter
to Bruxelles. The monsignor believes his Eminence
seeks to do Spain a mischief by provoking more
general war in the Germanies."

Jones nodded. "Definitely one for Rebecca. Larry,
I think your hopes of tidying up your hierarchical
headaches are still faint."

"Maybe," said Mazzare, "on the other hand, Mazarini works for the pope. Something might come of
it, after all."

4

"Your Eminence." Mazarini began to kneel, feeling slightly silly doing so for a cardinal younger than
himself.

"Come, Giulio, we are in private. My esteemed
uncles may have fine ideas about the dignity of car-
dinals, but I am not so grand. Come, sit by me.
Come." Cardinal Antonio Barberini the Younger might
disavow his grandeur of station but, like the rest of
his family, he had done well out of his uncle's secur-
ing of the Vatican.

Mazarini took the chair he was waved to. An easy

conversational gambit—"How is the cardinal finding Avignon?"

"Now that I am here? As ever I did. Charming. Rustic. Alas, French. Come, Giulio, you have not sought a private audience to inquire after my health and pleasure, eh? Out with it, Giulio, out with it."

Mazarini smiled. "The cardinal finds me transparent."

Barberini snorted. "Not only this cardinal. I was met at the border by one of Richelieu's intendants." The warmth had gone from Barberini's face.

"Your Eminence?" Mazarini made himself ask the question, although he knew what was coming.

"If you think our esteemed brother in Christ at Paris does not see and hear everything in this town you are not the man who was recommended to me."

Mazarini nodded. "I was waiting for a response."

"From Richelieu? You have it. His Eminence is displeased. Speaking for Rome, so is His Holiness. Speaking for his Holiness, perhaps helping pry apart France and Spain is no bad thing. Speaking for my dear uncle Maffeo, it would be good work but your timing is execrable."

Mazarini slumped in his chair. "Such was not my intention. I had thought France and Spain were about to be at each other's throats again."

Barberini smiled again. "Come, events make fools of us all, sooner or later."

"As they have of Richelieu." Mazarini grinned. "He would have had more for France by doing nothing."

"Or by helping the Swede." Barberini's moustaches twitched as he said that, as if he smelt something vile.

Mazarini nodded. "Although there he—he is helping the Swede?" He frowned.

It was Barberini's turn to grin. "No, I doubt it. I read your appreciation, good work, good work. Come, Richelieu is not so stupid as to think he can sway the Swede now the Swede has the Jew money, no?"

Mazarini sucked at his moustache for a moment. "I am pleased the cardinal finds my work useful. Has His Holiness any further directions as to my actions in Thuringia?"

Barberini pinched the bridge of his nose and sighed, deeply. "I cannot speak in detail, you understand? Uncle Maffeo may have raised me to the purple but he still expects me to be his little nephew. I think you should take care. When I left Rome my uncle was considering two million in subsidy to Wallenstein. Just, you understand, to balance the Swede. Olivares' lapdogs were snarling as usual about our lack of enthusiasm for the Habsburg cause. And the French army has yet to stir out of its winter quarters. Much could happen before springtime."

"So I may continue making preparations to open formal discussions later in the year?"

Barberini chuckled. "No, if you would be a peacemaker, you must wait for war. Best to wait for the die to be cast before you work your charms in the Germanies."

Mazarini felt his jawline grow numb with the effort of maintaining his face. He kept his voice slow and careful, his manner that of the patient, polite *uomogalanto*. "And while the cardinal awaits the development of the implications, how free a rein is Wallenstein to have to rape his way across the Germanies? How many converts for the Lutherans will satisfy the cardinal? How far past the right time to act does the cardinal wish me to wait?"

"As long as it takes!" Barberini slapped the arm of his chair. "As long as it fucking takes! Do you not see what Richelieu wants? Do you not? As soon as the Church moves to stop France, Louis of France becomes another Henry of England. How many do we lose then, Monsignor?" Barberini sighed. "Please, forgive me. I set a poor example, no?"

Mazarini waved the apology aside. "I provoked the cardinal. But, please, Richelieu threatens apostasy?"

"Come, does Richelieu ever threaten? Overtly, I mean? You know the man, Giulio. You know him, how he talks. How he can hardly control Louis at times, as if Caussin doesn't have *that* fool on a tight leash."

Mazarini raised an eyebrow. "We're counting on Caussin now? That prig?" He also had doubts that the popular opinion of Louis of France as a blithering, purblind, easily led idiot were entirely accurate.

"He is a good and pious man, else Richelieu would not have appointed him the king's confessor." Barberini waved a finger of admonition as he spoke and grinned at his own joke.

"The cardinal may joke, but Caussin is a good and pious and above all loyal man. That is his trouble. Richelieu does take some of his duties seriously, and the king's conscience is one of them."

"Yes," Barberini waved aside the minor matter of a monarch's conscience, "but we digress. We dare not prevail upon France lest they turn Protestant. We dare not prevail upon Spain lest they work a mischief on the church in the guise of their own piety. May god forbid a church run by Olivares and his lot, eh?"

Mazarini held his tongué with the first—insolent—reply that came to him. "We dare not," he said finally, "dare not."

"*Basta!* Don't be such a fool, Giulio. What we dare not is set the Church against what the two largest Catholic powers want. One of which is Spain, which runs the church in its territories how it damned well pleases."

"And the Catholics in Germany? Is it necessary to kill them to save them for the Church and the House of Habsburg?"

It was Barberini's turn to be silent while Mazarini glared at him.

Mazarini cracked first and sighed, deeply. "So I am called to my obedience. So be it. I will say I could do more—"

"I don't doubt it. Come, if it were only Uncle Maffeo and I perhaps you might be allowed to try, eh? For now, there were too many . . ." Barberini's forced bonhomie trailed off. "No, I mislike it, too. But do nothing, Giulio. To intermeddle and fail before the war begins, eh? You see?"

"So the possibility of embarrassment must take second place to the certainty of bloodletting?"

Barberini frowned. "I share your disappointment. But we are both bound to obedience."

Mazarini hung his head. "I know," he sighed. "I have a man in Thuringia. On his way back, more than likely."

"I know. Your messenger. Do not send him back with any message."

Mazarini looked the cardinal full in the face. "I understand."

The Rhone flowed slow and even, the litter of Avignon only thinly scattered in it. "Obedience," he said, and spat. The spittle drifted down to vanish, blown by the wind under the arch of the bridge.

The thin winter sun, not yet tinged with the warmth of spring, scattered and danced on the wavelets around the river boats. He mimicked Barberini's pompous tone. "Come, Giulio, you patronizing little bastard." He spat again.

He hawked up one more, this time for the House of Habsburg, and dropped a good one into a boat as it emerged under the Pont St. Benezet. Snickering like a naughty boy, he stepped back from the parapet. *Ah, if it was all that simple. Do the thing and escape notice after. The fat fool. And his*—back to the parapet for another gob of malice into the river—*dignity!*

"Monsignor?" The voice was German-accented. "Monsignor Mazarini?"

"Ah, Heinzerling. There I was, convinced my life was being written by Cervantes from his assured place in Hell, and you arrive to be my Sancho Panza."

"Monsignor?" Heinzerling was frowning.

"Did the paltry contribution of Spain to world literature pass you by, Father?"

"No, Monsignor, but—"

Mazarini waved it aside. "How was Grantville?"

Heinzerling grinned. "All the reports had and more. The priest there, Father Mazzare, invites you to visit him, and their dignitaries would welcome discussions provided there is no expectation of conclusion. I have here for you a letter from the priest Mazzare, a note of the words I had with the Jewess I spoke to who is in their council of government, notes of what I saw in the town, everything." He pulled out a small packet of papers, on which the rings of ale mugs were visible.

No doubt there would be fowl-grease and tobacco-scorches where he had composed the notes in taverns on the ride back. Mazarini gestured for the paper. "I shall look forward to reading this. Father Heinzerling, does the priest at Grantville need a curate? Can he afford one?"

"He is alone, yes. He seems rich enough to hire a curate, too. Why?"

"Because you did not meet me here, Father Heinzerling."

"But Deacon Bazin said you'd be—"

"Never mind that little turd. If he asks, I wasn't here. No, you go back to this Grantville, make yourself at home. Get a living of this priest who thinks de Paul is dead, and wait for word. While you're waiting, get letters to me in Rome, where I'm going, eh? You have the address of my usual correspondent there, yes?"

"Yes, but—"

"I cannot go to Grantville. I need a pair of eyes and ears there, and someone who will keep me informed. You're going back of your own free will because you missed me here, yes? I left word—I'll see Bazin later to leave it—that you were to follow me to Rome, but like the thickheaded German oaf you are you went back to this town of wonders in Germany, with that woman you think no one knows you keep, yes?"

"*Ja—*"

Mazarini waved to shut him up. "You've come out, missed me here and gone and got drunk, all right? That's the excuse you've used every other time you've been at home with the woman, yes?"

Heinzerling grinned. "Your spies are good."

"You have a lot to live up to, eh?"

5

Heinzerling returned to Grantville with what appeared to be a small party of refugees: a woman and three small boys.

"I have no response for you," he said to Mazzare. "The monsignor is recalled to Rome."

"Why?" Mazzare had had hopes of a response that would ease his own tension.

"I cannot say for sure. He did leave word that I might come to Grantville if I wished it, and would come himself when he might."

"What as?" Mazzare frowned. "You, I mean. His spy?"

Heinzerling shrugged. "He would have reports of me, *ja*. Will you have a curate in whose ears you might speak no secrets?"

Mazzare stared at him, hard. Then, coming to a decision, sighed. "Fine. I need the help. You can stay at least until Monsignor Mazarini arrives."

Heinzerling nodded. "And Hannelore can keep the presbytery. And clean the church."

"Ah," said Mazzare, "let us discuss Hannelore . . ."

✧✧ ✧✧ ✧✧

The months passed. Work, again, was the remedy for Mazzare's doubts. Grantville's population swelled. The expanding cordon of rumor and report was like an osmotic membrane, sucking in the frightened and unsettled, the hopeful and the greedy.

Mazzare was far and away the busiest of the pastors in town. His responsibilities to what had already been the largest congregation in town doubled and redoubled; more of the refugees, immigrants and outright carpetbaggers were Catholic—or at least decided to be so on arriving—than any other denomination.

On top of that, he was working as part of Grantville's corps of mechanics and teaching at the high school, evening classes for those who wanted to try their hand at the new trades the Ring of Fire had brought.

"I'm doing the work of a bishop, Simon."

"Put in for the promotion, then," said Jones, muffled inside another recalcitrant engine. "You got a ten-millimeter nut?"

"Sure." Mazzare rummaged in one of the drawers of his rollaway. "Joking apart, if we hadn't been such an ageing town, we'd have been in real trouble."

"Eh?" Jones stood up.

"Well, the Ecumenical Relief Committee. What'd we have done without all the old—"

"Battle-axes?"

"May you be forgiven, my son. Good word, though. Here's the nut."

"I know what you mean. I never thought I'd say this, but having a supply of fierce elderly ladies on hand was a godsend when it came to soup kitchens, if nothing else."

"I'm getting sidetracked again. We're getting to be a fair-sized deanery here and practically a diocese. It's more than six priests can deal with, never mind the two of us. And I'm worried about things getting, you know, tense."

"Tense? I haven't seen any of that sort of thing other than maybe some brawling now and then. As to the workload, I know what you mean. Well, I would, but we don't get half so many Protestant refugees and there's plenty of a whole lot of denominations hereabouts so we're not so stuck for hands."

"Speaking of denominations, how's the theological correspondence?"

"There, that's fixed." Jones stood up again, slipped his wrench back into its place in the roll. "We'll do the rest in the morning, huh? Too late now."

"Yes. The kids are asleep. Y'know, it still feels weird to say that. Coffee?"

"Kill for one. No, about the correspondence, we seem to have exhausted the real fruitcakes, but Al Green got a doozy this morning. Did he tell you?"

Mazzare worked the coffee machine, the newly-arrived Turkish roast temporarily overruling the smell of oil and hot metal. "I haven't seen him since, oh, must be last week sometime."

"Yeah, well, word got around that he's the Reverend *Doctor* Al Green, and so he's gotten a letter from the Earl of Carlisle's secretary. Apparently the earl's in Paris, helping Ussher with his researches, and does the reverend doctor have anything that might help?"

Mazzare pantomimed jaw-dropping amazement. "*That* Ussher?"

"The very same. He's glomming antiquarian documents from across Europe."

"Reassure me Al's not going to send him anything." Mazzare felt a genuine pang of alarm. The Reverend Doctor Al Green, while a fine man, was notorious for occasionally needing to take a little more water with it.

"Well, I offered him my copy of Hawking . . ." Jones cracked up.

Mazzare found Jones' humor infectious. "Simon Jones," he chuckled, "may you be forgiven. Mocking a harmless old lunatic so."

"Had a bit of fun at Ussher's expense, too. Anyway, speaking of theological debate, I understand your curate was disputing a point or two at the Thuringen Gardens last night?"

"Oh, I heard about that. A lively controversy, by all accounts. You hear how it turned out?"

"Indeed. God exists, by two falls to a knockout."

"Exactly." Mazzare grinned a fiendish grin. "Although what Gus got in the Gardens was nothing to what Hanni gave him when he got home."

Jones laughed again. "I'll bet. Seriously, how's he shaping up?"

"Not so bad, within his limits, once I cured him of a few bad habits."

"Such as?"

"Drunkenness. Lewd cohabitation. Foul language." Mazzare chortled. "I thought I had him broken of picking fights in bars, too. No, he's all right. Ah, that's brewed. About the only person that objects is Irene Flannery, bless her."

"Oh?"

"Bit of a story. Come on, let's sit on the porch with these." Mazzare poured coffee into two workshop-issue chipped mugs.

The evening was warm with just a hint of the cold night that the clear sky promised after the heat of the summer day. Father Heinzerling was already there, his heels on the porch rail and puffing smoke at the stars. "Hast fettled the engine?" he asked by way of greeting.

"Likely," said Jones, "try 'er in the morning, I reckon."

"How's the jaw?" asked Mazzare.

"Mending." Heinzerling grinned ruefully and lop-sidedly, rubbing at his bruised chin, "and a certain Scotsman will be more respectful of Catholic courage, *ja*?"

"Never mind the jaw, what about the eye?" asked Jones.

"Ah, now," said Mazzare, "while the jaw was got in defense of the faith, the eye was got for disobedience of Hannelore. Sympathy only where it is proper, Simon, and for just punishment he must suffer in silence."

They settled down again, stretching and shifting to get comfortable. Jones broke the silence first. "You know, if Gus' little fracas there was the worst of it, I don't think we need worry too much."

"You know me, Simon, I worry." Mazzare sipped at his coffee. "I don't think there was any malice in last night's nonsense, but I hear some ugly things."

"Oh?"

"Oh, the usual. All the best jobs are going to 'them,' we're not getting a fair shake. I'm hearing it from the Catholic side, of course, but I'll bet the same thing is going around among the rest of town. If it's just the creaking as we settle in here, it's nothing, but—" He gestured with his mug, waving at all the possible problems that waited to crystallize out of the clear air.

"You worry overmuch, Father Mazzare," said Heinzerling, tapping out his pipe on his bootheel. "There are those who will gripe if it would rain florins. With your leave, gentlemen, I shall take to my bed."

They bid him good night.

"So, Larry, what's the story with Hanni and Irene Flannery?" Jones leaned forward. He would cheerfully admit that, if he had a fault, he was an awful gossip.

Mazzare grinned. "Ah, now I first got a notion something was up when I turned up at the church and heard the shrieking."

"Oh, my." Jones was on the verge of cracking up. "I can imagine. You know, Irene Flannery has scared me all my life? I had her as a teacher. And I imagine Hanni didn't hold anything back—"

"No, not a bit. I do declare I learned more 'colorful idiom' in two different languages than I had ever hoped to in a lifetime." Mazzare shook his head and chuckled gently.

"Let me guess—once you intervened, they turned on you?"

Mazzare sighed. "That was the worst of it. That might have given them a point of agreement. Of course, they stopped the minute they saw I was there."

"A Father Ted moment?" Jones had bought videos of the Irish comedy as a present for Mazzare a few years before.

"Pretty much. Suddenly all sweet and meek for the priest. And now Irene says she's too old to keep the church any more, and we don't see her but for mass, and her neighbors say she's getting worse. It used to be just kids and footballs, but—" Mazzare bit his lip.

"She got worse?" Jones frowned.

"No joking matter, Simon. No, I think she'll get over it in time. She's about the only one who hasn't, anyway." Mazzare sighed and shook his head.

"Bit of a shock, suddenly having a married priest."

Mazzare grinned. "Not for most of my parishioners. Perfectly normal, at least to the older folks. The counter-reformation took a while to get out to here, and most of the older Germans can remember having married priests about the place."

"Well, Larry, I can find you—"

Mazzare laughed aloud. "Get thee behind me, Jones. I have seen enough of clerical matrimony to know better than to inflict it on myself at my age."

"What, four years younger than me?"

"Shut up, Simon."

6

It was months before Mazarini could get away from Cardinal Barberini's court to make the long ride to Grantville.

His first sight of the town, spread out in the evening sunshine before him, confirmed its alien origin as no amount of reports could have done. The geometry of the place had nothing to do with defense. No wall to huddle in, no easily defended spot. Just a place where roads met. He stopped to look over the town, comparing the place to the map he had had. He identified the carillon tower of St. Mary's, and smiled a moment at the memory of its former name. Then, his lathered horse glad of the slower pace, he dismounted and walked in.

The town was quiet, almost deserted, but that was to be expected if the American forces were away dealing with the Spanish threat that had been the main news at Paris when he had passed through. When he reached St. Mary's, he found Heinzerling saying an evening benediction.

"How are you keeping?" he asked, when Heinzerling had finished and the gratifyingly large congregation had gone.

"They have a phrase here: 'going native.' I think it fits me."

"About the only thing that still does, by the look of you." Mazarini appraised his former aide. He wore the weight like a prize boar. Called on to wrestle with Satan, Heinzerling could make Satan regret it.

"The living is good here." Heinzerling grinned, and shrugged. "Even a curate does well."

"How does the Society take your new status?"

"Well as can be expected. The Provincial asks I report regularly and fit in. They ask after converts, and I tell them of the increase in numbers here, which satisfies them well enough."

Mazarini raised an eyebrow.

Heinzerling shrugged. "Things are different here. The place is governed in the strangest way. There is more regulation of how one shits than of how one prays. When you get used to it, though—" He shrugged again.

"And so your converts?"

Heinzerling laughed. "This is a good place to live. People come here. Some of them are Catholic. So we have more each day at mass. Converts!" He waved a hand, "Oh, we have a few, *sicher*. We have a fine social center. Some come for that. The rigor of our doctrine and the holiness of our sacraments? No. The other churches do just as well, and to each his own."

Mazarini had known the genial German was capable of fitting in anywhere—sent among the Turk he would have made friends and found something kind to say of Mahomet—but had not quite expected this. Indeed, had not suspected it from the reports. He changed the subject. "Father Mazzare? He has not written since that first invitation to visit."

"As he was. At the moment, he is at the rectory, mending an engine with one of the Protestant priests."

Mazarini's bewilderment must have shown.

Heinzerling grinned. "There is a lot that has not gone into my reports. Father Mazzare's closest friend is a Protestant priest, and together they raise church funds by mending engines, which they enjoy. I should report this where it might come to the ears of the Holy Office?"

Mazarini could not help but grin. "I must meet Father Mazzare. But first, I need to speak with whoever is in charge of the troops here."

"This would be Dan Frost, *mein' ich*, he is the police chief here."

"The what?"

"Sort of like a town watch. Only not. I will explain later. You have news for him?"

"Indeed. I think Wallenstein may have sent someone this way. I passed what looked like three or four squadrons of cavalry, Croats by the looks of them, four days ago. I have been coming as fast as I could make post-horses go, so I will be ahead of them by perhaps two days. Can you summon a messenger?"

"I can do better. Here, come to the rectory. How is your English?"

"Poor. Why?"

"Ach, I shall translate." As they spoke, Heinzerling had led them across the grounds of the church to the presbytery. Once inside, and before Mazarini could spend any time gawking at the house, Heinzerling had picked up a peculiarly shaped object attached to another by a twisted cord.

"*Telefon*," he said.

"Ah, I wanted to see this. How is it done?"

"You press numbers to make another telefon ring. This number makes the one at the police station ring, and, ah," Heinzerling held the instrument closer to his ear. "Marlene? Father Augustus here."

Mazarini watched closely as Heinzerling held the instrument to his ear and mouth. He could just hear a voice from the thing, could better follow Heinzerling's much-improved English as he passed on the report of cavalry and their location.

Heinzerling turned again to Mazarini, now back in French. "Monsignor, it was three to four hundred, yes?"

"Yes, nearer four hundred."

Heinzerling passed that on to the invisible Marlene. "*Ja,*" he said into the phone, "the monsignor was once a captain of horse. He knows what he is talking about. Perhaps two days if they come straight here." Another exchange of pleasantries and Heinzerling put the phone down. "Done," he said. "Dan Frost will know of these Croats soon enough. There are plans in place for any raid."

"Excellent. Now, shall we discuss Grantville while we await Father Mazzare?"

Mazzare turned out to be all that the reports had said: tall, spare, silver-gray and black in his short-cropped hair and a touch of gold in his brown eyes: patrician was a word that might have been coined for him. Committed to his pastoral duties, continent in his vows and gentlemanly in his manner. By the standards of his own time, apparently, not unusual. By the standards of the time he was in, practically a saint.

Heinzerling, for example, had a woman in tow and three children, none of whom had formed any great bar to his remaining in orders. To Mazarini's surprise, Mazzare had insisted they marry. Over dinner that evening, Mazzare said: "Every other thing about this parish is irregular, so why not our curate?" There was little mirth in Mazzare's laughter.

The other irregularity was the presence at table of the pastors of four Protestant churches of Grantville, whom Mazzare had invited to meet the visiting monsignor. There was the Reverend Chalker, a Pentecostalist, the Reverend Wiley, Free Presbyterian—although not, apparently, a Scotsman, and the Reverend Doctor Green, a Baptist. These were familiar strains of heretic, able to give a—friendly enough—account of their heresies by reference to Protestant sects that Mazarini knew.

The Reverend Jones and his wife were remarkable, not least for Signora Jones being a minister herself. Their "Methodist" sect was a schism of the English heresy that would not be committed for another hundred years.

The meaning of the gesture—Protestant and Catholic clergy at table without even harsh words—was not immediately clear. Mazarini could not help but shake the feeling that it was purely a normal guest-list for such events. He put the thoughts aside and concentrated on enjoying Frau Heinzerling's cooking.

After dinner, Mazarini joined Mazzare in the garden behind the presbytery. The Protestant pastors had gone home, leaving promises of hospitality in the coming days, another wonder.

"I have made errors in my assessment of your situation." Mazarini had discovered early in the day that Mazzare's Italian, his own hesitant, new-learned English and the Latin they had in common were enough to communicate fluently.

"Easy enough to do. There'll be a lot of change in the Church over the next four hundred years, and St. Vin . . . St. Mary's reflects that."

"Not that. By the standards of these times you are a model of obedience to Rome." Mazarini waved a hand. "From what I see so far, I should arrange for Vincent de Paul to come here and see what he should be trying to achieve." He looked up at Mazzare's face, and grinned back at the frown. "I have the dubious honor to know him, but I haven't told him. The man's a nuisance as it is. Seeing his name on the front of a church would have made him more than mortal man could stand."

Mazzare laughed. "Most of the usual patron saints for Catholic churches in the twentieth century are either still alive, not saints yet or not even born." He frowned again. "Or politically sensitive."

"It must be difficult. No, to return to my confession of error, I had believed that His Eminence the Cardinal Richelieu was preparing to seek advantage from your presence. I had thought that he would seek a more general war with Spain."

"He's not?"

"No. It seems that between Grantville and its Jews, His Eminence feels Sweden is strong enough that France is better served by alignment with Spain. Which puts me in a hard place."

"Oh?" Mazzare's face was suddenly still. Unlike Jones, he had been known to play the occasional hand of cards, and was good at it.

"Yes. I am now in poor odor in Rome. With France and Spain now aligning, my efforts to hold a balance between them are no longer so highly thought of. I have been these past few months trying to keep on my political feet."

Mazzare let out the breath he had been holding in a sigh. "That's nothing we hadn't heard, of course. We have a force out to—we have forces out. We suspected something of this kind must have happened. And His Holiness?"

Mazzarini nodded. "Can do nothing for fear of the Spaniards. So long as we were providing a, a—"

"Level killing field?" Mazzare's tone was savage.

Mazarini, in return, was gloomy. "Yes, yes, *rem acu tetigisti*. A phrase of the twentieth century?" He thought for a moment of what Mantua had looked like after three years of bloody stalemate.

"Yes. An English diplomat," Mazzare spat the word, "sent to try and settle fighting in the Balkans."

Mazzare barked a short laugh. "I can excuse him a harsh word or two, if he was sent to do that. Even the Turks have trouble there. No, now France and Spain no longer need their killing field, His Holiness has less need of peacemakers. These three months past I am recalled to Cardinal Barberini's court. It is said to me that I were better to keep quiet for a time, since I have tried to make trouble for France and keep her from Spain's throat, not knowing they were pissing in the same pot." He snarled the last words, his waxed mustachios quivering in indignation. "So," he sighed, "I am come here, at your invitation. Perhaps there is something I can do."

Mazzare placed a hand on his shoulder. "We figured some of it out, you know, when Servien never turned up, or at least never announced himself. We'd heard he'd left Vienna after trying to make trouble for the Abrabanels and was on his way here, but we didn't have anyone on hand who'd recognize him." Mazzare's voice turned bitter. "All this time thinking the religion would cause the trouble."

"I will admit it is worse than I imagined it would be. There is talk of witchcraft"—he held up a hand to stop Mazzare's hot interjection—"Flummery. The talk of witchcraft is a pretext, as it usually is. The real issue is France, Spain, and the Spanish Road. I had thought that Richelieu would take advantage against Spain, but it seems that His Eminence has made an error."

"An error? We're a threat to him. We took his best ally against the Habsburgs and bought them out from under him."

"Which Richelieu should have seen as an opportunity to undo Spain. The fool." Mazarini gave vent to a stream of language in an idiom four centuries older than Mazzare had learned in Chicago yet surprisingly comprehensible. "That could so easily have been repaired," he said when he had run out of splenetic force. "France and Spain guided into deadlock with each other, Sweden allowed just enough to stop Wallenstein. It could have been done. I could have done it. This war could have been ended!" This last a shout, at the heavens, clear and starry and moon-bright, the half moon low in the east obscuring the earth with silver-gray shadows.

"And Rome?"

Mazarini sighed again. "Rome is under Spain's thumb. Now Richelieu is in with Spain, Rome must needs no longer intrigue against France and France will not help Rome against Spain. We must allow France her head, and no doubt they will cease to move against Italy."

"That isn't what I meant." Mazzare's voice was gentle, weary.

"It is not?"

"Where am I in all this?" Mazzare spoke quietly, pleading.

Mazarini placed a hand on his arm. "I am sorry, Padre. I do not know. I truly do not. No one is paying mind to such petty matters as religion. Or peace."

Silence fell. Mazarini made his excuses and retired to the presbytery's guest room.

Mazzare did not go to bed that night. Had anyone been up and about, they would have seen lights on in the church.

For a little while, at least, sitting in the presiding chair on the sanctuary—itself an anachronism in this century—he could be seen to be at peace. Over his shoulder, the crucifixion scene behind the tabernacle. In his lap, his well-worn rosary.

For some time after, sitting perfectly still, he stared across the sanctuary at the lectern, the missal open on it. Now he sat in a less composed fashion, his face closed and tight as he considered the sight of the book of liturgy.

And when he could bear that no longer, he simply stared, eyes unfocused, into the empty pews, his face candid in its misery as he awaited a dawn that had still not come when he turned off the lights and left the church.

Mazarini, as was his habit, arose before dawn and descended to find Mazzare, Heinzerling and the redoubtable Frau Hannelore Heinzerling in the kitchen.

Like breakfast tables since the dawn of time, there was little conversation among the adults while the children—three beefy little boys, the eldest about eight—chattered. Frau Heinzerling served up just about everything that it was possible to fry in heroic portions, and coffee and beer in similar quantities. Mazarini declined coffee and beer, but noted that

Mazzare was drinking coffee like his life depended on it.

"You like coffee?" Mazarini tried to open some form of conversation once breakfast had gone down and Frau Heinzerling had rounded the boys up for school. St. Mary's, it seemed, was a rich parish to afford schooling for three children.

"Didn't sleep much, last night," was the mumbled reply.

Mazarini noted a peculiar expression on Heinzerling's face. Reproach for his former master, concern for the American priest—it was hard to tell.

Another gambit, then. "Perhaps we might discuss how I am to spend my time in Grantville?" Something was troubling Mazzare, it seemed, and Mazarini thought that perhaps a practical topic would concentrate his wits.

At that, Heinzerling rose from the table. "I will go and open the church for morning mass, *ja*?" he said, and left.

"Doesn't want to hear anything he'd have to report," said Mazzare. His voice was as tired as his face. "The man's torn."

"You are troubled?"

"Somewhat."

"I will not pry. Perhaps I might presume upon you for introductions to Grantville's notables? If I can do nothing else, I can at least be plying my trade."

"Already tried. I called Rebecca Stearns, but she's gone up to the school for the morning, I was told. Everyone else is out of town at the moment." With a sudden burst of vigor, Mazzare wrenched himself from his chair. "Come on, I'll give you the ten-dollar tour. Need some fresh air, anyway."

It was a fresh, bright September morning, the pale moon still showing in the west, the sun low in the east. The town of Grantville, seen only briefly the day before, had some intriguing novelty on every street and corner.

The architecture was odd; severely plain in some instances, strangely fanciful in others and here and there, bizarrely, echoing classical Rome. Tastes in ornamentation were radically different from his own.

Mazzare was clearly well known. Those up and about were, in the main, women and the elderly. Most with a greeting or a wave or a nod for the American priest.

Children he saw assembling to be taken to school, and the notion of schooling for all was explained to him. It was more than even the Jesuits attempted.

Then he saw the buses, and was startled almost out of his wits. He had read of the engine-vehicles of Grantville, but the first encounter was a shock. In that shock, he made the mistake of asking Mazzare how the engine worked.

Half an hour later, and dazed by the flood of information and the first genuine enthusiasm the American priest had evinced in his presence, Mazarini was, if no wiser about the operation of the internal combustion engine, at least ignorant in more detail than before.

Their walk had taken them down by the creek that ran through Grantville when the alarms began to sound. It began with a wail, somewhere between a wolf and night wind in a chimney-cowl.

"Trouble," said Mazzare.

"What is that noise?"

"Siren." He said the word in English. "No, not the mythical creature. A machine for making noise." Mazzare turned and lengthened his stride.

"Oh." Mazarini had to walk more quickly to keep up with Mazzare, who stood a full hand-span taller than him. "Where are we going?"

"Downtown. See what's going on."

"We can help?"

"Straight away, no. But we need to know where our action stations are."

Downtown turned out to be the name for the part of town with the tallest buildings in it, and there was the busy, determined chaos of a wasp's nest going on in it. Mazzare spoke to several people to get the story, and then translated for Mazarini. It was, indeed, a cavalry raiding party, sighted on the edge of town near the school.

Mazarini followed Mazzare to help direct people as they came into the center of town. A man sporting a bronze badge had given the orders. He had been swearing sulphurously about the lack of warning. Apparently someone assumed that cavalry a hundred miles away two days before would not be a threat so soon and simply left a note on the desk of the Chief of Police—who had been too busy to notice it.

"Wallenstein," said Mazarini.

"You think so?" answered Mazzare. "No shortage of other bandits."

"Not with Wallenstein around. Better opportunities for loot and a stipend when pickings are poor."

"Whatever." Mazzare shrugged, began directing the streams of people toward doorways.

Mazarini felt his eyebrows climbing when he saw the people coming to take shelter. "They're all armed!"

Mazzare grinned over his shoulder, breaking off briefly from his work. "Welcome to America!"

The weapons were different, the soldiers nothing like those Mazarini had led in the Valtelline. Nevertheless, the ambush taking shape around the plaza was as old as warfare.

Heinzerling showed up at the head of a column of elderly women, half of them with the peculiar pistols the Americans favored.

And then came a shout. "Father Mazzare! We need your help." It was another man with a badge.

Mazzare strode off, Mazarini on his heels. The man with the badge strode along with him, explaining something in English, talking too fast for Mazarini to follow.

They came to a building that was a whirl of activity, more men—and women, here, too, with badges. There was a thunder of shouting in English and German both. Many of those doing the shouting were shouting into little boxes with sticks on them. Like the *telefon*, he thought.

Mazzare, oblivious to Mazarini now, had picked up a telephone and was talking into it, urgently but gently. Heinzerling had come along too. "*Scheisse,*" he said, "*typisch.*"

"What?" Mazarini was still confused.

"Frau Flannery. She was at mass this morning. She must have gone home instead of following me here."

"Who?"

In the background, Mazzare. "Irene, it's not safe, yes, I know, but you must . . ."

Heinzerling went on. "Widow. Older than Satan and just as pleasant. Took it badly when Hannelore began cleaning the church. Thought Hanni was not good enough to set foot in a church. Called her a whore. Hanni called her some bad names, too. Father Mazzare couldn't get them to see reason. I told Hanni to forgive and forget, but Frau Flannery stopped talking to anyone but Father Mazzare."

" . . . I know, Irene, but you'll be—yes, but there's no sense . . ."

Mazarini, trying to follow two conversations at once, stopped staring at Mazzare and asked, over his shoulder, "Why?"

Heinzerling's shrug was all but audible. "Who knows? She is a crazy old woman."

" . . . yes, Irene, I know to the minute how long it's been, but I can hardly hear it over the phone, you should come . . ."

"Is he doing what I think—"

"*Ja.*" Pause, for another shrug. "He feels bad that she feels unwanted, *mein' ich*. But Hannelore was fifty years younger and lives next to the church. She could still have helped, but—"

From Mazzare, resignedly, the Latin words of absolution. He put the phone down, his face gray. "Penance hardly seemed worth it." Louder, to one of the badged men. "She won't come, Dan. Won't be driven out of her home, she says."

"You did all you could, Father."

"I should go—"

The badged man, Dan, cut that off with a wave. "No, Father. Don't. She made her choice. Save those that want it." He strode away, barking orders—unmistakably in command.

Heinzerling, now, with more tenderness than Mazarini had thought the Jesuit had in him. "We should find a position on the plaza, Father."

The battle itself was short, noisy and one-sided. The three priests took station in an upper room, awaiting the signal. Heinzerling turned out to have an American pistol, a huge brute of a thing by the standards of such, machined of some black metal. Mazzare frowned, but said nothing.

Outside, Mazzare could see down the street to where the Croats were coming from, and saw Dan Frost the constable facing them down. *Good*, he thought, *draw them in. There is a man with courage, to die for his people. Would that constables in other towns were so conscientious.*

The constable drew a pistol, leveled it at the front rank of Croats.

The shooting, when it came, was a rattle of rapid fire, the crack and curls of blue smoke from the Americans answering the coughs and reeking clouds of the Croat pistols.

Mazzare kept to the back of the room, where the unarmed sheltered, comforting the frightened. Mazarini stood in the window, ignoring the imprecations to keep his head down—every inch the captain he had once been—and watched the slaughter in the street below for some minutes.

Like him, Heinzerling stood. Side on to the window

in the classic duelist's stance, returning fire and grinning the savage, tusky grin of a boar with the drop on the hunters.

The windows shattered in the storm of fire, the tinkle of glass inaudible in the rip of gunfire and the screams of wounded men and dying horses.

When it was clear that the battle was won, the street outside a bloody, shrieking shambles, Mazarini turned to find Mazzare holding a blood-soaked cloth to the back of a woman's head.

"Scalp wounds always bleed badly," offered Mazarini, "but are seldom serious."

"She's concussed. That"—Mazzare stabbed a finger at a heavy, brass-framed icon in the Eastern style—"fell off the wall."

Mazarini picked it up. It was painted on, of all things, black velvet. The saint's face was serene, slightly corpulent, and he was dressed in a white raiment adorned with jewels. The name written under the portrait was an odd one, the appellation even more so. *Elvis—Still the King*.

"What saint is this?" he asked, able now to converse normally with the guns all but silent.

It took some time to explain the slightly hysterical laughter to his satisfaction.

Irene Flannery's body was not found for hours. Cut down in her front yard, she had tried to drag herself back to her house to die, but had gotten only as far as a flowerbed. A riot of colorful growth like the rest of her garden, it had concealed her corpse from the first quick parties of searchers.

She was found, eventually, and only on Father

Mazzare's insistence was she brought to the church for burial.

The order of service was stilted. The passages of scripture, the prayers and invocations echoed in the empty church. The badged man, the "Dan" who had spoken with Mazzare after he had tried to save the old woman's life, turned up for the requiem mass.

He had taken no communion and left without speaking. The Protestant Jones had also attended and had followed the pitiful cortege to the graveside, his worried silence following Mazzare's grimness like the foam in the wake of a ship running before a storm wind.

Mazzare had spoken the words of the requiem mass in a cold tone, an iron tone that hammered the flowing Latin syllables and drew them out as a glowing, hot wire of condemnation.

His sermon had been harsher still, for all its quietness and plainness of manner.

"The Ring of Fire was an Act of God," he had begun, "and in His Act he has done nothing so capricious as the act that has brought us here today. Irene Flannery, in her lonely old age, felt rejected. Rejected even by the church she made the second home of her thirty years of widowhood."

Not, today, the literary form of the eulogy, deprecated in a catechism that would not be written for three hundred years.

"She was not alone."

There were only seven people and a corpse to hear him. Only the corpse did not flinch.

"We have been brought to a world in which religion is no more than gang colors."

The walk to the cemetery was silent. There had been neither gasoline nor spare horses for a hearse. Irene Flannery, birdlike in life like so many old women, scarcely outweighed her pine box, but the pallbearers' tread was heavy.

"A world in which people kill and die and nations stand or fall by the canting of theologians and the greed of statesmen."

Heinzerling had risen in the small hours to dig a grave in the pouring rain.

"It is not enough to say that religion is not to blame. That it was only a pretext."

Half of those present at the graveside wore vestments. The rain had made short work of all of them, and the wind flapped the sodden cloths in short, harsh volleys of cracks, the only salute Irene Flannery would get.

"Nor is it enough to say that she will be missed by no one. That she left no living relatives behind in America, had no friends here. The same can be said of millions."

Around the grave, four clerics and no mourners bar the pallbearers, three miners whom Mazzare had had to call out to help him and Heinzerling and Mazarini carry the coffin.

"That has never been an excuse for any murder. Who murdered her?"

After the fighting, Mazzare had moved among the dead and dying in the plaza, trying to administer the last rites, blessings, whatever might be wanted.

"The man so lost to his faith that he refused the rites of his own church?"

He had been spat at, cursed, insulted in all the

languages the Croats could manage. His countenance, grayed already by the carnage, had paled.

"No. But his guilt is no less for his lack of responsibility."

He had hardly spoken since then, had spoken two words to Mazarini when he finally walked away from the blood-soaked plaza.

"Poor bastards.

"They say that religion is only the pretext."

In the grave, already a hand's depth of water.

"But it is the fault of the religious who let it be so used."

The pallbearers, waiting to lower the stubborn old woman into the red clay, avoided meeting Mazzare's eye as he barked the words of the rite to the uncaring clouds.

"Irene Flannery was murdered by every man of God who turned his back on the things done in the name of his faith. That good men should do nothing. Indeed. We have all done that nothing, sinned in what we have failed to do."

The words spoken, the coffin lowered to its resting place, the cemetery fell silent other than the drumming of the rain on the coffin lid.

"She lived nearly ninety years, to die of the cowardice of men she would have trusted for the cloth they wore. She had a right, contrary as she was, to better. From me, from everyone professing a Christian faith."

Heinzerling picked up the shovel he had left thrust into the mound of earth. He stood, silent a moment, watching Mazzare gaze, empty-eyed into the grave, at the handfuls of earth on the plain, unseasoned pine board of the coffin.

"Should we take the churchmen of this time to task for their failure to see now what will be seen over the next three centuries?"

It was the last of the five graves left after the raid. The others were already starting to settle, a flush of green weeds appearing on the raw earth.

"Perhaps I cannot. I have, myself stood by. Not acted. Who am I to cast the first stone? But if I cannot, God will."

Heinzerling put down the shovel, and, with the others at the graveside, left Mazzare to stand, staring silently into the earth at the coffin of an old woman who had had no living friends.

"Without faith, the thing that gives meaning to religion, we truly have nothing here but a meaningless death."

Rain ran down Mazzare's face. Perhaps he wept. There was no one to see.

The kitchen was hot and fuggy with pipe-smoke and steam. Irene Flannery, unwaked before she was buried, was being drunk to now in scalding coffee and silence.

They heard the presbytery door open and shut. Long minutes passed. Jones, Mazarini and the Heinzerlings waited in silence.

Mazzare walked in to the kitchen. His face was calm. Water dripped from his hair, his clothes.

Under his arm, a stack of books. "Mazarini," he said.

Mazarini nodded.

"Larry," said Jones, "are you—"

"Never better," said Mazzare, "never better, Simon."

There was a small, cold smile on his face, his eyes clear and bright. "Can you carry a message, Legate Monsignor Mazarini?"

"Certainly."

"Here. The Papers of the Second Vatican Council." He slammed a heavy hardback in a gray dust-jacket onto the table. "The Catechism of the Catholic Church, 1992 Edition." A thick paperback volume, dog-eared and stained and fringed with yellow notes. Hammered onto the table. "The Bible. In English. An approved Catholic translation." This, more gently, on the table. "You won't recognize the names that go with the approval. Take my word that they're honest ordained bishops. Meantime, Father Heinzerling here will stop editing his own reports."

"Larry—"

"Father Mazzare—"

Only Mazarini was silent.

Mazzare held up a hand for silence. "Simon, Augustus, I've had enough of being quiet but I don't have a big enough voice. Monsignor Mazarini, you rode between the armies once, calling for peace."

Mazarini nodded, understanding what was asked of him. "I will fail, of course," he said. "Some things can only be done once."

Mazzare nodded. "Sometimes," he said, "failure counts."

𝕭𝖎𝖙𝖎𝖓𝖌 𝕿𝖎𝖒𝖊

Virginia DeMarce

1

Jeff Higgins climbed the stepstool and eyed the diminishing number of boxes stashed between the top level of the trailer's kitchen cabinets and the ceiling. It was odd, he thought, the things that brought memories from before the Ring of Fire back to him. He and his father used to tease his mother unmercifully for her tendency to buy foods by the case every time there was a special at the grocery warehouse in Fairmont. In the two months since he had married Gretchen, though, it sure had come in handy.

Grandma Richter was really the problem—the rest of them could and would eat almost anything that

Gretchen defined as food. Even Wilhelm was doing pretty well on solids, if you considered canned yams to be a solid food.

Grandma had fewer teeth than Wilhelm. Grandma had no teeth at all.

It wasn't that Grandma didn't eat with enthusiasm—she ate instant oatmeal with cinnamon apples, instant mashed potatoes with gravy, cups full of instant ramen noodles with flavoring (add boiling water). After two months of eating twenty-first-century America's versions of dehydrated and reconstituted goo, in addition to the ever-present pease porridge and boiled cabbage, she was, according to Gretchen, just about back to her normal size (wiry but no longer withered) and strength (Jeff's best estimate was, "tough as an old gourd").

Above and beyond all other forms of sustenance, she had taken to Stove Top brand. By his count, there were only three more cases, with six double boxes per case, which figured out as thirty-six more meals. *There's no doubt about it,* Jeff thought. *Grandma needs to get false teeth. She needs to get them right now, before Dr. Sims runs out of supplies.*

"Grandma, we need to talk about your teeth." Jeff had prudently waited until the household was fifteen minutes into supper to bring the matter up—the first quarter hour of every meal, as soon as the blessing had been completed, was devoted to serious eating. He opened his mouth, pointed, said, *"Zaehne,"* and pointed at her mouth. "You need to go to the dentist—to Dr. Sims—to get teeth, so you can eat regular food, not just soft food."

"What teeth? I lost my last tooth a dozen years ago. They say that you lose a tooth for every child. *Wahnsinn.* What did I have? Ten pregnancies, all my teeth gone, and not one living child to show for it: four miscarriages, two born too early to live, four that made it to the font but died before they were six years old." Grandma paused. "Not, mind you, that Annalise and Hans and Gretchen aren't as dear to me as if their father had been my own son."

Jeff eyed Gretchen rather warily as this spate of words descended upon him. His German had improved rapidly since being immersed in Gretchen's extended family, but Grandma's Oberpfalz accent resembled spoken Thuringian German only vaguely. After considerable participation by everybody around the table, he managed to determine three things. The first was that Grandma had been the stepmother of Gretchen's father, being too young by several years to be her actual grandmother. The second was that all seventeenth-century Germans defined the function of a dentist as pulling teeth, not repairing, much less creating, them.

The third thing that he determined was that Grandma thought he was making fun of her, which was not a good state of affairs—not good at all.

By the end of August, everyone in Grantville had learned to be wary of the high school library's collection of German-English dictionaries. The original Langenscheidt by means of which Jeff had proposed to Gretchen had been augmented by a ragtag collection of paperbacks formerly in the possession of private owners and a sizable number of travelers' phrasebooks, not to overlook the invaluable little picture book, *See It and Say It in German*, which had already been reprinted, the cartoons by way of woodcuts, and widely distributed, along with the companion volume created by substituting new subtitles *Sieht das und sprecht das auf Englisch*. The problems tended to lie in the way the language had changed during more than three hundred and fifty years.

The dictionary said that the term for dentures was "*kuenstliches Gebiss*." Cautiously checking further, he discovered that Grandma Richter, however, would hear "*Gebiss*" as a reference to the bit one attached to a bridle and placed in the mouth of a horse. That wasn't going to improve domestic relations if he said it to her . . .

Bridge? Well, the German word was "*Bruecke*," but in the seventeenth century, in both languages, the structure went across streams rather than between teeth.

"*Kuenstliche Zaehne*" would be understandable enough as applying to individual teeth, but would give someone who had never seen false teeth no idea how they might be set together on the plates to make dentures.

See It and Say It in German gave him an idea. *See it . . .* he thought. *Now, who . . . ?*

Henry Dreeson's bachelor Uncle Jim had come back from the army hospital after World War I with a glass eye. Jim had entertained the younger Dreeson relatives (including Henry) at family reunions and all-day-meetings at the church by popping it out and tossing it from hand to hand. He had frightened the more impressionable younger Dreeson relatives (not including Henry) by telling them that the eye could follow them around and report all of their misdeeds to their parents. On the theory that he wouldn't need it on the other side, one way or the other (if the preacher's conviction of a glorious bodily resurrection was right, it would be superfluous; if the argument of Robert Ingersoll and the other freethinkers that there was no afterlife was right, it would be unnecessary), Jim had directed that the eye be removed before his burial and given to his favorite nephew. Henry Dreeson carried it in his pocket as a good luck piece, often tossing it from hand to hand while he was thinking.

The more Jeff considered the matter, the stronger his conviction became that old Jim Dreeson's nephew was not a man who would mind taking out his dentures in public, mayor of Grantville or not. That took care of "who." "What" and "why" were already very clear in his mind, leaving only "when, where, and how" to be tackled. "When" was clearly ASAP, but would have to be pinned down. "Where" would have to be "not at home," because if he unexpectedly brought the mayor home for dinner, Gretchen and Grandma would skin him. As for "how," the most effective approach was bound to be the most direct approach. He set out for City Hall.

2

"Monday will be Labor Day—let's take the whole bunch to the Thuringen Gardens before it gets too chilly to have the kids out at night."

"What is Labor Day?"

"It will cost too much."

"Aw, c'mon, Mrs. Richter," protested Jeff's friend Eddie Cantrell, who, along with Larry Wild and Jimmy Andersen, lived in the trailer complex with Jeff and the Richter family. "All of us guys will chip in. You and Gretchen can feed the kids before we go, so they won't really be hungry—we'll just buy 'em a big bowl of pork rinds that they can snack on while they run around."

Jeff took care of the easy part. "Gretchen, Labor Day is an American holiday that celebrates the dignity of work and workers."

"It will cost much too much. This household should not spend money on such things until Jeff is properly of age and is a master in his trade."

"I *am* of age, Grandma. I've been of age for over a year. I just had my nineteenth birthday."

"Nineteen is not of age—twenty-five is of age."

"Listen, Mrs. Richter!"

"Eddie, you also are not of age. I cannot imagine what this place can be thinking of, allowing youth to be treated as if they were adults. You should properly still be under guardianship, all four of you."

Gretchen's younger brother Hans weighed in. "If *they* were subject to guardians, Grandma, *you* and Annalise, and Gretchen, and the kids, would be sitting over by the power plant in the refugee camp rather than comfortably around our dinner table."

"Hans, *sprich mich nicht so frech an.*"

Gretchen brought it to a close, to Jeff's relief. "*Genug*, that's enough. Labor Day would appear to be a worthwhile holiday. We shall go. Then no more extra spending until Christmas."

"Er, Gretchen . . . I don't think we've told you about Thanksgiving yet."

"Are we skipping Columbus Day this year?" asked Larry.

"Columbus Day doesn't count. We usually never even got off school."

"Are we doing Halloween?"

"That's *Allerheiligen*—the eve of All Saints' Day. It's a lot different here."

"We never got off school for Halloween, either. It's not even a federal holiday."

"We ought to have a Halloween party for the kids, at least. Andy Partlow has a pumpkin patch."

"*Worueber sprechen Sie, Hans?*"

"*Amerikanische Feiertagen.*"

"Look, guys. Let's get through Labor Day first."

Before the Ring of Fire, the principle of taking life one day at a time, or at least one holiday at a time, had, somehow, never seemed so wise.

"Okay, Eddie, what's the plan?"

"Hans and Annalise say that once you get a couple of pints into Mrs. Richter, she really mellows a lot."

"So?"

"So Mayor Dreeson doesn't bring out the false teeth until she gets to that stage."

"But we need to have him take them out before it gets too dark for her to get a really good look. They haven't wired lights for the outside seating, and the kids make too much noise for us to sit inside."

"We can leave here earlier—get the first pint into

her on an empty stomach, before Mayor Dreeson gets off work. Then we eat. Then it's bring on the dentures. Julie's bringing her dad. They're going to come in behind us and sit two tables away. As soon as Gretchen's grandma looks impressed enough, he pounces and goes off with her signature in his appointment book. He's bringing it with him. Just to make it official, he's bringing a stamp to plop down next to her signature. I've noticed that Germans would rather do almost anything than go back on something that's been officially stamped. Of course, it's a play stamp out of one of Julie's old toy boxes and has Tinker Bell on it—that's all we could find, but at least the appointment will be 'gestempelt.' If she does ask what it is, I'll tell her it's a heraldic bumblebee with a lot of symbolic significance."

"Eddie—I dunno. You're getting awfully devious these days."

"She'll just say that they cost too much, anyway," added Jimmy.

Jeff shook his head. "Anything that will keep Gretchen from having to put every bite that Grandma Richter eats for the next twenty-five years through the hand grinder is cheap, guys. I know that it's going to stretch things to the limit, but we'll manage to pay, on installments if we have to."

It took a certain political adroitness to get oneself elected mayor, even in Grantville. Henry Dreeson came into the Thuringen Gardens bearing a basket with two dozen freshly picked apples from the cherished Winesap tree in his backyard. After he had disposed of his share of the wurst and kraut, he distributed them, after which he made a point of mentioning his age, opening his mouth wide enough to show an unnaturally perfect set of teeth, and ceremoniously biting into one. (This was showing off, of course: ordinarily the course of prudence would have caused him to quarter and core it first. Luckily, the Fixodent held.) Then he paused and bent across the table solicitously.

"Would you like me to slice yours very thinly for you, Mrs. Richter? Thecla could take the slices inside and boil them for a few minutes to soften them down." He busied himself with arranging this, as the odor of fresh apple, with each thin slice, wafted from his pocket knife to Gretchen's grandma's nose. As her mouth watered, he pounced, "You really ought to see Doc Sims about getting a set of teeth, you know."

"How do you 'get' teeth?"

"Doc Sims makes 'em to fit your mouth—here, like this." Mayor Dreeson pulled out his teeth and handed them across the table. "See, uppers here, lowers here. They fit in like this." He took them back, demonstrated the insertion, and handed them across the table again.

Grandma Richter promptly popped them into her mouth.

The adolescent diners winced, flinched, or surreptitiously gagged, as best suited the temperament of each. The younger kids watched with genuine fascination.

Mayor Dreeson leaned across and said, "You won't have a proper fit with these, you know. They're made to fit my mouth and not yours. Here, wiggle those lowers a little." He stuck his finger into her mouth to reposition them a bit as he looked over his shoulder and called, "Hey, Doc."

As Julie giggled helplessly, her father, armed with the Tinker Bell stamp, advanced to clinch the deal. Mayor Dreeson retrieved his teeth and put them back in.

"That's really weird," Eddie said to Julie. "Isn't there a proverb or something about getting married to someone you wouldn't mind sharing a toothbrush with? What does it mean when you run into someone you wouldn't mind sharing your teeth with?"

Thecla emerged from the kitchen with a small bowl of boiled apple slices. Mug in one hand and spoon in the other, Grandma Richter settled down to consume mushy apples and beer. Mayor Dreeson was saying, "Your name's Veronica, is it? Mine's Henry. I used to be a big fan of Veronica Lake in my day."

3

"Really, Annalise. I mean, yeeecchhh. Ugghhh. Phewewww!" In spite of her status as a dentist's daughter and *ad hoc* dental receptionist, Julie was still thoroughly grossed out by her memory of the Thuringen Gardens episode.

"It worked. She's here." Annalise might have spent the last two years as a camp follower in Tilly's army, but, like Gretchen, she had absorbed the pragmatism that enabled people to survive in the small spot on the German map called the Upper Palatinate. She leaned forward, her chin on her hand, contemplating the rack full of back issues of *National Geographic*, *Rod and Gun*, and *Parenting* that adorned Dr. Sims's reception room. "Can I take a couple of these back for Grandma to look at while they're waiting for the mold to harden?"

"Sure. Can your grandma read English at all yet?"

Annalise grinned. "Better than she could a week ago. Mayor Dreeson climbed up into his attic and came down with a couple dozen Archie and Veronica comic books that his daughter Margie left behind when she married and moved to Ohio. We're making translations of the words for her. She reads them because the cover has her name on it."

"Well, I'm not surprised he had 'em. If anything was there when Mrs. Dreeson died, it's probably still there. I doubt that Mr. Dreeson ever does much cleaning in that old rattletrap of a place. He's always either down at City Hall or at the barber shop—or any place except his house. He keeps the yard and garden up nice, but inside . . ."

Attracted by the pictures of cute children, Annalise opted to supply Grandma with *Parenting*. "Some things are hard, though. What does it mean to 'enhance your child's self-esteem'?"

"In German? I dunno. I don't even know exactly what it means in English."

The outer door slammed. Julie looked up and shuddered. "But whatever it is, Maxine Pilcher has done it. Those kids of hers are the worst brats in town and here they come now. Two simple checkups, but we'll get tantrums."

Howls of fury echoed throughout the clinic as a thin, harrassed-looking woman forcibly dragged a five-year-old and a seven-year-old through the inner door.

Julie added hurriedly, "She's the kindergarten teacher, too, of all things for her to be!"

Almost all the German women who came into Grantville had immediately seized upon the canvas-tote-bag-with-two-handles as a wondrous advance of modern civilization compared to the shallow-basket-precariously-perched-on-one-hip-and-likely-to-tip. Since this was an item that multiplied in American closets at a rate second only to wire coat hangers, the local housewives had been more than happy to supply the perceived need. Annalise dropped a couple of issues of *Parenting* into hers (which commemorated the eleventh annual conference of community-based Black Lung clinics) and backed down the hall toward Room B where Grandma was sitting.

Joshua and Megan Pilcher shrieked, sometimes in unison and sometimes alternately. Maxine Pilcher wanted to know why her dental coverage wasn't still in effect. Julie outlined the difficulty of submitting bills to an insurance company in Cleveland when the dental clinic was in Thuringia and displaced four centuries in time. Mrs. Pilcher protested that she had paid her premium for six months in advance just in June. If the company wasn't going to pay, she wanted a refund. With commendable restraint, Julie wished her luck in getting it.

Megan and Joshua continued to wail, but Julie foresaw from bitter experience that although their mouths might be open now, the minute she got either one of them into the examining chair, the lips and teeth would be clamped shut.

The door of Room B opened. Veronica Richter advanced into Dr. Sims's waiting room.

◆-◆   ◆-◆   ◆-◆

"That was awesome, Mrs. Richter." Julie's voice resonated with sincerity. Megan and Joshua, under the close supervision of an ogre who lived in the supply cabinet in Room A and two trolls whose preferred mode of transportation from the bridge over the river into Dr. Sims's office was the water pick, had submitted to having their teeth cleaned with really surprising docility.

"She is a fool." There could be no doubt that "she" was Maxine Pilcher. "Gretchen is busy, *immer*, always. Jeff and the other boys are busy, always. Hans is busy, always. Annalise must go to school, always, always, always. All of Gretchen's orphans go to school. Even little Johann has started school. All the parents work; they must. So what do I have? I have all the tiny ones in the trailer court who are not old enough for school. I have Wilhelm, but also I have Frans and Peter. I have Sofia, I have Hedwig, I have Carolina. Six children I have, all day, every day. Do I have noise? Yes. Such is the way of nature. Do I have *that much* noise? No."

"Ummm." Julie wasn't quite sure how to ask this. "Do you really think that there's an ogre in the supply cabinet in Room A?"

Grandma Richter snorted. "Of course not. I am not an ignorant woman. I am not a stupid, superstitious peasant from some remote village. I am a townswoman, the widow of a printer. My husband was a *Stadtburger*, a *Druecker*. But some things I know, and one of them is that if a child believes that there is an ogre in my cabinet, he will not open it and get sick by eating the soap. If he believes that there is a troll under a bridge that has no railing, he will not run onto the bridge and fall off the side. If he believes that there is a snake-monster in the carp pond, he will not wade too deep and drown. The world has dangers for small children, many dangers. By the time they are old enough to realize for themselves that there are no ogres or trolls or monsters, they are old enough not to eat soap or fall in the water."

Somehow, this seemed to make perfect sense to Julie (who had, of course, heard the stories about the alleged disciplinary powers of Jim Dreeson's glass eye all her life). She filed the news away in the mental storage compartment known as, "stuff I may need to try some day."

"Now," continued Grandma Richter, "How much does this 'set of teeth' cost? Too much, probably, but I have signed a contract. Jeff talked about installments. I do not want installments if they charge interest. I will be no party to the practice of usury."

For just such occasions, Dr. Abrabanel had written, and supplied to all of Grantville's professional offices and businesses, a nice prepared statement, in German, which explained in detail that the charges for installment payments were not to be regarded as interest on the money involved, but as compensation for any inconvenience caused by the delay.

Julie read it out loud.

Grandma Richter didn't buy it for a minute.

"I wish," she insisted, "to pay when I get my teeth. Also, I do not wish to be dependent upon Jeff. I brought a proper dowry into my marriage. I have a life estate in my late husband's property. Now that the king of Sweden has pushed out the Austrians,

I have written to a lawyer to find out if anything is left. But I have no money now."

"Well," said Julie. "You're babysitting six kids already, just to be neighborly. Could you manage a few more? When both parents are working, they're happy to find reliable child care. They pay you; you pay Dad; everyone's happy."

On September 17, 1631, Grandma got her teeth. Although Grantville did not yet know that Gustav II Adolf had defeated Tilly at the Battle of Breitenfeld on that momentous day, Dr. Sims's decision to stay late at the office the night before in order to finish up the dentures probably had great allegorical significance. Veronica Richter would have considered the day to be one of momentous victory in any case. By combining her earnings from a week of completed sitting for eight additional paying children with a week of advance payments for eleven and the contributions from Jeff, Hans, Eddie, Jimmy, and Larry, she had paid for the teeth—without usury.

She had still to pay the Jungen back, of course—without usury. But that was household. That was what family was for.

She took on an assistant, but the three trailers, even when everyone else in the household was at school or at work, had room for only twenty paying children: no more. By early November, she had a waiting list as long as the list of those she had accepted.

"Think about it, Ronnie," Henry Dreeson said. "When you babysit kids out at the trailer park, all the parents have to go over there to take them and pick them up. You and Gretchen have a lot of mess to clean up before you can get supper and put your own kids to bed. If you take care of them downtown here, it will be a lot handier—Mom or Dad can just drop them off on the way to work, and there will be space for a lot more. You'll probably double your weekly income in no time. This old building isn't suitable for a store, because there's no street frontage—just a door. That's why it isn't rented. Can't imagine why anyone ever built it that way."

Larry Wild raised his eyebrow at Jimmy Andersen. It not only would never have occurred to him to address Gretchen's grandma as Ronnie—it would never have occurred to him that *anyone* might address her as Ronnie. Jimmy just shrugged.

The mayor pulled out his key ring. The building was one of those 1920s oddities that occur in towns without strict zoning codes. The street door opened into a corridor no more than three feet wide and a good twenty-five feet long, no stairway, no side doors opening into the neighboring buildings, no windows; just one bare lightbulb and another door at the back. That one, unlocked, opened into a single large room, about thirty feet by fifty feet, with a row of windows facing on the creek. Henry Dreeson stared at the contents with a broad smile. "Gawd, I'm glad I brought you guys down. I'd plumb forgotten that I had all that lumber I bought at George Trimble's auction sitting in here. I bet there's enough to frame a duplex."

At either end of the far side, there were doors opening out onto a landing and wooden steps leading down to a grassy area between the building and the creek. "It's flood plain down there—not buildable," said Dreeson. "Don't usually flood more'n about ten days out of the year, though. You can use it for a playground when it's dry enough.

"You won't have to pay rent if we go partners—no upfront capital involved. Set it up this way: I provide the premises and you provide the labor and do the bookkeeping. Get these fine, strong, young men here"—he slapped Larry on the back—"to clean it up for free. Divide the profits, fifty-fifty."

"No rent?" Grandma Richter pulled a spiral-bound tablet out of her tote bag and started to make calculations.

4

After the next Emergency Committee meeting, the mayor asked, "Becky, could I talk to you. Privately. Just for a few minutes?"

"Oh, of course."

"How does a man court a German lady? How does he do it right, I mean? Not helter-skelter."

"You put your money where your mouth is. No, better, you put your money where your mouth is going to be. You give her presents, proper ones, suitable to your rank, income and status; suitable to her rank, income, and status. For you? You need something valuable."

"I don't *have* anything valuable. I'm the mayor, but I'm the mayor of a dirt poor, scroungy, Appalachian coal town."

"Certainly, you must. Everyone in Grantville has things that are valuable. Look, tomorrow. Look at your house with all that you have learned about the costs of things in Germany while you have been arranging the supplies and provisions for this town. Just look."

"Would these work? They were never opened after Annie died. She'd bought them right before she had that aneurysm, just before Valentine's Day. They should still be fresh."

Rebecca looked at the little bottles he was showing her. Glass, with tightly fitting plastic screwtops, the three little bottles themselves were worth quite a bit. But the contents . . . cinnamon, nutmeg, ginger: there must be two ounces of each. "It is a gift worthy of being given by a prosperous merchant; truly it is."

"Maybe I could write a note to go with them in English. Paying my respects, and asking her to accept them in time for the holiday baking. If you could translate a copy of it into German? Ronnie doesn't read English very well yet, and I'd sort of rather not have her call on one of those boys to read it out loud. If she doesn't accept—well, I could always, say, I guess, that it was meant for all of them if they'd invite a hungry old bachelor to Thanksgiving dinner and treat him to some Christmas cookies."

Jeff had walked out to the road with the mayor, to engage in one of those interminable, "Well, I guess I should be going about now" conversations without which rural and small town America could not function. Grandma opened the little packet that Henry had pressed into her hand as the two men went out the door and gasped. "Maria Margaretha!"

Throughout Gretchen's life, the appearance of her

full baptismal name had heralded events of porten-
tous significance: she hadn't seen or heard it since
she signed "Maria Margaretha Richterin" on the
marriage register for Father Mazzare. She looked at
what Grandma was holding and her eyes grew wide.
"There's a note."

"We *must* discuss it with the whole household,"
Grandma was insisting. "It is a matter that will
concern us all."

"No Grandma." Gretchen was also insisting, even
more stubbornly. "We're Americans now. I decided
for myself. You decide for yourself if you will
accept Mr. Dreeson's offer to court you. Then, if
it happens—then we can talk about how it will
concern us all."

Dreeson offering to court Grandma Richter?
Every one of Ms. Mailey's repeated, urgent, anxious
lectures about cultural misunderstandings, repeated
like a hammer throughout the summer at every
available opportunity, came rushing into Jeff's head.
This had to be a monumental mistake. This had
to be a cultural misunderstanding of stupendous,
humongous, proportions. This could not have been
equaled by anything that had happened since the
Ring of Fire. *Oh, good grief,* he thought. *And it's
too late to do anything about it tonight.* He wasn't
looking forward to tomorrow.

But first, to find out what had brought it on. He
entered the kitchen. All this from three dinky little
bottles of spices? Mom hadn't gone in for cooking
from scratch, so there hadn't been any in the Higgins
trailer, but he had seen them in the stores. Racks

full of the things at what? He had no real idea. Two dollars a bottle, maybe? At least, he'd learned when to keep his mouth shut. He'd warn the mayor first thing in the morning. Then what? Of course, ask Becky. In a pinch, always ask Becky.

Jeff was the first one out the door the next morning. He was waiting when City Hall opened; he was in a chair outside the office before Mr. Dreeson arrived. "I thought I'd better flag this. Er—Gretchen and her Grandma got all excited about those bottles of spices."

His efforts were rewarded with a broad, relieved, smile. "Great, she's willing to consider the idea, then. I was afraid she wouldn't be. It'll be a big change for her, you know. If we can work it all out."

Never before in his life had Jeff Higgins understood the true depth of meaning signified by the simple word, "relax."

5

The license for the day care center was issued in mid-December. As soon as it was in hand, the great clean-up of the premises began. The grand opening was scheduled for January 1, to take advantage of the holiday and draw a bigger crowd.

"Do you ever get the feeling that we've been stung?" grumbled Larry.

"Shaddup and haul those two-by-fours out to the flatbed."

"D'you think he really forgot that he had this lumber here?"

"'Course not—he intended all along to get something extra out of this deal, and that was having his lumber carried down this stupid narrow hallway without having to hire anyone. I knew it the minute that he said 'plumb forgotten.' He only talks with that much local color when he has a reason to act like a good ole boy. He's the tightest man with a dollar anyone ever met. That's why they made him minister of finance."

"Oughta get along *real* good with Gretchen's granny, then."

"Lennox says that she's thrifty."

"Lennox admires thrifty. What d'you want to bet? If Dreeson hadn't beaten him to it, would he have shown up on our door with some kind of a nosegay?"

"Too late to bet. No way to find out."

But Larry had his revenge, both for the lumber hauling and for all the evenings for the past six weeks when he had cowered in the farthest corner of the third trailer while Mayor Dreeson entertained the Higgins household with his favorite 1940s videos on the VCR. Somehow, between the last inspection the night before the grand opening and the next morning, the entry door acquired an elaborate full-length exterior-enamel portrait of Veronica Lake with a lock of hair falling down over her eye and a sign on the wall next to the doorframe, in Gothic Fraktur, that proclaimed, "Ronnie's Day Care."

Veronica Richter was not amused. Neither, however, was she willing to pay for a completely unnecessary additional coat of fresh paint.

❦   ❦   ❦

Guided by Becky, Dreeson had continued to be a punctilious suitor. For Thanksgiving, there had been a 1950s silk headscarf, all pink and turquoise flowers and paisley, found in its original box; then paintings suitable for decorating the day care center ("wonder why we never threw out these old calendars?"); for Christmas, which Becky had warned him was not a big gift-giving day in Germany, a pair of quilted, insulated, footwarmers with cotton knit tops and also two linen handkerchiefs edged with Irish crochet in variegated thread; for New Year's, two pair of knit knee socks, with all sorts of fancy cables and feathery sorts of stitches, that, O blessings upon us, stayed up without garters. Each offering had been accepted graciously. The courtship was progressing. On Epiphany, January 6, 1632, he presented his chosen wife with a hand mirror. (Heavens! Is the man made of money?) To the full satisfaction of the future spouses, the match was agreed between them.

6

"The woman is totally insane." Maxine Pilcher had not attended the grand opening, but had certainly heard enough about it. "I tell, you, Anita, I could not believe the things she said to Megan and Joshua. I was surprised they didn't have nightmares for weeks."

"They didn't, though, did they?" Anita Barnes asked.

Since Megan had passed through her first grade classroom the year before, the prospect of the arrival of her colleague's second offspring next year was not one of the experiences to which Anita looked forward with happy anticipation. The Pilcher children did not strike her as having fragile egos. Nor, she thought, were any children of Keith Pilcher likely to develop them. She'd gone to high school with Keith. He had not suffered from undue sensitivity.

Maxine pushed on. "How can they possibly allow her anywhere near young children? The city council is completely crazy to have given her a day care license. It must have been all arranged under the table—she's the grandmother of Higgins' wife. He's in tight with Stearns and they're all hand-in-hand with Dreeson."

"It wasn't exactly a secret, Max. It was on the council agenda for two meetings. They put the agenda up on that bulletin board in the City Hall lobby. They publish it in the newspaper. They announce it on the radio. Rebecca Stearns reads it on her TV show. You absolutely have to go *out of your way* not to know what they're going to be discussing."

"I go to my book discussion group on Mondays."

"Your book discussion group reads Harlequin Romances."

"Don't knock it, Anita. Kelley Bonnaro had three titles that no one else did. She's sold the translation rights to a press in Muenster for enough money to add a room to her house for each title."

"She *what?*"

"Well, the authors sure aren't here to collect the money, so we figured that the owners might as well. Publishers are absolutely grabbing for them. The only thing was to decide how to share it out. We decided that anyone who had the only copy of a title got to sell it; for the rest, we put as many titles on the table at each meeting as there are women in the club and draw straws for who gets to sell which one."

"You gals are in *absolutely no* position to call anyone else crazy, no matter what they do. Does the cabinet know about this? Has the committee on foreign currency exchange approved this?"

"None of their business." Maxine returned to the topic at hand. "We've decided to do something about Mrs. Richter, though. Next week, we'll sacrifice our discussion group meeting. We're going to the city council meeting instead. Someone has to speak out about this."

"You and who else?"

"Well, Darlene. Jenny. The rest of them didn't really want to come."

"You and your sisters, in other words? What did Keith say about . . . this?" Anita managed not to say, "about this latest nitwit fit and start of yours."

"Well, I haven't told him. He has so much on his mind, you know. I think I ought to spare him my own troubles if I can possibly bear them alone." Maxine looked virtuous.

Anita thought, *You dwork! The only thing besides hunting that Keith ever had on his mind was his hair, and that's gotten pretty thin on top.*

The entire Monday Evening Book Discussion Club was sitting around the table in the conference room, looking rather defensive. "Maxine," said Melissa Mailey. "Would you please just explain. You don't have to justify it. Just explain it."

"We've got a right. When they came around to

collect for the National Library, or whatever the fancy name is now, they just laughed at our books and said we could keep them—a bunch of intellectual snobs, that's what all of you are out here at the high school."

"What on earth gave you the idea for selling the publication rights to them?" Melissa looked around the room and fixed her eye on a club member who had once been in her classes. "Kelley." Having undergone conditioning, Kelley scrambled.

"Ms. Mailey, it was when that guy from Amsterdam came to talk to Dr. Abrabanel. You know Susie Castalanni here. She has a complete set of first edition Betty Neels—real collectibles, valuable—all the ones about English nurses who marry Dutch doctors, more than forty titles, I think. Susie's *awfully* proud of it. She invited him to come see it. He was *real* happy to find out that in three hundred fifty years the Dutch and the English would still have their countries and their languages and their churches and live in peace and have good hospitals and not be harried by the Spanish Inquisition like the remnants of the Waldensians. Susie hasn't found out what a Waldensian was yet, but whatever happened to them, it wasn't good."

Kelley was forced to pause for breath. Maxine interrupted. "They're real respectable classics, too—not like some of the newer ones. No sex at all until the nurse and doctor get married and not very much after they do. Lots of descriptions of houses and furniture and landscapes. Shopping trips for new clothes. Pictures of ancestors on the wall. Being nice to your stepchildren. He thought that the Calvinist preachers would OK them just fine."

Kelley regained the initiative. "When he went back to Holland, a publisher up there sent a guy down to copy her whole set. They're going to publish them in English for export to London and translate them into Dutch. So we thought, if Susie can sell those, why can't we sell the rest of them? And we did. To the highest bidder. That's all there is to it."

"We reported it on our taxes, too," added Susie. Then, looking at the expressions of her fellow club members, she added in a more doubtful tone of voice. "Well, at least I did. You can look it up."

Nobody blamed Anita Barnes, of course, for dropping the news to everybody she met that Maxine was going to make a fuss about the day care center at the next city council meeting. She hadn't campaigned about it or said anything that a person could call criticism of another teacher. There sure was a big crowd, though—as city council meetings went. All the chairs around the sides of the room were full, with SRO in the back.

"Face it, there's no one in this town over forty whose grandma didn't say something of the sort to them. We all turned out all right." Karen Reading finished her thirty seconds at the microphone. Darryl McCarthy turned to the man next to him and whispered, "Hell, there's probably no one in this town over *twenty* whose grandma didn't say something of the sort to them."

"Will the audience please maintain silence. Everyone will be given a chance to speak in turn. If you want to speak, and didn't take a number at the door when you came in, please see one of the ushers now."

Quentin Underwood was acting as chairman *pro tem,* since Henry Dreeson, as a partner in the business, had recused himself.

It surely was not to be interpreted as a comment on the dialogue that Mayor Dreeson pulled his glass eye good-luck piece out of his pocket and absent-mindedly started to toss it from hand to hand. He did that all the time.

Nat Davis expressed the opinion that kids these days were too full of themselves anyway and didn't need their self-esteem enhanced. The German apprentices he had taken on paid more attention to him than the ones from West Virginia families. Ollie Reardon seconded him. The Baptist minister got up and read part way through a pamphlet on the importance of discipline, but ran out of time.

Maxine had spoken first. When she realized how many people were there, she had sent Darlene and Jenny back to trade in the low numbers they had picked up by coming-early-to-make-sure-they-were-on-time for higher ones, so they would have a chance to comment on the comments.

"We don't want our children exposed to it. It's not modern. It's not progressive. Disciplining children that way is cultural regression." Jenny glanced at the three-by-five card in her hand. "Er—I was supposed to say next that it's un-American, but I guess that I really can't, though, because Karen Reading was telling the truth: my grandma was always frightening us with ghosties and ghoulies and things that go bump in the night. You should have heard what she could make out of an acorn hitting the shingles or a squirrel in the chimney." Maxine's glare at her sister indicated that Jenny's contribution had not been up to the standard of debate she had hoped for.

"I guess maybe Maxine has reason to complain about what Mrs. Richter said at Dr. Sims's office," began the manager of the Dollar Store (who didn't sound very sure, even about this qualification, because Maxine Pilcher had brought her children into his territory on many occasions). "But that doesn't have anything to do with the center. If you don't want to send your kids there, you don't have to. Send them somewhere else. Find someone who's running a day care center that you like." He sat down.

"Actually, I mean, you know, well, when you come right down to it. It's not such a bad thing to have kids do what you tell them to." If Jenny had gotten a glare, Darlene got the kind of look that signified the beginning of a major family bone of contention—the kind with reruns at every holiday dinner for the next fifteen years. Darlene, of course, did not have an education degree: she had gotten married right out of high school and gone to work for the Grantville veterinarian. Veterinary assistants develop considerable respect for the value of discipline, even though they don't always articulate its theoretical basis very well.

By a unanimous vote, the city council reaffirmed the day care license that had been issued to Mrs. Veronica Richter.

7

Jeff had discovered that there was a big chasm that gaped between the stage when a match had been agreed upon by the parties involved and the stage when it was a done deal. There were a lot of conversations. Negotiating the marriage of a widow and widower of such prominence in the town bore more resemblance to a corporate merger than a proposal, even when both of the parties concerned were heartily in favor of the project. Necessarily, there would be feelers and tenders; offers and counteroffers; exploration of the options. Eddie, of all unexpected people, was invaluable—he was learning esoteric diplomatic arts from Becky and her father almost faster than they could teach him.

"It's hard for a man to maintain a proper housekeeping without a wife to manage things—there's a lot of scrubbing and stuff that ought to be done first. We could get a maid. My income runs to that."

"We will need a cook, also. To cook, with the business, I do not have the time. My own income, now, runs to paying the cook."

"It might be that I should help with the cook. It sort of contributes to a man's position to have a wife. Because I'm mayor, people have asked me to have dinners when we have out-of-town visitors, but I've put them off."

"It's only proper for you to host dinners, considering your office."

"I'd need to get a new suit if we gave dinners."

"Leonhard Kalbacher is a tailor of respectable quality. He opened a shop about three doors down from the museum a couple of months ago. A nice black worsted, with velvet facings?"

"Velvet facings? Er—Ronnie!"

"Velvet facings are very fine. America used them, too. I saw them on Professor Ferrara's suit the day the faculty came from the university at Jena to visit our *Hochschule*."

"Hell, that wasn't a suit. That was the academic gown Greg had to buy when he got his M.S. degree."

"It was a very fine robe, indeed. Dignified."

"Velvet facings?"

"It still doesn't seem just right to me for a boy as young as Jeff to be the head of a household. Probably, sometimes, I don't give him quite the deference that his position deserves."

"He's American, Ronnie. He isn't expecting your deference—not the way a German might."

"Well. Remind him that if we ever do get my late husband's property back, I only have a life interest. After that, it will go to Gretchen and Hans and Annalise, so there will be no harm to his children's inheritance. What will your family say?"

"I don't have any really close relatives left here—just a couple of my late wife's nephews and their families. Technically, they don't have anything coming from my side of the family, but I thought—if you don't mind—I'd just divide Annie's personal things between them, half of the trinkets for Lila and half for June. They weren't worth a lot back home, you understand, just some costume jewelry and such. But if we make it, if Grantville makes it, they'll all turn into 'valuable, irreplaceable antiques' in another twenty-five years. Which the boys know—they've seen as many tourist traps as I have. It's probably more than they'll have been expecting. And if we don't make it . . ."

"*Ja, wohl*. You ought to make sure that they understand that it will not hurt their prospects in the long run. It's always best to be on good terms with your kin."

"Yep. No matter what else comes and goes, family stays with you."

A few days later, Henry Dreeson had reason to reflect more deeply on his comment that family stays with you. "Hoo, boy, did it ever!" Or if it went away, it came roaring back in spades. It appeared that he had traded a deceased wife and one married daughter with a husband and two children in Ohio for . . . what? Well, Ronnie appeared to think that it would be his first duty as an adoptive step-step-grandfather to provide moral support, wise advice, useful contacts, and at least some financial backing for launching Eddie, Larry, and Jimmy into their careers. It did not strike him that Ronnie was the type to let a man shirk on his duty. *And that's not all,* he thought with a quirky grin. *No, that's not all.*

"It's a big old Victorian house. You'll have a lot more room than you do now, and fewer people."

"Certainly, but with the new baby coming, we should make more room for Jeff and Gretchen."

"You could bring Hans and Annalise along."

"It would certainly save time for Hans if he were living downtown, now that he's working for the newspaper. It would also improve Annalise's prospects, I think. Those boys are not doing her manners any good at all—she's becoming very outspoken, almost *frech*—fresh."

"Do you have any idea what Gretchen would say if we suggested this? I've sort of felt Jeff out about it. It seems okay with him."

"Gretchen is their sister. But under our old law, I would be their guardian. She was under age when their parents were killed. I would not fight her, though. Still, with a second baby . . . and they will be with us, right here in town. Without the war, they would both have gone by this age, Hans to an apprenticeship and Annalise into some form of service."

"So let's count on having them."

"I think that we should probably take the two oldest of the other children, also. It's a lot closer to the elementary school here. They can help me at the center when they get out of school in the afternoon."

"You will be closer to the center, too—not the long walk home after dark on winter evenings."

"Have you ever thought that we might expand to another location? There's plenty of need, and a good place would be over by the power plant. Appollonia Hirsch could be manager. She's learning fast."

"Well, I have an old garage on a lot over that way. If we tore it down . . ."

"I may have already done a few figures here, just thinking about possibilities."

There was a formal betrothal, of course: everything was to be done in the most proper order, suitable to the age and standing of the parties. It took place in late March, presided over by Father Mazzare and the Calvinist minister whom Henry Dreeson shared with Mike and Rita, who both solemnly accepted the words of promise *de futuro* (after cautiously looking up the

significance of the rite in advance and finding to their
surprise that both Mazzare's completely up-to-date ritual
and an 1894 Manual of the Presbyterian Church in
the USA once bought at an auction provided for such
a contingency). For the preparation of the marriage
contract, Jeff and Dr. Abrabanel represented the bride;
Mike Stearns and Quentin Underwood represented the
groom. All parties emerged with greatly heightened
respect for the negotiating abilities of the others.

All of the parties: even Grandma, who for the
first time referred to Jeff as "Herr Higgins" after
his triumphant, if mischievous, insertion of a clause
according to which, when Hans married, he and his
wife should receive the right to occupy an apartment
to be constructed on the third floor of the second
day care center building for five years at a fixed, very
modest, rent, with option to renew. Hans was not old
enough to marry yet, of course; Grandma was certain
of that. But he was also now of age by the American
laws, so it was best to be prepared.

The day care center had held a grand opening.
Henry Dreeson's house received what the entire
Higgins/Richter household came to think of as the
Grand Inspection.

- ❏ Soap
- ❏ Rags
- ❏ Whitewash
- ❏ Furniture polish
- ❏ Floor wax
- ❏ Laundry

"Oh, all those curtains and draperies; oh, that smell
of tobacco smoke; Henry, what is *this*?

"We cannot possibly marry until September. Everyone in Grantville is so busy, always, *immer, immer*. It will take a while to organize a cleaning crew to bring it up to the standard that will be properly, yes properly, expected of a Herr Buergermeister and a Frau Buergermeisterin."

"Nobody's ever objected to my house the way it is so far."

"Did your first wife keep it like this? I ask you?"

"Well, ummn, no."

"So. I am a townswoman, not an ignorant peasant. I know what is due to your position. I may never have expected to *be* a Frau Buergermeisterin, but I certainly know what is expected of one."

8

Every morning for several weeks, when she came down to open the center, she had spent a few moments glaring at Veronica Lake on the door. Then, for several more weeks, every morning, she had carefully ignored the door. On Monday of the eleventh week, the day after the signing of the marriage contract, she backed across the street to look at it more carefully, and came to a decision. While keeping most of the picture intact, thus saving on the expense of hiring an artist, a modest amount of overpainting could transform Veronica Lake into Saint Veronica and she would have her very own respectable patron saint for her business. A headdress, with a bit of the linen falling forward to cover that hair. A halo. Drapery fluttering across the neckline and arms; drapery down the bottom of the skirt. There was bound to be someone among the Germans in town who could do it. Almost the first thing any apprentice artist learned to paint was drapery. It should be done. There would henceforth be a pious matron of Jerusalem on her door.

She could reuse the sign. Whichever of those three young rascals put it up (and she had her suspicions), he had made it from nice cured wood with shaped edges, far too good to waste. "Ronnie's Day Care" was not suitable for Saint Veronica, but with a little sanding, she could turn it over and use the other side.

She paid extra to have the door taken off the hinges and carried to the back room of the store next door to be repainted. She was prepared to say that it needed to be repaired, if necessary, but always, *immer, immer,* everyone was so busy here in Grantville. Nobody asked.

Carefully, very carefully, she drew the letters. A printer's widow, that she was. A calligrapher she was not!

It was the first thing that she'd said when Jeff brought them there, she thought. She'd said that the building couldn't be a school—that there weren't enough noble children in all of Germany to fill it. She'd known at once that it couldn't be any ramshackle village school for peasant children, nor even such a one as they had in town. It had to be a great Akademie, a Gymnasium, for those who could pay and those lucky few who had scholarships. It was too late for Gretchen and Hans. They were too old. But her little Annalise, she would graduate there. Her granddaughter would be a member of the learned professions, like Ms. Mailey. Anna Elisabetha *Richterin, Lehrerin.* Maybe even *Professorin.* She would introduce her grandmother to her colleagues, *"Meine Grossmutter, Veronica Schusterin verw. Richter, verh. Dreeson."* Pride was a deadly sin, yes, so they said, but Veronica would have pride in her, no matter how many eons she must repent it in Purgatory. And she would have pride in all the children who followed her.

Carefully, very carefully, she placed the stencils for the letters on the wood.

"St. Veronica's Preparatory Academy."

She had made her letters a little too small. There was still a space at the bottom. Should she do them over?

She decided to give it more thought, and put the stencils for them back in the folder until such time as they would be needed.

The new sign did not escape notice. The first morning it was up, the center scarcely open for the day, it brought Maxine Pilcher through both doors and into the center itself.

"Preparatory Academy, Mrs. Richter? Preparatory Academy! Don't you think that's maybe a little pretentious?"

Grandma's answer was blank incomprehension of the last word.

"I mean it's too fancy. You're just being a show-off, calling a day care center a preparatory academy. What do you think you are doing?"

"Herr Higgins found it for me—the name. It is right."

"Listen to me."

"No. You listen. You can let the children in your class not learn. You *know* that whether they learn or not, they will still go to Mrs. Barnes in the first grade and then they will learn what you did not teach them. Or the year after. Or the year after that, perhaps. For American children, there will always be another year, it seems. You are all rich, so rich. My children have no such promise that they will have another chance."

"Mrs. Richter, the best modern theories of early childhood learning indicate—"

"*Akademies* we have in Germany. Or the *Gymnasium,* if you call it that, but it is the whole school and not where the young people play sports. Only through an *Akademie* can a boy of ordinary family advance, to become a member of the learned professions, to became an official in the chancery of a ruler. There are few scholarships, so few can advance. Most of the places are only for the children of the nobles, or the great families—the *Geschlechter*—the bankers and the wholesale merchants in the Imperial cities. And all of them boys, boys, boys, boys, boys. *Immer die Jungen. Immer die Knaben.*"

"Well, naturally, I don't have any objections to coeducation."

"I learned well in the town school. Could I go to an Akademie when I was ten? No. Could I become *ein Beamter*? No. *Ein Gelehrter*? No. I loved my schooling; I loved my reading. My parents wasted the money on my brother, wasted it. Hopeless, he was; spoiled, lazy too. All of his opportunities he frittered away. He came to no good end!"

"Mrs. Richter, just what do you think that you are doing?"

"I am making a Preparatory Academy. I am preparing

children for *Akademies*, and to do it I must use my ways, not yours. Boy children. Girl children. Poor children, of peasants and artisans. All of them! I shall take them when they are so little, the tiny ones. I shall teach them. They shall have no choice but to learn, to be ready when they are ten. The *Akademies* shall drown in children. It will be like the play-yard down by the creek that no one can build upon because the powerful water comes down from the mountains and would push all the buildings off their foundations. I shall flood them. They *will* take my children when the time comes, all of my children. Or they will be washed away."

9

"Well, no, Henry. I wouldn't mind being married by your and Mike's Calvinist preacher. I was baptized a Calvinist, after all."

"You were *what*? Ronnie, you had a saint painted on the door of the day care center."

"I was born the year before the old Calvinist prince died. Then his son inherited. He was Lutheran, like his mother—so I grew up a Lutheran, like the king of Sweden. Lutheran is how I learned the catechism. Lutheran is how I was confirmed and married to Stephan."

"Umm-hmm."

"But then he died, and the heir was Calvinist. But it took quite some time to decide and there were many fights between the Calvinist regent and the Lutheran *Adel*—the nobles. Finally, the ruler won.

That wasn't so long ago. Maybe twenty years, or not quite that."

"I see."

"But when we were taken away from the king of Bohemia after the Battle of the White Mountain, the Emperor gave us to Bavaria, so we all became Catholics a few years later. Gretchen and Hans remember a little bit about being Calvinist, but Annalise isn't old enough."

"So Calvinist is okay for the wedding."

"Yes. I was Lutheran longer than anything else, but Calvinist is fine. The American freedom of religion is much simpler, really. Sometimes it was quite hard to remember what answers a new pastor wanted to hear, from one year to the next."

10

It was bad, that Croat raid, but she lost no more of her children. Not even—*Gott sei Dank!*—Gretchen's foolish young Jeff, wounded though he may have been as a consequence of his stupid bravery. Dashing right out to get yourself shot at does not lead to having many descendants, no, not at all. But he was defending the children, so perhaps it was not so stupid after all.

As for her, she had seen nothing of it. After all, what could one old woman do to fight in a raid? With her little tiny ones, who had been dropped off early by working parents, already safe inside, protected by the stores in front and by the intercession of Saint Veronica, she had simply locked up and placed tables as barricades. The day care center had proceeded with its accustomed daily schedule throughout the gunfire.

The wedding took place, as planned, in September— on Labor Day. The feast included a basket of Henry's Winesaps, uncooked.

But already, the day before, the bride had come to another decision. She knew what to do with the extra space on the sign she had left unpainted. Carefully, very carefully, she drew a few more letters.

She thought they fit nicely, next to the bullet-ridden door where Saint Veronica proudly bore her battle scars.

"School Number 1."

Power to the People

Loren K. Jones

It was a typical Sunday at the Grantville Power Station. Claude Yardley, the senior operator on "C" Crew, was leaning back in his chair as always, watching the power plant's main board. Everything was as it should be, right down to that annoying little flutter in #2 Boiler's pressure. It had been there for years, and no one had ever found the cause. By now it was just one of those little idiosyncrasies of the plant that everyone ignored.

"Hey Nissa, how about bringing me a refill? Please?" he called to the back of the figure at the coffee urn.

"Does I looks like yo' nigga?" Nissa Pritchard sassed back without turning around. She was slightly older than Claude, and had risen through the ranks to become the senior instrument tech in the plant through pure cussedness. The fact that she was a black woman had hindered her over the years, and it was something that she never let the men around her forget.

"No, from this angle you look like my Aunt Diane. Don't throw that!" he quickly added as Nissa turned and raised the can of creamer that she was holding.

"I've met your Aunt Diane, Claude," she growled at him, eyes burning. Diane Yardley was a large woman, especially from the rear. "Are you calling me a fat-ass?"

Claude raised his hands defensively. "Never! Wouldn't dream of it."

"Better not. Union rules say that I can have your ass busted for harassing me about my weight. Besides, I lost five pounds this month." Nissa was bringing a thermos carafe with her as she returned to her desk. Claude held his cup off to the side, well clear of his panel and his lap. Nissa's sense of humor tended toward the physical. She poured the cup full enough that he had to carefully sip before he could move it much.

"Thank you very much, Madame Nissa."

"I ain't no madame, either. You better jus' watch yo' mouth, White Boy. Those size twelves of yours won't both fit." Nissa smiled to show that she was joking, though there had been times in the past that she hadn't. It had been the union's rules, not the EEOC or state snoops, that had seen to her rightful rise through the ranks.

"You're mean. No fun at all. Not like the old days." Claude pretended to pout, which only made Nissa laugh.

"The old days out by #1 Stack? We're both too

old for that crap any more. Damn the luck." Nissa
grinned and winked at Claude. Their brief affair had
ended almost as soon as it started fifteen years before.
They had both been married, but the temptations of
nightshift and the solitude of the area had been more
than they wanted to resist. Now, years later, they could
laugh about it. In private.

Claude sighed. "Time to take readings. You know, I
wish that they would get rid of this stupid paperwork.
The, computer logs everything instantly."

"If they got rid of the paperwork, they could justify getting rid of us." Nissa sighed. "I installed these
monitoring systems. Thought that they would be a
great help. Fah! Help to the company in justifying
minimum raises. Crap."

"Crap indeed, Nissa. Crap—" Thunder slammed
through the control room, and white light showed
around the rim of the door, interrupting Claude's
complaint.

"*Holy shit!* Loss of load! Loss of load!" Claude
shouted, grabbing for his controls. The old-fashioned
gauges on the wall mirrored the computer's reading.
They had been cruising along at fifty-eight percent
power, then suddenly nothing. Automatic systems
reacted before Claude could, cutting the flow of
steam to the main turbine in the blink of an eye.
Even so, the turbine was already turning at far above
its rated RPM.

"Initiate steam braking! Slow the turbine down!"
Nissa shouted as she ran her fingers over her board.
"All of the main breakers are tripped. I'm getting
ground-faults on all transmission lines. Phase-to-phase
in the south. Shit, what was that?"

"I don't know, Nis. Everything else seems okay, it's just the outgoing lines that are down. Call in help, Nis. Call Bill. I think he's in his office. I'm calling Northeast Grid Control. See if they know what happened." Claude was picking up his phone as he spoke, then tapping the hook. "My line's dead. How's yours?"

"External lines are dead. Not even a dial tone. Bill isn't answering his phone."

Claude grabbed his radio next. All of the men and women on the crew carried a five-watt hand-held radio. "We have an emergency. We have an emergency. All personnel report."

Nissa was sitting beside him, shaking her head. "I can't hear you, Claude. You aren't broadcasting." A sudden chill swept over her, and her eyes grew large with fear. "Oh, shit, Claude. EMP? Was there an attack? Oh shit oh shit oh shit," she began chanting, almost hyperventilating.

"Nissa! Shut up! It wasn't an attack! Look at your computer! Look at your watch! They're still working." Claude held up his wrist. "EMP would have taken these out too. Whatever it was, it wasn't nuclear."

"But what . . ." Nissa grabbed for the old intercom microphone and gingerly pressed the switch. "Testing. Testing. Can anyone hear me?"

"Yah, Nissa, I hear you," Rodman Shackleton's voice replied. "What the hell was that? What happened?"

"We don't know, Rod. Is anyone else with you?"

"Yep. Norris, Carney, Vaughn, Jeff and Latham," he instantly replied, drawing sighs of relief from the two in the control room.

"Where's here? Maintenance?" Claude asked over

Nissa's shoulder, pressing his hand down on hers to key the mike.

"Ten-four."

"Are you bastards playing poker without me again?" Nissa asked angrily.

There was a pause before Rodman answered. "Would we do that?" He sounded genuinely hurt, but the laughter in the background ruined it for him.

"Get up to control immediately. Grab anyone that you see on the way. Something happened and we can't contact anyone outside of the plant. Anyone who can hear this, come to control." Nissa let go of the mike and looked up at Claude. "What now?"

Claude looked at the plant layout on his board and shook his head. "Everything is shut down. We have to recover the plant first, then see about recovering the rest of the grid."

Pounding feet moments later announced the arrival of two of the other instrument techs on the crew. Leona McCabe and Darlene Braun had been in the instrument shop repairing a pressure gauge when the intercom had come to life. Both had listened and then run, taking the stairs two at a time to reach control. "Nis, what happened?" Darlene immediately demanded.

"Don't know yet. Find a perch and wait for the rest." Nissa pointed to the counter along the back of the room and the two women immediately complied. Gina Goodman entered right on their heels and joined them, glancing nervously at the big board. She was another of "C" Crew's four operators, and had been eating lunch when the call came. Five others followed her in and immediately began asking questions. "Wait for the rest," Nissa commanded, and they quieted.

More running feet announced the arrival of the men from the maintenance shop. Once everyone was present, Claude spoke. "All right. Here's what we know. We're out of communication with the rest of the area. Phones and radios don't work. Internet is gone as well.

"The main generator is down and is going to stay down. We're running on the emergency diesel for now. All of the outgoing lines show ground-faults, and a few phase-to-phase shorts. We have to get the field crews going and start isolating the problem, but we can't contact them. I want four volunteers to go get help. Operators and instrument techs only. I want the mechanics and electricians working the plant."

Selena Alcom and Paul Stancil immediately stepped forward, as did Dane Stevenson and Leona McCabe. Claude nodded. "Selena, go to Bill's office and see if he's still here. If he isn't, come right back." He nodded as she immediately went to find the plant manager.

"Leona, drive into town and see what gives with the phones. They have their own generator, so us being down shouldn't affect them. Someone should be there, even today." Leona nodded and turned to leave, but hesitated at the door.

"Claude, what if there isn't a town there?"

"There is! Don't talk that way or you'll scare someone. Like me." Claude's wide eyes made her almost grin, then nod before leaving.

"Dane, go to the police station. They should have some idea what is going on. Stay there until you find out what's happening. If no one knows, come back in three hours."

Dane nodded and left, ambling in his unhurried fashion even in what amounted to a major emergency. He only had one speed, unless there was beer involved.

Claude watched him go, shaking his head. "Paul, go to the service depot. See if there's anyone there and get them out looking for the downed lines. Since we don't have radio contact, tell them to come here and report. And tell them to go out in groups of three. They can't call in help, so they need to be able to handle whatever they find. Tell them to isolate any downed lines. Cut 'em high. We need to get the grid back up. Once everyone has reported, we'll bring the generator back up. Until then, everyone stays."

That pronouncement drew immediate protests from everyone. "I'm sorry!" Claude shouted. "I'm sorry. I want to go home and check on Beth and the kids too, but we have a responsibility to everyone. We have to get the power back on. For our families as well as everyone else."

Claude's shout had the desired effect, and the men and women began nodding. Paul turned and left as Claude began speaking again. "Everyone else start checking out the plant. Get the main turbine on the jacking gear." He paused and looked at his readouts. "It's down to less than fifty RPM already. Get the jacking gear going as soon as possible. We have to keep that baby turning so she doesn't warp." The four mechanics of the crew immediately went to do their job.

"The diesel generator is running, and I want someone

watching it. We are well and truly screwed if that thing stops. Take it turn and turn about. Operator, mechanic and electrician when we can."

"C" Crew immediately began their task, assuming the calm demeanor of experienced professionals as the minutes slowly ticked by.

Help arrived shortly after that in the form of off-shift personnel. When you work at the power plant and the lights go out, family members expect you to do something about it. And when you can't call in, you come in.

The first to arrive was Thomas McAndrew, an electrician from "D" Crew. He entered the control room in a foul mood. "What's going on? Jen is throwing a fit about not being able to chat with her mother online because the power's out."

"We don't know. Suit up, we need the help. The entire grid is down, and we can't contact anyone." Claude's terse report, spoken without turning, silenced Tom.

"Where do you need me?"

"Diesel. That's where the other electricians are." Tom nodded and left immediately.

Nissa stood and walked to the door. "I'm going down to the guard shack. I just realized that we haven't heard from Howard since whatever it was happened."

"No, Nissa, wait . . . Oh, damn it all anyway." Nissa hadn't even slowed down when he tried to call her back. Not surprising. Howard was an old man, old enough to be her father, and one of the few men that Nissa didn't tease. Howard had once used his nightstick on a man who was harassing her. The two of them had lied about it to keep him out of trouble, but the harasser's broken arm and cracked skull couldn't have been caused by the fall that they both swore that they had seen.

Nissa arrived at the guard shack in moments. Both gates were open, against company policy, but the shack was empty. Looking around, she spotted the one place that Howard was likely to be if he wasn't in the shack. The bathroom.

Walking over to the door, she knocked loudly. "Hey, you old fart! What happened, did you fall in?" Silence answered her. Knocking again, she pushed the door open a crack. "Howard? You in here?" Still no answer. Finally, she entered the men's room.

Howard was there. His pants were still around his ankles, but he had managed to pull his underwear up. He was crumpled in a heap on the floor, and there was blood around his head. *"Howard!"* Nissa shouted, going to her knees beside him. "Howard, are you okay?"

Nissa gently turned his head, but the first contact with his flesh made her scramble back. He was cold. *No. No, no, no! He can't be dead!* her mind screamed. Touching him again, she checked for a pulse. None. Scrambling to her feet, Nissa ran out of the men's room just as a pickup pulled up to the open gate.

"Help! Howard's down! We need to get an ambulance right away!"

The man in the truck stared at her for a moment before driving toward her. Nissa recognized Ross Flemming, a mechanic from "A" Crew. He slammed on his brakes and jumped out of his truck, leaving the engine running. "Where is he?"

Nissa turned and ran back into the men's room with Ross. Ross knelt by Howard's side and felt for a pulse. "No pulse. His skin is cool. I'm sorry Nissa. We have to call an ambulance, but I don't think . . ."

"_No!_ He has to be okay! He has to be!" Nissa shouted. Nissa grabbed Ross by the collar and dragged him to his feet. "Go get an ambulance! The phones are down. Go now! Go, for god's sake, go!" Nissa was crying and pushing Ross toward his truck as she spoke.

"Okay, Nissa, okay, I'm going. I'm going!" Ross climbed into his truck and drove away as fast as he dared. He was sure that it was futile, but he liked old Howard, too.

Others were trickling into the plant now as well, but Nissa didn't notice. She was sitting on the floor of the men's room, stroking Howard's curly hair.

Bill Porter's arrival in the control room ten minutes later was welcome, and he immediately called a meeting of the senior personnel. "Where do we stand?" he asked, looking around the conference room.

Claude stood as he answered. "We're self sufficient, but we don't know what happened to the grid, and we can't find out. There's no communication from outside of the immediate area."

Bill nodded. "Okay, I'm instituting Emergency Protocol One. Everyone needs to be here. We can't call, so I want one person to take the list and go get everyone. Most of the people who live in the local area are already here, but not everyone. I also want someone to go to the school and find the police chief. He needs to be informed about Howard." Bill paused and hung his head. Nissa had refused to leave Howard's side until the ambulance arrived.

"What about our families?" Gannon Emerson, "B" Crew's senior operator asked. "I don't want to leave Mary and the kids alone . . ."

Others immediately joined in, demanding that they be allowed to go home to their families. "Okay, okay, enough already. Whoever goes out will hit every house. Tell the families that they can come here."

"I want to go . . ."

"*No!* We need an operational staff. We'll get your families here as soon as possible," Bill interrupted once again. "We have a responsibility to the community . . ."

"We have a responsibility to our families first, Bill," Gannon continued.

"Then do them a favor and get their lights back on," Bill snarled. "We all need electricity. How many of you can cook right now?" His question silenced them. "How much of your food is going to spoil in the fridge and freezer if you don't have power? Think about it. I want any of you who used to work the lines to get out and grab a truck. We have to clear the faults and get the power back on. But I want "C" and "A" crews here. The rest of you grab your cars and get to the depot. Grab a service truck, drive to the end of a line, fix the problem, and come back here. Go home for your families if you want." Bill paused. "And someone stop in and tell Jill to come out here too."

The men and women who were from "B" and "D" crews immediately went to their cars. No matter what Bill said, families first. Even his.

It was completely dark before any of the field service crews returned. Men and women climbed wearily out of the trucks, stretching their aching backs and in some cases limping. Each crew reported on the lines that they had checked. And each report was eerily alike.

"The lines were cut, slick as a whistle. Just ended. So did the road, about where the lines would have been."

Once all of the crews had reported and all of the faults were clear, Bill ordered the main generator brought back on line. Two hours later, after carefully warming the turbine and bringing it up to speed, power came back to Grantville.

Gannon found Bill once the generator was on line. "Bill, I ran into some people who said that there was some trouble out south of town. A fire and then some fighting. Apparently Dan was shot."

"Dan? Dan Frost? The *police chief* was shot? Who's in charge? What happened?" Bill immediately asked, but Gannon was shaking his head.

"Don't know much more than that. The people that I talked to didn't either."

Bill looked around him at the plant that was his responsibility. "Tomorrow. It'll have to wait until tomorrow." Looking around, he took a deep breath to calm himself. "Maybe by tomorrow we'll have our answers."

⊰⊱   ⊰⊱   ⊰⊱

Morning brought more questions than answers. The story of the fight south of town had made its way to the plant with a speed that only urgent gossip can attain. The woman that Stearns and the men of the United Mine Workers of America had rescued told them that they were in Middle Ages Germany. Thuringia. A mutter of "Where the hell is Thuringia?" had swept through the plant. Worse was what they couldn't find out.

Where was the rest of the world that they knew?

Where was the United States?

And worst of all, where were their families?

Claude and Nissa sat in almost stony silence as they listened to what the various members of the plant crew had learned. They were lost, and alone. Both of them had lived out on Route 250. Beyond the cut. Bill Porter's family was also gone, left behind in Barracksville.

It was decided to turn some of the plant's unoccupied offices into bunkrooms until something could be done about the situation. The three were taken off of the watch rotation and unobtrusively watched. Each was encouraged to talk, to let the healing begin. Each saw a priest, but Claude was not a religious man and found little comfort in "God's Will."

Nighttime darkness and pilfered sleeping pills saw them to bed with the hopes that morning would bring better news.

Claude was missing the next morning. Nissa was the first to notice his absence when he failed to meet her for breakfast, and raised the alarm. A quick search of the plant showed that he had not gone alone. Ross Flemming's .300 Savage was gone as well.

Claude had stared at the ceiling for half the night before making up his mind to go. Rising quietly, he had dressed in the hall and headed for his car. He was just pulling up to the gate when his eye caught the silhouette of a rifle in the back window of a truck. A smile crossed his face when he realized whose truck it was. *Ross is going to be so pissed*, he thought to himself as he opened the door. A brief search under the seat yielded a box of ammo, as expected. Some people were just too predictable for their own good.

Claude had a destination in mind. He had been rolling the idea around in his head since the Ring of Fire, and the rumors that they had been hearing had convinced him to go. It was only twelve miles from the plant to home. Or at least where home had been. Driving up the road, he felt a tightness in his chest begin to ease. He was finally going home.

The end of Route 250 was abrupt and chilling. He had heard the stories of the line crews, but they hadn't prepared him for the reality. The road ended at the edge of a three foot tall cliff. The ground had crumbled a bit, but the edge of the pavement was cut in an almost glass-smooth line. The land beyond the cut was strange in the moonlight.

There should be hills there, he thought, *and the stream.* But there wasn't. Still, his sense of direction led him on, and his feet knew the distance. Forest that hadn't existed in West Virginia impeded him, slowing his progress. Bushes that he couldn't identify tangled his legs.

The sun was peeking over the horizon in the wrong place according to his senses, but it matched what they had been told was east. He slowed now, walking carefully and looking ahead at each clearing. He was depressed and homesick, but he wasn't suicidal. Not yet, at least.

His legs told him that he was near home. Just ahead was a shallow valley where there should have been a hill. Staying in the trees, he made his way to where his heart said home was.

An old oak had grown in his front yard. It had been there since before the area had been developed, and he had cherished the gnarled old tree like one of the family. But there was no tree here. A small meadow with a trickling creek ran through where his heart said his house should have been.

He drew a long, shuddering breath, never looking away from the empty space where his home should have been. Deep in his heart he had held out hope that he would find it. That Beth and the kids would somehow be there. Now he believed, and that belief was tearing him apart.

The sound of movement in the bushes caused him to snap his head up some time later. Searching the area with his eyes, he fumbled with the rifle in his hands. Thank god that Ross kept it loaded. He hadn't even thought to check. Clicking the safety off, he wrapped the shoulder strap around his hand as he brought the stock up to his shoulder.

The sound wasn't repeated, and he carefully eased back to the tree line, continuously scanning the area. The story of the German soldiers came to his mind, and sweat beaded his forehead. Taking one last look around, he began the trek back to the plant. Then it hit him. Where was the plant from here?

❧❧ ❧❧ ❧❧

Nissa was almost frantic as the day wore on. Claude was no wimp, but he was no Rambo either. Nearly fifty, with a beer belly and bad eyes, Claude wasn't exactly a prime specimen of American manhood, but he was the best friend that she had. All through her marriage it had been Claude to whom she had taken her troubles. He had been the sounding board for her sorrows, and had shared her joys.

Her marriage to Jim Pritchard had been all but over. Nineteen years with no children had left them more like friends sharing a house than lovers. It had only been her deep faith that had kept them out of divorce court. She wondered if him not even being born yet would suffice for "Till death do us part." Now, at age fifty, she was facing the loss of someone who meant more to her than her husband.

Nissa was facing off against half of the men in the plant with her fists planted on her hips and a snarl twisting her lips. "What do you mean? Won't any of you pussies go out and look for him?" she shouted, sweeping the men with a gaze that said just how little she thought of them.

"Now, Nissa, we understand how you feel, but . . ." Bill Porter began, but she shouted him down.

"Horseshit! That's horseshit, Bill. Claude is out there alone someplace, and you bunch of pussies won't even go look for him!"

"Where!" Latham Beckworth shouted back. "Where are we supposed to look, Nissa? No one knows where he went, and it's too risky to just go charging around beating the bushes. Claude is a grown man, and he's armed. Give the man some space. Maybe he just wanted to be alone for a while."

Nissa glared at Latham in silent fury. Still, even she had to admit that he was right. Claude was no child. Stamping away in frustration, she climbed to the highest point in the plant and began scanning the area with a pair of binoculars.

The day was wearing on toward noon as Claude made his way through the forest. He was thoroughly lost, alone, and hungry. Thirst had, fortunately, not been a problem. There were a number of small creeks crossing the area, and he had drunk his fill at each one. Unfortunately, he had no idea which plants he could eat, and he was not going to shoot a squirrel with a .300. There wouldn't be anything left but bits of hair and bone if he did.

Sounds filled the forest, but they weren't sounds that he knew. He found himself jumping at the calls of birds, and all but shouting at the chattering squirrels above him. Sounds that he had no way of identifying assailed him from every direction. Then a sound that he could identify caught his attention.

A roaring sound silenced the animals and made him turn to his right. That sound had no place in seventeenth-century Germany, but he knew it by heart. It was the sound of the steam pressure relief on the boilers being tested, and it was the sweetest sound that he knew.

The sound was repeated every half hour. It didn't last long, but it gave him a direction to go. His path was still far from straight, but within a few hours he sighted the edge of the land that had come with

Grantville. He could see the plume of smoke from the plant in the distance, and gratefully turned toward it. It was still a long walk to his car, but he was back.

Nissa saw him coming and all but ran down the stairs to reach the gate. She was there in moments, and her worry and fear had turned into anger by the time that he arrived. "Claude Yardley, you son of a bitch! What the hell do you think you're doing!" she shouted as soon as he pulled in and parked.

Claude waved his left hand over his head, but didn't shout back. He was too tired and relieved to shout. Walking toward the office, he was met by half the crew. Especially Nissa and Ross.

Ross was the first to reach him. "You bastard! You'd better not've scratched my rifle."

Nissa was right on his heels. "Claude, what the hell did you think that you were doing? Where did you go?" Her shout was muffled because she was burying her face in his shoulder. When she pulled her face back, there were tears running down her cheeks. "How could you leave me like that?" she whispered.

Claude was taken back by her last question. "I went home. Or at least I tried. I walked half the night away, following my nose to where home should have been. I thought . . . I don't know what I thought. I had to see it for myself, Nis. I had to see that the house really wasn't there."

"Selfish bastard," she said in an almost normal tone. "You could have told someone rather than have me worry myself to death."

"Sorry, Nis."

⟨≈⟩⟨≈⟩ ⟨≈⟩⟨≈⟩ ⟨≈⟩⟨≈⟩

It was days later that their answers were to come. Everyone who could be spared was at the high school for the town meeting. Sitting there, listening to the discussion, Claude stared at the podium with bleak eyes. Nissa was at his side, nearly as numb as he was. They were stuck in Germany, more than three centuries from their families. Nissa clutched Claude's hand as Greg Ferrara said those fateful words: "We're here to stay." A choked sob drew her attention back to Claude.

"I loved her, Nis. I really did."

"And I loved Jim. What now, Claude?"

Claude just shook his head. "I don't know. I don't even know if I care."

Nissa squeezed his hand and laid her head on his shoulder. "You care, Claude. We all care."

Claude nodded and stood to walk out of the gym. The commotion behind him didn't even make him turn his head as the mayor once again took the podium. Nissa stayed at his side, still clutching his hand.

They had come in Nissa's jeep, and Claude naturally took the passenger seat for the ride back. His eyes were haunted as they drove back out to the plant. All that he could think of was how alone he was.

The plant was running, but just barely. Looking up as they neared the plant, he saw the figures of three men walking along the highest catwalks. One of the first precautions that they had instituted was to have the workers arm themselves. The fear of someone going "postal" was overridden by the fear of the unknown. Claude and Nissa were off-shift, but with nowhere else to go they went to the control room. Sympathetic eyes met them as they entered, but no one spoke. There were no words. Of the seventeen people at the plant that day, only Bill, Claude and Nissa had been left alone by the Ring of Fire.

The two stayed, helping where they could, but as night came they felt their uselessness. By unspoken agreement they walked out and headed for the office.

Cots had been set up in the plant offices, and the two old friends stopped in the hallway outside the room that had been designated the "Women's Dorm." "Good night, Nis. I hope that you can sleep, 'cause there's no way that I can."

"You will. You can sleep standing up, Claude. But if you can't, look in on me. I'll probably be counting spots on the ceiling again tonight."

Bill Porter called a meeting just after supper the next day. The off-duty personnel were all gathered in the plant's lunchroom. "All right, people, listen up. After the town meeting yesterday it was decided that we would begin planning and building a smaller plant. One that will supply our needs, but isn't so large that it will eat us alive. This is Andy Frystak and Scott Hilton." He nodded to the two men sitting behind him. "They are both steam engine buffs. Our basic plan is to build a steam engine and generator that is capable of supplying ten to fifteen megawatts. That may not sound like much compared to our two hundred megawatts, but it's more than enough to handle the area and any reasonable amount of growth."

A man at the back stood and raised his hand. Bill nodded for him to speak. "How are we going to do that? We don't have the facilities to wind a generator that big?"

Bill nodded. "Not at the moment, but that doesn't mean that we can't build them. Look, people, I figure that we have eighteen to twenty-four months before this plant becomes a monument to the future. And I'm not talking about one generator. I want two, maybe three, to give us some backup. Remember, we're all that we have. Even the diesel isn't going to do us much good once it's out of fuel. And that's another thing. Fuel. As of last night fuel, gas and diesel, became a vital resource. No driving into town. No driving home. Sorry, but the new U.S. Army has first call on the gas."

After the meeting Claude and Nissa walked out of the office side by side, but not touching. "A ten to fifteen meg plant. That's barely enough to . . ."

"It's enough for Grantville," Nissa interrupted. "Even with growth, our load is going down, not up. No new appliances. Fewer lights. Hell, Claude, where are we going to get light bulbs? Someone is going to have to build a plant to build them. By the time that we need more than fifteen meg . . ."

"We'll be dead and buried," Claude said morosely.

Claude and Nissa were both being kept under close supervision, as was Bill. Claude's little escapade had brought everyone's attention to the stark realities of their situation; the three of them were alone, with no home to go to.

Claude immersed himself in his job. The plant had been his home away from home for years, and he knew it better than just about anyone else. Now he haunted the catwalks and workshops. He did everything that he could to avoid returning to the office that was his bedroom. It was only when he could no longer keep his eyes open that he would leave, but he often came back just hours later. Sleep was a reluctant lover who kicked him out of bed as soon as she could.

Nissa was in better shape. Always self-sufficient, she became almost cold. Her emotions ran to the extremes, with bouts of rage alternating with bouts of crying. But in between she was all but a mannequin walking around the plant. It was only around Claude that she began to show some signs of life.

Claude and Nissa had been partnered in the control room for six years, and it was there that they began to recover their spirits. Other workers occasionally heard the sound of crying from behind the closed doors. Less often, they heard laughter.

It was after the first big battle that Nissa and Claude began to really take notice of the world outside the plant. The new U.S. government had built a refugee center next to the plant to take advantage of the waste heat from the boilers. After the battle, the prisoners that were brought to the refugee center were, for the most part, pathetic. Nissa stood on the middle level of the #2 Boiler catwalks and watched them as they sat in the sun. Few of them really looked like soldiers. Most of them looked like farmers, and all of them looked thoroughly miserable. The bright lights at night left them confused and dazed. The loud voices that came from high in the air left most of them terrified. And the armed men who surrounded them simply stared, never answering even the most innocent question.

The refugee center had been equipped with several makeshift water heaters that had been built using spare heat exchangers and pumps from the plant. Low-pressure steam was piped over and run through the heat exchanger shells while water from the plant's fire main was passed through the coils. Hot water, a most uncommon luxury, was available for everyone. Even the soldiers.

Claude returned from the refugee center chuckling. Nissa looked at him with a question in her eyes, and he burst out laughing as he explained. "They just made all of the soldiers take a shower. Talk about a bunch of miserable mo fo's. I swear, most of them would rather've been shot!"

Nissa grinned, more from seeing the life come back to Claude's eyes than from his story. "I wish that I could've seen that."

"I'll bet! Couple of hundred naked men to ogle. Wouldn't have been right though. It was bad enough that the army guys were watching 'em. Worse than prison. One of the Scots was there and said that most of the prisoners were convinced that they were being condemned and wailing about the Inquisition. It seems that their own people are likely to turn against them and denounce them if they appear too clean. Be the first time that I've ever heard of someone being shot for not stinking."

Nissa's eyes clouded for a moment. "They wouldn't be shot. They'd be tortured and then burned at the stake."

Claude calmed down immediately. "Oh. Didn't know

that. Still, from what I've heard, burning would be too good for some of them. Did you hear about the family that hid their girls under a shithouse to save them from the 'friendly' troops?"

Nissa nodded. "There's a long history of that, Claude. I've been talking to Ms. Mailey, the history teacher. Seems that the losing side's baggage becomes the property of the winning side. Including any women and children that are there. What she describes sounds a lot like slavery to me. White men taking white girls as sex slaves and drudges. Makes me sick to think about it."

"Well, those boys down there ain't taking nobody for nothing, I can tell you that. Even the toughest are a bit timid in the face of a twelve-gauge shotgun."

Now Nissa did grin. "Especially bare butt naked."

Claude nodded. "I need to get something to eat. Coming?"

Nissa nodded and joined him on the short walk. "I'm getting sick of this place," she murmured.

Claude nodded but that was all the answer that he could manage. They made their way to the plant break room and grabbed a couple of sodas. The machines were running low, and they were all too aware that when they were empty, they would never be refilled.

"I've been thinking about home, Nis. A lot." He paused to look around. "This isn't a home. This is . . . work. I . . . I need someplace to call home."

"Claude, please don't. You're tearing yourself apart, and me, too."

"Sorry, Nis. I'm really sorry. I'm really depressed." He paused to sigh deeply. "I'm really lonely."

"You're really going to get smacked in the nose if you keep that up," Nissa said softly. "I'm depressed enough without your help."

"So what do we do?"

"We? What's this we shit, White Man?" Nissa grinned as she spoke, uttering the punch line of a joke that was almost as worn out as she was.

Claude gave her a lopsided grin. "Us. I've been thinking about us lately, Nis. About how we used to be. You know, Bill has turned his office into an apartment of sorts. He already had a fridge and coffee maker, and his office has a private bathroom. He has to shower in the locker room, but that's not a big problem. I was thinking about doing something like that."

"Oh? And just where do you plan to do this?" Nissa asked, curious in spite of herself. Claude rarely talked about plans that he hadn't thoroughly thought out.

"Well, I want a place with a private john. I hate having to walk down the hall to piss in the middle of the night."

"Where, Claude?" Nissa said softly.

"A nice, big place. Not as big as a real apartment, but with enough room for a king size bed." Claude grinned and winked at Nissa as he mentioned the bed.

"Where?" she growled.

Now Claude was grinning. "Well, it has to be close. Don't want to walk to work in the snow, you know."

"Yardley!"

"Upstairs."

Nissa just looked at him for a moment. "Ya ain't getting Bill out of his office, Claude."

"Nope, sure ain't."

Nissa's eyes narrowed with real anger. "Talk or die, Yardley."

Now Claude laughed. "Remember when this was going to be the central plant of a huge power corporation?"

"Before my time, but go on," she answered softly, intrigued.

"Well, there are other offices upstairs besides Bill's."

Now Nissa's eyes grew from slits to round orbs. "You're insane."

"Yep. Ain't it great! The CEO's office is just sitting there, ready for us to move in."

Nissa eyed him carefully. "Us, Claude?"

"Us, Nissa. I'm not talking anything permanent, unless that's what you want." There was a twinkle in Claude's eyes as he continued. "What d' ya say? Wanna shack up?"

Nissa's laughing assent was punctuated by her punching his chest.

A Matter of Consultation

S.L. Viehl

"Now I know how Hansel and Gretel felt." The spring breeze had Sharon Nichols buttoning her jacket as she eyed the forest. Her paramedic training hadn't covered hikes through the woods. "How did they find their way out? With a trail of bread crumbs?"

"They torched the witch and ran." Anne Jefferson also scanned the tree line. A registered nurse, she'd grown up in the backwoods of West Virginia, and unlike her friend felt almost at home. "Not an option today."

Ragged stumps lined either side of the forest path, but the woodcutters had barely made a dent in the dense groves of oak and birch. According to rumor, none of the locals went into Thuringenwald unless they desperately needed firewood, venison, or the witch.

Their patients didn't need chopped wood or deer meat.

"One thing." Sharon glanced sideways at the nurse. "Becky said if she lives in a gingerbread house, she's got dibs on the chocolate. *All* the chocolate."

Anne grinned. Some of their needs were serious, while others—like Rebecca Stearns's pregnancy cravings—were just plain painful. "Fair enough, but if she's got anything that even remotely resembles coffee, it's mine."

The forest canopy made the air lacy with sunlight and shadow, as disparate as the well-endowed, dark-skinned Sharon and the pale, redheaded Anne. Oddly, the sight of a black woman and a white woman together didn't seem to shock the natives as much as what they wore. Their clothes, like both women and a huge chunk of the town of Grantville, West Virginia, had traveled back in time to land in the middle of seventeenth-century Germany.

Time would eventually catch up. In three hundred and seventy years.

The carpet of twigs, dead leaves and moss grew thicker, and made crunching sounds beneath Sharon's sneakers. "You really sure this witch can help us?"

"Mathilde said Tibelda was the only decent healer the prostitutes in Jena had, before the burghers drove her out." Anne didn't think much of those upstanding citizens, not after hearing what they'd done to many of the refugee women from Palatinate. "Her knowledge of the area alone could save us a lot of time and foraging."

"I hope so." Sharon ducked to avoid a low-hanging branch. "Why does she live all the way out here by herself?"

"Remember how twitchy these people are." Anne paused to adjust the straps on her backpack. "A cow drops dead, the local healer gets blamed, then someone starts piling up wood and asking who wants extra crispy or original recipe."

"Better keep that in mind, nurse." Sharon tilted her head and squinted. "I think I see something up there."

The cottage that appeared around the next bend wasn't made of candy, but the mud-brick walls and thatched roof looked solid enough. A large patch of ground on one side had been cleared to make way for a thriving garden. As they drew closer, Anne smelled freshly cut rosemary, and spotted some familiar white and pink flowers in the garden's front row.

"See those?" She pointed out the blooms. "That's yarrow. It's an excellent astringent and coagulant, and even works as bug repellent. This is definitely the place."

"Why do we need her?" Sharon asked as she went to knock on the front door. "You know more about plants than anybody."

Anne thought of her grandmother, who wouldn't be born for three centuries. "We need her. This is her turf, not mine."

The door opened an inch, and a suspicious eye peered out. "*Was willst du?*"

"*Guten morgen, Frau Tibelda.*" Being more fluent in German, Anne handled the introductions. "*Mein name ist Anne Jefferson, könnten sie mir bitte helfen?*"

The door opened to reveal a gaunt, elderly woman wearing a plain peasant's dress. A faded cloth covered her hair with the ends knotted under her prominent chin. She gave both women the once-over, uttered something scathing, then shut the door.

Sharon frowned. "What was that?"

"She said she doesn't perform abortions." Now Anne hammered on the door. "*Bitte, Frau Tibelda, ich bin Englisch Krankenpflegerin!*"

"You dress like harlots," Tibelda said through the door, in heavily accented but understandable English.

"We're not. Please, open the door."

The gap and the eye appeared again. "What do you want?"

"Some help." Anne brought out their bribe—dried parsley, one of the last bottles in stock at the Grantville A & P. "This is for you."

Tibelda emerged and took the bottle. "It should be dried on the stem, not crumbled." She opened it and sniffed. "Too old." She thrust it back in the nurse's hand. "Go away."

"Wait!" Sharon caught the door before it slammed shut. "Mathilde said you took good care of the women in Jena. There are other people who need your help, and they can't take no for an answer."

Either Mathilde's name or the compliment appeared to mollify the old woman, for the door swung inward.

Sharon and Anne walked in. Crude furnishings within the cottage provided Spartan comfort, while bunches of flowers and herbs hung suspended from the network of boughs supporting the roof thatch. Another door at the back of the cottage stood open, revealing a well-stocked pantry. The air smelled fragrant and delicious, thanks to something bubbling in a pot hung over the hearth.

A thin pallet occupied one corner, while a simple cross nailed to one wall provided the only decoration.

"Just like Granny's." Anne's eyes grew misty. "Right down to the simmering stew pot."

Sharon gave her friend's arm a squeeze. When Grantville had been wrenched from the year 2000 and thrown back through the Ring of Fire to 1632, Anne had been shopping in town. She'd lost her entire family, including her beloved grandmother, who'd lived only twenty miles away.

Tibelda went to stir the pot. "Where are the people who need me?"

The two women exchanged a look before Anne began with, "You may have heard about Grantville—"

"The place of endless wonders, and witchcraft." She snorted. "I've heard."

Anne wondered if the old woman resented the competition. "People who have lost their homes and families to the war have taken sanctuary with us. Most of our refugees arrive wounded."

"War destroys everything." Tibelda didn't sound impressed.

"We've used our own supplies up 'til now to help these people, but we're running low now," Sharon said. "Especially on medicine."

Tibelda sampled what was in the pot. "So you need my herbs."

"We need your *knowledge*," Anne corrected her. "I know a lot about herbal medicines, but nothing about what grows here or can be had from traders. You do. We'd like you to come back to Grantville and teach us."

Tibelda removed a handful of leaves from a pocket

in her girdle, and tossed them in the pot. "You could be witch-hunters, sent to test me."

"Show time," Sharon murmured.

"Frau Tibelda, watch this." Anne removed a syringe and a small vial from her pack. While she prepared the injection, the paramedic rolled up her sleeve and tied off her upper arm.

The sight of the needle seemed to mesmerize the old woman. "What are you doing?"

"Proving we aren't witch-hunters." Anne slid the slanted needle tip into Sharon's vein and depressed the plunger. "Would they do something like this?"

The old woman came closer, so engrossed she spoke in rapid German. "So small—like a bee sting. Why does she not drink from the bottle instead? Why put it in her arm? How do you distill it to make it so clear?"

"She wants to talk shop, right?" At Anne's nod, Sharon grinned. "We've got her."

"*Alte Hexe!*" Someone pounded on the front door. "*Aufmachen! Du wirst mir helfen!*"

Sharon rose, still holding her arm. "What's that mean?"

"Someone else wants help, and they're not asking nicely." Anne swept everything off the table and into her pack. "Do you have a back door?"

"No, hide, in here. Quickly!" Tibelda shoved Sharon in the pantry. Before she could do the same with Anne, the door flew open and three men strode in. From their rough, sweat-stained clothes, bleached hair, and ruddy skin, the nurse guessed they were farmers.

Very *upset* farmers.

The largest began gesturing wildly while speaking in

German too rapid for Anne to follow. When Tibelda shook her head, he shouted *"Ist Drud!"* and came after her.

"Hey." The nurse shoved him back, and he stared at her with almost comical disbelief. *"Hau ab,* you jerk."

"Do not do this. They need our help."

"What for? They look healthy enough."

"A man in their village is dying." The old woman didn't blink as the other two men brandished crude but very lethal looking scythes. "And they won't take no for an answer."

The jolting ride to the village in the back of the farmers' cart didn't seem to bother Tibelda, who sat in calm silence. Anne alternated between glaring at her bound wrists and wondering how long it would take her friend to get help.

Thank God Sharon had the good sense to stay out of sight. "Why didn't they tie you up?" she asked the old woman.

"I did not punch any of them in the face."

"True." She sighed and rubbed her bruised knuckles. She'd never hit anyone before in her life, but she'd never been shanghaied by men with razor-sharp weed wackers, either. "Do they usually kidnap you when someone gets sick?"

"Drud's wife sent them. She knew I would not come to the village willingly."

"Really." Anne eyed the scythes propped on the shoulders of the men guarding them. "I take it she doesn't like you much."

"No." Tibelda's mouth twisted. "She doesn't."

By the time they arrived at the village, Anne's hands and backside were numb. "Finally. Can someone untie me now?" Everyone seemed to be ignoring her, and she turned around.

Two well-dressed men emerged from one of the farmhouses. The older of the two men sported a snow-white goatee, expensive black robes and a skullcap on his balding head. The younger man's traveling clothes were not as fine, but he had an appealing smile and shrewd dark eyes.

"Who are those guys?"

"They brought Drud here," Tibelda said. "One of them is a physick."

"A doctor? Then what the heck do they need us for?"

Her companion sniffed. "They say he does nothing for Drud."

"Terrific." She tried to rub the back of her neck and nearly dislocated her shoulder. "So he's either a lousy doctor, or a lazy one."

Tibelda shrugged. "Most of them don't bathe or cure people."

"I see the prodigal farmers have returned, and with such interesting companions." The elder man spoke German with a distinct accent—or sneer, Anne couldn't decide which. Whatever it was, it sounded British.

"I speak English," she told him. "Who are you?"

He showed some mild surprise, then inclined his head a degree or two. "William Harvey, physician in ordinary to His Majesty, King Charles of England."

Anne barely noticed the farmer untying her wrists. *He can't be* that *William Harvey. Can he?* "Are you the

Dr. Harvey who was—who wrote that blood circulates through the body?"

"Yes." He frowned. "You have read my books?"

"Not exactly." Anne skipped the explanations as she grabbed her backpack and climbed off the cart. "I'm Anne Jefferson."

"Lady Jefferson." The younger man stepped forward and offered a more courtly bow. "I am Adam Olearius, scholar and ambassador for the Duke of Holstein."

"Anne is fine." Probably another loser from Jena, Anne thought, and addressed Harvey again. "Doctor, what are you doing in the middle of Germany?"

"Until recently I accompanied the king's cousin, His Grace James Stewart, the Duke of Lennox, on his tour of the Continent." Harvey invested each word with weighty significance. "His Grace sent me from Belgium to Holstein, to meet with the duke and Ambassador Olearius before he begins his tour of Persia. Why is that woman glowering at me?"

"This is Frau Tibelda. She's, uh—"

"I can speak for myself." The herbalist marched past Harvey. "But not to him." She entered the house, the three farmers trailing her.

"She's a little cranky." Anne shrugged. "Being abducted at scythe-point does that to people."

"My condolences." He plucked a bit of straw from his sleeve. "I understand she is a healer of some sort."

"Yes." She'd dealt with enough snotty doctors in her own time to recognize professional contempt. "She's the local expert on herbal remedies."

The skin around his nose drew up. "You brought an *herbalist* to treat this man?"

"It wasn't my idea." She gestured toward the farm-house. "Go talk to the three stooges."

Olearius cleared his throat. "We have heard rumors of extraordinary folk come to the south of here." He eyed Anne's backpack with barely concealed curiosity. "Would you be citizens of this new United States of America?"

"Tibelda isn't—yet—but I am." She gave Harvey a deliberate smile. "I'm also a registered nurse."

The older man's white brows rose. "Nurses of this region are required to be registered? Like Jews? How novel."

A distraught wail from inside the home made Anne move. "Excuse me. I should go check on the reason I was kidnapped."

The two dignitaries escorted her into the farmhouse, which like Tibelda's cottage consisted of one room. Unlike the old woman's home, it was much larger, with stone walls and a packed-dirt floor strewn with clean straw.

Someone had been making cider, and the smell of apples was strong. Larry, Curly and Mo sat at one large center table, muttering as they passed around a jug of something that probably wasn't cider. Baskets filled with grain and root vegetables sat stacked against the walls, while cooking pots and utensils crowded shelves near a large hearth. The blazing fire added heat to the warm glow of candles and oil lamps.

Anne's mouth hitched. *Farming sure pays better than witchcraft.*

Tibelda crouched by the hearth, sorting through bunches of herbs from her satchel. On the other side of the room, a peasant woman knelt and prayed at the foot of a wood frame bed.

Anne went to the bed and pulled the heavy cover-let back. "This the patient?" Without waiting for an answer, she put her backpack beside the enormous man sprawled on the straw-filled mattress and took out her stethoscope.

Harvey joined her. "Are you a giddy midwife, to administer to him with such unseemly haste?"

"Not now, doctor." Anne glanced at the peasant woman. *"Wie heißen Sie?"*

"Uli." The woman sniffled. "I speak English."

Harvey blocked her view with his bulk. "I've already personally examined this man."

"Good for you." Anne leaned over to look around him. "Uli, how long has he been like this?"

"Since this morning, when those men brought him home." She bowed her head over her clasped hands. "Drud is never sick. Never."

From her place by the hearth, Tibelda made a scoffing sound. "He is probably drunk."

The peasant woman stiffened. "He never drinks!"

"Ladies, please, no bickering." Anne depressed Drud's tongue to check his throat. *Airway's clear, no obstructions or inflammation.*

She didn't realize she'd spoke out loud until Harvey asked, "What has his throat to do with anything?" When she didn't reply, he tapped her shoulder. "I asked you a question."

Oh, sure, explain standard traumatological procedure to a man who thinks leeches are a cure-all.

"Let's chat later, shall we?" She rolled a black cuff around Drud's upper arm. "BP's two-ten over one-twenty. Pulse's irregular, two-fifteen." She moved the diaphragm of her stethoscope from his arm to his chest. "Tachy, fluid in his lungs." She reached automatically for drugs she didn't have, then exhaled her frustration. "I need some digoxin or lidocaine, he's going to stroke out on me."

Adam Olearius came to stand beside her. "Can they be obtained locally? I can ride back to Jena."

"No, not from Jena." She slung her 'scope around her neck and straightened. "I can't risk moving him. We need to get a doctor out here."

The farmer Anne had dubbed as Curly stalked over, looked down at Drud, then shouted at Tibelda in German. Her response was equally blunt.

Adam's dark brows drew together. "Perhaps I should ask Drud's neighbors to accompany me."

"Ambassador, don't encourage this nonsense." Harvey turned to Anne. "As for you, young woman, I *am* a doctor."

Now he'll want to bleed him or something. "Right." She took out a styrette and jabbed Drud's finger, then squeezed a drop of blood onto a chemstrip.

"Pricking the finger is not enough," Harvey told her, his expression smug. "Shall I demonstrate the proper method of opening a vein for you?"

See? "Thanks, but we'll skip that for now." After the strip showed normal, she put a hand on Drud's brow. "Blood sugar's okay, but he's burning up."

The great anatomist stalked off in a huff, but Adam bent closer to study the chemstrip. "That scrap of paper indicates he has the fever?"

"No, this does." She pressed a digital thermometer to Drud's ear canal, then read the display. "Temp's a hundred and three. Could be viral pneumonia, with cardiac comp." Anne jerked the linens off the bed, startling Curly. "Uli, open all the windows and bank that fire. You"—she dropped the linens in Curly's beefy arms and gave him a push toward the table—"move. Adam, I need the cleanest water you can find, and Tibelda, start boiling some more."

Uli took care of the windows, while Curly went back to drinking with Larry and Mo. Adam returned with a bucket drawn from the village well, and Tibelda brought it with some well-worn, folded linen to Anne. In a low voice, she said, "I have tincture of meadwort, to drive the fever out."

Anne knew meadwort contained salicylic acid, but Drud needed a cardiac glycoside, not an aspirin. Still, if she could get his temperature down, it would take some stress off his laboring heart. "That would help."

"You are wasting your time, young woman," the English physician said from his chair by the hearth. "Your theatrics are certainly entertaining, but useless."

"You being an authority on that, I suppose?" As Anne began bathing Drud's fever-flushed body, she looked for signs of injury or disease, but found none. She hadn't packed more than the basic medkit before leaving town, so there was little more she could do. She eyed the man beside her. "Ambassador—"

"Adam, please."

"Adam, I need someone who can speak English to go to Grantville and get me a doctor and some supplies. Right now. And guess what?" She patted his lean cheek. "You're elected."

"The man will be dead before sunset." Harvey sounded like a judge pronouncing sentence.

Drud's wife dropped the pot she carried. Water went everywhere. "No!"

"Calm down, Uli, we're going to get a second opinion." The nurse took out a notepad and scribbled down a brief explanation along with a list. Then she gave Olearius directions, ending with, "When you get there, ask for Dr. James Nichols and give him this note. Tell him to throw all of it into the fastest truck Mike's got and hightail it back here, okay?"

"You have a lovely hand, but what is . . . a de-fibrill-ator, an IV rig, sa-line, EKG,"—Adam struggled over the words—"portable battery pack?"

"I don't have time to explain, but it's what I need. Oh, wait." She took the list back and added another item. "Ask James to scrounge in the ER, see if there's any digoxin left."

Harvey snorted. "For God's sake, man, you can't be seriously considering this—she's just a woman. She may have some amusing toys, but she knows nothing about proper methods of treatment." He said as much in German to the farmers.

Larry, Curly, and Mo eyed the nurse with identical expressions of angry doubt.

Anne decided the level of testosterone in the room needed immediate reduction. "Doctor, I have an M.S.N. degree from Johns Hopkins, and seven years experience working in a two-thousand bed hospital. Before I landed in the middle of this godforsaken place and time, I was studying for my P.A. in critical care obstetrics. I come from a long line of women healers, too—my mother is a midwife and my grandmother, like Tibelda, is an herbalist. My great-grandmother took care of Rebel soldiers during the Civil War." From Harvey's bewildered expression, she realized he didn't comprehend half of what she'd said. "Look. If he's dying, it doesn't really matter what I do, right?"

Adam murmured something indistinct to Harvey, who waved a languid hand. "Oh, very well, Adam, if you wish to be sent on a fool's errand, go."

Before the ambassador left, Tibelda blocked his path. "Is something amiss, madam?"

The old woman glanced over her shoulder at Anne and Harvey. "If you can find a priest there, bring him back, too."

After Olearius left, Anne had Tibelda administer the meadwort as she continued bathing Drud, and gradually his temperature dropped. Uli had resumed her fervent prayers, while William Harvey observed from the hearth, silent but bristling with indignation.

Larry, Curly and Mo disappeared briefly, only to return and take up their vigil at the table, passing around two more jugs and an enormous joint of some kind of meat.

At last Anne felt safe enough to leave her patient under Tibelda's watchful eye. She took the notebook she was using as a chart and went to Harvey. "Doctor, Uli said you brought Drud home. Where did you find him? Was he conscious? Did he complain of any chest pain or nausea?"

"Oh, you wish to consult *me* now?" His upper lip curled. "I, who never attended Jonathan Hopkins's school?"

"I apologize, I didn't mean to insult you." She'd have to play Stupid Helpless Female for awhile, to appease him and get the information she needed. "Please, help me out here."

He steepled his fingers and considered that for a moment. "We came upon his cart, which had gone off the road," he told her. "The man was sitting beside it, short of breath, but in no other apparent discomfort. He remained lucid enough to direct us here, but his subsequent utterings were quite unintelligible."

"The fever must have made him delirious." Anne bit her lip. Drud's wife continued to insist he'd been in perfect health until today. "This doesn't make sense."

"I have no wish to disparage your efforts, young woman—misguided though they are—but I examined him quite thoroughly." Harvey nodded toward the bed. "The man will be dead before nightfall."

"No!" Uli reached out and seized the herbalist's hand with both of hers. "Tibelda, you can save my husband! A stimulating tonic—you can make that for him, that will work!"

Anne knew many aggressive drugs that came directly from plants—like the heart stimulant atropine, derived from belladonna, AKA deadly nightshade. "What's in this tonic?"

"Come here, Miss Jefferson." Harvey led the nurse to Drud, and placed her hand over the man's heart. "Do you feel how rapidly it beats?"

Anne gathered what was left of her patience. "I know his heart rate is too fast."

"I am an expert on the function of this organ. Not only is it beating too quickly, but the rhythm itself is irregular." He tapped Drud's sternum. "This indicates that the heart is either diseased or damaged, and doomed to fail."

His diagnosis was surprisingly accurate, she thought

as she removed her hand. "So you're convinced the patient is in a terminal decline."

"I am certain of it, my dear. I have treated many patients with these exact symptoms, and all of them died." His tone went from pitying to adamant. "This woman's ridiculous potions cannot repair a damaged heart."

Uli wailed again, and Curly staggered over to pull her from the floor and guide her to the table.

"I'm not so sure about that, Doctor." Despite the great man's intuition, and lack of supplies, Anne couldn't give up on Drud. *You're a nurse. Treat the symptoms, and let James Nichols worry about the disease.* "Tibelda, tell me what ingredients you use to make your tonic."

"Sage, dandelion roots, and humility flower." As she named them, the old woman produced each from her satchel.

Anne took the flower and studied the dried stalk. "Was this white and bell-shaped, and did it grow in a shady place?" Tibelda nodded. "Thought so. Granny called it Dead People's Blossom."

"That is lily of the valley!" Harvey sputtered the words. "It's deadly!"

"Dr. Harvey, this plant has been used medicinally to treat cardiac disorders for centuries, even before now." Anne crushed the end of one stem, and held it to her nose. The fragrance assured her it had been dried properly. "A correct dosage will increase the efficiency of Drud's heart muscles without increasing his need for oxygen." Which was a reasonable substitute for her longed-for digoxin.

"An incorrect dosage will kill him!"

Anne remembered to count to ten. "Tibelda, has anyone ever died after taking your stimulating tonic?"

"No."

"Then would you be so kind as to make some up for us?" Before Harvey could protest, she lifted her hand. "Please, unless you have a better idea, let's give this a shot."

"That woman's presence is an insult to me and my profession. I will not be a party to this farce a moment longer." Harvey swept out of the house.

With him gone, Tibelda's shoulders rounded, and she seemed to shrink. "The English physick grows angry. Angry men are dangerous." She glanced at the three villagers gathered around Uli at the table. "Very dangerous."

"Don't worry, the cavalry is on the way." She handed the dried stalk back to the herbalist. "Show me how you steep it."

The simple process took less than a half hour, and Anne watched as Tibelda administered her brew to Drud. By then Larry, Curly, and Mo had silently left the house, while Uli paced back and forth by the bed, until it became apparent there was to be no miraculous change in her husband's condition.

"His breathing does not ease." Uli clasped her husband's limp hand between hers. "You must make a stronger tonic."

"It takes time, Uli," Anne said. "Give it a chance."

"You can see it was not enough." Drud's wife turned on the herbalist, and grabbed her hands. "You can't let him die. You know what they will do if you fail."

"Yes." Tibelda eased out of Uli's desperate grip. "I will try again."

Anne had faith in the herbalist, but caught the flicker of fear on her face. "What happens if we fail?"

Tibelda wouldn't meet her gaze. "Something bad."

Anne checked her watch. Sharon was on foot, and Adam might get lost on the way to Grantville. Neither of them might return for several hours. If Drud's condition deteriorated any further, he might not last thirty minutes. She didn't have time to worry about the *something bad*. "I'll give him another bed bath while you make it up."

The old woman left the house for a moment, then returned with some flowers and leaves and went to the pot of water boiling over the fire.

The nurse glanced over her shoulder. "What's that?"

"Fairy's glove, to ease his chest." Tibelda crushed some leaves before immersing them in hot water. "How is the fever?"

Anne took Drud's temperature. "Climbing again."

Tibelda cooled the second tonic by pouring it from one pot to another, then brought it to Anne. They had to dribble it between Drud's parched lips, a little at a time, but had gotten two-thirds of it in him when the door flung open.

"I have returned," Harvey announced.

"I'll notify the press." As Drud coughed, Anne took the cup away. She didn't see the English physician go to the table and examine Uli's ingredients.

"What have you done?" He stalked over and grabbed Anne's arm, giving her a hard shake. "This moronic hag means to kill him! Give me that!"

With difficulty, Anne held the tonic out of his reach.

"Hands off. Let us do . . ." she trailed off as the three stooges and a sizable number of villagers entered the farmhouse. "What's going on?"

Tibelda seemed frozen.

Harvey turned to the people and pointed an accusatory finger at the two women. "They have poisoned this man!" He strode back to the table, grabbed a handful of leaves, and shook them. "Here is what they have used to hasten his end!"

Uli pushed her way through to the front, then stared in horror, first at Tibelda, then Harvey.

The crowd made a collective, ugly sound, then several voices cried out "Witches!" and "Murder!"

Drud's wife flung herself on top of her husband, while Tibelda backed up until her thin shoulders hit the wall.

Anne stepped between the mob and the herbalist. "We are not witches and we are not poisoning this man. Tell them that, Dr. Harvey."

"I have proof of the poison right here." The physician put on his judge face. "You may not be witches, but women like you kill more patients in a month than I can save in a year."

"Yeah? And how many do you bleed to death, doc?" Anne held the cup out toward the villagers. In German, she repeated, "I'm a trained nurse. This is *not* poison."

Curly lifted a ham-sized fist and shook it at her. "Save your assurances for God, witch!"

"You need proof?" There was only one way to handle their disbelief—the same way she had Tibelda's. "Fine. Cheers." Anne lifted the cup to her lips and drank the rest of the tonic.

"Maybe you should drive, Sharon," Father Mazzare said as he held onto the pickup truck's roll bar with a white-knuckled hand.

The paramedic patted Hans Richter's strong arm. "Slow down, Hans, you're scaring the priest."

"Jeff says I am good driver," Hans said proudly. Jeff Higgins, the American boy who had saved Hans, his sisters, and his nephew during "the Battle o' the Crapper," had since become both brother-in-law and personal hero to the young printer. He glanced at Sharon. "You wanted to get back fast, you said, *ja*?"

"Fast, *ja*. With concussions, *nein*."

Hans chuckled and eased his foot off the accelerator. For the beautiful dark angel who'd awakened him to his new life, he'd do just about anything. "Okay, I slow down."

Father Mazzare muttered a short, fervent prayer of thanks.

"Almost there?" Gretchen yelled through the window from the back of the truck.

Sharon checked through the window, saw the lights of the village and gave her a thumbs up. She watched as the German girl adjusted the belt around her curvy hips. "Did your sister have to bring a gun?"

Hans's grin faded. "The Committees of Correspondence recommend it, but Gretchen would carry her pistol no matter what is said. Anne and the old woman were kidnapped. She is also concerned about this English doctor Adam brought out of Jena."

Sharon knew a concerned Gretchen was no one to mess with. "Just see to it she doesn't create more patients for Balthazar."

She glanced back to see how Balthazar Abrabanel was faring, but Rebecca's father seemed to be enjoying himself immensely. With her father tied up in surgery, he'd not only insisted on returning with her but riding in the back of the truck as well, probably to keep Adam Olearius company.

The ambassador, on the other hand, had not recovered from his brief whirlwind tour of Grantville, and hung on with his expression still dazed.

A little payback for how we felt, being dropped here. Say hi to the twenty-first century, pal.

When they stopped just outside the village, Sharon saw a crowd of people clustered outside the farmhouse Adam indicated as Uli and Drud's. She helped Abrabanel down from the truck bed, then went to retrieve the medical cases.

Gretchen led the group in. No one paid any attention to them, which puzzled her until she saw Anne being dragged out of the house between two farmers. Her light brown eyes narrowed as she saw the terrified old woman already bound to one of the two crude wooden stakes erected in the center of a heaping pile of firewood. "*Was machst du da für scheiße?*"

No one wanted to look at her, and several women muttered to each other in low voices.

"We burn the witches," one of the men called out at last.

Sharon, busy carrying medical supplies from the truck, also came to an abrupt halt. "Jesus." She put down her bags and headed for Tibelda. "I abandon you for a couple of hours, Jefferson, and look what happens—you have a barbecue without me."

"Next time," Anne said, sounding breathless but relieved, "*I'm* hiding in the closet."

One grim-faced farmer moved to stop Sharon, but Hans got between them and unconsciously imitated his beloved brother-in-law. "Don't even think about it."

"We have no quarrel with you." The man flung a hand toward the farmhouse. "They tried to poison Drud, and for that they will burn. It is justice." He went after Sharon again.

Hans pushed the farmer back, and used another of Jeff's favorite phrases. "Over my fucking dead body."

Gretchen turned her lethal gaze on the man. "You kidnapped these women and forced them to help you. Now you intend to burn them for trying. This is your idea of justice?"

"They have been of little help, I assure you," a snide voice said.

The Teutonic goddess swiveled and watched the older man approach. "You would be the English doctor."

"I am William Harvey," he said. "As I've told these good people, I don't believe these women are witches. Mentally deprived, perhaps, and criminally negligent, surely, but—"

"But you would have watched them burn." Gretchen studied him for a moment. "What does that make you?"

Twin red spots appeared on the great man's cheekbones. "You do not know whom you are addressing, madam."

"I know exactly what you are," she said flatly. "Do you know who *I* am?"

Apparently the villagers did, for her expression made everyone shuffle back. One of the peasants bumped into Harvey, who tripped over the hem of his robes. As he tried to regain his footing, the physician doubled over and howled.

"Oh, for crying out loud." Sharon finished untying Tibelda before she ran over to Harvey, whose face was contorted with pain. "What did you do? Stub your toe?"

"My gout." He pulled back the tattered hem and displayed a badly swollen foot. "I must soak it in cold water at once, or I will be lame for weeks."

Hans helped Sharon support Harvey as he called two of the sturdiest village men to take him. Still cowed by Gretchen's presence, the crowd dispersed as the men led Harvey to a neighboring home.

"I think we can go in now," Hans's sister said. "Hans, stand guard."

Inside, Sharon saw Anne sit down by the fire, while Father Mazzare joined Uli at Drud's bedside and Gretchen spoke to a much calmer Tibelda.

Adam went to the hearth to speak to Anne. As soon as he touched her hand, his head snapped up. "Lady Sharon, come here, quickly."

Sharon caught the urgency in his voice and hurried over. Anne sat very still, and was dead white. "Honey, what is it?"

"We had a bit of a crowd control problem." She spoke slowly, as if getting out each word took tremendous effort. "I had to take some of Tibelda's tonic, to prove it was harmless." She swallowed. "Surprise, it's not."

Sharon checked her pulse, which was practically nonexistent. "Overdose?"

"Not sure." Anne's voice dropped to a whisper. "My heart rate's dropped, and I've got one hell of a migraine. I've been so dizzy and nauseated that I can't stand up straight. Where's your Dad?"

"He was operating, so we drafted Dr. Abrabanel." Sharon waved Balthazar over. "Got another patient for you."

Anne related the circumstances while the elder Abrabanel performed a brief exam. He left her to pick up the leaves Harvey had thrown on the floor, and examined them for a moment before he returned.

"I fear this was not caused by lily of the valley, Anne." He displayed a dark green leaf tinged with purple. "This, I believe, is the source of your illness."

At the sight of the plant, she stirred. "Is that what I think it is?"

"*Digitalis purpurae.*" Balthazar gave her a sympathetic smile. "A very dangerous substance for a healthy woman to digest."

"Foxglove—Jesus Christ, no wonder I can't move. She called it fairy's glove, and I thought it was a diuretic." Anne closed her eyes. "Maybe Harvey is right."

"Tibelda." Sharon's voice snapped across the room. "Come here. Now."

The old woman reluctantly left the priest and came to the hearth. "She was not supposed to drink the tonic herself."

"Will it kill her?" Sharon demanded.

"I don't know." Tibelda lifted her chin. "I do not give it to people who are well."

"What concentration did you use, and how many

leaves?" Balthazar listened as the old woman gave him her measurements, then nodded. "That would be sufficient for someone of Drud's size. Anne, as long as you do not take another dose, the effects will wear off. However, you must rest and someone should stay with you. Sharon, I will need you here with me."

"Allow me the honor, sir." To Anne, Adam said, "The villagers have made rooms available for Dr. Harvey and me, and I insist you take mine for as long as you need it."

"Insist all you want." She swayed as he helped her from the chair. "Just hold on to me or I'm going to fall flat on my face."

Hans stood by Sharon to watch them go. "They look good together, *ja*?"

"Sure they do," she said. "Not everyone falls in love at first sight, like Jeff and your sister, though."

He gave her an odd look. "Are you so certain of that?"

"This is silly, Ambassador. Put me down, I can walk."

He shouldered the door to his room open. "I thought we agreed you would call me Adam."

"Put me down, Adam."

"Dr. Abrabanel insists you rest, Lady Anne." Olearius carried her the last few yards to his bed. "You do not wish to make more work for him, do you?"

"No wonder you're a diplomat." As he eased her down, she struggled to sit up. "No, let me. I'll lose consciousness if I'm prone."

"Prone to what?" He sat down on the edge of

the mattress. "Independence? Stubbornness? Deter-mination?"

"All of the above." Anne edged backward until her shoulders rested against the mound of pillows he piled behind her. "I meant if I lie down, I'll fall asleep."

"Sleep then, my lady." He smoothed some rumpled hair away from her cheek. "I will watch over you until you awake."

"I don't need a baby-sitter either." She caught his hand, and focused on the fine scars crisscrossing his palms and fingers. "Where did these come from?"

"Sharpening quills, scraping vellum, grinding inks." He made a seesaw gesture. "A scholar's work is oftimes hazardous."

"Tell me about it. I nearly poisoned myself in the name of nursing today." She licked her lips. "Lord, I'd kill for a cup of coffee right now."

"No need to plot a murder." Adam disappeared for a moment, then brought back a steaming cup.

The rich, familiar smell made Anne blink. "I'm hallucinating." She took the cup, inhaled, then took a cautious sip. "I'm not hallucinating. Oh, my God. This is real coffee." She sipped again, and moaned. "Adam, I'm in love with you."

Amusement made his eyes gleam. "On so short an acquaintance?"

"Forget that. This is honest-to-God coffee here." She took a third sip, then forced herself to hand the cup back to him. "I can't believe I'm saying this, but I can't drink it, not on top of Tibelda's tonic. I'll throw up."

"Perhaps later, when you are feeling better." He

set the coffee aside. "You have a fondness for the brew, then?"

"I was a confirmed addict, until we ran out about a month ago. Where in the world did you get it?"

"Dr. Harvey introduced me to the drink in Holstein." Adam reached behind her to adjust a pillow. "Apparently he carries a prodigious supply of the beans, wherever he goes."

She wondered what Harvey would take in trade for his prodigious supply. Maybe Mike Stearns wouldn't miss one or two of the town's pickup trucks. "What did you think of Grantville?"

"I saw so many wondrous things, my head fair spins." He tapped his temple. "It is a marvelous place, but you are all so very far from home."

"This is our home now." Anne looked out through the small window at Uli's farmhouse. Tibelda reminded her so much of Granny, and over the past months Sharon had been like a sister to her. Even the lofty Dr. Harvey had brought something back to her life—pride in her work and her heritage.

The coffee didn't hurt, either.

"I am glad you feel that way." Adam watched her eyelids droop. "Does your husband share the same sentiments?"

"No husband." Anne yawned, then lifted her left hand and languidly wiggled her ringless fingers. "No time . . . for . . . one. . . ."

As she fell asleep, Adam caught her hand and gently lowered it to rest at her side. "Ah, but Lady Anne, you are in a different time now."

⋘⋙   ⋘⋙   ⋘⋙

Despite his aggravated gout, Harvey refused to be kept from the patient, and limped in several hours later. Since Drud's heart rate had improved, and his fever remained low-grade, Balthazar called everyone to the table. Father Mazzare tactfully invited Uli for a walk and guided the peasant woman out of the house.

"Sharon has stabilized the patient, and will monitor him so that we may concentrate on diagnosing his condition," The physician scanned the faces around him. "Dr. Harvey, you have far superior knowledge of anatomy, while Frau Tibelda understands the nature of botanical medicines. I myself have studied a wide variety of healing practices used in many different lands and have learned much from my new colleagues in Grantville. If we consult together—"

"With her?" Harvey rose to his feet, gasped, then dropped back in his chair. "It is our duty to drive women practitioners out of our profession, man, not collaborate with them!"

"If it wasn't for Frau Tibelda, Drud would be dead," Anne said from the doorway. She still looked shaky, but the color had returned to her face, and her voice was much stronger. "I didn't keep him alive until you got here. The medicine she made did."

When Harvey glanced at Balthazar, he nodded.

"Very well." The English physician regarded the herbalist with thinly veiled dislike. "We will consult on the matter . . . together."

Anne thought of morning ward rounds as they went together to examine Drud. Balthazar listened as she described the patient's progression, and showed him the makeshift chart she'd kept on his vitals. Sharon had performed an EKG earlier, and explained the results to Tibelda and Harvey.

"An incredible device." Harvey examined the paper strip. "It also supports my diagnosis. As you can see"—he pointed to several clusters—"the lines that are shorter, here, here, and here. This can only be attributed to dysfunction."

"The lines are the same, at the same spaces," Tibelda said. "Would they not grow more shallow as his lungs seize?"

Balthazar examined the tape, then consulted the vitals on Drud's chart. "You are both right. The lines do indicate a dysfunction, but one that is regular. This condition may have originated much earlier in his life, and been of some duration."

"Wait." Anne recalled something the English physician had said. "Dr. Harvey, you told me you'd seen a lot of people with this condition die. How old were they?"

"Most of them were children or adolescents." Harvey's shrewd eyes moved to the patient. "Now that I think of it, I've never actually treated a middle-aged person with this type of dysfunction."

Anne took a quick breath. "A congenital heart defect, like abnormal walls, or valves, or vessels. That's it. He's had this from birth, Dr. Abrabanel."

"Corrective surgery or implanted devices sustain patients in your time, Anne, but as for the present"—Balthazar shook his head—"such a defect means retarded growth and development, and an early grave. Even if Drud somehow survived childhood despite this, as an adult his health would have rapidly deteriorated."

"Perhaps not." Tibelda looked thoughtful. "Anne, what manner of defect would make Drud this way?"

"It could be aortic valve stenosis—having two flaps in a valve in his heart, instead of three. Over the years, the flaps tend to become calcified, and that causes regurgitation of blood into the ventricle. In other words, his heart doesn't pump enough blood out." She rubbed the back of her neck. "But Balthazar is right, it doesn't fit. An untreated defect would become very serious in adulthood. Drud's symptoms appeared out of nowhere."

The old woman turned to Drud's wife, who had silently returned with Father Mazzare. "Tell them, Uli."

"I don't know what you mean, old woman."

"No one cares about that"—Tibelda shook her head—"but I took the fairy's glove from your own garden."

Suddenly Uli became very interested in examining the floor. "I grow it because it is pretty."

"Tell them!"

The command made Uli explode. "I grew the plant and made your tonic and gave it to Drud! I put it in his cider! Every day!" The farmer's wife clenched her fists, then she seemed to crumple. "He forgot to take the cask I put it in when he went to Jena two days ago. When they brought him back, they wouldn't leave. I didn't know what to do. I couldn't tell them."

"Well, why the hell not?" Sharon demanded. "Do you have any idea how much time it would have saved us?"

"Do you think I wish to be branded a witch? Like her?" Uli gestured wildly at Tibelda. "Live, like her?

Hiding in the forest? I have Drud, and friends here! I would be despised, driven from my village!"

Anne felt the dregs of her migraine flaring up again. "But you had no problem with using her to clean up your mess."

"What else was I to do, when he came?" Uli pointed toward Harvey. "He would not go, he would not leave Drud alone. He would have had them burn me."

"This man might have died . . . simply because of my presence?" Harvey looked stricken.

Sharon touched his hand. "You didn't know."

With visible reluctance he turned to Tibelda. "I owe you an apology, madam."

"Do not strangle yourself on the words, physick." The old woman waved her hand. "I have no need of them."

Father Mazzare went to Uli, and took her hands in his. "I believe she needs more from you, my child."

The peasant woman cringed. "She hates me."

"No," Tibelda said, in an unfamiliar, gentle voice. "I have never hated you. I have always protected you, child."

Uli slowly walked over to kneel before the herbalist. "I've pretended for too long, but I was so afraid. You know that, don't you?" She buried her face in Tibelda's skirt and sobbed. "Forgive me, Mother."

As the Grantvillians stared, the old woman rested one hand on her daughter's head, and carefully stroked her hair.

Two days later, Drud had recovered enough to be moved, and the entire group relocated themselves and their patient to Grantville for further treatment at the hospital. By then Tibelda and Uli had reconciled, and were in agreement with James Nichols' decision not to perform heart surgery.

"Your daughter's herbal treatments have been successful for the past twenty years," Nichols told Tibelda. "I see no reason to discontinue the medical regime, unless you do?"

Pleased at being treated as an equal, the herbalist shook her head. "It is as you say, physick. Now, what is this about working in a lavatory?"

"Jeff Adams is setting up a *laboratory* where he can work with you on developing new medicines," Nichols said, and smiled as he took the old woman's arm. "Let me show you around."

Anne Jefferson was already working on Uli, and nearly had her convinced to move to Grantville, and begin interning as a nurse in Anne's fledgling training program. "You already know a lot about cardiac care," she pointed out. "And Drud is interested in joining our construction crew."

"I would like to stay close to my mother," Uli admitted. "And if we live here, we need not worry about being burned as witches if anything goes wrong."

She laughed. "No, you'll probably be drafted to help fix it."

Anne left work that evening to find the ambassador waiting patiently outside the hospital's main entrance. "Adam, what are you doing out here?"

"I wanted to bid you farewell before I leave." He sketched an elegant bow. "Would you allow me to escort you home?"

"Okay." She took his proffered arm and tried not to feel depressed. The man was an ambassador, after all, and travel went with the job. "So, are you excited about the trip?"

"The duke has requested I forego the second half of my journey after I complete my mission in Persia. He is quite interested in pursuing new trade with you Americans." He guided her around a puddle on the street. "I should be returning to Germany in a few months."

"I see." She felt better, for some reason. "Will you be stopping by Grantville on your way back?"

"Perhaps." Adam sounded amused. "Is there a specific reason that I should?"

"Maybe." She felt her face grow hot as she recalled what she'd said to him over Harvey's coffee. She'd only been joking at the time, but now . . . "I think it would be a good idea. Seeing as your duke is interested in trading with us and all."

Adam, ever the diplomat, only smiled.

Before he left Grantville, William Harvey took a brief tour with Anne Jefferson that concluded at the high school principal's office with an introduction to Ed Piazza.

"I'm sorry I have to run, but my shift at the hospital starts in twenty minutes." She hesitated, then held out her hand. "After everything that's happened, you probably won't believe this, but . . . it was an genuine honor to meet you, sir."

"You are a very uncompromising woman, Miss Jefferson. You've insulted me, overruled me, and completely undermined my position against women practicing medicine." Harvey brushed a dry kiss over her knuckles. "The honor, I believe, is mine."

As the bemused nurse left, the principal exchanged a glance with Harvey. "Hell of a woman, isn't she?"

"Utterly terrifying. I shall not feel safe or competent again until there are at least two hundred miles between us. Now, for the last of my tasks." He placed four books on Ed's desk. "Dr. Abrabanel said I could inquire as to whether copies of these medical texts could be made for me here."

The principal, who had become Grantville's unofficial director of information and resources, put aside a schedule of projects for the school's machine shop and examined the books on modern diagnostic and surgical methods. "Sure, we can do that."

"Thank you." Harvey also produced a scrap of paper. "I must hasten my return to England, so when your monks have completed making the copies, would you send them by courier to this address in London?"

"Um, we don't use monks anymore, sir." Ed managed to keep a straight face as he picked up the books. "Come with me and I'll show you."

After escorting Harvey to the head librarian's office, Ed demonstrated how the school's copy machine worked. "We have to conserve its use these days, but doing the books are no problem. Especially after your generous gift of coffee, and telling us where to find the Turkish traders to buy more."

"I have never seen grown men weep like that." The English physician shook his head. "Over a beverage, no less. It was most disconcerting."

Ed thought of the precious half-pound of beans locked in his office safe, and grinned. "We get very sentimental sometimes." To the librarian, he said, "Would you copy whatever Dr. Harvey needs?"

The principal excused himself to return to his office, and the librarian got started on the books. Disturbed by the unfamiliar sounds from the incredible but eerie machine, Harvey left the room to examine the shelves outside. The sheer number of books collected by these Americans still stunned Harvey. And the quality—every volume was meticulously bound, worthy of a monarch's library—yet left out in plain sight, where anyone could take them.

"God in Heaven. They should hire monks, if only to stand watch over this place," he muttered as he removed one book and caressed the smooth binding. He opened it carefully, flipped through the pages, then a passage caught his eye. Harvey groped blindly for a chair, sat down, and began to read.

Ten minutes later, he approached the woman at the copier. "Dear lady, would it be a terrible inconvenience for you to copy a few pages from this book as well?"

The librarian checked the spine. "Trevelyan's *History*?"

"I think the king would be charmed to see what future scholars have written about him, don't you?" Harvey pointed to the corners he had folded over. "Just these pages I've marked, if you would."

"No problem." She added the book to the stack and went back to work.

A new influx of refugees fleeing Tilly's battle lines kept the town's physicians on double shifts, so Rebecca Stearns volunteered to retrieve her father's medical books from the high school library.

"I need to walk, Anne says. James, too," she told

her father when Balthazar Abrabanel protested. She caressed the protruding curve of her lower belly. "It is good for the baby."

It was also good for her, she thought on the way, as the queasiness from her first months of pregnancy still returned on occasion. A daily cup of Tibelda's chamomile and mint tea helped, but not as much as the fresh air and exercise. Besides, as she constantly reminded her big, tough husband Mike, she was pregnant, not made of porcelain.

Thinking of Michael made her dark eyes grow dreamy as Rebecca walked into the high school library. Just that morning the former union leader, now Grantville's main domestic crisis manager, had spread his large hand over her stomach. He'd given her a slow smile as he'd felt their child kick. *You'd better not be made of porcelain, sweetheart, or this kid is going to make some cracks.*

"Morning, Mrs. Stearns," the librarian greeted her as she walked in the office. "What can I do for you?"

"I'm here to pick up my father's medical books." She spotted them on a shelf beside the copier, but didn't recognize the history book on top. "I don't think this one is his."

"Oh, that belongs to the library. That English doctor who was here last week had me copy a couple of pages for him." The librarian took it and placed it on the to-be-shelved cart. "I heard he nearly killed someone, but he seemed like a nice old man."

"Dr. Harvey is a very nice man. He merely gave the wrong advice." Rebecca retrieved the book and flipped it open to a dog-eared section. "You copied these pages, here?" At her nod, Rebecca skimmed the text, then closed her eyes for a moment. "Do you know why he wanted them?"

The woman thought for a moment. "I can't remember, exactly. He said something about a king. Why?"

"That nice old man is not only the most celebrated anatomist in England, he also happens to be personal physician to King Charles." Rebecca showed the first marked page to the librarian. "The same King Charles who will lose his head in 1649, as it says here."

"Oh, geez." The librarian clapped a hand over her mouth. "He'll tell him, won't he?"

"As loyal as Dr. Harvey is to the crown, yes, I am sure he will." Rebecca closed the book. "And I fear this time, the advice he gives will have far more lethal consequences."

Family Faith

Anette M. Pedersen

Johannes Grünwald shivered in the cold gray dawn and tried to stifle a cough. The down-hanging branches of the big conifer sheltered him somewhat from the cold, but a thin layer of ice was visible on the small puddles of water in the wagon-track, and despite the layers of rags wrapped around him he was chilled to the bones. He had grown up here on Grünwald-an-der-Saale, his father's small estate, and knew the area like the back of his own hand. There were several warmer places nearby, but before seeking a better shelter he had to talk with his old playmate Frank Erbst.

Frank was the son of the old reeve, and for the first sixteen years of their lives the two boys had been each other's best friends. Then Johannes had left to stay with his mother's family in France, where his remarkable talent for painting and drawing could be

trained better than on the small estate at the edge
of the Thuringen Forest. Frank now ran the estate
for Johannes' older brother Marcus, who preferred
the life of a Protestant professor of theology at the
university in Jena.

Johannes had not visited the estate since becoming
a Jesuit priest seven years ago, but the old reeve had
always walked to the piers at the river landing first
thing in the morning, and Frank would undoubtedly
do the same. From beneath the conifer Johannes could
see and hear who came along the track between the
river and the estate, without being seen himself, so he
muffled the sound of the cough and tried to burrow
deeper into the dry needles. He had walked all night,
as he had walked most nights of the late summer and
autumn. Despite the cold he soon slept.

As the sun rose above the forest on the other side
of the river, it quickly melted the thin layer of frost
on the ground. The tall trees were nearly naked in the
early November morning, but the yellow leaves of the
brambles glowed in the sun, and along the track small
water-drops sparkled on the knee-high seed-heads of
the grasses. The old dog shook the droplets from his
graying head and sniffed into the wind before slowly
approaching the big conifer.

At the first bark from the dog, Frank Erbst left
the track and hurried toward the tree while lifting the
gun from his shoulder. Old Wolf's barking was mixed
with yips and sounded joyous rather than angry, but
with all kinds of people displaced by the war it was
better to be careful.

Beneath the sheltering branches of the big tree

Wolf was wagging his tail till he nearly fell over, while trying to lick Johannes' face. At Frank's command the old dog went to him and sat down with the tail still wagging. Johannes crept out from his shelter and stood before his old friend with a tentative smile on his face.

"Johannes," said Frank, hardly believing his eyes.

"Well, yes. I don't intend to stay, but do you know what has happened to Martin and his family?"

Frank's responding hug squeezed Johannes' ribs and started a new coughing fit. When the fit passed ,Johannes was wrapped in Frank's coat and the two men sat down on a log, passing a small bottle of brandy between them.

"Of course you must stay, Johannes, this is your home."

Johannes looked at the red-haired bear of a man beside him. "No, not anymore. Had Lucas still been alive it might have been possible. After Papa's death, Lucas' devotion to any religion would always come a distant second to his place as head of the family. Marcus, however, is a devoted orthodox Protestant, and being a professor in Jena means much more to him than the position he inherited."

"You might be right," said Frank, frowning towards the river flowing north to Jena. "Marcus has grown more stiff-necked than ever since his wife died. But Marcus also hasn't been here since Lucas' funeral. He would never know."

"Perhaps, but there is another problem," said Johannes with a slight smile. "People around here know who and what I am, and I made some very bad enemies after Magdeburg. Besides, neither Protestant nor Catholic soldiers are likely to show much mercy towards a excommunicate Jesuit. Or to those who shelter him. And before you protest my old friend, remember your family."

"Oh, we are fairly safe these days," said Frank. "Largely thanks to old Wolf there."

"Of course, I remember Wolf," said Johannes, reaching out to put his hand on the head of the dog. "But is he really that fierce? He was bred as a hunting dog, and I trained him so myself on my last visit."

Frank grinned in answer. "When Lucas and his heir died, and Marcus hired me to run the estate, I started a few projects of my own. One of them was breeding and selling hunting dogs to both Protestant and Catholic nobility. Grünwald-an-der-Saale is now very well known to both armies for its excellent hunting dogs, and only out-and-out bandits don't fear the wrath of the officers enough to leave us alone. Old Wolf has probably done more to keep the estate safe with the puppies he has sired than the fiercest guard-dogs ever could. But joking aside, Johannes. If you are really in danger, you could go to Jena. Marcus'll protect you if you ask."

"Probably. I'm just not certain I really want to live *that* badly. I would, however, like to stay in one of the cabins till this cough I'm plagued with has passed. And I really want to hear everything you know about Martin."

By noon, Johannes was installed in a cabin overlooking the river valley, with old Wolf for company. The cabin was little more than four walls and a sod-roof dug partly into the hillside. Inside, a fireplace would keep out the cold and a heap of boughs covered with old blankets formed a sleeping place. Otherwise, the only furniture were two rough benches and a rickety table placed in front of the shuttered window-opening.

Frank ordered Johannes to sit on the bench nearest the fire, and started brewing a tisane and heating an old pot filled with stew.

"Was not your wife curious about the stew?" asked Johannes.

"Elisa? No. Our oldest daughter may present us with a grandchild any day, and none of the women can think of anything else." Frank's broad grin showed his pride as well as his worry.

"Your first grandchild?"

"Yes. Elisa was a farmer's daughter. She gave me five children in as many years. The three daughters are all married, but they haven't been in much of a hurry to make us grandparents."

"Are you happy here? Running the estate for Marcus?"

"Yes. Marcus has always had a very rigid mind. He is, however, neither unkind nor unfair. And besides, employing the son of his father's reeve to run the estate for him fits his creed of people doing God's will by filling the place they have been born to." Frank smiled wryly. "I get that particular sermon every time I go to Jena. We mainly talk by letters, though. The few times a year I visit, I can live with a sermon or two."

"You've always been far more easygoing than me," said Johannes. "I never understood the pride that kept Lucas and Marcus from playing with you and the other children on the estate. As heir and the oldest Lucas may have felt it beneath his dignity to join our games and pranks, but even before Marcus went to study in Jena, his dogmatism always irritated me. Had it not been for his love for his wife, Catherina, I would have doubted he even knew the meaning of the word compromise. You do know Catherina was a Catholic?"

Frank shook his head, "No, but I know his son Martin is." He gave Johannes a mug filled with the fragrant tisane. "I'm leaving the herbs here with you. It is mainly thyme, but with some of the southern herbs you gave me at Martin's wedding. You can make a second portion from the same herbs. Drink it hot, but no more than three times a day."

Johannes obediently drank and said, "Once you hoped to study medicine."

"Going to a university to become a doctor was always an impossible dream for the son of a reeve. For a while I hoped an apothecary might be willing to take me on as an apprentice, but we could never spare the money for the fee. Still, I've learned a lot from reading on my own, and the seeds and recipes you've sent me over the years have been most useful."

"And now your herbs may help me regain my health. Bread upon the water."

"Bread upon the water indeed," answered Frank. "Now eat the stew before we start on the news. Elisa doesn't expect me before dark, and I want to hear about your life before I tell you what I know."

Once the plates were empty, Johannes sat fiddling with his spoon. "I don't want to talk about my own life. I suppose you've heard what happened at Magdeburg last May."

"Yes," said Frank quietly. "Louisa, Martin's wife, told me you were there."

"Then they made it to Jena?" Johannes looked up quickly. "And Martin lives?"

"Yes, but there are complications. Please go on."

"I don't know how much you know about this, but when Marcus went to study at the university in Jena, he became the special protégé of the strongly orthodox Lutheran Professor Johann Gerhard. Despite this he married Catherina, a devout Catholic, and allowed her to raise their only son Martinus in her faith. For all his aloof behavior, I suppose Marcus must have loved his little dab of a wife very much. He certainly became more cold and dogmatic than ever, when she died of the same fever that had killed Lucas and his family." Johannes stopped his tale while Frank rinsed out the mugs and filled them from a jug of wine.

"Young Martin grew to his father's size, but with Catherina's cheerful and gentle temper. He stayed to study in Jena, and in all matters, except religion, he was his father's dutiful son. Turbringen—and the other universities specializing in students from the nobility—offers a full range of military training for its students. Jena University, boasting of its theological scholars, has never tried to do so. Still, after the death of Lucas, Martin managed to acquire at least the most basic of the skills of war necessary to a nobleman. During his weapon-training Martin met and made friends with Helmuth Eberhart. It must have been a case of opposites attract. As far as I can see, the two men have nothing in common except both being minor Thuringian nobility and heirs to small estates. Did you ever meet Helmuth?"

"Yes, I saw him at the wedding and a few times later. We never spoke."

"I met him only at his and Martin's double wedding, but everything I've heard about him supports my opinion of him as a short-tempered, hot-headed enthusiast, who never gives the smallest thought to the consequences before leaping into action. A bigger contrast to the gentle and studious Martin I can barely imagine." Johannes shook his head and went on.

"The brides were two sisters from Nancy in France. Their mother had been Mama's closest friend there, and after Papa's death she had come with her two daughters to keep Mama company for a while. Martin's bride, Louisa, seemed a very calm and serious young girl, while her one year younger sister Anna impressed me as the most frivolous little flutter-head I'd ever met. Anna was also an unusually pretty young girl, and her flirting combined with Helmuth's temper alternatively scandalized and amused the entire town for months before the wedding. Louisa was far less pretty than her sister and probably the most practical-minded female I had ever met. I suppose you saw them, while they stayed with Mama?"

"Yes, and I completely agree with you."

"Well, according to Martin both marriages were quite happy, while the two couples lived in Jena. And had it not been for Marcus they might still all have been safely there. Do you know why they left?"

"Not in any detail."

Johannes sat for a while drinking from the wine before taking up the tale again. "The way the changing political alliances of this war has been supposed to change people's religion as well has created a lot of problems for the parish priests. Some have just gone on as they always have, regardless of the decrees of the princes. Others have found it necessary to flee, and now wander around looking for a new place. Still others just change as the wind blows. This can work in the countryside, but would never do in a town. I could come to Protestant Jena, even during the war, by invitation from the university, to 'assist' Marcus' mentor Professor Gerhard in his research on theological questions. That I timed those visits with family affairs was no problem, but Martin and Louisa, who lived in Jena, had to pretend to be Protestants. And that meant having their children baptized by a Protestant priest. And to promise in church to raise them in the Protestant faith. Is Loewthall still priest for the estate?"

"Yes. And people may choose if they want the old or the new rituals." Frank smiled. "Do you want to talk to him? He is a man of many faiths."

"No. I have nothing to say to a man of any faith." Johannes drank again and held out the mug for more wine before saying more. "A year after the weddings— well, eight months for Anna, but I'm told it *was* a small baby—both sisters had borne a son. Martin had intended to work around the baptism problem by arranging for the ceremony to take place at the estate, using Mama's wishes as an excuse. When Marcus overruled his son and arranged a ceremony in Jena, even asking Johann Gerhard to witness and permit the child his name, Martin for the first time in his life rebelled against his father. The baptism took place, but afterwards Martin and Helmuth both left Jena with their families. Taking service as officers at Tilly's army must have been Helmuth's idea. Martin's faith in the Catholic church has always been strong, but I had told him some of the things I'd seen since the war began. He could not possibly have thought such a life would suit him. At least I hope so. Perhaps I should have told him more."

Frank kept silent, while Johannes sat a long time staring at the flames in the fireplace. When a log shifted, it seemed to startle him and he went on in a rush. "I expect you know that Martin lost a leg at Magdeburg. Louisa came to me for help, but by then I'd been confined to quarters with a guard outside my door, and there was little I could do to help her. Conditions at the field-hospitals were—as always—horrible, but she had stayed with Martin to nurse him, leaving little Johann with Anna in the camp outside the town. Martin had survived the amputation and overcome the following wound fever, but the horrors surrounding him made her fear for his sanity. We decided that the best thing to do, would be trying to get Martin back to Jena. The boats and river-barges carrying goods along the Saale river went no farther than Halle, so it would be dangerous, but it was the least strenuous way for Martin to travel. And besides, a wagon and an escort all the way would cost more money than either of us had."

Johannes drank again. "Louisa wanted to leave Johann with Anna. None of us really liked this, but Louisa felt that keeping track of an energetic four year old, while caring for Martin and handling all the travel arrangements, would be too much for her. Anna, on the other hand, had long since found some camp-followers to help look after her own son. Not that she didn't care for him, but to Anna her husband and her own pleasures came first."

Johannes stopped his rush of words, and said slowly,

"In a way I envy people like Anna—and Helmuth too. Once I condemned such lack of reflection, the frivolity and seeming absence of the finer emotions. But Anna really loves life. Her sense of humor may have lacked refinement, but it enabled her to see the horror around her, and still look at life with joy. As officers, Helmuth and Martin usually had a farmhouse or at least bigger tents placed apart from the camp with the soldiers they commanded. But as they were young and without political connections, their troops were among the worst in the army. I went to visit her and Louisa several times during the siege at Magdeburg. We talked about faith. About God's purpose."

Johannes stopped again. Then he shook his head and went on. "Still, no soldier would dare harm the child of an officer. And besides, little Johann's sunny temper can melt all but the hardest men. He surely melted the heart of his Uncle 'Annes the few times we met." Johannes smiled. "Is Johann in Jena too?"

Frank shook his head.

"What happened?" Johannes' voice sank to a whisper.

"In early September, I had a letter from Marcus telling me to come to Jena," said Frank. "Louisa and Martin had made it there, but Martin was in a bad shape from fever, and nobody could find little Johann. Louisa had left Johann with Anna, as she told you she would, and Marcus had sent a messenger to Helmuth in Tilly's army, now camped near Leipzig. Helmuth was to bring Johann to Leipzig, and from there a friend of Professor Gerhard would arrange an escort to Jena. But the messenger brought back only a short letter. Helmuth had been killed in a skirmish near Magdeburg, and Anna had died from a fever shortly afterward. The group of soldiers Martin and Helmuth had commanded was no longer a part of the main army, and what had happened to the two boys nobody knew."

Frank drank the rest of his wine. "Tracing that group of soldiers, and especially those camp-followers Anna had hired, seemed to be the only chance for finding the boys. Marcus now wanted me to use my Catholic contacts to do so, and before leaving the estate I sent off the first letters to people who might be able to help. We have now traced the soldiers and the camp-followers to a place called Grantville. We don't know for certain that the boys are there. Or even if they survived the fever that killed Anna. The main problem with finding out is Marcus, but that's a long story and I better get back to Elisa." Frank put a hand on the shoulder of his friend. "Drink the rest of the wine and get some sleep, Johannes, you need it. I'll be back tomorrow."

After Frank left, Johannes remained sitting at the table drinking the wine and gazing at the fire until only embers remained. When he curled up between the blankets, and old Wolf went to lie beside the bed, he patted the blankets and said, "Come here old man, I can use the extra heat."

After a few moments he continued, "I like it here. I should never have left this place. Perhaps I can become a hermit. Would you like to be a hermit's dog?"

Old Wolf sighed and closed his eyes, and soon two sets of snoring filled the cabin.

The next morning, Johannes woke to the sound of somebody chopping wood. His head felt as if it was being used as the chopping block, and the sour taste in his mouth made him stumble through the open door and head for the small trickle of water running from a shale outcrop.

"Good morning." Frank's cheerfulness seemed out of place in the gray November morning. "I've brought you breakfast."

"Don't be obscene."

Frank laughed, "You always were a slug-a-bed, Johannes. However did you manage to get up in time for mass at daybreak? No. Don't answer me. Congratulate me instead, I am now the grandfather to a big bouncing red-haired baby boy."

"Congratulations indeed, Frank." Johannes smiled and went to give Frank a hug. "But should you not be with your family today? Play with the boy? Or at least stand and admire him?"

Frank's grin grew a little sourly. "No chance for that today. Every woman from miles around is gathered around the baby and his mother. Chattering like magpies, too. I'll go down later."

Inside the cabin Frank built up the fire and made the tisane, while Johannes opened the shutters and let in the light.

"I brought along an extra gun for you," said Frank. "It's an old one, but you might need it."

"No!" Johannes jerked around. "I'll never touch a gun again."

Frank looked surprised at his friend. "I don't mean for hunting. You are in no shape to do so. But there are all kinds of people moving around the forest these days. You might need it for protection."

"No! No more deaths." Johannes pulled the fingers of his shaking hands through his hair.

"Be sensible Johannes," Frank looked worried now. "No more deaths might well mean no more deaths but yours."

"Then so be it," Johannes' voice grew firm. "At least I won't have to look at my own corpse."

"As you will, but come sit down. Are you sure you don't want any food?"

"Quite sure, but you promised to tell me what you knew about little Johann. I've been trying to remember a town or place named Grantville but with no success. Is it in France?"

"No, it's between here and Jena."

Johannes frowned. "Frank, that's ridiculous. It might have been seven years since I was here last, but I spend several months in Jena five years ago. Nobody mentioned starting a new village or estate."

"It's true though," said Frank. "It seems a group of foreigners settled there sometime last spring. I haven't been there myself, but I spoke to some of them in Jena last month. They call themselves Americans. Clever people, too."

"And what do they have to do with Marcus and Johann?" Johannes asked.

"I managed to trace the group of Catholic soldiers Martin and Helmuth had commanded to Badenburg not far from Jena," Frank said. "There they had been part of an army defeated and nearly wiped out by Protestant troops reenforced with soldiers from Grantville. The Grantville soldiers—the Americans—had several kinds of new weapons, and it was them, rather than the Protestant troops, that saved Badenburg. No one at the time had ever heard of Grantville, but the Badenburg leaders were desperate. Besides, the changing political and religious alliances have forced many people to move for one reason or another. You must have met some, Johannes."

"Sure. A Hungarian Protestant took care of me when I caught fever on my way here. He was a Calvinist and on his way to Holland, where he hoped to find employment. But please go on."

"While I was in Jena a couple of months ago, another Catholic army threatened the town, and the Americans again offered to help. Not surprisingly the offer was accepted in the end, but when the town leaders first asked the university for the opinion of the professors the replies ranged from eager cries of "new knowledge" to vehement "vile sorcery." And, as you can probably guess, your brother Marcus was strongly in the second group."

Johannes nodded. "But surely even Marcus cannot have become so rigid as to let that stop him from finding Johann?"

Frank grinned a little, "No, but things got worse for your brother. The Americans completely beat the army threatening Jena, and with seemingly few losses. They left a few of their soldiers in Jena to help the City Watch maintain order. Just a few men, nothing like an occupying army. And the only payment they asked for was trade and an exchange of knowledge and skills. Seemingly a most innocent request, but after a few weeks it had the entire faculty of theology in a state of absolute fury. That the Americans were republicans was bad enough, since God had surely created kings to rule and peasants to serve. But the new ideas and chances for knowledge had completely won over all the brightest students, and that was absolutely intolerable."

Frank was now grinning broadly. "One night even Marcus lost his temper—and dignity—and threw an inkwell at one of Professor Gerhard's favorite students. The student, Peder Winstrup, was defending the contact with the Americans with the argument that any knowledge about the world would lead to a better understanding of God. After all the Bible said· that God's mercy spanned the world, so if one knew exactly how big the world was, one would know more about God."

Frank laughed out loud at the memory and Johannes joined more quietly.

Then Frank grew serious again and said, "It was only a few days later we finally found out that the captive soldiers from the battle at Badenburg had gone to Grantville, not Badenburg. Unfortunately your brother's dislike for the Americans had by then hardened to considering them anathema. He not only forbade me to go to Grantville, he also ordered me back to the estate. Not even a last chance to find his missing grandson could make Marcus consort with such Devil's spawn."

"And Martin?"

"Martin has not recovered completely from the fever he contacted on his journey to Jena, and he is slowly getting weaker and weaker. He tried to reason with his father, until Marcus refused to go near him."

"Stiff-necked idiot." Johannes frowned. "But surely Louisa would not just accept that."

"No," said Frank, "and neither did I. Before returning to the estate I first contacted Helmuth's parents. They are in favor of the Americans, and would gladly go to Grantville. Unfortunately neither of the Eberharts have seen any of the two boys since they were babies, and in the end we decided that Louisa and Helmuth's father should go to Grantville together. Louisa didn't like leaving Martin, but finding Johann is quite likely the only thing that can make Martin live, too. And if the boys are not in Grantville, there are no more leads to try. My last task before leaving Jena was making contact with one of the American soldiers. The man could not help with information about the boys, but he promised that Louisa and Herr Eberhart would be quite welcome to search in Grantville. He also promised to introduce Louisa to a woman named Gretchen, who knows both those camp-followers from Badenburg who stayed in Grantville and those who left."

After Frank had stopped talking both men sat silent for a while.

Finally Frank broke the silence. "If the boys are still alive, I believe we'll find them in Grantville, but I must admit I don't understand your brother's definition of faith. Or of family. Perhaps you can explain it to me, Johannes."

Johannes shook his head, "I never understood Marcus either. I once thought I understood faith, but it turned out I didn't. As for family? Well, I care about Martin and his family, but you are so much closer to me than anybody else. We haven't spent very much time together since I first went to France, but it seems to me that no brother—and certainly none of mine—could have been more pleased to see me."

"There is nobody I would have been more happy to see, Johannes, but remember that you are quite a lot younger than your brothers, while you and I were born only two days apart and spent nearly every moment of the day together from the day we could walk."

"Yes, and quite a lot of nights too. Do you remember how I used to climb down the wall from my bedroom window?" Johannes asked.

"Yes, and I never understood how you could do it. The only time I tried something similar I fell and broke an arm."

"Well, that particular skill may have saved my life this summer. I don't want to talk about Magdeburg, but, as you probably know from Louisa, I was arrested for heresy and blasphemy, and placed under guard. Father Vincent tried to convince the rest that I was sick, and would regain my senses if sent to the peace of a monastery. Father Francisco—as always—opposed him and wanted me burned as a heretic for my insults to the church—and to him. I was far from the first priest to suffer a crisis, and while most just sink quietly into black melancholia, it is becoming a problem. So for a while I was merely locked away, and—aside from those coming to interrogate, argue or just shout at me—I was left alone.

"Father Vincent was the one who gave me most of the recipes I've sent to you. He is from northern Italy and—I suspect—more than a little influenced by the humanism once popular there. He often works with the hospitalers, and sort of took me under his wing when I was first sent to draw pictures of the war.

Father Francisco, on the other hand, is a Spaniard and strongly connected with the inquisition. The two of them almost never agree on anything, but though Father Francisco usually wins, it doesn't seem to slow Father Vincent the slightest."

Johannes paused before going on, "I managed to escape from Magdeburg before they got around to torture me, though. In June, as always after a major battle, fever spread around the area. I took advantage of the fewer guards, and escaped one night, simply by climbing out the window and down the rough stone wall. Just the way I used to do as a child to join you catching crawfish in the ponds and all the other things we used to do. Do you remember the kobold trap in the ravine, that caught Frau Messel?"

"Yes, and also the beating I got afterwards," said Frank wryly. "But how did you get here from Magdeburg?"

"I walked." All traces of humor had disappeared from Johannes' face. "Once out of Magdeburg I walked south towards Jena. The area is filled with abandoned farmhouses, some just standing empty, and I could usually find edible plants growing round the house. Others were burned and plundered. Often, much too often, with the corpses of the previous owners inside." Johannes tried to smile. "It wasn't the corpses, as such, that bothered me. Only, sometimes the corpses showed beyond any doubt exactly how those poor people had died. I couldn't take that. At first I just dug their graves, and prayed for their souls with a sincerity I had never felt as a priest. But after a very bad house, the nightmares started haunting me until I feared going to sleep. I caught a fever and that wracking cough you are trying to cure, while standing outside a farmhouse in a thunderstorm, fearing what might be inside would break my sanity.

"I knew I had to find someone to talk to, but Father Francisco would surely have sent out soldiers to search for me. I could not approach a church of any faith, and trying to find Martin and Louisa would endanger them. Marcus? You are probably right that Marcus both could and would protect me, but we have never been able to talk of anything but the most commonplace without quarrelling. Meeting that Hungarian traveler saved me in more ways than one. Still, if I never see another corpse from now until Judgement Day, it'll still be too soon."

Again both men sat silent, until Johannes spoke again, now in a lighter voice. "Once past Jena, I dared not let anyone see me, so I walked at night when the moon was up, and hid during the day. It took me until now to get here."

"And the future?"

"I don't know." Johannes drank the last of the tisane and looked down into his empty mug. "I cannot stay here, where people know I used to be a Jesuit, but there is nowhere I want to go, and nothing I want to do."

Frank smiled and pushed two bundles across the table to Johannes. "I can do nothing to give you back the faith in God you seem to have lost, but perhaps this will change your mind about wanting nothing. I must go now, but if nothing else, eat the food in the big bundle. I'll come back tomorrow."

After Frank left, Johannes sat staring at the two bundles, before reaching out to open the biggest. Never taking his eyes from the oblong roll of the smaller bundle, he broke off pieces of bread and ate them slowly. Closing the food-bundle again he hung it from a peg, and with unsteady hands he reached to open the second bundle. Sheets of fine white paper lay on the rough table along with big feathers and ink.

At the sound of a broken sob, old Wolf came, and looked up at the shaking man as if to ask a question.

"Look, Wolf," whispered Johannes. "For this I traded my home and family. My faith and everything I was or could have been. Marcus might have been the only devoted Protestant in the family, but even Mama worried, when her brother entered me in a Jesuit school. She only reluctantly accepted that it offered the best teachers. Me? I was so absorbed by learning how to draw and paint, that I never even questioned going to her family in France. I'd barely noticed the religious teachings until I found myself a priest. Even my quarrels with Marcus seemed unreal. I suppose I defended the Catholic faith so strongly, more because my brother irritated me than because I felt very strongly about the theological differences. Only my drawings were real. Only while painting did I really live."

Carefully Johannes cut a feather, and made the first lines on a sheet. Jagged lines as if of flames followed each other across the sheets until darkness forced him to stop.

Johannes built up the fire and closed the shutters against the darkness outside. Then he sat down at the table and looked at the sheets of paper now filled with drawings and words.

> *In my dreams Magdeburg is still burning, and so it still is in my drawings. As a boy I dreamed of painting the glories of Heaven in glowing colors in the churches. When told my talent was better suited for copperplates and broadsheets, I accepted this, still certain that my talent was a gift from God, and that I was using it for His purpose.*
>
> *But at Magdeburg there could have been no God's purpose. No Glory. Nothing right! Denouncing my fellow priests and superiors as hypocrites, and accusing them of doing Satan's work in God's name had me branded as a heretic. But they had claimed those people had died and burned for the glory of God and the true faith. This could not possibly be!*
>
> *I no longer know what I am, or what I believe. The faith that once made me certain, that I knew what God wanted from me, is as burned as those people in Magdeburg. As dead as those children I saw in its gutters.*

The old dog put his head on the knee of the crying man, and when getting a hug in return, tried to lick away the tears. Rising, Johannes rolled together the sheets, wrapped them in rags and hid them in a hollow between the wall and the roof.

The next morning there was no sign of Frank Erbst around the cabin. Old Wolf was restless and kept sniffing into the wind blowing from the valley, so Johannes took him to the ledge from which they could see the estate. The dog whined, and Johannes put his hand upon its head.

Normally few people came to the small estate, but today many were moving around. Mainly on the estate and along the roads, but also into the Thuringen Forest. There were horses and wagons, people looking like soldiers but with no banners to identify them.

The old dog whined again and looked up at Johannes.

"There are no fires, Wolf." Johannes spoke as much to calm himself as for the dog. "And people seem to move about in an orderly fashion. I don't think they are bandits, so Frank and his family are probably safe. But how about you and me? The existence of the cabin is no secret, and the trail here isn't hidden. Sooner or later those soldiers will get here."

Johannes sighed, "I suppose we can try hiding in the forest until they have left, but I'm still frail, and who knows how long they'll stay. Perhaps we should just stay at the cabin. Disciplined soldiers, Protestant or Catholic, might not know who or what I used to be, and might leave a harmless old man and his dog alone. With the drawings hidden there is nothing to show I'm more than just an old refugee with no possessions of any value. Of course, if they are one of those rowing bands of riffraff plundering the countryside in between serving in one or the other of the armies, we'll probably both be dead before nightfall, and I probably by torture. But they *do* look well organized. What do you think, Wolf?"

The old dog looked up at the man, and whined again.

"That's not very helpful."

The man and the dog went back to the cabin.

❊❊❊   ❊❊❊   ❊❊❊

Taking the old pot from the fireplace, Johannes went to the small spring and placed the pot beneath the trickle of water, before sitting down and waiting for it to fill. The stone he was sitting on was cold, but the sun had broken through the low clouds. It warmed his face and made the autumn colored shrubs glow.

Like fire.

The bright blue sky above the rocks and the forest made Johannes long for the colors and paints he had left behind when first sent to draw The Glorious Victories of God's Holy Army over the Heretic and Damned Protestants. Painting the sufferings of Protestants and Catholics alike had been no problem, though letters had to be added to show who were what. But Glory! Or Holiness! Those had become increasingly difficult to see.

Like fire. The colors of fire.

"No. Like harvest. God's harvest."

The sound of his own voice woke Johannes from his reverie, and he looked around in confusion. The pot was full, and he took it back to the cabin. Wolf had placed himself at the top of the narrow trail from the cabin to the valley. His ears were raised and he stood sniffing into the wind, but when Johannes called he came with no protest.

Inside, Johannes stirred the fire and placed the old pot on its hook above the fireplace, before sitting down to dry his feet and stare at the flames.

"The fires! The fires at Magdeburg. They were caused by people, not by God. God's colors are those of the harvest." At the sound of Johannes' whisper

Wolf looked up, but Johannes fell silent again, and the old dog laid his head on his paws.

Drops of boiling water hitting the fire startled Johannes back to the present. He crushed some of the dried herbs into a mug and poured on the boiling water. Then, stirring the tisane with a twig, he again sat staring into the fire.

Painting God by painting His creation.

The words of Johannes' old teacher suddenly sounded in his mind. Father Baptiste's hands had been shaking so badly he could no longer hold a brush, but he had taught his pupils to see the beauty of the smallest leaf. Taught them to paint what they saw. To paint Truth. He had shared his pupils' joy, when their results had been good. And their sorrows, when eyes and minds wanted more than the hands could give.

In the brash ignorance of his youth the young Johannes had asked if Father Baptiste did not miss painting his own pictures. After all he had once painted an altarpiece for a royal chapel. Father Baptiste's gentle answer, that his pride in his pupils brought him more joy than the empty hubris of his own accomplishments ever had, sounded like nonsense to the young Johannes. It still didn't make sense, but thoughts about painting and creating now tumbled through Johannes' mind. If the soldiers killed him today, what would he be leaving to show he had ever lived? Had he nothing to teach to others?

Taking the big cloth-wrapped bundle from its peg Johannes put the dark rye bread, apples and a piece of honeycomb on the table. At a sound from outside he went to the door, but there was no one in sight, and Wolf remained calm.

Leaving the door open, Johannes sat down and started to eat. Old Wolf moved closer to the fire and split his attention evenly between the food and the open door. Johannes scraped honey from the comb into the tisane, before throwing the rest to old Wolf. Then he drank the tisane and poured more hot water into the mug. He packed away the rest of the bread, and went to stand in the open door. Old Wolf joined him, but just sat down looking alert.

Suddenly Wolf growled and stared towards the trail to the valley with his hackles up. Johannes went outside and listened. When hearing the sound of men and horses on the track to the cabin, he sat down on a rough bench by the cabin wall, his eyes meekly on the ground. A short command made the old dog lie down by his side, still bristling and looking towards the sounds.

The soldiers would come now; they were only minutes away. Perhaps what would happen would give him back some idea of God's will. Of what God wanted from him. As living or as dead.

The purpose of life is living.

The memory of Anna's simple words made Johannes' head jerk up.

Anna dancing with her son on her arm amid the ruins and cruelty of the war.

Father Vincent's pain and Father Francisco's triumph.

Teaching and Creating.

Fire and Harvest.

"No! Not like this." Johannes hurried into the cabin, grabbed the drawings from their hiding place and spread them across the table. If even one of the soldiers looked at them and remembered, then they would not be wasted. Even if burned immediately afterwards.

And those words he had spoken in Magdeburg. About doing Satan's work in the name of God. They might be the only thing resembling a sermon from his heart that he had ever spoken. But he would be speaking them again to whoever now came to the cabin. Speaking them as he died.

Johannes hurried outside, taking a deep breath to speak to whoever waited there.

His jaw dropped at Frank Erbst's cheerful—if slightly out-of-breath—greeting.

"Good morning, Johannes. Come meet Harry Nielson and Magnus Fries. They are some of the Americans I told you about."

When Johannes came to himself again, he looked up at Frank's worried face.

"Thank God, Johannes. I thought you'd died." Frank held his small bottle of brandy to Johannes' mouth.

"I'm fine. I'm fine. I just didn't expect you. I expected somebody else." Johannes took the bottle and drank deeply.

"The Devil himself, from the look of your face." The oldest of the two American soldiers smiled down at Johannes. "More people are coming to Grantville— our town—every day, so we need more food to see everybody through the winter. We gather food from abandoned farms, and trade with those who have anything to trade. Your friend, Frank Erbst, wants us to take you with us, when we go back. We have room for anybody. Do you want to come?"

"Yes." Johannes stumbled to his feet. "Yes, I'll come. I just want to get some papers in the cabin."

The first thing Johannes noticed about Grantville was the activity. He had seen more people on streets in market towns, but never a place with so many things going on at once. Many he did not see the purpose for, but whatever these people were doing, they seemed very enthusiastic about it. The Americans he had traveled with had called Grantville a "boom-town." Odd word. But somehow very fitting.

"We sent a message ahead about you," said Magnus Fries. "Father Mazzare is expecting you. He is our Catholic priest."

Johannes shook his head. "I told you, I am no longer a member of the Catholic church."

"That doesn't matter, you can stay with him until you find a place of your own. And besides, he wants to see you."

"Oh."

Father Mazzare met Johannes and Magnus at the door of his church, and when Johannes looked into the smiling eyes of the priest, he immediately felt less worried.

"Father," Johannes blurted out. "Do you understand God's purpose?"

"No. And I personally doubt anybody truly can. But sometimes His Mercy is unmistakable. Please come in." Still smiling, Father Mazzare stepped aside.

❦❦❦   ❦❦❦   ❦❦❦

Inside the church a small boy left his mother to run down the aisle, shouting "Uncle 'Annes, Uncle 'Annes!"

When the Chips Are Down

Jonathan Cresswell &
Scott Washburn

The tool bit reached the shoulder of the shaft and the steel chip it was peeling off suddenly widened. A screeching noise hammered at Larry Wild's ears. Frantically, he hit the panic button on the lathe, remembering a split-second too late that—

Bang! The tip of the cutting tool shattered as the lathe slammed to a halt. Larry stared glumly at the ruined tool bit. Nat Davis was heading his way and Larry could hear the lecture already. From the expression on his face, the owner of the machine shop was pissed, pissed, pissed.

"—many times do I have to tell you, Larry? Carbide's fragile, dammit, you can't slam it around like you can high-speed. You stop a cemented carbide tool in the middle of a heavy cut and you'll bust it nine times out of ten! You're supposed to stop the feed *before* you hit the shoulder and ease it in by hand."

Angrily, the middle-aged man pointed to a small wheel on the side of the lathe. "That's what *that's* for."

Larry looked at the machine shop's proprietor sheepishly. "Sorry, Mister Davis."

Davis looked as though he was going to explode; but after he took a few very deep breaths, the red color slowly faded from his face. "Larry, you can't treat a piece of precision machinery like one of your damn video games! This is the third time you've done this. Take it *easy*, for Pete's sake. Learn how to do it right before you start trying to do it as fast as possible. Look at this! The tool's busted—and there's no way to repair it. Not cemented carbide—and that's the last thing we can afford to be wasting. There's no way to replace carbide in the here and now. Not for years, anyway."

"I'm sorry," Larry repeated dully.

Davis snorted. "Sorry doesn't cut it around here . . . Look, kid, it's almost quitting time. Why don't you go home before you wreck anything else?"

Oh, and I guess you were born knowing how to do this? thought Larry; but he just muttered, "I didn't do it on purpose."

Relenting, Davis clapped Larry on the shoulder. "I know, I know. But go on home anyway. We can try it again tomorrow."

"Okay. Good night, Mister Davis."

"'Night, Larry."

As he headed toward the shop's exit, Larry brushed the metal shavings off himself. He started to remove the safety glasses but decided to wait until he'd left the shop itself. The last thing he needed was *another* lecture from Nat Davis.

A few more steps took him out of the shop and into the December twilight. It got dark early these days. Cold, too. He pulled his bicycle out of the rack and started pedaling toward town. He felt a little silly riding his old bike, but with the gas restrictions, he couldn't use his dirt bike anymore. One more irritation. It seemed like life had become just a collection of irritations now. Since Grantville had been deposited in seventeenth-century Germany, things had gotten worse and worse.

Oh, it had been exciting enough at first. The realization that they had actually traveled through time and space had fascinated Larry. And then there were the battles and Jeff's wedding to Gretchen Richter and the influx of refugees and all the other new things. But now that winter was here, there were no more battles; just a daily grind with everyone trying to survive.

And everyone trying to do their part.

Larry hadn't been sure what his part should be. Before the Ring of Fire, he'd had some hopes of going to college. That was now on indefinite hold—instead, he'd become a motorcycle scout for the Grantville army. But the campaigning season was over, and he needed something else to justify the food he was eating. He needed a job.

But he was starting to suspect that "machinist" was not something that suited him.

Today's mishap was one of a series. Nat Davis had been remarkably patient with him, but Larry wasn't sure how much longer that would last. And, for all its intricacy, Larry found the work pretty boring anyway.

Larry cycled slowly into the center of town. The trailer where he lived lay on the far side, about a four-mile ride. Normally, he would have made it in about twenty minutes, but today he was slowed by crowds of people on the streets. He coasted to a stop and looked around. Dozens of people balanced on ladders, stringing lights and hanging wreaths. Hundreds of others, many of them German refugees, stood and watched.

Christmas decorations, he thought in surprise. *Christmas is only a week away. That's not enough warning—guess they forgot you have to start advertising it in August.*

Larry shook his head. He hadn't even thought about Christmas. It had always been a big event in his family, although with little money, presents were few and simple. But they still managed to make it a holiday. They would decorate the trailer and the little pine tree that grew outside. They would walk around the neighborhood and sing carols. His mother would make that great stuffing of hers to go with the turkey. And her pumpkin pie . . . he could almost taste it.

Almost before he realized it, he was wiping away tears. There wouldn't be any Christmas with his family this year—or ever again. His mom and dad and sister were centuries away—forever out of his reach. "I miss you guys," he whispered. He had cried once before when it had sunk in that he would never see them again. But then he had been busy with lots to do and forced it from his mind. Now the loss came back to him—worse than ever.

His private mourning was jarred by a cry of amazement and pleasure from the watching crowd. Someone had plugged in a big batch of the lights and now hundreds of them sparkled along a row of houses. The Germans pointed and gasped and the smaller children shrieked in delight. He was surprised that anyone was taking the time to do this now, with so much work to do. They'd almost completely ignored Thanksgiving in the desperate scramble to find food and housing for so many refugees before the weather turned bad. But now things had slowed down . . .

"Hi Larry!"

He jumped in surprise and jerked around. Bonnie Weaver, a girl from his high school class, smiled at him from a few feet away. He liked her and they'd dated a few times, but with his after-school job at the machine shop, he hadn't even talked to her in weeks. Had she seen him crying . . . ?

Sorry doesn't cut it around here. "H-hi, Bonnie. Where are you going?"

"Choir practice," she said brightly. "We're getting ready for the big Christmas celebration."

"What big celebration?"

"Where have you been? Everyone's been talking about it for weeks! I think it was Rebecca Abrabanel's idea, believe it or not, but everyone's getting involved."

"I . . . I guess I've been busy."

"The choir has been translating some of the carols into German and we've been practicing them. Want to come along?"

"I can't carry a tune in a sack," muttered Larry.

"Well, you ought to get involved in something,

Larry. Gotta go! See you later!" Bonnie skipped off down the street.

Larry stared after her for a few seconds and then pushed his bicycle into motion and slowly wove his way through the crowd. *Christmas!* He couldn't remember ever having *less* interest in Christmas than he had right now.

He worked his way through town and headed for his home. It was completely dark now, but roads had little traffic anymore, so he didn't worry that the light on his bike hadn't worked for years. Last week's snowfall had been plowed, but he still worked up a sweat in his parka. A few minutes later he turned into the driveway that led to the trailers he called home. Lights shone in all the windows; most everyone would be home by now.

He propped his bike against one of the trash cans and walked up the steps to the left-hand trailer. This was the "bachelor's quarters" for the extended family that now lived in all three trailers. Larry, Jimmy Andersen, Eddie Cantrell and Hans Richter all shared it. Jeff and Gretchen and the baby and little Johann had the one in the middle, and Gramma and the other girls had the far one. It was a bit crowded—okay, a *lot* crowded; but still, better than coming home to an empty house. And the women surely cooked better than any of the boys . . .

To his surprise, the only person inside was Jimmy, hunched over the computer and working the joystick madly. He didn't even look up. He wore two lumberjack shirts and fingerless gloves; the trailers were heated by natural gas now—Jimmy's standing joke about that had worn pretty thin—and they got chilly at night.

That was fine for the Germans in their sleep-heap, but there was no way Larry would even think about *that* as a solution.

Larry shucked off his parka and tossed it in a corner. "Where's everyone else?"

"Hans had an appointment at the clinic," said Jimmy, still not looking up. "Not sure where Eddie is. Dinner's in an hour."

Larry grunted. Hans had been badly wounded a few months earlier in the fight that had brought Gretchen and her family to these trailers. He had only gotten out of the hospital a few weeks before, and crowded their own trailer even more, although at least he didn't move around a lot. Larry walked over to stand behind Jimmy and look over his shoulder.

"Playing *OrcSmasher* again? Aren't you sick of that?"

"Of course I'm sick of it! I'm sick of all these crummy games! But the nearest game store is three hundred and fifty years away, and my time machine is broken."

"I hear you—watch out for that *Skraknar* behind you."

"Crap!" exclaimed Jimmy as he lost half his hit points. "Stop distracting me!"

"I'm not, you're just a weenie."

"Oh yeah? Hell!"

"Game over, bro'."

"Yeah, yeah," said Jimmy in disgust. He pushed his chair away from the computer, scowling. Then he pointed. "Have you noticed the way the screen flickers lately?"

"I guess so. It's been doing that for a while."

"It's not going to last much longer. I'm not sure I'll be able to fix it. What'll we do when it craps out on us?"

"Find another one, I guess."

"Where?"

"From some computer that's broken but still has a good monitor! How the hell should I know?"

"This really stinks, y'know," grumbled Jimmy. "Old games, out-of-date equipment, and pretty soon we won't even have that anymore. How the hell do the locals stand it?"

"Don't know what they're missing, I guess," shrugged Larry. He turned and went over to a shelf and plucked out a video tape. He turned back to the television and stopped in his tracks.

"Where's the VCR?" he demanded.

"Oh, Gretchen borrowed it earlier. She wanted to show some cartoons to the kids."

"Why didn't she just use the one in their trailer?"

"Don't you remember? Johann dumped his oatmeal down the tape slot last week."

"Oh, right. Think you can fix it?" asked Larry. Jimmy was pretty good with electronic gizmos. *His* afternoon job was in the school's computer lab.

"Dunno. It's gummed up pretty good. I'll have to strip it down completely and see."

"What's on the school station?" Larry turned on the television set and after a moment grimaced. "Not *The Seven Samurai* again! What's with those guys? They've got other tapes than that!"

"Hey, Reverend Jones is in charge of the afternoon programming. What do you expect? Anyway, the samurai are pretty cool."

"Not cool enough after a dozen times." Larry turned off the set, sighed and flopped down on the sofa. *What a pain. Old computer games, no VCR. Reruns. Christmas.* "What's for dinner?"

"What do you think? Venison, bread and boiled turnips."

"Ick. I'm getting tired of that."

"A long way 'til spring. Better get used to it."

Larry sat there grumbling to himself. After a while he noticed his stomach grumbling, too—but not for boiled turnip. There had to be something better . . .

Why the hell not? At least there's one thing I can enjoy.

Larry got up and went to his bedroom. He opened up a dresser drawer and rummaged around in the rear of it, pushing aside his stash of girly magazines to reach for . . . for . . .

"Where are they?"

He pulled the drawer all the way out. *Gone!* He slammed it shut and stormed back into the living room.

"*Who ate my cheese curls!?!*" he roared. Jimmy jumped in his chair.

"What cheese curls?" he asked with a totally unconvincing veneer of innocence.

"The ones in my drawer! I was saving half a bag! Where are they?"

"They were stale anyway," mumbled Jimmy.

"I like 'em stale! And they were *mine!*"

"Chill out, man," said Jimmy. "It's nothing to get wound up over." But Larry *was* wound up—as wound up as the shrieking lathe that he'd mishandled. *I make an honest mistake and get reamed for it—and he steals my stuff and tells me to chill?*

"There aren't any more at the stores, they're all gone! They were the *last ones*! The last ones in the whole goddam world! And you *stole* them, you son of a bitch!" Suddenly all the frustration and anger of the day boiled up in Larry—and unfortunately for Jimmy, he was the only possible target for it. Larry stepped forward and punched an astonished Jimmy square in the face, spilling him out of his chair. He lunged after him, but the toppled chair was in the way and then Jimmy recovered enough to fend him off with a few frantic kicks.

"Are you crazy?" he shouted, scrambling to his feet with blood gushing from his nose. Larry waded into him; in a moment both boys were throwing punches like windmills and cursing like sailors. They tripped over the chair and rolled around on the floor, still punching and kicking. They collided with some furniture and there was a loud crash and tinkle—*oh, perfect,* thought Larry as a fist rang off his skull, *that's the TV gone.*

Suddenly, something bristly slapped Larry's head and he heard a shrill German voice close at hand. "*Dummkopf! Dummkopf!* Halt!" He rolled away from Jimmy and there was Gramma whacking at him with a broom. Larry rolled further away, cringing, and she turned and whacked at Jimmy for a while. "Halt! Halt!"

"Okay! *Okay!*" shouted Jimmy. "I've stopped! Now *you* stop!"

Gramma stopped her whacking and glared at the two boys. She spouted off a string of German that they couldn't follow. Then she tossed the broom at Larry and pointed to the broken drinking glass where it had fallen. "Swine! Pigs! Clean up!" She turned and stalked out of the room, slamming the connecting door to the next trailer behind her.

The boys lay there and glared at each other. Larry spat out a straw.

"You are nuts, you know that?" said Jimmy, wiping his bloody nose on his sleeve and frowning at it.

"Yeah, I probably am," grumbled Larry. He got up and grabbed the broom. Jimmy flinched reflexively, but Larry merely began sweeping the glass into a pan with as much dignity as he could muster for the chore, secretly relieved that the crash had only been the glass and not the TV after all. Then the trailer's door swung open and clipped his elbow, re-spilling half the fragments. Eddie Cantrell leaned around the panel.

"What's all the *dummkopf*-halting about?"

"I ate his cheesh hurls," said Jimmy thickly, holding his head back and forcing a plug of tissue up one nostril.

Eddie whistled. "And you lived to talk about it? Lucky boy! Larry has killed men for less than that!"

"Well, he nearly hilled *be*."

Larry finished his sweeping, dumped the glass in the trash can and flopped back on the sofa. He patted at one cheekbone; there was no blood on his fingertips, so it just *felt* as though it had been split. "Give me a break. I've had a bad day."

"What was so bad about it?" asked Eddie.

"Oh, Mister Davis yelled at me when I screwed up . . . and Bonnie Weaver was . . . and this big Christmas celebration . . . and . . . and he ate all my cheese curls."

"Oh, well, no wonder you're being such a jerk," said Eddie. "Who wouldn't be in your place?" Larry glared at him.

"So what do you guys want to do tonight?" continued Eddie.

"How abou' some *Dunheons & Drahons*?" suggested Jimmy to the ceiling. "We habn't played tha' for a long time. . . . Ah, sproo this." He pried out the tissue and wiggled his nose gingerly with two fingers.

"Not much fun with just three people. You think we could get Jeff interested?"

"Are you kidding?" snorted Larry. "The only thing Jeff wants to do anymore is make love to Gretchen. He's got no time or energy left for *kid stuff*." The bitterness in his voice made the others look at him in surprise.

"Hmm, maybe we could get Hans interested when he comes back."

"I tried," said Eddie. "He can't understand the point of the whole thing. He does like the miniatures though. He tried painting a few before the paints all dried up. He's pretty good. . . ."

"Hell, I don't feel like playing anyway," said Larry. "I don't know what I want to do. We can't even watch TV."

"Yeah, I really miss that," admitted Eddie. "No football, even. I wonder who's going to win the Super Bowl this year?"

"I wonder who won this year's World Series . . ." Jimmy blinked. "That year's. Oh, hell, you know."

"I wonder if *Voyager* is ever going to make it home?"

"I sure wish *we* could get home. I . . . I miss my folks."

"Yeah."

The three boys sat in silent gloom, thinking of all the things they had left behind. Of all the people they would never see again. They were just seventeen.

"I sure could go for a Big Mac," said Eddie, suddenly.

"Oh, don't start on that!"

"And those incredible fries . . ."

"Stop it, Eddie, I'm warning you . . ."

" . . . and a triple-thick shake . . ."

"*Stop!*" shouted Larry and Jimmy in unison.

"Okay, okay."

"I'd just settle for some stale cheese curls," grumbled Larry. "But I can't have *those* either."

"Maybe we could make some," said Jimmy after a moment.

"What? How?"

"I don't know. They gotta make them somehow. What are they made of?"

"Cheese. And curls."

"They're mostly corn, I think. You still got the bag with the ingredients listed on it?"

"It's in the recycling bin. I'll go get it." Jimmy hastened out the door without even putting on his coat. The town was not actually recycling very much at present, but every bit of metal or plastic or paper was to be saved. They might or might not find uses for those things, but it was a sure bet that they could not get any more.

After a few minutes Jimmy returned, shivering, with a flattened-out snack food bag. He brought it over to the light and they squinted at the tiny print.

"Corn meal, partially hydrogenated soybean oil, cheese flavoring and salt. No preservatives added," read off Eddie.

Jimmy looked uneasy at that. "How old were they?"

"Years," Larry said deadpan. "What's that other list of stuff below it?"

"The 'cheese flavoring.'"

"Ick. Looks awfully complicated."

"Yeah," agreed Larry. "And how do they make these things out of corn meal? It doesn't look like corn to me. They're all puffed up."

"I think they get shot out of some machine and then deep fried or something."

"It says 'baked' on the front of the bag."

"Okay, baked then. But we don't have the machine to make the things in the first place."

"Hell, so much for that idea." The boys all flopped back in their seats.

"What about something else?" asked Jimmy after a while. "Corn chips or something?"

"We don't know how to make those either. There must be some sort of fancy processing involved to make corn come out like that."

"What about potato chips?" said Larry. "They've got to be pretty simple. Just slice up potatoes real thin and fry 'em."

"That might work. I've seen recipes for homemade potato chips," said Eddie.

"Probably still a lot of work," said Jimmy. "Hardly worth it just to make some chips for the three of us."

"Well, we could make them for the whole family," said Larry. "None of the Germans have probably ever tasted a potato chip. We . . . we could do it as a Christmas present."

"Cool! That's a great idea!" Jimmy and Eddie started talking about what they would need and how they could get it, but an idea started growing in Larry's brain. He remembered the people putting up the lights in town. He remembered Bonnie Weaver . . .

"Say guys . . ."

"Yeah?"

"What about making a lot of potato chips? I mean a *whole lot* of potato chips?"

"What for? They'd just get stale," said Eddie. "Better to make smaller batches every now and then."

"No," said Larry, firmly. "We are going to make a lot of potato chips. Enough for the whole town! And we're going to make them in time for Christmas!"

The first requirement was potatoes—although as Larry found, the first *problem* was rationing. "Sorry, son. They've all been collected to make a seed crop. Mister Hudson's orders." He wasted an evening going from store to store; and it seemed the only variety left now in stores was in the way that their owners told you *no*. All right, what about local producers? Potatoes were pretty common, right? He wasn't looking for pickled artichokes, after all. But no one he asked seemed to know *anything*.

He thought about asking his teachers during the next day. But if this was to be a surprise—the sort of surprise that impressed a girl like, say, Bonnie—then he could hardly stick up his hand and ask a *teacher* about making potato chips. . . . At the end of classes he borrowed a book from the school library, *Applied Agronomy: The Potato*. It was possibly the dullest thing he had ever voluntarily taken home to read.

"The potato has a series of ploidy levels . . ." *What the hell is that? Jeez, I miss the Internet! No search engines in books.*

Noises from the next trailer made it clear that both Jeff and Gretchen were home; Larry tried to block them out and concentrate on his reading. The information he could puzzle out looked promising; potatoes had terrific yields per acre. *Twelve tons? That's a lot of chips! Forget just snack foods, we could feed a huge number of people!*

But the rest of it . . . "In Lemhi Russet potatoes, gene escape by pollen is unlikely, unless sexually compatible relatives are in the immediate proximity." *Well, that's definitely a yes.* Larry winced at a particularly enthusiastic bellow in German. *Extended family living, they call it. Yep, I'm getting extended already—that was a five on the Richter scale. Where's Gramma when you need her?*

Now *there* was an idea. Gramma might be a terror with a broom, but she ought to know whether there were any potatoes being grown in the region. She lived in the third trailer, so Larry would have to duck out into the early evening chill and that seemed like an even better idea just at the moment. He folded the book shut on his finger and slipped outside, scurried to the last trailer in the row, and knocked at its door.

Gramma peered around the panel. "*Was?*"

"*Guten abend,*" ventured Larry. "Ah . . . Do

you know about any potatoes near here? Farms? Gardens?"

"*Was?*" repeated Gramma blankly. She didn't invite him to step inside.

"Do. You. Know . . ." Larry said carefully. "About. Potatoes." He opened the textbook, and pointed to the picture of a potato.

Gramma's eyes widened in recognition. *Hey, we're getting somewhere!* She slammed the door; he waited, shivering, for a few seconds. Then she opened it again much wider in order to swing the broom fully through the doorway.

"Hey!" yelled Larry. He dropped the book to cover his head from the blows. "What—"

"Swine! Pig! *Ist skandal!*" She added a string of German syllables. "*Raus!* Scram!"

Larry stumbled down the steps and grabbed the textbook. The door slammed loudly, a universal language. He dusted snow off the book—and straw off himself—then stamped back to his own trailer to get his parka and bike. *That's it. I've had it.*

Time to go to the top on this; in fact, it was the last straw.

The corridors of the high school milled with people who, like Larry, had some kind of petition for their leaders. Several languages filled the air. He used his status as a combat veteran to get through, and his shoulder when necessary. The meeting that had attracted the crowd was just finishing up; after a few minutes of jostling, the doorman—another underemployed motorbike scout—nodded slightly. Larry slipped past him into the meeting room.

Willie Ray Hudson, the farm czar, was shrugging into a Peterbilt jacket older than Larry; he looked as worn and creased as the leather. "Mister Hudson?" asked Larry. "Ah, can I talk to you a moment? I think it's important."

Hudson cocked his head and stared at him. "You been fightin', son?"

"Just a disagreement." Larry cleared his throat. "Mister Hudson, a few of my friends and I want to make something special for the Christmas feast, and we thought that potato chips would be good. But I don't know if anyone around here grows pota-toes . . . and some people get kinda, um, strange when I ask them about it. And this book I was reading about potatoes said that they could feed . . . uh . . ."

"A whole lot of people?" finished Hudson. "Bet they quoted twelve tons an acre, didn't they? Well, son, that's with fertilizer, irrigation, and spraying Lorox twice a week. Here, we'd be lucky to get two, three tons an acre. This is *farming*, not agribusiness."

"Oh," said Larry, somewhat taken back. He hadn't exactly thought that farmers were dumb—but they didn't go to college either, did they? He could feel himself blushing.

"But there's no point anyway," Hudson continued. "Sure, it'd still be a good yield, but we can't get 'em to grow the damn things. The locals think 'taters are animal fodder—or worse." He turned, although not far enough that Larry could slip away. "Hey, Melissa!"

The slender woman sorting folders at the table's head looked up. "Yes?"

"How'd that Prussian guy get his peasants to grow potatoes?" *Sounds like a joke,* Larry thought.

Melissa Mailey sniffed. "Frederick the Great? He cut off their noses if they refused to. Inspired leadership." She resumed her work.

Typical seventeenth-century punchline, though. Or was he eighteenth . . . never mind. "Maybe we could persuade them instead?" offered Larry.

"We're trying to stop people from killin' each other over which Bible they thump," said Hudson wearily. "Vegetable tastes aren't exactly top priority."

"Well, I don't need a *lot* of potatoes. A couple of bushels at most. And maybe if they eat something that tastes better than boiled turnip, they'll change their minds . . ." But Hudson was shaking his head.

"Nobody here I know of has any potato *seed*, Larry. We need to keep the potatoes we *have* to plant 'em as cuttings, so we can grow more potato plants. Otherwise, the only potatoes around are somewhere in the Andes, and we aren't goin' there anytime soon. Hearts and minds is all very well, but when . . ."

Melissa stopped next to them as though the phrase had physically hooked her. She had a parka slung over her arm and a scarf already wrapped around her neck. "Willie Ray, you're going to freeze like that," she said sharply.

"Aw, it's not cold," said the farmer, looking down.

"There might be influenza this winter. Don't wear yourself down when you don't have to." She looked at Larry. "Men. Have you been fighting, young man?"

Damn you, Jimmy. "Just a scuffle, ma'am. I was asking Mister Hudson about potatoes. My friends and I want to make potato chips for the Christmas feast."

"Sounds great! What's the problem?"

"No potatoes," said Larry. "I asked Gretchen's grandmother, but she just yelled at me."

She frowned. "Well, what was she yelling?"

"It was all German. *Teufels-wurzel,* I remember that . . ."

Melissa turned and waved vigorously. "Becky! Hey! I need some translating."

Larry bowed instinctively as Rebecca Abrabanel joined them. She just *did* that to him somehow. "Larry here's running into some language problems," Melissa added. "Larry, you know Rebecca, right? Everybody does."

"Hi," he managed. *I just wanted to ask about potatoes . . .*

"You have been fighting, I see. What is the language?" The National Security Advisor had donned a woolen shawl; now she slipped it free again with a graceful tilt of her neck.

"German, what else? *Teufel* . . . something. Larry?"

"Uh . . . *Teufels-wurzel,* I think."

"Devil's root," said Rebecca. She glanced to Willie Ray, then back to Larry. "You are discussing agriculture? Devil's Root is a common term for what you'd call *potato.* It is used by apothecaries, and even *eaten* in England and Holland, but I do not recall that it grows here."

"C'mon, Larry," urged Melissa. "Think. What else did she say?"

"Ah . . . *Verke* . . . *her, ter* . . . then *Knave* or something like that."

Rebecca lifted an eyebrow. "*Verkehrter knabe* would be 'perverted boy.' Just what sort of conversation were you having, Larry?"

Larry knew the school floor *couldn't* open beneath him and swallow him; he just wished that it could. "I asked Gretchen's grandmother about potatoes. That's all! And she went Jeet Kune Do on me!"

"Went . . . ?"

"Hit me with her broom. A lot."

"Ah." Rebecca nodded. "You are . . . off the hook, as Michael says. Potatoes are very exotic here. They are believed to be *Aphrodisiakum*—an aphrodisiac, a sexual stimulant, like rhinoceros horn—but that is superstition. My father says that rhinoceros horn is *much* more effective."

Larry opened his mouth, thought, and closed it again.

Hudson grinned sympathetically. "You should have heard what they called *me* when I tried to suggest planting 'em in gardens."

"This is rather interesting," mused Rebecca. "*Missgebildete Schmutzknolle?* Ugly dirt-tuber object? That's a common one as well. Do you recall it?"

"It was hard to hear, uh . . . with the broom and all."

"Jeez, you must have gotten her riled up," muttered Hudson. "Look, son, I appreciate your stopping by, but there's a rationing system for a reason. I'm not breaking it just for some snack foods. Go shoot yourself a deer."

Rebecca looked back to Hudson. "I am distracting you, I'm sorry. Good night, gentlemen."

As Hudson and Larry made replies, Melissa jumped into the gap. "Now just hang on, Willie Ray. Potatoes could be a useful crop, right?"

"Well, yes, but—"

"And if people eat tasty snacks made from potatoes, they'll *like* potatoes, right?"

"Melissa," said Hudson with heavy patience, "you're not runnin' rings around me on this one, okay? We got to have *some* priorities. Snack foods just aren't in there."

"Mister Hudson . . ." Larry gestured at his own face. "I got this from fighting over a bag of cheese curls. She's right—people really *like* junk food."

Hudson's face tightened stubbornly. "It's a *seed crop*. You don't eat that."

"If we don't get people to plant the seed potatoes by this spring, won't they just rot anyway?" said Melissa. "It took Frederick the Great *years* to make them do it. Better the carrot than the stick—even better *carrot sticks*, of course . . ." Melissa still hadn't quite made the mental adjustment from *calories make people fat* to *calories allow people to survive.* "But junk food's powerful stuff—it conquered the world in our time, and they won't have any built-up immunity to it. Now, we can't spare sugar for anything nonessential—"

"Now *that's* right," put in Hudson. "Salt we can get, but I can't grow sugarcane in central Europe without a greenhouse." He shook his head ruefully. "Got me agreeing with you already, don't you?"

"No *sugar?*" blurted Larry. Sure, it was being rationed, but—none?

"There's only a few plantations nowadays," explained Melissa. "Refined sugar's still about as expensive as cocaine was in our time. Pretty much the same kind of people running things, too—the world's first drug lords. But just wait until we get some sugar beets growing here!" She bit off the rant. "Sorry. Long day. Anyway, salt we do have. If you can make the chips, and get people to change their minds about potatoes by tickling their taste buds instead of cutting off their noses, it's worth doing. Come on, Willie Ray! He only needs a bushel or two."

"All right," muttered the farm czar. "I'll give you a slip for *one* bushel. But it isn't gonna work."

Melissa looked at the door; figures could been seen milling behind the reinforced glass pane. She reached up to lay her hand solemnly on Larry's head, then grinned. "Gotta go. Larry, you are now officially in charge of . . . Project Quayle. May you do better at it than *he* did."

A few minutes later a pleased but puzzled Larry slowly pushed his way through the crowd, clutching the precious authorization slip. *Quail? Why would she name a potato chip project after a bird?*

It took all three of them to carry a bushel of potatoes back home from town; then Larry discovered they'd forgotten to give the storeowner the ration slip, and had to ride back with it, then meet the others in town again. Two different stores had no cooking oil at all. Night had fallen before they started peeling, and the moon was up before they managed to get an even slice.

And it was one-fifteen in the morning when Larry stumbled, choking, out of the trailer, Jimmy and Eddie treading on his heels with Hans slung between them. The half-moon barely threw enough light to show the clouds of smoke billowing from the open trailer door. Larry wiped his eyes, coughed rackingly until nothing seemed to be shaking loose anymore, and turned back to the others.

"Okay," he wheezed, "so that's what they meant about *smoke point.*"

"I guess that oil's no good," said Eddie. They'd had to settle for olive oil at the store; the high-temperature oils had all been requisitioned for emergency diesel fuel. Eddie's hopes for "Italian flavor" chips had clearly been a little optimistic.

"Jimmy, go back and open all the doors and windows," said Larry. "Hans, you okay?"

"Okay, okay," said Hans. He sat on the ground with his legs stretched out, still blinking in surprise, while Eddie braced him upright. They'd bundled him outside wrapped in the blanket he was sleeping in—Larry was relieved to see he wasn't coughing hard. That wouldn't be good for someone with a wound still healing.

"Why me?" grumbled Jimmy, but he pulled his shirt over his face and darted inside.

"Fire? Is fire out?" asked Hans anxiously. "The other trailers—"

"It wasn't a fire," said Larry. "I don't know why Jimmy wasted that extinguisher—crap, those things are priceless now! The oil just started to smoke. A lot. The stove's turned off, and the oil's cooling down now. It's *okay*, Hans. We'll go back inside in a minute." The windows were rattling open one by one.

"Okay," Hans repeated. He wrapped the blanket closer and settled down to wait. At least he *had* a blanket; Larry was freezing already after the boiling confines of the trailer's kitchenette. In a minute or two, though, they could go back in, close up, and crank the heat.

Jimmy trotted down the steps, coughing pointedly. "All done, Darth Tater. Got any holes to dig—bales to tote?"

"Kicking of butt are you seeking, young Jedi," sing-songed Larry. "I think there's another extinguisher in the shed; go get it."

"What, so we can eat smoke again instead of chips?"

Larry bunched his fists. "Jimmy, do you remember the *last* time we had an argumen—" He stopped in midword as a smoke detector started keening. "*Shit!*"

"Didn't you turn it off?" said Eddie.

"I took out the damn battery myself!" Larry followed the sound with his eyes. *The second trailer.*

"Jimmy," he said carefully, "did you open *all* the doors?"

"Sure, like you said."

"The *connecting* door?"

"But you said *all*—"

"You moron!" howled Eddie. He stood up abruptly; Hans wobbled, but braced himself on the ground with one palm. "They're gonna be out here any second! Jeff's gonna kick—"

"Jeff's off doing a courier run," snapped Larry. "*Gretchen's* gonna kick our butts." He walked grimly towards the noise and the second set of steps, framing an apology in his mind. Behind him, Eddie and Jimmy railed at one another, voices rising like baseball players grabbing the bat before a game; but he was starting to feel concerned.

Something's wrong. There's no lights going on in there. They can't sleep through that! God, there can't be enough smoke to—

It hit him as he set one foot on the steps. *Night. Smoke in the house. A wailing noise. Jeff's away. Loud voices outside.* The memory of a stone-faced Gretchen, standing with folded arms as she waited for the mercenaries to come, flashed into his head. *Oh, shit!*

"Hans!" he shouted—just as Gretchen slammed out of the darkened door with a blanket wrapped over one shoulder and a pistol gripped in both hands.

Larry recoiled a pace, skidding in the snowpath. There wasn't enough light scattering from his own trailer to show him or the figures behind him very clearly—but there was damn well enough moonlight to shoot by. *She'll see Hans on the ground, surrounded by figures—targets, just like me!* He was already raising both hands palm-out. "*Gretchen!*" he shouted, his voice breaking as it hadn't for two years. "It's me, Larry! Gretchen, it's *okay!*"

She was down on one knee on the front stoop; her arms foreshortened as she swung the pistol onto Larry below. The faint light that caught her face showed as much expression on it as a steel lathe spindle might have. This close, the nine-millimeter slugs would blow clean through his chest, splintering bone like balsa wood. Gretchen was a crack shot, too; once Jeff had shown her how to use the pistol, she'd taken to it with a passion.

Hans called out in English behind him. "Gretchen, is okay! Me, friends, all okay!"

Larry was frozen from his guts outward, much colder than the air accounted for. Instinct screamed at him to turn and run, but that would be the worst thing he could do—and even more importantly, he wouldn't let himself die like a coward in front of his friends. That had kept him from running on a battlefield before; now it kept him alive. Gretchen blinked hard once, twice, and suddenly became just an angry human being. She lifted the pistol's muzzle, and Larry took a long and shaky breath.

"It's okay," he husked, and swallowed. "Just a cooking mistake." *Shit, what a stupid way to get killed.*

Feet thumped to the ground on the third trailer's opposite side. Larry glimpsed motion between the foundation blocks. *The kids? They went out a back window? Oh, God, that's why she went out the front. While she's being killed by the men who set her house on fire, they might get away. It's a German fire drill.* He rubbed at his face. *I'll never complain about my childhood again, ever.*

"*Was?*" snarled Gretchen. "*Cookink?*" Her brother called out something in German. Presumably he'd shouted first in English because that was less of a threat. Her eyes scanned along the treeline while she sorted out what he'd said; then she safed the weapon and got to her feet. Larry turned away sharply. Part of him wanted very much to stare at places the blanket didn't cover—but the rest was still thinking about survival, not reproduction.

At least the threat of gunshot wounds had stopped Jimmy and Eddie's arguing, although the smoke alarm continued to wail. Hans looked startled, but unharmed. The trailer door banged shut, and Larry turned back again as Gretchen yelled out the opposite window at the kids. He crouched to look through the blocks; they'd popped up in the snow-dusted underbrush just short of the trees, their faces pale blobs lifted to her voice. They'd been low-crawling, and he'd wager that they hadn't looked back once until she called. *That's one damn scary fire drill.*

A thud came faintly from the trailer, then another. The electronic wail stopped abruptly. Gretchen opened the door and flung a handful of plastic shards onto the plowed driveway. She'd wrapped the blanket properly this time; Larry rose from his crouch and stepped forward. *Blame Jimmy? No.* Jimmy could be a jerk sometimes, but he was still Larry's friend.

"I'm really, really sorry. It was an accident. I—" He twisted aside as the kids pounded up the steps and glued themselves to Gretchen like limpets. One of them was carrying Gretchen's baby, who seemed to have slept through the whole adventure. Now that the emergency was over, two of them were crying, and guilt gnawed at Larry as he looked at them. *You must have been scared half to death. Arson's part of warfare for you.*

He'd seen far worse in battles, but for all its crowding and irritations, this was his *home*—and they were his family now. "I'm sorry," he repeated softly. "It shouldn't be like that here."

Eddie and Jimmy took up the chant behind him. "Sorry, sorry . . ."

"Sorry doesn't cut it around here!" shouted Gretchen. "Look at zem!"

Larry nodded, although his mind muttered *Does everyone in town say that when I screw up?* "There's no fire. No fire. Just some oil that got too hot and made a lot of smoke. We'll clean up anything we have to."

"Uh, maybe the kids would like some Italian chips?"

"Shut *up*, Jimmy."

Gretchen sniffed. "You all say *sorry* to Jeff, ven he gets back in mornink! Maybe he just hit you with hand, not hit you with motorbike!" She ushered the kids inside with her left hand. She still held the pistol in her right; the edge of her palm was bleeding from a small cut. Larry was very glad that the smoke alarm's housing had taken the worst of her anger. "Cooking *always* makes fires. If kitchen burns, houze burns—you must watch, always! You are all stupid!" She slammed the door behind her.

"I guess we are," said Larry to the door. He turned and sat down hard on the steps; his legs were a little shaky. *What a Goddamned stupid way to get killed that would have been, all right.* He rested his head in his hands. "Okay. Eddie, you help Hans back inside and close the windows. I'm gonna sit here until I decide not to rolf; then we figure out how to get some real oil before Jeff gets back, because about the only thing that's gonna stop him from killing all of us slowly and painfully is a handful of fresh potato chips."

"What do you mean all of *us*?" said Jimmy. "It was *your* idea—"

Larry glanced to the end trailer as its door opened. Gramma stood in the opening, holding her broom at high port. At least she hadn't tried to go out through the windows . . . Between the wisps of smoke still eddying around and the light silhouetting her, she looked like a bad remake of *The Terminator.* "Yeah, you're right, Jimmy," he said slowly. "Go help Gramma sweep up the smoke alarm bits, and maybe you can stay in her trailer overnight."

"Sounds good to me," grumbled Jimmy. "You guys

are bad news to be around." He trotted down the trailers. "Hi, Gramma! Give me the broom."

Larry settled his head again and closed his eyes. Whiskery thuds and yelps and guttural curses sounded to his left; he found it kind of soothing while he thought. *No stores open this time of night.* Grantville wasn't quite the sleepy town it had once been; merchants locked up their stores now, and the gas station—where the diesel substitute oils were kept—was actually guarded. Larry wasn't going to run a risk of getting shot *again* for the damn potato chips.

Jimmy slammed their trailer door in a delayed echo of Gramma slamming hers. Larry looked up and realized he was shivering with cold. *Time to go in and admit it; I haven't got a clue. Sorry, guys, we'll draw straws to see who Jeff gets to beat up in the morning. . . .*

"Sorry doesn't cut it around here," Larry said aloud, and snorted. Nat Davis would laugh his head off at this scene . . . His jaw sagged open. *Hang on. We use lube oil to cut gears. And the lathes need oil. What if Mister Davis grabbed some of that stuff in case he needed it later?*

Larry didn't have keys to the shop. But there was that window at the side alley, the one that Mister Davis always cursed because it wouldn't shut properly . . . and that he never had time to fix. *It wouldn't be stealing—we'd just borrow it for a while. It's not like we'll use it up.*

He jumped down from the steps and hurried to his trailer. The doorknob wouldn't turn; he rattled it with increasing force. *"Hey!"*

"Go away," said Eddie's muffled voice. "No one's home. We've cashed in our chips."

"If *you*—" shouted Larry; then he lowered his voice. "If you guys want something better to do than a D & D game, I need a couple of Level Four Fighter-Thieves for a quest."

The door edged open. "Huh?" said Eddie.

It took them three hours—plus the fifteen minutes it had taken Jimmy to find his ninja mask in the litter of his room; he'd refused to go without it—two frostbitten fingers, a set of flashlight batteries, one skinned knee, and a fuming half-hour putting all the drill bits back *into* the storage bin that Eddie had knocked over before they switched on the lights; but when they finally staggered home with six one-quart containers of canola oil, Larry knew that it had been worth it.

Then the *real* work started. *Batch Two*.

"I didn't know you could get blisters from peeling things," complained Jimmy.

"Shut up. Keep peeling, it's almost dawn."

"Never mind!" yelled Eddie from the living room. The kitchenette wasn't big enough for three to work in—not with a pot of hot oil on the stove. "I've already got enough sliced for a batch. Is the oil doing okay?"

Larry stirred the big pot doubtfully. "Looks pretty hot. All right then, *load*!"

The cooking rig was an old oversized egg basket, with additional levels of mesh provided by screening pulled out of the bathroom window and wired in place. As Jimmy had pointed out, mosquitoes were a distant problem compared to Jeff. They arranged the slices within; Larry thought he saw a wisp of smoke and hastily backed down the burner, although the connecting door was duct-taped around its seal now. "Let's try two minutes of cooking."

The resulting chips could have been used *themselves* for lubricant. "Okay, too long. *Load!* Half a minute."

Jimmy crinkled up his face at the first bite. "Pthaw!" He flicked the half-chip at the window; it stuck. "Ugh. That can't be good."

"One minute, then." Larry was sweating, and it wasn't entirely from the burners. "*Load!*" A minute later the basket came out of the oil. The things inside actually, sort of, looked like potato chips . . .

Another anxious minute while they drained and cooled. Jimmy snagged one, blew on it and popped it into his mouth. It crunched in a very satisfactory manner.

"Not bad! Bland, though."

"Crap, we forgot the *salt!*" Larry dug a shaker from a cupboard and unscrewed it. "I think there's enough here for now. Get them salted fast, before they cool off. *Load!*"

They didn't stop for breakfast; semi-failed batches kept all of them nourished. By the time it was fully light and Jeff's motorbike rumbled into the driveway, there were several bowls stockpiled.

Larry turned off the burner. "Show time, troops."

"He's gone inside their trailer," reported Eddie, holding the Venetian blind open with two fingers; he *was* a scout, after all. "Maybe he'll want to wash up, eat breakfast first . . . Uh oh. Guess not." He released the blind and strolled casually toward the bathroom.

"*Oh* no you don't," said Larry. "That's not why we took the screen out. All for one, one for all."

"Gretchen did it for *her* folks," muttered Eddie; but he slumped onto the sofa with the others. "Is the door open?"

Jeff slammed the panel inward, catching its expected rebound from the computer desk with his arm.

"Is now." Larry leaned forward. "Hi, Jeff! Sorry about the trouble. We're . . ." He trailed off. *Courier duty? Looks like mud wrestling instead.* Jeff was slathered in road gruel from boots to cap; he'd taken off his goggles, leaving a raccoon mask of clean skin around his eyes. He'd also taken off his gloves, Larry noted, as Jeff cracked the knuckles of first one hand, then the other. The room got more crowded as he advanced into it.

Hans was back in the third bedroom. They'd asked him to speak to Gretchen, but he'd explained that the phrase *death wish* had originated in German. . . .

"You. Stupid. *Shit*heads. What were you *doing*? You scared the crap out of my entire family. You scared my *kids*."

Jimmy opened his mouth, but said nothing. *Thank God for that*, Larry thought. They *were* Jeff's kids now, no matter whose genes they had. "Jeff, we're all really sorry about that. It was our fault—*my* fault. We were cooking . . ."

"*Sorry doesn't cut it around here!*" bellowed Jeff. "Would've served you right if she *had* shot you, you stupid jerk! You know what they've *been* through?"

"Yes," said Larry evenly. "I was there at that battle. We all were."

Jeff checked momentarily at the mention of

Gretchen's rescue. "Yeah, you were. So you should know better! Waking her up like that—smoking up *two* trailers—we need a new smoke alarm, and they're *goddamned* expensive now—"

"Pretty much ruined a broom, too," muttered Jimmy.

"You're right," agreed Larry as Jeff stooped, closed a hand in Larry's shirt, and lifted him to his feet. "Absolutely right. Here, have a potato chip." He edged a bowl between them.

"What? There's no chips since—" Jeff looked down. "Where'd you get these?"

"We made 'em last night," said Eddie proudly. "We're gonna make enough for *everyone*."

"Probably taste like crap." He scooped up a handful. "Hmnoh. Y'know why Gretchen didn't whale you, Larry? In German families, the husband does all that stuff . . . Hmnoh. Not bad. Y'see, I *know* Gretchen can take care of herself, but I still gotta do the right thing. Hmnoh. Six hours riding with nothing to eat . . . C'mon outside a minute."

Larry sighed and put the bowl down. "No, bring that," said Jeff. He dragged Larry onto the stoop and down the steps, taking fistfuls of chips with his off-hand, until they both stood on flat ground; then he let go, his breath smoking in the freezing air. "Here, gimme those."

Larry complied. Jeff grinned and took the bowl—

—with his *right* hand. Larry didn't even see the left hook coming. He was just suddenly *there* on the cold, hard ground, his head ringing. Some pretty-looking red clouds filled the morning sky. *Is that a hawk circling, or a vulture?* Jeff looked awfully big, standing up there. . . .

"Hmnoh. That settles that," said Jeff. He turned. "Hey, *kids*! Gretchen! *You gotta try these!*"

Larry leaned against the row of lockers and let the chattering crowd flow past him. Conversations just didn't sound the same after cell phones had stopped working—they all had at least *two* sides. His eyelids drooped. *God, I'm tired. Two more classes, some more fun at the machine shop, then home and more chip-making . . .*

"Larry!" He jerked upright. "Oh, your face looks awful! Were you fighting again?"

"Uh, sort of, Bonnie. So, how are you doing?"

"Never mind that!" She twisted out of the crowd's current. "Is it *true*? You're making *potato chips* for the feast?"

"Well, it was supposed to be secret, but I guess I can tell you." A few feet behind her, Eddie bounced on his toes to be seen over the crowd, dragging one hand's edge repeatedly across his neck. *What's with him?* "The prototypes have been a success, my minions served me well—and we're gonna change German agriculture, one chip at a time."

"*Great!*" Bonnie squealed. "I'll tell all my friends so they can be first in line! Oh, this is gonna be great!" She dove into the crowd.

"Didn't you see me?" snapped Eddie a moment later. "You told her anyway, didn't you?"

"Well, why not? You're just ticked 'cause you don't have anyone to impress yourself."

Eddie pressed his palms to his forehead. "I've been

trying to get you for— Never mind. We're screwed. Why'd you have to go and—"

"What?"

"Don't you listen to what they tell you here? *Do the math*, Larry. It took us *two hours* to make a few bowls of chips—and Jeff and Gretchen ate all of them already! There's gonna be *four thousand people* at the feast. We can't make nearly enough in four days! Are you gonna tell ninety-five percent of 'em that 'there's no chips left, try again next year'?"

He felt a sinking feeling. "We'll get faster at it."

"Not that much. None of the Germans are gonna help, either. Maybe some of our people would . . ."

Larry frowned. "They're all *our people* now, Eddie."

"Sorry," said Eddie, looking as though he meant it. "But they're all gonna be *hungry* people, too." He looked over his shoulder. "Damn! I'm late. Look, just stop telling everyone, okay?"

"Okay." But it wasn't okay; and Larry brooded on that for the rest of classes, for his shift at the machine shop, and for the slow ride home. He wiped out twice; the roads had melted during the day and were already refreezing at dusk, making them treacherous. After the second fall he just lay there a while until a truck rumbled up and someone asked him something loudly in German. He staggered to his feet. "I'm not hurt, just tired. Thanks. *Danke*."

"Naw, he's sayin' to get out of the *way!*" yelled the driver of the truck. One of the figures in the open back stooped and straightened; a shovelful of sand fanned over Larry's feet.

Well, that figured.

Lights glowed in all three trailers when he wobbled into the driveway. *At least we won't wake anyone up. Eddie's right, but we've gotta keep trying.* He trudged up the steps. *Why is there a brick in the doorway?* He looked to his right; the other two doors were also chocked open. He shrugged and pushed open the door.

A row of hulking garbage bags barricaded the living room. *Are they throwing out my stuff? Jeff said it was settled!* But the bag that toppled against his leg hardly seemed to weigh anything. It rustled when he touched it. *Chips?*

Then he saw the kids sitting beside a composting bin, peelers flying like cavalry sabers—Johann and the girls, plus another boy he recognized from down the street. They hardly glanced up as the door clunked against the brick behind him. Hans' voice sounded from the kitchenette. *"Driese!"*

"I'm out!" called Eddie from the next room. Johann jumped up with an armful of peeled potatoes, scurrying around the corner. Larry followed him in a daze. Eddie sat cross-legged on the floor; Johann dumped the potatoes beside him. "Thanks, Johann. Hi, Larry!" He held up an orange plastic food-slicer. "Found this baby in the shed—whoever lived in this trailer before us *already* thought like we do, and they didn't throw out *anything*." He skimmed a potato into a blizzard of slices. "I'm just not as fast as Gramma with a knife. Look at her go!"

Larry leaned past Eddie to look through the open connecting door. Gramma stood at a counter that had been covered with a plank; her dark iron cooking knife hammered out a volley on the wood, and a potato dissolved under it. She caught Larry's eye, grimaced, spat out *"Teufelwurzten chippen! Ist skandal!"* and looked down again.

"Einse!" barked Hans. Larry turned and stumbled four steps to the kitchenette. Gretchen had just lifted a cooking rack from one of three pots at full flame; she held it over a fourth—unheated—pot to drain, blew a strand of hair out of her eyes, and looked witheringly at him. "Stupid men," she growled. "Not to *use* kitchen right." She shook the drained chips out onto a towel, then dropped the rack onto the counter. The half-familiar neighbor behind her—Traudi?—dealt fresh chips into it.

"Triese!" cried Hans, wedged into a corner of the kitchenette and holding three wristwatches. The open window beside him wafted in cold air—*ah, that's what the brick's for. Why didn't we think of that?* Gretchen lowered the freshly loaded rack into a pot and drew another out. "Jeff *likes* po-ta-to chips much," she said. "Und Jeff is husband, und you Jeff's *kamerade*, zo I make chips. But not stupid way! Jeff talkink about man Henry Forhd . . ."

Melissa will kill Jeff if she finds out, thought Larry dazedly. *Death by liberal feminist.* "Ah, where is Jeff?"

"In *our* kitchen, mit *Grossmutter* und Jimmy, und Dolores und children from next . . . road. Need strong arms, to lift *chippenmaaschen* so many from kettle."

All right, maybe not . . .

"Billy Wallins from Reynolds Crescent is in the last trailer with his wife and kids," put in Eddie. He massaged his slicing hand while he paused. "They brought all their cooking pots—"

"Edvard! Schnell!"

"Yes'm." Eddie bent to his task.

"Driese!"

"I'm out! Johann!"

As he watched in amazement, another trash bag filled with chips was added to the pile. *This timeline's United States is gonna be unstoppable*, thought Larry.

By the next day they had used the last potato. A rough guess told them they had enough chips for about a quarter of the people who were going to be wanting them. A quick trip and a generous sample of their work, and an enthusiastic endorsement by Gretchen convinced Willie Ray Hudson to write out another slip for three more bushels. He even authorized the gas for a pickup truck to deliver them to the trailer. *Nothing succeeds like success, I guess*, thought Larry, shaking his head.

Two days to go and fortunately there was no school. They cut back on the frantic production pace a little so there was some time to sleep. Still, they were hard at it on Christmas Eve.

"Hey, guys, it's snowing!" said Jimmy, looking out the window during a break.

"Hard?" asked Larry.

"Coming down like gangbusters right now."

"Damn, if we get a lot of snow it will screw up the celebration!"

"And no weather forecasts so we don't know what's coming," said Eddie. "What a pain not knowing what the weather's going to do tomorrow." Several of the Germans looked at him like he was insane.

About two in the morning, the last potato was

peeled, sliced and cooked. Almost every cubic foot of all three trailers was packed with bags of chips. They couldn't leave them outside for fear the raccoons would get into them.

"How are we gonna get them all to the school tomorrow?" asked Jimmy.

"We'll figure that out in the morning," yawned Larry. "Assuming we can get to the school at all with this snow. Right now, I'm going to bed. Great job everyone!"

Christmas morning dawned clear and bright. Larry guessed that there was about three inches of fresh snow on the ground. Not too bad, but it was going to make it harder to get their chips over to the school. He was still worrying about the logistics when the roar of a diesel engine outside caught his attention. He squeezed past the mound of bags in the living room and opened the trailer door. Outside was one of the town's two dump trucks. This one had a plow fitted to the front of it. He thought it might be the one that had almost run him over the other day. The driver was swinging down from the cab.

"Hey! I understand you've got a special delivery for the school?"

"Sure do!" cried Larry. "And Merry Christmas!"

The high school was the only building in town big enough to handle the crowds—barely. Naturally enough, the food would all be served in the cafeteria, although people would have to find other places to actually eat it. As Larry gently tossed bags of chips down from the back of the truck, he could see that he and his fellow-chippers had not been the only ones laboring through the night to get the feast ready. Hundreds of other people were already bustling about, making sure there would be enough for everyone. He and the other *chipmeisters* were assigned spots in the serving lines and they piled up their bags behind them so they could keep the serving bowls filled. By about ten o'clock, most of the preparations seemed to be complete. Larry could see a huge crowd forming outside, as nearly the entire population of Grantville—new and old—converged on the school.

But before the feast there was something far more important to do.

An announcement over the school's loudspeakers sent everyone heading for the football field. It was cold outside, but not really bad: bright sun, no wind, and snow beginning to melt here and there. Crews had already swept the snow off the bleachers, leaving dry seats. Larry and Jimmy and Eddie and Hans and Jeff and Gretchen and Gramma and all the kids grabbed a section for themselves and huddled together near the forty-yard line. At midfield a podium had been set up on a platform, framed by an arbor of evergreen branches. Folding chairs lined the field in front of the podium, but most folks were heading up into the bleachers where their feet could stay out of the snow. Another, higher platform stood behind the podium; the choir had assembled there. He could just make out Bonnie Weaver.

Mike Stearns appeared, ushering the movers and shakers from the town and the community toward the metal seats. Larry grinned when he saw a few of them glance towards the bleachers enviously. Sometimes rank's privileges were uncomfortable ones . . .

Rebecca Abrabanel came over to Mike, spoke with him and pointed. Larry followed Becky's gesture and saw a small group clustered by the south goalpost. He recognized Becky's father and Mr. and Mrs. Roth and a few others. He puzzled for a moment; then nodded. *Jews at a Christmas celebration. No wonder they're hesitating!*

But Mike Stearns walked briskly over to them and took Mrs. Roth by the arm and led her and the others over to the folding chairs. Larry had seen military formations maneuvering on the field before, and there was a certain military precision in what happened next. The group were seated, but somehow there were no unoccupied sections big enough for all of them. They had to split up—just enough to create a mingling, a merging. *No ghettoes here in Grantville! Not even temporary ones!*

Finally, everyone had found a seat. The stands were filled with people and the blending of brightly colored synthetic fabrics with dull wools and leathers made a patchwork pattern in the morning light.

The people of Grantville were assembled. All of them.

The crowd fell silent as three small groups of people entered the field. Father Mazzare, wearing colorful robes, strode in from one sideline. Reverend Jones, in more sedate clothing, approached from the other. And a third group was coming in from the north goal. The first two groups had people carrying books and small crosses. The third had someone carrying a small menorah. There was a stir in the assembled crowd and Larry realized he was witnessing something that must have taken *a lot* of planning.

All three groups met in the center of the field and bowed to each other; and four thousand people looked on in utter silence.

A man from the third group came forward and hesitantly approached the microphone; Larry didn't recognize him. He must have been one of the German refugees. No, refugee no longer—one of the new citizens of the town. He glanced back at Father Mazzare and Reverend Jones; the two men smiled and gestured for him to go ahead. The man began to speak, and after a momentary flinch when his voice boomed out from a dozen loudspeakers, he went on. Larry could not understand the words, but he recognized that it was Hebrew he was hearing; and the effect on the Jews seated in front of him was plain. Rebecca clutched at her father and the Roths seemed to be crying, too.

The man finished and stepped back. Father Mazzare took the microphone and Larry was a bit surprised when he could not understand him either. He was speaking in Latin. He spoke for perhaps five minutes and at least a few of the people in the crowd seemed to be reacting to it.

Then it was Reverend Jones' turn. When he stepped up to the microphone, he held out his hand and Rebecca Abrabanel came forward to stand beside him.

"My friends, welcome," he said. "And a very Merry Christmas." Rebecca leaned forward and repeated it in German.

"This is always a very special time of year," continued

Jones. "But this year's Christmas is perhaps the most special since the very first, so many years ago. This is the first Christmas since the Ring of Fire." He paused while Rebecca translated.

"Many of us have wondered what the Ring of Fire was. How did it happen? Why did it pick us? Why did it bring us here? How did so great a power leave us alive and unharmed? I cannot answer those question, my friends, I can only tell you what I believe in my heart.

"I believe that we have witnessed the Hand of God in this thing. He has brought us here for a purpose. It is not for Man to question God's Purpose, but there are some things we can try to understand. His hand has brought us here. All of us. American and German, Jew and Gentile, Catholic and Protestant. We have all been brought here, to this time and this place to serve His Purpose.

"What that purpose will ultimately be, we can only imagine. But we have begun a great task here. We are building a place where people can be free; truly free. A place where people, no matter their origins, can live and raise their families and serve God as they see fit. A place free of the fear and superstitions of the dark past. A place where people can worship God as they please."

A place where they won't be spooked by potatoes, thought Larry.

As the reverend's words sank into the English-speaking listeners, and as Rebecca translated it for the Germans, the impact spread through the crowd. Larry felt it, too, even though he did not at first have the words to describe it; and then he realized he did.

A place for me.

"We must become a single people," continued Jones. "Rich in our diversity, but unconquerable in our unity. As we have begun, so let us continue. I ask Almighty God for his blessings. May He guide us to a bright new future. Amen."

Four thousand people echoed with one voice; but it seemed to Larry that the six adult voices on both sides of him were particularly strong. Or perhaps it was just that he'd heard them a little more clearly than any of the others. . . .

He shook his head ruefully. *C'mon, it's just Christmas feelgood crap, isn't it?* He *knew* where his family still was, and it wasn't here—or *now. Still, two different timelines, both of them real; maybe there's room for two different families. . . .*

Jones stepped back from the microphone and the choir began to sing. It was a sweet, sweet sound. All the traditional carols were sung, first in English and then again in a German translation. Or in the case of "Silent Night," in the English translation and then the original German. Soon everyone was joining in.

Larry told himself he was singing along with Bonnie, down in the choir; but by the fourth carol, he'd admitted it; he was singing with his folks. His *family*. Not a perfect one for sure, not even one he'd have chosen if he could—*but then you never get to choose, do you?*

During breaks in the singing, the clerics did more formal services. Father Mazzare held mass; Larry had to bite his tongue to keep from laughing at the thought that if they had substituted their potato chips for the Communion wafers, they might see a mass conversion. Gramma leaned forward to glare at him from two seats away. *Damn, she's a telepath!*

By the time it was all done, it was nearly noon and most of the people were getting pretty chilly despite the warm sun. A call blared over the speakers for all the food serving people to man their stations.

"That's us folks!" Larry called to the family. They made their way down off the bleachers and headed for the cafeteria.

The chips were a great success.

It took several hours to serve everyone, but each and every person who wanted them got a large handful of potato chips to go along with the turkey and ham and venison and stuffing and turnips that were being handed out. They kept telling people "no seconds" until everyone was served, but Larry noticed that a few faces in the line seemed awfully familiar. In the end it didn't matter, there were plenty for all and even some left over for the dance.

"Well, congratulations, Larry," said Melissa when she came up. "Project Quayle has accomplished its mission. Willie Ray is being mobbed by German farmers asking about potatoes."

"That's great!" said Larry. "But all we were really trying to do was have some chips for Christmas."

"You did that, too, Larry. Everyone's really enjoying them. Merry Christmas."

"Merry Christmas, Miss Mailey."

After the meal, music and dancing filled the gymnasium. They could only fit a fraction of the people in at a time, but they had cranked the heat up to the point that people gladly went outside after staying a while. They also lured people out by having the gift exchange outside. Larry wasn't sure whose idea the exchange was, but it seemed like a good one. It was just a big pile of stuff. Clothes and blankets and old toys and nicknacks. Anyone who had something to give added it to the pile. Anyone in need could take from it. The exchange went on all day.

Once the last of the chips had been distributed, Larry slipped away; he'd been tracking Bonnie as best he could in the crowd, and after a few minutes of squeezing past enthusiastic—and unskilled—dancers, he managed to cross her path.

"Oh Larry, isn't this a great day?" she asked when she saw him.

"One of the best. The choir sounded wonderful."

"Thank you! And your chips were fantastic!"

"A lot of people chipped in to make them. . . ."

"Ugh," said Bonnie; then she grinned. "Want to dance?"

"Sure."

It was a very nice day—scarcely even dimmed by Nat Davis' comment about wanting to do a lubricant inventory at the shop—but eventually it drew to an end. People started drifting off toward their homes as the early night came on. Larry had lost track of the rest of the family but he was in sort of a daze anyway. Bonnie had kissed him goodnight.

He hitched a ride home on one of the buses that was shuttling people back to town. He was surprised to see that only the lights in his own trailer were on.

He was even more surprised when he saw that the only one there was Jimmy. He had disappeared early on, and Larry had been wondering where he had gotten to. Most surprising of all, Jimmy was back in the kitchen, slicing up another few potatoes he'd found somewhere. A funny odor wafted through the trailer. . . .

"Hey, Jimmy! Aren't you sick of making potato chips? What are you working on now?"

Jimmy didn't even look up. "Sour cream and onion flavor," he said.

American Past Time

Deann Allen & Mike Turner

Billy stood on the mound and sweated in the glare of the afternoon sun. His game was on and he knew it, but he couldn't help feeling a little nervous. It wasn't from checking the stands to count the major league scouts with their laptops and cell phones—not anymore. He had just never pitched in front of so many people.

It was the Fourth of July, the first big baseball game since the Ring of Fire, and it seemed like half the town had turned out to watch, refugees included. He hadn't expected that. The Americans heading toward the high school had attracted notice, and now the refugees formed their own crowd along the fence surrounding the athletic field.

Or maybe it wasn't so surprising. The Germans had been working like bees, putting up new shelters and other projects in the town, and working the nearby farms to make sure the crops survived. They needed the holiday as much as the Americans. And they seemed to grasp the game of baseball.

That was no surprise, either. It really was a simple game: you throw the ball; you hit the ball; you catch the ball. Simple. It didn't even surprise him that everyone was pretty well-behaved, despite that things were getting rather drunk out. What did surprise him was that every single refugee was completely and vocally behind the UMWA!

Conrad had never seen anything like this *baseball*. The numbers being posted on the large board outside the fence had something to do with the players' actions, but he did not quite understand what they meant. It didn't seem to matter, though. The little ones especially were having a grand time, cheering whenever anything happened on the field, shouting encouragements to the miners that Conrad doubted most of them understood. He was surprised at the grin plastered on his own face. The UMWA team needed all the encouragement it could get, facing the young man throwing for the school team.

The young man—boy? he was certainly no older than Conrad—was tall and thin, but threw the white leather ball with the force of an arquebus, and far more accurately. It was deceptive, for he moved with a casual and easy grace until he released the ball, which seemed to explode from his hand in a blur that ended in a loud *thwok!* into his teammate's glove that Conrad could hear even over the noise of the crowd.

He wondered what it would be like, trying to hit

that ball. It was fast. Oh, it was fast! But not so fast he couldn't see it, couldn't track it with his eyes as it flew across the field. He looked at the man now trying to hit it—trying and failing. *He digs his toes into the dirt, shifts his weight as he swings the club. It's not all in his arms.*

Thwok! The ball was past the man before he'd even begun to swing. He stood straight and stepped outside the lines drawn on the ground with white powder. He bumped his club against the ground, seeming to mutter to himself. Then he spat in the dirt, stepped back inside the lines, and readied himself.

The young man leaned forward and looked intently toward the . . . *plate.* He nodded at something and stood upright. A moment's pause, then he kicked out a long step while pushing off with the rear foot, snapping his hips around as his hand arched over his head, his wrist snapping to loose the ball just as his body reached its full extension.

The miner swung, and Conrad knew he would miss. *That throw was slower than the others. It looked the same, but it was slower!* The loud *thwok!* came again and the older man crouched to the rear of the group around the plate stood and shouted something.

Players from both teams swarmed onto the field, shaking hands and patting backs. The people who had been watching from the tall, scaffold benches also moved out on the field, smiling and talking loudly. The game was over, and everyone seemed to be still having fun.

Conrad certainly was. *I could have hit that ball. I know I could!*

<>-<>   <>-<>   <>-<>

Billy wiped the sweat from his sunburned neck, heaved the last sack of vegetables onto the bed of the pickup, and waved to the scrawny German in its cab. The truck lurched forward with a loud grind of the gears that made Billy mentally deduct a good fifty bucks from its Blue Book list price, then it roared off toward the rutted dirt road by the farm Billy and his crew had spent most of the day harvesting.

"You folks done here?" Mr. Hudson's voice came from behind Billy, and he nearly jumped. The old farmer stood across the dirt track, looking pleased.

"Yes, sir, I think we are."

Mr. Hudson nodded. "We'll have the crops in in plenty of time. I didn't think we'd do nearly this well. Gather your crew up for me, would you, please?"

Billy dutifully gave out a whoop and circled his arm over his head, and the mixed group of Americans and refugees who had been working the field began to gather around. A couple of the older refugees and not a few of the Grantvillers looked about wiped out.

"Nice work, folks," Mr. Hudson said. "Most of the other crews are finishing up, too, so go ahead and take the rest of the afternoon off. I'd say you've earned it."

A tired cheer went through the group. The man in charge of the crew read haltingly from his cheat sheet of German phrases to fill in the local workers, and another quiet cheer went up. After days on end of the breakneck pace of the harvest, both the townsmen, who were unaccustomed to the work, and the refugees, many of whom were still recovering from borderline starvation or old injuries, welcomed the unexpected break.

Billy grabbed up his backpack with the remains of his lunch and other such necessities as his folks insisted he take with him when out "on crew," and headed along the windbreak of trees lining the field toward the forested hills beyond. This patch of woods was pure Grantville for quite a ways, and Billy was glad of it. There were a lot of things he missed from before the Ring of Fire—real baseball most of all—but at least his personal favorite swimming hole wasn't one of them.

If anything, the displacement had improved the place. Before, the hole in the creek bed with its sheltering boulder would have been half-dry this late in the summer, but now a new and larger stream fed into the creek. It might cause some excess flooding, come spring, but it kept the water flowing nicely.

Billy stepped around the fallen hickory tree that edged the pond and looked at the sun-drenched boulder that held back the clear stream water, forming the surprisingly deep little pool. The sun twinkled invitingly off the water as he hung his pack on a root sticking out of the tree base like a coat hanger. Grinning in anticipation, he bent to untie his shoes.

The icy chill of the water was welcome after all that hot work, but it didn't encourage him to stay too long. After a short bask on the sunny rock to dry himself, Billy got dressed and set out for home. He hopped over a narrow place just downstream, and trudged up the opposite hillside to cut a corner off the path to his house on this, the now-south side of town. As he descended the far slope, he heard voices ahead. It sounded like kids playing.

He came out of the woods into a hay field on the

edge of town, and found the kids. They were refugees, and they were playing ball on the stubble of the freshly mowed hay. Billy grinned in amazement. Nearly two dozen Germans, most about his age, were playing by-God baseball! Or at least making a good go at it.

They were playing gloveless, with a sturdy club making a reasonable bat and a largish ball made of what Billy guessed was brown leather. Flat stones marked the bases. The pitcher was throwing overhand with great enthusiasm, but seemed to be having trouble finding the plate. No one was umpiring, at any rate, each batter getting three swings or hitting the ball. There was much argument and confusion, the boys jabbering loudly in German and having a lot of fun. It looked just like the sandlot games Billy had played when he was ten.

He joined a group of boys alongside the field, recognizing several of them from the work crews. They were smiling and shouting what sounded like advice to the players. A few girls were in the group, paired off with boys or watching over some younger kids who were playing under the trees along the field's roadside edge.

One of the boys smiled at him as he joined the group, and stuck out his hand. "Hallo. *Ich heisse* Conrad."

Billy took his hand and shook it firmly, feeling slightly foolish, and said "Billy."

The German boy grinned at him, and motioned to two of his companions who promptly joined them. Conrad introduced them with broad gestures and a clear "Karl" and "Wilhelm," along with a gabble of fast-paced German that Billy could not quite catch, despite the fact that every kid in Grantville was struggling to master the language. Billy would hear a familiar word and miss ten more while he tried to place the first. The gestures came across much easier.

The Germans conferred together for a moment, then Conrad shouted something out onto the field. Several of the players shouted back. Conrad turned to Billy and said, "Please," and motioned toward the field. All eyes turned to him and the action stopped. Billy felt oddly exposed as the boy pitching motioned him forward, and Wilhelm trotted out to join him. Billy put his backpack on the ground, and ambled onto the field. He wasn't exactly sure what they wanted, but he was beginning to suspect. Wilhelm conferred for a moment with the younger boy who had been pitching, who then nodded eagerly and handed the ball to Billy.

It was leather, like boot leather, and very soft— stuffed with rags, maybe. A few threads dangled from the unevenly stitched seams. It was slightly larger than a softball.

It's a good thing it's so soft. They'd tear their hands up with a regulation ball. Billy had seen kids play bare-handed occasionally when he was little, and he knew the only way to catch a hard ball that way was on the bounce, and not always the first. This one they could probably catch straight off the bat—assuming anyone could get something that size over the plate in the first place. But it's what they had. So . . .

Billy nodded. The two boys smiled, jabbered happily, and went to stand with Conrad. Karl picked up the bat, and stepped up to the makeshift home plate.

Billy approached the mound with the ersatz base-ball in hand, and felt his slightly smug pitcher's look coming onto his face. The smugness was fully justi-fied. Few high school juniors grabbed the interest of even one major league scout, much less several. For him, Yankee Stadium had been both a dream and a definite possibility.

Now he had a hay field, and a ball the size of a grapefruit—with the consistency of one gone past prime. *What the hell, the thing's brown. They won't be able to see it worth a damn, anyway.* He stopped at the low clear place the Germans had been pitching from, and carefully kicked some stray dirt into a pile in the center of the area. Stepping onto the mound, he turned to face the batter.

Karl grinned at him with the loglike bat hitched over his shoulder. One of the younger boys stood a few feet behind him, ready to field the pitch. Billy pointed to him and made motion to back up. After the youngster had retreated several feet, Billy signaled that he was fine, and started his pitching motion.

He opened with an easy side-arm throw, sort of a fastball but not too fast, to see how the ball handled. The ball went far to the side of the plate. Fortunately, the outside, and the catcher fielded it on the bounce and sent it back.

Billy nodded to himself. "Okay. I can throw this ball. Nothing fancy. Just a clean throw." Kicking off easily, he unleashed another side-arm fastball. Right down the pipe and a little high, but Karl swung mightily at it, eyes shut and shoulders straining, and managed by sheerest accident to catch the bottommost corner of the ball. Which sent the ball back over the catcher's head and into a nearby clump of bushes.

That was the highlight of the next few batters. Karl took two more swings but never got close to the ball again. The next batter, a younger boy Billy had never seen before, tried to hit the ball while diving backward out of the way. At least he kept his eyes open. Billy decided to slow down on the smaller kids a little, but the next still proved no match.

Then the teams traded places, but Conrad motioned Billy to stay on the mound. It seemed fair enough to him. One of the older boys from the work crews led off and Billy increased the speed a little. The boy took a swing late and Billy decided to try a curve. The big soft melon ball broke only about six inches, but the German youth still had no luck hitting it. Nor did the younger boy who followed him.

The bright core of fun at playing started to fade. *These guys are no challenge. They're pathetic. My arm will turn to spaghetti before one of them hits me.* He looked around the outfield. The dozen or so kids in it were standing talking in pairs, or sitting on the ground playing with straws or with their chins on their fists. Looking next to the batter's box, Billy saw Conrad step up to the plate. He perked up a bit. Conrad was as big as he was and probably older. With shoulders. *Hmm . . . Maybe.*

Billy tried another curve. Harder. This one broke better and Conrad swung at it hard but awkwardly. Flatfooted. Billy noticed he never took his eye off the ball, but the curve flummoxed him and the ball sailed past.

Billy motioned his catcher back a few more feet

on the next pitch. Conrad had set up a little closer to the plate, but Billy had a feel for the ball now. He let loose an overhand fastball a little inside, and watched Conrad jerk the bat inward and down, grazing the top of the ball and bouncing it to the catcher.

Billy threw the next pitch almost exactly the same except half speed. Conrad, now set up a little more off the plate, over-swung and missed entirely.

After one more desultory inning, most of the kids had had enough and the game more or less broke up.

"Well, that was fun," Billy muttered under his breath as he watched the German kids moving away in small clusters. He guessed baseball was not much of an attraction anymore. Well, no one but a hardcore fan liked a pitchers' duel. Especially with only one pitcher. *And I'm the only hard-core fan or player left. Yippee.* He slumped over to where he'd left his pack. Conrad waved to him from a cluster of the bigger kids, who did not look like they were leaving just yet. The big German kid approached him with a strained look on his face.

"How?" he began in uncertain English. "You . . . ?" and completed the question with a throwing motion. Billy sighed and nodded, holding out his hand for the ball. *Maybe if I show them some stuff, and they have the gumption to practice it, they won't be so totally hopeless.*

He beckoned them all into a semicircle, and began to demonstrate baseball pitching mechanics in mime. He showed both his usual overhand delivery, and the sidearm throw he used sometimes when he was tired or the other team had him figured out. They watched him intently, pointing to something he'd done and arguing with each other, or trying to catch his attention and mimicking his movements to see if they were doing it right.

He pulled his baseball out of his pack and handed it around, showing its hardness and how he gripped the seams, then switched to their cloth-stuffed ball, and mimed out his approval of its density from a fielding standpoint. He showed them his glove, removing it from its usual place nestled snugly in his pack. They oohed and ahhed as if he'd pulled a rabbit out of a hat.

Then a couple of them started arguing over something, which got the rest jabbering again, most eagerly nodding, a couple still looking a bit puzzled. Then they all moved out to take positions and try out what they'd learned from Billy's impromptu baseball clinic. He put his ball and glove back in his pack, slung it over his shoulder, and got out of their way.

Conrad stopped him before he left, though, gesturing toward the plate. *What now? Batting lessons?* But the German boy wanted something else. He made it clear when he crouched behind the catcher, then looked back at Billy and pointed to the ground where he stood. Billy couldn't help but chuckle. *Now they want me to be the bad guy!*

Standing back there, trying to judge balls and strikes, it didn't take him long to realize that batting lessons were also needed. But what the hell, it was sort of like playing baseball. And it was better than going home.

"And then they had me umpire!" Billy said.

His mother laughed and handed him another

biscuit. "I bet it wasn't easy explaining strike zones to them."

"No, it wasn't. I could only think of about one word in ten that I needed. I really—"

"Then you should have paid more attention to your language lessons in school," his father said, frowning.

Billy gritted his teeth. "That's what I was going to say."

"You need to get your head around reality, Billy. Playing baseball is no excuse for not being here to do your chores."

"What chores? Polishing cars that no one'll buy because they nationalized all the gasoline? I did my chores for the day! I worked my butt off on that farm and earned some time off! You got a problem with that, take it up with Mr. Hudson! What were you doing all day?" He knew that was a mistake as soon as he said it. He looked at his plate and started shoveling food into his mouth.

"What was I doing? I was trying to find some way to make a living, to keep food on this table and a roof over your ungrateful head, *that's* what I was doing! I have two trucks from the army that need suspension work, and I needed you *here* to help with them, not gallivanting off in some hay field, pissing away time that could be spent helping this family!"

"Then you should have damned-well said something about it!" To hell with supper; he'd go hungry before he put up with another second of this. *Dammit, Dad, you used to be proud of me!* He shoved back from the table to leave.

"Billy, sit down and finish your supper," his mother

said. "After working the farm all day, you should know we can't afford to waste food. And don't swear." She turned to his father as he sat back down. "Keith, that is enough. He did his work for the day. He earned his afternoon off. If you didn't tell him you had things for him to do, that's your fault, not his."

"He should know there are always things to do," his father grumbled, but stuffed a large bite in his mouth, and chewed it angrily.

"Be that as it may, he was doing other things we've been told need to be done. Working on his language skill, for one. Do you think he can be teaching those boys, and playing with them, and *not* pick up more German? For another thing, he's finding common ground with them, which may be even more important here and now than working on those trucks. The more things we can find—or create!—in common with the people around us, the less the army will have to defend us against, and the more people it will have to do it with. So don't think of it as wasting his time. Think of it as . . . improving foreign relations."

His father swallowed his latest over-large bite. "I still need him here!" He jabbed his fork at his plate for emphasis.

"Well then, I suggest you put him on the payroll and pay him for the work he does for you, since that will be time taken from other useful things he could be doing. You can make up a work schedule, and go over it with him in the mornings before he leaves."

Billy smothered a snicker at the look on his father's face—if he hadn't just swallowed, he might have choked. He looked like he might, anyway.

Billy's mother smiled much too sweetly. "That will,

of course, also serve several purposes. It will teach you to talk to Billy, and schedule things, instead of just assuming he can read your mind, and taking his help for granted." She turned that smile on Billy. "And it will teach you the discipline and responsibility that comes with having a real job."

Billy looked at her, looked at his father, thought of having him as an actual *employer,* and quickly swallowed the bite he was chewing before he choked on it.

The work on the trucks took up three evenings, and even with the mechanics from the mine workers to help, it was just as heavy and dirty as the work in the fields, if not more so. They wound up dog-robbing heavier leaf-springs from old farm equipment to support the armor hanging on the trucks. The shocks were a hopeless cause—no matter what they put on, the extra weight and nearly nonexistent roads would soon trash them. The army would be in for rough rides in the near future. But the contract was done, and Billy's evenings would be free until his father found another.

Billy and his mother watched as his father dutifully entered Billy's pay into the account books, then they went to the bank to transfer the money into Billy's savings account. His father goggled a bit at the amount already in there from Billy's work on the harvest crews. Billy suppressed a smirk until he noticed his mother wasn't suppressing hers, at all.

They left the bank with his father shaking his head. His mother looked across the street, smiled to herself, and said lightly, "Excuse me. I'll meet you back home." She started across the street. "Miss Abrabanel? Could I have a moment of your time, please?"

Billy looked at his father; his father looked back. They both shrugged, two men together, baffled by the ways of women.

After dinner, Billy called some of his teammates and arranged for them to meet at the hay field after the work crews knocked off. With gloves, balls, and bats.

The next day, Billy, Vern, Steve, and a couple other team members gave a clinic on the fine art of baseball, passed out gloves, and coached two separate games on opposite ends of the hay field. The refugees were joined by several of their Grantville peers. Strangely, Billy's mother and Miss Abrabanel showed up and watched for a while, talking and occasionally gesturing at the players. They didn't stay long, and Billy soon forgot about them. The games went on until it got too dark to see the ball, and the youths found themselves walking home in the near-inky blackness of night.

Even with his father having a claim on his time, and the abysmal lack of talent among the Germans, the remainder of the summer passed much easier for Billy. Something like baseball was better than nothing at all.

"Pass the sausage, would you, Billy?"

"Sure, Dad." He handed the platter across the table. "Oh. I was talking with Mister Kinney, today. He's worried about Joey, what's going to happen to him, and I was thinking . . . well, Todd's working out okay, isn't he?"

"Yeah, he's a good worker. Why?"

"I thought that since Todd's doing well, maybe there might be a job that Joey could do? He's going to need to be able to support himself, too. I mean, he's nowhere near as smart as Todd, and he probably couldn't help with actually making the nails, but maybe he could dump them in the barrels, or bring bar stock, or help Todd keep the shop cleaned up? There's a lot of stuff to do that doesn't take any real skill."

His father sighed. "What do you want me to do, hire every Special Ed kid in the area?"

"You've hired one, already," his mother commented. "Why not another?"

"Martha, I am not a charity! Georg had a lot of doubts about hiring a 'simpleton' like Todd. He'll give me hell about even thinking of hiring someone he'd class as the village idiot! I may supply the building, but he's the one who actually runs the business."

"Surely a used car salesman can sell him on the idea. . . ."

"If you'll recall, one thing I like about this new business is that I don't have to feed people lines of bullshit anymore, so do tell me why I should feed a line to my partner. And I sold new cars, too!"

"Nobody says it has to be a line, Dad. Just see if there's anything he can do. Todd really likes Joey, and when Joey's around, I've never seen Todd lose focus like he does around other people. It's like he's looking out for someone who's worse off than he is. So it might even make Todd a better worker."

"And if you or someone else can't find a job for Joey," his mother said, "the churches are going to have to set up a charity for him. Or the government will have to start a welfare program. His parents aren't going to be around forever. Which would be better, for him to be a productive citizen, or a charity case?"

"All right, all right, quit ganging up on me! I'll talk to Joey's parents and see what he can do. *If* he's got the ability to hold a job, I'll bring it up with Georg." He snorted, then muttered angrily, "Hell, I'll even put it in terms of charity. Christian charity. It's about time all this religious hoo-hah was good for something besides an excuse for killing people."

"Thanks, Dad."

"Don't thank me, yet; I haven't done anything."

Billy shrugged. "You said you'd look into it. That's all I asked."

"I . . . um . . . hmm . . . You're welcome." He cleared his throat, then turned back to his plate with a puzzled frown.

Huh. Weird reaction. Billy wondered about it for a second, then shrugged it off. He reached for the bowl of porridge, and served himself some of the ubiquitous glop, when he saw his mother glance at him with a pleased, and rather proud, smile. Wondering what in the world had brought that on, he started eating, bending over his bowl with a puzzled frown on his face.

WHACK! Conrad hammered the ball with a swing of the white ash bat worthy of a Teutonic war god. Billy's head tracked up and over his shoulder. Quickly. The ball wobbled as it arced high into the air. The crowd of children roared in astonished approval as, despite its great altitude, it cleared the tree line to the north for a home run.

Vern's head was shaking in disbelief, and Billy grimaced at the grinning teenager rounding the base paths at a lope. The locals seemed to be learning baseball all right. Too darn fast. That was the second solid hit Conrad had had off him today, and the longest hit Billy could remember seeing off anybody, anywhere. *What's he been doing, sneaking lessons with the army from Mr. Simpson?* Wilhelm was still off in the trees looking for the ball when Conrad crossed home plate.

As the storkish Saxon was mobbed by his elated teammates, Wilhelm finally emerged from the forested slope. Billy held up his glove to signal Willi to throw the ball in, but the outfielder held onto it and trudged up to Billy in the diamond's center. He drew near, and silently held out the baseball. One seam was split down an entire side, and its yarn insides trailed out like some soldier's innards after a hard battle. From the pale look on Wilhelm's face, it might have been a soldier.

Vern ambled up to the plate, took one glance at the split ball, and said, "I have another in my game bag."

"This was my last one that isn't autographed," Billy said. "How many are left?"

"Some, I'd guess, around town."

Billy frowned and said nothing. There was nothing to say.

Vern put a hand on his shoulder. "Hey, we're aiming for eighteen-hundreds tech, right? The game got started back then, so we just roll the equipment back to match." He grinned. "Walter Johnson started on dead balls, and you pitch like him, so you'll match, too!"

Yeah, right. Go back to dead ball days, go back to sandlot games. Glorified Little League, that's all it'll be. Ever. He stifled a sigh and nodded, forcing a smile for Vern's sake, knowing his friend would be hurt if Billy didn't at least pretend he'd been cheered up.

The day had started bad enough. "I will *not* accept any 'the dog ate my homework' excuses!" Miz Mailey had said at the beginning of the year. How about a "the cat shredded my report then used it for a litterbox" excuse? He'd even brought the two pages that weren't fouled to prove it.

Then the day got worse. The bus passed huge smears of blood all over the road, and what he could swear was a pile of bodies just off the shoulder. Someone on the other side of the bus had seen a dead horse. What the hell was going on?

He found out soon after arriving at school, and suddenly the shredded report wasn't very important anymore.

The line moved up. Billy heard the younger students pounding up the stairs. No one called them down for running in the halls today. Desks and cabinets screeched across the floor—metal to barricade the stairs. Metal to block bullets. The line moved up. Another senior took a baseball bat from Mr. Trout. A club to fend off swords. Wood to block bullets. The line moved up. Smooth wood pressed into his hands. Snakes started crawling in his stomach.

"Herr Trout!" Conrad's voice came over his shoulder. "*I* take the bat; *he* takes the balls." The lanky German eeled past Mr. Trout into the athletic equipment locker, reappearing the next moment with the bucket of baseballs. He plucked the bat from Billy's hand, and hung the bucket over his arm. The snakes quit crawling.

"Conrad, are you nuts?" Mr. Trout said. "They'll be wearing armor and helmets!"

"Open-faced helmets, sir," Billy replied. "No, he's right. Randy Johnson keeps a bucket of balls beside his bed for home security and never had a break-in. Nobody wants a ninety-five-mile-an-hour fastball in the teeth."

Mr. Trout nodded shortly. "All right, if you think it'll do you more good. Just don't hit anybody standing in front—" He stopped with his mouth open, then closed it. "Never mind. You don't hit anything you don't aim at." He turned to hand out the last two bats, and the boys headed for the gym.

Conrad looked at Billy. "This is true? You hit only where you aim?"

Billy smirked slightly. "Yeah, pretty much."

"Ah. So the time you almost took off my nose was deliberate?"

Looking at Conrad standing there with a bat in his hand, Billy took the better part of valor. "That . . . was one of the not-quite times."

Conrad cocked an eyebrow. "Try not to have any not-quite times today."

This time the snakes didn't crawl; they simply bit. Billy jerked his head in a nod. "Yeah."

Half a dozen students ran the north bleachers out from the wall with a rumble like distant thunder. Or the pounding hooves of approaching cavalry. The gym doors shut behind them with a hollow boom, then came the rattle-clatter of Jeff Higgins setting the top and bottom catches, and running a chain through the handles to padlock them shut.

Mr. Trout chivvied kids up to the top levels of the bleachers, looking like he was herding cats for a second as Gena bounded off the end of the middle level and into a corner behind a different set of bleachers. She returned shortly with the long, heavy handle from one of the janitor's big push brooms. Mr. Trout motioned her upward when she took a lower level. She turned a narrow-eyed look at him and spun the broom handle so it hummed.

"Brown belt, sir. Remember?"

"Okay, front row of the top, but top! Please?"

She nodded and backed up three more rows. That left Billy standing between her and the bigger boys armed with bats.

Shouts sounded outside in the foyer, followed by gunfire from another part of the building. Mr. Trout hurried the students upward. Jeff stepped back toward the center of the room and jacked a round into his shotgun's breech.

Then the distant shooting stopped. The shouts moved closer. The noise just outside increased. Glass smashed. The doors shook as something started bumping into them. More shouting. The bumping stopped. The smashing sounds didn't. Then . . .

Boom! The doors shuddered as something slammed into them. Some of the kids started yelling. Vern, Conrad, and others stood on the lower rows of seats, bats in hand, between them and danger. *Ka-boom!*

Billy clenched his teeth to keep them from chattering, crouched down, and started sorting through the balls in the bucket, shoving the hardest ones into his pockets and shirt. *If . . . when they get through, I can't be stooping down to get these.* He just wished he'd thought to go to the bathroom before all this started. He *really* needed to pee!

Ka-boom! The doors bent inward. More kids started yelling, shoving their way toward the top of the bleachers. Mr. Trout went to stand with Jeff and readied his pistol. *Ka-boom!* Gena twirled the broom handle, swallowed hard, and stepped down to stand behind Vern and Conrad. Billy gripped a ball and made sure his others were in easy reach.

Ka-boom! Ka-boom-crack! Boom-crack! Crack-slam! The doors splintered and burst. The shouts rose to a triumphant shriek as the Croats poured into the gym.

The racking boom of Jeff's shotgun filled the gym with sound and emptied the front line of Croats with torn and dying bodies. He stepped back to reload and Mr. Trout started firing.

Billy threw at one man on the edge of the crowd— the rest were too close to Jeff and Mr. Trout for a clear throw—but his foot slipped on the slick wood and the ball went wide, bouncing off the wall and rolling into a corner. He swore and grabbed another. This time it flew straight, but bounced off the chest armor of the man it hit. He grabbed a third ball and looked up just in time to see a saber come down on Mr. Trout's head. The next one went into his neck and he fell, blood flying.

Jeff took down that man and many others in a roaring storm of gunfire that ended all too quickly. He turned the shotgun into a club against the Croats' sabers, bashing one in the face as another came at his back. That one caught a major-league-grade fastball square in the head that knocked him flat.

But there was nothing Billy could do about the new group that came howling in through the broken doors, nor the Croat on the other side who sent his saber smashing into Jeff's shoulder and drew back for the killing blow.

Then there was nothing for Billy to do at all but watch in sick fascination as the new group began taking the Croats apart, starting with the one standing over Jeff. The giant in the lead of the new force split the man's head like a cantaloupe, and stood there shouting to his men who quickly drove the Croats into the back corner of the gym, while some made a protective line in front of the students on the bleachers.

And then the slaughter began. It didn't end even when the last two dozen or so Croats threw down their weapons and held up their hands. They just went down to savage cries that sounded like "Hack 'em all!" When the last Croat lay dead on the blood-smeared floor, then it ended. Only then.

And Billy quietly walked over to the end of the bleachers, knelt down looking at some part of the floor that wasn't covered with blood, and was not so quietly sick all over it.

"What happened?!" Steve stared in wide-eyed horror at their bloody clothes.

"Hey, bro, settle down," Vern said. "It ain't ours. Jeff Higgins got cut really bad, and we had to do first aid on him." He looked down at himself, then closed his shaking hand into a fist. "Damn, I'm glad I took that EMT course!"

"Certainly I would never have known to do most of that," Conrad said wonderingly. "You are sure he will not be crippled from it?"

"Nah, the docs will stitch him up and he'll be fine."

"But Mr. Trout . . ." Billy said hollowly. "God damn those bastards!"

"Mr. Trout?" Steve looked back and forth between them.

Vern nodded heavily. "They killed him."

"They damn-near cut his head off, is what you mean!" Billy said, wiping sudden tears from his eyes.

Steve swallowed hard, then squeezed his eyes shut. "Dammit, I should have been in there with you. I could've done something!"

"No, you didn't want to be there, Steve," Vern said. "Believe me, you didn't!"

"And you wouldn't have been able to do anything," Billy said. "They came in a rush, went right at Jeff and Mr. Trout. You'd have been standing up there with the rest of us, holding nothing better than a bat. I had baseballs, and I couldn't really hit the ones in the middle, and those were the ones that . . . did the damage.

"Then it didn't matter who could've done what, because those other men came in. What's-his-name . . . Captain Gars' men. They shoved the Croats back against the wall and cut them to pieces."

"Yeah," Vern said. "Screaming something like 'hack them to paté,' and that's just what they did." He started to shake, and whispered, "Even after they tried to surrender . . ."

Billy reached up and put his hand on Vern's shoulder.

"And that's why you didn't want to be there, Steve. I saw that and lost my breakfast."

Vern took a deep breath and straightened. "Well, I know what I'm going to do—start paying more attention to those militia training sessions. There's no way in hell I'll ever stand there again with nothing but a bat in my hands when some pack of bastards is trying to kill us all."

"A gun is well and fine," Conrad said. "But a saber will not run out of bullets. I intend to speak to Colonel MacKay about lessons on that, as well."

Billy reached into his pocket and pulled out a ball. He turned it in his hand, looking at it. "I think I'll join you," he said quietly.

"Are you crazy?" Steve exclaimed. "You said you never wanted to be in the Army, just like me!"

"Yeah, that was before I realized that a baseball is a really piss-poor weapon to be holding when someone's shooting at you, or coming at you with a big friggin' sword. If you really want to be able to do something next time, Steve, you'll go to those training sessions, too, 'cause that's the only way I can think of to do anything but die."

"Your parents are gonna have a cow, y'know," Vern said.

"Let 'em. Me, you, Gena, Conrad, and a couple of others were the only kids in there who weren't screaming their heads off and trying to hide in the woodwork. If my folks can't see that it's better for the many to defend the few, than the other way around, that's their problem. I'm eighteen, now. I can join the militia or the Army on my own say-so. Don't know that I'll ever sign up, for real, but I do want to know how to use something besides this. . . ." He bounced the ball in his hand. "When the shit hits the fan, again."

Billy rolled his head, trying to relieve some of the tension in his neck and shoulders. His elbow felt like someone had tried to dislocate it. Someone had. Himself. The last two pitches—a curve and a slider—had been murder this late in the game, but they'd psyched Conrad out, coming from opposite directions to cross the plate cleanly in the strike zone.

Billy grinned wanly as Karl waggled two fingers wildly around for the sign. He did not have much left and the call was perfect. His high kick obscured the plate for a moment as he reared back to let go what was to all appearances a screaming fastball that looked to sail up high in the strike zone.

Conrad swung hard, only to nearly stumble as the ball fell almost vertically into Karl's mitt. The gangly German stared, perplexed, as Mr. Simpson called strike three. A perfect fade-away.

Billy blew a sigh of relief. Conrad had gotten two hits off him this game—a single to center field, and a triple when the ball took an utterly crazy bounce into the far right-field corner. With him gone, Billy's biggest worry was gone, as well. In the bottom of the ninth, with one out, one man on second base, and his team up by only one run, he'd had to go all out to keep the German from driving in another run and tying the game. Or worse, getting a home run, as he had a disturbing tendency to do.

A big German started toward the plate, a man Billy had never seen before. Conrad stopped on his way back to the dugout and spoke to him quietly. Billy used the time to move his arm around, working out some of the soreness. The audience did a somewhat ragged wave. For which side, he couldn't tell. The once-wooded dell where they now played did weird things to cheers, but the school field bleachers wouldn't hold everyone who'd wanted to see the game—people had come from other *towns*. So an area that had been cleared for building materials and firewood had been chosen, and boards set across the stumps for seating. The slope let everyone see the field, and had room for even more people than had showed up.

The batter stepped up to the plate. Billy rolled his shoulders one more time and stepped up to the pitching board. One more out and he'd be done. Three pitches. He could do three pitches. The man on second didn't look like he was going to try anything. Billy looked for the sign.

Heat. Good. I could throw that in my sleep. Karl wasn't as experienced a catcher as Vern—who now sat in the Army dugout—but he was shaping up fast. Good call. Get the guy thinking about the ball's speed, instead of its location and direction. Billy wound up and let fly with a fastball right up the center.

Then shoved his glove in front of his face as the ball came screaming off the bat straight at his head.

Or so it seemed. He missed catching it by a foot, and quickly turned to watch it sail into the middle of the center outfield seating, causing a mad scramble among the audience.

The guy on second gave a whoop and headed for home. The batter loped around the bases with the world's most surprised grin on his face.

Billy stood on the mound with his head back and his eyes closed. The only thoughts in his mind were things that would get his mouth washed out with soap by his mother, if he ever said them in her hearing.

He felt a hand on his shoulder. "Ach, bad luck," Karl said. "That's all it was. You threw a good game."

Billy let his breath out in a sharp hiss, but still couldn't think of anything to say that wasn't foul. What was the use? He was the only real pitcher in existence, and with the piss-poor—hell, practically nonexistent!—competition around here, he was losing his edge to the point where any schmuck could hit him. *Screw it. Baseball is dead. I'm just going through the motions out of habit.*

Someone came up on his other side. Conrad. Who stood there with a crooked grin on his face. "You were careless, Billy. You were ready for me, but you thought no one else could hit you, and so you were not ready for my student!"

Student. Great. Bad enough my talent's rotting on the vine, now he's training other people how to embarrass me by proving it. "Aw, blow me," he said, and turned toward his dugout. Karl followed. So did Conrad.

Mr. Simpson came ambling over from home with a kind of wistful grin on his face. As he drew abreast of the younger men he laid a hand on Billy's shoulder, resting its mate on Conrad's. "Gentlemen, that was a good game. Come on down to the Gardens, I'm buying the first round."

"Thanks, sir, but I don't really—" Billy began, as the others accepted eagerly.

"Don't tell me you're going to mope about it! So

you lost a game. Big deal!" Mr. Simpson snorted softly. "If we were keeping stats, your earned run average would be . . . one-point-oh-oh-what? So come on and have a free beer."

Billy shrugged and nodded. "Okay. Thanks."

"Great! I'll meet you all there!" He patted their shoulders and went off to talk to Captain Heinrich.

Billy packed up his gear and headed up the footpath leading out of the dell. As he reached the top, the lowering sun shined straight into his eyes, and he stopped and turned away for a moment to let the dazzle subside. There was still quite a crowd down there, milling around and talking. From here, the board seats didn't look as ratty—he could barely see the stumps—and nearby trees threw shadows across the field. If he squinted his eyes, he could almost imagine it was a real stadium.

He shook his head and started the walk home, wondering what he'd do for the rest of his life. Nailmaking was okay, but, geez, it was boring!

Billy sat in the chair Karl pulled out, and nodded thanks to the waitress as she handed him the promised free beer. He still didn't really want to be here, but Karl had been waiting for him outside his house, and had practically dragged him to the Gardens. It didn't help that Conrad was sitting at the same table, laughing and accepting congratulations for his team.

"Great, everyone's here!" Mr. Simpson said loudly. Some of the noise died down. He lifted his mug. "To the Army!" Everyone cheered and drank the toast. Everyone but Billy, who drank because it was expected, but couldn't muster more than a weak smile he was sure looked fake.

"To Viktor!" Conrad called, and led the cheers that followed.

The German batter stood up from another table and waved the noise down. "*Nein!* Not for me. I was only doing what Conrad taught me. Give him the credit, for it is his, and well-earned!"

When that round of cheers died down, Coach Benton stood up. "And to Billy, who is not only the best pitcher in the United States, but has added another two miles an hour to his fastball!"

Billy's head whipped up so fast he almost cricked his neck. "*What?!*"

Coach leaned over the table. "Ha! Didn't know I'd clocked you, did you?" he said with a huge grin. "I even bet you thought you were losing your edge for lack of competition, didn't you?"

"I . . . ah . . . yeah."

"Because Conrad and now Viktor can hit you? Because you're so blasted arrogant that you think you must be getting worse instead of them getting better?" There didn't seem to be any way to answer that, but the narrow-eyed look and quiet snort Conrad gave him told Billy the truth was plain as day on his face.

"Billy, if Nolan Ryan never had batters who could challenge him—and beat him, now and then—he'd have been nothing but a circus freak. If baseball is going to be popular, we'll need German superstars, too. And here's Conrad, the very first!" The crowd cheered again.

"Two teams don't make a league!" Billy growled.

"Nobody else is playing, so it isn't very popular, is it?"

Coach stood up and looked at him. "I guess you haven't heard, then." He turned and looked over his shoulder. "Hey, Tom!" he called to Mr. Simpson. "Billy here says two teams don't make a league!"

"Well, I admit Badenburg isn't ready, yet, but Jena wants a game with Army next month. Every one of them was at the game, today, checking out what they'll have to face."

Do four teams make a league . . . ? Yeah, they do. Damn. Baseball isn't dead! Billy stared at his beer, knowing the voice inside himself whining that he didn't want to be one star among many was just a lingering remnant of brat. *I'd have had to share the spotlight with lots of others, if none of this had ever happened. Shared it and been proud of it.*

The beer pitcher appeared in his view as someone refilled his mug. Conrad set the pitcher down and lifted his own mug, smiling. "I get the bat, you get the ball," he said quietly. "And perhaps someday, between us, we'll find or create the one who gets the glove."

Billy looked at him, saw the sincerity and enthusiasm shining in his eyes, the love of the game that Billy had known so well for so long, and had almost given up on. The new flag of the United States hung on the wall behind Conrad. The same stripes, but fewer stars. It really did look better with more than just the one star off in a corner by itself. *One state doesn't make a new U.S. One person doesn't make a team. Or a sport.*

He remembered that last look back at the field where they'd played. The crowd still milling around, the low hum of their voices reflecting from the dell's bowl to wash over him. The way the board seats fell away in a seemingly smooth sweep. The long, pillar-like shadows from the trees that lay across the infield. *And if you look at it just . . . so . . .*

He grinned, lifted his mug, touched it to Conrad's, and drank to future superstars. *How about that? Maybe Yankee Stadium isn't impossible after all.*

Skeletons

Greg Donahue

Dave woke up when the front door slammed. He sat up off the couch and pushed his glasses back in place. A book fell off his chest and onto the floor. Scooby sat up and barked once before running into the kitchen.

Dave muttered as he picked up the book and placed it on the coffee table. He looked at his watch. Gerd was probably getting home from his shift. "Hey buddy, how was work?" Dave shouted towards the door.

"It vass gut," Gerd hollered back from the kitchen. He appeared at the doorway with two beers. He handed one to Dave before taking a seat in the La-Z-Boy opposite the couch. "*Aber*, I am worried. I mean, but I am worried."

"Talk to me, Goose," Dave replied before taking a drink. Gerd first saw *Top Gun* two nights ago, and it had enchanted him. He was heartbroken to learn that apparently no one in Grantville possessed an aircraft.

"You know they let all men from Jena come here?" Gerd asked, calming down a bit after sipping his beer. Scooby, Dave's Great Dane, sat completely still, hoping Gerd would share the beer.

Dave was still getting used to his boarder's version of English. He had met Gerd a couple of months ago while helping recruit labor for his tree-trimming crews. Gerd was one of the few who spoke any English at the time, and Dave grew to like him. He offered to let Gerd stay with him after about two weeks of working together. Gerd had happily accepted, anxious to leave the growing refugee camp.

"I'm sorry, what?" Dave asked slowly.

Gerd had a look of concentration on his face before continuing. "The man all taken from battle at Jena. They come here and join Army, or work with us. I heard today at work."

"Oh, right," Dave replied. "We could certainly use them. So why are you worried?"

"These man are trouble. Gretchen kicked some out after Badenburg. How you know if they start trouble this time? Who kicks them out?"

"I'm sure some will start trouble. We gave you and the others a chance, and it worked out great. It's how we do things," Dave said, trying to keep his wording simple.

"Right, but these men . . . we must be careful," Gerd finished by setting his empty bottle on the coffee table. Dave knew Gerd liked a lot about Grantville, but the German was never shy about his feelings of the beer Dave and the other Americans had brought with them. Gerd had made no small ceremony of the day Dave ran out of beer. Dave was shocked with how quickly Gerd and his co-workers had started brewing their own.

"Look, America was formed in no small part by groups of unwanted people. In fact," Dave stood up and took his empty bottle into the kitchen, "several of . . ."

"I know, I know. I hear this from you before," Gerd followed him and put his bottle in the recycle bin. "What we have for dinner?"

Dave, relieved that Gerd moved onto another subject, smiled. "We're about out of the usual." He scratched his chin, then pointed at Gerd. "We will feast like men! Wait here!"

Dave left Gerd standing in the kitchen, waiting and looking slightly confused. Scooby, either picking up on the conversation, or just happy to be in the kitchen, started pawing at his bowl.

Dave returned with a shotgun in one hand, and a scoped rifle in the other. He tossed the shotgun to Gerd. Gerd fumbled and almost dropped it. He held the shotgun gingerly, as if Dave had handed him the fire of the gods. Scooby, seeing the weapons and knowing meat was coming, grabbed his bowl in his mouth and sat at the sliding glass door, pawing at it.

"We will stalk our prey like cats, strike like eagles and feast like pigs!" Dave shouted, thumping the rifle to his chest. He laughed at the look on Gerd's face. Dave handed him a box of shells. "Guess you'd better have a lesson first." Dave walked out the sliding glass door and into the woods behind the house.

Gerd followed, carefully holding the weapon as if expecting it to start firing off dozens of rounds at the slightest touch. "No more vegetables for dinner, thank God."

"So you ended up shooting your dinner?" Mathias asked, tugging on a branch as Gerd sawed away.

"Yes. I think Dave was looking for deer or something. A boar charged, and I dropped it with one blast from the *shotgun*," Gerd replied, with the last word in English. The limb broke free and fell to the ground. "A very impressive weapon; it stopped the boar cold. We had it cleaned and cooking within an hour."

"Nice! Mr. and Mrs. Sizemore haven't needed to go hunting yet. They had plenty of food stored away. I sure hope they eventually let me try, especially with one of his firearms," Mathias replied as Gerd helped him drag the branch over to the pile of detritus. "I think, however, that Mr. Sizemore would rather I save ammunition and use the bow he has. The damned thing looks like some torture device. Pulleys and wires everywhere, rails for holding the arrow, and other parts I can't recognize. It is extremely quiet and easy to use, though. An intriguing weapon." Mathias was staying with an older couple that took him in as a son.

"You'd love the shotgun. Smooth and very powerful. Not that I needed to, but I had it reloaded and ready to fire before the boar hit the ground. It's a wonder any of us survived the battle," Gerd said, remembering the leg wound he received that frightful day. "I wonder how bad the Americans chewed up the men marching on Jena."

"The way I hear it, not too bad, actually." One

of Mathias' hosts, Mrs. Sizemore, was also an excellent source of rumor, gossip and news. Gerd found that Mathias wasn't shy in sharing any of it with his coworkers. "There is some girl who is supposed to be an incredible shot with a rifle. She apparently took out most of the officer types before anyone knew what was going on. They folded before really going nose-to-nose with the Americans."

"Lucky for them." Gerd started sawing on another limb. "When are the prisoners coming here?"

"They're already here, but not as prisoners," Mathias replied.

"How do you always know these things?" Gerd asked, a little exasperated.

"I suffer through hours of conversation with Mrs. Sizemore to get a few details. Mr. Sizemore says he let me stay with them just to 'run interference on the wife' as he put it."

Gerd laughed, understanding the meaning if not the translated idiom.

Hermann sipped his beer slowly, keeping his eyes on the crowd. Pieter and Jan were also eyeing the crowd. Most of the men from Jena were packed into Thuringen Gardens for their first night off after being inducted into the American Army.

"What an unusual place," Pieter said softly.

"What an unusual week," Hermann added. A few days prior, he had barely escaped death. Most of the other men on horseback, especially those with plumage on their heads, were swatted down by an unseen and unheard weapon. Hermann had immediately sensed the trend, dove off his horse and hid

among the men. In short order, they had all sur-
rendered under the best of terms. At the time, he
actually looked forward to fighting with the obviously
wealthy and powerful Americans. His first impression
was fast changing. "Naïve bastards."

"Sir?" Pieter asked, cocking his head to the side.

"The Americans, naïve," Hermann repeated. "They
could take any city, crush any army, and here they
are, letting us sit on our asses and drink beer while
they worry about refugee camps."

"Weak," Jan commented. He was always short on
words, and those he did speak were often in agreement with Hermann. Hermann favored his efficient
brutality over his "intellectual" dialogue.

"That's right my nearly mute friend, weak," Hermann
said, pointing to his beer, "so get us some more."
Hermann cuffed Jan and sent him on his way.

"I have to say, this could be a most profitable
diversion, sir," Pieter said, once Jan had left.

"What diversion is that, Pieter?" Hermann
replied.

Pieter smiled. "Our temporary stop in Grantville,
sir. There are some things here that would be in
extremely high demand in other parts of . . . well,
anywhere, really."

"How do you propose we liberate the naïve Americans of some of their underutilized valuables? More
importantly, how do we get out of here without having
them looking for us with their damned vehicles?"

"As I said, sir, a profitable *diversion*."

"What's the matter?" Mathias asked. Gerd had talked
his coworker into joining him at Thuringen Gardens

for some drinks before heading home for the day. Apparently, most of the new arrivals from Jena also had the same idea.

"Why did you stop? Do you see one of those underdressed American women?" Mathias looked out in the crowd.

"Oh shit," Gerd muttered.

"I don't see her! Who are you looking at?" Mathias started jumping a little to look over the crowd.

"Stop, you fool!" Gerd growled, grabbing Mathias and dragging him to the side. "I see Hermann."

"Who the hell is Hermann?" Mathias protested, yanking his arm free from Gerd's grip.

Gerd took a moment to breathe deep before continuing. "Of course, you wouldn't know him. I suffered under him all of the winter and spring, before joining up with you guys."

"What, do you owe him money or something?"

"No," Gerd replied. He looked back over to the table where Hermann was sitting. His right-hand man Pieter was where he always was, next to Hermann. Hermann's two other favored thugs, Jan and Christopher, were nowhere to be seen. "He is one of the most vile men I have ever known. A bastard's bastard. What the hell is he doing here?"

"I imagine he was brought back after the battle at Jena," Mathias replied, giving Gerd a concerned look. "We've both known our share of bastards. What's the problem?"

"Let's get out of here. They are trouble, and I don't want him to see me." Gerd turned around and took off at a fast walk without waiting for Mathias.

❧❦ ❧❦ ❧❦

Dave awoke to the sound of Scooby barking. He realized his watch alarm was beeping. It usually served to wake Scooby up, and Scooby in turn would wake up Dave. He rubbed his eyes and put his watch on.

"Stupid damned Ring of Fire," he muttered as he skulked into the kitchen. Everyone had been working hard ever since the Ring of Fire, and his tree-trimming crews were no exception. He hadn't had a day off since, but set his alarm early this morning to get one last good breakfast in before the cereal ran out.

Dave pulled open the cupboard and pulled out the last box of cereal. He got the milk out of the fridge. It wasn't the pasteurized, homogenized two-percent milk he was used to, but it was white, wet and helped the cereal go down.

"Come on, *schlafkopf*!" he hollered. "This is our last day of Lucky Charms for the rest of our lives!" They had agreed to make it a special occasion as the last of the cereal was consumed.

Dave got out two bowls and two spoons. He filled both with cereal and threw the empty box away. "I don't want to start without you, hurry up!" Since Gerd was moving slow, Dave figured he had time to get some coffee going. Coffee was running out too, so he decided to add it to their last "twentieth-century breakfast" for the foreseeable future.

"God damn it, wake up!" Dave yelled. He had already downed a cup of coffee with no peep from Gerd. "The best part of waking up, my ass," he muttered while walking to the living room. He turned on the stereo and set the volume to an uncomfortable level. A Rolling Stones' song started, causing the walls to buzz.

Gerd stumbled out of his room a minute later, punched several buttons on the stereo before finally hitting the power, and flopped into a chair at the kitchen table.

"What the hell's wrong with you? Stay up late with a lady friend?" Dave asked, pushing a coffee mug towards Gerd.

"*Nein*. I sleep bad." Gerd picked up the cup and held it both hands. "Remember our conversation about new men from Jena?"

"Mmhmm."

Gerd got quiet and looked away quickly. Dave was about to say something before he continued. "Well, I . . . met some guys at Thuringen Gardens. They keep me up all night."

"Ah, some drinking buddies!" Dave said with a smile. "We could use some more drinking buddies. Invite them over."

Gerd almost dropped his coffee mug. "I . . . I didn't catch their names. Probably won't see them again."

"Hmm, okay," Dave said, setting his mug down and grabbing a spoon. "This is the last of the Lucky Charms, man, enjoy it while you can!"

Gerd finally managed a smile. He picked up his spoon and started on his bowl.

"This will do nicely!" Pieter said, with a savage grin. He racked the slide on the shotgun.

The three of them were sitting around a small fire on the edge of the refugee camp. Most of the inhabitants had quickly learned to keep their distance from the three men. It was evening, and they had spent the day familiarizing themselves with the tools of the American Army.

"I don't understand what that Simpson man meant when he called this the 'Elmer Fudd Special,'" Hermann said, holding up the large double-barreled shotgun issued to him. Tom Simpson spoke fair German, but during the weapons issuing process, he didn't elaborate on the strange term. Hermann, thinking it was probably the name of the inventor, and wanting to keep a low profile, hadn't asked. "However, it will indeed do nicely."

"Nice," Jan growled, sticking his large finger in the barrel of the weapon issued to him.

"Unfortunately, they are keeping a tight hand on the ammunition," Pieter added. They were not issued ammunition, and were instead given spent shells to practice operating the weapons.

"Only for these shotguns. We have all the powder we need for our pistols." Hermann gestured, with the shotgun, to their wheel locks. The wheel locks were normally a hot commodity, and Hermann had felt fortunate to have just one, prior to Jena. In one violent moment, he and his comrades learned how obsolete the pistols had become. As such, the Americans had no use for them, and Hermann had taken several from other fallen mercenaries.

"Not too tight," Jan said, smacking his fist into his other hand.

"What was that, you lout?" Hermann said impatiently. Hermann made it a point to always act annoyed at everything Jan said or did.

"I think he meant we could get ammunition easily, for the new guns that is," Pieter replied for Jan.

Jan nodded.

"Do you care to tell us how?" Hermann poked Jan with the end of his shotgun.

"There," Jan said, pointing to some of the American houses visible from their fire.

Hermann was about to tear into Jan about how all the Americans have ammunition because they all have weapons, but stopped himself. If Jan thought he could get ammunition from an American home, Hermann was inclined to let him try. Jan had a way of getting things done. If not, Hermann knew he had one less person to split any loot with.

Hermann sat back a moment in thought. He looked at Pieter and considered the plan Pieter brought up at the beer garden. Pieter returned the look, nodded and winked. Hermann smiled, glad that at least one of his smart men was still around. Christopher, unfortunately, did not survive the battle at Jena. Pieter's original plan, slightly modified to allow time for Jan to get ammunition from an American home, would work nicely.

"No, NO!" screamed the old man.

Gerd hesitated, earning a backhand from Hermann.

"You gutless cur, he's obviously hiding something!" Hermann snarled.

Jan pulled back on the old man's arms tighter and smiled. "Do it."

Gerd tried to postpone the inevitable by reheating the knife over the candle.

"For God's sake, young pup," growled Hermann. He grabbed the hand Gerd was holding the knife with. "The longer you wait, the longer this old bastard suffers."

Hermann guided, by force, Gerd's knife-wielding hand towards the man's stomach. He slowly pressed the knife in. The hot tip sent an acrid smell of burnt hair, skin and blood into the air. Hermann released his grip.

"Pull it out and heat it again," Hermann said, sounding bored.

Gerd pulled the knife out, and stuck it back over the candle, blood sizzling. He felt like he was going to throw up at any moment.

"Please," the old man whispered.

"What?" Jan said, driving his knee into the man's back.

"Please," came another weak whisper.

"Speak up." Hermann grabbed the man's thinning hair and lifted his limp head.

"Please, no more."

"Gerd, give him a reminder." After a moment's hesitation, Hermann turned to face Gerd. "I don't want to tell you twice."

Gerd stuck the knife slowly in the man's stomach.

"Where is it, you bastard?" Hermann yelled at the old man. "Where's your stash? Give it up! Give it up! Give it up . . ."

" . . . get up! Man, get up! I'll sic Scooby on you!"

Gerd woke up with a flinch. Dave stopped shaking him.

"What the hell's been going on lately?" Dave asked, opening the blinds in the room. "You've been over-sleeping and looking like hell."

Gerd sat up and rubbed his eyes. "*Was ist* . . . what time is it?"

"You're not late, but only because I bothered to check on you," Dave answered. "Still don't have a lot of time. We're going to start clearing some trees to the north. Looks like they might run a line up to Jena."

Gerd got out of bed without comment and lumbered to the bathroom.

"Good morning to you, too." Dave went to the kitchen, concerned, and started preparing breakfast.

"Remember, don't make a sound, and avoid anyone. No need to make them look for murderers," Hermann whispered. He handed a matchbook and sack to Jan.

"Nice." Jan took the sack and matchbook with a smile.

"When you find enough shells, pick a shed, not a house, to light. We don't need to give them a reason to look for a murderer or an arsonist, make them think it was an accident," Pieter added.

Jan stood up and walked quickly to the first house. Hermann and Pieter stayed behind cover, with an axe handle, to quietly take care of any witnesses. Hermann had picked midmorning rather than night to make their move, as the houses would likely be unoccupied. He also wanted daylight to navigate quickly out of town.

Jan disappeared around the back of the house. After a few long moments, he walked quietly out the front door. He had the sack in his hand, with something in it, and smiled.

"He's really good at this, you know," Pieter whispered.

Hermann nodded. "He only needs the occasional flogging to keep him on his toes."

Jan continued to the next house and took much longer. Hermann was about to send Pieter to go and get him, when he finally appeared at the front door. He shook his head and pointed to the bag. It didn't look any fuller.

Jan hurried to the back of the third house they had cased. After a few moments, he quickly walked back the way he came, shaking his head, indicating with his free hand that someone was sleeping inside.

Hermann waved Jan over to a house farther down the street. Jan nodded and proceeded towards it at a fast walk. Hermann and Pieter crept through the edge of the woods, keeping pace.

"He needs to slow down, he's too obvious," Pieter hissed.

"He'll be done soon enough, get ready to move." Hermann hustled over to their gear, as Pieter followed.

Jan was in and out of the last house before they had gathered all the gear. He had a huge smile on his face and the sack had several more boxes in it. He disappeared behind the house for a minute before returning. A small wisp of smoke was coming from the backyard.

"Hurry," Jan said as he approached.

Hermann grabbed the sack as they hustled into the woods. It held five boxes of shotgun shells. One of them was labeled "20 Gauge" and the rest "12 Gauge." When they were issued their weapons, they were told that the weapons were made for 12-gauge shells. Hermann would have normally backhanded Jan for something like that, but he was too happy to have four boxes of usable ammunition.

"Perfect. Let's get out of here, we have a package to pick up," Hermann whispered. They headed northwest.

"This is not rocket science!" Dave hollered.

Gerd sighed and lowered the .22 rifle. Of the ten soup cans on the ground fifty yards away, only one had any holes in it, and only two holes at that. Fifteen spent .22 cartridges were on the ground next to him. "*Ja ja*, I know, and Germans make rocket science. You say that before!"

"Tell you what, forget about the .22. You do fine with the shotgun anyways." Dave had spent the afternoon after work trying to teach Gerd marksmanship with a rifle, so Gerd could help hunt as well. He was fast deciding it was a wasted afternoon. Gerd had done well enough by killing a boar with a shotgun slug a few days ago.

"Mathias say the Sizemores have a bow. I can use that, and not use ammo. I can ask him tomorrow."

Dave made an overdramatic display of slapping his forehead. "I haven't used that thing in years!" He turned and ran into the garage, leaving Gerd outside, unloading the remaining .22 cartridges. After rummaging in the garage for a few minutes, he seemed to find what he was looking for.

"Got it!" Dave ran out with a crossbow. "Oh, crap, I'd better get the foam target for it, so we don't ruin all the bolts." After a few more minutes of rummaging,

Dave came out and quickly had the crossbow ready and the target set up.

He handed Gerd the crossbow. "I hope you have a strong back, it's set pretty tight. It doesn't use sights like the rifle, but a bead and . . . damn dude!"

Gerd yanked the string back and locked it with little apparent effort. He slid a bolt into place and sighted on the target. Gerd fired and the bolt hit a few inches high, but horizontally centered. "Much better."

"Definitely," Dave added. "Again."

Gerd repeated the process and put the next one directly in the middle.

"You'd better stop before you Robin Hood my bolt and ruin it," Dave laughed.

"Can you tighten it? These little wheels make easy to pull back," Gerd said, pointing to the cams.

"Uh . . . sure. I think I have some Allen wrenches handy. However, I think the bolt might punch through a deer if we do that, and I don't want to lose any. Let's leave the setting where it is, gorilla boy." Dave took the crossbow back from Gerd.

"Mathias is coming over tonight. He is bringing some ladies from the camp, and some more real beer!" Gerd said as they walked back to the house. Mathias and the Sizemores lived fairly close to the camps. He was always meeting women there and trying to get them to meet his friends.

"What was wrong with my beer? I still don't understand why you're so happy it's gone."

Gerd smiled and didn't answer.

Hermann, Pieter and Jan had been moving for over an hour without being seen by anyone. They had heard some strange sirens on some vehicles heading back in the direction of the houses Jan had robbed, but nothing else. Hermann saw one of the vehicles, a red one. One of the many markings on it had the word "Fire" in English, raising Hermann's hopes that the American police were not involved. Jan, despite his typical brutality, was a remarkably hands-free thief. It was possible no one would know they were robbed for hours, even days.

"*Ja. Ich verstehe*," Gerd said into the phone.

"Did Mathias get stood up?" Dave asked, while Gerd was on the phone. He must have detected the obvious disappointment in Gerd's voice.

Gerd nodded. "Sorry."

"Damn!" Dave put the box of Twister back in the closet. "The beer and Twister combo would have worked, too, I know it!"

"*Ja . . . Ja . . . tschüs*," Gerd said into the phone, and hung up.

"So what happened?" Dave asked.

Gerd suppressed a smile. Dave was learning German, but much slower than Gerd was learning English. He could still safely rant in German without Dave picking up on too much.

"He say there was a fire several houses down, in someone's shed, this morning. He was helping rebuild it. Also, someone rob two houses, maybe more. They were checking all the houses."

"Well, let's head to T-Gardens. Maybe we'll meet some ladies there." Dave stood up and grabbed his jacket.

"I, uh . . ." Gerd hesitated. He didn't want to risk

running into Hermann and his thugs there. "If these house robbed by someone, maybe we should stay?"

"It was probably just kids, stole some cigarettes and lit the barn up by accident. I'm not worried about it, Scooby has it covered." Scooby, hearing his name, ran to the kitchen full of hopes.

"All right, but . . ." Gerd sighed. He really didn't want to have anything to do with Hermann. "Bring your pistol. In case they not kids, I don't want to get robbed on the way. Also one less thing to steal."

Dave shrugged. "Well, I don't mix beer and guns, but I'm on a mission to find women tonight. I don't want beer goggles interfering with that anyway."

Gerd smiled. He inwardly hoped that Dave would meet Hermann tonight. More to the point, he hoped Dave's .357 would meet Hermann. "All right, let's go."

"What are you worried about, anyway? You pull that crossbow back like it's a slingshot! You could throw some young punk across the street."

Dave decided Gerd was right. They should have stayed home. He was sharing a table with Gerd, three lovely ladies, and Johann, one of the Germans newly inducted into the Army after Jena. It was all probably a perfect evening with friends new and old, except the only other person who spoke English was Gerd. He was too busy flirting and having fun to translate for Dave.

Dave's hopes flared a little when he spotted Tom Simpson. Granted, Tom didn't have any women with him, but he spoke both English and German and was a fun guy. Dave waved him over.

"Hey there L-T!" Dave shook Tom's hand. "Congratulations on a successful military campaign. Care to reap the rewards of peace by helping me chat it up with some of these ladies?"

Tom shook his head. "I'd love to, but I'm here on official business."

"That's a damned shame. What's going on?"

"A few of the new arrivals from Jena failed to muster this morning. They probably deserted, but in case they're screwing around here, we need to grab them. They have some weapons with them. Some of our weapons, that is." Tom was scanning nearby people.

"No shit, huh? There was a fire this morning and some break-ins, you think it might be them?"

"Could be," replied Tom. He turned to the other people at the table and asked them, in German, if they knew or saw anything. Dave was pleased he picked up most of Tom's German. He knew he was a little slow in learning the language. The ladies shook their heads, while Gerd paused before shaking his head. He looked a little ashen.

Johann stood up, in respect for his new superior, before replying with a *nein*.

"All right," Tom said, turning back to Dave. "The bastards probably just took off with a couple of shotguns. We didn't give any ammo to them yet, though. They're likely halfway to Leipzig by now. Damn it!" Tom gnawed on his lower lip hard enough that it looked painful to Dave. "Well, we're going to keep searching around here. Keep your eyes open. They won't be in any uniforms or camouflage, but will have our shotguns. None of them speak a lick of English, to my knowledge."

"All right, hope it works out." Dave shook his hand again.

"Catch you later, thanks." Tom stormed off through the crowd.

Dave and Johann sat back down. Johann started talking with one of the women again. Dave looked across the table, and noticed a face missing.

"Hey, where did Gerd go?" Dave exclaimed. Johann knew little English, but understood the meaning and shrugged. The other ladies did the same. "That's odd. I hope he comes back with some pretzels."

Dave wasn't too worried, Gerd was having fun talking to one of the girls, and would surely be back to pick up where he left off. Dave decided to try again with one of the other ladies.

"So, uh . . . *Wie heisst du?* Whoops, my bad. *Wie heissen Sie?*"

Dave got concerned about Gerd after about an hour and a half. He called back to the house, with no answer. He spent another fifteen minutes walking around the area looking for him, with no luck. Dave decided to head home before the sun set.

When he opened the front door, Scooby was there to meet him.

"Gerd!" Dave hollered. "Where the hell are you?"

He went through all the rooms and around the outside of the house looking for Gerd, with no luck. He finally plopped on the couch and turned on the TV. The marquee said that *Memphis Belle* would start in an hour. Dave hoped Gerd would show up by then. As much as his German friend loved *Top Gun*, he should like tonight's movie. Of course, Dave recalled, it pitted Germans and Americans against each other.

The thought abruptly vanished when loud whining came from the kitchen. Dave stood up and walked towards it.

"I fed you this afternoon, butthead," Dave grumbled. When he got in the kitchen, Scooby was sitting and pawing at the back door, whining and wagging his tail. His bowl was in his mouth. "Ohhh SHIT!"

Hermann heard Jan's quiet whistle. He and Pieter shuffled across the road to Jan's position. The sun had been down for about a half hour, and they were beyond the lights of Grantville. They had followed one of the American highways out, keeping a slow pace, out of sight in the adjacent woods. They finally had to cross it to keep heading northwest. There was no indication the Americans were looking for them, but they kept quiet anyway.

"How much farther do you think?" Hermann whispered.

"Not sure. This is still American land that was put here from the Ring of Fire," Pieter replied. "If what they told us is right, we'll be in German land shortly. The effect ends three miles from the center of town."

"The outhouse we want is about two leagues west of Jena."

"We're on track, sir. We will most likely get there before dawn."

"We may need daylight to find our little treasure." Hermann starting walking, smacking Jan into motion as he passed by.

Pieter and Jan fell in behind him.

"This works out well. We only have to split it three ways, not five. Gerd and Christopher aren't joining us," Hermann snorted. "Poor Christopher is dead and Gerd ran off like a girl months ago."

"He was weak. Good riddance." Pieter spat.

"No," Jan stated flatly.

Hermann turned to look at Jan. He stared for several moments before finally backhanding Jan. "Do I always have to prompt you? Will you *ever* just spit it out without encouragement?"

Jan rubbed his chin and smiled. "I saw him."

Hermann stopped and pointed his shotgun in Jan's face. "For God's sake, man. I think you like it when I hit you. No more games, talk!"

Jan lost the smile. "When we were in the Gardens. He was there. I don't think he saw me."

"Or the rest of us?" Pieter asked.

Jan shrugged.

"Damn!" Hermann hollered. "He might have already grabbed it!"

"I doubt it, sir. He's too soft, and probably has nightmares about that old man. If it is indeed gone, we can always sneak back into town and beat it out of him."

Hermann nodded. "I think I'll send Jan by himself. He'd attract less attention. We'll worry about that if we can't find the sack. We still need to get away from town."

"No, it's not a missing persons issue. He took off. He took my shotgun, too, and who knows what else!" Dave shouted into the phone.

"So this is a robbery? He lives with you . . ."

"Look, who else is on duty?" Dave got frustrated.

"Fred Jordan."

"Put him on." Dave rubbed his temples. Hopefully Fred would see it as a more urgent situation.

"Fred here, what's up?"

"Fred! My boarder, Gerd, has taken off with my shotgun."

"When did you last see him?" Fred asked.

"We were at Thuringen Gardens. I turned to talk to Tom and he took off. I came home an hour or so later, and he wasn't here, and neither was the shotgun."

"Okay. Any idea where he might have gone?" Fred continued, the sound of scribbling audible in the background.

"Not really. I don't think he really had much to drink, either." Dave was glad he didn't have any. He wanted a clear head.

"Does he have any beef with Tom? Did you or Tom say anything that might have pissed him off or something?"

Dave paused for a moment before answering. "No, I don't think he had any problem with Tom. I'm thinking," Dave sighed. "Tom mentioned some missing men from Jena. New guys brought into the Army. He thought they might have deserted."

"All right. I heard that from Tom as well. They sent out a few guys on bikes, but didn't see anything. His boys in Jena have been told to be on the lookout, in case the deserters went that way. You think he joined them?"

"I really have no idea," Dave sighed, knowing the frustration in his voice was too obvious.

"Hey, we'll figure this out, try to relax a little. Tom was going to send some of the new recruits on a combined field exercise and search party. I don't think they're going to find much on foot, though. This counts as enough of an emergency to use the truck. I'll be at your place at dawn. Be ready to roll when I get there." Fred hung up the phone before Dave could say anything else.

Dave went to the closet in his room and yanked the door open. He pulled his M-1 Garand out of the back and headed for the kitchen. He field stripped it and began cleaning.

Hermann squinted in the near darkness. The moon was out, but not full.

"I think we just head west from here," Pieter whispered. The area looked familiar. A faintly visible road wound its way east and west.

"We'll wait here until morning. We won't be able to find the loot without light, and I'd rather sleep now so we can grab it, leave, and get as far away from Grant-ville as possible."

Gerd's legs burned like fire. He didn't know how much of a head start Hermann and the rest had, but he was determined not to miss them on account of not running fast enough.

He had scouted the route once before. It was shortly after Gretchen had set most of the detained soldiers free. He was given the benefit of the doubt at the time for being new to that group of mercenaries. Luckily, no one seemed to know about the horrors he was complicit in committing with the likes of Hermann. Before being picked for Dave's tree-trimming crew, he took a day to find the sack of gold and other trinkets that he helped steal from the old man west of Jena. Jan had hidden the sack in an outhouse, so that Hermann and others wouldn't be forced to "share" with other mercenaries, or have it outright stolen. Gerd had located the sack, and then left it in place, buried in the same sort of filth that desired it. Gerd still had no idea where the old man got all the loot from. It didn't matter if the old man had ten times as much, Gerd thought, it wasn't worth taking a soul. Taking a soul and damning another, he thought.

Gerd ignored the burning in his legs and kept running.

Dave was restless the whole night, and didn't sleep. He had cleaned the Garand four times, and the pistol twice. He heard a car pull up in front of his house as he started to work on the pistol again.

"I don't know when I'm coming back, Scoobs. This is your lucky day." Dave pulled out a large chunk of cooked boar from the freezer and tossed it on the floor. The sun had just peeked over the horizon and Dave heard a honk from outside. He came out of the door with his Garand in hand, and got in the police four by four. Fred put the truck in gear and floored the gas.

"Which way are we headed?" Dave asked.

"For now, we'll just take the highway out. I don't think we need to head to Jena, given that Tom's already got a small garrison up there," Fred replied.

"I hope we just find him walking down one of the highways, though he's been gone long enough to be in German lands by now. We'll hit some of their roads, too, and see what we see. The woods are too dense to really drive into, and there's too much area to cover. If he's not walking alongside a road, this is a lost cause."

"The way I hear it, Tilly's army is north of here. If the deserters don't join back up with them, they'll probably head roughly north, over familiar ground. I can't even guess what Gerd has in mind." Dave slapped a clip into the rifle and pulled his hand free as the bolt slammed shut.

"Damn, man, you going to open up on him with that antique? I hope I never piss you off!"

"Probably won't." Dave smiled. "However, he is armed, and so are the deserters. I'm not sure if he's rushing to join up with them or what. He might even have a grudge against them."

"How much would it bother you if he shot those deserters if, say, they killed his wife or daughter? The way I hear it, many of the guys in these mercenary armies are as much victims as perps," Fred offered. "I'm not sure what Dan or the others would do with him if that's the case. A jury of our peers would let him go."

"Don't talk around it, I heard about that Gretchen thing." Dave smiled. "Frontier justice had a bit of a rebirth after the Ring of Fire."

Hermann saw Jan waving them forward. He and Pieter hustled up to Jan's position. The small cluster of houses was much as they left them months ago, except the houses had long since stopped burning, leaving charred skeletal remains. The rising sun cast long shadows across the ravaged crossroads. The only untouched structure was a lone outhouse.

"Funny the men didn't burn that," Pieter commented.

"Some things are indeed sacred, especially to a soldier," Hermann replied.

The three of them made quick work of tearing the outhouse away from the underlying pit. Jan set his shotgun on the ground and stared inside the hole, with his hands over his eyes.

"Still too dark." Jan stood up and let out a deep breath.

"See if you can't find a large stick or board to fish it out with." Hermann pointed to both Jan and Pieter.

Pieter returned quickly with a hoe retrieved from one of the collapsed barns. "This should work."

Jan took the hoe from Pieter and started poking around in the pit. When he had hidden the bag, he'd tied a rope to it to help later pull it out. He dug around for several minutes before Hermann interrupted.

"Is it in there or not?" he asked.

Jan stood up and shrugged. "Still too dark to tell."

Hermann let out a sigh. "I'd like to know if we have to send you back to Grantville to beat some answers out of our friend Gerd. Would you rather dig in filth all day looking for a sack that isn't there, or be beating the piss out of Gerd by noon?"

Jan smiled. "Beating Gerd."

"That's right. So tell me, will Gerd have the sack, or is it still swimming here in this shit?"

Jan didn't answer. He got back on his belly and continued looking for the sack.

"Got it," Jan said with little emotion, five minutes later. He stood up and pulled the hoe out. A rope was looped around the end.

"Excellent!" Hermann almost grabbed the rope with his bare hands, before remembering where it had been sitting for many months.

Jan took his shirt off and wrapped it around his hands. He grabbed the excrement-soaked rope and pulled out the sack. The sack was equally soaked. Still working with his wrapped hands, he managed to untie the sack. Inside was another, much less soaked sack. Jan threw his shirt down and grabbed the second sack. He pulled it free and set it on the ground with an audible clink.

"Ah hah!" Hermann clapped his hands and laughed.

"Don't worry, my friend, we'll be able to buy you another shirt!" Pieter squealed, patting Jan on the back.

The sound of the bolt flying through the air might have registered in Hermann's mind, but it was moving too fast and too quiet for any of them to even realize what it was before it hit.

Jan staggered back while clutching his lower stomach. The bolt had punched clean through, instantly staining both sides of his undershirt with his own blood.

Gerd set the crossbow on the ground and picked up the shotgun. Instinctively, he had wanted to shoot Hermann first. Logic dictated that Jan, being the most dangerous in a fight, took the first hit.

He sat perfectly still. During their brief hunting trip, Dave told Gerd that camouflage coveralls made a man virtually invisible. The less he moved, the better the concealment. Gerd, having survived the battle at Badenburg, was already a true believer in the American camouflage.

Hermann and Pieter ran for one of the burnt outbuildings while Jan fell to the ground. Pieter fired an unaimed shot into the woods on Gerd's left, sending hundreds of small pellets ripping through the leaves.

Gerd smiled. During his brief shotgun lesson with Dave, Gerd was told to use birdshot only when hunting birds. He had ended up killing their dinner with a slug. Hermann the pig, Gerd thought, will get a slug as well.

Hermann and Pieter dove behind a section of collapsed roof as Gerd lined up his shot. He heard rapid talking followed by a moan from Jan. His fallen form raised an arm and pointed directly at Gerd. Gerd was about to shoot Jan again when Pieter leaned around the piece of roof and fired right where Jan pointed.

Gerd yelped as a couple of sharp stings bit into his shoulder. He clenched his jaw and lined up his shotgun with the piece of roof Pieter and Hermann were using for cover. He fired three rapid shots before pressing himself behind a tree. His shooting was rewarded with a startled grunt of pain from behind the roof.

Two rapid booms accompanied a shower of pellets, but the tree Gerd was behind provided plenty of protection. He slid three more slug shells into his shotgun before breaking cover and charging Hermann and Pieter's position. He had seen Hermann's doubled-barreled shotgun, and knew he would still be reloading. As he approached, he saw Pieter lean back around the roof, shotgun first, with his face partially covered in blood and splinters. Gerd fired from the hip. The shot went high, but forced Pieter to duck back behind the roof.

Gerd racked the slide on the shotgun, and ran to the opposite side of the roof. He turned the corner to find Hermann facing him, his double-barreled shotgun open as he fumbled to put more shells in. Gerd fired from ten feet away. The slug blasted dead center through Hermann's chest, and he collapsed to the ground in a mangled heap.

Pieter scrambled to turn and face Gerd, his backside covered in Hermann's blood. Gerd racked the slide. Pieter dropped his shotgun and threw his hands up. He had managed to make it to his knees. His face was covered in splinters and was bleeding in several places.

"Mercy, my friend," Pieter said quietly.

"You . . . you . . . bastard!" Gerd spat. Some part of him was wishing he had something better to say. His finger crept into the trigger.

"I never made you do . . ." Pieter's reply was cut short by a boom.

For the shortest of instants, Gerd thought he had fired. There was a numbing slap on his left thigh and Pieter went down hard, face first. Gerd struggled to maintain his footing as his thigh began to burn and seize up. As Pieter fell, Gerd saw Jan behind him, smiling and holding a smoking wheel lock. Gerd quickly put the shotgun to his shoulder and fired. The slug caught Jan in the chin and scattered his smile, along with the rest of his head, across the remains of the outhouse.

Gerd crumpled to the ground, his thigh oozing blood. A gurgling bloody cough came from Pieter's fallen form.

"Killed by the maniac Jan," Gerd snorted. He unzipped the coveralls and pulled them past his waist. He removed his belt and did his best to staunch the bleeding.

"Both of us," Pieter hissed through spit and blood. He let out a string of hacking coughs, forming a foamy pool of blood on the ground.

"I think not. You may have saved my life, just by being in the way." Gerd grunted as he tightened the belt over a rolled-up strip of cloth on the wound.

"Pigs."

"You and your two dead friends, sure!" Gerd laughed. He picked his shotgun back up and laid it across his lap.

"No, pigs!" Pieter gurgled. He used his head to nod in the direction Gerd came from.

Gerd looked over his shoulder and saw several wild pigs trotting from the woods. Using both his hands and one good leg, he spun around to face them. Pieter hacked out rough laughter.

"What are you laughing for? I've still got some fight in me. You don't." Gerd wasted no time, using his three-"legged" crawl, in distancing himself from Pieter. He topped off the ammo in the shotgun, and held it at the ready. He had two shells left in his pocket.

The animals approached Hermann's corpse first. They sniffed it briefly before taking a few tentative bites. Pieter's hacking cough and desperate attempts to move got their attention, and they approached him.

Gerd thought he might enjoy watching the pigs eat the bastards that had damned him. Hearing Pieter's screams changed his mind, quickly. He fired one round into Pieter's side, instantly silencing him. The shot sent the pigs running.

Gerd allowed himself to relax for a moment. He didn't feel his soul was any more or less damned, but he sensed profound satisfaction and closure, knowing all others involved were dead.

The pigs quickly regrouped. Gerd shuffled over towards the outhouse pit. He knew Jan's discarded shotgun would have more shells in it, even if they were likely birdshot. He propped his shotgun on his good knee, forcing himself to keep an eye on the pigs as they split their work between Hermann and Pieter.

Jan had one more wheel lock pistol hanging from his belt. Gerd took it. He struggled to his feet, and took a few tentative steps. He leg throbbed with deep, dull pain. He limped away slowly, looking over his shoulder. Several of the pigs started to follow him. He fired the wheel lock at one, missing. The pigs scattered. They quickly gathered again at the fallen bodies, apparently deciding Gerd wasn't worth the effort. He slung the shotgun over his shoulder, and concentrated on walking.

"What do we have here?" Fred brought the truck to a slow stop.

The small crossroads they approached contained the remains of a few burnt houses. There were several carcasses strewn about. They looked like men, given only that they had bloody clothing more or less on them. There were several pigs gnawing on the bodies. Some ran back into the woods at the sight of the truck

"If Gerd doesn't magically float down on a cloud and into the truck in five minutes, I say we get the hell out of here!" Dave clicked the safety off his Garand.

"You don't have to tell me, mister," Fred pulled his .45 from his holster.

The two got out of the truck and slowly approached the pigs. One turned to face them and Dave fired, dropping the squat animal where it stood. The remaining ones scattered.

"Any of them Gerd?" Fred asked quietly.

"I don't think so. These guys are all dressed like Germans. Gerd was fond of jeans." Dave started approaching one that appeared to be missing a head. As he did, his foot snagged on something. He looked down to see a crossbow bolt stuck in the ground. An aluminum one. "He was here."

"Check this out!" Fred said excitedly. He was tapping a sack with his foot. Several of the contents had spilled out. They all shined brilliantly. "If Gerd was here, why did he kill them and leave this stuff?" Dave didn't answer.

Dave and Fred gathered the shotguns left on the ground and put them in the four by four. Dave put the sack in the truck as well. It smelled like it had been marinating in the outhouse for some time.

"Jeff is going to get a kick out of this," Dave giggled, pointing at the sack.

"Out of *that*?" Fred waved his hand in front of his nose. He bungied the sack down tight.

"Yeah, *that*. Amazing what wonderful treasures can be found in German outhouses."

Fred let out a tired laugh and motioned Dave inside the truck.

"We've retrieved most of the weapons, and found the deserters. I don't think we're going to find Gerd unless he wants to be found. Sorry, Dave, but we've got to head back into town and let Tom know. I can't justify burning any more gas over this whole ordeal," Fred said.

Dave nodded without comment.

Gerd had been convinced for the last hour that his next step would send him falling to the ground, and that he wouldn't be getting back up. It had been slow but steady going all morning, but as the afternoon wore on, he was beginning to have doubts about his leg. It was with great relief that he found the edge of the American road. Somehow, leaving behind the brutal world of mercenaries, torture and nonstop war had a physical effect he could feel. Over the months, the perfectly cut dirt wall had been smoothed out to a dirt slope connecting the German landscape with the American one. He eased his way down the slope, grunting with each step.

He wasn't sure how soon it would be before an American vehicle would travel by and see him. *Not soon enough*. The bleeding from his wound had stopped, but his leg was still swelling and seemed to get more tender with each step. As he had done for the past hour, he overrode the pain with willpower, and hobbled on.

Ten minutes later, biology overrode willpower, and Gerd found himself hurling towards the ground. He caught himself in the tumble, and managed to prevent any further injury. He tentatively worked his injured leg. It didn't budge, and he was instead rewarded with intense pain.

Gerd took off his shirt and bundled it under his head before zipping up Dave's hunting coveralls. He considered leaving the top unzipped and pulled down, knowing his white chest would catch a driver's attention much easier than the camouflage coveralls, but the afternoon sun was making its way to the horizon and was taking the temperature with it.

The events of the day, and being finally off his feet, quickly caught up with him. Gerd recalled something he read from Dave's small collection of textbooks from, as Dave called it, his "aborted college days" from the late twentieth century. He knew his body was on a collapse from an adrenaline surge, and he realized he'd had nothing to eat since the previous night. *Gute Nacht, Gerd,* was the last full thought he remembered before losing himself in the gentle shuffle of leaves and trees lining the American road.

"No, NO!" screamed Dave.

Gerd hesitated, earning a backhand from Hermann.

"You gutless cur, he's obviously hiding something!" screamed Hermann.

Jan pulled back on Dave's arms tighter and smiled. "Do it."

Gerd tried to postpone the inevitable by reheating the knife over the candle.

"For God's sake, young pup," growled Hermann. He grabbed the hand Gerd was holding the knife with. "The longer you wait, the longer Dave suffers." Hermann guided, by force, Gerd's knife-wielding hand towards Dave's stomach.

Gerd jerked the knife away from Dave's stomach and shoved it into Hermann's chest. "What in the hell are you sick bastards thinking?" Gerd screamed. He rammed the shotgun that suddenly appeared in his hands against Jan's face and pulled the trigger. Gerd was slightly surprised, as Jan's head exploded exactly as he knew it would.

"Mercy, my friend," Pieter oinked through his snout, as Gerd swung the shotgun towards him. Hermann's corpse turned into a pig and started nibbling on Pieter. "Mercy," Pieter said again, before being consumed.

"Let it go, Gerd. Let it go and come with me," Dave said. He turned and started walking out of the house and towards Grantville. "Let it all go, Gerd. Have a beer, watch a movie with me and Scoobs, and just leave all this behind."

Gerd struggled to follow Dave to Grantville, but found he couldn't walk fast enough, much less run. His leg wouldn't cooperate. Dave walked farther, looking over his shoulder and beckoning to Gerd.

Jan's headless form sat up and somehow started speaking, very loudly. "FRED DAMN NEAR RAN OVER YOU, YOU'RE ONE LUCKY SON OF A BITCH!"

Gerd sat up in a flinch. He was in the back seat of a police four by four, and Dave was in the front passenger seat and was still talking.

"If we hadn't driven by, you might have been lying there a bit longer. By the looks of your leg, you couldn't afford a bit longer. How in the hell did you make it this far on that leg anyhow?" Dave's voice betrayed an enormous amount of concern.

Gerd rubbed his eyes hard. Sleep was still drawing him in, and he tried to fight it off. "What happened?" He felt his voice come out in a croak.

The man driving the truck spoke up. "We might ask you the same thing, Gerd." Gerd remembered his name as Fred, one of Grantville's deputies. "We had three dead men back there, or what the pigs left of them. You didn't make off with their weapons, or that sack full of goodies. In fact, given where we found you, I'd say you were trying to hobble your way back to town. What gives?"

Gerd sat up slowly, shifting his weight to his right side as his left leg quickly reminded him of the lead ball still inside. "They were murderers. Thieves, rapists and murderers."

"Not to mention burglars and arsonists." Fred grumbled. "I take it they did their murdering before the Ring of Fire. You knew them from Tilly's army?"

Gerd nodded.

"Dare I ask how you became aware of their crimes?" Fred shifted his gaze from the road to the rear view mirror, looking right at Gerd.

Gerd shook his head.

"Punished outside Grantville for crimes committed outside Grantville. Hell, crimes committed before

Grantville even existed," Dave said. Gerd caught Dave giving Fred a knowing look.

Fred's mouth bunched up in a suppressed smile and he shook his head. "As much as I criticized it before the Ring of Fire, I'm starting to miss the American criminal justice system."

Reverend Jones opened the door to find a large, dirty sack sitting at the stairs. A young man was walking away and towards a police truck.

"Hey, there! What's this about?" Reverend Jones asked.

The young man got into the truck before answering.

"Don't ask. It ain't a perfect world. Just put it to good use, Reverend." The truck pulled away.

It ain't a perfect world, the minister thought. *That would be a good intro into my next sermon.*

He leaned over to pick up the sack, and was caught off guard by the odor.

"Thanks Ms. Nichols," Dave said. "Don't be too gentle on him, though."

"He's a cutie; I can't make any promises!" Sharon replied, before turning to Gerd. "What happened to you, anyway?"

"I . . . uh . . . plead the fifth," Gerd stammered.

"Hey Gerd!" Dave hollered from the truck.

"Yes?" Gerd replied.

"If you have any other dark secrets in your past, can you get them sorted out before you come home? I'd just as soon not risk getting in the way!" The truck pulled away before Gerd could respond.

"Dark secrets, huh?" Sharon asked, dubious, as she led Gerd into the first aid tent.

"I plead the fourth? I thought it *was* the fifth! The sixth then?"

A Witch to Live

Walt Boyes

A. M. D. G.

He looked at the letters he'd just written at the top of the page. "*Ad Majorem Dei Gloriam*," he breathed. "To the greater glory of God." He calmed himself as he had been taught in his novitiate, and began to write.

"Father Friedrich von Spee, of the Society of Jesus, to His Excellency, Mutius Vitelleschi, Father General of the Society," he wrote.

Branches slapped her face, roots grabbed at her feet. Veronica ran, exhausted and terrified. The forest was dark and there was no moon. She could hear the baying of the dogs behind her. Were they getting closer? She couldn't tell. She ran on. Her breath was tearing in her lungs. The pounding of her heart felt like hammer blows throughout her body. Behind her, the baying grew louder.

Suddenly she broke into a clearing. She had been braced to push branches out of her way and their sudden absence sent her sprawling. She spat the dirt and leaves from her mouth and scrabbled to her feet, swaying. She turned and faced back the way she'd run. Her face shaped a rictus of terror. She slowly backed up as the first dogs broke through the brush into the clearing.

She put up her arms to try to defend herself against the fangs of the dogs and kept backing up. She started as her back came up against something. It was the stump of a tree. She whirled around it, trying to keep it between her and the dogs. The stump was thin, only about a foot in diameter, and broken off just above her head. It was too small to hide behind, and too short to climb. The dogs snapped and snarled around her.

Voices and then horses and men carrying torches burst from the forest. A troop of cavalry surrounded the clearing and a couple of troopers took their crops and beat the dogs off the woman. The packmaster collected the dogs to one side of the clearing as two of the riders dismounted.

"Well, Father Eberhardt, what have we here?" The taller of the two spoke. He was tall, run to fat, and wearing a back and breast that could have used a polish. His pot helmet was still lashed to his saddle horn. "The witch, as I live and breathe!" In the torchlight, she could see the grin on his face, and her heart stuttered in her chest.

"Veronica Junius; the witch indeed," Father Eberhardt replied, pulling out his prayerbook. "Get her tied up and we can take her back."

"What for? We've got a nice stake she's hugging there. Let's burn her right here and get it over with."

"Captain, please," the priest bridled like a banty rooster. "There are forms we must follow. She has been found guilty of witchcraft, yes. But only in an ecclesiastical court. She must be relaxed to the civil arm, tried again and then you can burn her. Tomorrow. In Würzburg."

"What? And give that damned Jesuit, Von Spee, a chance to try to get her off? You heard what he wrote in his devil-inspired book, didn't you? She's a witch! She needs to burn! You know what she knows! We will take her to Suhl!"

Eberhardt spluttered as the soldier's fist grabbed his soutane and lifted him partway off his feet.

"Do you want to try me, priest? I want her dead, and His Excellency wants her dead. I have my instructions from the bishop. We will take her to Suhl, and burn her there. She has no friends in Suhl." The priest nodded and the captain released him and turned away.

"Get ready to move out!" he commanded. "We've a long way to go!"

The priest and the captain mounted. Two burly troopers muscled the woman onto the priest's horse behind him, and tied her to the saddle. The packmaster busied himself rounding up the dogs.

The troops dressed lines, and the captain motioned them forward.

<∞-∞>   <∞-∞>   <∞-∞>

Father Spee was still writing. "It is with a chastened heart that I accept your rebuke, Father General. I will amend myself so that in the future I will keep better control over such writings as *Cautio Criminalis* so that they are not printed against my wishes. But, with respect, Excellency, I must tell you that nothing in the work is false. I have attended the confessions of over two hundred witches up to now, and I have never heard one confess except after torture and the rack."

Von Spee put his pen down. He stood in his bedroom. It was spare, small and had a simple crucifix on the white, stuccoed wall as its only decoration. There was a bed against one wall, several shelves of books and papers, and the desk at which he had been writing. He stretched his neck, thought about sitting down and completing his letter, and then decided against it. He went to the bookshelf and took down a thin, well-thumbed volume. He looked at the title, *Spiritual Exercises* by Ignatius Loyola. How many times in his forty years of life had he read the book, done the exercises? He could not count.

"Eternal Lord of all things," he read, "I make my oblation with Thy favor and help, in presence of Thy infinite Goodness and in presence of Thy glorious Mother and of all the Saints of the heavenly Court; that I want and desire, and it is my deliberate determination, if only it be Thy greater service and praise, to imitate Thee in bearing all injuries and all abuse and all poverty of spirit, and actual poverty, too, if Thy most Holy Majesty wants to choose and receive me to such life and state."

Friedrich von Spee closed the book, put it back on the shelf, and taking his breviary, went down to the chapel to pray and to reflect.

The chapel was dark, with only a few candles and the Presence lamp lit. Through the tall, narrow, stained-glass windows, the late afternoon sun made colored pools on the floor. Von Spee breathed deeply as he entered. He loved the smell of the chapel. The scent of years of melting beeswax and incense was to him the odor of sanctity. He moved quietly down the main aisle, paused before the altar to genuflect, and knelt at the altar steps. As he knelt, he began to relax his mind, as he had been taught, and prepared to pray. He was grateful for all of the years of the discipline of the Society and the *Spiritual Exercises*. His mind quieted, and he grew still.

Von Spee remained kneeling motionless before the altar for several hours. He really did not notice the passage of time. In his mind, he saw again the images of the trials of the witches he'd seen. He saw the brave, the timid, the intelligent and the foolish all reduced to terror by application of the proper instruments of persuasion. He heard again the confessions to the judges. He saw the victims, for that is what he knew them to be, as they went to their deaths. He heard again many of them cursing God as they died.

"Lord Jesus," he prayed silently, "give me the strength to continue. Give me the courage to witness, and to comfort these poor innocents."

As he prayed, a sense of calm, of peace descended on him. Finally, he felt a sense of release. He stirred, stood, genuflected, and walked briskly down the aisle. He signed himself as he pushed open the heavy chapel door. There was the sound of activity coming from the gates. Curious, he moved to the top of the stairs.

The courtyard gate opened to admit a party on horseback. It was dark, and the group was preceded by linkboys with torches. As they moved into the courtyard, the light from a torch illuminated the face of one of the riders.

"Johann!" Von Spee rushed down the stairs into the courtyard. "My friend, I have not seen you in too long! What brings you to Würzburg?"

"It is you I have come to see, Friedrich." The man swung down from his saddle, and gripped von Spee's forearms in greeting.

"Come in, come in, then. We are just sitting down to supper, have you eaten?"

"Not yet. I was hoping to beg a meal and a bed from you this evening."

"No begging needed. We can talk during our meal."

Von Spee motioned to a young man in the robe of a novice.

"Albert, this is His Excellency Johann Philip von Schönborn, from Mainz. Father von Schönborn is secretary to the prince-bishop. He is an old student of mine from when I taught at the seminary in Trier. Have his horses and his party seen to, please. I will show him to his room."

The novice motioned to the guardsmen and the servants to follow him. Attendants took the horses off to the small stable on the first floor of the residence. The guards closed the courtyard gate after the linkboys were paid and sent off.

Von Spee turned and ascended the stairs, von Schönborn behind him.

Supper was light, as was common in a Jesuit residence. There was a plate of meat and some vegetables, some bread and a light wine, followed by fruit and cheese. Although born to noble families, neither priest missed the extravagant meals of court life. Both were spare and thin, Father von Spee to the point of gauntness.

"I have been using some of your hymns in the services at Mainz, Friedrich," Johann said around a slice of apple. "You have a way with words and the people seem to enjoy singing them. When will you print them in a songbook?"

"Probably never. They are simply scribblings, of no real account." Friedrich carved a piece of cheese, and stared at it. "And besides, I've just gotten into trouble for a book that *was* printed." He popped the piece of cheese into his mouth.

"Ah, yes! The *Cautio Criminalis*."

"Yes, that."

"You know, Friedrich, pardon me for saying this, but you are not looking well. How old are you now, forty?"

"Yes, yes, I am forty."

"Yet your hair is already gray, like an old man! And you keep yourself fit, too. So what is the problem, my friend?"

"It is the witchcraft trials, Johann. I do not know how much more of this I can stand."

"What do you mean?"

"It is regret that has turned my hair all gray," Friedrich said, looking at his hands, "regret that I have had to accompany so many witches to the place of execution and among them I found not one who was not innocent."

Johann stared at his older friend. "Not a single guilty one?"

"No."

"I have read your tract. Do you really believe that it is the torture that gets them all to confess? And that they are confessing false things to keep from being tortured again?"

"That is what I believe. It is not possible that so many people of stature, such as the nephew of the bishop of Bamberg, and the chancellor and several burgomasters there, could all be witches!"

"Do you not believe in witches, then?" Johann asked, his winecup poised.

"Of course I do! The Bible says they exist, and the Church says they exist, and I firmly believe they do exist. It is just that . . ." Friedrich's voice tailed off. He looked past Johann to a point in space.

"That what?" Johann prompted.

"I do not see how hanging someone from the ceiling with weights on their feet and bouncing them at the end of the rope can possibly be used to tell if they are lying or not!"

"Yes, I don't like the strappado either. Or the screws. Or the rack. But what else is there to do?"

"Look, Johann, you were good at logic when I taught it to you," Friedrich leaned forward intensely. "Is it logical to assume that someone who is being tortured will eventually tell the truth if they are tortured enough, or is it more logical to assume that they will say anything, anything at all, simply to stop the pain?"

Johann looked away. The silence grew intense. Finally he spoke.

"Have you heard about this new city that has appeared in Thuringia? It appeared like magic, they say, and is filled with warlocks and witches."

"You can't catch me out like that." Friedrich laughed, finishing his wine. "I have been writing to a friend of mine who is at the University in Jena."

"You have Protestant friends?" Johann said, eyebrow raised.

"Of course. How else to know the enemy?" Friedrich replied, smiling. "The city is called Grantville, which is English, and the people call themselves Americans and claim to have come from a time in the future when the New World is highly populated. Professor von Muenster, in Jena, has even been there, and says that though the things they have, and their works, are marvelous, they are artisans of great power, not warlocks."

"How did they come to be in Thuringia?" Johann replied.

"None of them knows. It is considered by them to be a miracle. Von Muenster writes that they have a very clear set of laws, and they are a republic, like the Dutch."

"What do they think of witches, then?" Johann asked.

"They don't believe in them," Friedrich said starkly. "They don't believe in them at all."

He paused, sitting still for a moment, then he turned to his friend.

"Johann, what if they are right? What if there are no witches? What if all the people we've burned are innocents? I have seen more than two hundred people burned! How can I face Almighty God with that on my soul, if there are no witches?"

"Ach, Friedrich," Johann said. He paused, then he breathed deeply.

"Now I must tell you the reason for my visit," he said slowly.

Von Spee looked at him, horror slowly dawning in his eyes.

"Eberhardt, the bishop's inquisitor in Bamberg has chased down the daughter of that man, Junius, who was the burgomaster of Bamberg before he was burned. He is taking her to Suhl, and will be trying her again there. He aims to burn her in Suhl because she has too many friends in Bamberg. My master the prince-bishop was informed of this by one of his intelligencers. He has sent me to ask you to go there and make sure that the trial is conducted properly."

Von Spee rubbed his face with one hand, and pushed back his hair.

"Why me? I am not in good odor with either the bishop of Bamberg or my own father general at the moment. You know his true mind, what does the prince-bishop expect me to do at Suhl?"

Johann looked at him, light from the table candle glittering reflected in his eyes.

"He too has read your tract. He is concerned as we all are, that innocent people may be suffering the vilest torture. And even though the Protestants also hunt witches, he is concerned that these trials are giving the Holy Office a terrible reputation. The Church, he says, should not compel its children to obey out of fear of torture."

He met von Spee's eyes. "He is a good man, Friedrich. He needs you to go, and report to him."

Von Spee straightened in his chair. He looked

off into space for a few moments, and then sighed deeply.

"Very well, I shall go to Suhl. But I am going for myself, not for the prince-bishop, or the Society of Jesus. I am going for Friedrich von Spee, nothing more. And if she is innocent, I will not let her burn."

Johann nodded. "I think," he said slowly, "that my master will be pleased."

Von Spee blew out his breath. He rose.

"I must see to some things, if I am to leave in the morning, Johann."

"I believe that I and my guards will ride with you. We will have access to extra horses, and we will keep you safe," Johann said. "In the morning, then."

"In the morning, Johann."

Friedrich von Spee sat at the outside table at the Inn of the White Swan in Suhl, watching. He and von Schönborn had arrived earlier that morning. Von Schönborn was at the episcopal palace, delivering papers and seeing to the guardsmen. Friedrich had taken a walk through Suhl. They had arrived before Eberhardt, for which he was grateful.

An enormous American officer leaned over the left fender of a big metal vehicle and wiped his wet rag on the glass. The big metal wagon was standing in front of the inn where they were staying. Von Spee stared at it, thinking that it reminded him very much of the woodcuts he had seen of a Bohemian war wagon. There was another officer, not so large, using a brush and a bucket filled with soapy water on the wheels and the sides of the wagon.

The huge soldier had taken the armor off so he

could wash the curved glass window in the front of the wagon and get the mud and smoke and guck off it.

"Hey Tom," the other soldier called, "Want a beer?"

"Sure, Heinrich, I'm just about finished here. We've got us a nice, clean APC. Just gimme a minute to put this back." Tom lifted the huge metal plate and set it gently down over the window of the war wagon. Heinrich tightened the bolts on the right side of the truck, while Tom did those on the left. "Tom" had an unusual accent but his German was fluent, von Spee noted, while "Heinrich" was clearly a native speaker. The only word von Spee could not understand was "aaypaysee" but it was clear that it was the name of the war wagon.

Finished, the two American soldiers strode to one of the other tables outside the inn and sat down not far from von Spee. Von Spee had his breviary out but was not reading. Fascinated, he just sat and listened. The barmaid brought beer, smiling.

"I'm glad you did that, not me," Heinrich said, blowing the head off his beer and taking a drink. "You are stronger than two oxen! And I hope to the Good God that you don't ever get mad enough at me to forget I'm your commander!"

"Me? Violent?" Tom slurped his own brew. "How could you ever think that? I am wounded, Captain! Wounded!"

"You are a big bullshitter, Tom Simpson. After you picked that one drunken bastard up and tossed him right through the door of this very inn, you can say that to me?" Heinrich declaimed.

"Yeah, well." Simpson drank his beer.

"You know, Heinrich, this garrison duty beats the

hell out of marching around, and it sure beats fighting, but it is awful damn boring."

"*Ja,* Tom, but you know, it isn't going to be boring forever."

"You think they'll come through Suhl?"

"I don't know, but it is a good bet."

"When will they come?"

"Who knows? Don't get all, how do you Americans say it, all stressed out, *ja,* that's it . . . don't get all stressed out over it, eh? They will come when they come. It is our job to be ready."

"Yeah, well, I guess I ought to go out and see how the breastworks are coming."

"Tom, stop. Listen to me. Our men know what they are doing. You know that. What do you think they will do if you keep going out and looking over their shoulders?"

"I guess they'll think I'm nervous."

Heinrich nodded. "That's right. And you are. But you can't let them see it. So have another beer, and let's finish cleaning up the APC."

"*Hauptmann* Heinrich! Captain!" One of the sentries at the breastworks was running toward them. "Soldiers! Some *soldaten* coming are!"

"Who are they?" Heinrich asked.

"Don't know," the runner panted. "They have no banner. It is a small troop, but they have dogs and a woman with them."

"A woman?" Heinrich asked. Von Spee tensed, knowing who the soldiers and the woman must be.

"*Ja, Hauptmann!* She is riding behind one of the men."

Abruptly, Heinrich stood.

"We will come. Tell them to keep them at the gate. But do not fire on them!"

"*Ja, Hauptmann!*" The runner tore off back toward the American emplacements.

"Good, now Tom, let us go finish our beer, and then make an appearance."

"I see," said Tom. "It wouldn't do for either our men, or our visitors to believe that we were too anxious. Did I get it right?"

"Right in one." Heinrich smiled.

"Should we take the APC?"

"I don't think so. Let us walk."

"Suits me, Captain," Simpson said.

Von Spee waited until the two officers had gotten a couple of buildings down the street, and then he stood and tucked his breviary into the sash of his cassock, and quietly followed the soldiers.

The commander of the troop of soldiers was arguing with one of Heinrich's guards when Heinrich and Tom arrived at the gate. The American troops stood, and saluted as Heinrich walked up. Von Spee stopped, and stood in a doorway far enough away so he would not be noticed.

"What is going on, Sergeant Massaniello?" Heinrich asked, pleasantly. Simpson stood behind him, a little to one side.

Sergeant Massaniello, the soldier in command of the detachment, reported.

"This gentleman wishes to enter Suhl, sir!" Massaniello spoke in heavily accented German, obviously a courtesy to the strangers.

"And why does he wish to do that, Sergeant?" Heinrich asked, also in German.

"It appears that they have caught themselves a witch, sir, and they want to bring her in and put her on trial."

Tom Simpson began to look very angry. Von Spee sharpened his gaze, and looked closely at the huge American. Simpson started forward. Heinrich held up his hand. Simpson stood still. Heinrich thought, then he moved forward.

"*Guten Tag*," he said. "Good day."

"I am Captain Wolfgang, *Ritter* von Brun," the mounted commander replied. "I am the Commander of the Guard of His Eminence, Bishop Friedrich von Hatzfeld, of Würzburg-Bamberg. This is Father Joachin Eberhardt, the bishop's inquisitor."

Heinrich smiled. "I am Captain Heinrich Schmidt, of the Army of the United States. This is Lieutenant Thomas Simpson, and Sergeant Lawrence Massaniello. Welcome to Suhl, *mein Herr Ritter*. May I ask your purpose in coming here?"

"Father Eberhardt and I would like to use the courtroom here in Suhl, and the town square."

"For what?"

"We have apprehended a notorious witch, already tried before the ecclesiastical court in Bamberg, and we want to relax her to the secular authorities and burn her."

Von Spee noticed that all of the Grantville men were standing now, intent on von Brun. Each of the American soldiers appeared to be carrying an odd type of arquebus, small, and very light. Friedrich saw that all the guns were pointed at the incoming troop.

"Fine then," Heinrich said. "You may safely leave her with us. It appears that you may not have known

Suhl has been accepted as one of the United States. It is very recent, so. We will have her sent to Grantville for the trial. You need not accompany her further, if you wish." Von Spee found himself moving forward, slowly, almost without his own volition. He stopped himself and stood still. No one had noticed him standing there.

"What do you mean, you will have to send her to Grantville? The woman is guilty, and she must burn. We will stay with her until this is done."

"Perhaps Father Eberhardt would like to come with her, but there is no need for you to trouble yourself further, *Herr Ritter*."

"Why are you interfering? All we want to do is to burn this witch! Why is this causing a problem?"

"It is not our policy to permit armed troops of foreign princes on United States soil, Captain. If you wish to enter Suhl, you must do so unarmed."

"This is preposterous! If I wish to enter Suhl I *will* enter Suhl. I am the *Ritter* von Brun. I don't have to give up my weapons to any jumped-up peasant in rusty armor!"

"But I am not a jumped-up peasant," Heinrich said, still pleasantly. "I am a sovereign citizen of the United States. Suhl is now part of the United States. And in the United States, *Herr Ritter*, my blood is as good as yours."

"Then perhaps we should do something about this United States of yours. Stand aside. I will enter Suhl." The *Ritter* was incensed.

"Your pardon, *Herr Ritter*, but unless you agree to disarm, you will not." There was steel in Heinrich's voice. Von Spee watched as unobtrusively each of the troopers had moved into positions of high alert. The Bamberger horses stamped and neighed nervously.

"I see six of you, and there are more than a dozen of us," Captain von Brun declared.

"I would think again," Heinrich began.

Friedrich would always remember how suddenly it happened. It was like a hot rock dropped into a cooking pot.

Veronica began to struggle with the priest she was riding behind.

One of the Americans raised his rifle. A Bamberger trooper pulled one of his horse pistols, fired at the American and missed. The American fired back and didn't miss. Von Brun drew his saber, preparing to ride Heinrich down. Even though Von Spee was standing directly behind Heinrich, he felt paralyzed.

A small hole appeared in von Brun's forehead as the back of his head sprayed away on the trooper behind him. Tom Simpson held a squarish silver handgun with smoke coming from the hole in the muzzle. The *Ritter* von Brun slid out of the saddle. Von Spee vomited. He'd seen death before, but usually in the hospitals where he regularly served as a nurse. Never before had he seen such an explosion of violence.

"Everybody stand still!" Heinrich ordered. "You," he pointed at one of the Americans, "get the woman. You, take the priest. Bring them along. Tom, make sure that these soldiers are disarmed and find housing for them. Oh yes, and see if any of them would like to join the United States Army."

"*Jawohl,* Captain!" the enormous lieutenant replied.

"And find someplace to bury the *Ritter* von Brun."

Heinrich snorted, turned and strode back down the street into Suhl toward the inn. He immediately ran into von Spee, still paralyzed, standing over the puddle of his vomit in the street.

"Who are you?" Heinrich demanded.

Von Spee shook himself. He wiped his mouth with a handkerchief from the sleeve of his cassock, hawked, spit into the handkerchief, and met Heinrich's eyes.

"I am Father Friedrich von Spee, of the Society of Jesus. I have been sent to Suhl by the prince-bishop of Mainz to witness the trial of a woman from Bamberg. I believe that is the woman, there." He pointed to Veronica. "It is my charge to see to it that no innocents are burned as witches any longer." He held his head proudly, and stared at the American captain and at Father Eberhardt. Eberhardt glared back. Heinrich slowly nodded, thoughtfully.

"Come along, then."

By the time Simpson and Massaniello had sorted out the bishop's soldiers, and brought Father Eberhardt and the woman to the square in front of the inn, a large crowd had gathered.

Heinrich had brought together the tables from the inn and moved them out into the square. He was sitting, waiting. Von Spee sat beside him. The crowd parted and Johann von Schönborn and his guards marched to the table. Along with him was the burgomaster of Suhl. The burgomaster sat next to von Spee at the table.

The American troops lined up at one side of the table, and the prince-bishop's guard, unarmed but in armor, took the other side. Tom Simpson walked around behind the table and stood at Heinrich's side. Von Schönborn stood just behind von Spee. Eberhardt and Veronica Junius stood before the table facing them.

Heinrich nodded to the burgomaster, who began to speak.

"We have not yet learned to be truly Americans," he said. "But I have been studying the Constitution very hard, *ja*. And it is part of our new Constitution that nobody can be forced to confess against his or her own will. Since Fraulein Junius has been tortured, we must assume that her confession to the crime of witchcraft was forced. Captain Schmidt has suggested that it would be best if we sent this woman to Grantville where she can be tried again according to our new laws, and I have agreed. So be it done."

Eberhardt began to protest, but it was soon obvious that no one wanted to listen to him.

"Massaniello, take Fraulein Junius and Father Eberhardt to Grantville and turn them over to Dan Frost and Father Mazzare." Heinrich spun around, pointing and giving orders. "Tom, take the bishop of Bamberg's guards back to the checkpoint and send them on their way back to Bamberg, as soon as His Excellency here can have a copy of his judgment ready for them to take with them."

He turned to von Spee and von Schönborn. "And what will you do now, Reverend Sirs?"

Johann smiled, and looked at Friedrich. "I must be back on my way to Mainz immediately, Captain."

Von Spee looked at his hands thoughtfully. "I have a letter to finish," he said, "but I think I will accompany Fraulein Junius to Grantville if I may." He looked at Heinrich for permission.

"Yes," the American captain said, "I think that would be wise."

"Father, Father! Father Mazzare! Where are you?" The elderly woman, with von Spee behind her, barged into the garage of the rectory. There was another one of the metal vehicles, with a man's legs sticking out from under the front part.

The man started, banged his head on the underside of the vehicle, muttered some words Von Spee didn't understand, then came out from under the vehicle. Von Spee stood in the doorway watching as the man, covered with grease, sat up on a peculiar rolling cart.

"What is it, Mrs. Flannery?" The man—Father Mazzare, apparently—rolled off the odd, low-slung cart and got to his knees, holding his head.

"Oh, Father," Mrs. Flannery gasped, holding her palm to her mouth. "What happened?" She ran to him and helped him up.

"Nothing, really. You startled me when you came in, and I banged my head on the engine mount. I'll be fine in a few minutes. Yeah, fine."

She muttered to herself.

"What? I didn't hear you, Mrs. F," Mazzare said.

"I *said* that it just isn't seemly for a priest of God to be getting all dirty and greasy working on the underparts of cars. That what I said! And that's what I believe, too!" Her glare was trying to melt him into a puddle on the floor.

"Yes, well, so you've said before," Mazzare sighed, and pushed himself to his feet.

"But what brings you looking for me, Mrs. F? I thought you were too angry to be here."

"This gentleman here asked me to come fetch you for Dr. Adams. Sergeant Massaniello has brought in another one."

"Another one?" Mazzare looked nonplussed. "Oh, you mean another poor woman who's been accused of witchcraft. I'll get changed and go. Is she at Dr. Adams' office?"

"Yes. But Father, what are we going to do if one of these days we get a real one? A witch, I mean."

"Mrs. Flannery, I'm surprised at you. There's no such thing as witches."

"Not in our time, maybe. But there must have been witches back in this terrible time. After all, they were burning a lot of them. It seems to me that there just has to be some truth to it."

"I've never heard of any," Mazzare replied, shaking his head. "Please tell Dr. Adams it'll be about an hour. I need to take a shower and shave, and get dressed."

"You'll wear your cassock, Father?" the old woman encouraged.

"Yes, I'll wear my cassock! The poor woman who's been accused will probably have a hard enough time believing I'm a priest without it."

"Well, then I'll go tell Dr. Adams. Good night, Father."

"Good night, Mrs. Flannery."

Mrs. Flannery turned and shepherded von Spee before her. Friedrich said nothing, and turned obediently back into the rectory. As he and the old woman moved down the hallway to the door, he heard the American priest singing, horribly off key.

"I am I, Don Quixote, the Lord of La Mancha! My destiny calls and I go!"

Friedrich von Spee smiled as he puzzled out the words of the song. He had always enjoyed the exploits of the Dubious Knight. He was beginning to feel even a stronger kinship with the addled old hidalgo. Or was it more likely a kinship with Sancho Panza? He hurried to follow the bustling old woman out into the night.

Massaniello paced the front room of Dr. Adams' combined house and clinic. At the sound of the knock, he strode to the door and opened it.

"Hi, Father, come on in."

Mazzare entered and shook the big coal miner's hand.

"Sit down, Father," Massaniello offered. The priest sat in one of the armchairs in the sitting room. Massaniello sat down, too.

"How is she?" the priest asked.

Massaniello took a deep breath.

"Well, she was running to Grantville when they caught her," he began.

"She wasn't running very fast, I'll bet." A deep voice interrupted from the door of the clinic.

Mazzare turned toward it. Dr. Jeffrey Adams strode through the door into the parlor with his hand outstretched. The messenger Mazzare had seen at the rectory entered the parlor behind him. Chief of Police Dan Frost came in last of all.

"Father Larry, how are you?" Adams greeted him. Frost nodded at the priest.

"I'm fine, but what about our newest immigrant?"

"She's under sedation. She's been hurt, badly. She has

really been through the ringer, Larry. I never thought
I'd actually see what happens when you put somebody
on the rack. Oh," Adams added gesturing toward von
Spee, "this is Father Friedrich from Würzburg. He came
with Fraulein Junius. My German is still horrible, but
I think he is her defense attorney."

Von Spee shook Mazzare's outstretched hand, his
brow furrowing at the strange legal reference. His
spoken English was really terrible. He could read
it, but had never had the chance to speak it much.
He wasn't sure what "attorney" meant, but he had
decided to be her defender, so he kept his questions
to himself.

"Who is this woman, Father Friedrich?" Mazzare
asked.

Von Spee was folding and refolding a piece of
paper in his hands, like it was a worry stone. Mazzare
spoke slowly, and von Spee had very little problem
understanding what Mazzare wanted to know.

"She is Veronica Junius, daughter of Burgomaster
Junius from Bamberg," he replied.

"What happened?"

"Well, Burgomaster Junius got accused of witchcraft
about four years ago, along with some other high officials in Bamberg. They all confessed and were burned.
So the bishop seized Junius' property and she wound
up in the gutter. She went to Würzburg to try to start
over, but she fell into hardship there."

Massaniello took up the tale. "After the burgomaster determined what the facts were, he sent her back
here to Grantville to be officially retried under our
laws. Captain Schmidt sent me with her." He looked

at the Grantville priest. "We had a chance to talk a little on the ride back from Suhl. Heck, she could be my daughter."

"How did she come to be accused of witchcraft herself?" Dan Frost inquired.

Von Spee replied, "I don't know all of the . . . how you say it, details? Yes, details. Somebody found out who she was, and told Father Eberhardt, the bishop's inquisitor from Bamberg. He came to see her in Würzburg, and accused her of all of the usual things they accuse witches of doing. She says she denied doing any of it, but of course, he wouldn't believe her."

"And . . ." Mazzare cocked his head, wincing a little.

"Just so. They put her on the rack until she confessed. But one of the guards was friendly, and didn't think she was guilty, and looked the other way while she escaped. She appears to have been running to United States territory when they caught her."

Frost spoke. "As soon as she is well enough, we'll have a hearing. This Father Eberhardt from Bamberg is insisting on it. Father Friedrich here is, too. But she isn't in good shape, physically."

"I imagine she isn't in a great mental state, either," Mazzare said, shaking his head.

"Not after what they did to her." Von Spee said, "She tells me that they tried her under torture for three days before she could escape. Of course, each day worse than that before."

Mazzare turned to Adams. "Can she talk to me?"

"I think so. Come with me."

Adams turned and led the way into the clinic, with everyone trooping in behind him. It was a small white room, with two beds and some medical equipment on stainless steel carts.

The woman was in one of the beds. Her face was swollen and it was full of lacerations. Von Spee thought the newer scrapes probably came from the woman's dash through the woods to Grantville.

"Do you understand me well?" Mazzare asked in hesitant and newly learned German.

"*Ja.* And I can *ein wenig* English speak," said the young woman.

Mazzare took a deep breath. Von Spee could see that Mazzare was not comfortable with the idea of interrogating someone accused of witchcraft.

"I am Father Mazzare, the Catholic priest in Grantville here. How are you called, and from where do you come?"

The odd constructions of German made Mazzare sound stilted to his own ear, but Von Spee realized that it was easier to understand the English words when Mazzare used German-like grammar.

"I am Veronica Junius, and I come *aus* Bamberg," she replied.

"Why were those men chasing you?"

There was silence. She looked away.

"Veronica," Mazzare said softly, "were you accused of being a witch?"

She looked at him. The pause lengthened. He held her gaze.

"*Ja* . . . I mean, yes," she said softly, finally.

"Were you practicing witchcraft?" Mazzare asked.

"*Sheiss* no!" she retorted, animated for the first time. "I'm not a witch, I'm a whore!"

Behind him, Massaniello broke up. He tried to

stifle his snigger, but failed, miserably. Dr. Adams started to chuckle, then Mazzare, and finally Veronica did too. Von Spee looked a little blank, parsing the statement in his mind. His English was poor, yes, but he finally got the joke, and he smiled.

"Well," the American sergeant choked out, "at least, in English, it starts with the same letter!"

As the laughter died, Mazzare gestured for focus, and went on.

"What did you do that got you accused?"

Veronica tossed her nondescript brown hair. "It was not what I did," she replied, "but who my father was, that got me into trouble."

"Mmmm?"

Her story came out in a rush. "*Ja,* my father was Junius the burgomaster of Bamberg. They . . . they burned him. But he was innocent! He never was a witch! I swear it! And I never was. After they killed him, and the bishop took our house and our business, I went to Würzburg. But I didn't have any money, and the families I knew didn't want to know me anymore."

"So you became a prostitute," Mazzare said quietly.

"Yes." Her language, Mazzare noted, was becoming better and more educated by the minute, like she was taking off a disguise.

"That is all right, my child," Mazzare said. "We sometimes have to do very terrible things in order to survive. God, I am sure understands."

Suddenly, von Spee pushed forward, and handed her the paper he'd been folding and refolding.

"I kept this for you," he said.

"Oh, Father Friedrich," Veronica said, "thank you. I thought it was lost. And then nobody would believe me."

She handed the paper to the Grantville pastor. Mazzare looked at the shaky German handwriting. He looked around the room.

"Father Friedrich, can you read this?" he asked. "It is hard for me to make out."

"*Ja,* I can read it," von Spee said. "Please excuse my English. I speak much better Latin and Italian." He cleared his throat.

"'Many hundred thousand good-nights, dearly beloved daughter Veronica. Innocent have I come into prison, innocent have I been tortured, innocent must I die. For whoever comes into the witch prison must become a witch or be tortured until he invents something out of his head and—God pity him—bethinks him of something.'"

Friedrich somehow kept reading, slowly, and in almost a monotone, punctuated by the sobbing of the woman in the bed. He read on and on, until the end.

"'Dear child, keep this letter secret so that people do not find it, else I shall be tortured most piteously and the jailers will be beheaded. So strictly is it forbidden. . . . Dear child, pay this man a dollar . . . I have taken several days to write this: my hands are both lame. I am in a sad plight . . . Good night, for your father Johannes Junius will never see you more. 24 July, 1628.'"

There was silence, except for Veronica's sobbing.

"You see, Father," she said through her tears, "he was innocent. There is a scribble in the margin, Father Friedrich. Can you read that, too?"

"*Ja.* 'Dear child, six have confessed against me at once: the chancellor, his son, Neudecker, Zaner, Hoffmeisters Ursel and Hoppfen Els—all false, through compulsion, as they have all told me, and begged my forgiveness in God's name before they were executed. . . . They know nothing but good of me. They were forced to say it, just as I myself was . . .'"

Veronica looked hard at Mazzare.

"They had a chance to steal a fortune," she said. "So they accused rich and powerful men, and tortured them until they confessed, and stole their goods and homes. And their families were put out in the street like me."

"And even then it wasn't enough, Father. They sent Eberhardt to find me. He tracked me down from Bamberg to Würzburg, and arrested me for being a witch. I told him I wasn't a witch but he wouldn't listen.

"But Father, even if it damns me to say this, I must. That Father Eberhardt, I'd put a spell on him, all right, if I could, but I don't know any."

"I see," Mazzare said.

Mazzare brushed his hair back from his face with both hands. He sighed, and said, "Veronica, you're safe here. We don't burn witches in Grantville. We don't believe in torture in Grantville. We don't really even believe in witches in Grantville! We will have a trial, as soon as you are well, and then you will go free."

Von Spee stared at him.

Mazzare morosely sipped his tea and read his breviary at the kitchen table in the rectory. He'd invited von Spee to spend the night at the church, and the two of them had said an early mass and come back into the kitchen for tea. Neither man spoke much as they waited for Hannelore to fix breakfast.

The screen door banged, and Mazzare looked up. Simon Jones barged into the kitchen, smiling. Mazzare's friend, fellow auto mechanic and the town's Methodist minister began pouring himself a cup of tea.

"The Good Lord knows I hope we can talk the Turks into selling us more coffee beans," he said, by way of greeting. "They are still pretty expensive for coffee every morning."

"The Good Lord is getting more help along those lines from the Abrabanel family, from what I heard," Mazzare replied. Von Spee' eyes widened. Like every Jesuit, he knew his politics, and he knew who the Abrabanels were. It was not widely known that they were supporting the United States. Interesting, he thought, very interesting indeed.

"I hear you were out late last night with a beautiful woman," Jones needled.

"That's not very funny, Simon!" Mazzare said. "You know Vincent de Paul? The guy this church was named for? Well, he is still alive, campaigning over there in France to keep priests out of the whorehouses, did you know that? The Church in this time has much to answer for, I think."

"Whoa, there, my friend," Reverend Simon Jones put up his hands. "Easy. I was only kidding."

Jones noticed von Spee. He smiled at him, and looked questioningly at Mazzare.

Mazzare said, "Father Friedrich, this is Simon Jones. He is a Protestant minister here in Grantville, and my good friend." Wondering, but remembering his own friendship with Professor Muenster in Jena, Friedrich shook Jones's hand. Mazzare was continuing to speak.

"It's this whole darn witchcraft thing. We got another one last night. A young woman named Veronica Junius from Bamberg. It seems her father was burned for witchcraft, so they assumed she was a witch, too, and they were all set to burn her at the stake! For real! Tom Simpson shot the leader just as he was going to put his sword through Heinrich Schmidt's head."

"Yeah, they did it a lot in this century, here and in England. And in America, too . . . remember the Salem witch trials? It wasn't just the Catholics, you know."

"Well, we've got to do something about it, Simon." Mazzare looked straight at his friend. "It's like the Church thinks that every woman is the 'wicked witch of the west' nya-ah-ah! Too bad we can't get them to think about Glinda the Good Witch instead."

"Um, why can't we?" Jones said, slowly, thinking. "What?"

"Well, you have a tape of *The Wizard of Oz*, don't you? Why don't we have Becky show it? And we can have a discussion afterward with young Miss Junius and Melissa and maybe Gretchen or one of her friends from Jena."

"Okay," Mazzare said. "That works for inside the United States. Now we have to figure out what to do outside the United States."

Friedrich von Spee was completely confused by the back and forth. He had no idea what the two Americans were talking about. He started to interrupt, but Mazzare suddenly stiffened, and rose half out of his seat.

"Wait a minute," he said.

Mazzare got up and went into his study. He returned with a large volume.

"Catholic Encyclopedia," he said. "I want to look something up. Let's see. 'Witchcraft' . . . yes, here it is. I thought I remembered it."

"What did you find, Larry?" Jones stood and peered over his friend's shoulder.

"This. Look here. 'Friedrich von Spee: a poet, opponent of trials for witchcraft . . .' He sounds like a pretty good guy. I think we need to find him."

"Um." The sound came from von Spee.

The two Americans looked at him. He came forward, and as he did so, they noticed he was shaking.

"May I please see that book?" Von Spee's voice quavered, and he took the book from Mazzare.

He looked at the cover, then he turned to the page Mazzare had been reading from, and read haltingly aloud.

"Friedrich von Spee. A poet, opponent of trials for witchcraft, born at Kaiserswerth on the Rhine, 25 February, 1591; died at Trier 7 August, 1635." Friedrich swallowed heavily, and kept reading. " . . . During the storming of Trier by the imperial forces in March, 1635, he distinguished himself in the care of the suffering, and died soon afterwards from the results of an infection contracted in a hospital. He was one of the noblest and most attractive figures of the awful era of the Thirty Years' War . . ."

He looked at Mazzare and Jones.

"It . . . it is not every day that a man gets to read the judgement of history upon him," Friedrich said.

The two Americans sat, staring at him.

"I am sorry not to have properly introduced myself last night, Father Mazzare," he continued. "*I* am Friedrich von Spee."

Friedrich von Spee crumpled up the letter he had started to write so few days before. He went to the window and stared out of it, at nothing.

"Not my will, but thine, almighty Father," he said to himself, softly.

He returned to his desk, took out a new piece of paper, lifted his pen, and began to write.

"AMDG. Father Friedrich von Spee, of the Society of Jesus, to His Excellency, Mutius Vitelleschi, Father General of the Society," he wrote. "It is with a chastened heart that I accept your rebuke, Father General. I did not intend the *Cautio Criminalis* to be published. But, with respect, Excellency, I must tell you that nothing in the work is false. I have attended the confessions of over two hundred witches up to now, and I have never heard one confess except after torture and the rack.

"I have just returned from the new town of Grantville, which I am certain you have heard of by now. I am now convinced that all of the witches I have seen burned have been completely innocent.

"I have brought back with me to Würzburg copies of some books that were given to me by Father Mazzare, the priest in Grantville. They have a marvelous machine that flashes a strong light at the pages of a book and produces an exact replica without a printing press. Father Mazzare showed me the workings, and explained them so far as I was able to understand them. It is an entirely mechanical device, and nothing of witchcraft. Father Mazzare himself is a scientist and artisan, I believe. I have put together a package of some of these copies to include with this letter.

"I am asking for your permission to publish the *Cautio Criminalis* in my own name, and with official imprimatur. I am certain that your permission will be forthcoming once you have read these books.

"Father General, I beg you to permit me to continue as I have begun, for as a priest of God, and a theologian, I can do no other."

The Three R's

Jody Dorsett

Bishop Comenius put down the page of the book he was working on. Swedish was not his best language, and he had to be very precise in what he was doing. He hoped that writing textbooks for the Swedes would pay his way, and the Church desperately needed more money to help the Brethren scattered across Poland and the rest of Northern Europe. Since the publication of his work *Janua linguarum reserata* several years before he had received many requests for his time. Now that he had recently been elected bishop of the Unitas Fratum he hoped those contacts would help him save the Church.

That effort consumed much of his time; more still was taken up earning a living. He had barely enough time for his personal work, the *Didactica magna*, a revolutionary concept of universal education. He had no way of knowing when, or if, he would get it published. His fear of the Brethren fading away occupied his every spare thought. These works were the beginning of what he was slowly coming to accept was a long-term vision. The planting of seeds.

His ruminations were disturbed by a knock at the door of his study.

"Bishop?" The young minister quietly asked, interrupting as gently as he could. "There is a man here to see you . . . Jan Billek?"

"Deacon Billek? Here? By all means, send him in Timothy, send him in!"

Jan entered the garret room, his body filling the doorway. He looked much the same as he had the last time they had seen each other, only much grayer. Comenius rushed forward and grabbed the hand of the man. "Praise be, that I get to see you again, Jan Billek!"

"Yes, Bishop, it has been quite awhile."

They both stopped and looked at each other. Remembering the horror after White Mountain and Bloody Prague, the time following Tilly's victory and the capture of the barons. The time when Liechtenstein had declared the Brethren apostate, banished them from Bohemia, and turned the Brethren into penniless, desperate refugees. Burned their Bibles, hymnals, and catechisms, and placed them in the position they were in now—the head of the church an exile in the Netherlands, and the congregations reduced to running or hiding.

"What brings you, Deacon Billek, from far away Poland to here? It was surely an arduous journey."

"I came to speak to you about the future of the Church, my Bishop."

"I've read your reports from Lissel. I hope you have received my observations?"

"Yes, Bishop. I have read your letters, and they give us strength. It has given us hope these last many years, that now you will one day get us the help we need to bring the Church back to its home."

Comenius sat back down in his chair. Not long ago he had taught and fought vigorously for not only the evangelical expansion of the Church, but the need to ally with others. He had felt that there was, or at least should be, a common bond between the Protestant nations and people. It was one of the reasons the synod had selected him. Now, away from the halls of academia that he had trod for so long, he realized that theory and practice were quite different. That realization had made his publishing efforts even more important to him. He had committed himself to finding a savior for his people, and would seek it where he could, but his heart was committed to an effort that would take years.

"I know you hope that, and I petition for aid from all I can, but help is not forthcoming. And you must know from my letters, that I have begun to plant what I hope are the seeds of rebirth for the Church. That when the time is right, it will grow again. You and your fellows' acts of distributing the printed Word to the people, even if they hide them away, is a great help." Comenius paused, then forged ahead. "But anything else might bring about the destruction of the Church. We *must* wait."

"Sir, perhaps not." Jan went to the window, and looked out of it. "You've heard that Wallenstein's army was routed at the Alte Veste? Wallenstein himself badly wounded—some rumors say mortally."

"Yes, I have heard."

Billek turned from the window and looked at the last bishop of the Church of The Brethren. "Wallenstein's army is smashed, true, but so long as the Habsburgs rule Bohemia, we will find no succor at home. But that victory over the Habsburgs has made me think of these new folk. The 'Americans,' as they seem to be called, whom the rumors say were instrumental in his defeat. Perhaps they might help us. I don't know how much you know about them, or even if you have considered contacting them."

"All we hear are wild rumors, Deacon Billek. That they are 'witches' and other such nonsense. Nothing is really known of them, and I hesitate to contact an unknown."

"I have tried to glean a little about them. One of the first things I found was that the Jesuits are also collecting information. That must be a good sign."

Billek and Comenius exchanged a hard smile at the thought of the Jesuits having consternation over the appearance of the new folk.

"Hmmp . . . Another foe for them, you think?"

"I don't know. But what I have found out is very interesting. Although they are allied with the Swedish Lutherans, they apparently believe in complete religious tolerance. They are highly educated, and have great command of the physical sciences. And they have interesting ideas of freedom for every person. I am reminded of Zizka, and the early Church. None could stand before them."

"I see." Comenius was intrigued. Education and tolerance were some of the seeds he wanted to plant. Perhaps there was something here after all.

"What is that you want me to do, Deacon Billek? I can hardly show up at their court with no prior knowledge, and ask them for aid."

"That's why I'm here, my Bishop. I want to go there. Give me a letter of introduction as your emissary. I will find out enough about them for you to determine if you wish to pursue further talks with them yourself."

Comenius didn't respond at once. He was torn between the sudden flare of hope, and the experience of rejection. He also didn't want to lose Billek. He was one of his rocks in Poland, and he kept the Church alive, even if hidden. But Comenius also knew that every day Billek spent outside of the Protestant countries he was at risk.

"All right, Deacon Billek, you'll have your letter. But I ask one favor in return."

"What might that be, my Bishop?"

"That you consider receiving your ordination and taking a congregation."

For the first time since he entered the room, Jan smiled.

The first part of Jan's journey was not as hard as he feared. Comenius' contacts with the Swedish court helped get him first to Sweden, and then to Germany. He was able to accompany a Swedish supply column until he was close enough to the area of Thuringia that he believed held the Americans. The last leg was a different story.

When Jan entered the region that lay close to the country of the Americans, he was appalled at the devastation. It was worse than anything he had seen in

Bohemia or Poland. Whole areas in central Germany were almost devoid of people. Struggling groups of refugees abounded, and towns were not pleased to see strangers. The constant reports of bands of brigands forced him to move at night. He had learned to travel at night during his travels back into Bohemia, but he didn't like it. It took longer to travel.

Then, suddenly, everything changed. While the country he was in still showed the ravages of war, the roads began to show cart traffic, and clots of people traveling in apparent relaxation. Jan walked along the road and listened to the people. Some were refugees on the edge of collapse, following the rumors of a safe haven. However, there were many others who were in better shape. These were apparently traveling to the town called Grantville not out of necessity but because they were on some business or other. This was the type of group he wanted.

The group he approached allowed him to join without too much of a glance, since he only carried a small bag and a walking staff. Despite his size, his lack of weapons seemed to gain him acceptance in a group all too familiar with what even the smallest band of armed men could do.

Shortly after noon on the next day, the small band he had attached himself to came to a halt. In front of them was a small tollbooth, and men in strangely colored garb surrounded it. Some held familiar muskets, but others held what were surely weapons but unlike any that Jan had ever seen before. The group was formed into a queue. Jan could see that each was asked a question, and then directed off to another area.

When he reached the front of the queue, he was confronted by a man with blazing red hair, a full beard and mustache. He wore the oddly colored clothing that many of the others wore, but his boots were those of a cavalryman and he carried a brace of pistols on his belt. Jan took him to be one of the officers. He then asked, in the most atrocious German Jan had ever heard, "Lord, yer a big 'un. Be yer here fer business, or be yer fleeing?"

"I come from my bishop. But . . . perhaps there is another language that we may speak in, that you may be more comfortable in?"

The answer was clearly longer, and different, than the man had expected, and it took him a moment to parse it out. Then he grinned and replied, in some of the worst English Jan had ever heard: "If yer speak English it would be a vurra good thing. We don't get many past here that speak naught else but German. You say you come from yer bishop. Are ye a Catholic then?"

Jan couldn't help but chuckle a bit. "Hardly, sir, I come from Bishop Comenius, of the Unity of Brethren. I wish to present my papers to your court."

The red-haired man blinked. "Yer wanting to present papers to our *court?* Hold on a minute, laddy . . . you'll be needin' to speak to someone other than myself."

The red-haired man went to one of the tents that were behind the tollbooth. He opened the flap and went inside. Shortly he emerged with another, a very young man who wore spectacles such as Jan had never seen before, and who carried a sheaf of papers in his hand.

As they walked back towards Jan the young man

flipped through the pages and then apparently found what he was looking for. The two came to a stop and the young man spoke, with an accent Jan had never heard before.

"Lieutenant McAuliffe here says you are a representative of Bishop Comenius. The Unity of Brethren. If the information I have is correct, that's what we'd call the Moravian church. Back where we come from. Uh, I guess I should say 'when' we come from."

It was Jan's turn to blink. *"Moravian" church? What sort of name is that?*

But, whatever it was, it seemed to satisfy the young man. Indeed, he gave Jan a smile that was downright friendly. "Moravians were well spoke of, in our time and place. So, welcome. We usually don't receive such august personages mixed in with a group of refugees. What's your name?"

"I am Deacon Billek, and these are my papers." Jan handed over the letter he had pulled from a pocket in his cloak.

"I'm Marty Thornton," the young man introduced himself. He opened the letter and began to read it. "What exactly is your business here?"

"I wish to present my papers to the court, as I told the first gentleman."

Thornton made a sound somewhere between a snort and a chuckle. "Well, that would be the first problem. We don't *have* a court. We aren't ruled by an aristocracy here."

So Jan had heard, from some of the refugees, but he'd discounted it as wild rumor. "I . . . I didn't know," he almost stammered. "I am here to make arrangements for my bishop to meet your rulers."

Thornton stared at him. Jan could practically hear his thoughts. Billek clearly wasn't a peasant, yet neither did he dress or act in the manner of the nobility and merchants. "If you are a diplomatic representative, where is your entourage?"

"I don't need one. I am but a deacon of the Church of the Brethren, the Unitas Fratum. Such would be a waste, and it would also be dangerous. There are not many outside of England, Sweden or the United Provinces who are friendly to us."

"Well, we certainly know how that feels," said Thornton with a wry grin. He look back down at the letter. "Well, why not? This certainly seems authentic. Come with me to the tent, and I'll call for someone from Ms. Abrabanel's office to come down and meet you."

Jan was picked up by several men in a sort of carriage that he had never seen before. Seeing new mechanical marvels was something that he figured he would have to get used to. The knowledge also made hope swell in his heart. These strange folk might be the answer that the Church needed to survive.

The ride into town further encouraged him. The streets were a bustle of activity, and he heard several different languages spoken or shouted as they drove. The road itself amazed him. It was smooth and continuous, and there were no wheel ruts or loose stones. They passed several churches, only one of which seemed to be Catholic, and that interested him even more than the road. He was tempted to ask if what he'd heard about their religious tolerance was true, but the men he was with had not introduced themselves, nor spoken more than a few words.

The carriage came to a halt in front of a brick and glass building. The glass in the front was the smoothest and clearest Jan had ever seen. Through it he could see desks with people sitting at them, some speaking into odd-looking horns. The men escorted him across the floor, past several small offices with glass fronts and then down a corridor to a large office with a very large desk. Behind it sat a beautiful woman with lustrous black hair. Though she was quite young, she seemed to radiate a kind of quiet confidence. Jan knew he was about to speak to one who held the reins of power in this strange place.

"I am Rebecca Abrabanel," she introduced herself, after reading the letter. She smiled a bit wryly and added: "I hold the somewhat peculiar title—office, I should say—of 'National Security Adviser.' I am not actually certain if I am the one who should really be speaking to you, but since no one else knows either, I suppose it will be me. That is generally how my title seems to operate." She glanced back down at the letter. "This says you are Deacon Billek, the personal representative of Bishop Comenius, leader of the Unity of Brethren. It is written in Latin. Do you speak Latin?"

"I speak it and write it, yes. I am also knowledge-able in several other languages."

"I see," replied the Abrabanel woman in excellent Latin. "Would you like something to drink? Something to eat?"

"A little water will suffice."

"Besides opening communications between the bishop and us, what else does your bishop ask?"

"I come to offer my bishop's congratulations on

your recent victory over Wallenstein. I also will ask for
time to appear at . . . whatever you call a court . . . for
him to speak."

"What sort of things might Comenius wish to
say?"

"I cannot speak thus for my bishop. But we wish
to see if the Brethren can find a friend in your
people."

"Deacon Billek, it is my understanding that Comenius acts alone in his representation of the Church.
How long have you been a diplomat for him?"

Jan paused. He was no diplomat, and began to
fear he would make a hash of this conversation. The
Church needed friends, and being too obtuse might
put this woman at odds. That was not the way he
wished the Church to begin with these folk.

"Lady Abrabanel, this is the first I have done so for
my bishop. I have known Bishop Comenius for a long
time. He and I understand each other. He is seeking,
as we speak, support from the Swedish court for our
people. I urged him to speak to you, but he wants
more information before he would make such a journey.
It is not safe for him, except in a few places. I felt
that we could not wait. Liechtenstein has scattered us
to the winds, taken our property, and destroyed our
Bibles. We need a friend who can help us."

"Deacon, we are a friend to all who are a friend
to us, but whether we can help you . . ." She paused,
then continued. "We are having a meeting tomorrow morning of the cabinet. We will take up several
issues. I can't speak for our government in this,
other than to tell you that I would not hold hopes
for much assistance beyond that which we offer any

who flees depredation. Our own resources are limited and already tightly stretched. Still, you may wait and speak to our cabinet—or you may leave your letter and return and tell Bishop Comenius that we would love for him to visit us."

The room seemed to narrow in on Jan, and his vision became like a tunnel. His hopes fell. He closed his eyes, and took a few breaths. There was still that faint chance that the others on the cabinet might be more receptive, and as long as there was hope, he would continue. "I will stay and address your council, if that may be arranged."

Jan walked through the crowd of people on the streets of Grantville in almost a stupor, the wonders that surrounded him no longer registering. He knew, in his heart, that these people represented the only hope that his people and his Church had for survival. He prayed for strength and guidance. In his wandering, he found himself in front of a tavern. One of the people from the ministry had told him he could get food there and directions to a place he might sleep.

He entered the tavern. It was quite busy by the front bar, the large room full of smoke and laughter in English and German. He spied a small table in the corner and sat, looking around him. He didn't see the withdrawn manner he had come to know through most of his travels in central Germany. Soon a young woman appeared before him. She didn't have the look of the typical serving wench he was accustomed to in such a place.

"Yes, may I help you?" Jan asked.

The girl giggled. "That's what I'm supposed to ask *you*. What can I get you?"

"Ah. Some food and mild beer would be fine."

"Our daily special is hamburger steak with beets and turnip greens and a liter of small beer. How about that?"

"Yes, that's fine." Jan wasn't sure exactly what he had ordered. But being surprised was no longer a new thing for him. When she returned with his drink, she dropped a slip of paper off. He picked it up and read it, mildly surprised that it was a tally of his food and drink, and obviously written by the girl. Even the servants could read in this land, it seemed. The thought brought both pleasure and disappointment. Like all of his church, Jan believed that reading and writing were the keys to salvation.

And so he ruminated on the mystery of being so close to salvation, but having it held out of his reach. He sat in front of his food for hours, barely picking at it, and sipping his beer. After he had waved the serving girl off several times, she told him to simply call her if he needed anything.

A brown-haired man in a leather jacket finally interrupted him. It was one of the men who had driven him to meet Rebecca Abrabanel.

"Hey, pal, you look like someone killed your puppy."

"I'm sorry, what do you say?"

"My partner and I have been watching you," the man said, with a nod toward someone sitting at a nearby table. Jan saw that it was the other fellow who had been on the carriage with them. "We figured that anyone who looked that sad, for that long, couldn't be a spy."

"A spy? You make a joke. Why would you think I'm a spy?"

"Well, you weren't exactly the typical refugee or diplomat."

"I see. I suppose I am a little bit of both. And really, not much of a diplomat," Billek replied with some sadness.

"Why don't you let us join you?"

"Certainly. Perhaps I could use some company, and I can learn more about you people."

The man in the leather jacket pulled up a chair and motioned for the other to join him. The man who walked up also had the small spectacles that Jan had seen some wear. He had a face that was lined with smile lines, eyes that were lively and intelligent, and was carrying a glass of beer in his hand.

The man who was sitting grimaced a little as he shifted in his chair and introduced them. "I'm Skip and this is Red."

"Pleased to meet you," said Red. "I gather your meeting didn't go as you would hope?"

"Yes. Lady Abrabanel held out little hope for me. But I still will press on with your cabinet. Maybe God will put the words in my mouth that I need to get your help."

"Red, the deacon here describes himself as sort of a refugee. He don't look like one to me. Especially as big as he is."

"Oh, I don't know, Skip. The Brethren got hammered pretty bad by the Habsburgs. Victims of a hostile aristocracy. Shit, it's bad enough having an aristocracy, let alone one that targets you. That's why most of them wound up in America, back—" He waved the beer glass about. "Then. There. Whatever. 'Moravians,' they were called then. I used to have some Moravian neighbors, in my hometown."

"Ah, hell, here we go . . . Red on the soapbox again." Despite the grimace, Skip seemed more amused than anything else. "Ah, not to change the subject, Deacon Billek, but why don't you tell us about yourself there. I haven't met any of the Brethren before—and neither has Red, neighbors or no."

Jan began with his early studies at the Brethren school. He found it a good way, when he was out in the villages, to slide in a little theology when talking to people. But soon he found himself going into deeper detail than he thought. Red and Skip asked questions that brought him out. He spoke to them of the hope they had had after Emperor Maximillian II had approved the National Protestant Bohemian Confession, which opened all of Bohemia for them to preach and set up congregations. His joy in bringing the teachings, both of Christ and of worldly education to the people. He spoke of the horrors of Bloody Prague and the Brethren's expulsion from Bohemia. Finally, he spoke of his efforts to keep the faith alive. The secret meetings and the hidden printing presses. The raids by the bullyboys of the local nobility or bishop.

Suddenly, he realized that the men he was speaking to weren't smiling anymore, nor had they asked any questions. "What is the matter, have I offended you?"

"Nope, I guess I'm a little embarrassed by the actions of the Church. I'm a Catholic, myself, but I can't stand how they operate in this day and age. It's not part of *our* customs and traditions." Skip then stood up. "Look, I gotta go, the wife's waiting. You guys stay, if you like. I'll see you in the morning."

After he left, Jan turned to Red.

"Are you a Catholic too? I did not mean to offend."

"No, Jan, I am not a Catholic; I'm not really religious at all. Your stories reminded me of what I did before I came to Grantville. I was a union organizer. I guess I went around and preached a different sort of gospel, and got into the same sorts of trouble you did."

"And what do you do now, here in Grantville?"

"Oh, I was working in the mine. But there are plenty of stronger backs than me now. I work full time for the government; most of the union officers do." Then he started laughing; a deep, heartfelt laugh.

"What is so funny?"

"Oh, me—working for the government!" replied Red. "Look, you got a place yet? I live by myself, and have a spare couch you can sleep on. I'll tell you all about it, if you'd like."

"Thank you, the Brethren often rely on the kindnesses of those we meet. Just as we gladly give it."

As they walked to the edge of town and up the hill towards Red's home, Jan took the opportunity to ask Red more about how things worked in Grantville. He was fascinated by their conception of "democracy," especially the notion of a written constitution that guaranteed each person's freedom. As they neared the house that Red pointed out was his, they heard a series of shots. Jan hunched and looked around. Shots, to him, meant an army; and that was always bad.

Red laughed again. "Don't worry, Jan, that's my neighbor Bobby Hollering. He's one of our gunsmiths, and he always has something cooking. Would you like to see it?"

Jan nodded, and Red led him down a narrow lane to a house with a small barn close by. It was to the barn that they went. Standing at the door was a heavyset fellow with a musket in his hand. But out of the side of the musket a bar of iron protruded. The man was preparing to fire at a bail of hay at the back of the yard when Red called to him.

"Hey, Bobby. What the hell *is* that thing, anyway?"

The man named "Bobby" turned toward the pair and put down his weapon. "It's my new improvement that I'm going to present at the meeting tomorrow. They're finally going to let me argue my case. Actually, I stole the design, but it's really cool. Wanna see?"

The man's enthusiasm was palpable. He picked the weapon up, pulled back the hammer and fired. As soon as the shot went off, he brought the weapon down, pulled a lever, slid the iron bar, cocked the hammer, and fired again. He did this seven times.

"See, Red! Seven shots in about a minute," Bobby said through a pall of smoke. "Using an old musket! They gotta take this one. We'll really be able to fight with these . . ."

How long he might have gone on with this enthusiasm, the two would never know. For at that moment, the door to the house opened and a woman stepped out, scowling a bit. "Bobby, put that thing down and come hold your son while I finish supper."

With the same enthusiasm he had just displayed for his weapon, Bobby put down the gun and called back to the house. "Yes, honey! I'll be right there. Are you coming tomorrow, Red?"

"Yeah, Bobby. Me and the deacon here will be there. He's going to speak too."

Bobby looked at Jan as if seeing him for the first time. "Okay, great. I'll see you then."

As the man jogged to the house, Jan asked Red: "Isn't he a little old to be a father?"

Red laughed. "As you'll see tomorrow, he's unstoppable. Let's get to the house."

The meeting of the cabinet began at midmorning. There were quite a few petitioners there, all of whom wanted the cabinet's permission to do something. Most were small matters: permits to build houses, new enterprises to start, that sort of thing. All were questioned, and if they could justify the need and benefit, and demonstrate that it would not divert too many resources, they were generally approved by a voice vote.

The last two were Bobby Hollering and Jan. Jan was to be last.

The central figure in the cabinet was a man named Mike Stearns. He looked down at Bobby and said: "Okay, Bobby, let's hear it."

"The slide rifle was first invented by Browning. It is easy to make . . ." Bobby went on for quite awhile, impervious to the glazed looks that soon began to cross the faces of some of the members. Finally, when he seemed to pause for breath, Mike interrupted him and informed him that it was soon time for a lunch break.

"We'll get back to you after recess; we'll discuss your proposal over lunch. I'm sure you have a write-up on this thing, so pass it up. Meanwhile, we need to hear from Deacon Billek, a representative of Bishop Comenius of the Church of the Brethren."

Jan had thought all night long what to say. He decided to use an abbreviated version of the tale he had told Red and Skip the day before. It had moved them; maybe it would have the same effect on the cabinet. He was used to speaking in front of people. As he spoke, he could tell he moved a few of the people who would decide the future of his people. When he concluded, he saw Mike whisper to a few. Then he stood.

"Thank you, Deacon Billek, that was a powerful speech you made. Again, like Bobby, you'll have to wait for our decision after we return this afternoon. We'll see any interested party back here at half past one."

With that, Stearns banged his gavel and he and the others rose and filed from the room.

Red walked up to Jan. "So, Jan, if the cabinet decides not to go any further with your request . . . what'll you do?"

"I will go back and tell my bishop what has happened. Then I shall return to Poland and continue my work. Planting the seeds of the future of the Church is a job for the bishop. I only want to see the Church and its people survive as best they can."

"Okay, I certainly understand that. I gotta go talk to that young lady over there." He nodded toward a young blond woman standing toward the rear of the room. "Gretchen just got back from one of her trips, and I need to speak to her. I'll see you when the cabinet session begins again."

Jan couldn't eat. He went back to his seat, and prayed that the coming hours would show him God's will for the salvation of the people. He sat by himself, and the intensity he gave off kept the others away. With a passing of time that surprised him, soon the cabinet returned. He looked around, and found that there were only a few people there. Bobby and some of his friends and associates, and Red, Skip and Gretchen in the back.

Mike Stearns began brusquely. "Bobby, your gun is an ingenious weapon. Yes, we agree that we could convert enough to supply the home guard. But that's it—and at what cost? We have extremely limited resources. Our greatest resource is the skill and knowledge that folks like you possess. We need you to continue your work in training our friends—that means the Swedes, first and foremost—to make the modest improvements that we can afford to do for a *lot* of soldiers. We have to have a plan that gives us the greatest impact over the whole thing. We appreciate you and your boffins. We would be lost without you.

"Furthermore, what if we lose some of those things? As you say, they are easy to make once you know how. And we don't have the capacity to compete with some of our potential enemies. We aren't ready for an arms race of that kind, yet. One day, we will be able to build that and all the other inventions you and your team have uncovered. But not now. I'm sorry, Bobby . . . I know you are disappointed."

Now, it was Jan's turn.

"Deacon Billek, as you just heard me say to Bobby, we have limited resources. We all feel for the plight of your people. We will welcome any of your people that you send. They will find a good home in our area. And freedom. But we can't offer you any more than comfort when they get here. We have nothing to spare to help them anywhere else. We certainly can't make any sort of offer to free your land."

Jan's head dipped in despair, though he had known the probable outcome. It seemed that God favored the bishop's plan after all. Jan also knew his own purpose, still.

"Thank you for your time, sir. I will tell Bishop Comenius of our speech here. Perhaps some of the Brethren may make it to your land, where you will find us to be a valuable addition to your community."

Jan picked up his cloak, his bag, and his staff, and moved towards the door. As he approached it, Skip, Red, and the woman with them moved towards him. Red held out his hand, and Jan took it.

"Jan, are you really going to go back to Poland?"

"Yes. I will tell the bishop, and the people, of your offer. We have prospered in sanctuary before; perhaps we will do so again. I will go to help those who cannot come, and to keep spreading the ministry as best I can. The only way evil can be stopped is to witness against it. Thank you for your help."

"Ah, Deacon," interjected Skip, "have you ever heard the expression 'the Lord helps those that help themselves'?"

"What do you mean?"

"What he means, Jan," Red interjected, "is that

we have a little proposition for you. Why don't we go outside and talk about it?"

Mike Stearns and Rebecca Abrabanel stood in the window of his office watching the ox cart being loaded on the street below. Red and Jan were piling in sacks and boxes, while Bobby and one of his friends lifted an anvil into the back of the cart.

"Isn't it a little risky, sending them out like this?" Rebecca asked.

"I guess, but it isn't the first time we've sent people into hostile terrain—either us, or the UMWA back where I came from—and it won't be the last. Besides, Billek would have gone anyway."

"What about Red?" Rebecca asked.

"Red didn't come to Grantville expecting to stay this long. He came to get back in touch with his roots, and work with the local. He was taking a break from what he does best. He has no kin here, and certainly didn't expect the Ring of Fire to keep him."

"And what does Red do best, Mike?"

"He makes trouble."

"Well, that's the last of it," Bobby said, wiping the sweat from his brow. "I hope that you can make use of it, and I'm sure Mike is happier I lose my home shop—it'll keep me focused."

With that, and a flurry of farewells, Red and Jan headed the ox cart out of town. Skip and Bobby watched them until they couldn't see the cart anymore.

"Skip, what are the deacon and Red going to do out there in Bohemia?"

"Oh, they're going to be teaching the three R's, Bobby," Skip said with a rueful chuckle. "Call it 'reading, righting and revolution.'"

Here Comes Santa Claus

K.D. Wentworth

When Julie Mackay initially proposed it, the First Annual Grantville Christmas party seemed a bit of unnecessary fuss to Mike Stearns. Not to mention that it was a misnomer: it would actually be the *second* Christmas since the Ring of Fire. In December of 1632, Mike had vastly more important things to think about, not the least of which was the future of their infant United States in war-torn Europe.

Besides, all the children in Grantville who had been orphaned, either the American ones by the Ring of Fire or the ensuing battles, or German ones by the chaos of the Thirty Years War, were being well looked after anyway. But Julie, heading toward motherhood herself in the coming new year, was adamant. These were all American children now, she said, and American children should have a proper Christmas, one with Santa and all the appropriate trappings. She meant to show this strange new world of theirs just how it was done.

For just a second as Mike stood there on the street, looking down at her, homesickness glimmered in the former cheerleader's blue eyes. Mike saw all that had been left behind, the many comforts and people this displaced populace would never possess again.

"We should start out as we mean to go on," she said stoutly. "Tradition is important. The fact that we didn't do it the first Christmas we were here doesn't count. We were too busy then just staying alive."

Mike's will crumbled. Perhaps a small celebration of the season would not be amiss. If they were circumspect, it wouldn't deplete their limited resources too badly, and, after all they had been through since the Ring of Fire, spirits could use some lifting. "All right," he said, "if you don't get carried away. It's going to be a long winter, you know. We can't waste food and supplies."

Julie beamed, her enthusiasm contagious. "I'll take care of everything," she said, "the presents, the decorations, the food. We'll have it one week from today, on Christmas Eve. There's just one hitch—we need someone to play Santa." Her eyes measured his six-foot frame. "How about you?"

Mike turned and quite wisely fled.

Accompanied by two of his handpicked men, General Gottfried von Pappenheim, the trusted top subordinate of the duke of Friedland, Imperial General Albrecht von Wallenstein himself, approached the outrageous new settlement known as "Grantville" on foot. He was a tall man, barrel-chested with a strong profile and prematurely white hair, though he was but four and thirty. On his face, he bore a distinctive birthmark, which looked for all the world like crossed swords. More than one had sworn that birthmark glowed red when he was angry.

Two of his men, handpicked for this mission, Otik Zeleny and Meinhard Durst, strode along at his back, clad in shabby farmers' smocks. Pappenheim knew all three of them looked entirely too well fed to be what they claimed to be, but there was no time to starve themselves and they settled for clothing too large for their frames to achieve the look.

The day here in Thuringia was cold, but fine, the sky arching overhead like a vault of shimmering blue glass in a cathedral. Armed guards with curiously sleek muskets patrolled the borders of the town, but allowed the three to pass without even paying a toll after they were found to be unarmed and asked for sanctuary in low German.

They were posing as poor refugee farmers, as per Wallenstein's specific orders. The general himself had been transported back to his estates in Bohemia in order to receive the best medical care. He had nearly died not long before, at the battle of the Alte Veste, when his jaw had been broken by a bullet from a gun fired from so far away, no one could even detect the shooter.

As they walked slowly down that strange gray road, Pappenheim couldn't keep from bending down to examine it. The unfamiliar substance was hard as rock, yet seemed to have been laid down in malleable form somehow, then smoothed like butter before it solidified.

His right-hand man, Durst, the sober veteran of innumerable years of fighting, also bent and ran calloused fingers over its unyielding surface.

Pappenheim shook his head. "The Croats told me, but I didn't really believe them. If it were indeed made of crushed rock, as it appears to be, how did they get it to bond in this fashion? Amazing," he murmured. "I have seen nothing like it anywhere."

Another of those devilish carriages roared past and Pappenheim did not suppress his shudder. The ignorant peasant he was imitating would have shuddered too. The upstarts who populated this town reportedly had countless such vehicles that moved without benefit of horse, not to mention lights not generated by fire and stoves that cooked without flame. The list went on and on.

His orders were to find the one called "Jew Lee Mackay," who was, by all reports, the marksman whose aim had been so devastating to General Wallenstein at the Alte Veste. One of his subordinates had beaten the name out of several refugees who had lingered for a time in this bizarre town, but then, frightened by its outlandish ways, returned to their farms. He still wasn't sure he believed the witless peasants.

"Jew Lee Mackay" was a strange name, made all the more puzzling by the peasants' insistence that "Jew" meant the same as the German word "Jude" in the newcomers' garbled version of English. That the shooter might be a *Jude* surprised Pappenheim. Most realms who allowed *Juden* to live within their borders forbade them to possess firearms. Pappenheim had never known a *Jude* who was proficient with weapons, much less a miraculous marksman.

But, beyond that, it was said this *Jude* was female, and though the females of this outlandish bunch seemed to put their hands to much that was traditionally male, he had trouble believing any woman could be so skilled in arms or steady of nerve—or that any self-respecting man would yield his place in combat to her.

At any rate, Wallenstein had been adamant: Find this mysterious Jew, Lee Mackay, and complete their mission.

A knot of young boys stood on a corner just ahead, arguing cheerfully in German about something. Pappenheim glanced over his shoulder, but none of the local inhabitants was paying them any undue attention. He headed toward the boys. The folk of this place spoke a bastard form of English so these children must be refugees. Perhaps they could point them toward this particular Jew.

He stopped behind the tallest, who looked thirteen or fourteen, a big yellow-haired lad just beginning to put on flesh after obvious long starvation.

"We are looking for the *Juden* of this town," Pappenheim said, giving the boy a stern look. "Where is their quarter?"

A shorter redhead with his arm in a sling looked from face to face. "There are no such quarters here," he said. "The townspeople do not consider such things when assigning living space."

"Besides," said the yellow-haired one, "why should you care? You do not look *Judisch.*"

Durst stepped forward and backhanded him so that he fell onto the hard road. "Insolent pup! No one cares what you think!"

"Klaus!" The red-haired boy dropped to his knees.

A trickle of blood ran from the fallen one's lip, but his blue eyes were like stone as he took his friend's proffered hand and lurched back onto his feet. "This is Grantville," he said, and there was a flash of pride in his face. "No one has the right to do that here! No one is better than anyone else. Here, we are all equal." He glanced at his companions and they moved in to stand at his side. "Stearns has said!"

Durst snorted. "You—a common field brat, whelped under some bush by the look of you, equal to me, or anyone else for that matter?"

The boy flushed and he clenched his fists as a metal vehicle pulled up and stopped. A man with closely cropped hair stepped out. He was dressed in some sort of uniform that Pappenheim had never seen before and carried one of those small but deadly looking American pistols in a holster on his hip. "What is going on, Klaus?" the man asked, in badly accented German. "These men making trouble?"

Klaus dabbed at his lip with the back of his hand and Pappenheim could see how badly the boy wanted the speaker's respect. It was not in him to admit how easily he'd been struck down.

"They want directions, Mr. Jordan," he said finally, not meeting the fellow's eyes, "but we have been trying to tell him that here in Grantville we have no special quarter for *Juden.*"

"Oh." The man nodded as though all that made sense. He turned to Pappenheim. "Okay, this is the way it is: no one here cares if you are a *Jude* or a Catholic or a Protestant. All are welcome. Go down this road until you come to the school. It's a big brown-and-white two-story building. They will you feed there and tell where you can sleep tonight."

Remembering his supposed identity as a poor peasant farmer, Pappenheim dropped his gaze. "Thank you, sir. It is very good of you to give us sanctuary."

The man waved them on, then the humming vehicle lurched back into motion and rumbled down the road.

"He thought we were *Juden*!" Durst stared after him, both angry and dumbfounded. "Does he not know what *Juden* look like?"

"Perhaps not," Pappenheim said. "By all reports, these people are very strange."

Klaus and his two friends had withdrawn across the road and now watched as the three men started toward the building that must be the promised school, just visible in the distance.

"What about them?" Zeleny jerked his chin toward the trio.

"Field brats," Pappenheim said. "It won't matter what they do or do not say. No one will care." He felt for the package tucked into his waistband beneath his filthy peasant smock. Soon enough, they would find this Lee Mackay, as ordered.

After Julie consulted Victor Saluzzo, the man who had replaced Len Trout as principal of the high school after Trout had been killed in the Croat raid a few months earlier, he gave her free access to the Christmas decorations. Armed with the key to the storage room, she dug through box after box, discovering wreaths and strings of lights, along with decorative candy canes as tall as her knee and smiling plastic Santa faces.

"The kids are going to love this!" she told herself, surrounded by boxes of ornaments and plastic tinsel.

She sat back on her heels, thinking. She was fuzzy on the details, but, as far as she knew, Christmas at this point in history had developed few of the traditions that so flavored the celebration in her own century. Maybe she could ask Gretchen Higgins, her closest friend among the locals, how people in this area liked to celebrate, but she was fairly certain the Christmas tree had first been used in Germany. Perhaps that was the one point where her culture and this one overlapped.

So, she told herself, shoving a box aside, the school's tired old artificial tree would not do for this party! She would send her husband Alex out for the tallest, greenest real tree they could find. Closing her eyes, she imagined the majestic evergreen out in the middle of the gym floor. It would smell divi—

"So here you are." A voice broke into her reverie. "An' just what is all this rubbish for?"

"Alex!" She came to her feet and threw her arms around her husband. "Just wait until you hear what I've got planned!"

"Dinna tell me." He smiled beneath his trim ginger mustache. "I have married myself a woman who is a better shot than I'll ever be and my puir heart canna take nae more shocks, at least not until after the bairn is born."

"Oh, that won't be for months," she said. "You'll have lots of shocks to get through before that."

"No doubt," he said, running his fingers through her hair fondly. "Of that, I think we can be sure."

"We're going to have a Christmas party," she said, "for the orphans, and anyone else who wants to come. I hope the whole town will be there." Her face sobered. "This Christmas is going to be hard for us, since it's our first holiday away from our old lives—well, our second, but last year we were too frantically busy to think much about it." She thought of her elderly grandmother, who lived in Virginia along with her aunt and uncle and six noisy cousins, none of whom she'd ever see again, and swallowed hard. "Lots of folks will be missing their families this year. I think we need to celebrate together and be glad for what we still have."

"Well, I'm certainly that glad for what I have!" He pulled her into his arms and nuzzled her neck with great enthusiasm.

The resulting tingle ran all the way down to her toes. "Hey!" she said, but made no move to hold him off. "I can't think when you're doing that."

"I should hope not!" he said indignantly. "Anyway, thinking is highly overrated. Mike Stearns himself told me so, and you know how wise he is."

Julie grinned. "Now," she said, firmly extracting herself from her husband's embrace, "you have to help me plan this Christmas party."

"Well, I know aboot Christmas, of course," he said. "What Christian does not, but a party? Christmas is a time for sober reflection and worshipping in church back in Scotland, and not much else, unless you're a papist."

A furrow appeared between Julie's eyes. She'd forgotten. Her dear sweet Alex was a Calvinist, though mostly lapsed, by his own admission. Calvinists and probably most Protestants had likely frowned upon anything that smacked of pagan origin, like a tree or decorations. They tended to be adamant about anything that smacked of idol-worshipping.

"Okay," she said, "I'll plan it myself. You can do all the fetching and carrying and hanging, not to mention the cutting down of the tree. I'll handle the rest."

His brow furrowed. "Cutting doon of the tree?"

"You'll see." She held up a string of red and green lights and sighed. "I just hope we have peace for Christmas, whatever else we manage. There are still enough stragglers from Wallenstein's and Tilly's armies roaming the countryside out there to make trouble."

"That, wife," Alex said, "unlike fancy parties, I do know aboot." He enfolded her in his arms again. "Whatever else comes, I swear I will keep you and our wee bairn safe."

Otto Bruckner and Anton Berg, officers in Emperor Ferdinand's army, skulked around the perimeter of the strange town for hours, but in the end found no way to sneak in carrying their casks of gunpowder. People were entering Grantville, yes, quite frequently, and without a toll, but some of them were also being searched. It might be possible to spirit in something as small as a knife or even a pistol, if one were careful, but an ungainly object like a wooden cask was another matter.

"This settlement was not here two years ago," Bruckner told his subordinate, as they finally retreated to bury the two precious casks beneath a lightning-split oak out to the north of town, out of sight of the frequent patrols. "I spent a number of days in the area. This was mainly woodland, and the few surrounding farms were poor. The peasants had nothing worth stealing, other than the occasional daughter."

Berg, newly assigned to his command, snorted. "I doubt any of their filthy piglets would have tempted me."

Bruckner ignored the implied refinement of Berg's taste. Though Berg was his subordinate and younger than himself, he was of a noble family.

Relieved of the weight of the casks, the two made a last check of their clothing. Before setting off to see what they could learn of these devilish "American" upstarts, they had exchanged apparel with several like-sized members of their footguard. The boots were worn to holes in the soles, the nondescript trousers and shirts tattered, the linen unspeakable. Soldiers in the field for months at a time sometimes bettered their situation by robbing corpses, but this area had been at war for many years now and apparently no one better shod or dressed had made themselves useful by dying within recent memory.

Bruckner did not have orders to do anything but scout the area. But since it took days of riding on the fleetest horses available to take a message to Vienna, then return with its answer, he'd decided to act on his own. Bruckner was confident the emperor would be generous to an officer who had taken the initiative to wound this new enemy at its very heart.

Two kegs of gunpowder could be very effective, when positioned properly and detonated. If they could just find a suitable target, they might well strike a quick blow for the empire and use the ensuing confusion to steal some of these remarkable munitions and perhaps even one of these bizarre iron carriages that moved faster than any horse, and, unlike living flesh, never tired.

Such a carriage stood in the middle of the main road into the town as they approached. "Halt!" A pair of men emerged from behind it, their shoulders broad, their muscles heavy with years of work. They were clad in curiously splotched garments and most obviously were not of peasant stock. No peasant ate well enough to put on that kind of muscle and fat.

"What business you have here?" said the foremost, a man with a heavy jaw but no beard or mustache at all so that he had the aspect of a youth, even though he was well advanced in years.

His German was so heavily accented as to be barely intelligible. These troops had been imported from very far away, Bruckner told himself, perhaps even as far as England. He snatched off his battered hat and then held out otherwise empty hands. "We only look for food," he said, keeping his voice faint, as though he were either ill or weak with hunger. "Soldiers burned our homes, killed our families, and took what little we had." He glanced out of the corner of his eye at Berg, who quite plainly had never put hand to plow in his life. "But we are hard workers. Will you take us to your lord so that we may put ourselves into his service?"

They would see through this ruse, he told himself, as cold sweat pooled between his shoulders. Anyone with half a brain would have the wit to see that he and Berg with their well-trimmed beards were of the aristocracy. They would be taken before the local lord all right—then put to death. This was utter foolishness. They never should have come—

"Hold out arms," the second man said. When Bruckner didn't obey at once, the guard seized his shoulders and spun him around. Bruckner had to resist the urge to whirl and strike him with a ready fist. No one laid hands on him in such a disrespectful fashion!

For the emperor, he told himself with gritted teeth. Focus on the rewards that would flood his way when Emperor Ferdinand learned of his initiative and cleverness. Hands patted the length of his body, straying into territory entirely too personal. He stiffened but kept his eyes focused downward on the bizarre gray ground.

"Good," the gruff voice said. "Around turn."

Over to the side, Berg looked as furious as he himself felt, evidently having been searched as well.

"Walk this road down," the man said, still mangling German, "until school in the center, brown and white, two stories. They take care of you there."

Berg straightened his grimy smock. His aristocratic blue eyes were glacial. "That is where we will swear allegiance?"

The shorter guard smiled grimly. "Something like that. We have room as long as you work. Everyone in Grantville works."

"That is all we want," Bruckner said. "Thank you." He took Berg's arm and dragged him in the indicated direction. He smiled and Berg smiled back with his strong crooked teeth as they stalked toward the school.

❖❖❖   ❖❖❖   ❖❖❖

Word of the party had spread by the next day, so that offers of help as well as inquiries came flooding in. Julie was hard put to sort them all out. She finally set up a command center at the school, using the consumer science room on the ground floor—the class used to be called "Home Ec" and that was the way Julie still thought of it—to receive donations and organize the tasks.

Gretchen Higgins, married to Jeff Higgins, a local boy, was among the first to drop in. Julie looked up as her friend appeared in the doorway. Gretchen was pregnant too, and due at about the same time, though like Julie, she wasn't really showing yet. The statuesque blonde put down her son, young Wilhelm, who was flourishing in his new home, and he toddled toward Julie on chubby, unsteady legs.

Gretchen smiled broadly. "We are having a party, *ja?*"

"You bet!" Julie gestured to her. "Come in and give me a hand!"

"I know little of parties," Gretchen said, striding across the room. She was tall and vibrant, her honey-blond hair clean and shining, her light-brown eyes dancing. "But I will do whatever you want."

"Well . . ." Julie nibbled on the end of her pen. "I'm trying to decide what local customs to include."

Gretchen pulled out an orange plastic chair and sat across the table from Julie, her brown eyes now puzzled. "Customs?"

"What people do for Christmas," Julie said. "Presents and decorations, trees, stuff like that."

Gretchen rubbed her forehead, concentrating. "It

has been long since we thought about anything but trying to keep alive." She sighed and closed her eyes. "But when I was little, I remember putting out shoes for presents." She opened her eyes and met Julie's. "Is that what you mean?"

"Shoes?" Julie shook her head. That sounded Dutch. "Well, never mind. I'm probably trying too hard. We have plenty of decorations and we'll just make it up as we go along. If we leave out something local, we can put it in next year."

Gretchen nodded, then rose to capture Wilhelm before he toppled a pile of Home Ec books. "So what do I do?" she said over her shoulder.

"Well, we need presents," Julie said. "I had Melissa give me a count of orphans and we're already up to two hundred thirty-three. You could go door to door and see what folks could spare in the way of toys and clothes and anything else that kids would like. Most of the local children arrived with so little. They could use almost anything."

"Okay," Gretchen said and swooped Wilhelm up. "Whatever we find, bring back here?"

"Yes." Julie stood and then leaned down to tickle the boy under his chin. His dazzling blue eyes crinkled and he crowed with laughter. One of these days, she told herself, she would have a baby of her own and it still made her head swim to think about it. "Thanks for helping."

"No problem," Gretchen said, sounding uncannily like her young husband, Jeff. "I'll get a lot, you'll see. We will have a good time!"

Julie had no doubt about that. She'd already seen Gretchen in action often enough to have a good idea what her friend was capable of. "You go, girl!" she said softly as the door closed, then turned her attention to the next on her list of knotty problems:

Where to find turkeys?

And who could she get to play Santa?

After two days in Grantville, Gottfried Pappenheim had been able to ascertain several facts. First, there were indeed a number of Jews in this outlandish town, as reported, but they were scattered throughout, as the boys had maintained, not sequestered in their own ghetto. No one seemed to make any fuss here about who was Catholic, Lutheran, Calvinist, or Jew. In fact, no one had even asked them to state their religion since they'd arrived. Several churches already existed within the city limits, although nothing as grand as the cathedrals in other cities, and a Jewish synagogue was currently being constructed.

Second, the marksman whom they sought actually was female, as reported. He found this harder to accept than the existence of these bizarre metal carriages constantly rattling about, but everyone who professed to know anything about the attack at the Alte Veste agreed: Jew Lee Mackay had done the shooting and she was a woman, a young one at that. Several even maintained she was presently with child and had been so even at the Alte Veste.

On the morning of the third day, Pappenheim motioned his two men outside after they had broken their fast in the huge dining hall of the refugee center attached to the school. The sky was gray, ominous with snow, and it was so cold, their exhaled breath hung like low clouds in the air.

He could still taste the breakfast served this morning. The food was extraordinarily good here, if sometimes strange. He rubbed his hands together in the cold, then stared ruefully at his blistered palms. In payment for food and bed, they had labored the last two days with other refugees to build a fortress guarding the northern approaches to the town. The Americans, clearly enough, were taking no chances of being surprised by another Croat cavalry raid.

Their hands were raw, their backs sore, but no one else seemed to mind the hard work so Pappenheim and his two companions had been careful not to utter any complaints themselves.

"I know now where she is," Durst said, blowing on his hands to keep warm.

Pappenheim narrowed his eyes. "The Jew?"

Durst nodded. "One of the cooks told me when I took my plate back to the scullery."

Pappenheim's hand went to the package concealed beneath his grimy farmer's smock. "Where is she then?"

"She is married to the headman of the village, a man named Michael Stearns, and serves herself as 'National Security Advisor.' She also, apparently, has the title of 'Senator,' whatever that means."

Unlike Durst, who was not well educated, Pappenheim recognized the term "Senator." It was a title the ancient Romans had used, although whether it meant the same thing here was impossible to determine. But the other . . . *National Security Adviser?*

"What exactly does that mean?" Pappenheim stared at Durst. The man looked ridiculous as a peasant, something like substituting a slavering war dog for his mother's pampered spaniel and imagining no one would notice.

The shorter man waved his hands. "I do not know, but the cook said she was the most important Jew in all of Grantville. So that must be the one we're looking for."

"Did she say where we could find this Jew?" Zeleny asked, his hands tucked beneath his armpits for warmth.

"They have a house near the center of the town, the cook told me." His face was rosy with cold. "A very nice house, apparently, since she described it to me rather enthusiastically. But I didn't dare ask her for directions. That would have made her suspicious. But I know what it looks like well enough, I think, to be able to find it if we can go to the town."

"We'll have to slip away," Pappenheim said. He raked fingers back through his white hair, now clean thanks to the marvelous "showers" provided in the refugee center. "The work crew will be going out soon."

"They never count," Zeleny said, "and it's a large work crew. I do not think we will be missed."

With Pappenheim leading the way, they edged around the massive building so that they were out of sight of the peasants gathering to work. In less than an hour, they were threading their way through the wood and brick domiciles that characterized this town.

"Fine work," Zeleny murmured, running his fingers over the magnificently regular red bricks. "I wonder who heads their guild?"

Pappenheim scowled. "Keep your mind on our mission. Who cares about bricks?"

Zeleny, whose father had been a guildsmen in

Rothenberg, ducked his head and closed his mouth, but Pappenheim could see the wheels turning in his obstinate head. It was almost as though this place were haunted, or possessed, like the old tales of faeries. According to them, if a man once tasted faery food, he was ruined for the real world. That was what Grantville was like.

It took them some time, but eventually they found the right residence. It fit the description, at least. And it was still early in the morning. Early enough that the residents would probably still be at home.

Pappenheim made sure Wallenstein's package was readily to hand, then marched up the steps, his head held high, and knocked on the door.

After a moment, it opened and a beautiful black-haired woman gazed at him with dark-brown eyes. "Yes?" she asked, in flawless German.

Pappenheim cleared his throat. Could this beauty possibly be the infamous marksman of Alte Veste? "We seek the Jew Lee Mackay, and we were told she lived here."

The woman blinked in surprise. "Julie Mackay?"

"Yes," Pappenheim said stiffly. His nose felt numb with cold.

"Oh, Julie does not live here," the woman said, shivering. "This is the home of Michael Stearns." Somewhere in the house, the thin wail of a baby began. She glanced over her shoulder, then looked at her wrist. "Julie should be at the school before too long, in the room called 'consumer science' on the first floor. Did you want to help with the party?"

Pappenheim blinked. "You are not the Jew Lee Mackay?" She certainly looked like a *Jude*, he thought.

The baby's crying grew louder. "No," she said with a trace of impatience. "Julie is at the school. You will have to excuse me." And she shut the door in his face.

"The school," Durst said, disgusted, after Pappenheim came down the steps and reported the conversation. "But we were just there!"

"We must go back then," Pappenheim said. He shook his head. "What does 'consumer science' mean? Sometimes I think these Americans are not sane at all."

Hard labor most certainly did not agree with Bruckner and, after two days, Berg was beside himself at the very thought of spending even one more hour sorting rock and fitting appropriately sized chunks into the walls of the growing fortress.

He glowered as they were herded along with the rest of the peasants out to the perimeter of the town. "I will not demean myself in this way anymore!" he said under his breath to Bruckner.

"They do not watch us so carefully now," Bruckner said quietly. "Have you noticed?"

Berg's lip curled as a small girl with blond plaits waved at them from the steps of a nearby house. "I have noticed that my back hurts!"

"I think we could sneak into the woods and retrieve our casks of gunpowder, if we picked the right moment. Then we could hide them near the wall and come back for them when it is dark tonight."

"Oh." Berg nodded. "I suppose so."

Bruckner scratched his neck. "I hear there is to be a party on Christmas Eve, in the great hall at the school. Everyone is invited, even peasants like ourselves."

"That is ridiculous," Berg said. "They should go to mass on Christmas Eve."

"A number of orphans will be at this party," Bruckner said. "People are being encouraged to bring presents for the poor children who have lost their family."

"Presents!" Berg glanced at him, cheeks ruddy from the cold. "You expect me to bring a present for some sniveling houseless brat?"

"We have very little, you and I. We are poor peasants, remember? Little more than the clothes on our backs and those two casks, but I think we should try to do what we can."

"The casks." Berg's eyebrows rose and understanding dawned in his face. "If we brought them disguised as presents, no one would ask questions."

"I imagine not." Bruckner smiled thinly. "Imagine how surprised the orphans will be."

Three days before the party, Julie shut herself up in the Home Ec room in despair. Although Jeff Higgins had agreed to oversee the hanging of the decorations and his wife Gretchen was efficiently collecting presents, no one in the entire town of Grantville would agree to play Santa! All the available men were either too shy, too short, too busy, too skinny, too young, too—something! The excuses were endless. She'd play Santa herself, if she thought she could pull it off, but this was important. As nearly as she could tell, local children knew nothing of her time's archetypal jolly old gent. If she settled for some poor excuse, the legend she was trying to establish would be warped forever.

She'd begged the doctor, James Nichols, last night, and he'd laughed in her face. "No," he'd said, his dark face apologetic. "I'd rather stitch up a hundred men than face a roomful of orphans and try to do the *ho-ho-ho* thing. Surely you can find someone else."

But there wasn't anyone. Michael Stearns had been but the first to turn her down. Her own husband Alex had been the second, pleading his Calvinist ties. "Dammit!" She folded her arms and put her head down on the shiny table. "How hard could playing Santa be?"

Someone knocked on the door.

"Go away!" she called, too close to tears to want to see anyone.

"Ve vant help vith partee," a deep voice called. "This right place, *ja*?"

Julie brushed the unshed tears out of her eyes. It was just the pregnancy hormones that were making her so emotional, she told herself, and besides, by the accent, these were obviously locals. She couldn't turn them away.

"*Ja*," she said, rising, then went to the door and unlocked it. "Come right in and—"

The door swung open to reveal three men waiting out in the hallway and the rest of her words died in her throat. Two of the men were unremarkable, just more refugee farmfolk, it seemed, one short and swarthy, the other pale, both clad in dingy peasant smocks.

But the third!

"Hallelujah!" she said, taking the center man's arm and pulling him into the light from the windows. It was as if Santa himself had come knocking on her door. He was tall, well over six feet. Best of all, even though he looked to be in his thirties, he had a head of white hair and a lovely beard. She resisted the urge to reach out and stroke it. "I'm Julie Mackay and you've just saved my life!"

True, that weird birthmark didn't really fit on Santa's face, but you couldn't have everything.

"*Ja,* Jew Lee," the man said. "Ve come find you."

She walked behind him, admiring the breadth of his shoulders. "You certainly did!"

The white eyebrows knotted together. "Ve haf orders—"

"Mike sent you, didn't he?" She beamed. "This is so wonderful! I must remember to thank him. You'll make a splendid Santa!"

The man fumbled at his smock.

"Yes," she said, "you're right. You really should try on the suit, but not in here." She hurried over to the cardboard box languishing in the corner and pulled out the traditional red flannel suit trimmed in white. "Take it down to the bathroom and see how it fits." She pushed the shirt and trousers into his arms. "We may have to alter it a bit, but I'm betting both pieces fit perfectly—after we add a few pillows."

"Pil-losss?" The man's brow knitted, then he turned to his companions, speaking in rapid German. By now, Julie's own German was rather good, but the language had so many dialects that she couldn't really follow what he was saying. Something about—a message?

"Don't worry," she said. "Mike didn't get around to telling me you were coming, but I know you'll be perfect." Taking his arm, she led him to the door and pointed. "The bathroom is down the hall, to the left. You can't miss it."

Her new Santa blinked down at her, perplexed, and seemed disinclined to leave. "Ve haf orders," he said again.

"Not now, you don't. Whatever Mike told you, I'm overriding him. President or not, Christmas comes first." She glimpsed Victor Saluzzo's worn blue suit jacket as he entered the hallway on the way to his office and waved. "Mr. Saluzzo!"

His head turned.

"I've found my Santa!" She pointed at her man.

Saluzzo's affable face broke into a smile. "Splendid!"

"But," she continued, "he doesn't speak much English and I can't understand his dialect. I need someone to help him try on the outfit."

Saluzzo nodded and headed toward her.

"*Nein,*" her Santa said, trying to wave him back. "I haf for you somesing, Jew Lee Mackay. You must—"

"Later!" Julie said merrily, giving her candidate over into Saluzzo's capable hands. "For now, go down to the men's room and try that on."

The tall man's blue eyes darted to his companions. "But—"

"Go!" She fixed him with a steely glare. "I'm too busy to argue!"

Saluzzo grinned. "Come on," he said. "I don't know about you, but, where we come from, there's no arguing with a pregnant woman once she takes that tone of voice!"

Julie leaned limply against the wall and watched their halting retreat. Her Santa kept looking back at her, something plainly on his mind. There was no telling about what. Well, it was probably nothing.

At any rate, she had her Santa! Now all she had to do was to make sure Jeff Higgins hung the rest of the decorations in the gym and Gretchen located enough presents for the list of orphans.

She charged out the door, her energy renewed. After finally finding a Santa, that should be a cinch.

In the end, Bruckner was surprised how easy it was to bring his nebulous plan to fruition. Instead of having to ferret out where and when this celebration was, a woman actually came out to the fortress and asked the workers for donations to be given to the orphan children of the town.

"For fatherless urchins?" Berg muttered, his aristocratic face smudged with mud. "They cannot be serious!"

Bruckner put down the rock he had been fitting into the cursed wall and dusted his blistered hands off. "Shut up," he hissed.

"We will both bring something," he said over his shoulder to the lovely peasant with the statuesque frame and shining dark-gold hair. Indeed, by the cleanliness of her person and the way she carried herself, she might easily have been mistaken for a duchess, if not for the hideous garb of this region. "We have very little, but we will do what we can."

He had to sigh, looking at her. She looked quite magnificent. The woman wore tight dark-blue trousers, just like a man, and a long flannel shirt beneath a sleek jacket that looked very warm. Though Berg was openly staring, she seemed totally at home in the bizarre garb.

Berg managed to make a effort to maintain their disguise. "What kind of donation do you require of us?" he asked, a bit sourly.

"Whatever you think a child might like," she said. "Toys would be nice, if you could fashion any, but old clothing to be made over or blankets, anything you could spare." Her light-brown eyes were shrewd, as though she wasn't fooled at all by their impersonation of farmers. Bruckner had the sudden intuition this Valkyrie had experienced things that no young woman of good breeding would encounter.

Then she took him totally by surprise. "Can you find a way to wrap your donation?" she asked.

Bruckner blinked, then glanced aside at Berg. "Wrap?"

"It is the custom of Grantville," she said, "to give presents at this season covered in something, so that their nature is not readily apparent. Then, I am told, the child is allowed to 'unwrap' it. I gather it was usually done with paper, in their—" She hesitated, her gaze faraway. "In their old home."

She shrugged, which only served to emphasize the ampleness of her very healthy figure. "At any rate," she said, "you can use whatever is at hand. If you can't find paper, some sort of cloth, perhaps, or cast-off clothing, but Julie is very determined. She wants everything 'wrapped.'"

"Then we will wrap," Bruckner said. "What time does the festival start?"

"Sundown on Christmas Eve," she said, "in the great hall at the school. What they call a gymnasium, which means something different than it does to us. You are staying right next to it in the refugee center."

"Yes, I know it," Bruckner said. He had wandered into the school several times, and peered into the huge room on the lower floor with its gleaming wooden floor and strange rope baskets dangling from boards nailed to columns. Once, when he looked in, youths were bouncing large orange balls, shouting with great abandon and running about. The activity was clearly popular—a game of some sort, obviously—but he found it perplexing.

"Bring the presents before the party starts," the woman said, then worked her way down the incomplete construction, asking the rest of the workers for their help, just as she had asked them.

The day of the party had dawned frosty and bright. Outside, a foot of snow already covered the ground, so Julie knew they would have a white Christmas for sure. Alex had guard duty with his cavalrymen that day, but had promised he would be off in time for the gift distribution this evening.

She picked up a cut-paper "snowflake," crafted by refugees. Unfortunately, it resembled an elephant more than an ice crystal.

Not that it really mattered, she told herself firmly, as she hung the "snowflake" on the magnificent tree set up in the center of the gym. She just wanted everyone to be together so they wouldn't focus on all they had lost. Though admittedly not everyone looked at it her way, she felt most had gained as much through the Ring of Fire as they'd been forced to leave behind. She had a sense of really being needed in this world, of coming into her own, despite her youth. Back in America, it would have been years before she could have had this much responsibility.

And then of course there was Alex, her wonderful husband, and the baby. Her hand crept to the new roundness of her abdomen. Next Christmas, they would share the wonders of the season with their child and she was surprised to find how eager she was for his or her arrival, when she'd never even thought she wanted children before this. For now, she would have to settle for making the best Christmas she could for Grantville's current population of children. Fortunately, Gretchen had gone over her quota on the gift gathering, so if a few unexpected guests turned up, it would just be the more, the merrier.

Hank Jones, one of the miners, called her over to admire the UMWA banner they were hanging on the wall. She was just having them move it over a few feet, when her dad stuck his head in the gym and waved. "Need any help, Jules?"

"You bet!" she said.

Her dentist father, Henry G. Sims, looked good, she thought, as though this century agreed with him. And maybe it did. Back in their own time, people took dentists for granted, made jokes about them, many avoiding them like the plague until they had no choice.

Here, the locals were literally lining up for Dr. Sims' services, despite the distressing lack of anesthetics. Next to their physicians, Doctors Nichols and Adams, he was the most sought after professional they had brought into the past. Even her Alex had gone to him and had his teeth worked over before he'd summoned the nerve to propose to her.

"Hang these up along the wall," she said to her father and pointed at an armful of sweet-scented pine boughs.

He picked one up and sniffed. "There's really something to be said for the real thing, isn't there? I can't remember when I smelled anything this wonderful."

She laughed. "You're just saying that so I'll forgive you for not playing Santa!"

"Maybe." He grinned and moved off toward the wall.

She put her hands on her hips. Now, just where was her German Santa Claus, Gottfried, anyway? She'd left instructions for him to arrive early.

Gretchen sailed through the door, holding her son Wilhelm in one arm and using the other to sweep her younger sister and a whole host of children before her. "We come early," she said to Julie, her cheeks red with the outside cold. "They all want to help."

The kitchen volunteers were already loading long cafeteria tables with food and drink and the children's eyes gravitated to the piles of iced Christmas cookies. "All right," Julie said, "but no snacking before the party begins."

Gretchen rattled off a string of insistent German. The wide-eyed children nodded, then headed for the Christmas tree instead, chattering like sparrows. Immediately, a slender little girl pulled off a gleaming gold ornament and dropped it, then stared in tears at the shards on the floor.

Julie sighed and went to fetch a dustpan. While she was on her knees sweeping up, three men appeared in the doorway, one of them Gottfried. His red Santa suit was hung neatly over one arm.

"It's about time," she said, dustpan in hand. The shards slid together with a clink. "Why aren't you dressed? The children are already beginning to arrive."

Gottfried glanced at his companions. "We talk," he said, using German this time. "Now."

"Not now," Julie said as another group appeared in the double doorway, their arms full. "Go put your suit on!"

"No, we talk." His blue eyes were fiercely insistent. "They say you are the shooter—"

"Look," she said, "I don't have time! I have to organize the presents into appropriate age groups, as well as boy and girl things." She pushed him toward the door. "Dress now. Talk later!"

With a forced smile, she turned to newcomers who had evidently brought presents for the children—five live chickens, a handcart full of potatoes, and a kid goat. The benefactors, Franz, Anna, and Ernst, siblings from a local farm just outside the town, seemed quite elderly and all smiled gap-toothed smiles at her.

"How—lovely," she managed. "Just set them down by the tree." She watched them hobble away, wondering just how they were going to wrap any of that.

Over the next two hours, the pile of gifts increased to include handcarved spoons, two rusty keys, an ax handle, a bag of goose feathers, a broken eating knife, several dozen candles, and innumerable bundles of firewood. Julie retreated to the wall where she watched the ongoing parade of dead hares and foxes, dried fish, vegetable seeds, and farm implements with growing amazement. Those few items that were wrapped, as requested, came covered mostly in hay or straw. The goat kept escaping to nibble at the hem of her dress.

The problem was quality, not quantity. Before too long, Julie had to start telling people to store the presents in the Home Ec room.

She shook her head. Toys—she'd told Gretchen to ask for toys, dolls, carved soldiers, balls, that sort of thing, but she'd obviously failed to communicate the concept.

It's all my fault, she thought miserably. *I messed up and now the orphans' first real Christmas is going to be ruined!* She felt tears coming on in earnest and didn't know what to do. She had to stay and do the best that she could, but the children were going to be so disappointed!

And, on top of everything else, Santa Gottfried had never come back, after she'd dispatched him to get dressed. She was either going to have to look for him herself, or find someone else who would.

"Pliss," a gruff voice said at the door. "Vhere put?" Two scruffy looking wind-burned peasants stood in the doorway, each holding a cask wrapped in a shirt.

Sauerkraut, she guessed. Wonderful. "In the room down the hall!" she said, pointing and trying her best not to snarl. The two ambled away, as she turned to find Santa and wring his neck.

Bruckner worked to contain his glee. There was a room right across the corridor from the one being used to store presents—unlocked and unoccupied. The perfect place for the casks. Close enough to the gymnasium to do the needed damage, but far enough away that no one would smell the burning fuse until he and Berg made their escape and it was too late to stop them.

"Come on," he said in a whisper, elbowing the door open. "We must hide these in here out of sight and lay the fuse."

Berg nodded, but his attention was clearly back

on the strange flameless lights that illuminated the gymnasium, as well as the steaming platters of food being carried in from the dining hall next door. Music was playing, as good as the finest musicians he'd ever heard, but none were in sight. "How do they do it?" he wondered. "Is it witchcraft?"

A dark-headed toddler of about three came running down the corridor and threw her arms around Bruckner's legs, dimpling up at him. "Are you Santa Claus?" she asked in German.

"No!" He shifted his weight to break her hold. "Let—go!" he said in a fierce whisper.

The girl laughed and pressed her cheek against his leg. "I am a good girl, Santa," she said. "I get present!"

"How—nice." Bruckner's skin crawled as he handed his cask off to Berg and then pried the tiny fingers off his trousers. "Now, run along and play."

Her face contorted and then she dissolved into wailing tears. "Did you forget my present?"

"Shhh!" Bruckner glanced around, afraid of drawing too much attention. Fortunately, they were alone and Berg had already taken the second cask into the room, closing the door behind him. "I am sure you will get a lovely present, when this Santa fellow arrives, if you just do not cry!"

A tall young woman came into the corridor, saw the wailing child and angled toward them without hurrying to sweep her up into her arms. "Hush, Berta! Whatever can you be making such a fuss about?" Her light-brown eyes regarded Bruckner over the child's dark curls.

He realized with a start it was the same woman

who had been soliciting gifts out by the fortress. "I am sorry," he said stiffly. "This child is mistaken. She thinks I am someone called 'Santa.'"

"Oh, Berta." The woman chuckled, taking the little girl by the hand and turning away. "This is not Santa. Julie told you—Santa wears a beautiful red suit and has a long white beard and merry eyes." She gave Bruckner a not entirely friendly glance over her shoulder. "And he is much nicer. Julie says he loves little girls."

A moment later, they were gone. Bruckner cracked open the door and slipped through. The room was dark, but there was enough light from the windows for him to spot Berg in a corner, already beginning to lay the powder fuse.

"I hate peasants," Berg muttered when Bruckner joined him in the shadows. "They are stupid and carry disease."

Bruckner began opening the second cask, mopping at his forehead with the back of his sleeve. He could hear people pouring through the school doors now, men, women, and children. The noise outside grew louder with every passing moment. Soon everyone would be too preoccupied to notice them at all.

"As soon as they start serving the banquet," he said, "we will strike a spark, and then slip away."

Berg nodded and settled on the floor in front of the casks to wait for the right moment.

Fortunately, Julie found Gottfried and his two friends in the cafeteria next door, sitting at one of the few tables that hadn't already been moved into the gym, and drinking hot tea. To her relief, he was wearing the red Santa suit, though not the hat. "What are you doing in here?" she burst out at the sight of them. "You're supposed to be next door playing Santa! Where's your hat?"

"I did not come to wear a silly hat," Gottfried said firmly. "I came to talk with you."

"Not now!" Julie hauled at his arm, but he was rock solid, impossible to move. "The children are all here. In a moment, they'll serve the food, and then after that, you're on!"

Gottfried's brows knotted. "On what?"

"Never mind," she said. "We're counting on you!"

"I want to talk about the Alte Veste," he said. "You were there, yes?"

The strange birthmark on his face, she suddenly noticed, seemed more prominent than she'd remembered. It looked almost like two crossed swords. "What?" she said, as his words came together inside her head. "The Alte Veste? What does that have to do with anything?"

"You were the shooter, yes?" His blue eyes were fierce now.

"Who are you?" She edged back out of reach.

"You shot Wallenstein." His tone was more sure now, his manner businesslike. He stood and towered over her, his body looking rock-hard. Her heart raced. How could she have seen Santa Claus in this man? He was more like a pit bull!

"I'll get Mike," she said, trying to keep her voice steady. "He can tell you about the Alte Veste, if that's why you're here." She turned and almost ran away.

Footsteps clattered after her across the floor as they followed.

In the gym, food was now being served on pink plastic cafeteria trays to the tune of "Rudolph, the Red-Nosed Reindeer." Children were squealing with delight as adults led them to their place and sat them down with the biggest portions they'd ever been served in their short lives.

As Julie dashed through the double doors into the gymnasium, she saw three Grantville boys trying to rig up a harness for a gift suckling pig out of school jump ropes, while a pair of wondering little girls in red Christmas frocks were on their knees, staring in rapt fascination at three speckled hens scratching in vain at the polished wooden floor. Mike Stearns was standing with his wife Rebecca and their new baby daughter over on the far side of the room, looking contented.

"Mike!" She waved, trying to keep the panic out of her voice. Gottfried and his friends were only three men and she hadn't seen any obvious weapons. Maybe Mike and some of the other men could get them out of here before they caused trouble. "Mike, I have to talk to you!"

Her father was standing close to the Christmas tree with her Uncle Frank, admiring the lights, and she tried to get their attention too. "Dad! Uncle Frank! Over here!"

The trio entered the room, their eyes searching her out. No! she thought hard at heaven. Please! Not here, not now, just when everyone is so peaceful and happy!

"What is it, Julie?" Mike said, his eyes twinkling. "I already told you I won't play Santa."

"I already have a Santa," she said, the breath wheezing in her chest, "and he's asking me about the Alte Veste!"

"What?" Mike glanced up at the approaching men.

"They know I was the sharpshooter at the Alte Veste," she said as her father and uncle reached her side. "I think—they must be part of Wallenstein's army."

Mike reached under his jacket and she saw the sleek deadly shape of his pistol tucked into a shoulder holster. "It's all right," he said, stepping in front of her. "Nothing is going to happen."

Julie caught at his arm. "I know this is serious, but please don't let them spoil the party."

Gottfried stopped a few paces away, and drew a small box out from his Santa suit. "Jew Lee Mackay," he said, his tone very firm—like that of a man who has put up with as much nonsense as he can tolerate. The other two flanked him like an honor guard.

"Hello, Santa," Mike said evenly. "It's about time you showed up."

"*Santa!*" A trio of Grantville children, who recognized the suit, squealed and launched themselves across the gym floor. "Where's your bag?" they asked, their voices echoing. "Where're your reindeer?"

Scattered applause rang out and more children sprang up from their places at the long tables. "Santa! Santa!"

Gottfried stared down at them, evidently unnerved.

"What's your business here, Santa?" Mike had his

hand on the .357 magnum under his suit, but hadn't drawn it out yet. "Only our friends are invited to this party."

Gottfried straightened and nodded at Mike, then turned to Julie. "I am General Gottfried von Pappenheim," he said. "I have been sent by Imperial General Wallenstein to find the one who shot him at the Alte Veste."

Mike's gun came out. Julie glanced at her uncle and father, who had also drawn guns. The image of Wallenstein's shattered body falling was vivid in her mind.

"The duke of Friedland instructed me—" Pappenheim broke off, his head suddenly swiveling toward the entrance to the gymnasium. His nostrils flared, as though scenting something.

Bruckner had the door open, ready for their escape. He could hear children in the gymnasium shouting. *"Santa! Santa!"*

Berg cursed, as a third spark flared and died.

"Idiot!" Already the room stank with burning gunpowder from Berg's fumbling efforts to light the fuse. The smell—if not much smoke, yet—was drifting down the corridor

He took the flint away from Berg and knelt down. The casks were in the corner, now on their sides, with a powder train leading to them.

He gripped the steel and flint carefully and struck a spark. For a moment, the powder hissed but, again, the flame didn't catch. Unfortunately, the long days the casks had been buried had allowed some dampness to penetrate.

Berg grasped his shoulder and pulled him around, pointing out the door. "Look!"

The tall, powerfully built man in the red suit was striding down the corridor, sniffing with his nose. He spotted Bruckner and Berg almost immediately.

He smiled and kept striding toward them. About the coldest smile Bruckner had ever seen. And, behind him, other men were starting to come into the corridor.

Desperately, Bruckner looked down at the cursed fuse. No hope for it. They'd just have to escape.

He and Berg scrambled out of the room and began running down the corridor. With a muffled curse, the white-haired man dashed after them. Glancing over his shoulder, Bruckner could see other men coming after him—and they were holding firearms.

They almost made it out of the building before being tackled from behind and sent sprawling across the hard floor. Berg was cursing, but the blow had knocked the wind out of Bruckner and he was having trouble breathing.

Someone flipped him over on his back and stared down at him with cold blue eyes. The muzzle of a pistol was shoved into his neck. "Who in the hell are you?"

He could only shake his head and try to make his lungs work. Rough hands hauled him to his feet and then held him there when his legs buckled. The blue-eyed man lowered the pistol but kept it in his hand.

To his left, he could hear Berg complaining of the rough treatment and invoking the prestige of his ancient lineage.

Red invaded his field of vision and he tried to make

his eyes focus. "There's gunpowder in that room!" someone was shouting in German. "They were going to blow up the school!"

The blue eyes were very hard. "Who sent you?"

He tried to take a deep breath and this time succeeded in drawing a moderate amount of air into his shocked lungs. "We are from Emperor Ferdinand," he said weakly. "We are of high rank and will surely be ransomed, if you preserve our lives."

The man in the red suit came up. "Nonsense. The emperor will disown you immediately. To save himself money, if nothing else. I sense two young officers haring off on their own, trying to curry favor and rise in rank."

He had a birthmark on his face and now it seemed to blaze red, like two crossed burning swords. Bruckner blinked. He had heard of such a famous mark once, somewhere . . .

"So, General Pappenheim," the blue-eyed man said. "It seems we are in your debt."

Pappenheim! Bruckner's knees went weak again. Though he had never had the honor of meeting the famous general, everyone who had fought in this war knew of him. He was something of a legend. What was he doing here with these damned Americans?

Berg had a cut over one eye where he'd struck the floor and his lip had already swollen to twice its size. "I demand to be ransomed!"

A squealing pig came racing down the corridor, followed by a bevy of laughing children.

The two would-be assassins were turned over to the custody of Fred Jordan and another deputy, who handcuffed them and hauled them away—none too gently. One of them was still shrieking a demand for ransom. The other seemed in shock and said nothing.

Julie, on the other hand, was full of questions. She came over to Pappenheim, who was now back in the gymnasium handing out presents from under the tree after it had become apparent to him the children wouldn't take no for an answer. Over in the corner, toddlers were building a fortress out of potatoes.

"I don't understand," she told him. "Those two meant to kill us, but you stopped them, so that can't be why you're here."

He looked baffled. "I told you." He passed out a doll made out of straw to a beaming two-year-old led up by Gretchen. "Wallenstein sent me."

"I shot Wallenstein," she said numbly. "I hit him twice! I saw him fall!"

Gretchen brought another child forward, a five-year-old with eager eyes. Pappenheim picked up a dried fish wrapped in yarn and handed it over. The child rattled off a string of incomprehensible dialect. Gretchen smiled. "He says he'll name it Fritz. It looks just like his uncle!"

The general shook his head and moved on to piles of vegetable seeds in burlap bags. "Wallenstein was wounded, true, very badly. Now he wants to change sides. The emperor is no longer pleased with him, after the Alte Veste—and then the duke read one of the books we stole from you which says the emperor will have him assassinated."

Another happy child raced off. "So the duke decided to make a secret treaty with you Americans and King Gustav of Sweden."

"But he tried to kill our kids—and I did my best to kill him!" Julie protested. "Came that close, too! He can't just turn around now, say all is forgiven, and become our ally."

Mike Stearns had been standing nearby, listening. "Why not?" he asked. "I'll sup with the devil—if it means breaking Bohemia from Austria and tying that bastard Ferdinand into a knot. I won't think twice. Gustav Adolf won't even blink an eye."

She was trying to think of an answer to that when Pappenheim gently disentangled a little girl who was trying to climb into his lap, reached into his voluminous red Santa pocket and pulled out the same small wooden box she'd seen him carrying earlier.

"I brought this from Wallenstein, at his command," he said earnestly. "For the Jew Lee Mackay who shot him. Though it seems you are not actually a *Jude*, after all." He handed it to Julie. "There is a condition to the alliance."

"I knew it," her Uncle Frank said. "Leopards don't change their spots. What does the bastard want—half of Thuringia?"

Julie opened the lid. Inside the box, nestled on a bed of blue silk, was the deformed shape of a rifle bullet, the same caliber she had used at the Alte Veste. It was threaded onto a golden chain. Beside it rested the remains of four shattered teeth.

"Oh—my—God," she breathed.

Gretchen peered into the box. Her light-brown eyes crinkled at the corners and her face was suddenly merry. "Ha! He wants magic, General Pappenheim, doesn't he? The magic of new American teeth!"

Pappenheim nodded. "That is his condition for the

alliance. Not negotiable. American dentist to come to his estate—or he will come here—so he can chew again."

Julie looked at her dentist father, who was as amazed as she was. "Well, Dad," she said. "I guess the alliance is up to you."

She could see the wheels turning inside his head as he tried to make sense of this upside-down world in which they found themselves, where the most sought after Christmas presents of the day were apparently a suckling pig and a pile of potatoes, dentists were held in higher accord than emperors, and a cavalry general was Santa Claus.

She snuck a second peek at the gruesome teeth. It would take some getting used to.

The Wallenstein Gambit

Eric Flint

Chapter 1: The Bohemian Opening
March, 1633

1

"So what's this all about, Mike?" asked Morris Roth, after Mike Stearns closed the door behind him. "And why did you ask me to meet you in Edith's home?"

Grantville's jeweler looked around the small living room curiously. That was the part of Mike's request that Morris had found most puzzling. By the early spring of 1633, Stearns was usually so busy with political affairs that people came to see him in his office downtown.

As soon as he spotted the young man sitting in an armchair in the corner, Morris' curiosity spiked—and, for the first time, a trace of apprehension came into his interest. He didn't know the name of the young man, but he recognized him even though he wasn't in uniform.

He was a German mercenary, captured in the short-lived battle outside Jena the year before, who'd since enrolled in the army of the United States. More to the point, Morris knew that he was part of Captain Harry Lefferts' unit—which, in reality if not in official parlance, amounted to Mike Stearns' combination of special security unit and commandos.

"Patience, patience," said Mike, smiling thinly. "I'd apologize for the somewhat peculiar circumstances, but as you'll see for yourself in a moment we have a special security problem to deal with." He glanced at the man sitting in the armchair. "I think the best way to make everything clear is just to introduce you to someone. Follow me."

Stearns turned and headed for the hallway, Morris trailing behind. Edith Wild's house wasn't a big one, so it only took a few steps before he came to a closed door. "We're keeping him in here, while he recovers from his latest round of surgery. Edith volunteered to serve as his live-in nurse."

Morris restrained his grimace. Edith Wild was capable enough as a nurse, so long as it didn't involve any real medical experience. Like many of Grantville's nurses since the Ring of Fire, she'd had no background in medical work. She'd been employed in a glass factory in Clarksburg.

Her main qualification for her new line of work,

so far as Morris could tell, was that she was a very big woman, massive as well as tall, and had much the same temperament as the infamous Nurse Ratchett in a movie he'd once seen, *One Flew Over the Cuckoo's Nest*. Not the sadism, true. But the woman was a ferocious bully. She was normally engaged in enforcing Grantville's public health laws, a job which required a firm hand given the huge influx of immigrants who had a seventeenth-century conception of sanitation and prophylaxis.

A "firm hand," Edith Wild certainly had. Morris had, more than once, heard Germans refer to her as "the Tatar." When they weren't calling her something downright obscene.

And who is "he"? Morris wondered. But he said nothing, since Mike was already opening the door and ushering him into the bedroom beyond.

It was a room to fit the house. Small, sparsely furnished, and just as spick-and-span clean as everything else. But Morris Roth gave the room itself no more than a cursory glance. Despite the bandages covering much of the lower face, he recognized the man lying in the bed within two seconds.

That was odd, since he'd never actually met him. But, perhaps not so odd as all that. Like many residents of Grantville, Morris had a poster up in his jewelry store that portrayed the man's likeness. True, in the form of a painting rather than a photograph. But he could now see that it was quite a good likeness.

He groped for words and couldn't find any. They'd have been swear words, and Morris avoided profanity. The poster in his shop was titled: *Wanted, Dead or Alive.*

The man was studying him with dark eyes. Despite the obvious pain the man was feeling, his expression was one of keen interest.

Abruptly, the man raised a hand and motioned for Morris to approach him.

"Go ahead," said Mike, chuckling harshly. "He doesn't bite, I promise. He couldn't anyway, even if he wanted to. His jaw's wired shut."

Reluctantly, much as he'd move toward a viper, Morris came over to the side of the bed. There was a tablet lying on the covers—one of the now-rare modern legal tablets—along with a ballpoint pen.

The man in the bed took the pen in hand and, shakily, scratched out a message. Then, held it up for Morris to see.

The words were written in English. Morris hadn't known the man in the bed knew the language. He wasn't surprised, really. Whatever other crimes and faults had ever been ascribed to that man, lack of intelligence had never been one of them.

But Morris didn't give any of that much thought. His attention was entirely riveted on the message itself.

    CHMIELNICKI
    I CAN STOP IT

For a moment, it seemed to Morris Roth as if time stood still. He felt light-headed, as if everything was unreal. Since the Ring of Fire, when Morris came to understand that he was really stranded in the seventeenth century, in the early 1630s, not more than a week had ever gone by without his thoughts turning to the Chmielnicki Massacre of 1648. And wondering if there was something—anything—he could do to prevent it. He'd raised the matter with Mike himself, several times before. Only to be told, not to his surprise, that Mike couldn't think of any way a small town of Americans fighting for its own survival in war-torn Germany in the middle of the Thirty Years War could possibly do anything to stop a coming mass pogrom in the Ukraine.

"How?" he croaked.

Again, the man scrawled; and held up the tablet.

> COMPLICATED
> STEARNS WILL EXPLAIN
> BUT I WILL NEED YOUR HELP

Morris looked at Stearns. Mike had come close and seen the message himself. Now, he motioned toward the door. "Like he says, it's complicated. Let's talk about it in the living room, Morris. After the extensive surgery done on him, the man needs his rest."

Morris followed Mike out of the bedroom, not looking back. He said nothing until they reached the living room. Then, almost choking out the words, could only exclaim:

"Wallenstein?"

Mike shrugged, smiling wryly, and gestured at the couch. He perched himself on an ottoman near the armchair where the soldier was sitting. "Have a seat, Morris. We've got a lot to discuss. But I'll grant you, it's more than a bit like having a devil come and offer you salvation."

After Morris was seated, he managed a chuckle himself.

"Make sure you use a long spoon."

Seeing the expression on Mike's face, Morris groaned. "Don't tell me!"

"Yup. I plan to use a whole set of very long-handled tableware, dealing with that man. And, yup, I've got you in mind for the spoon. The ladle, actually."

"He wants money, I assume." Morris scowled. "I have to tell you that I get awfully tired of the assumption that all Jews are rich. If this new venture of ours takes off, I might be. Faceted jewelry is unheard-of in this day and age, and we should get a king's ransom for them. But right now . . . Mike, I don't have a lot of cash lying around. Most of my money is invested in the business."

Mike's smile grew more lopsided still. "Wallenstein's no piker, like the rest of them. He wants a lot more than your money, Morris. He doesn't want the gold from the goose, he wants the goose himself."

Morris raised a questioning eyebrow.

"Figure it out. Your new jewel-cutting business looks to make a fortune, right? So where's that fortune going to pour into? Grantville—or Prague?"

Morris groaned again. "Mike, I'm over fifty years old! So's Judith. We're too old to be relocating to—to— A city that doesn't have modern plumbing," he finished, sounding a bit lame even to himself.

Stearns said nothing, for a moment. Then, harshly and abruptly: "You've asked me four times to think of a way to stop the coming massacres of Jews in the Ukraine. Probably the worst pogrom in Jewish history before the Holocaust, you told me. This is the best I can manage, Morris. *I* can't do it, but Wallenstein . . . maybe. But it's a hell of a gamble—and, frankly, one which has a lot more parameters than simply the Jewish problem in eastern Europe."

Morris' mind was finally starting to work clearly again. "To put it mildly. Am I right in assuming that Wallenstein came here secretly to propose an alliance? He'll break from the Austrian Habsburgs and take Bohemia out of Ferdinand's empire?"

Mike nodded. "That—and the best medical care in the world. Julie's bullets tore him up pretty good, Morris, and the man's health was none too good to begin with. The truth is, Doctor Nichols—he did most of the actual surgery—doesn't think Wallenstein's likely to live more than a few years."

"A few years . . ." Morris mused. "Do you think—?"

"Who knows, Morris? Immediately, the alliance is a godsend for us, as weird as it looks. I've discussed it with Gustav Adolf and he agrees. If Becky's mission to France can't get us a peace with Richelieu, we're looking to be at war again soon. A revolt in Bohemia—sure as hell with Wallenstein in charge—will at least take the Austrians out of the equation. As for the Ukraine . . ."

He shrugged. "We've got fifteen years, theoretically—assuming the butterfly effect doesn't scramble so-called 'future history' the way it usually does."

"It'll maybe scramble the timing," Morris said grimly, "but I doubt it'll do much to scramble what's coming. The Chmielnicki Massacre was centuries in the making, and the ingredients of it were pretty intractable."

Mike nodded. Morris knew that after the first time he'd raised the subject with Mike, Stearns had done some research on it. He'd been helped, of course, by his Jewish wife and father-in-law. By now, Morris thought, Mike probably knew more than he did about the situation of eastern European Jewry.

"Intractable is putting it mildly. If it were just a matter of religious or ethnic prejudices and hatreds, it'd be bad enough. But there's a vicious class factor at work, too. Polish noblemen are the landlords over Ukrainian peasants—whom they gouge mercilessly—and they use the Jews as their rent collectors and tax farmers. So when the Ukrainian peasants finally revolted under Cossack leadership—will revolt, I should say—it's not too hard to figure out why they immediately targeted the Jews."

Morris sighed. As much as he was naturally on the side of the Jews in the Ukraine, he knew enough about the situation not to think for a minute that there was any simple solution. In fact, he'd once gotten into a ferocious quarrel with one of the Abrabanel scions who, like a number of the young Jews who had gravitated into Grantville, had become something of a Jewish nationalist.

Arm the Ukrainian Jews! the young man had proclaimed.

"For what?" Morris had snarled in response. "So they can become even more ruthless rent collectors? You stupid idiot! Those Ukrainian peasants are people too, you know. You've got to find a solution that they'll accept also."

He stared at the large bookcase against one of the walls, where Edith kept her beloved collection of Agatha Christie novels. For a moment, he had a wild and whimsical wish that the great detective Hercule

Poirot would manifest himself in the room and provide them all with a neat and tidy answer.

Neat and tidy . . . in the seventeenth century? Ha! We never managed "neat and tidy" even in our own world.

"All right," he said abruptly. "As long as Judith agrees, I'll do it. I'll try to talk Jason Gotkin into coming with us, too, since he was studying to be a rabbi before the Ring of Fire."

Having made the pronouncement, he was immediately overwhelmed by a feeling of inadequacy. "But—Mike—I don't . . ."

"Relax, Morris," said Mike, smiling. "You won't be on your own. Just for starters, Uriel Abrabanel has agreed to move to Prague also."

Morris felt an instant flood of relief. Rebecca's uncle was probably an even more accomplished spymaster and political intriguer than her father Balthazar. And if he was elderly, at least he didn't have Balthazar's heart problems. So far as anyone knew, anyway.

"Take those young firebrands around Dunash with you, also."

Morris grimaced. Dunash Abrabanel was the young man he'd had the quarrel with. "I'm not sure they'll listen to me, Mike. Much less obey me."

"Then let them stay here and rot," Mike said harshly. "If nothing else, Morris, I want to give those fellows something to do that'll keep them from haring off to the Holy Land in order to found the state of Israel. I do *not* need a war with the Ottoman Empire on top of everything else."

Morris chuckled. "Mike, not even Dunash is crazy enough to do that. It's just a pipedream they talk about now and then, usually after they've had way too much to drink."

"Maybe so. Then again, maybe not. They're frustrated, Morris, and I can't say I blame them for it. So let's give them something constructive to do. Let them go to Prague and see if they can convince Europe's largest Jewish community to throw its support behind Wallenstein."

Morris was already thinking ahead. "That won't be easy. The Jews in Prague are Ashkenazim and they're Sephardic. Not to mention that Prague's Jewry is orthodox, which they really aren't—well, they are, but they often follow different—and . . . Oh, boy," he ended lamely.

"I didn't say it would be easy, Morris."

"Dunash will insist on arming the Jews."

Mike shrugged. "So? I'm in favor of that anyway. As long as those guns aren't being used to help Polish noblemen gouge their peasants, I'm all for the Jewish population being armed to the teeth."

"Will Wallenstein agree to that? As it stands, Bohemian laws—like the laws of most European countries—forbid Jews from carrying weapons."

Mike jerked a thumb at the bedroom door. "Why ask me? The man's right in there, Morris. Negotiate with him."

After a moment's hesitation, Morris squared his shoulders and marched into the bedroom.

When he came back out, a few minutes later, he had a bemused expression on his face.

"Well?"

Mutely, Morris showed Mike a sheet of paper from

Wallenstein's legal pad. When Mike looked down at it, he saw Wallenstein's shaky scrawl.

AGREED
JEWS MAY BE ARMED
BUT MUST SUPPORT ME
OR I WILL BURN DOWN THE
GHETTO

"He's not the nicest guy in the world," Morris observed. He folded up the sheet and tucked it into his short pocket. "On the other hand . . ."

Mike finished the thought for him. "He's ambitious as Satan and, whatever else, one of the most capable men in the world. Plus, he doesn't seem to share most of this century's religious bigotry. That doesn't mean he won't burn down the ghetto. He will, Morris, in a heartbeat. But he won't do it because you're Jews. He'll do it because you failed him."

Judith agreed more quickly than Morris would have thought. Indeed, his wife began packing the next morning. But the first thing she put in the trunk was the biggest ladle they had in the kitchen.

"We'll need it," she predicted.

2

"It looks a little weird without the statues," mused Len Tanner, adjusting his horn-rim glasses. He leaned over the stone railing of the Charles Bridge and looked first one way, then the other. The bridge was the main span across the Vltava River, and connected the two halves of the city of Prague. It had been built almost two centuries earlier, in the fourteenth century—though not finished until the early fifteenth, moving as slowly as medieval construction usually did—and had been named after the Holy Roman Emperor who commanded its erection. The *Karlüv most*, to use the proper Czech term, although Tanner said they hadn't given it that name until sometime in the nineteenth century. In this day and age, it was still just called the Stone Bridge.

Watching Tanner, Ellie Anderson almost laughed. Something in the little twitches Len was making with his lips made it clear that he'd have been chewing on his huge mustache, if he still had one.

But, he didn't—and wouldn't, as long as Ellie had anything to say about it. However many of Len Tanner's quirks and foibles she'd grown accustomed to and decided she could live with, that damned walrus mustache was not one of them. She preferred her men clean-shaven and always had, a quirk of her own she suspected came from memories of a great bearded lout of a father. Dim memories. He'd been killed in a car wreck when she was only seven years old, caused by a drunk driver. Him. It was a one-car accident and the only other casualty had been the oak tree at the sharp bend in the road near their house.

Fortunately, the oak tree had survived. Ellie's memories of the oak tree were a lot more extensive, and a lot fonder, than those of her father. Years later, she'd even built a treefort in it. The neighbors had been a little scandalized. Not so much by the implied disrespect for her father—truth be told, nobody in that little eastern Kentucky town had had much use for Dick Anderson—but because it was yet another display of the tomboy habits that had already made her the despair of the town's gentility.

"Gentility" as they saw themselves, anyhow. Ellie had thought then—still did—that the term was ludicrous applied to seven matrons, not one of whom had more than a high school education and only two of whom had ever been anything more than housewives and professional busybodies.

She wondered, for a moment, what had happened to any or all of them. She hadn't been back to her hometown in ten years, since her mother died of cancer and her two brothers had made it clear they'd just as soon not be burdened with her company. Since the feeling was mutual, she'd simply come in for the funeral and left the same evening.

And what do you care, anyway? she asked herself sarcastically. *They're a whole universe away, so it's a little late to be thinking about it now.*

But she knew the answer. Hers had been a self-sufficient life, and she was not sorry for it. Still, it had often been a lonely one, too.

It wasn't now, because of Len Tanner. Ten times more aggravating, often enough, but . . . not lonely.

"Looks weird," he repeated.

"Oh, for God's sake, Len! Doesn't it strike you as a little eccentric to call a city 'weird' because it doesn't have statues from three and half centuries later, in another universe, that only *you* remember because—far as I know—you're the only resident of Grantville weird enough to go to Prague on vacation?"

The jibe, not to Ellie's surprise, simply made Tanner look smug.

"Not my fault the rest of 'em are a bunch of hicks. 'Vacation,' ha! For most of 'em, that meant fishing somewhere within fifty miles or—ooh, how daring—a trip to the big city called Pittsburgh." Again, his lips made that *wish-there-was-a-mustache-here* twitch. "Ha! I remember, back when Mike Stearns went to Los Angeles for three years. Everybody else in Grantville—'cept me—thought he'd gone to Mars or something. The only 'furrin country' most of those boys had ever been to was Vietnam. And that was hardly what you'd call a sight-seeing trip."

It was one of the many odd little things about Len Tanner, Ellie reflected. To her surprise, she'd discovered that he was probably the most widely traveled man she'd ever known. Tourism was one of Len's passions. His main passion, probably, leaving aside that grotesque mustache. For his entire adult life, every vacation he'd gotten—and he'd always been willing to work extra hours to pile up vacation time—Tanner had gone somewhere outside the old United States. Some of them pretty exotic places, like China and—

Ellie chuckled. One of Tanner's little brags was that he was the only American veteran in Grantville who'd made it all the way to Hanoi. True, he was a veteran of the Grenadan conquest, which the Vietnam vets in town didn't consider a "real war." Still, they didn't begrudge him the boast. They even chuckled at it, themselves, partly because most people who got to know him tended to like Len Tanner, and partly because . . .

He was a lonely man, and, what was worse, a

man who was uncomfortable in his loneliness. So, for years, his friends and drinking buddies had indulged his little oddities.

Loneliness had been at the heart of his compulsive traveling, Ellie suspected. Tanner had adopted tourism as a hobby, the way other lonely people adopt other things. And if it was a more expensive hobby than most, it had at least made Tanner less parochial-minded than most people of Ellie's acquaintance. He actually *had* seen the "big wide world," even if his ingrained awkwardness with learning foreign languages always kept him at a certain distance from the people whose countries he'd visited.

Now, Tanner was staring up at the Hradcany. The hill upon which Prague Castle was perched overlooked the entire city. It wasn't much of a hill, really, but it hardly mattered. The *Prazský hrad*—to use the Czech term for "Prague Castle"—seemed to dominate everything. It was an ancient edifice, begun in the ninth century A.D. by the rulers of the Slavic tribes who had migrated into the area a century or two earlier, and added to in bits and pieces as the centuries passed. But, always, whether the rulers of the area that eventually became known as Bohemia were Slavic princes or German Holy Roman Emperors, the seat of power was in Prague Castle.

"At least that's still pretty much the same," Tanner said. "Except for that stupid, boring façade they added in the eighteenth century. Good riddance—or riddance-never-come, I guess I should say." He exuded an air of satisfaction, studying the hill. "Even when I visited it, though, that gorgeous cathedral was the centerpiece. Now, even more so."

Ellie wouldn't have used the term "gorgeous" to describe St. Vitus Cathedral, herself. As far as she was concerned, the immense Gothic structure that loomed over the entire Hradcany belonged where everything Gothic belonged—in a romance novel, preferably featuring sexy vampires.

Womanfully, though, she restrained herself from calling it "ugly and grotesque." One of Tanner's many little quirks was that he invariably defended—ferociously— each and every architectural or artistic endeavor of the Roman Catholic Church. That was to make up, she'd once accused him, for the fact that he was never found in church more than once a year.

I ain't a "lapsed Catholic"! he'd responded hotly, at the time. *Just, y'know, not around as much as maybe I oughta be.*

Well, that's one way to put it, Ellie had retorted. *Is that why Father Mazzare greets you with "howdy, stranger"?*

Remembering that minor fight, she smiled a little. She and Tanner bickered a lot, but, truth be told, he really *was* a hard man to dislike. Once you got to know him, at least. Most of his vices and character flaws he wore on his sleeve. What lay underneath—assuming you could cut your way through that damn crust—was . . . really pretty nice and warm.

At least, Ellie Anderson thought so. More and more, in fact, as time went on.

As was her own nature, the surge of sentiment made her brusque.

"C'mon, Len! Let's quit gawking at the sights.

We're supposed to be on a secret mission for Morris Roth, remember?"

Tanner gave her a sour look. Then, bestowed a look considerably more sour on the squad of men who were following them. Lounging along behind them, it might be better to say. The four mercenary soldiers in Pappenheim's pay somehow managed to make their way across a bridge as if they were loafing in an alehouse.

"Some 'secret' mission," he grumbled. "With those clowns in our wake. Why don't we just put on signs saying: *Attention! Dangerous furriners!*"

She took him by the arm and began leading him along the bridge, toward that part of Prague known as the *Staré Mesto*—which meant nothing fancier than "Old Town"—where the eastern end of the Charles Bridge abutted.

"Jesus! Were you just as suspicious of tourist guides, too, back in your globe-trotting days? You know damn good and well—ought to, anyway, as many briefings as we had to sit through—that nobody in this day and age thinks of anybody as 'furriners.' Well. Not the way you mean it. A 'furriner' is anybody outside of your own little bailiwick. So who cares if they're 'Czech' or 'German' or 'French' or 'English'—or even 'American,' for that matter? That's the business of the princes, not the townfolk."

By the end, she was almost grumbling the words herself. Tanner's quirks, harmless as they might be, *were* sometimes annoying.

"I never trusted guide books. They don't pay the guys who write 'em to tell the truth, y'know? They pay 'em to sucker in the tourists."

Her only response was to grip his arm tighter and march him a little faster across the bridge. And maybe tighten her lips a little.

Stubbornly, Ellie continued her little lecture. "So nobody—except you—gives a fuck about whether we're here on a 'secret mission' or not." She jerked her head backward a little, indicating the castle behind them. "Not even Don Balthasar de Marradas gives a damn what we're doing here. If he's even noticed us at all."

Len's good humor returned. "How's he supposed to? He's too busy squabbling with the Count of Solms-Baruth over which one of them is _really_ the Emperor's chosen administrator for Prague. Gawd, there are times I love the butterfly effect."

Ellie grinned. Grantville's knowledge of central European history in the seventeenth century was spotty and erratic, as you'd expect from the records and resources of a small town in West Virginia that had neither a college nor a business enterprise with any particular reason to develop a specialized knowledge about central Europe, even in their own time much less three or four centuries earlier. But, there were occasional exceptions to that rule, little glimpses of historical detail—like islands in a sea of obscurity—usually engendered by some individual interest of one or another of Grantville's residents.

And, as it happened, Prague in the middle of the seventeenth century was one of them. That was because, some years before the Ring of Fire, Judith Roth had developed an interest in genealogy. She'd traced her ancestors back to the large Jewish community which had lived in Prague since the tenth century and had enjoyed something of a "golden age" recently because of the tolerant policies of the Austrian Habsburg Emperor Rudolf II, who'd reigned from 1576 to 1612.

Judith's interest in genealogy had lapsed, eventually. But she'd never bothered to erase the data she'd accumulated from her home computer's hard drive. Eventually, some months after the Ring of Fire, it had occurred to her to look at it again.

Melissa Mailey—for that matter, the entire executive branch of the U.S. government—had practically jumped for joy. Most of the information, of course, concentrated on Jewish genealogy and history. But, as is invariably true when someone does a broad and sweeping search for data on the internet, there was a lot of other stuff mixed in with it, mostly disconnected and often-useless items of information.

One of those little items—the one that was causing Tanner and Anderson to enjoy a moment's humor as they crossed the Charles Bridge—was that Johann Georg II, Count of Solms-Baruth and one of the Austrian emperor's top administrators, had died in the plague that swept Prague in the spring of 1632.

But that had been in a different universe. In this one, he was very much alive a year later, in the spring of 1633. Apparently, following Gustavus Adolphus' victory at the battle of Breitenfeld in September of 1631, the influence of the newly arrived Americans on events thereafter had been enough to send a multitude of ripples through "established history." Small ones, at the beginning, as was always true of the butterfly effect—so named after the notion that the flapping of a butterfly's wings could eventually cause a hurricane.

But big enough, obviously, to allow one Count Johann Georg II to survive the disease that had felled him in another universe.

Good for him, of course—but now, also, good for those who were secretly scheming with Wallenstein to overthrow Austrian rule in Bohemia. Because the Count of Solms-Baruth was a stubborn man, and refused to concede pre-eminence in Bohemia's administrative affairs to the Emperor's favored courtier, Don Balthasar de Marradas. The enmity between Count Johann Georg and Don Balthasar went back to 1626, apparently, when Wallenstein had selected the count over the don as his chief lieutenant in the campaign against the Protestant mercenary Mansfeld.

Neither Tanner nor Ellie knew much of the details, which were as tangled as seventeenth-century aristocratic feuds and vendettas usually were. All that mattered to them was that Solms-Baruth was tacitly on Wallenstein's side, and he was doing his level best to interfere with Marradas' ability to retain firm Austrian control over political developments in Prague and Bohemia. Which, among other things, meant that the two of them could carry out their special project in Prague—even go on side expeditions like the one that was taking them across the Charles Bridge—without any real fear of being stopped and investigated by Austrian soldiery.

In fact, the only soldiery in sight were the four men in the squad following them—who had been given the assignment personally by Wallenstein's general Pappenheim, and had an official-looking document signed by the count to establish their credentials should anyone think to object.

"There are times," Ellie mused, "when the Machiavellian' scheming and plotting of these fucking seventeenth-century princes and mercenary captains reminds me of the Keystone Kops more than anything else."

Tanner came to an abrupt halt. "Think so?" He pointed a finger ahead of them, and slightly to the left. "We'll be coming to it soon, on our way to the Josefov. The Old Town Square—'Starry-mesta,' the Czechs call it, or something like that. That's where Emperor Ferdinand—yup, the same shithead who's still sitting on the throne in Vienna—had twenty-seven Protestant leaders executed after the Battle of the White Mountain."

Now he swiveled, and pointed back toward the Hradcany. "The guy who did the executing was—still is—one of the most famous executioners in history. Jan Mydlar's his name. When I was here, I saw his sword hanging in one of the museums in the Castle. They say he could lop a man's head off with one stroke, every time."

The finger lowered slightly. "They stuck the heads on spikes, right there, all along the Charles Bridge. They left them there to rot, for years. Only took the last down maybe a year ago."

He turned and they started walking again. In silence.

As they neared the end of the bridge, Ellie cleared her throat. "Whatever happened to that guy? The executioner, I mean. Jan Whazzisname."

Tanner shrugged. "Not sure. Maybe he's still alive."

Ellie gurgled something inarticulate. Tanner gave her a sly, sidelong glance.

"Hey, sweetheart, cheer up. The funny thing is, according to the story Mydlar was something of a Bohemian patriot himself. They say he wore a black hood that day—in mourning, so the story goes—instead of the flame-red hood he normally wore. So who knows? If he's still around, he might wind up working for us."

"Like I said," Ellie muttered. "The Keystone Kops. Okay, sure, on steroids."

Chapter II: Pawn to King Four
April, 1633

1

By the time the expedition finally set out for Prague, three weeks after his meeting with Mike Stearns and Wallenstein, Morris was feeling a bit more relaxed about the prospect. A bit, not much.

What relaxation did come to him derived primarily from the presence in their party of Uriel Abrabanel. By temperament, Rebecca's uncle was less given to sedentary introspection than his brother. True, Balthazar Abrabanel had spent much of his life working as a spy also. But he was a doctor by trade and a philosopher by inclination—more in the nature of what the term "spymaster" captures.

His brother Uriel had had no such side interests, beyond the financial dealings that were part of being a member of the far-flung Abrabanel clan and integral to his espionage. He'd spent much of his earlier life as a seaman—a "Portuguese" seaman, using the standard subterfuge of secret Jews anywhere the Spanish Inquisition might be found—and, though now in his sixties, he rode a horse as easily as he had once ridden a yardarm.

"Oh, yes," he said cheerfully, "they're a lot of hypocrites, the English. Jews have been officially banned from the island for centuries, but they always let some of us stay around, as long as we—what's that handy American expression?—ah, yes: 'kept a low profile.' Not only did their kings and queens and dukes and earls always want Jewish doctors, but they also found us *so* handy to spy on the Spanish for them."

Morris tried not to make a face. Even two years after the Ring of Fire, with the attitudes and sensibilities of one born and raised in twentieth-century America, he found it hard to accept the position of Jews in the seventeenth century. What he found harder to accept—and even more disturbing—was the readiness of Jews in his new universe to accommodate to that seventeenth-century reality.

Uriel must have sensed some of his distaste. "Whatever else, Morris, we must survive. And the truth is that, for all their hypocrisy, the English are no real threat to us. Not the Stuarts, nor the Tudor dynasty before them. The real enemy . . ."

His voice trailed off, as Uriel studied the landscape ahead of him. His eyes were slitted, though there was really nothing in that central European countryside to warrant the hostility. By now, having skirted Saxony, they were through the low Erzgebirge mountains and beginning to enter the Bohemian plain.

"The *Habsburgs,*" he said, almost hissing the words. "There is the source—well, the driving engine, anyway—of Europe's bigotry in this day and age. The Austrians as much as the Spanish."

"I would have thought you'd name the Catholic Church. From what I hear, the Austrian Emperor has treated the Jewish community in Prague rather well."

"That's because he needs their money to keep his war coffers full. As soon as the war's over, Ferdinand will treat the Jews in Prague just as savagely as he treated the Utraquists and the Unity of Brethren. Watch and see."

Uriel shrugged. "I am not fond of the Roman Catholic Church, to be sure. But then, I'm no fonder of most Protestant sects either. No pope ever fulminated as violently against the Jews as Martin Luther. Still, religious intolerance we can live with. Being fair, it's not as if there aren't a lot of Jews who are just as intolerant. The real problem is when that intolerance gets shackled to a dynasty driving for continental power. Which, for centuries now in Europe, has meant the Habsburgs first and foremost."

Morris glanced to his left, where a number of horsemen were escorting several large wagons. Uriel followed his gaze, and a slight smile came to his face.

"Ah, yes. The Unity of Brethren. It will certainly be interesting to see how they finally—"

Again, he groped for an American colloquialism. Uriel was very fond of the things.

"'Shape up,'" Morris provided.

"Indeed so! Such a splendid expression! 'Shape up', indeed."

Morris shook his head ruefully. The political situation he was about to plunge into in Prague was a genuine nightmare. Since the Habsburg armies had conquered Bohemia, after the short-lived period from 1618 to 1621 during which the Bohemians had tried to install a Protestant king against Ferdinand's wishes, the Austrian emperor had ruled the province tyrannically. In particular, he had introduced a level of brutality into religious persecution that had not been seen in Europe since the campaigns of the Spanish Duke of Alva during the first years of the Dutch revolt.

It was said that, upon hearing the news of the Catholic victory at the Battle of the White Mountain, a priest in Vienna had taken the pulpit to urge Emperor Ferdinand II to follow the Biblical precept: *Thou shalt break them with a rod of iron; thou shalt dash them into pieces like a potter's vessel.*

Ferdinand had needed no urging. He was a bigot by nature, who was a genuine Catholic fanatic, not simply a monarch using the established church to further his political ends. In point of fact, it was also rumored—apparently based on good information—that Pope Urban VIII had several times tried to rein in the Habsburg emperor's religious zeal. But, to no avail. Stalin's notorious wisecrack from a later century—*how many divisions has the Pope?*—would have been understood perfectly by rulers of the seventeenth century, the Catholic ones perhaps even better than the Protestants. Like Cardinal Richelieu in France, Emperor

Ferdinand felt he was simply following Christ's advice to give unto Caesar that which was Caesar's.

And he was Caesar, and Bohemia was his, and he intended to make the most of it. Thus, he had:

—executed dozens of Protestant noblemen who'd led the short-lived revolt;

—banned the Utraquist and Calvinist and Hussite sects of the Protestant creed outright, and made it clear to the Lutherans that they were henceforth on a very short leash;

—abolished elective monarchy and made the Kingdom of Bohemia henceforth hereditary in the Habsburg line;

—had the Letter of Majesty, the Bohemians' much-cherished charter of religious liberty that had been captured in the sack of Prague, sent to him in Vienna, where he personally cut it into pieces;

—with his Edict of Restitution in 1629, seized Protestant churches and church property and given them to the Catholic church;

—seized the estates of "rebels," bringing into his dynasty's possession the property of over six hundred prominent Protestant families, fifty towns, and about half the entire acreage of the province;

—allowed his soldiery—mostly Bavarians in Bohemia and Cossacks in Moravia—to ravage and plunder the peasantry and the small towns, more or less at will, thereby saving himself much of the need to actually *pay* his mercenaries;

—ruined the economy of Bohemia and Moravia by severely debasing the currency in order to buy up still more estates;

—transformed the once-prosperous peasantry and

urban commoners of the region into paupers, and created a handful of great landowners to rule over them (of whom none was greater and richer than Wallenstein, ironically enough in light of current developments);

—and . . .

Oh, it went on and on. True, Morris would admit— even Uriel would—Emperor Ferdinand II of Austria did not really make the roster of Great Evil Rulers of History. He just wasn't on a par with such as Tamerlane and Hitler and Stalin. But he was certainly a contender for the middleweight title of Rulers You'd Like to See Drop Dead. A narrow-minded, not overly intelligent man, who could invariably be counted on to follow the stupidest and most brutal policy offered to him by his multitude of advisers and courtiers.

Yes, stupid as well as brutal. A stupidity that was evidenced in the fact that the mission Morris was on was designed to break Bohemia away from the Habsburg empire again—permanently, this time, if all went well—and the instrument of that break would be the very man whom Ferdinand himself had raised up from obscure origins because he was the most brutally capable mercenary captain of the day and age.

Albrecht Wenzel Eusebius von Wallenstein. Born in the year 1583 into a family of the minor Protestant Bohemian nobility, and orphaned at the age of thirteen. Today he was the greatest landowner in Bohemia—possibly in the entire Austrian empire except for Ferdinand himself—as well as the duke of Friedland, a member of the Estate of Princes of the Empire, recognized as the duke of Mecklenburg by the Habsburgs (if not, of course, by the Swedish king Gustav Adolf who today actually controlled Mecklenburg), and prince of Sagan.

Thinking about Wallenstein—and the big ladle Judith had stuffed into one of their trunks—Morris grunted.

"What do you think of him, Uriel?"

Abrabanel had no difficulty understanding the subject. "Wallenstein? Hard to say." He paused for a moment, marshalling his thoughts.

"On the one hand, he is probably the most completely amoral man in the world. I doubt if there is any crime he would shrink from, if he felt it would advance his purposes."

"No kidding." Morris scowled. "He's the stinking bastard who ordered his Croat cavalry to attack our school last year. Tried to slaughter all of our children!"

Uriel nodded. "Indeed. On the other hand . . . There is a lot to be said for him, as well. It's no accident, you know, that he wound up becoming something of a folk hero in German legend."

He barked a little laugh. "Not an unmixed admiration, of course! Still, what I can tell of reading your books from the future, the Germans came to grudgingly admire the man in the decades and centuries after his death, much as the French never stopped grudgingly admiring Napoleon. The German poet and playwright Schiller even wrote several plays—in the next century, that would be—about him. Odd, really—a Corsican folk hero for the French, and a Bohemian one for the Germans."

The scowl was still on Morris' face. "Big deal," he

said, adding somewhat unkindly: "That's just because the Frogs and the Krauts don't have too many genuine heroes to pick from."

Uriel's easy smile came. "Such terrible chauvinism! Of course, that term does come from a French word, so I suppose there's some truth to your wisecrack. Still—"

The smile didn't fade, but the old spy's dark eyes seem to darken still further. "Do not let your animosities get the best of you, Morris. This much is also true of Wallenstein: a peasant on one of his estates is in a better situation than peasants anywhere else in the Austrian empire. Wallenstein is shrewd enough to know when *not* to gouge, and he even fosters and encourages what you would call scientific farming. He opposed the Edict of Restitution and, by all accounts, is not much given—if at all, beyond the needs of diplomacy—to religious persecution. If he is amoral, he is not *im*-moral."

"They say he believes in astrology," grumbled Morris.

"Indeed, he is quite superstitious." Uriel's smile broadened, becoming almost sly. "On the other hand, they also say he treats his wife very well."

Morris grunted again. "Um. Well, okay. That's something, I guess."

They heard the sounds of a horse nearing and twisted in their saddles to look backward. The motions were easy and relaxed, since both men were experienced riders. In Morris' case, from an adult lifetime of being an enthusiast for pack-riding; in Uriel's, from an adult lifetime that had had more in the way of rambunctious excitement—including several desperate flights on horseback across the countryside—than most city-dwelling Jews of the time ever experienced.

The same could not be said for the man approaching them, and neither Morris nor Uriel could restrain themselves from smiling. Jason Gotkin, though in his early twenties, was not at all comfortable on horseback—and showed it. He rode his mount as gingerly, and with the same air of uncertainty, as an apprentice liontamer enters a lion's cage.

Seeing their expressions, Jason flushed a little. When he finally came alongside—it might be better to say, edged his horse alongside with all the sureness of a cadet docking a boat—his words were spoken in something of a hiss.

"Look, I was getting a degree in computer science and was trying to decide between a life spent as a software engineer or a rabbi. I was *not* planning to become a cowboy."

Uriel's smile widened into a grin. Among the uptime hobbies that Uriel had adopted since the Ring of Fire, reading westerns was one of them. He was particularly fond of Donald Hamilton, Luke Short and Louis L'Amour.

"I should hope not! Leaving aside your pitiful manner on horseback, you can't—what's that expression?— hit the broadside of a barn. With a rifle, much less a revolver."

"Software engineer," Jason hissed again. "*Rabbi.*" He scowled faintly. "The average rabbi does not pack a gun. Not even in New York—and wouldn't, even if it weren't for the Sullivan Act."

Morris' gaze slid away from Jason and drifted back

toward the rear of the not-so-little caravan. There, almost at the very end, was the small group of horsemen centered around the figure of young Dunash Abrabanel. None of them rode a horse any better than Jason. But, unlike Jason, all of them were armed to the teeth. They looked like a caricature of highwaymen, in fact, they had so many firearms festooned upon their bodies and saddles.

Morris sighed. "We're nearing Bohemian territory, if we're not already in it. They're going to have to hide the guns, Jason. Whatever Wallenstein's promises, until he carries out his rebellion Imperial law still applies."

"Either that or agree to pretend they aren't Jews," grunted Uriel. The humor that had been on his face was gone, now. This was a sore subject with him, and one on which he and Dunash's little group had already clashed several times. Many times in his life, Uriel had passed himself off as a gentile of one sort or another. Once, he'd even successfully passed himself off as a Spanish hidalgo.

"Stupid!" he said, almost snarling. "They are no more observant—not any longer—than I am. Much less my brother Balthazar. And even in the days when we were, neither of us hesitated to do what was necessary. So why do they insist on flaunting their Jewishness, when it is pointless?"

Morris started to sigh again, but managed to restrain himself. Jason was apprehensive enough as it was, without Morris making his own nervousness about their project apparent.

It was hard. Even in the age from which Morris had come, the urbane and cosmopolitan world of America at the turn of the twenty-first century, there had been divisions between observant and non-observant Jews, leaving aside the disagreements between the various branches of Judaism. In the seventeenth century, those tensions were far more extreme.

Not, perhaps, for the Ashkenazim of central and eastern Europe, cloistered as they were—corralled by the gentiles surrounding them, more properly speaking—into their tight ghettos and shtetls. There, rabbinical influence and control was powerful. Even enforced by law, since in most places—Prague being no exception—the gentile authorities gave the rabbinate jurisdiction over the members of the Jewish ghettos. But for the Sephardim, since the expulsion from Iberia, it was far more difficult. The Sephardic Jews had been scattered to the winds, and although many of them had managed to retain their traditions and customs and ritual observances, many others had not. So, the issue of how to handle nonobservant Jews—any number of whom had even officially converted to Christianity—was always difficult. In practice, Amsterdam being one of the major exceptions, most Sephardic rabbis and observant communities had adopted a fairly tolerant and patient attitude.

Morris and Judith Roth were themselves Ashkenazim, but their attitudes had far more in common with the cosmopolitan Sephardim they'd encountered since the Ring of Fire than the Ashkenazim of this day and age. And now, unwittingly, the arrival of a half-dozen modern Jews into the seventeenth century had introduced a new element into the equation: the twentieth-century ideology of Zionism.

"Zionism," at least, using the term loosely. Not

even Dunash proposed to launch a campaign to create the state of Israel in the middle of the seventeenth century. His own Abrabanel clan would squash any such notion instantly, since their own survival and well-being depended largely on the tolerance of the Ottoman Empire. Murad IV, the current sultan ruling in Istanbul, bore not the slightest resemblance to Lord Balfour. "Murad the Mad," they called him, and for good reason. Though astonishingly capable for a ruler who was obviously a sociopath, one of his principal amusements was wandering about Istanbul personally executing inhabitants he discovered violating his recently decreed hardcore Islamic regulations.

So, the zeal of Dunash and his young comrades had been turned elsewhere. Toward the great mass of Jews living in eastern Europe, and the alleviation of their plight. They had been more enthusiastic about Wallenstein's scheme than anyone. Even Wallenstein himself, Morris suspected. If a Jewish homeland could not be created in the Levant, who was to say that somewhere in eastern Europe . . .

It was a tangled mess. Morris had supported the state of Israel, was a U.S. army veteran himself, and had no philosophical attachment to pacifism. But he also did not share Dunash's simple faith in the efficacy of violence as a way of solving political problems. In the end, he thought tolerance and a willingness to accept a compromise were far more practical methods than shooting a gun.

Not, admittedly, that shooting a gun isn't sometimes necessary to get the other *guy to accept a compromise,* he reminded himself.

He put the thought into words. "Look at it this

way. Maybe having them along will help the others involved see things the right way."

Uriel looked skeptical. "*Pappenheim?* And what do you propose for our next trick? Intimidate a wolf with a stick?"

Pappenheim himself came out to meet them, as they neared the outskirts of Prague. Wallenstein's chief general rode down the line of the little caravan, inspecting them coldly. Looking every bit, Morris thought . . .

Like a wolf on horseback.

There was no other way to describe him. Pappenheim was just plain scary. Melissa Mailey had a copy of C.V. Wedgwood's classic *The Thirty Years War,* and Morris had read the passage in it describing Pappenheim. In fact, he'd reread the passage in the copy of the book which he now owned himself, produced by a seventeenth-century printing press, just before leaving on this expedition. Morris had an excellent memory, and now, watching Pappenheim trotting down the line, he called it up:

The heaviest loss Wallenstein had suffered at Lützen was that of Pappenheim. Reckless of his men, arrogant and insubordinate, Pappenheim was nevertheless the soldier's hero: tireless, restless, the first in attack, the last in retreat. Stories of his fantastic courage were told round the camp fires and he had a legend before he was dead—the hundred scars that he boasted, the birthmark like crossed swords which glowed red when he was angry. He flashes past against that squalid background, the Rupert of the German war. His loyalty to Wallenstein, his affection and admiration, had been of greater effect in inspiring the troops than Wallenstein probably realized. The general owed his power to his control over the army alone, and the loss of Pappenheim was irreparable.

But Pappenheim hadn't died at the battle of Lützen in this universe, because that battle had never been fought. He was still alive, still as vigorous as ever—and still Wallenstein's right hand man. Come out to meet Wallenstein himself, who was hidden in one of the covered wagons since his trip to Grantville had been kept a secret.

Morris watched as Pappenheim exchanged a few words with Wallenstein, who had pushed aside for a moment the coverings of his wagon. Then, watched as Pappenheim inspected the rest of the caravan, examining the peculiar new allies whom Wallenstein had brought with him.

Pappenheim spent not much time studying the men from the Unity of Brethren. Those, he was familiar with. Though now defeated and scattered, the spiritual descendants of Huss and Jan Zizka were a force to be reckoned with. One which had often, in times past, proven their capacity to break aristocratic forces on the field of battle.

He spent more time studying Dunash Abrabanel and his little band of Jewish would-be liberators. Pappenheim wasn't exactly sneering, but there was enough in the way of arrogant condescension in his face to cause Dunash and his followers to glare at him.

Morris decided he'd better go back there and defuse the situation. With the ease of an experienced horseman, he was soon at Pappenheim's side.

"Is there a problem, General?" he asked, keeping his tone level and mild.

Pappenheim swiveled to gaze at him. Up close, Morris could see the famous birthmark. It didn't really look like crossed swords, he thought. Just like another scar.

"You are the jeweler, yes?" Since it wasn't really a question, Morris didn't reply.

Pappenheim grunted. "There are times I think the Duke of Friedland is mad. Nor do I have his faith in astrologers. Still . . ."

Suddenly, his face broke into a grin. It was a cold sort of grin, without much in the way of humor in it.

"Who is to say? It is a mad world, after all."

2

"Well, will it do?" asked Len, a bit gruffly.

"It will do splendidly," Uriel assured him. He cocked an eye at Morris and Jason. "Yes?"

"Oh, sure," said Morris, looking around the cavernous room that served the—small palace? mansion? it was hard to say—as something of a combination between an entry hall and a gathering place. Not for the first time, he was struck by the conspicuous consumption that was so typical of Europe's nobility of the time.

He reminded himself that there had been plenty of conspicuous consumption by rich people in the universe they came from, also. But at least they didn't—well, not usually—have people living in hovels next door. Not to mention—

He moved over to one of the windows and gazed out at the street beyond, almost glaring. Across the narrow passageway rose the wall of Prague's ghetto, sealing off the Jewish inhabitants from the rest of the city. The *Josefov*, that ghetto was called. Somewhere around fifteen thousand people teemed in its cramped quarters, the largest ghetto in Europe. It was quite possibly the largest urban concentration of Jews anywhere in the world, in the year 1633, except maybe Istanbul.

Jason came to stand next to him. The young man's gaze seemed filled with more in the way of dread—anxiety, at least—than Morris' anger.

Morris smiled crookedly. It was hard to blame Jason, of course. Morris could glare at the injustice embodied in that ghetto wall till the cows came home. *He* wasn't the one he was trying to wheedle and cajole and finagle into becoming a new rabbi for its inhabitants. A Reform rabbi-to-be, with precious little in the way of theological training, for a community that was solidly orthodox and had a long tradition of prestigious rabbis to guide them. Rabbi Loew, in fact—the one reputed by legend to have invented the golem—had been Prague's chief rabbi not so long ago. He'd died only a quarter of a century earlier.

"They don't even *use* the term 'Orthodox,'" Jason muttered. "In this day and age, there's nothing 'unorthodox' to give the term any meaning. In our universe, the term didn't come into existence until after the Reform movement started in the nineteenth century. In the here and now, Jews are Jews. Period."

He gave Morris a look of appeal. "They'll just

declare me a heretic, Morris, and cast me out. So what's the point?"

Morris jabbed a stiff finger at the street separating their building from the ghetto. "You're *already* out of the ghetto, Jason. So how can they 'cast' you out?" He glanced at the two gentiles in the room. "That's why I asked Len and Ellie to find us a place just outside of the Josefov."

Jason gave the two people mentioned a questioning look. "Is there going to be any kind of . . . you, know. Trouble about this?"

Len shrugged. "From who? Don Balthasar de Marradas? Yeah, sure, he's officially in charge here in Prague—so he says, anyway. But most of the soldiers and officials in the city are Wallenstein's people, from what Ellie and I can tell. And the ones who aren't are too preoccupied dealing with Wallenstein to be worrying about whether a few Jews are living outside the ghetto."

"They wouldn't know the difference anyway," added Ellie. "Not with you guys."

She hooked a thumb in the direction of the Hradcany. "Don't think they won't learn soon enough that some more Americans have arrived. They're not *that* preoccupied. Whatever else is backward about the seventeenth century, spying sure as hell isn't. By the end of the week—latest—Marradas will have his fucking stoolies watching you, just like they do us."

Morris found Ellie's coarse language refreshing, for some odd reason. He was one of the few people in Grantville who'd always liked Ellie Anderson, and had never found her brash and vulgar personality off-putting. And, in their current circumstances, he thought her *go-fuck-yourself* attitude toward the world was probably . . .

Dead on the money.

"Dead on the money," he murmured, repeating the thought aloud. "Stop worrying, Jason. Ellie's right. They'll spy on us, but what they'll see is Americans, not Jews."

"What about Dunash and the others?"

Morris shrugged. "What about them? The plan is for them to find quarters in the ghetto anyway, as soon as possible. They'll be officially coming here every day to work in my new jewelry establishment. Even in the here and now, Jews are allowed out of the ghetto on legitimate business."

"Especially when the soldiers stationed in the area to check stuff like that are handpicked by Pappenheim," Ellie added cheerfully. "Nobody fucks with Pappenheim. I mean, *nobody*. The one and only time a Habsburg official gave Pappenheim a hard time since he arrived here, Pappenheim beat him half to death. The way the story goes, he dumped the fuckhead out of his chair, broke up the chair and used one of the legs to whup on him."

Morris couldn't help smiling. Pappenheim was scary, true enough. But if there was one lesson Morris had drawn from his studies of history, it was that bureaucrats, in the end, killed more people than soldiers. Way more. If Morris had to make a choice between this century's equivalents of General Heinz Guderian and Adolf Eichmann, he'd pick Guderian any day of the week.

No "if" about it, really. He *had* been given the choice, and he'd made it. Whatever new world Wallenstein and his ruthless generals made out of Bohemia and eastern Europe, Morris didn't think it could be any worse than the world the Habsburgs and their officials had made—not to mention the Polish *szlachta* and the Russian *boyars*.

Wallenstein, whatever else, was looking to the future. He'd get rid of the second serfdom that was engulfing eastern Europe and its accompanying oppression of Jews, if for no other reason, because he wanted to build a powerful empire for himself. Of that, Mike Stearns was sure—and Morris agreed with him. Wallenstein had said nothing to Stearns—or Torstensson, Gustav Adolf's emissary in the negotiations—about his plans beyond seizing power in Bohemia and Moravia. But neither of them doubted that Wallenstein had further ambitions. He'd try to take Silesia, for a certainty—he was already the ruler of Sagan, one of the Silesian principalities—and probably other parts of Poland and the Ukraine.

In short, he was—or hoped to be—a seventeenth-century Napoleon in the making. That could obviously pose problems in the future. But for Morris, as for most Jews, Napoleon hadn't simply been a conqueror and a tyrant. He'd also been the man who broke Germany's surviving traits of medievalism, had granted civil rights to the Jews—and had had a short way with would-be pogromists.

Jason was still worrying. "If they know we're Americans—even if they don't realize we're Jews—won't that cause trouble in its own right?"

Ellie's grin was lopsided and a tad sarcastic. "Where the hell have you been for the last two years? In the here and now, people don't give a fuck about 'patriotism.' Ain't no such animal. You're loyal to a dynasty—or work for one, at least—not a country. Wallenstein's paying us the big bucks—he is, too, don't think Len and me didn't stick it to him good—and so everybody assumes we're his people."

Morris nodded. "I don't think the word 'patriotism' has even been invented yet. She's got the right of it, Jason. The Habsburgs will be suspicious of anyone connected with Wallenstein, right now, because of the strains between them. But until and unless they're ready to move against him, they won't meddle much with us."

"Nothing dramatic and open, anyway," added Uriel. "Though I'd keep an eye out for a stiletto in the back in dark corners. And we need to make sure we hire a trustworthy cook or we'll need to hire a food-taster." He grimaced. "Food-tasters are expensive."

Jason gave Morris a meaningful look. Morris sighed.

"Oh, all right, Jason. We'll start eating kosher."

He wasn't happy about it. Still . . .

The dietary restrictions of Orthodox Judaism irritated Morris, but they weren't ultimately that important to him. Compared to such things as separate seating for women in the synagogue, no driving on Shabbat, family purity laws, women not being allowed to participate in the service, the divinity of the oral law—oh, it went on and on—keeping kashrut barely made the list.

"It's a good idea, Morris," said Jason softly. "At least that'll remove one obstacle. And the truth is, it's a safer way to eat anyway, in a time when nobody's ever heard of FDA inspectors."

Then, he looked faintly alarmed. Morris chuckled harshly. "Yeah, I know. You can't cook worth a damn, kosher or not. Neither can I."

Morris looked toward the bank of windows on a far wall. Somewhere beyond, over one hundred and fifty miles as the crow flies, lay Grantville—where his wife was getting ready to join him with the rest of the workforce that was moving to Prague.

"Judith is gonna kill me," he predicted gloomily.

"Nonsense," pronounced Uriel. "Hire cooks from the ghetto. You have no choice anyway, under existing law. It is illegal for a Jew to hire Christian servants—and you'll need servants also, living in this almost-a-palace. Or Judith will *surely* murder you."

"That's a good idea," Jason chimed in eagerly. "It'll help dispel suspicions of us, too, if people from the ghetto get to know us better. If you have cooks and servants coming in and out of the house every day, as well as jewelers and gemcutters coming to the workplace . . ."

That just made Morris feel gloomier. "Great. So now I've got to be an exhibit in a zoo, too?"

"Yes," said Uriel firmly.

Chapter III: Fianchetto
June, 1633

1

"Please come in, Bishop Comenius, all of you."
Morris waved his hand toward the many armchairs
in the very large living room.

Morris still thought of it as a "living room," even
though he suspected that "salon" was a more appropriate term. Despite having now lived in this mansion
in Prague for a number of weeks, Morris was still
adjusting mentally to the reality of his new situation.
Three months ago, by the standards of the seventeenth century, he had been a well-off man. Today,
after the results reported by his partners Antonio
Nasi and Gerhard Rueckert in the letter Morris had
received two days earlier, he was a wealthy man—by
the standards of any century.

Seeing the entourage Comenius had brought with
him and who were now filing into the room—a room
that was already occupied by a large number of
people—Morris was glad that the room was so enormous. It was a very proper-looking room, too, since he

and Judith never used it as a "living room"—for that, they maintained a much smaller and more comfortable room on the second floor of the mansion—and the small army of servants they had recently acquired kept it spotlessly clean.

That was another thing Morris was still trying to get accustomed to. Servants. And not just a cleaning lady who came in once a week, either, but a dozen people who came and went every day. In fact, they would have *lived* in the mansion except that, following Uriel and Jason's advice—which was the law, anyway—Morris had hired exclusively Jewish cooks and servants. By the laws still in force in Prague, they were required to return to the ghetto every night, just as they were required to wear distinctive insignia identifying themselves as Jews whenever they left the ghetto.

Morris did not share the ferocious egalitarianism of such people as Gretchen Richter and her Committees of Correspondence, although he was, quietly, one of her chief financial backers. He wasn't even as egalitarian as some of the more diehard members of the United Mine Workers and their growing number of spin-off unions. Still, he found the situation somewhat embarrassing—and was growing angrier all the time at the restrictions placed on Jews in his new day and age. The restrictions were being ignored in his case, true, since Morris fell into the informal category of a "court Jew." But they still left a smoldering resentment.

Seeing the last man filing into the salon after Bishop Comenius, Morris felt the resentment vanish.

"Hey, Red! Long time. I was wondering if you were still alive."

Red Sybolt squinted at him. "Hi, Morris. Oh, yeah, I'm still around. Still kicking, too." He jerked a thumb at the very large man by his side. "Hell, even Jan here is still alive, which is a real miracle given how crazy he is. Things got hairy now and then, especially in Saxony, but the worst that happened is my glasses got busted. I still haven't managed to scrounge up a new pair."

Morris had always liked Bobby Gene "Red" Sybolt. He wasn't sure why, exactly, since on the face of it Red and he shouldn't have gotten along all that well. Just for starters, Red was one of those union activists who, though not really a socialist himself, had been influenced by socialists he'd run across in the course of his activities before the Ring of Fire. In his case, by the Socialist Workers Party, which had, off and on, had a certain presence in northern West Virginia going back to the late 1940s. One of the things Red had picked up from the SWP was a hostility toward Zionism. And while Morris had been uneasy about some of the policies of the state of Israel toward Palestinians, both he and his wife Judith had always been supporters of Israel.

But Red was such a friendly man that it was hard for anyone to dislike him. Even Quentin Underwood, the hardnosed manager of the mine Red had worked in for a while, was known to allow that "the damn commie" was personally a decent enough fellow. And Morris knew that Red's anti-Zionism was not a veiled form of anti-Semitism. It was simply a political opposition to what Red considered a colonial-settler state. As he'd once put it to Morris:

"Where the hell did Europe get off exporting its

anti-Semitism problem onto the backs of the Arabs? I got no problem with the Jews having a homeland. Since it was the Germans massacred 'em, they should have been given Bavaria. Or Prussia. Instead, the British offered them a choice between Palestine, Kenya and Madagascar. Guess what those all have in common? Natives of the swarthy persuasion, that's what. Typical British imperialism! Lord Balfour said it all: 'We will create for ourselves a loyal Jewish Ulster in the Middle East.'"

Morris had disagreed, of course. But it had been a friendly enough argument, as his arguments with Red usually were. And, besides, in one of those odd quirks of human personality which made the real world such an interesting place, the radical Red Sybolt had also been the only inhabitant of Grantville before the Ring of Fire except Morris himself who had been genuinely interested and knowledgeable about gems and jewelry.

Red claimed that was due to the residual bad influence of his ex-wife; Morris suspected it was due to the residual regrets Red had concerning the lifestyle he'd chosen for himself. The life of an itinerant union organizer and "hell-raiser" did not lead to expansive bank accounts. Red had spent many hours in Morris' jewelry store discussing gemstones, but he'd never bought so much as a single gold chain.

"Did the faceted jewelry make as big of a splash as I told you they would?"

Morris smiled wryly. In another of those little ironies of life, it had been Red Sybolt who brought to his attention the fact that faceted jewelry was first introduced into the world in the *second* half of the seventeenth century. Simple faceting and polishing had been done for a long time, to be sure—which meant that the needed tools and experienced workers would be available—but the art of gemcutting had not advanced much in almost two centuries. People in 1633 were still accustomed to nothing fancier than polished stones and, at most, the simple design of the "Old Single Cut," which dated back to the fifteenth century. The first real advance in gemcutting wouldn't come until the middle of the seventeenth century, with the introduction of the Mazarin Cut.

In short, Red pointed out, Morris had had the great luck of arriving in the right place at the right time—riding just ahead of the wave. The tools and skills were in place, all that was needed was the addition of Morris' knowledge. For a few years, if he played it right, Morris and his two new partners would be in a position to make a fortune.

So it had proved—as the letter upstairs verified. It had taken Morris and his partners a year before they could begin producing modern-style faceted gems. Morris knew the theory, yes; but he had the skills of an uptime jeweler, which was not the same thing as an experienced gemcutter. They'd had to hire and train seventeenth-century jewelers, which had taken time. Fortunately, two of the jewelers they'd taken on had turned out to be very adept at grasping the new ideas. So adept that both of them had been given hefty shares of stock in the company, lest they become disgruntled and take their skills elsewhere.

"Yes, you were right." Morris grinned. "Sure you don't want some stock? My offer's still good."

Red shook his head fiercely. "Get thee behind me, Satan! Me? What kind of respectable agitator owns stock in a company which is no doubt plunderin' the poor?" But he was smiling as he said it, and, after seating himself in one of the expensive armchairs, luxuriated visibly in its comfort.

"Okay," he admitted, "plunderin' the idle rich is probably more accurate. Still, I wouldn't feel comfortable with it." He gave Morris a nearsighted squint. "Mind you, I *will* expect some hefty donations to the cause."

Morris looked around the room, all of whose inhabitants except him were now seated. "*Which* cause, Red?" he asked mildly. "I see at least . . . what is it? Four or five present."

Red's smile widened. "Bit of a problem, isn't it?" His own eyes moved across the room, and if he was nearsighted and without glasses, he seemed to have no problem at all assessing its occupants.

"Yup, quite a collection. You got your Committees of Correspondence—that's me—your Brethren, and I figure at least three different varieties of Zionism. Not to mention the other budding exploiters of the downtrodden—hey, Len, Ellie, how's it going?—and, lounging just outside the front door, I figure at least two flavors of military dictatorship we poor lambs seem to have allied ourselves with. Three, if you count that pig·Holk, even though he's too stupid to even make a respectable fascist."

At the mention of Holk, Morris grimaced. So did Jan Billek.

"His troops have been ravaging northern Bohemia just as badly as they did Saxony," Jan growled, in his heavily accented English. "Even though they are supposed to be 'protecting' it."

Morris had no trouble believing him. In preparation for his relocation to Prague, he'd studied what he could find in Grantville's libraries as well as Judith's genealogical data. One of Grantville's bibliophiles had donated a copy of some plays written by the eighteenth-century German writer Schiller. Morris had read the following passage in one of them, *Wallenstein's Camp*:

> *In Bayreuth, in the Vogtland, in*
>   *Westphalia;*
> *Wherever we have survived—*
> *Our children and grandchildren,*
> *Will still be telling stories,*
> *After hundreds and hundreds of years,*
> *About Holk and his hordes.*

Heinrich Holk was one of the major military commanders of the Habsburg forces now stationed in Bohemia. He was the worst type of condottiere in the Thirty Years War—a breed of men who were none too savory to begin with. A one-eyed, primitive, drunken mass murderer; a scourge who persecuted and mistreated the people he was charged with protecting; and a dishonor to the imperial army. Holk, born into the family of a Danish Protestant official, had not only changed his allegiance several times during the course of the Thirty Years War, but also his faith—which, admittedly, was nothing especially unusual for the time. Wallenstein had done the same, early in his career, converting from his native Protestantism to Catholicism in order to ingratiate himself with the Habsburgs.

Unlike Wallenstein or such men as Tilly and Pappenheim, however, Holk did not have any significant victories to his credit. His military prowess was demonstrated only by raids, plundering and atrocities, and he had been defeated on several occasions—by Wilhelm Christian of Brandenburg near Magdeburg, in 1630; later the same year by the Swedes near Demmin; and again by the Swedes at Werben in 1631. Not to mention that Holk had failed to bring his troops to meet Tilly's in time for the battle of Breitenfeld, which had been partly responsible for Tilly's defeat there at the hands of Gustavus Adolphus.

Unfortunately, Holk's services were much in demand, because whatever his multitude of faults Holk was also a thoroughly competent commander in the major criterion by which that was usually judged in the Thirty Years War: he could hold together a random heap of mercenaries with consistent firmness. But he did so by making his army a refuge for the dregs of loot-hungry, brutal soldiery.

Morris was still a bit mystified why Wallenstein accepted the crude Holk as one of his top subordinates. As a rule, Wallenstein was a better judge of men—at least their capabilities, if not their morality. Morris thought it was probably due to the simple fact that Holk seemed to admire Wallenstein, which he demonstrated by imitating his master in Holk's own gross and coarse manner. Like Wallenstein, he threatened to punish people "through taking them by the head"—which meant hanging them, in the slang of the time. And when a subordinate reacted sluggishly to orders, Holk accused him of having the "inborn speed of Saturn"—another one of Wallenstein's favorite expressions.

Morris knew that in the history of the universe they had come from, after Pappenheim's death at the battle of Lützen, Holk had become Wallenstein's prime factotum. Whatever else, Wallenstein had been able to assign tasks to Holk with the certain knowledge that whatever could be done by harshness and brutality would be done well. Or thoroughly, at least. But without Pappenheim's ability to generate genuine loyalty in the army, and Pappenheim's sense of strategy, Wallenstein had soon fallen foul of the Byzantine factionalism within the Habsburg forces. Not that Wallenstein hadn't been guilty of the same factionalism himself, of course—but with Holk instead of Pappenheim to rely on, he had been outmatched.

"What's Wallenstein going to do about him?" demanded Red. "If this keeps up, Morris, there won't be much left of northern Bohemia. Wallenstein—there, at least—will be 'King of Nothing.'"

Morris almost snarled: *Why ask ME?*

But he didn't, because he knew the answer, as much as it discomfited him. In the months since he'd arrived, Morris had indeed become Wallenstein's "court Jew." It was an odd and informal position, but one which was not all that uncommon in the Europe of the day. Despite all the restrictions and sometimes-savage persecution of Jews, most of the European courts had a few wealthy and prominent Jews in their entourage. For the most part, of course, that was because Jewish money and medical skill was wanted by Europe's monarchs and high nobility. But there was more to it than that, at least for some of Europe's Christian rulers, especially the smartest ones. Being "outside the loop," their Jewish courtiers could often be relied upon for better and more objective advice. Queen Elizabeth of England, when she'd been on the throne, had often consulted with her Jewish doctor Roderigo Lopez on her diplomatic as well as medical affairs.

And . . . from what Morris could tell, Wallenstein even seemed to *like* him. It was hard to be sure, of course, with a man like Wallenstein. But Edith Wild had told Morris that Wallenstein spoke well of him in private. And Edith—talk about miracles!—had somehow managed to become one of the few people whom Wallenstein trusted. Edith herself thought that was because, after an initial period of hesitation—even veiled hostility—Wallenstein's wife had taken a liking to her. If not for her own sake, then because Edith was keeping her husband alive. And, in fact, under Edith's bullying regimen, Wallenstein's shaky health had improved. Rather dramatically, in fact. Edith even managed to intimidate Wallenstein's pestiferous astrologers into not contradicting her medical and dietary advice. (And there was a true miracle. Seventeenth-century astrologers, as a rule, made the "snake-oil salesmen" of Morris' time look like downright saints and wise men.) Finally—oh, the world was a wondrous place—it had turned out that Wallenstein had developed a fanatic enthusiasm for the multitude of Agatha Christie mysteries that Edith had brought with her to Prague. *All that keeps me alive!* he'd once sworn to Morris, to all appearances dead seriously.

"I'll talk to him," Morris said gruffly. "Though I'm not sure if he'll listen."

"What *is* he up to, anyway?" Red asked. "There are rumors flying all over, but nobody really knows what he's planning."

Morris shrugged. "Don't ask me. Uriel might be able to give you a good educated guess, but he had to go back to Grantville on mysterious business of his own. Whenever I ask—very diffidently, let me tell you—Wallenstein just gets grimmer than usual and more or less tells me to mind my own business. 'Soon,' is all he'll say."

Morris had been about to sit down himself, but instead he moved over to one of the windows and gazed up at the Hradcany across the river. He couldn't see Wallenstein's own palace, from here, since it was perched in the Malá Strana at the bottom of the hill instead of the summit. But St. Vitus Cathedral, which dominated the Hradcany, always reminded him of Wallenstein. For all of Wallenstein's forward-looking temperament, there was ultimately something Gothic about the man.

Ellie Anderson seemed to be sharing his thoughts. "Fucking vampire," he heard her mutter.

For some odd reason, the image of Wallenstein lurking in his palace like Count Dracula cheered Morris up. Granted, Dracula was a monster. But at least he wasn't *stupid*.

Morris turned away from the window. "Enough of that. Wallenstein will do whatever he'll do, and whenever he chooses to do it. We have no control over that, so let's concentrate on what we can control. Influence, at least."

He knew why Comenius and Billek had come. Comenius, to pay his official regards, since the central figure in the Church of the Brethren had just arrived in Prague. But he was really here to lend his authority to Jan Billek—and Red's—long-standing proposal with regard to the paramilitary forces that were being quietly organized to support Wallenstein when the time came.

Morris had wrestled with his decision for days. More precisely, he had wrestled with his reluctance to have a confrontation with his own people. But, now, the decision came into clear and hard focus. He braced himself for a brawl.

"Red and Billek are right, Dunash. Your people and those of the Brethren should form a joint unit. It's stupid to do otherwise."

Dunash Abrabanel shot to his feet. "Our interests will be pushed aside—as always!"

"Shut up, you—" Morris caught himself, almost laughing, before he added: *young whippersnapper!*

Still, his jaws were tight. "What the hell do *you* know about it, Abrabanel?" He glared at Dunash and the young Jews sitting around him—all except Jason Gotkin, the only young up-time Jew in their midst, who was seated off to the side, a bit isolated from the others.

"What do *any* of you know about military affairs?" Morris demanded. "In the world I came from, the worst enemy the Jewish people ever faced was not defeated by Israel. Nor could he have been, even if Israel had existed at the time. He was defeated by the great armies of the United States, England and Russia—all of whom had Jews serving in them. The Russians, especially. There were over two hundred Jewish generals in the Red Army. Berlin was first penetrated by Russian soldiers under the command of one of them—and Auschwitz was liberated by another."

He lapsed into one of his rare uses of profanity. "*So shut the fuck up!* Not one of you has any real idea what to do with those guns you festoon yourselves with, like a bunch of would-be bandidos. I leave aside what Pappenheim had to say."

The one and only time that Pappenheim had observed Dunash's band of youngsters attempting what they called a "military exercise," his comments had been vulgar, brief and to the point. Most of which he had uttered as he trotted his horse away, shaking his head in disgust.

"Look, Dunash, he's right," said Red mildly. "The truth is, the Brethren aren't really what you'd call 'seasoned soldiers,' either. But at least they're familiar with firearms, and a lot of them have seen some actual fighting. Most of all—" He hesitated a moment, gauging Dunash's temper. "Most of all, they aren't arrogant."

He left unspoken the obvious implication: *like you are.* "That's why they've agreed to let some of Wallenstein's officers train them."

Dunash said nothing, but his jaws were even tighter than Morris' felt. Red kept on, talking smoothly. Morris decided to let him handle it. Whatever Morris sometimes thought of Red's political opinions, the fact remained that Red—not Morris—was the experienced organizer in the group.

"Look, I'm not too fond of the situation either. Neither is Jan or any of the Brethren. But the truth is that Wallenstein—probably Pappenheim, actually—seems

to have been careful in their selection of officers.
They're really not too bad."

Jan Billek nodded. "Two are quite good. I even
have hopes of converting one of them."

"And look on the bright side," Red continued.
"Officers be damned. We'll be the grunts with the
actual guns in our hands, if push comes to shove.
Neither Wallenstein nor Pappenheim—sure as hell
not the officers directly over us—have any doubt at
all what'll happen if they order us to do something
we don't want to do."

He and Jan exchanged a meaningful glance. Morris'
anger faded, replaced by his earlier good humor.
"Ha!" he barked. "Red, should I start calling you
'commissar'?"

Red smiled a little sheepishly. "Well . . . the word
doesn't mean anything, in the here and now. But,
yeah." He gave Billek another glance. "Actually, you
oughta apply the title to Jan. He's really the one all
the Brethren soldiers listen to."

Jan's face was stolid, but Morris thought he detected
a little gleam somewhere in the back of his eyes.
"Indeed," he said. "And why should they not? Good
Brethren, so they understand the difference between
'orders' and 'what should be done.'"

Suddenly, to Morris' surprise, Jason Gotkin spoke up.
"Do it, Dunash. They're right and you're wrong—and
the truth is, I think it'll help you recruit more Jews
from the ghetto, anyway."

Dunash seemed to be even more surprised than
Morris was.

"How so? An exclusively Jewish force—"

"Will seem crazy to them," Jason interrupted

forcefully. "Cut it out, Dunash. How many have you managed to recruit so far, since you've been here? All of five, I believe—three of whom are orphans, two of those too young to use a gun—and of the other two, one of them is not much more than the village idiot. You know as well as I do that the only recruit you've gotten in three months who'll be any use is Bezalel Pitzkler."

Jason's eyes examined the eight young men sitting around Dunash. "At that rate—one real recruit every three months—you won't be able to field more than a squad when the balloon goes up. What's the point?"

"We have special weapons!" one of Dunash's followers said stoutly.

Morris had to fight down a sneer. Red didn't even bother. "Oh, swell. 'Special weapons.' Which translates to: maybe three dozen rockets you got smuggled into Prague, supplied by sympathizers in Grantville—do notice that I'm not inquiring as to the particulars, but I somehow doubt that Mike Stearns or Frank Jackson authorized that—and none of which you really know how to use."

"Do you?" demanded Dunash.

"Me? Don't be silly. Rockets are dangerous. Besides, I'm a man of peace. Well, a man of words, anyway. But I know someone who *does* know how to use them, and he happens to be a friend of mine—well, associate—and he's willing to come here for a bit and teach us. I hope you noticed the functioning pronoun there. *Us.*"

Red leaned back in his seat, spreading his hands in something of a placating gesture. "Dunash, if it'll make you feel better, you and your guys can stay in charge of the rockets. As well as that pickup truck that you've also managed to smuggle into this city, piece by piece, to use as a jury-rigged katyusha—a truck which you have no fricking idea in the world how to assemble. Or drive, even if you did manage by some kinda miracle to put it back together in working order."

Red looked smug. "I, on the other hand, am a crackerjack auto mechanic. I've rebuilt more cars and trucks than I can remember. And I *do* know how to drive."

"In a manner of speaking," Morris muttered under his breath. He'd driven with Red, on two occasions in the past. And while the union organizer wasn't quite as reckless as the now-infamous Hans Richter, riding in the passenger seat of a vehicle driven by Red Sybolt was no pleasure for anyone other than a daredevil. Or teenagers, among whom Red had always been surprisingly popular for a man in his forties.

"That's the deal, Dunash," Red went on. "You can keep the rockets, and I'll volunteer to show you how to put together the truck—even get you some fuel, which you haven't given any thought to at all. And I'll drive it for you when the time comes. But you give up the idea of a separate Jewish combat unit and integrate yourselves with us."

Dunash was still looking stubborn, but his cousin Yehuda spoke up. "Who is 'us,' exactly?"

Red hooked a thumb at Billek. "The Brethren, mostly, other than some people from the CoC we've managed to get started here in Prague. By now, me and Jan—mostly him—have managed to recruit about four thousand volunteers from the Brethren. Half of them are already in Prague, with the others on the way."

Four thousand. Red let the words hang in the air, for a moment. Four thousand—as opposed to Dunash Abrabanel's handful. For that matter, Morris didn't doubt for a minute that Red would provide more people from his newly organized CoC than Dunash had following him. Say what you would about Red Sybolt, the man was a superb organizer.

"We will be buried," hissed Dunash.

For the first time since he'd entered the room, Bishop Comenius spoke. "No, you will not be 'buried,' young man. I give you my word on that. My oath before God, if you will accept it."

Comenius was, by nature, an immensely dignified man, and even Dunash was visibly affected by his words. The more so after the bishop rose to his feet.

"I am recognized by all the Brethren as the foremost religious authority in our church." To the side, Deacon Billek nodded firmly. "Tolerance was one of our watchwords from the beginning of our faith. And now that I have had a chance to study what would have happened in the world of our future, my faith has been fortified."

He turned and pointed to Len Tanner and Ellie Anderson. Then, to Morris himself; then, to Jason; and finally, to Red Sybolt. "Consider, if you will, these five people. One, a Catholic noted for his lapses; two, a man and a woman who believe in no God at all; one, a Jew who is considered a heretic by most other Jews living today; the last, a young Jew who is trying to decide whether he can be a rabbi in these times, because he is no longer sure exactly what he believes."

Morris was astonished by Comenius' accurate assessment of five American strangers whom he had never met before. Obviously, the Brethren (with Red's help) had an excellent espionage service in all but name. True, it wasn't *quite* accurate. Except for a few places like Amsterdam, most rabbis were loath to proclaim someone an actual "heretic," since Jews didn't place the same emphasis as Christians did on doctrinal purity. What most of them would have said about Morris was that he was "practically an apikoros"—an uncomplimentary term indicating someone who was much too loose and self-willed in his interpretation and application of customs and observances.

"Yet in the world they came from," Comenius continued, "it was people such as this who built a nation which, in the fullness of time, provided a sanctuary for my people as well as yours. Most of the world's Brethren wound up living in that 'United States,' as did the single largest grouping of the world's Jews. There is a lesson there for any of God's children, in whatever manner they see that God. Unless you are blind. Which I am not. Freedom of religion must be the banner for both of us—a banner which, by its nature, must be held jointly."

He sat down. "That is my pledge—and the pledge of the Unity of Brethren. You will not be 'buried.' Unless you are buried by our enemies, along with us ourselves."

The decision hung in the balance. Then—and this surprised Morris more than anything that happened that morning—Dunash turned to Jason.

"You will be our rabbi, if anyone is to be. You are sure of this?"

Jason was obviously as startled as Morris was. But he still managed to nod as firmly as Billek.

"Yes, Dunash. It's—ah—kosher."

2

Over dinner, Comenius raised the subject that Morris had suspected was his primary reason for coming. Normally, he would have had to suppress a sigh, but in this instance . . .

Rich, remember. You are now stinking rich, Morris Roth, so stop thinking like a small town jeweler. Judging from the letter I got from Antonio and Gerhard—and I think they're right—within five years I'll be one of the richest men in Europe. Especially if I divest and diversify intelligently. Our monopoly on faceted jewelry will bring us a fortune for a few years, but it won't last.

"Yes, Bishop, I will finance your proposed university."

The words came out more abruptly—even curtly—than Morris had intended. The thought of his new wealth still made him feel awkward and out of place. The last thing Morris Roth had ever expected, in all the years he'd spent as the jeweler for a small town in northern West Virginia, was that someday, in another universe, he'd become the equivalent of the founder of a new house of Rothschild.

Comenius looked a bit startled. "How big—I mean . . ."

Morris smiled wryly. "How big a donation? If you give me two months—let's say three, to be on the safe side—to have the funds transferred, I can finance the entire thing. Enough to get it started, at least. I assume you intend to locate the new university here in Prague, yes?" He shifted in his seat, feeling awkward again. "There will be some conditions, however."

"Of course." Comenius inclined his head, inviting Morris to elaborate.

"First. I'll agree to have theological schools attached to the university, so long as there are no restrictions with regard to creed. That will include a Jewish rabbinical seminary."

He looked over at Jason, whose expression was a little strained. Forcefully, Morris added: "Yes, I know the rabbis currently in Prague will probably want no part of it. That's their problem, not mine. If they want to stick to their yeshivahs, so be it. Even if it's nothing more than a plaque on a door, with nothing behind the door, I want some building in the university—or part of one, anyway—set aside for that purpose."

He turned back to Comenius. "But the university itself will be secular. Open to anyone, regardless of creed, and unaffiliated to any religion. Agreed?"

Comenius nodded. "Yes. But that still leaves the question of how the theological schools themselves will be regulated. Herr Roth—"

"Please, call me Morris."

"Ah, Morris. You will find it difficult—perhaps not impossible, but difficult—to find anyone who can serve as the regulating authority of this university who is *not* affiliated, in one manner or another, with an existing creed. Most of the scholars in—ah, how strange the

thought—in 'this day and age' are religious figures."
Comenius hesitated a moment. "Unless you choose to
select someone from your own people."

Morris chewed on the problem, for a moment. He
considered, and then discarded, various possibilities
from the American uptimers. The problem was that
any of them he could think of who'd be qualified,
even remotely, to become a university president—or
"rector," to use the seventeenth-century term—were
overwhelmed already with other responsibilities. And
if any of them were available, the top priority anyway
would be the new university that was taking shape
in Jena, which was, after all, part of the CPE rather
than a foreign country.

"No . . ." he said slowly. "It'll have to be someone
from this day and age."

Comenius nodded again. "So I thought. But, as I
said, such a person will most likely be affiliated already
with one or another creed. If they have authority over
the theological schools . . ."

Morris grunted. "Yes, I understand the problem.
Fine. We'll set it up so that the religious schools have
complete control over their own curriculum and methods of instruction. They'll also have complete control
over hiring and firing their teachers. The only authority
the university will have over them will involve such
things as the building code, fire regulations, sanitation,
and so forth. How's that?"

Comenius looked a bit dubious. "Workable, perhaps.
There will still be a great deal of suspicion."

Morris had to restrain himself from slapping his
hand on the table. There were things he liked about
seventeenth-century Europeans. Most of them, anyway.

There were also some things he detested. One of them was their seemingly inveterate and obsessive religious sectarianism.

"Let them be suspicious," he growled. "The way I look at it, Bishop, the main point of this university— one of them, at least—is to start overcoming those suspicions. In practice, which is always the best way to do it."

He gave Comenius something just barely short of a glare. "Understand something, Bishop. I *know* a secular university will work—and way better than the alternatives you have today. *I know it*—because I've seen it. My own kids went to West Virginia University, which was a far better university than anything you've got in Europe today. And in the world I come from, WVU was just considered a middling-rate university."

Judith interjected herself. "Morris, don't be so hardnosed. A lot of those universities got started as religious ones, remember. Including Harvard and the University of Chicago, if I remember right."

Morris suspected he was looking mulish, and the suspicion made him still more mulish. "Yeah, I know. I also know how long it took to haul them kicking and screaming into the modern world. Harvard didn't even go coeducational until—"

He broke off, rubbing his face. "Oh, hell, don't tell me."

Comenius' brow was creased with a frown of confusion. "I am afraid my English is perhaps not as good as it should be. What does that term mean? 'Coeducational,' I think it was."

Morris glared at the table. "Well, that's the second thing . . ."

❖❖❖   ❖❖❖   ❖❖❖

Eventually, they got past that hurdle. But only because Morris finally agreed—under Judith's coaxing—that the university would have two colleges, one for men and one for women, with separate faculties. He did manage to hold the line on a common curriculum—"I want women *educated*, damn it; I'm not shelling out money for a lousy finishing school"—as well as a common library. And he took a certain sly pleasure in having gotten Comenius to agree to a coeducational "student union"—mostly, he suspected, because Comenius didn't quite understand what was involved.

That would be a fight in the future, he was sure, but Morris was willing to deal with that when the time came. Somewhere in the middle of construction, he suspected, once Comenius finally realized that Morris proposed to have young men and women socializing and dining together at all hours of the day and night with no real supervision or chaperonage. But since Morris would control the purse strings, he imagined the construction workers would obey him.

The rest of it went smoothly enough. They settled on the name "University of Prague," which wasn't a problem since the only existing university in the city was named the Karolinum—or "Charles University"—founded in the fourteenth century by the same Emperor Charles who'd had the city's great bridge erected. The Karolinum was located in the southern part of Staré Mesto, so they agreed to find land for the new university somewhere in the northern part of Old Town, even though that would be somewhat more expensive. Morris was pretty sure that a certain amount of friction between the two universities was bound to happen. The Karolinum was no "cow college." Even after the ravages of the past fifteen years, it was still considered one of the premier universities in Europe. In the long run, he thought having two major universities in Prague would simply enhance the city's prestige—and its prospects. But in the short run, competition between the two universities was likely to be a source of trouble. He saw no reason to aggravate the situation by placing them cheek-to-jowl.

Besides, a location in the northern part of Old Town would have the further advantage, to his way of thinking, of being close to the Josefov. Already, in the few short months since he'd become resident in Prague, Morris had come to realize that the Jewish inhabitants were going to be at least as resistant to change as the gentile ones. In some ways, more so, even in ways that objectively benefited them. Morris thought that having a university open to Jewish students just a short walk from the ghetto would have a nicely subversive effect.

Of all the things he missed about the universe they'd lost forever, the thing he missed the most was the atmosphere in his old synagogue and the Hillel House attached to the campus at WVU. That relaxed, sophisticated, cosmopolitan modern Judaism that he'd grown up with and cherished. He knew that Jason had come to have a real respect for some of the orthodox rabbis he'd encountered in Prague's ghetto. But, to Morris, they were as much a part of the problem as the Cossack butchers who would soon enough be slaughtering tens of thousands of Jews in the Ukraine. Their stiff necks bent over, endlessly studying the complexities of the Torah and the Talmud and the midrash, completely oblivious to the disaster that was beginning to curl over them. Morris had every intention of undermining their control and authority over the largest Jewish community in Europe, as best he could, using any legitimate means at his disposal.

Comenius had tentatively advanced the idea of naming it "Roth University," but Morris declined the honor immediately. He said that was because he thought it would create unnecessary problems by having the university too closely associated with its Jewish founder. But the real reason was simply that he found the idea too self-aggrandizing and presumptuous. In times past, in the universe he'd come from, he'd been known to make wisecracks about the swelled egos of the men who'd founded "Carnegie-Mellon Institute."

Judith had given him something of an odd look, then. Morris wasn't sure—he'd find out soon enough, of course, once they were alone—but he thought he was probably in for a little lecture on the subject of false modesty.

So be it. In times to come, he might get comfortable enough with his new status to consider the possibility. Morris had a feeling this was not going to be the last university he provided the financial backing for—assuming, of course, he and Judith survived the years to come. If this new world had greater opportunities than his old one, it also had much greater dangers.

The last item remaining was the first: who would they find to become the rector of the new university?

By the end of the evening—quite a bit early on,

in fact—Morris had already made up his own mind. So as soon as Comenius raised the subject again, he had his answer ready.

"I think it should be you, Bishop."

Comenius, startled, began to say something by way of protest. Morris raised his hand.

"Hear me out, please. Yes, I know you're the central leader of the Unity of Brethren, recognized as such all over Europe. You're also famous for being an advocate of educational reform. To the best of my knowledge, you're the only person in this day and age who's actually written books on the subject. Well, okay, outside of the Jesuits. But while I'm perfectly willing for the new university to have Catholic students—Jesuit teachers, for that matter—there's no way I want a Jesuit in charge of it. Not in today's political climate, anyway. So I think it makes perfect sense for you to do it. As far as the religious issue goes . . ."

Morris shrugged. "You said it yourself, Bishop—we'll face that with almost anyone we select. The advantage to it being you is twofold. First, you've become just about as well-known for advocating religious tolerance. And second—not to put too fine a point on it—the Brethren are a relatively small church. Certainly compared to the Catholics or the Lutherans or the Calvinists. So you won't seem as much of a threat to anyone, even leaving aside your own views on toleration."

Comenius was still hesitant. Morris regarded him for a moment, and then added: "And, finally. I think you and I can get along pretty well. Better than I think I'd get along with anyone else."

Comenius stared at him for a moment. Then, with a wry little smile, inclined his head. "So be it, then. I can hardly refuse, since without you none of this would be possible at all."

Judith was giving Morris that same odd little look. This time, he understood it completely.

Okay, fine. Yes, I'll have to get used to it. But I draw the line at the "Baron" business. I am NOT a Rothschild. Just a Roth.

3

After dinner, most of the guests left. The only ones who remained behind, at Morris' quietly spoken request, were Ellie Anderson and Len Tanner.

"So. Why'd you ask us to stay, Morris?" Ellie's question was asked with a tone of voice that indicated a certain suspicion on her part. Of course, Ellie was usually a little suspicious of most things.

In this case, however, with good reason.

"*That's* why I asked, as a matter of fact. I'm hoping to talk you into staying."

For a moment, both Len and Ellie looked a little confused. Then, as his meaning registered, Ellie gave Len a quick, hostile little glance.

"Did you put him up to this?" she demanded.

Len looked aggrieved. "I had nothing to do with it! This is the first time Morris has ever raised the subject."

Morris found the interchange both interesting and heartening. He'd had no idea that Len had given some thought himself to remaining in Prague.

"He's telling the truth, Ellie. This is the first time I've ever brought it up."

Ellie transferred the hostile look to him. "The answer's 'no.' Prague's okay, I guess, but I have no intention of staying here after we get this job done."

"Why not?" Judith asked. "It's not as if you have any family in Grantville." Diplomatically, she did not add what she could have: *or all that many friends either, when you get right down to it.* Ellie's abrasive manner didn't bother either of the Roths, but the woman's temperament was not one that had ever made her very popular.

Diplomacy, as usual, was wasted with Ellie. "Or any friends either," she snorted, half-barking the words. "So what? Grantville has toilet paper."

Len made a face. Ellie scowled. "Okay, fine. It's that crappy stuff that they're starting to make in Badenburg, which is all there is since the modern stuff ran out. So what? It's still toilet paper and it still beats the alternatives."

She raised her left hand and began ticking off fingers. "Two. It's got modern plumbing. Fuck squatting over a hole. Here, even in Wallenstein's palace, that's about all you've got. Three. It's got electricity—I am *so* sick and tired of reading by lamplight at night."

"Prague will have all of those things before too long, Ellie," Morris said mildly. "And if it really bothers you that much, import what you need in the meantime."

"With what money?" she demanded. "AT&L is still scraping by and will be for at least another year. We can't even afford to pay Dougie to start running the company full time, which is a fucking waste because he'd be great at it. Instead, half the time he's galloping off into the countryside somewhere running messages for the king of Sweden. He'll get killed, you watch. If Wallenstein hadn't come up with the dough for this special project here in Prague, I'm not sure we wouldn't have had to close our doors. That's the only reason Len and I agreed to come here at all. We didn't have any choice."

"With what money? With the sudden influx of money you'll get from *me*. From the new company—or subsidiary, if you prefer—that I propose to form here in Prague. Call it AT&L Bohemia, if you want. I'll put up all the capital and you give me forty-nine percent of the stock—you can remain in control of it, I don't care—and agree to live here for another, say, five years. If you're still unhappy five years from now, fine. You go back to Grantville, if you want. No hard feelings."

Ellie and Len stared at him. Morris found himself swallowing. "Me and Judith would miss you guys. We really would. Right now, except for the two of you and Jason, we really don't have anybody to talk to here in Prague who . . . You know. Understands us."

"How long do *you* plan on being here, Morris?" asked Len.

Morris and Judith looked at each other. Judith shrugged. "Who knows?" she mused. "Either a very short time—if Wallenstein's plans go sour and we wind up having to run for it—or . . . probably the rest of our lives. Except for trips."

Morris rose from the table and went over to one of the windows. Pushing aside the heavy drapes, he stared out over the city. At night, in the seventeenth century, even a large town like Prague was eerily dark to someone accustomed to American cities at the turn of the twenty-first century. A few lamps in windows, here and there, one or two small bonfires in open areas, not much more than that. The Hradcany, at a distance, was just a formless lump of darkness, with the towers of the cathedral barely visible against the night sky.

"We've got fifteen years to prevent one of the worst massacres ever perpetrated on my people," Morris said quietly. "And I'm just a small-town jeweler who really doesn't have any idea how to do it—except, maybe, do what I can to turn Bohemia into a country that can start drawing those Jews—some of them, anyway—out of the line of fire. And, maybe—most of this is completely out of our control—help build this into a nation that can intervene ahead of time."

"You're talking about *Wallenstein*, Morris," Ellie pointed out harshly.

Morris' lips twisted into something that was half a grin, half a grimace. "Ah, yes. Wallenstein. Actually, this was his idea in the first place. Trying to get you to stay here and set up a telephone company, I mean. Just like I know when I go talk to him tomorrow about the new university the bishop and I want to establish that he'll agree immediately. That's an idea he's also raised with me, on several occasions."

He turned away from the window. "In fact, I won't be surprised if he provides the land and the building for both projects, free of charge—assuming you agree to stay."

Len and Ellie were back to staring at him. "Look," Morris said abruptly, "Wallenstein wants it all—a modern nation that will give him the power he needs to become the historical figure he thinks he deserves to be. In some ways, he's a raving egotist, sure enough. But he's *smart*. Bohemia is not big enough for him, unless he modernizes it. That means the whole works. An electrified capital city, one of the world's premier universities, factories, you name it—yes, and toilet paper. Why else do you think he's agreed to remove all religious restrictions, even on Jews? The goodness of his heart? Not hardly. It's because—I'm as sure of this as I am of anything—he plans on grabbing most of the Ukraine and probably a good chunk of Poland and the Balkans. Maybe even part of Russia, who knows? And the only way he can do that, starting with little Bohemia as his power base, is to make Bohemia the Japan of eastern Europe. And he can't do that without stripping away all the medieval customs and traditions that get in the way."

Morris barked a laugh. "He spent a lot of time in Edith Wild's house in Grantville himself, you know. I've heard him complain about the lack of toilet paper here in Prague several times."

"So have I," muttered Len, giving Ellie a glance. "I also heard him pissing and moaning about no electricity, too."

Ellie's face looked pinched. She'd undoubtedly heard the same thing from him. Morris knew that Wallenstein spent a lot of time with Ellie and Len, watching them as they set up a telephone center in his palace. Not so much because he was trying to oversee the work, about which he knew effectively nothing, but simply because he was interested. Wallenstein was a curious man, interested in many things. Except when his shaky health was acting up, or he was distracted by his obsession with astrology, Wallenstein's mind was always alert and active.

The pinched look on Ellie's face went away, replaced by . . . something else. She cocked her head sideways a bit.

"I'm curious about something. It sounds like—no offense—you're almost planning to set up Bohemia as a counterweight to the CPE. Even a rival. Doesn't that bother you any?"

Morris shrugged. "Some, sure. But I talked to Mike about it before we left Grantville, and he agrees that it's the only way to do it. That's not just because of the Jewish question, either. Mike's thinking about the whole picture."

"What Wallenstein *wants* is one thing," Judith chipped in. "What he winds up with . . . well, that's something else. He's not the only player in the game."

Mention of the word *game* jogged Morris' mind. Like him, Len was a chess enthusiast. "Think of it as a *fianchetto*, Len. You move up knight's pawn one rank, creating a little pocket for the bishop. Then the bishop sits there, protected, but ready to attack at a diagonal."

"Yeah, I know. I like the maneuver myself. But what's the—oh."

"'Oh,' is right. And that's just what Wallenstein might be saying, one of these days. Chess is just a game, so it has firm and hard rules. Real life doesn't. A bishop can take out its own queen, in the real world, if that ever proves necessary. Try to, anyway."

While Len chewed on the analogy, Morris returned to the table and sat down again. "It's a race, really. That's how Mike puts it. A strange kind of race, because we're trying to beat the same man we're allied with—without ever attacking him directly. He'll try for one thing, but the means he has to use for his ends can turn around and bite him on the ass. In our world, the Japanese wound up being saddled by a military dictatorship as they modernized. But who's to say the same thing has to happen here? Maybe it will. Then, again, maybe it won't."

Honesty forced him to say the next words. "It'll be dangerous, I admit. You'd be a lot safer staying back in Grantville."

Oddly, that did it. Ellie sat up straight. "You think I'm *afraid* of these assholes? Bullshit. Len, we're staying."

"Yes, dear," he murmured.

"And stop smirking."

"Hey, look, they got the best beer in the world here, just like they did four hundred years from now. You admitted it yourself, just the other day."

"I said, *stop smirking.*"

The last conversation Morris Roth had that day was the one he hadn't foreseen or planned on. After everyone had left and he and Judith were getting ready for bed, his wife said to him:

"There's one last thing, O great Machiavellian prince of the Jewish persuasion."

"Yes?"

"I want you to stop bullying Jason."

Morris stared at her. Judith was busy turning down the covers, but she looked up at him squarely.

"Yes, you *are*," she said firmly. "He's just a young man

who wants to become a rabbi, Morris. That's *all*. There's at least one of those rabbis in the ghetto whom he likes a lot, and wants to study with. So let him do what he wants, instead of trying to force him to be your Reform champion who'll slay the dragon of Orthodoxy. Let him study and decide for himself what he thinks. And if he winds up becoming an Orthodox rabbi, so be it."

Morris felt his jaws tighten. "You really want to listen to him at prayer, thanking God for not making him a woman?"

Judith shook her head. "That's neither here nor there, Morris. No, of course I don't. So what? I know how much you miss Rabbi Stern and our old synagogue and Hillel House. So do I. But you can't force Jason to become something he isn't. He's not even twenty-three years old, for Pete's sake. Steve Stern was a middle-aged man with all the confidence of someone who'd studied the Torah and the Talmud for years and was an experienced rabbi. How can you possibly expect Jason to substitute for him? Just because *you* want to launch a Reform movement two hundred years ahead of schedule? Well, then, why don't you do it yourself, big shot? Instead of trying to jam a kid into it, while you turn yourself into another Rothschild."

Morris winced. That struck . . . a little close to home. As much as Morris prized his Reform beliefs, he knew perfectly well that he'd be completely over-matched if he tried to cross theological lances with Orthodox rabbis.

Judith smiled. "Thought so. You chicken."

She straightened up from the bed. "Has it ever occurred to you, even once—because I know it has to Jason—that maybe, just maybe, you ought to apply

your fancy chess terms to this situation also? Who is
to say, Morris Roth, how Judaism will develop in *this*
universe? They don't even use the term 'Orthodoxy'
in the here and now. Maybe . . ."

She waved her hand, half-irritably. "I don't know.
Maybe everything will shape up differently. Maybe it
won't. What I *do* know is that you've got one unhappy
kid on your hands, and you're driving him away with your
pressure and your demands. Leave him alone, Morris.
Let Jason Gotkin do whatever Jason Gotkin winds up
doing. You never treated our own kids the way you're
treating him. So why are you doing it to someone who's
become something of an adopted son?"

Morris thought about it, for a moment. Then, heaved
a deep sigh. She was right, and he knew it.

"Okay. I guess I look a little silly parading around
as 'Baron Roth,' huh?"

His wife looked at him calmly. "No, actually, that's
not true. Give it a few more years, and I think you'll
have the role down pat. Come as naturally to you as
breathing. Surprises the hell out of me, I admit, being
married to you for over thirty years. But . . . there it is.
Morris, if we survive, you will—we will, I guess—become
the new Rothschilds of this universe. So what do you
say we don't screw it up? I'd hate to be remembered
as a pack of overbearing bullies. I really would."

4

"We cannot postpone a decision on this matter
forever, Isaac." Mordechai Spira spoke softly, as was
his habit, but firmly nonetheless.

His friend and fellow rabbi sighed and looked out the window of his domicile. Beyond, the narrow and crooked street was as crowded as it usually was at that time of the morning. Prague's Jewish population was really too big for the Josefov's cramped quarters, and it showed. People were almost living on top of each other.

"Things are still very tense, Mordechai," Isaac Gans pointed out. "Between the mess with Heller and then—just what was needed—the strains with Auerbach . . ."

Mordechai nodded, understanding the point. Prague's last two chief rabbis had been something of a disaster for the Jewish community. Heller had fallen afoul of the Habsburgs and had wound up being cast into prison in Vienna. Mordechai thought Heller was personally blameless in the matter, having simply had the misfortune of being politically inept in a tense political situation. The Habsburgs had imposed a harsh tax on Prague's Jewish community in order to help fund their military activities in the savage war that had been rolling across Europe for over a decade. Forty thousand thalers! Heller had tried to resist, and then, when resistance proved futile, had done his best to collect the tax fairly.

But . . . he had enemies, and they had taken advantage of the situation to lay accusations against him before the emperor. In the end, his supporters in the Jewish community had been able to get his death sentence commuted, though only because Ferdinand II's greed was such that he had been willing to ransom him for another 12,000 thalers. Still—and probably for the best, all things considered—Heller had not been able to return to Prague. He'd accepted instead a position in the rabbinate of far-off Nemirow.

Probably for the best, Mordechai reflected. It was hard to say. Alas, he'd been replaced by Simon Auerbach, who, if he had better political skills had been a much harder man for Mordechai and other rabbis to get along with. Auerbach had been a renowned Talmudist, true enough. But he was one of those men whose great learning was coupled to a harsh and inflexible temperament. Throughout his career he had clashed with those around him—at Lublin, with Meïr ben Gedaliah, another famous Talmudist; later, at Posen, with the city's rosh yeshivah, Benjamin of Morawczyk; and, soon after his arrival at Prague, he'd had a quarrel with Heller himself.

Auerbach had died, a year and a half earlier. But he'd done enough damage in the two short years he'd been at Prague that it was still felt, especially coming on top of the continuing strains in the community over the Heller imbroglio.

The current chief rabbi was a mild-mannered sort of fellow, thankfully. Alas, he was one of those people whose mild manner was principally due to his reluctance to make any decisions. Not a good characteristic for the chief rabbi of the largest Jewish community in Europe—at any time, much less these.

"Still," Mordechai said abruptly, "a decision must be made. We cannot continue to simply ignore Jason Gotkin."

"We haven't *ignored* him, Mordechai," protested Gans.

Spira waved his hand. "Stop avoiding the issue. First of all, even in social matters we've avoided him. And the Roths, even more so. Yes, we speak to Jason in the street. But have you invited him to your home for Shabbat dinner? No. Neither have I. Neither has anyone. It's grotesque. A *schande!*"

He waited a moment; Issac looked away.

"No," Mordechai repeated. "A complete breach with our customs. And, as I said, neither have I—despite the fact that I like Jason Gotkin. Quite a bit, in fact." He chuckled softly. "And don't forget that *I* have three unmarried daughters."

Gans started to grimace; but, then, as his innate fairness and good humor rallied, the grimace shifted into something of a sly smile. "Well, true. And I imagine Sarah in particular would take a fancy to him."

Mordechai must have looked somewhat alarmed, because Isaac's sly smile started bordering on a grin. "Yes, I know she's your favorite, even if you'll never admit it. But that's because she's sprightly. Just the sort of girl to find an exotic fellow like Gotkin of interest. He's a rather handsome boy, too, you know. To be sure, his Yiddish is somewhat pathetic."

"His Hebrew isn't," Mordechai pointed out, forcefully. "In fact—spoken, at least—I suspect it's better than yours or mine. Or any other Jew's in the world today."

Isaac rubbed his forehead. "Do you really believe it, Mordechai?"

"Say better: is there any way to *doubt* it, any longer?" Spira's eyes moved to a table in the corner of the room, atop which sat a book whose appearance was unlike that of any other Mordechai had ever seen. He'd lent it to his friend Isaac a week earlier, after Jason Gotkin had lent it to him.

On one level, the book was simply another edition of the Tanakh—the Jewish version of the ancient holy texts which, in a slightly different variant, Christians called "the Old Testament." Jason had told Mordechai that he'd had it in his possession when the mysterious event had taken place which had brought him and his town into the world from . . . somewhere else. "In my bags in the trunk of my car," as he'd put it, whatever that meant.

Mordechai rose and went over to the table. He opened the book and began fingering the pages. He'd lent it to Isaac, in part, because Isaac knew how to read English—a language of which Mordechai himself was completely ignorant.

"Leave aside the pages and the printing, Isaac— though I know you've never seen anything like it." He swiveled his head around, to regard his friend. "It *is* the Tanakh, yes?"

Gans nodded.

"The Tanakh. In *English*. At a guess, Isaac, how many copies of an English Tanakh—in any edition, much less one so fine as this—do you think exist in the world?"

Gans looked away, staring back out the window. "I suspect that is the only Tanakh anywhere in the world, printed in English."

"The world *today*, Isaac. Our world. This one. Which means—to me at least—that the boy must be telling the truth. The rest—"

He waved his hand at the window. "—all of it, this new Confederated Principalities of Europe, Gustavus

Adolphus grown so mighty, Wallenstein's disaster at the Alte Veste, the political turmoil. All of that I might possibly ascribe to something else. Those are things of the *goyishe* princes." Then, softly: "But how can I explain such a fine edition of the Tanakh, printed in a language which very few Jews in the world today use? Except some Sephardim, and they would have no more use for an English Tanakh than we do."

He closed the book and returned to his chair. "We are rabbis, Isaac, not princes. All that faces us, right now, is that a Jewish boy who is—in any manner that you or I can determine—qualified to do so, wishes to join the yeshivah. He does not even ask for financial support, though he is entitled to it. On what grounds can we deny him that wish? For weeks now, I have searched the Talmud and as much of the commentaries as I could, and found nothing."

"Nothing? He is probably a heretic, Mordechai."

"Be careful, Isaac," replied Spira softly. "Yes, he comes *from* what appears to be heresy—to me as well as to you. *Appears* to be, I remind you. Heresy is not that simple to judge, as you well know. And so what? Has he told us he wishes to advocate heresy? No. He simply wishes to study. On what grounds can we refuse him—without, ourselves, abandoning the traditions we would accuse him of having abandoned?"

Isaac went back to his window-watching.

"And what is so fascinating out there?" demanded Mordechai. "Besides too many Jews in too little space, as always. Stop avoiding this, Isaac. In the end, it is our souls that are being tested here, not the soul of Jason Gotkin."

Gans sighed. "True enough. Very well, Mordechai. I will support you in this. But I warn you, I do not think we will be able to convince the rosh yeshivah."

Spira shrugged. "No, I don't expect we will. But with your support, no one will oppose me if I begin instructing the boy myself. And I already have a chevrusah for him."

Gans burst out laughing. "Mordechai, you schemer! I assume you asked young Hoeschel. I think that boy would accept any challenge."

"Schmuel is a bold one, true enough," allowed Spira, smiling. "But he's met Gotkin, you know, several times. He likes him and tells me he would be quite happy to become Jason's study partner."

Now that he'd finally made his decision, Gans seemed to relax. That was his usual pattern, Mordechai knew—and the reason he'd begun with him. Isaac Gans was perhaps the best scholar among the rabbis in Prague; careful and deliberate in coming to a conclusion, but firm and confident about it thereafter. His support would mean a great deal.

"And why shouldn't he?" said Isaac. "He *is* a nice boy, whatever else may be said about him."

He was smiling slyly again. "You watch. The first time you invite him to Shabbat dinner, Sarah will start pestering you the next day. As sprightly as she is, she'll be hard to resist, too. Especially after she enlists your wife—which she will. You watch."

Mordechai Spira did his best to look stern and patriarchal. Master of his house. But Isaac's smile just kept widening.

5

That same morning, in Vienna, a prince of the goyim came to a decision.

"Very well. I agree. We have no choice, any longer."

Emperor Ferdinand II eyed General Piccolomini skeptically. He didn't trust the mercenary, though he understood the man's reasons for refusing to remain in Prague. Piccolomini had once been one of Wallenstein's closest subordinates. But had he remained within Wallenstein's reach, after the Alte Veste, the Bohemian magnate would surely have had him assassinated. By now, the emperor was sure—so was Piccolomini—Wallenstein had obtained his own copies of books from Grantville. In another universe, Piccolomini had been one of the chief conspirators in the plot that had resulted in Wallenstein's assassination.

As he still was in *this* universe, to be sure—but now he proposed to keep his distance.

"It will work, Your Majesty," Piccolomini assured him. "Wallenstein is on his guard, yes. But he also listens to his astrologers—and two of them are now on the imperial payroll. With their influence, Rossbach has ingratiated himself with Wallenstein. He assures me he can manage it."

"How much?" the emperor grunted.

Piccolomini understood the terse question. "He wants

thirty thousand thalers—but he will settle for twenty, I think, if your Majesty makes him a Freiherr."

Ferdinand grunted again. Then, decided he could live with it. If the imperial purse was too straitened, when the time came, he could always simply refuse to pay the full amount. What could Rossbach do, after all?

"And Pappenheim?"

"Rossbach says he will do his best, but—" Piccolomini made a face. "Assassinating Pappenheim is a different matter. Risky, much riskier. Unfortunately, Pappenheim doesn't listen to astrologers. And, up close . . ."

He shrugged. So did the emperor—although, in his case, the gesture was one of a man relieving himself of a load. Who was to say? If Rossbach made the attempt on Pappenheim, either he would succeed or he would fail. Mostly likely, he would fail.

So be it. Wallenstein would still be dead, which was the key thing. And the emperor would be relieved of the burden of paying 20,000 thalers to his assassin.

"Let it be done, then," he commanded.

"He won't *listen* to me, Edith," complained Isabella Katharina. Wallenstein's wife shook her head. "Those damned astrologers! All he listens to! And they are telling him he has nothing to fear in the year ahead."

Edith Wild scowled and glanced at the door. Her bedroom directly adjoined the suite that served Wallenstein and his wife as their living quarters in the palace. That was due to Isabella Katharina's insistence that Wallenstein's nurse be readily available in the event his poor health suddenly deteriorated. In the months since she'd arrived in Prague, Isabella had come to trust Edith's advice far more than she did those of her husband's doctors. Much less his astrologers.

Smart woman, thought Edith. "What does Pappenheim say?"

"My husband won't listen to him either. I spoke to Gottfried myself, and he says he can do nothing beyond make sure that a guard is always stationed at the entrance."

"Well, that's true enough. He can't very well force the Duke to accept guards in his own suite."

Isabella seemed close to tears. Edith patted her on the shoulder. "All right, then, you'll just have to rely on me, if something happens."

As much as Isabella trusted her, the look she gave Edith now was definitely on the skeptical side.

Edith sniffed, and marched over to the chest in the corner that held her clothes. After rummaging in the bottom for a moment, she brought out something and showed it to Isabella.

"This'll do the trick."

Now more intrigued than anything else, Isabella came over and stared at the thing.

"Is that one of your American pistols?"

Edith grunted. "Don't call it a 'pistol.' It's a revolver. Smith and Wesson .357 Magnum Chief Special. Holds five rounds, 125 grain. Kicks like a mule and it'll damn near blow your eardrums, but it'll drop an ox. I wouldn't have bought it myself, it's my son's. But he gave it to me after the first time he fired it on the shooting range." She sniffed again. "I hate to say it, but he's something of a sissy—even if he does like to hang out with those bums at the Club 250, pretending otherwise."

She was wearing seventeenth-century-style heavy skirts with a separate pocket underneath, attached by a drawstring. Using a slit in the skirts designed for the purpose, she slipped the revolver into the pocket. "Anyway, relax. If anybody gets into the Duke's rooms, I'll see to it they don't leave. Except in a coffin."

Isabella gazed up admiringly at the large American woman. "What would we do without you?"

"I don't know," grunted Edith.

It was the truth, too. There were ways in which taking care of Wallenstein and his wife was like taking care of children. Still, she'd grown very fond of the two of them. The Duke himself was always courteous to her—far more courteous than any "fellow American" had ever been, she thought sarcastically—and Isabella had become a real friend.

Edith Wild hadn't had many friends in her life. That was her own harsh personality at work, she understood well enough. She'd never really been sure how much she'd like *herself*, if she had any choice in the matter. So it was nice to have a place again in life, and people who treated her well.

"Don't worry about it," she gruffed. "I like it here in Prague, and I plan on staying. Anybody tries to fuck with the Duke, they're fucking with me."

"You shouldn't swear so much," chided Isabella. The reproof was then immediately undermined by a childish giggle. "But I'm *so* glad you're here."

Chapter IV: En passant
July, 1633

1

"I feel silly in this getup," Morris grumbled, as Judith helped him with the skirted doublet. "Are you sure? I mean, I've gotten used to wearing it—sort of—when I go visit Wallenstein in his palace. He dresses like a peacock himself and insists everyone does at his little courts. But I'm just going next door!"

"Stop whining, Morris," his wife commanded. She stepped back and gave him an admiring look. "*I* think you look terrific, myself. This outfit looks a lot better on you than a modern business suit ever did."

She was telling him nothing more than the truth, actually. Judith thought he *did* look terrific. Her husband had the kind of sturdy but unprepossessing face and figure that a drab up-time business suit simply emphasized. Whereas that same figure, encased in the clothing worn by seventeenth-century courtiers, looked stately rather than somewhat plump—and it was the shrewdness and intelligence in his face that was brought forward, rather than the plain features, when framed by a lace-fringed falling collar spilling across his shoulders and capped by a broad-brimmed hat.

"The plume, too?" he whined.

"I said, 'stop whining.' Yes, the plume too." She took him by the shoulders, turned him around, and began gently pushing him toward the door of their suite. "Look at it this way, Morris. For years I had to listen to you crab and complain about how much you hated wearing a tie. Now—no ties."

He hadn't quite given up. "Damnation, I'm just going across the street—barely inside the ghetto—to visit Jason in the new community center."

They were outside the suite that served them as their private quarters, and moving down the hallway toward the great staircase. Judith was no longer actually pushing him ahead of her, but she was crowding him closely enough to force him forward.

"Which you have never yet visited," she pointed out. "Not once in the two weeks since it was finished and Jason started working out of it. Even though you paid for the whole thing—buying the building, refurbishing it, and stocking it with what's becoming a very fine library as well as a kitchen for the poor."

Now, they were starting down the stairs. Judith wasn't crowding him quite as closely any longer. Not quite.

"I won't feel comfortable there," he predicted. "Especially not wearing this damn getup. When I went to Hillel House—"

"This is *not* Hillel House in Morgantown, Morris," Judith pointed out firmly. "And this is *not* the twenty-first century. Everybody in the ghetto knows you're the benefactor who financed the new community center—just like they know you're the source of the not-so-anonymous funds that went to help refurbish the Rathhaus and improve the Old-New Synagogue."

They'd reached the bottom of the stairs. Morris turned around and planted his hands on his hips, almost glaring at his wife.

"Yes? And did they use the money the way I wanted?"

Judith gave him a level look, for a moment, before responding. "Yes, as a matter of fact, they did. Avigail and Hirshele thanked me for it just yesterday. They say the seats in the womens' section of the synagogue are much improved—and the air circulation even more so."

That only made Morris look more sour yet. "Swell. So I'm aiding and abetting 'separate but equal'—which it never is."

It was Judith's turn to plant her hands on her hips. It was a gesture she did a lot more authoritatively than he did.

"Morris, cut it out. You're fifty-three years old and I'm only a year younger than you are. Neither one of us is going to live long enough to see a tenth of the changes you'd like to see—and you know it as well as I do. So what do you say we keep our eyes focused on what's really critical?"

She was actually a little angry, she realized, not just putting on an act. "What do you think those Jews are, over there in the Ukraine, whose lives you want to save? A bunch of Mendelssohns and Einsteins and Oppenheimers? Hundreds of thousands of budding Stephen Jay Goulds, champing at the bit to study evolution and biology? They're every bit as set in their ways and customs as the crankiest rabbi here in Prague—a lot more so, in fact. So?"

He looked away. "I just don't like it," he murmured.

Judith shook her head. "Husband, I love you dearly but sometimes you are purely maddening. What's *really* going on here is that you just have a bad conscience because you know you've hurt Jason's feelings by not showing up sooner at the community center. And now—*men!*—you're taking it out on everybody else. Starting with me. So cut it out. Just do your duty and march over there. Wearing your Jewish prince outfit."

She took him by the shoulders and spun him around, facing the door to the street. A servant was standing by, ready to open it. Judith was a bit startled to see him, only realizing now that he would have heard the whole conversation.

How much of it he would have understood, of course, was another question. So far as she knew, Fischel spoke no English at all.

So far as she knew—but she'd never asked. Mentally, she shrugged her shoulders. Nothing had been said that would come as any surprise to anyone, after all. Unlike Morris, Judith never let her own attitudes blind her to the fact that seventeenth-century traditional Jews—and certainly their rabbis—were no dummies. By now, months after the Roths had arrived in Prague with a big splash, the people of the ghetto would have made their own assessment of these exotic foreign Jews.

Well, perhaps not "assessment." Not yet, anyway. But Judith was quite sure that she and Morris had been studied very carefully by their servants—and their observations faithfully reported to their rabbis.

"Go," she commanded.

After Morris left, Judith went to the kitchen—insofar as the term "kitchen" could be used to describe a huge suite of interconnected rooms on the lowest floor devoted to the storing, preparation and serving of food for the inhabitants of a small palace. And not just food for the lord and lady of the mansion, either, and the guests who came to their now-frequent dinners and soirees. Judith was well aware that the midday meal that the cooks and servants made for themselves was their biggest meal of the day—and that they quietly smuggled food out every night, for their families back in the ghetto. Quietly, but not particularly surreptitiously. Judith had made clear to them, long since, that whatever disputes she might have with aspects of their beliefs and customs, she was a firm believer in the Biblical precept about not muzzling the kine that tread the grain.

Avigail, as usual, was tending the big hearth in which the actual cooking was done. Even after the months she'd been in Prague, Judith was still always a little startled to see that hearth, and the profusion of kettles hanging over it and smaller skillets nestled directly in the coals. It was such homely things as the absence of stoves that really drove home to her, more than anything else, that she was now living in a different universe.

Avigail straightened up and smiled at her. "Good morning, gracious lady."

Avigail spoke Yiddish, not German, but Judith had no trouble understanding her. Except for some loan words, the languages were almost identical. The spoken languages, that is. Yiddish was written in Hebrew characters, which Judith couldn't read at all. One of the reasons Judith had hired Avigail was because the woman could read German also, which allowed Judith to leave notes for her when need be.

Now, she wondered what *other* languages Avigail might speak. Judith knew the woman was fluent in Czech also. But—

She blurted it out. In English. A language she had just assumed—without ever asking—would be completely foreign to the cook.

"Avigail, do you speak English?"

The cook hesitated for a moment. Then, her face a bit stiff, replied in heavily accented but quite understandable English: "Yes, gracious lady. I do."

Judith suddenly realized that the normally-bustling and busy kitchen had fallen very quiet. She scanned the room and saw that all five of the cooks and helpers present were staring at her. All of them with that same, slightly stiff expression.

"Do *all* of you speak English?"

Again, that hesitation. Then, again, nodding heads.

For a moment, Judith wavered between anger and . . .

Well . . .

She burst out laughing. "Does *every* servant in this house speak English?"

Nods. A bit hastily, Avigail said: "Young Jacob upstairs, not so well." She pointed with a ladle at a teenage girl standing in a corner near the pantry. "And little Rifka over there, even worse. Lazy youngsters, they don't do their studies like they should."

Judith had to fight to bring her laughter under control. "Their 'studies,' no less!"

She shook her head, grinning. "They must have scoured the ghetto to find this many English-speakers. Avigail, if you have any questions—or if the rabbis do—you need only ask. I really have no secrets. Neither does my husband."

There didn't seem anything else to say. Still grinning, she left the room.

After she was gone, Avigail and the three women who'd been employed since the first days after the Roths arrived, turned their heads to regard Rifka. The young woman was new to the household, having only started working there the week before. Their expressions were identical: that of older women finally and fully vindicated in front of skeptical and callow striplings.

"You see?" demanded Avigail. "Did we not tell you?"

"I will study harder," Rifka said meekly.

"That's not what I meant!" snapped Avigail. "And you know it perfectly well."

She sniffed, turned away, and went back to work with her ladle. It had a very long handle, because the hearth was large and the fire was hot. But the ladle in Avigail's mind had just grown shorter still. By now, it was not much longer than a spoon.

2

The first thing Morris saw when he entered the community center—the first thing he really noticed, at least, because of his nervousness—was the rabbi standing next to Jason and another young man.

He assumed he was a rabbi, at least. Partly from the clothing the man was wearing, but mostly from certain indefinable things about the way he carried himself—and the very evident respect with which Jason and the other youngster were listening to what he had to say.

Morris found himself almost gritting his teeth. He had a better knowledge of history, in general, than most residents of Grantville. And because he'd always been especially interested in Jewish history, he had a particularly good knowledge of that subject. He felt like shouting at the three of them: *Your damn rabbinate didn't start running the show until not much more than a thousand years ago! Those old men in Babylon who started throwing their weight around after the destruction of the Second Temple. Our history goes back at least two thousand years earlier than that. Ask David and Solomon—or Abraham and Moshe—if they kowtowed to a bunch of old men with long beards and stupid hats!*

But, he didn't. It would have been unfairly one-sided, as well as rude and pointless. And, besides . . .

Well, the fact was that the rabbi in question was not particularly old. In fact, he looked to be younger than Morris himself.

Nothing for it, then. Morris took a deep breath and marched over.

Seeing him come, Jason smiled widely. It was the biggest smile Jason had given Morris in at least two months, and Morris felt himself warming. As Judith had said, since the Ring of Fire Morris had come to look upon young Gotkin as something of an adopted son. The estrangement that had grown between them since their arrival in Prague had been painful.

The rabbi turned his head and regarded Morris. He obviously knew who he was, even though they'd never met. Morris was not surprised. This was not the first time, by any means, that Morris had entered the ghetto. He'd made a number of trips—right into the center of the Josefov—to meet with Dunash and his people. And, every time, although people had not been rude about it, Morris had been quite aware that he'd been carefully and closely observed everywhere he went. And was just as sure that the people who watched him passed on their observations to their rabbis.

As he neared, the rabbi smiled politely and addressed him. "Good morning, Don Morris. Since I have never had the opportunity, let me take it now to thank you for your generosity in providing for this center. And your many other generosities."

The rabbi's German was excellent, if oddly accented to Morris' ear. By now, Morris' own German was almost fluent. What he found more interesting, though, was the way the rabbi had addressed him. *Don Morris*—as if Morris were a Sephardic hidalgo. True, it made a certain sense, because most court Jews in the first half of the seventeenth century were still Sephardic rather than Ashkenazi. Still . . .

Morris decided it was a workable compromise, for him as much as the rabbi. Although there were some differences in the way Sephardim and Ashkenazim observed their faith, which resulted in friction and even occasional clashes, neither one of the branches of Judaism considered the other to be heretics. Not to mention that Italian Jews, in this day and age, constituted something of a third tradition of their own.

Truth be told, the friction between Ashkenazim and Sephardim was due more to social factors than religious ones. Sephardim, as a rule, were more comfortable with cultural accommodation to gentile society—and, as a rule, considerably wealthier than most Ashkenazim. So, they tended to look down on Ashkenazim as the equivalent of "country rubes"—a disdain which the Ashkenazim returned in kind, much as Morris' hillbilly neighbors made wisecracks about city slickers. But, since he'd arrived in his new universe, Morris had discovered that the interaction between the two—and with the Judaeo-Italians—was quite a bit more extensive than his study of history had led him to suspect.

Besides, the man was being courteous. Whatever his underlying attitudes, Morris had never found it possible to be rude to someone who was not being rude to him.

He nodded. Graciously, he hoped. "My pleasure, rabbi. Ah—"

"This is Rabbi Spira," Jason said promptly, almost eagerly.

So. This is the one.

Morris had to fight down a momentary surge of jealousy. Although Jason had been veiled about it, Morris was well aware that the young man had come to develop a deep admiration for Mordechai Spira—and something that bordered on filial respect.

Now that Morris had finally met the man, he could understand that better. As much as Morris was inclined to dislike zealots—and he considered all Orthodox rabbis to be zealots, by their nature—he couldn't miss the intelligence in Spira's eyes. Nor the quite evident warmth and kindliness in them, either. Jason had told him, more than once, that even when Rabbi Spira corrected him for his errors, he invariably did so with good humor. Even wit.

For Morris Roth, "witty Orthodox rabbi" had always been something of an oxymoron. Unlike Jason, who'd lived in Israel for a year as a student, Morris and Judith had never done more than visit the country for a couple of weeks at a time. Morris had not had much contact with Orthodox Judaism in the United States he'd come from, since his area of the country was dominated by Reform Judaism. So his main personal impression of Orthodox rabbis came from what he'd seen in Israel—which, to him, had been their constant interference in Israel's politics, their narrow-minded obsessions, the readiness with which they threw their political weight around. He'd been particularly angry at their refusal—well, some of them—to allow their adherents to serve in Israel's armed forces, at the same time that they demanded those armed forces be used to carry out policies *they* wanted.

He had to remind himself—as Judith reminded him constantly—that they'd left that world behind. There was no Israel in this universe. Not yet, at least; and not for some time to come, if ever. The rabbinate that existed here was one that had been shaped by the life of Jews in central and eastern Europe's ghettos and shtetls. It simply wasn't fair for Morris Roth to pile atop Mordechai Spira's head all the sins of a rabbinate in a different time, in a different universe.

He began to say some words that would have been simply friendly. But he'd barely begun before he heard noises coming from the entrance. The sounds were very faint, seeming to come from a great distance, but Morris thought he recognized them.

Gunshots. Then, a moment later—

Lots of gunshots.

"It's starting," he said. "Finally."

3

Ellie leaned back in the chair before the console, and took a deep breath.

"Well, Duke, there it is. Finished. Finally."

Wallenstein examined the telephone center, his eyes bright with interest. "And you have the people trained to operate it, yes?"

Ellie nodded. "Three, so far. Enough to keep shifts going round the clock—for a while, anyway. You'll need to give them some time off, though, now and then."

Wallenstein was frowning a little, as he often did listening to Ellie's idiosyncratic blend of German and English. Belatedly, she realized that the expression "round the clock" wouldn't have meant much to him. True, they had clocks in the seventeenth century. But the devices were rare and expensive, too much so for their habits to have entered popular idiom yet.

Wallenstein shrugged irritably. "I see no problem." He jerked his head toward a door. "They will sleep here, anyway."

The new telephone center, at Wallenstein's insistence,

had been built directly adjoining his personal suite in the palace. He'd even had living quarters connected to it prepared for the eventual telephone operators. Ellie thought that was an odd arrangement. But, given Wallenstein's shaky health—not to mention the terrible wounds that Julie Mackay had inflicted upon him at the Alte Veste, which he would never fully recover from even with the help of American medical care—she could understand it. Wallenstein had to spend a lot of his time, now, resting in his bed. But with a telephone literally at his fingertips, he would have the wherewithal to continue managing the empire he intended to build for himself. Ellie and Len had already built and put in place a direct phone connection between Wallenstein's bed in his private room and the telephone center itself.

By now, Ellie had gotten to know Wallenstein well enough not to be afraid to contradict him. The Duke of Friedland was insistent upon his privileges, and had a very harsh way with anyone who was impolite to him. But he did not bridle at being opposed over a matter of substance, as long as it was done respectfully and not too insistently. And, fortunately, he cut more slack for Ellie than he did for just about anyone else except his wife Isabella and his nurse, Edith Wild. And Pappenheim, of course.

Ellie shook her head. "Duke, this is not that simple a system to operate. It takes a lot of mental alertness—at least, assuming you wind up using it as often as you think you will. What I mean is—"

There was an interruption at the door. More precisely, in the large room beyond that served Wallenstein's private suite as an entry salon. A man was pushing his way in, overriding the protests of the guard stationed at the entrance to the suite. There seemed to be several men standing in the corridor beyond, as well.

Ellie recognized him. It was Eugen Rossbach—*Ritter* Rossbach, as he insisted on being called—one of the mercenary captains who had attached himself to Wallenstein's service. Wallenstein was rather partial to the man. Ellie despised him, herself—but then, admittedly, Ellie despised most of the mercenaries who surrounded the Duke of Friedland. Perhaps oddly, Pappenheim—in some ways the most frightening of them all—was the one she disliked the least.

Wallenstein, now frowning fiercely, stepped out of the small telephone center into the main salon. "What is it, Rossbach? I am occupied at the moment."

Rossbach, still fending off the protesting guard with one hand, waved a document with the other. "Yes, my apologies—but you must see this immediately! It's from the emperor!"

Ellie rose and came to the doorway. Wallenstein took a step forward to take the message, which Rossbach extended toward him.

It suddenly dawned on Ellie that the three men with Rossbach were coming into the main salon, now that the guard was distracted. *Why?*

One of them—then the other two—reached for their swords. Without thinking, Ellie grabbed Wallenstein by his collar and yanked him backward.

The Duke cried out in protest. Rossbach snarled. Then—Ellie never saw the stabbing itself—the guard suddenly screamed and staggered forward. Behind him, as he fell to his knees, she could see one of Rossbach's companions with his sword now in his hand. The tip of it was covered in blood.

Wallenstein cried out again. A curse of some sort, Ellie thought. Rossbach shouted something, dropped the document and drew his own sword.

Ellie hauled Wallenstein back into the telephone room. He stumbled on the way and fell backward, landing on his rump. She just had time to slam the door shut in Rossbach's face.

Then, fumbled to find the lock which—

Didn't exist.

Goddamit! There'd been no reason, after all, to put a lock on that door. In fact, Wallenstein would have been furious if they'd done so. It was *his* telephone center, not that of the men who would be operating it for him.

She heard Rossbach's fist slamming the door. Then, a moment later, a much heavier *wham* as his boot slammed into it.

Ellie's fear and fury were, for a moment, penetrated by an absurd impulse to cackle with laughter. *That idiot Rossbach thinks the door IS locked.*

But it probably wouldn't take him long to figure it out. And besides—another *wham*—even if he didn't, that door wasn't really that solid. He'd be able to kick it in easily enough.

Wallenstein was now rising to his feet. Unfortunately, in his own personal suite, the Duke wasn't carrying his sword. They were both unarmed.

"Bullshit!" Ellie snarled. She stooped over and rummaged through the big tool chest that had been in the room for weeks now. An instant later, she came up with a modern Crescent wrench—Len's

12-incher—as well as the two-foot cheater pipe he used for extra leverage when he needed it.

She tossed the pipe to Wallenstein and hefted the wrench. It wasn't much, but it would have to do.

Wham!

Wham!—and the door came off the hinges. Rossbach and another man started pushing through the doorway, their swords level.

WHAM! WHAM!

Both of them sailed through the opening, as if shot from a cannon, their swords flying out of their hands. Wallenstein clubbed Rossbach down, but Ellie missed the other man. Her swing had been wild, accompanied by a shriek of fear as she dodged the sword sailing ahead of him. Now it was her turn to fall on her ass.

It didn't matter, though. The swing had been more of a reflex than anything else. She'd seen the erupting exit wound on the man's belly. That *WHAM* had been a gunshot.

She stared through the open, shattered doorway. She could see Edith Wild standing in the salon, now. The big woman's face was contorted with anger and she was holding a modern-style revolver in both hands. The two remaining assassins were out of Ellie's range of view. But she could just imagine how astonished they were. Ellie was astonished herself.

WHAM! WHAM!

Now that Ellie wasn't completely overwhelmed by adrenalin, the sound of the gunshots seemed ten times louder. Edith must have been nearly deafened. Each shot from the short-barreled revolver was accompanied by a bright yellow muzzle flash. The gun bucked in

Edith's big hands—so badly that Ellie was pretty sure the second shot had gone wild.

But Edith didn't seemed fazed at all. The snarl stayed on her face and she brought the gun back into line.

"The Tatar," indeed. *Don't fuck with Nurse Ratchett.*

Ellie heard a man shout something. A protest of some kind, perhaps, or a plea for mercy.

Fat lot of good it did him. **WHAM!**

Ellie shook her head to clear it. When she looked up again, Edith was no longer in sight. Hearing some sort of noise—she couldn't really tell what it was, her ears were ringing so badly—Ellie scrambled over on her hands and knees and stuck her head out the door.

Edith's last shot had gone a little wild too, it seemed. The man had only been wounded in the shoulder—from what Ellie could tell, nothing more than a flesh wound—and Edith's gun was out of ammunition.

Fat lot of good it did him. *Don't fuck with Nurse Ratchett.* Edith had wrestled him to the floor and was now clubbing his head with her revolver.

Thump. Thump. Thump. Thump.

Wallenstein stuck his own head out the door, crouched a little higher than Ellie. "Rossbach is dead," he announced.

He studied Edith at her work for a moment, then straightened and helped Ellie to her feet. When she looked at him again, to her surprise, Wallenstein was smiling thinly and stroking his badly scarred jaw.

"A pity there are so few American women," he announced. "If I had an army of you mad creatures, I could conquer the world."

Pappenheim charged into the salon, his sword in his hand. Behind him came at least half a dozen soldiers. When he saw Wallenstein, obviously unhurt, the relief on his face was almost comic. It was odd, really—not for the first time, the thought came to Ellie—how much devotion a man like Wallenstein could get from a man like Pappenheim. She didn't think she'd ever really understand it.

But, she didn't need to. The fact itself was enough. Wallenstein was still alive and kicking and now Pappenheim was on the scene. Which meant that—finally—all hell was about to break loose.

"Best stop her, Gottfried," said Wallenstein, pointing to Edith. The nurse was still clubbing the would-be assassin, though he was now completely limp and lying on the floor. "It would help if we could get him to talk."

Even ferocious Pappenheim seemed a little daunted by the project. After a moment's hesitation, he sheathed his word and walked over, taking care to remain outside of Edith's reach.

He knelt to bring himself into her field of view and gave Edith his most winning smile. Which, on Pappenheim's face, looked about as out of place as anything Ellie could imagine.

He extended his hand in a carefully nonthreatening plea for restraint. "*Bitte,* Frau. We need the man to talk."

Edith let up on her thumping and glared at Pappenheim. Then, gave the assassin one final thump and rose heavily to her feet. "All right. But he better never try it again."

Pappenheim studied the man's bloody head. "No fear of that, I think."

Now Isabella came piling into the room, shrieking with fear, and practically leaped into her husband's arms. As he comforted her, Wallenstein gave Ellie a meaningful glance.

"Yes, boss," she muttered. She went back into the telephone center and started making the connections.

As Ellie expected, it wasn't long before Wallenstein came in. He was a considerate husband, but some things that man would always insist on doing himself.

"The first time it is used," he confirmed. "I will do so, and no other."

Ellie had already made the connection to the barracks adjoining Wallenstein's palace where he kept his trusted officers and troops. (Except Pappenheim and the *most* trusted ones—they lived in the palace.) Len was handling the phone center in the barracks itself, and they'd had time to exchange a few words.

Wallenstein leaned over and spoke into the tube. "Do it," was all he commanded.

Pappenheim crowded in, giving the telephone equipment no more than an interested glance. "I will see to Marradas myself."

"Make sure there's not another miracle, Gottfried."

The smile that now came to Pappenheim's face didn't look out of place at all.

⟨⊱⟩⟨⊰⟩   ⟨⊱⟩⟨⊰⟩   ⟨⊱⟩⟨⊰⟩

Ellie never saw it herself, since she spent the next many hours closeted in the telephone center. But she heard about it. In the famous "defenestration of Prague" that had been the incident usually cited as the trigger for the Thirty Years War, the Catholic Habsburg envoys thrown out of a high window in Prague Castle by rebellious Protestant noblemen had landed in a pile of manure. Their survival had been acclaimed as a miracle by the Catholic forces and had been disheartening to the Protestant rebels.

Marradas fell about the same distance—seventy feet—after Pappenheim threw him out of a window in the castle. But, as commanded, there was no second miracle. Marradas landed on a pile of stones on the street below—placed there by Pappenheim's soldiers at his command, while Pappenheim kept the screaming and struggling Spanish don pinned in his grip for ten minutes until the work was finished.

4

Ellie heard about it from Morris Roth, who had watched it happen—at a distance, through binoculars, from the room in the uppermost floor of his mansion that gave him the best vantage point.

Morris had gone back to his mansion as soon as he realized the coup was underway. Jason had followed him along with, somewhat to Morris' surprise, Mordechai Spira. The rabbi had not even taken the precaution of wearing the special badge that Jews were required to wear under Habsburg law whenever they left the ghetto.

For the first few hours, it was hard to tell exactly what was happening. Morris had tried to reach Len and Ellie with the CB radios they'd brought with them to Prague, but there was no answer. That meant neither of them were in their private rooms in Wallenstein's palace. They always left their CB there, hidden in one of their chests, since the existence of the radios was supposed to be a secret from their new allies. None of them really thought that Wallenstein was fooled any, but since he also never raised the issue, they'd decided that maintaining discretion was the best policy. Soon enough, no doubt, now that the conflict was out in the open, Wallenstein would start pressuring his American allies to provide him with more in the way of technological advancement.

But their protracted failure to answer was enough by itself to confirm Morris' guess. That had to mean that both of them were busy in the new phone centers, which Wallenstein would be using to coordinate the first stages of his coup d'etat.

The defenestration of Marradas took place early in the afternoon. A few short minutes later, a new standard began appearing, draped over the walls of every prominent building on the Hradcany—even the cathedral. Morris didn't recognize it, but he was sure it was the new coat of arms that Wallenstein had designed for himself.

Duke of Friedland, Prince of Sagan—and now, King of Bohemia and Moravia.

Morris lowered the binoculars. "Well, that's it. For the moment, anyway."

He heard Mordechai Spira clear his throat. "We will not take sides in this, Don Morris. None of us have any love for the Habsburgs, but . . . Wallenstein . . . It was he, you know, who had poor Jacob Stein guarded by dogs under the gallows while he extorted eleven thousand florins from us."

"Yes, I know. But the fact was that Stein had broken the law—even if unwittingly—and there are plenty of goyishe princes who would have executed him *after* squeezing the silver from us. And it is also a fact that Wallenstein eventually exonerated Hanok ben Mordechai Altschul, who had also been accused, when many a goyishe prince—most of them—would never have bothered distinguishing a guilty Jew from an innocent."

He turned his head and looked at Spira. The rabbi's eyes were a little wide. "You know the history of it?" he asked, obviously surprised.

"I know a great deal of history," Morris said harshly. He was on the verge of uttering some bitter phrases—more than phrases, entire paragraphs—on the ineffectual role generally played by Orthodox rabbis when the Nazi Holocaust swept over eastern Europe's Jewry.

But, thankfully, he managed to swallow them. Mordechai Spira seemed a well-meaning man, and young Jason liked and admired him—and, most of all, it was simply unfair to blame a man or even a group of men for the faults and failures of other men in a completely different time and place.

"I know a great deal of history," Morris repeated, but this time softly, almost sighing the words. "I only wish I knew what to do with that knowledge."

Inadvertently, his eyes drifted eastward. Spira's eyes followed his gaze.

"You are worried about the Ukraine, I know. Jason has told me."

"Will you help me, then?"

The rabbi hesitated, but not for more than a second or two. "I will do everything I can, Don Morris, which I feel I can do in good conscience."

Morris thought about it. "I guess I can live with that."

He went back to studying the city with his binoculars. "I do not know what is going to happen now, Rabbi. But you are not pacifists."

"No, we are not."

"You will defend the ghetto, whether or not you take sides in this business." It was a command, not a question. "I do not know if there will be trouble, but there may be. Not from Wallenstein or Pappenheim, but the Habsburgs. Or, for that matter, who knows what Holk and his butchers will do, when they get the news."

"Yes," replied Spira. "We will do our best, at least. Though we have no weapons beyond tools and kitchen knives."

Morris chuckled, and lowered the binoculars. "That's what you think. Show him, Jason."

Ten minutes later, Mordechai Spira's eyes were wider yet. Jason and Dunash's people—who'd arrived at the Morris mansion just moments earlier—were hauling the muskets out of the crates in the basement and stacking them against the walls.

"I was able to bring two hundred, which was all Mike Stearns told me he could spare," Morris explained. "These are the new flintlocks. You'll need to have

Jason explain how they work. They're not really much different from matchlocks, just better. I assume that in a ghetto of some fifteen thousand people, there have to be at least a few hundred who've handled firearms before."

Spira nodded. "Oh, yes. Many are here from the small villages, where things are less regulated. And there are at least a few dozen former seamen."

"We can help too!" Dunash said eagerly.

Morris glared at him. "You *are* taking sides in this business, young man—and you have commitments already. Red and Billek are counting on you to man the katyusha. So get your ass out of here."

Dunash hesitated. But Jason spoke up, very firmly. "Do as he says, Dunash. All of you."

The young Abrabanel firebrands and their new recruits—there were almost twenty of them, now—immediately left. The rabbi turned his head to watch them go, before bringing his gaze to Jason. It was almost as he were examining him.

Then, he smiled. "I have great hopes for you, young man. I think you will make a splendid rabbi."

Now he looked at Jason's chevrusah. "Spread the word, Schmuel. We want only men who know how to use guns. No point in trying to teach complete novices."

After Schmuel raced out, Spira chuckled. "Such as myself. Tell me, Don Morris, are you familiar with guns?"

Before answering him—by way of answer, rather—Morris went to another crate and drew out a different weapon. This one, unlike the others, was encased in a fancy covering rather than simple cloth.

He unzipped the guncase and drew out the rifle.
"This is a much better gun than those flintlocks, Rabbi.
I've owned it for many years. It is called—well, never
mind. Yes, I know how to use it. I was a soldier in
the American army, some years ago. In fact, I'm quite
a good shot."

Spira seemed to be examining him, now. Morris
shifted his shoulders uncomfortably. "Look, Rabbi,
it's not just my military training. In the world I came
from my wife and children and I were the only Jews
in our town. And it's a mountain country town, where
everybody hunts."

He looked down at the rifle, caressing the sleek
stock. "The strange thing about it—perhaps—is that
I never actually hunted myself. Hunting is not part
of our traditions and customs."

Spira nodded. "No, it is not. We may only eat meat
which has been properly slaughtered by a schohet."

Morris smiled wryly; almost bitterly. "Ah, yes, all
those rules. Most of which I do not agree with but still
often find it hard to ignore completely. Like hunting."
He raised the rifle a bit, as if starting to bring it to
his shoulder, and then lowered it again.

"But, you see, Rabbi . . . it would have been
standoffish for me not to join my friends in their
favorite sport. So, I did, even though I never shot
any deer. I just went along. I always enjoyed the
outdoors anyway. And—I don't know—I suppose just
in order to prove that the reason I didn't wasn't
because—well—"

He shifted his shoulders again. "I was one of the
best shots on the rifle range and everybody knew
it. So my friends—yes, gentile friends, I had lots of

them—still do—would tease me about it. But not much, and not hard, and only in fun."

He gave Spira something of a challenging stare. Spira looked away, but Morris didn't think it was because the rabbi was afraid of the challenge, or trying to avoid it.

"There are many wise and wonderful sayings in the midrash, Don Morris. 'When in a city, follow its customs' is one of them."

Morris swallowed. He'd heard that one before, from his rabbi Steve Stern, in a universe now impossible to reach.

Spira brought his gaze back. "But I think there is perhaps an even more apt saying—though not from the midrash. It is one of your American folk sayings, Jason tells me."

The rabbi gestured toward the west, where, faintly, the sounds of fighting could still be heard across the river. "We will not takes sides in this affair. But, however it is settled, we will be guided by the wisdom of the ancient Babylonian sage Schmuel. 'The law of the kingdom is the law.' That will suffice for you, I think, in the immediate period."

"Yeah," Morris gruffed. "I can live with that. For a while, at least. So can Wallenstein."

Spira nodded. "And, in the meantime, Don Morris—"

"I prefer to be called just 'Morris,'" he stated abruptly.

Spira nodded again. "As you wish. And, in the meantime, Morris . . . don't be a stranger."

With that, smiling, the rabbi turned away and headed for the stairs. "Now," he said over his shoulder, "I'd best see after young Schmuel—who is no sage. Indeed, he can be excessively enthusiastic. Please come with me, Jason, I could use your help."

Morris stayed alone in the basement after they left, silent, for perhaps five minutes. Then he began loading the rifle.

"Did you think it was going to be simple?" he muttered to himself. "You dummy."

Chapter V: Castling
July, 1633

1

For the next two days, while Wallenstein and Pappenheim fought a chaotic and swirling series of small battles in and around Prague with military units who opposed the rebellion—or simply wanted to remain neutral, which Wallenstein wasn't going to tolerate—Morris Roth remained in his mansion. He stayed on the uppermost floor most of the time, except for brief snatches of sleep; moving from window to window, rifle in his hands, keeping watch on the streets below. He hadn't planned it that way—certainly Len and Ellie hadn't, when they purchased the building on his behalf—but because of its location just outside one of the main gates in the ghetto wall, his mansion served the Josefov as something in the way of a ravelin. An exterior little fortress from which enfilade fire could be brought to bear on anyone attempting to assault the fortress itself.

He only used the rifle once, during those two days. That was on the evening of the first day, just before sundown, when a small band of ruffians—possibly soldiers operating on their own, possibly just criminals; it was hard to tell—advanced toward the ghetto brandishing a haphazard collection of swords, pikes and arquebuses. Morris warned them off when they were fifty yards away. When the only response he got was a small volley of arquebus fire that did no damage at all beyond making a few pockmarks in the thick walls of the mansion, he shot three of them.

One round each, good center mass shots. Not hard to do, at that range, especially for a good shot like Morris. All of them fell in the street, in the space of less than ten seconds. The rest promptly fled.

One man had been killed instantly; the other two were mortally wounded, dying within minutes. One of the men managed to crawl perhaps twenty feet before he finally collapsed.

Morris slept hardly at all that night. Early in the morning, Judith found him back at his post, rifle held firmly in his grip. He avoided her eyes, though, when she approached and placed her hand on his shoulder.

"Talk to me, Morris."

"What's there to say?" he asked, shrugging. "I'm a small-town jeweler who hasn't even been in a fist fight since I was a kid in boot camp. Over thirty years ago. Yeah, sure, I was in Vietnam. Big deal. I spent my whole tour of duty as a supply clerk in the big army base at Long Binh, and I didn't get there until long after the Tet Offensive."

While he spoke, his eyes kept ranging across the streets below, looking for possible threats. He never looked at Judith once. "I guess you could call it 'combat duty,' since I always knew that some of the explosions and shots I heard during the night was stuff aimed into the base rather than our own Harassment and Interdiction fire. But nothing ever landed close to me—and I never once had to fire my own weapon at any enemies I could see." Very softly: "I've never even shot a deer before, much less a man. Then stare at their bodies afterward, while they bleed to death."

Judith gave his shoulder a little squeeze; then, disappeared for a while. When she returned, she had Mordechai Spira in tow along with another rabbi who seemed to be a close friend of his. A man by the name of Isaac Gans. The two of them kept Morris company the rest of the day. There was little conversation, because Morris was not in a mood for talking. Still, he appreciated their presence. Not so much for anything they said or did, but just for the fact of it.

Neither Spira nor Gans was wearing Jewish insignia. During the afternoon of the day before, just a short time before Morris had his confrontation with the band of thugs, a small squad of soldiers led by a sub-officer had placed posters on buildings near the ghetto—as well as two posters flanking the entrance to the ghetto itself. The posters were proclamations by Wallenstein. The first proclamation announced that he was now the king of Bohemia—and Pappenheim was the duke of Moravia.

There were many proclamations on those posters. Among them, Wallenstein had kept the promise he'd made to Morris long months before, in a small house in Grantville. Freedom of religion was guaranteed. Distinctions between citizens (that was a new word, just in itself—*citizens*) would no longer take religious affiliation into account. And, specifically, all restrictions on Jews were abolished.

It was pretty impressive, actually. At least, the words were. A lot of the language was cribbed from texts of the American Revolution as well as the *Declaration of the Rights of Man* adopted in 1789 by the National Assembly during the French Revolution. One, in particular, was taken word-for-word from the French declaration:

No one shall be disquieted on account of his opinions, including his religious views, provided their manifestation does not disturb the public order established by law.

True enough, there was wiggle room there, if Wallenstein chose to exercise it. "Disturb the public order" could become a weasel phrase easily enough, in the hands of an autocrat.

Which Wallenstein would be. His proclamations, needless to say, did not include the *political* aspects of the French and American declarations. The rights and liberties of citizens would be respected—or so, at least, Wallenstein proclaimed. But political power would remain in the hands of the new king. There was a provision for the formation of a National Assembly, but it was obvious that Wallenstein intended it to remain purely advisory.

So be it. What Wallenstein intended was one thing; what eventually resulted, another. And, in the meantime, at least Jews no longer had to wear badges or distinctive yellow hats whenever they left the ghetto. They could build synagogues anywhere in Prague—in all of Bohemia and Moravia, in fact—and could henceforth own the guns to protect them, if need be.

There was one part of the proclamation that almost made Morris laugh. Wallenstein had also ordered the dismantling of the wall of the ghetto. And, sure enough, Dunash and his firebrands immediately began eagerly tearing down one little section of the wall near the quarter of the ghetto where they lived—ignoring the protests of most of their neighbors.

Their *Jewish* neighbors, for whom the wall was something of a comfort as well as a curse. The neighbors had even gone to register a protest with the rabbis.

The chief rabbi had hemmed and hawed. But most of the other rabbis—led by Spira and Gans, according to Jason—decided soon enough that the wisdom of the ancient Babylonian sage still applied: *The law of the land is the law.*

So, Dunash and his men had been able to proceed in the work cheerfully and unmolested.

But only for two days. In midafternoon of the third day, having established their control of Prague itself, Wallenstein and Pappenheim took most of their soldiers out of the city, marching to the southwest, to meet an oncoming army dispatched by Ferdinand II.

There was to be a second Battle of the White Mountain, it seemed.

The day after Wallenstein and Pappenheim left, Holk—who had been ordered to guard the northern frontier against any possible Saxon interference— announced that he was marching into Prague instead. "To secure the city from disorders," he was reported to have said. Or words to that drunken effect.

Whether he had decided to throw his lot in with Emperor Ferdinand, or simply couldn't resist the opportunity to loot a major city, no one knew. To the inhabitants of Prague, it hardly mattered. Not even the still-considerable body of residents who were Habsburg loyalists wanted Holk around. Nobody in their right mind, except his own thugs, wanted Holk anywhere nearby.

Morris got the news from Red Sybolt and Jan Billek.

"Is it true?" he asked.

"Seems to be," said Billek. "There is already a small stream of refugees coming into the city from the north. They believe it, certainly—that is why they are trying to get out of Holk's path."

Morris leaned out the window, scowling toward the north. "What does Holk think he's doing? If Wallenstein wins, he's dead meat."

"Does Holk 'think' at all?" Red shrugged. "He's a drunk and a thug, Morris. For all we know, he didn't decide anything at all. Maybe his own soldiers put him up to it, and he doesn't dare refuse them. Sacking a big city like Prague when it's got no real army to defend it is the kind of opportunity every mercenary dreams about in the Thirty Years War. Look at it from their point of view. At the very least, they'll have two or three days to plunder and pillage before Wallenstein and Pappenheim get back and they have to run for it. You think the average mercenary—sure as hell in Holk's army—thinks in the long run? 'Planning for the future' for guys like that means 'gimme what I want—now.'"

Morris brought his head back, still scowling. "All right. It'll be up to you and Jan, then. Wallenstein didn't leave more than a thousand soldiers here. Good thing he didn't take your Brethren volunteers with him, too."

Red smiled lopsidedly. "Pappenheim still doesn't trust us. Not our loyalty, just how much use we'd be in a battle. He's more set in his ways than Wallenstein, you know—and with Wallenstein in the shape he's in, Pappenheim will have to do the actual commanding on the battlefield."

Morris' smile was even more lopsided than Red's. "I never thought I'd say this, but I really wish—*really* wish—Wallenstein had stayed behind. What a world! To think I'd ever find Wallenstein's presence a comfort." He shook his head. "But . . . there it is. I surely would."

He glanced up at the Hradcany. "What about the soldiers he did leave behind?"

"Oh, I think we can count on them, well enough," Billek assured him. "Pappenheim left one of his protégés in charge—young Kastner, I do not think you know him. His unit is one of the best, actually. Wallenstein and Pappenheim want something to return to, assuming they win their battle. There are still plenty of Habsburg loyalists in the population, especially among the Catholics."

"Why'd they take almost everybody with them, then?"

"Morris, be realistic," said Sybolt. "If you were Wallenstein, you'd do the same thing. If he loses this upcoming battle against the Austrians, he's finished. He's burned all his bridges behind him, now. It's not as if he figured on Holk running wild, after all—and even if he did consider the possibility, so what? If Wallenstein whips the Austrians and comes back to a wrecked and plundered Prague, he's *still* the king of Bohemia. Cities can be rebuilt, too, you know. Look at Magdeburg."

Morris took a deep breath and let it out slowly. "True. Tough on the people living in the city, though."

"Yup. Unless they protect themselves. Speaking of which, what are your orders?"

"*My* orders?" Morris stared at him. "I'm not in charge here."

Red chuckled. "Morris, sometimes you're a real babe in the woods. What does 'in charge' have to do with anything? Nobody put Holk 'in charge' either—but he's still on his way."

Sybolt stepped up to the window and studied the Hradcany for a moment. "Kastner's just a youngster, Morris. He hasn't got the confidence to take charge of the whole city. What he'll do is fort up in the castle and the key buildings in the Malá Strana below the hill—including Wallenstein's palace, of course—and just be satisfied with fending Holk off."

"He is right," said Billek. "And Holk will make no real effort to take the Hradcany. He and his men are looking for loot, not a protracted siege." He came forward and joined Sybolt at the window, examining

the city. "From the direction they are coming, they
will strike Prague on the west bank of the Vltava
first. Then, they will recoil from Kastner's men in the
Hradcany and the Malá Strana and head for Stone
Bridge. Most of Prague is on this side of the river.
Not the richest part, to be sure, but Holk and his
men are not fussy looters. And this is the soft part
of the city."

Billek glanced at the two rabbis standing not far
away. The faces of both Spira and Gans were calm
enough, but tight with worry. "Especially the Josefov.
Jews are not armed and everyone knows it. They will
begin their plunder and ravages in Old Town and
move north to the ghetto."

Morris was no military man, but, as he studied
the layout of the city, he decided that Red and Jan
were right. Given the nature of Holk and his army,
that was exactly what they'd do.

"We should try to trap them on the Stone Bridge,"
he said abruptly. "Never let them get across at all."

Then a bit startled by the sureness with which he'd
spoken, Morris added: "I think."

"Well, so do I," said Red. "So does Jan—we talked
about it on our way over here. Good thing we've got
a smart boss."

"Who made me the 'boss'?" Morris demanded. "I
still don't understand—"

Billek interrupted him. That was unusual, for the
normally reserved and polite leader of the Brethren.
"Do not be stupid, Morris," he said forcefully. "*Don
Morris,* rather."

Billek nodded toward the two rabbis. "The only
way this plan will work is if the Jews hold the eastern

side of the bridge and keep Holk pinned on it. While we Brethren and Red's CoC volunteers hammer them from fortified positions in the Malá Strana. We have most of the guns and will do most of the killing. But the eastern end of the bridge *must* be held—and firmly."

Spira and Gans looked startled. Billek shook his head. "As Red says, we must be realistic here. Who else *except* the Jews will hold the eastern end of the bridge from Holk—hold it at all, much less firmly? Except for the Brethren, the Christian population on the east side of the river is still confused and uncertain. They won't fight—not most of them—not against such as Holk. They will simply flee the city."

Morris felt his jaws tighten. "Whereas the Jews don't have any place to run to. If they try to leave the city, in this chaos, they'd likely be plundered by"—he almost said *the stinking goyishe villagers on the way*, but didn't—"you know, everybody. Just about."

Billek said nothing. After a moment, to Morris' surprise, Red grinned cheerfully.

"Hey, Morris, look at it this way—it happened once before, didn't it? Well, in a manner of speaking."

Morris couldn't help but smile himself. *Talk about a topsy-turvy world!* In the universe they'd come from, in the year 1648, a Swedish army had marched into Prague and taken the Hradcany and the Malá Strana on the west bank of the river. Convinced that they'd do better even under the heavy hand of the Habsburgs than at the hands of a conquering Swedish army—by the end of the Thirty Years War, Swedish armies were no more disciplined than anybody's—the Jews of Prague's ghetto had joined

with Catholic students and burghers to fight off the
Swedes when they tried to cross the Stone Bridge
and pillage the eastern half of the city. It had been
the last major battle of the Thirty Years War, in
fact. It didn't end until nine days after the Peace
of Westphalia was signed—and the Swedes never
did make it across the bridge.

Less than a hundred years later, under Empress
Maria Theresa, the Habsburgs repaid the loyalty of
Prague's Jewry by expelling them from the city.

"Right," Morris growled, his smile fading. "Let's
do it again—and we'll hope, this time, it turns out
better in the long run."

He turned away from the window and faced the
two rabbis. "Will you agree?"

Spira and Gans looked at each other. Spira nodded.
Gans shrugged. "Do we have a choice? Not that I can
see. And I am sure all the other rabbis will agree."

"You will be in command, yes, Don Morris?" asked
Spira. He gave Billek and Red a somewhat apologetic
glance. "Our people will follow you. Not . . . others."

"See?" Red demanded, smiling wider than ever.
"Like I said, you're the boss."

"Make sure you are on a horse," Billek added.
"Biggest horse you can find. And wear something
suitable."

2

Morris had been prepared for a brawl with Dunash.
He was sure the young militant would try to insist
that he and his men should remain with the other

Jews on the east bank, rather than fighting with the Brethren as they were supposed to do.

But, to his surprise, Red Sybolt scuttled the problem before it could even emerge.

"We may as well keep me and Dunash and the katyusha on this side anyway, Morris. Those rockets are about as accurate as spitting in the wind. If we fire them at the bridge from the Malá Strana, we're as likely to kill our own people over here as Holk's people on the bridge."

Red pointed across the river. "The Brethren will be sheltered in fortified positions over there. At the beginning, for sure. So they'll be safe enough from friendly fire, since those warheads really aren't that powerful. We designed them as antipersonnel weapons. A small charge and a lot of shrapnel, basically."

"Jan's okay with that?"

"Yeah, he and I already talked it over." Red's easy grin was back. "Besides, the truck's in your basement, remember? That was the only place secret enough to assemble it under Wallenstein's nose. Well, under Marradas' nose. I'm pretty sure Wallenstein knows we have the thing. It'll be hard enough to haul it out of there, much less try to get it across the river and under shelter. The Malá Strana doesn't have too much in the way of garages, you know."

After he thought it over, Morris decided Red was right. If nothing else, even if the katyusha proved ineffective in the battle, just having a fabled American war machine show up in the midst of the motley "army" assembling on the eastern end of the bridge would do wonders for morale. Especially with Jews manning the thing.

Besides, he was tiring of fighting with Dunash. "Okay, done."

He had a bigger problem with the horse. Big enough that he even lapsed into profanity for a moment. "Where the hell did you get this thing? I didn't think Clydesdales even existed in this day and age." A little whine came into his voice. "And how am I supposed to even get onto it, anyway? Especially wearing this stupid getup. With a winch?"

He was coming to detest Red's grin. "Why not? According to a movie I saw once, that's how the old knights got lifted onto their horses." Red gave the horse in question an admiring look. "And quit exaggerating. It's not a Clydesdale, not even close. Just the second biggest horse Pappenheim owns. He took the biggest one with him."

Morris grimaced. "Oh, swell. Now I'll have Pappenheim furious with me, on top of everything else. Do they hang horse thieves in Bohemia? I'm sure they do."

Red shrugged. "If you keep Prague intact, I really don't think Pappenheim's going to mind much that you used one of his horses to do it. Look, Morris. Nobody ever said being a champion wasn't risky."

"Champion." Oh, swell. Like I need a hole in the head.

Gloomily, Morris went back to studying the horse. He was a good horseman, to be sure—within the limits of what "good horsemanship" meant for an American whose experience was almost entirely with the sort of horses one encountered on riding trails and pack stations. Whether that would translate into being able to control a seventeenth-century warhorse . . .

◁▷-▨◇   ◁▷-▨◇   ◁▷-▨◇

A bit to his surprise, it did. The warhorse was more spirited than Morris was accustomed to, but on the other hand it had been trained to remain steady in the middle of a battlefield. Once he got accustomed to it, in fact, he found himself enjoying the experience. It really was quite a horse.

And, there was no doubt of one thing: as silly as he felt, riding a horse while wearing the fancy garb of a seventeenth-century nobleman, his appearance before the crowd now erecting barricades at the eastern end of the Stone Bridge had an impact. He even got cheered. A very big cheer, in fact. Jason had told Judith that the story was already widely spread of how Don Morris had slain goyishe bandits seeking to victimize the ghetto, with his powerful American arquebus. As many as ten bandits, in one version of the story.

As big a cheer as it was, though, it was not as big as the cheer the katyusha received, when Red and Dunash's people finally managed to get it out of the basement—they used dozens of people with ropes to just *lift* it out—and Red drove it slowly forward onto the little square abutting the bridge.

Morris was startled when the initial cheer evolved into a chant: *APC! APC!* He wouldn't have guessed that the population of far-off Prague—certainly not the Jews in its ghetto—would have ever heard of that acronym. It was ironic, of course, since the "APC" was nothing of the sort. True, Red had mounted some thin armor plate to protect the engine and the driver and gunner in the front seat. But the thing was no solid and heavy coal truck. It was just an old Dodge Ram with a jury-rigged and flimsy-looking rocket launcher fixed in the bed.

It didn't matter. None of Prague's civilians had ever seen an American war machine before, but they'd heard the rumors. For them, "APC" was more in the way of a spoken talisman than anything else. And this was an age when most common folk believed in the power of talismans and amulets. That was as true for the Jews as the Christians, although the forms were different. The so-called "Book of Raziel the Angel"—the *Sefer Raziel ha-Mal'akh*—hadn't been produced yet in printed form, but parts of the ancient manuscript went back to Babylonian Talmudic times. It had drifted around the world's Jewish communities for centuries, never really approved by the rabbinate but never banned either. Morris wouldn't have been surprised to discover that a goodly percentage of the Jews building the barricades had little metal or paper amulets under their clothes, using the formulas of the *Sefer Raziel*.

When Red finally brought the pickup-cum-katyusha to a halt, after positioning it in the firing slot left open in the barricades, he rolled down the window and gave Morris an admiring look.

"I do declare, perched way up there on that great big horse—hell of a nice plume to the hat, too—you look like the spittin' image of a hidalgo. Damn near a conquistador, in fact."

"My family came from Krakow," Morris groused. "The closest I ever got to Spain was eating tapas once in a restaurant in Philadelphia."

"Don't knock it, Morris. All that matters is that you look and act the part. They've got a recognized leader now, instead of everybody fumbling around wondering who's in charge. That'll help steady everybody's nerves—a lot—as long as you don't get yourself shot."

For some odd reason, the warhorse had a delayed reaction to the Dodge Ram. It was accustomed to the sounds of gunfire, not internal combustion engines, to be sure. But Morris never did figure out why the blasted critter chose the moment when Red turned *off* the motor to start getting jittery.

Very jittery. Morris had a few tense and interesting moments, though he managed to stay in the saddle. He did lose the hat, though.

"Or fall off the horse," Red added sarcastically.

3

That evening, after looking for Len all over the Hradcany, Ellie finally figured out where he'd be. She realized it within seconds after she returned to the rooms in the castle that the young commander Kastner had assigned to them. Kastner, worried lest Wallenstein's precious American technical experts might get hurt in the fighting, had insisted that Ellie and Len move from Wallenstein's palace into the greater safety of the fortress above.

There'd been no point arguing with him. Kastner had no idea how the telephones worked, so he had no intention of trying to use them. In what was coming, Len and Ellie would just be fifth wheels on a cart. So, Len grumbling the whole time, they'd spent the morning hauling their belongings up the hill. Then, having made the last trip alone for a few final items while Len stayed behind in order to arrange their new living quarters, she'd come back to find him gone.

She'd spent most of the afternoon searching for him, growing increasingly worried. But when she finally returned, half-exhausted from endless hiking, she noticed that the lid to one of the chests was cracked open. That chest was normally kept locked, because it was the one where they kept their personal weapons.

She opened the chest and looked. Len's 12-gauge was missing.

What could he possibly—?

—I'll kill him if the idiot—!

Oh.

It all fell into place. Not sure whether she was more relieved than exasperated, Ellie closed the chest and sat down on it. For a moment, half-slumped, she tried to decide what to do. For that matter, what to think.

Then, shrugging, she got up and left. That was her man, when it was said and done. Quirks and foibles and all.

Although even for Len, this is a doozy.

She found him where she'd thought she would—the one place it had never occurred to her to look the entire afternoon. The place she must have circled at least four times while she searched for him. Impossible not to, of course, since it dominated the Hradcany.

Len was sitting in one of the rear pews in the huge Gothic cathedral. Just staring at the altar, his shotgun across his knees. Ellie was sure he'd been there the whole afternoon. The handful of priests watching him were still nervous, clearly enough, but it was the kind of nervousness that had worn itself down after a few hours. A few hours while the bizarre intruder—monster from another world, with a monstrous weapon—just sat there and did nothing.

She slid into the seat next to him. "You might have left me a note, dammit!"

Len looked uncomfortable. "I started to write one, but . . . I don't know. I didn't know what to say. How to explain it."

Ellie sighed. Then, felt all her exasperation going away. That was the nature of the man, after all. She reached out her hand and stroked the back of his neck.

"'S okay. I shoulda figured you'd unlapse your own way. You weird duck. What? You figure on protecting the cathedral all by your lonesome?"

She gave the priests a skeptical glance. "I don't think they'd be much help, if Holk's hordes came pouring in. Not that they will, without taking the Hradcany from Kastner. Which they won't."

Len flushed. "It's the principle of the thing, Ellie. Kastner's people didn't want me underfoot anyway, so I figured . . . Look, religious freedom's for everybody. That means Catholics too, even if the bums running the show here screwed up. And this cathedral's ancient. It's a *holy* place, even if I don't think much of the current tenants."

His hand tightened on the stock of the shotgun. "So anybody tries anything . . ."

"Ha! Saint Len and the Dragon, is it?"

Len's flush deepened. His eyes now seemed riveted on the altar.

"Will you marry me?" he asked abruptly. "I've been thinking about it all afternoon."

She studied him for a moment. "I'm not getting married in a fucking church, Len."

"You shouldn't swear in here."

"*Not* in a fucking church. I can't stand churches."

Len took a deep breath, sighed. His hand finally left the stock of the shotgun and came up as if to stroke his absent mustache.

Feeling the bare skin, he sighed again. "You are one hard woman, Ellie Anderson."

There was nothing much she could say, since that was true enough. So she said nothing.

Neither did he, for maybe five minutes. Then, finally, he looked at her.

"Was that a 'yes'?"

Ellie chuckled and went back to stroking his neck. "Yes, Len, that was a 'yes.' Just not in a fucking church. If you can't live with that, you can't live with me."

She looked at the altar, then at the priests. "But I don't mind if you decide to pull crazy stunts like this, now and then. So I figure we're square."

"Okay." He stroked his nonexistent mustache. "I can live with that."

4

The first detachments from Holk's army started showing up in the outskirts of the city early the next morning. By midmorning, they were exchanging shots with Kastner's men forted up in the Hradcany; by noon, with his men forted up in the Malá Strana.

By mid-afternoon, most of Holk's ragtag army had poured into the city's west bank—as undisciplined as you could ask for—and decided they'd had enough of cracking their heads against Kastner's troops.

Holk himself showed up then, on his own big warhorse, and led the charge. He waved his sword to the east, very dramatically. *That way! To the Stone Bridge!*

Tanner stayed in the cathedral the whole time, Saint Len faithfully at his post in case the dragon showed up.

Ellie, on the other hand, joined the soldiers on the walls of the Hradcany. She had a better vantage point to see what was happening than Morris and Red did, across the river. So, using her CB, she kept them informed all day of the movements of Holk and his men. Insofar as that rabble could be said to have "maneuvers" at all, other than the mercenary equivalent of Brownian motion.

When Holk showed up, though, waving his stupid sword, she put down the CB and drew her pistol. Then, cursing a blue streak, clambered up on the wall and emptied the entire clip at him.

"Where'd you go?" Red asked her, when she got back on the CB. Ellie explained in a few curt sentences, about every other word of which was short and had an Anglo-Saxon pedigree.

"Fer chrissake, Ellie—with a 9mm automatic? What're you, nuts? That's gotta be at least six hundred yards. You'd be lucky to hit the river at that range."

"It's the principle of the thing," she stoutly insisted.

Chapter VI: Discovered Check
July, 1633

1

By the time Holk finally got his men organized—
using the term loosely—it was almost sundown. He
began to send men onto the Stone Bridge, but the
small detachments retreated quickly once they started
getting peppered by shots fired from the flintlock-armed
men now perched behind the barricade.

So far as Ellie could tell, looking down on the bridge
from the distance of the Hradcany without binoculars,
that initial volley—using the term loosely—didn't do
more than scare off the thugs. She didn't think a
single one of them had even been wounded.

Ellie was sure Morris hadn't ordered the volley. The
Stone Bridge had a span of some five hundred yards,
with a little dogleg in it about one-third of the way
across from the west bank. The flintlocks had started
firing as soon as Holk's men made it to the dogleg and
came in sight of the barricades—a range of well over
three hundred yards. Maybe James Fenimore Cooper's
fictional marksman Natty Bumpo could hit something
with a flintlock at that range, but ghetto-dwellers with
meager experience with firearms hadn't much more
chance than Ellie had with her 9mm.

Red confirmed her assessment. *"Naw, just buck*

fever. Morris is fit to be tied. Good thing he ain't a cursing man. He's doing a pretty good job right now of flaying them alive with proper language. He's even waving his sword around."

Ellie stared at the now-darkening western bank, dumbfounded. "Morris has a *sword?* Where the fuck did he get a sword?"

Red's chuckle crackled in the CB. *"Judith had it made up for him, believe it or not. Presented it to him this morning, scabbard and everything. She even had a special scabbard made up so he could sling his rifle on the horse."*

Ellie burst out laughing. "Judith Roth—the gray eminence. It's like they say: 'behind every successful man there's a woman.'"

"No shit. And you should see the collection of women she's got around her, right here on this end of the bridge. Every prestigious matron in the ghetto, near as I can tell. Oh, sure, they're all being proper as you could ask for—but you can't fool me. Patriarchy be damned. That's the biggest collection of political clout in one city this side of old Mayor Daley's grave."

A moment later he added, in the satisfied tones of an longtime union agitator: *"We're pretty well organized over here, actually. If Morris can just keep those eager beavers from wasting all the ammunition. And if he can keep from stabbing himself with the sword. He handles it like a butcher knife. Except he ain't an experienced butcher. Personally, I wish he'd start swinging the rifle around. THAT he knows what he's doing with."*

Ellie shook her head firmly, even though Red couldn't possibly see the gesture. He was perched in the cab of the Dodge Ram, over half a mile away. "It's the principle of the thing, fella. You don't rally troops with a rifle. You do it with a sword. Haven't you ever seen any movies?"

Had Judith Roth heard the exchange, she would have disagreed. She was watching Morris also, and while she'd have admitted that he wasn't exactly handling the sword with panache, he was doing a fair job with it nonetheless. There was certainly no danger that he'd stab himself. Cut himself, maybe. Judith had made sure that the sword's tip had been blunted when she ordered it made.

Still and all, everything considered, she thought he looked superb. The horse was magnificent, Morris himself looked very distinguished in his nobleman's garb—the big plumed hat helped a lot—and nobody watching on this side of the river really had any more idea than Morris did how a sword should properly be held anyway. It was enough that he had one and was swinging it around authoritatively while bellowing authoritative-sounding orders.

Most of all, he didn't look afraid. Not in the least. In fact, he looked downright fearless.

And that was such an odd sensation, for Judith. That her husband was a brave enough man, in those myriad little ways with which people confront the challenges of daily life, Judith had known for many years. But that was the quiet courage of a husband and a father and a countryman, not the same thing at all as the dramatic valor of a commander on the battlefield.

She wasn't really that surprised that Morris could

do it. But she was well-nigh astonished that he could do it so well in public.

One of the women standing next to her, on the far side of the little square where the barricades had been erected, spoke softly in her ear. "I am very glad your husband is here, gracious lady. And you also."

That was Eva Bacharach, a woman just about Judith's age. Her brothers Chaim and Napthali were noted rabbis, and Eva herself was the widow of a rabbi who had died almost twenty years earlier. Since her husband Abraham had died, Eva had raised their three daughters and one son, somehow managing at the same time to gain quite a reputation in the ghetto as a noted Hebraist and a scholar in her own right. Even the rabbis were known to consult with her on difficult textual problems.

When Judith first learned that, from another woman in the ghetto, she'd been so surprised that her expression must have shown it. The woman had chuckled and said dryly: "Gracious lady, we are in Prague, not Amsterdam."

That short phrase had crystallized Judith's growing conviction that her husband's projected head-on collision with orthodox Judaism needed to be sidetracked before the inevitable train wreck ensued.

Prague, not Amsterdam.

Amsterdam's rabbinate was notorious all over Europe for pigheadedness, intolerance and authoritarianism. Whereas the rabbinate of Prague had been shaped, in the previous century, by one of the few rabbis of the era whose name would be remembered for centuries: Judah Loew ben Bezalel, also known as the Maharal. A man who became a legend in his own time for his learning and wisdom—a legend which only grew after his death. One of the great rabbis of the early modern era, a shaper of the orthodox tradition—yet also conversant with the scientific knowledge of the time and on friendly terms with many of its great scientists. One of his disciples, David Gans—a cousin of Mordechai Spira's friend Isaac—had studied for a time with Tycho Brahe.

The Maharal. Eva's grandfather, as it happened. And one of Judith's own ancestors.

Judith turned to look at Eva. "I am very glad we are here also. And will be staying. But—please—call me Judith. We are related, you know."

Eva's eyebrows went up. "Oh, yes," Judith said. "I am one of your descendants, Eva Bacharach. Very distant, of course. And also a descendant of your grandfather—I can remember how excited I was when I learned *that*."

Judith laughed softly. "In the world I came from, they even made what we call a 'movie' about him. True, it was because of the legend that grew up that he created the golem. But I knew enough to understand how much more important he was for all his other work."

"The golem!" Eva choked. "That silly story! Do you mean to tell me that—that—in some other world, wherever that may be—people actually *believe* it?"

Judith wagged her head in a semi-jocular manner. "Maybe yes, maybe no. It's one of those stories that people want to believe, even if they really don't."

Now Eva was laughing softly also. "My grandfather would have been mortified! Ha! The golem!"

When the laughter ebbed, Eva cocked her head

and regarded Judith a bit sideways. "The rabbis will probably need to spend a hundred years—maybe two hundred—chewing on the significance of that other world of yours and what we should think about it all. But since we are women, we are not under their obligations. Much easier for us.".

"Yes, I agree. Much easier. Quicker, too."

Eva nodded sagely. "Yes. Much quicker."

Perhaps twenty yards away, on the same side of the square as Judith and Eva, Mordechai Spira and Isaac Gans were also watching Morris.

"We will not be able to ignore this man," Mordechai stated, quietly but firmly. "Never think it, Isaac."

His friend and fellow rabbi made a little snorting sound. "I didn't think we would. Or should, for that matter. By now, I don't think even Joseph ben Abraham Khalmankhes retains that delusion. Certainly none of the other rabbis do."

Mordechai nodded. "Good. The beginning of wisdom is like everything else. Always the hardest part."

"It won't be so bad," Issac predicted. "In some ways, even good. Complicated, though, yes."

Spira chuckled. "'Complicated,' applied to this problem, is like saying the sun is bright. Just for a start, do we decide to accept or not those books of young Jason's? It is one thing to respect wisdom. But are we also obliged to respect the wisdom of another universe altogether?"

"You know my opinion. Does not the midrash say that the Holy One, Blessed be He, created many universes before this one? Could He not continue to do so?" Gans shrugged. "How can it matter how many universes there are? There is still only one God."

"Yes, I know your opinion—and I am inclined to share it. Still . . ."

Mordechai Spira shook his head. "I am not one of those Amsterdam blockheads who finds heresy everywhere he looks. But I started reading that translation you made for me of that one book of Jason's—the one by Mordechai Kaplan—and . . ."

Gans smiled slyly. "It's interesting, though, admit it."

"Oh, yes. 'Reconstructionist' Judaism, if you will! The number of schisms our descendants seem to have managed to find." Again, he shook his head. "Almost as bad as Christians."

"On the other hand, there is a lot to admire also. And, whatever else, if Jason's commentaries add to our understanding of Him and his Holy Torah, we must respect them. Subject them to searching analysis and criticism, to be sure, as Rabbi Moshe ben Nachman did to even Maimonides' work. But respect them nonetheless." Isaac's smile widened. "And the truth is, I am particularly taken by the works of the Chasidim that Jason had with him."

Mordechai cocked a questioning eyebrow. Isaac made a little apologetic gesture with his hand. "Sorry, I haven't had time to translate those yet. But—"

He was interrupted by a commotion on the southern side of the square. As the crowd there parted, Mordechai and Isaac could see that a large group of young men was advancing—somewhat tentatively, almost diffidently—toward the Stone Bridge. All of them were armed, though only a few of them with firearms.

They were all gentiles, clearly enough. After a moment, Isaac identified them.

"Christian students. From the Karolinum."

Mordechai brought his eyes back to Morris Roth. The American don was now trotting his horse toward the oncoming students. He had sheathed his sword and was not projecting an aura of menace. But he nonetheless managed to look authoritative. Very authoritative, in fact.

Spira found himself quite thankful that Don Morris was handling the situation, which could easily become tense. Then, found himself pondering his own reaction.

Indeed, it was so. Don Morris could not be ignored. Nor should he be, even if it were possible. For good or ill, Spira was quite sure that the man would bestride their world in the years to come. Whether as a champion or a menace—or both—remained to be seen. Supported, perhaps; combated, perhaps. Most likely both, Mordechai suspected, at different times. But whatever else, never ignored.

Mordechai and Isaac were too far away to hear the exchange between Don Morris and the Christian students from the Karolinum. But, within a short time, the resolution was obvious. With Don Morris on his warhorse prancing in their lead, the students came to join the Jews already on the barricade.

"So it is," Mordechai stated. "It will be complicated. But you were saying something?"

As he watched the students begin intermingling with the fighters on the barricade, Isaac spoke softly. "There is a lot of wisdom in those pages Jason brought to us, Mordechai. The wisdom of the Chasidic folktales, in particular, I think will serve us well in the time to come."

"And what do those stories relate?"

"I will give you two. In the first, a simple wagon-driver stops his cart at the side of the road to speak the Hebrew alphabet, one letter at a time. 'God,' he cries out, 'I don't know the prayers, so I am sending you the alphabet. You must know the prayers. Make them up out of the letters I am sending.'"

Mordechai barked a laugh. "Oh, I like that! And the other?"

"Ah, that one is my favorite. It seems one day a disciple came to complain to his teacher. 'Rabbi, some of the congregants are gossiping in the midst of prayer!'"

Spira smiled crookedly. "Not such a different world after all, then. And the rabbi's response?"

"'O God,' said the rabbi. 'How wonderful are your people! Even in the midst of gossip, they devote a few moments to prayer!'"

Shortly thereafter, the first campfires began springing up on the opposite bank of the river. Holk and his men were settling in for the night, it seemed, and would make no further attempt to storm the bridge until the next morning.

At sundown, Mordechai Spira returned to his home in the ghetto. The fighters would remain on the barricades, keeping watch through the night, with Don Morris there to lead them and keep them steady. But there was no reason for him to remain. Mordechai would return before daybreak, to do what he could.

But he wanted to spend this night—perhaps their last—with his family.

Over the dinner, he told the stories to his wife and children. And was still smiling himself when he finally went to bed.

The rabbi slept soundly that night, but Holk and his mercenaries did not. Jan Billek took advantage of the darkness to move his Brethren forward, from the positions they'd initially taken farther south in the Malá Strana. From their new positions, skirmishers were able to harass Holk's mercenaries all through the night. Occasionally with gunfire, but usually with grenades and swords, in constant probing sallies.

It was a bitter, nasty sort of fighting. And if none of the Brethren were as nasty as Holk's men, they were considerably more bitter. They had been victimized for years by such men, and were finally able to take some revenge.

They were also a lot more determined and resolute. Holk's ruffians had come into Prague expecting an easy and pleasant few days of murder, rape, arson and looting. They had not expected to spend their first night in the city worrying about getting their throats cut by dimly seen figures lunging from the darkness—or getting shredded by bomblets suddenly launched into their campfires.

Not all that many of Holk's men were actually killed or wounded that night. Less than a hundred. But none of them slept well, and a considerable number didn't sleep at all.

Except Holk himself. He was drunk by sundown, and comatose by midnight.

2

"*Okay, Red. Tell Morris they'll be coming any min-ute. Holk's done with the cursing and he's starting to threaten people with his sword. No, I take it back. I can't see too well from here, but I think he's put the sword away and now he's threatening them with a wheel-lock pistol.*"

"Thanks, Ellie, I'll tell him." Sybolt leaned out of the cab window and hollered the news to Morris. Then, quipped to Dunash in the passenger seat: "It's the old story. 'Go get 'em, boys! You first!'"

Dunash was too nervous to appreciate the jest. The young man was doing his best to retain his composure—and doing quite well at it—but only by adopting a stern and stiff demeanor. Butter wouldn't melt in his mouth. In fact, Red thought, you could probably use it for an icebox.

"Relax, old son. This is gonna be a cakewalk. Trust me."

Dunash made no reply for perhaps half a minute. Then, abruptly, almost harshly: "Why would anyone walk on a cake? And what does that mean, anyway?"

Red shook his head ruefully. "Gawd, all the work it's going to take me to recover my reputation as an endless source of wit and wisdom. Oh, well. What it means, Dunash, is that we're going to win this battle. Easily."

"Why do you think that?"

Red pointed at the roof of the cab. "Because of

this thing. Mind you—in general, that is—I think it's about as useless a gadget on the battlefield as you could imagine. I guess the Russians did pretty well with katyushas in the Second World War, but they used jillions of 'em. Just one? Pointless."

Dunash was inordinately proud of the katyusha. "Why?" he asked, in a very aggrieved tone.

"It's an area effect weapon, Dunash. Rockets—sure as hell these—aren't that accurate. If you've got a ton of them the way the Russkies did, that's one thing. Saturation bombardment, they call it. But just one? Pointless. On a battlefield, that is."

"Then why did you—"

"On a *battlefield*, I said." Red jabbed his finger at the quarter-inch steel plate that covered the windshield except for small viewing slits left for the driver and the gunner. "But that's a bridge, not a battlefield. A bridge that's the only way to cross the Vltava without boats—which Holk didn't think to bring with him, and he can't round up now that he's here because Jan and his boys made sure all the ones in Prague were taken up the river."

Red leaned forward over the steering wheel and peered through the viewing slit. "A bridge that I figure is not more than fifty feet wide and at least five hundred yards long. With no cover on it anywhere—not even the statues that Len says used to be on it hundreds of years from now—and only that one little dogleg way over to the other side of the span. Oh, those poor bastards. They've gotta cross about a quarter of a mile in plain sight with only maybe fifteen of them—okay, make it twenty with that mob—in the front line."

He leaned back, very satisfied. "Would *you* want to be one of those fifteen or twenty guys? I sure as hell wouldn't. Not with two hundred flintlocks and a fair number of old-style arquebuses banging away at me." He rapped the roof of the cab with his knuckles. "Not to mention after this baby cuts loose."

"Morris won't let them fire until they get within a hundred yards," Dunash pointed out. "So what does the rest of that distance mean?" Sourly, he looked at the firing switches mounted on the dashboard in front of him: "And you won't let me fire this until they get within *fifty* yards."

"All it'll take, boy. You watch." He opened the door to the cab and began climbing out. "But now that you bring it up, I better make sure those hotshots of yours didn't fiddle with my instructions."

They hadn't, although Red was sure they'd been tempted to. Most down-timers, in his experience, even ones with considerable military experience, tended to exaggerate the capabilities of American weapons. Enthusiasts like Dunash's followers, even more so. But the young men tending the rocket launcher in the bed of the pickup had left the settings alone. Even though it must have aggravated them to see that Red had lowered the elevation until the rockets were pointed at the ground right in front of the truck.

Well, almost. Red estimated that the rockets would hit somewhere between fifty and a hundred yards ahead. Exactly what he wanted.

"Those rockets could hit the Hradcany from here!" one of them complained, as Red started to clamber down out of the bed.

Once he was back on the ground, Red squinted at

the fortress in question. He was still without glasses, so it wasn't much more than a blur to him.

"Oh, sure, they can fly that far. But *hit* it? Be a pure accident." He pointed toward the Malá Strana. "They'd be just as likely to hit Wallenstein's palace. Just do it my way, boys. Holk's got as much chance of getting across this bridge as a pig does of flying. You watch."

After he got back into the truck and closed the door, Red cocked his head and smiled at Dunash. "Pigs *can* fly, you know."

Dunash frowned; as often, not sure whether Red was kidding or not.

"Sure they can," Red insisted. "Throw one off the highest wall in Prague Castle sometime and see for yourself."

The CB squawked. *"They're starting the charge, Red! They're on their way!"*

His eyes came back to the firing slit, as he reached for the CB. "Yup, that pig'll fly. All the way to the ground."

Only seconds thereafter, Morris could see the first ranks himself, charging across the bridge. Using the term "ranks" very loosely, of course. Holk's men just looked like a mob.

For a moment, he reached for the sword, ready to start swinging it around again as he bellowed mean-ingless but reassuringly martial words. But, as if it had a mind of its own, his hand went to the stock of his rifle instead.

He decided his hand was smarter than his brain. So, he drew the rifle out of the saddle holster his wife had had made for him. Then, with motions than were much surer than those with which he held a sword, jacked a round into the chamber and propped the butt of the rifle on his hip.

And said nothing. He just couldn't think of anything to say, since it was all too obvious. The brigands were coming and he intended to shoot them down. Simple as that. What was there to say about it?

His hand *was* smarter than his brain. Morris Roth had no way of knowing it—and never would—but the easy and assured motion, and the silence that followed, had precisely the right effect on the men on the barricades. Almost all of whom had been nervously watching him, once they realized the fight was finally underway.

In truth, it had a much more profound effect than any amount of sword-waving and speechifying could have had, at least with that assemblage of warriors-that-weren't. Shopkeepers, butchers, bakers, students—rabbinical students, some of them. With the exception of a few of the former seamen, who'd dealt with pirates, almost none of them had ever been in a battle before of any kind—much less a pitched battle against an army with as ferocious a reputation as Holk's. True, the tactical situation was completely in their favor, but they didn't really have the experience to know that.

But Don Morris did—or so, at least, they blithely assumed. He'd *told* them they could win, hadn't he? In speech after speech given the day before. And, now that the fury was finally about to fall on their heads, wasn't Don Morris sitting on his saddle not more than ten yards behind the barricade, as calm as could be? Not even bothering with his sword—not even *aiming* his rifle. Just . . .

Waiting.

He didn't speak until Holk's forces were within two hundred yards. "Fire when I do!" he commanded. Quite sure, this time, that he would be obeyed.

Red glanced into the side mirror of the pickup. "Shit," he snarled. "Dunash, tell—"

He opened the door. "Never mind, I'll do it myself."

Hopping out of the truck, Red took several steps toward the rear, making broad shooing motions with his arms. "All of you get the hell out of the way!" he bellowed. "The backblast on these rockets is fierce!"

A number of women and children and old men had started crowding in behind the pickup to get a better look at the oncoming soldiers. They didn't really understand what Red was shouting at them, but they got the gist of it well enough. A moment later, Red had a clear firing lane again.

He clambered back into the truck.

"They're almost here!" Dunash hissed.

Red squinted through the slit. "Oh, bullshit. I can't see the whites of their eyes."

He glanced over and saw that Dunash's hands were twitching, as if they couldn't wait to flip the firing switches.

"Whites of their eyes," he growled. "You don't flip those switches till I say so."

❦ ❦ ❦

The day before, just to be sure there wouldn't be a problem, Morris had fired the rifle while in the saddle. The warhorse hadn't even flinched.

When the first of Holk's men was within one hundred yards, Morris brought the rifle butt to his shoulder. He'd removed the telescopic sight the day before, seeing no use for it in the coming fray. Peering over the iron sights, he saw that his guess had been correct. At that range, firing into that mob, he could hardly miss with a blindfold on.

He squeezed the trigger. Oddly, as he did so, thinking only of the horse.

I wonder if Pappenheim would sell it to me?

3

The stern control Morris had managed to gain over his motley troops had its effect. This time, the first volley was actually that—a volley. A single, hammering blow at the enemy, shocking men with its power even more than the actual casualties inflicted.

The casualties themselves were . . . not as good as they could have been, had experienced troops fired that volley. Many of the shots went wild, more than usual with such inaccurate firearms.

So, Holk's men reeled and staggered, but they came on nonetheless, almost without breaking stride. Granted, these weren't men of the caliber of the great armies of Tilly or Gustavus Adolphus. Holk had known what he was doing when he delayed his arrival at Breitenfeld. On *that* battlefield, his thugs would have been coyotes at a wolf party. Still, they were mercenary soldiers with fifteen years of the Thirty Years War under their belts. They'd charged into gunfire before, and knew that the only way to get through it was just to plunge ahead, pikes leveled.

They were all pikemen in the front ranks. The clumsy arquebuses of the seventeenth century would have been almost useless in this kind of charge across a long and narrow bridge. And pikes always had the advantage of sheer terror, in a frontal assault. Outside of a cavalry charge, there was perhaps nothing quite as intimidating as the sight of hundreds of pikes, each of them almost twenty feet long and tipped with a cruel foot-long blade, charging directly at you.

Of course, it would have helped if Holk's men had been able to level the pikes. But, in that pressing mob, with no ranks being maintained, that was impossible for all but the very foremost. The first thing a pikeman learned was that a pike could easily kill or main the man in front of him, if not handled carefully. Those who didn't learn it—and quickly—found themselves out of the army. Sometimes, in a coffin. The term "fragging" didn't exist yet, but nobody had to teach seventeenth-century mercenaries how to deal with a fellow soldier who was a danger to his mates—or a sub-officer, for that matter.

The second volley was more ragged, but it struck even harder. The range was shorter. Fifty yards. Holk's men were definitely staggering, but still they came on. They had no choice, really, since by now there were thousands of men behind them on the bridge, pushing them forward.

"Okay, shoot," Red said quietly.

Dunash's fingers flew to the firing switches.

That volley broke the charge. To Holk and his men, it seemed as if a dragon had suddenly belched. Licking down the bridge with a tongue of fire that just seemed to engulf men whole. Swallow entire *ranks* of them.

The katyusha was firing the second generation of rockets that Grantville had been able to manufacture in quantity. It was a variation on the old nineteenth-century Hale 24-pounder rotary rocket—2.4 inches in diameter, slightly less than two feet long, with a maximum range of 4000 yards. The propellant as well as the warhead were black powder. The rockets were fired from a single-level rack, twelve tubes mounted side by side on an adjustable framework fixed into the bed of the Dodge Ram.

Red had foreseen the impact of the rockets fired at such close range on such a narrow target. The maximum flight time for a Hale rocket was about twenty seconds, most of it ballistic. At that point-blank range, the Hale rockets struck the advancing troops in split-seconds. But what he hadn't foreseen—was almost aghast when he witnessed it—was the effect of the stone retaining walls on either side of the bridge.

The rockets struck the paving of the bridge, just as Red had foreseen, between fifty and a hundred yards ahead. Some of them exploded instantly, but not most of them. Red had chosen to use contact fuses for this battle instead of the self-lit fuse that had been the standard for the old Hale rockets. But since the somewhat jury-rigged contact fuses available in this day and age made him nervous, he'd adjusted them to fire only in the event they made a direct hit.

Which most of them didn't. They struck the stones at a low glancing angle and kept on, sailing and skidding down the bridge—caroming off the low walls—until they finally ran out of fuel and momentum or hit something solid enough to explode. The narrowness of the bridge concentrated the impact, but it was the walls that channeled it into sheer havoc.

Without uptime propellant the black powder rockets were occasionally prone to explosion—CATO, as the rocket club kids called it ("Catastrophe At Take Off")—caused by an unforeseen bounce or bump that cracked the grain. Then the rockets were little more than large bombs, more black powder burning than could be safely ejected as the pressure rose. Red preferred not to have twenty pounds of black powder exploding near his head, so he'd inspected them carefully. One of them did burst, nonetheless. But that fact didn't make the charging enemy infantry any happier. The rocket exploded some fifty feet in front of the truck and became a huge ball of fire and flying debris hurtling towards Holk's troops at hundreds of miles per hour. A shot of grape from a six-pounder couldn't have been more effective. Grape didn't set the recipient on fire.

Two of the rockets, on the other hand, never exploded at all. Red later found one of them lying on the stones not more than fifty yards from the other end of the bridge. But that didn't matter, either. All twelve of the rockets in that volley did their damage, even those two—and far more damage than Red had foreseen. It was as if the dragon had a dozen serpent tongues, licking down the great Stone Bridge for hundred of yards, racing the length of the span up to the dogleg in less than two seconds. Hissing with fury, belching smoke, upending dozens of terrified men for every one they killed or wounded—which meant dozens of pikes flailing about, gashing and bashing and wounding still more.

The sheer weight of the charge would probably have kept it going, struck only by bullets. Men at the front being shoved forward willy-nilly by those at the rear. But the dragon-tongues ravaged the men in the first hundred yards, paralyzed and confused those behind them—and gave those at the very rear the time to do what soldiers rarely have in a frontal assault.

Time to think things over.

Even the best mercenary soldiers are not given to mindless obedience to orders. And Holk's men were far from the best. The charge staggered to a halt, and the men at the rear began coming back off the bridge. That relieved the pressure on those ahead of them; and, inchoate rank after rank, Holk's charge started disintegrating.

It took time, of course. Perhaps fifteen minutes, in all. But the critical furious momentum of the initial charge had been lost, and Holk's officers were neither good enough nor respected enough to rally the army. They did manage, four times, to paste together small charges from those men toward the front who could be convinced or cajoled or bullied into it. But the first three of those charges were driven off, easily enough, by the flintlocks and the arquebuses.

By then, Dunash's rocketeers had been able to reload the katyusha, and the dragon belched again. The fourth charge was shredded, and Holk's men had

had *enough*. This was even worse than the Hradcany. They hadn't signed on to fight a damn dragon.

So, back they came, in a hurry, leaving hundreds of dead and dying and wounded behind them on the bridge. Two of the corpses were those of sub-officers, too stupid or inexperienced to understand when it was time to stop trying to force mercenary soldiers to do something they really, really, really didn't want to do any more. One of them bled to death from no fewer than five stab wounds.

4

"For Chrissake, Red, it's obvious even from here. Tell Morris to quit screwing around with his stupid modesty act and start waving his hat. And while he's at it, do the Roy Rogers bit with the fucking horse. Y'know, rearing up on the hind legs. Whatever they call that silly stunt, I don't know. I can't stand big fucking animals. Damn things are dangerous. Even cats make me nervous, with their fangs and shit."

5

After Red whispered in his ear—well, shouted in his ear—Morris did take off his big, wide-brimmed plumed hat and wave it around, acknowledging the enthusiastic roars of approval from the crowd. He drew the line, though, at rearing the horse.

It didn't matter, really. Ellie was too nervous about a lot of things. After that sunny day in Prague, in

July of the year 1633—as Christians counted it; for the Jews who made up most of the crowd it was the month of Av and the year was 5393—it wouldn't have mattered if Don Morris had fallen off the horse entirely—or lost his hat in the river.

Don Morris, he was; and Don Morris he would always remain. For them as well as their descendants who heard the tale. It had been a long time, after all—a very long time—since the Ashkenazim of central and eastern Europe had had a martial hero of their own. The ancient Hebrews had had a multitude, of course; and the Sephardim, in their Iberian heyday, more than a few. But for the Ashkenazim of Europe, for many centuries, heroism had been something that could only be measured by martyrs.

Martyrs were to be cherished, certainly. But it was nice—delightful, in fact—not to have to do it again.

And who was to say? Perhaps never again. There were those other men, after all, who would outlive Don Morris. The much younger Jews who looked very bold and handsome, perched up there on that strange thing that was so much bigger and more deadly than a mere horse. And didn't seem to be afraid of it at all.

Perhaps the golem was not simply a silly legend. The Maharal had been a *very* wise man. One of the wisest, even in a city of wise men like Prague.

6

As usually happens in history, the famous Battle of the Bridge didn't have a neat ending. Holk and his men never tried to charge across the bridge again. But they did remain in Prague for days thereafter, burning and plundering what they could in the Malá Strana.

One part of the plan had not worked. Billek and his Brethren had tried—quite valiantly—to trap Holk's army on the bridge and slaughter them wholesale. But Holk had twice as many men in his army as he could get onto the bridge in one charge, and if he was a drunk and a brute he was not actually incompetent. So, he'd stationed half his army to protect the western entrance to the bridge, and the Brethren were unable to drive them off. Indeed, they suffered fairly heavy casualties in the attempt.

And continued to suffer them, the next day. The crude fact, soon evident, was that Billek's inexperienced volunteers simply couldn't stand toe-to-toe with Holk's toughs in a pitched battle. They tried, the next morning, fighting in the open in the streets, but by noon Billek realized his mistake and ordered a retreat. Thereafter, in the days that followed, the Brethren went back to their tactics of harassment and fighting from well-fortified positions.

At that, they were extremely capable—just as their Hussite ancestors, from the shelters of their armored wagons, had been very good at breaking noble cavalry. They couldn't defeat Holk—couldn't even drive him off—but they could certainly bleed him. And, what was most important, bleed the morale of his army.

Morris, during those same days, lapsed frequently into profanity. Understandably enough, having driven off the charge across the bridge on the first day and being in no real danger thereafter, the Jews of the ghetto were reluctant to get involved in the fighting still taking place in the Malá Strana. That was a goyishe battle in a goyishe part of the city where few of them had ever gone, and fewer still had ever lived. All of Morris' attempts to plead and convince and cajole them—even curse them, which he did more than once—had little effect.

But Dunash and his young firebrands came into their own, during those same days. They *did* participate in the fighting. First, at irregular intervals, by racing onto the bridge—almost all the way across, on one occasion—and firing rocket volleys at Holk's encampment. Then, racing off before Holk's cannons could retaliate. (Holk had finally brought in his artillery, three days too late to do any good.)

Secondly, perhaps more importantly, every day after sundown at least some of Dunash's men made their way across the river in a few small boats that they'd kept safely hidden away. Once there, they joined the Brethren in their nightly harassment of Holk's forces. In purely military terms, they were not much of a factor. But the political effect was significant—and, by the fourth day, was starting to result in a steady trickle of recruits to Dunash's miniature army. In any population of fifteen thousand people, there are a fair number of bold youngsters who don't see things the way their sage elders do.

Most of the Malá Strana was in ruins, by the end, though civilian casualties were minimal. Fortunately, the inhabitants of that section of Prague had fled before Holk arrived. For that matter—much to the disgruntlement of Holk's troops—they'd taken their valuable belongings with them. The destruction wreaked by Holk's army during the week it spent in Prague was not so much due to looting, as such; it was simply the mindless destruction and arson visited upon a town by frustrated and angry troops. Who became even more frustrated, the more they wrecked and burned, because their own living quarters and rations got steadily worse as a result.

Holk would have tried to restrain them, had he not been Heinrich Holk. Being Holk, it never once occurred to him to do so.

Then, a week after the siege of Prague began, word came from the southwest. A second battle of the White Mountain had indeed been fought. Actually, the battle was fought a good twenty miles away from the White Mountain, but since victors get to name battles, "the Second Battle of the White Mountain" it was.

It seemed that Wallenstein thought it made a nice touch, to inaugurate the new kingdom of Bohemia and Moravia.

Oh, yes. He'd won. Pappenheim and his dreaded Black Cuirassiers had pursued the retreating Austrians for miles, slaughtering pitilessly.

"Practicing for Holk," Pappenheim was reported to have said afterward.

The news arrived in the morning. By late afternoon, Holk's army was out of Prague, racing for the north. Holk, it was said, had already opened negotiations with the Elector of Saxony, John George, looking for a new employer. And shelter from the coming storm.

7

But there was no storm on the day that Wallenstein and Pappenheim finally returned to Prague—other than a storm of applause from the residents of the city who greeted his victorious army, on both banks of the river. Whatever private reservations any of them had regarding the change of power, nobody was willing any longer to speak out in open opposition.

Not even the Catholics in the city. First, because the Jesuits dominated the Catholic church in Bohemia. Wallenstein had always been partial to the Jesuits, and had sent them a friendly private note assuring them that they would be able to remain in Prague unmolested—provided, of course, they agreed to cease and desist their activities against Protestants on behalf of the Austrian Habsburgs.

The Jesuits hadn't decided yet, how they would react to that last provision. But they didn't have to fear for their own lives in the immediate period.

The second reason they decided to stay, however, and abide by Wallenstein's conditions—at least for the moment—would have amazed Ellie Anderson. Whatever she thought of Len Tanner's behavior during the siege, the Jesuits had reacted otherwise. Quirky—even foolish—he might have been. But, as the days passed and the pudgy American kept returning to his self-assigned post of duty in the cathedral, always with that bizarre weapon in his hands, the Jesuits came to the conclusion that whatever Wallenstein might think, his new American allies had their own opinions. And, whatever else, were clearly stubborn about them.

That was an interesting datum, with interesting possibilities for the future. The Jesuits in Prague duly recorded their impressions in several letters they sent to their Father General in Rome, Mutio Vitelleschi. They did so, of course, in the full knowledge that Vitelleschi was close to the Pope and would pass along their letters. The gist of them, in any event. So, the Jesuits would be patient. They were trained, and accustomed, to thinking in the long run.

Most of the crowd gathered to cheer Wallenstein's army, however, were Protestants of one sort or another—counting the Brethren and the Utraquists in their number, although they predated Martin Luther— and the Jews. Those people were far less ambivalent about the situation. Granted, Wallenstein was still an enigmatic figure, and a somewhat unsettling one. But the Habsburgs weren't enigmatic at all. Most of Prague's residents had had more than enough of the royal bigot Ferdinand II, sitting on his throne in Vienna.

And, finally, there was this: Wallenstein did not return alone. He had Pappenheim, of course, but he also brought with him tangible proof that his new regime had secured at least one redoubtable ally: the United States in Thuringia, if not perhaps the entire Confederated Principalities of Europe.

The proof came in the form of two APCs that Mike Stearns sent to Bohemia the minute he got word from Morris Roth—yes, there had been a long-distance radio stashed in that great mansion's basement, along with so many other treasures—that the political crisis had finally erupted and it was time for the United States to forego all secrecy. The APCs had not arrived in time to play any role at the second battle of the White Mountain, but they did arrive in time to join Wallenstein's triumphal procession back into Prague.

The only unfortunate episode in the day's celebrations—and that, only mildly unfortunate—was that the biggest cheer of all was not reserved for Wallenstein himself. That cheer erupted, quite spontaneously, when the two APCs from Grantville rumbled onto the Stone Bridge from the Malá Strana side and were met halfway by the katyusha coming from the east bank. Now that they could see what a *real* APC looked like, almost dwarfing the katyusha drawn up before it, Prague's citizens were greatly heartened. Their own little one had driven off Holk, no? Who knew what the big ones could do?

Best of all, perhaps—at least for fifteen thousand of the city's residents—was that the katyusha was festooned with banners. One—the largest, of course—was Wallenstein's new banner. But there was also, resting alongside it, the banner of the Josefov. The central image on the flag was that of a hexagram—a symbol that had, in another universe, evolved over the centuries into the Star of David.

There was something very fitting about it all, they thought. So far as anyone knew, Prague had been the first city in Europe whose Jews were given the right to fly their own flag. They had been given that right in the Christian year 1354—by the same Emperor Charles IV who had built the Stone Bridge it was now flying over, and which that katyusha had so valiantly defended.

Uriel Abrabanel had returned also, with the APCs. He'd come onto the bridge with the war machines, but he'd kept going, walking all the way across.

Morris came out of the crowd to greet him. "'Bout time you got back," he grumbled. "Where were you when all the dust was flying?"

Uriel grinned, quite unabashed. "I was busy. Never mind with what, I won't tell you. Besides, flying dust is no place for a proper spy. That's the business of princes and soldiers—and hidalgos, I hear."

"Just what I need. More rumors." Morris made a face. "So? Are you staying?"

"Certainly. Spies are all mercenaries at heart, you know. I also hear that the new hidalgo in Prague is a very generous patron."

Morris sighed. "Et tu, Brute? Soak the rich Jew, that's all anybody thinks about. Even other Jews."

"Stop whining. You need a good spy. Better yet, a good spymaster."

Morris thought about it. Not for very long. "Boy, isn't that the truth? Okay, Uriel, you're hired."

Chapter VII: End Game
August, 1633

1

"That is a ridiculous price for that horse." Pappenheim was smiling when he said it, though. A rather cold and thin smile, true, but—

From Pappenheim, that was good enough.

"All I can afford," Morris insisted. "It's not the horse that's the problem, Gottfried, it's the cost of feeding the great brute."

"And that statement is even more ridiculous. Not about the horse's appetite—I know what that costs—but the rest of it."

Pappenheim's eyes ranged up and down Morris' figure, examining his apparel. "What, no pearls? They're quite in fashion, I'm told, in Paris and Vienna—and you needn't worry about the sumptuary laws any longer, because the King of Bohemia has abolished all of them."

Morris was tempted to state that was because Wallenstein was a clotheshorse himself, but he wisely refrained. It *was* an autocracy, after all, even if Morris Roth was about as well-respected and well-regarded a courtier—in Bohemia, at least—as any in Europe. And he didn't even have to fawn all over his monarch to maintain the status. Clotheshorse or not, Wallenstein was far more interested in results than flattery.

Pappenheim rose from his chair. "Oh, let's be done with it. Morris, I give you the horse as a gift. In fact, I'll even include a full set of cuirassier armor to go with it. In recognition of your valor at the bridge."

He grinned at Morris' startled expression. "Don't worry. I promise I won't hold it against you if you never wear it. Miserable heavy stuff, I'll be the first to admit."

"It's not you I'm worried about, Gottfried," Morris replied. "It's my wife. She'll never let me leave it stuffed safely away in a chest. You watch. The first big ceremonial occasion—eek."

How Pappenheim could manage a grin that wide, and that cold, Morris would never understand.

"Indeed so," said the Duke of Moravia. "The coronation is less than two weeks from now. Still, that's more than enough time for me to have the armor ready. Do try your best not to trip during the procession, Morris. You'll never get up again, not at your age. Without a winch."

2

That night, Jason came back from his first Shabbat dinner at the home of Mordechai Spira.

He seemed in a peculiar mood, and said very little before he went to bed. Morris didn't notice, but Judith did.

The next morning, she pressed Jason about it.

"I don't know. It's hard to explain. A lot of it I liked—a lot. The discussion was almost exhilarating at times. The rabbi was at his best, too. I learned a lot and I laughed a lot at the same time. But . . ."

He ran fingers through his hair, which had gotten very long. "I don't know if I'll ever get used to men dancing alone. And it was weird, having the women do all the serving and cooking as if they were menials. Although I was even more surprised—pleased, but surprised—when the women participated in the Talmudic discussion after dinner. I didn't think they would."

Judith was surprised herself, hearing that. Although . . .

She reminded herself not to make the mistake her husband Morris was prone to making. People are not categories, not even categories to which they belong. Unusual rabbis were still rabbis, after all. So why should it really be that surprising—in the same city which had produced a woman like Eva Bacharach—that the wife and daughters of Mordechai Spira would be unusual women?

"One of the rabbi's daughters even made a joke in the course of it," Jason continued. "Pretty funny one, too."

His eyes got a little unfocused. Judith had to struggle not to smile.

"Tell me about her. The daughter, I mean."

Jason mumbled some vague phrases. The only ones that weren't hopelessly murky had to do with the girl's eyes—very bright, apparently—and the fact that her name was Sarah.

But Judith let it go. There was no reason to pursue the matter with Jason, at the moment, since it obviously made him uncomfortable. Eva Bacharach would be coming for a visit later that day. Judith could find out everything she needed to know from her.

"I just don't know what to think," he complained. "Everything seems gray, and complicated. It's confusing."

"And you think that'll change? It won't. Trust me. But for the moment—"

She gave the young man a very warm smile. "Welcome to your life, Jason Gotkin."

3

In late afternoon, Mordechai Spira visited his friend Isaac Gans.

After seeing Mordechai to a chair, Gans sat in his own.

"And?"

"You were quite wrong, Isaac. Sarah didn't start pestering me until after lunch."

"Ha!" Isaac chuckled. "That's because she spent the whole morning conspiring with your wife."

"I know," said Mordechai gloomily. His eyes moved to the books on Isaac's study table. "It's a puzzling and tangled problem, given who the fellow is. But I'm sure I can find something in the Talmud—perhaps the responsa—to guide me properly."

"Of course you can. Everything pertaining to proper conduct is contained somewhere in the Talmud or the midrash or the responsa. I'm more the scholar than you are, though I don't have your stature as a judge." Stoutly: "So I will be glad to help!"

Gans leaned forward, spreading his hands wide. "But

we must begin by facing the truth, Mordechai my old friend. We're rabbis. Studying the sacred texts takes time—hours and hours, days and weeks, poring over the words—and we are dealing with women."

Spira grimaced ruefully. "They're quick."

"Indeed. And so, I think, are these new times. We will just have to do our best."

"Always."

American freedom and justice versus the tyrannies of the seventeenth century

1632 by Eric Flint
Paperback • 31972-8 $7.99

"This gripping and expertly detailed account of an episode of time travel that changes history is a treat for lovers of action-SF or alternate history . . . it distinguishes Flint as an SF author of particular note, one who can entertain and edify in equal, and major, measure."
— *Publishers Weekly*, starred review

1633 by David Weber & Eric Flint
Paperback • 7434-7155-5 $7.99

The greatest naval war in European history is about to erupt. Like it or not, Gustavus Adolphus will have to rely on Mike Stearns and the technical wizardry of his obstreperous Americans to save the King of Sweden from ruin, but caught in the conflagration are two American diplomatic missions abroad. . . .

1634: The Galileo Affair by Eric Flint & Andrew Dennis
Paperback • 7434-9919-0 $7.99

The Thirty Years War continues to ravage 17th-century Europe, but a new force is gathering power and influence: the Confederated Principalities of Europe, an alliance between Gustavus Adolphus, King of Sweden, and the West Virginians from the 20th century . . .

And don't miss the Ring of Fire series anthologies:

The Ring of Fire edited by Eric Flint
Hardcover • 7434-7175-X $23.00

Grantville Gazette edited by Eric Flint
Paperback • 7434-8860-1 $6.99

- -

Available in bookstores everywhere

Or order online at our secure, easy website:
www.baen.com

If not available through your local bookstore send this coupon and a check or money order for the cover price(s) + $1.50 s/h to Baen Books, Dept. BA, P.O. Box 1403, Riverdale, NY 10471. Be sure to include full name & address for shipping. Delivery can take up to eight weeks.

16th-century Europe ...
the intrigue, the courtesans,
the magic, the demons ...

a historical fantasy series from masters of the genre

◇◇◇

The Shadow of the Lion

Mercedes Lackey,
Eric Flint & Dave Freer   0-7434-7147-4 ◆ $7.99

Venice, 1537. A failed magician, a fugitive orphan, a reluctant prince, a devious courtesan, and a man of faith must make uneasy alliance, or the city will be consumed by evil beyond human comprehension.

This Rough Magic

Mercedes Lackey,
Eric Flint & Dave Freer   0-7434-9909-3 ◆ $7.99

The demon Chernobog had almost seized absolute power in Venice until the guardian Lion-spirit awoke to protect his city. But the Lion's power is limited to Venice, and Chernobog has allied with the King of Hungary in besieging the island of Corfu to control the Adriatic. Far from the Lion's help, Manfred and Erik organize guerrillas, as Maria discovers the island's ancient mystic powers. If she can ally with them, she may be able to repel the invaders—but not without paying a bitter personal price.

A Mankind Witch

Dave Freer   (HC) 0-7434-9913-1 ◆ $25.00

In an alternate world where magic works, the Holy Roman Empire still rules Europe, and the Renaissance has come, with very different results. Norway is still pagan, and a sacred relic, the Armring of Telemark, has been stolen from Odin's temple. Without it, truce-oaths cannot be renewed and bloody war with the Empire will follow. Signy, the older stepsister to the King Vortenbras is accused. When she disappears, most think it proof of her guilt. Her only partisan, the Corsair-Captain Cair, knows that she had been carried off and is determined to find and rescue her; he will not only find that magic is very real, and dangerously so, but that he himself has a natural talent for it.

◇◇◇

Available at local bookstores everywhere!

Or, use secure, easy *online ordering* at:
www.baen.com

If not available through your local bookstore, send a check or money order for the cover price(s) + $1.75 s/h to Baen Books, Dept. BA, P.O. Box 1403, Riverdale, NY 10471. Include a full name & address for shipping. Delivery can take up to eight weeks.

CLASSIC MASTERS OF SCIENCE FICTION BACK IN PRINT!

Randall Garrett — edited by Eric Flint

Lord Darcy	0-7434-7184-9 ◆	$7.99

James Schmitz's stories — edited by Eric Flint

Telzey Amberdon	0-671-57851-0 ◆	$7.99
T'NT: Telzey & Trigger	0-671-57879-0 ◆	$6.99
Trigger & Friends	0-671-31966-3 ◆	$6.99
The Hub: Dangerous Territory	0-671-31984-1 ◆	$6.99
Agent of Vega & Other Stories	0-671-31847-0 ◆	$7.99
Eternal Frontier	0-7434-7190-3 ◆	$7.99

Keith Laumer — edited by Eric Flint

Retief!	0-671-31857-8 ◆	$6.99
Odyssey	0-7434-3527-3 ◆	$6.99
Keith Laumer: The Lighter Side	0-7434-3537-0 ◆	$7.99
A Plague of Demons & Other Stories	0-7434-9906-9 ◆	$7.99
Future Imperfect (trade PB)	0-7434-3606-7 ◆	$14.00
Legions of Space	0-7434-8855-5 ◆	$7.99
Imperium (HC)	0-7434-9903-4 ◆	$25.00

Murray Leinster — compiled & edited by Eric Flint

Med Ship	0-7434-3555-9 ◆	$7.99
Planets of Adventure	0-7434-7162-8 ◆	$7.99

Christopher Anvil — compiled & edited by Eric Flint

Interstellar Patrol	0-7434-8848-2 ◆	$7.99
Interstellar Patrol II (hardcover)	0-7434-9892-5 ◆	$26.00

Howard L. Myers — compiled & edited by Eric Flint

The Creatures of Man	0-7434-9900-X ◆	$7.99

Gordon R. Dickson — compiled by Hank Davis

The Human Edge	0-7434-7174-1 ◆	$6.99

for more books by the masters of science fiction and fantasy,
ask for our free catalog or go to www.baen.com

Available in bookstores everywhere

Or order online at our secure, easy website:
www.baen.com

If not available through your local bookstore send this coupon and a check or money order for the cover price(s) + $1.75 s/h to Baen Books, Dept. BA, P.O. Box 1403, Riverdale, NY 10471. Be sure to include full name & address for shipping. Delivery can take up to eight weeks.

Andre Norton ✪

"The sky's no limit to Andre Norton's imagination . . . a superb storyteller."
—The New York Times

Star Soldiers   0-7434-3554-0 | $6.99

A grand tapestry of the far-flung interstellar future, in which the first starships from Earth have burst out into the universe. (Previously published in parts as *Star Guard* and *Star Rangers*.)

Time Traders   0-671-31829-2 | $6.99

The U.S. and the Russians race back through time and across interstellar space, struggling for control of an advanced alien space craft.

Time Traders II   0-671- 31852-7 | $7.99

The fates of two worlds depend on Time Agents Travis Fox and Russ Murdoch, castaways in time.

Warlock   0-7434-7151-2 | $7.99

Three novels, *Storm Over Warlock*, *Ordeal in Otherwhere*, and *Forerunner Foray* set on the planet Warlock, secretly ruled by the matriarchial Wyverns, an alien race with mental powers beyond human comprehension.

Janus   0-7434-7180-6 | $6.99

Two novels, previously published as *Judgment on Janus* and *Victory on Janus*. This is their first combined publication.

Darkness & Dawn   0-7434-8831-8 | $7.99

Previously published as two novels, *Daybreak 2250 A.D.* & *No Night Without Stars*.

Gods & Androids   0-7434-9911-5 | $7.99

Contains the novels *Androids at Arms* & *Wraiths of Time*.

Dark Companion (hardcover)   0-7434-9898-4 | $26.00

Includes the two novels *Dark Piper* & *Dread Companion*, published together for the first time.

Available in bookstores everywhere

Or order online at our secure, easy website:
www.baen.com

If not available through your local bookstore send this coupon and a check or money order for the cover price(s) + $1.75 s/h to Baen Books, Dept. BA, P.O. Box 1403, Riverdale, NY 10471. Be sure to include full name & address for shipping. Delivery can take up to eight weeks.

• BOLO: The Future of War •

What is a Bolo? The symbol of brute force, intransigent defiance, and adamantine will. But on a deeper level, the Bolo is the Lancelot of the future, the perfect knight, sans peur et sans reproche. With plated armor, a laser canon, an electronic brain, and wheels.

The Compleat Bolo by Keith Laumer

0-671-69879-6 • $6.99 ☐

Two complete novels by Keith Laumer. "Without a doubt, Laumer's best work."
—Anne McCaffrey

BOLO STORIES BY OTHER AUTHORS,

Bolos: The Honor of the Regiment 0-671-72184-4 • $6.99 ☐
With stories by David Drake, Mercedes Lackey & Larry Dixon, Mike Resnick & Barry Malzberg, and others. Edited by Bill Fawcett.

Bolos II: The Unconquerable 0-671-87629-5 • $5.99 ☐
With stories by S.M. Stirling, William R. Forstchen, Christopher Stasheff, and others. Edited by Bill Fawcett.

Bolos III: Triumphant 0-671-87683-X • $5.99 ☐
With stories by David Weber and Linda Evans. Edited by Bill Fawcett.

Bolos IV: Last Stand 0-671-87760-7 • $5.99 ☐
With stories by David Weber, S.M. Stirling, Steve Perry & John DeCamp, and others. Edited by Bill Fawcett.

Bolos V: The Old Guard 0-671-31957-4 • $6.99 ☐
With stories by J. Stephen York & Dean Smith, Wm. H. Keith, Jr., and others. Edited by Bill Fawcett.

Bolos VI: Cold Steel 0-7434-3559-4 • $7.99 ☐
With stories by Linda Evans, Steve York, and Dean Wesley Smith. Edited by Bill Fawcett.

Bolo! (HC) 0-7434-9872-0 • $25.00 ☐
A new Bolo novel by *New York Times* best-selling author David Weber.

Complete Bolo novels by William H. Keith, Jr.:

Bolo Brigade	• 0-671-87781-x	$5.99 ☐
Bolo Rising	• 0-671-57779-4	$6.99 ☐
Bolo Strike	• 0-671-31835-7 (HC)	$19.00 ☐
	• 0-7434-3566-4 (PB)	$7.99 ☐

**Let Real SF Writers Take You
Across the Space Frontier to the Stars!**

COSMIC TALES:
Adventures in Sol System

Edited by T.K.F. Weisskopf

Cosmic Tales: Tales of hope and adventure that will remind you of the reasons human dare dream of the next great frontier. Join us as humanity moves out once again into the infinite ocean of space, this time to stay!

All new stories of the conquest of the solar system & the future by: Charles Sheffield, Gregory Benford, John Ringo, James P. Hogan, Wen Spencer, Margaret Ball, Jack McDevitt, Allan Steele, Mark L. Van Name, Debra Doyle & James D. Macdonald, Dave Freer & Eric Flint, fact & fiction by space scientist Travis S. Taylor, and fact & fiction by computer scientist and inventor Paul Chafe.

COSMIC TALES:
Adventures in Sol System
0-7434-8832-6 • 416 pp. • $6.99

COSMIC TALES II:
Adventures in Far Futures
0-7434-9887-9 • 480 pp. • $6.99

Available in bookstores everywhere

Or order online at our secure, easy website:
www.baen.com

If not available through your local bookstore send this coupon and a check or money order for the cover price(s) + $1.75 s/h to Baen Books, Dept. BA, P.O. Box 1403, Riverdale, NY 10471. Be sure to include full name & address for shipping. Delivery can take up to eight weeks.

WEBSCRIPTIONS:
The Last Word in EBOOKS

FREE EBOOKS FOR YOU!

Just type in the first word from page 224 of the volume now in your hands and email it to EBOOKS@BAEN.COM and you will receive immediate no-strings access to a full month of publications from your favorite publisher.

(Ahem, "favorite publisher": that's us, Baen Books. ;)